My skin shrank as ~~~~~~~~~~~~~~~~~~~~~~~~~~~~~~g-
nized the odor of dea~~~~~~~~~~~~~~~~~~~~~~~~~~nt
like it. This hut would never be livable again.

Along the rim of the inner wall lay two human corpses directly in front of me, shrouded in a milky spun-cotton material. I steeled myself and started toward them. Something bumped my forehead. I jolted back and looked up.

I'd been bumped by a naked human foot. In the middle of the hut, suspended from a construction ring, hung a dead woman dangling by the neck. Her face was mummified, yet there was still a clear expression of desperate sadness in the set of the jaw, even though the jaw was twisted askew by the rope.

No, it wasn't a rope . . . it was the braided shreds of her clothing.

The nearest body on the ground was wrapped loosely in that odd grayish shroud, like the forms outside. His skull and chest were large, bones bulky and obviously masculine. And there was a hole in the chest the size of a bowling ball.

"Rory?" Clark called. "You okay in there?"

"Come on in, but be prepared."

Once he got past his initial reaction, I said, "They're all the same. Chests exploded. Except this woman up hanging here. I think she hanged herself to avoid what happened to the others."

"What are they doing in here?" he asked. "It's the same out there. Two other huts have bodies. They couldn't get out, and nobody else could get in. Is it possible they locked themselves in?"

"How many bodies are in the other huts?"

"Four in one and three in the other."

I gazed up at him. "You know what happened to them, don't you?"

Other Aliens novels from DH Press

Aliens: Original Sin
by Michael Jan Friedman

ALIENS™

DNA WAR

DIANE CAREY

Based on the motion picture
from Twentieth Century Fox

DH PRESS
Milwaukie

ALIENS™: DNA WAR
© 2006 Twentieth Century Fox Film Corporation. All Rights Reserved.
TM indicates a trademark of Twentieth Century Fox Film Corporation.

Book design by Debra Bailey
Cover painting by Stephen Youll.

Published by DH Press
A division of Dark Horse Comics
10956 SE Main Street
Milwaukie, OR 97222

dhpressbooks.com

First DH Press Edition: May 2006
ISBN-10: 1-59582-032-9
ISBN-13: 978-1-59582-032-7

Printed in USA
Distributed by Publishers Group West

10 9 8 7 6 5 4 3 2 1

CHAPTER ONE

"The damned thing knows how to fly!"

"Throw your coat over it, Rory!"

"I'm no zoologist. Throw your own coat!"

I was caught in a cyclone with a hellhound. Caught in darkness as if we were wrapped in a red cloak. Mechanical thunder, bumping and falling, the din of conflict—we were having a visitation from the gods of panic.

Clark could yell all he wanted. I was diving under the table. When I got there, the magnetologist was already taking up the space. I had to pitch myself backward behind the galley hatch. Normally I'm pretty hard to scare, but I'd never seen anything this horrifying in my whole life.

Warning lights cast patches of red and yellow on the stark exposed piping and caseless electrical and magnetic conduits, and turned human faces into tribal masks. Were the strobing lights really supposed to help? The ship was panicking for its life.

Everything on this container ship was weird to me, but this moment was the weirdest so far. This bloodcurdling scarecrow was strafing us while the crew barked back and forth about losing altitude and crashing into the planet—not the kind of thing you want to hear when you've been asked to come along on a nice quiet ride. The thrusters screamed in our ears, fighting outside forces they were never built to fight. We were almost ready to settle into orbit when this monstrosity broke out and scared the pilot by landing in his hair. He went sideways and so did the ship.

The thing with wings twisted in the air over the table and flew straight at me. Instinctively I blocked it with my arms as wide black wings flayed my head and hands. Then it got caught for a hideous moment between me and the metal galley door. In a panic, it throttled me with its wings before flapping up and out over the top of the door. I swear it turned inside out and flew backward, laws of physics be damned. I didn't want that monster anywhere near me.

Around us, the ship's boxy body rattled with mechanical effort and physical battering. Every inch of the hull was under strain as we cut through the upper atmosphere. This wasn't supposed to be happening. I can almost fly a paper plane, but even a dope like me knows when the thing I'm riding on is in trouble. Good thing I'm not a genius in avionics. I'd've really be scared.

"Pocket, open the hangar bay hatch and let this thing fly in there!" Clark called to the first mate. "Pocket, where are you?!"

"He's underneath me," Gaylord, the magnetologist, reported from under the table.

"Then you get up and open it!"

"I don't want that thing in my hair!"

"Atmosphere in forty seconds! Emergency ignition! Barry, emergency ignition! Pocket, crawl out of there right now!"

"It's on me! Gaylord, get it off me!"

The bosun's shriek almost matched the creature's decibel level. "I'm not helping you till I get my six hundred!"

"I won that bet!"

"You tricked me!"

"Where did I get this reputation?"

"Maybe from all the gambling!"

Not being a member of the crew, I had the luxury of ignoring their frantic dialogue during my attempt to melt into the wall. Being the captain and all, Clark was trying to direct the chaos.

"Theo, what's the count?" he called to the first mate.

"Full atmosphere skim if we don't fire the planetaries in thirteen seconds." Somehow Theo's aristocratic English accent gave an elegance to the panic.

"Barry, we're going directly to landing mode!" Clark called. "Blow the relief valves!"

On the helm station above us, Barry, the pilot, shouted, "Keep that thing off me! I can't work!" He was four feet above us on the control balcony, which put him right in the flight path of the hyperkinetic attacker.

The scramble intensified. Forms ducked past me and scratching over me, and somebody stepped on my hand. I guessed the new jolt of movements meant they'd reached a point where they were more scared of getting sucked into the planet without engine control than they were of the weirdie in the air.

"Is there no one to shoot that thing?" the first mate shouted. "Where are the Marines?!"

"I can't do this alone!" Barry called from the helm.

"Gaylord, get up there and help Barry blow that valve—" Clark's voice was drowned out suddenly by a roar of engine surge.

The bursts and spasms of the ship, complicated by the screwball lunatic in the air, made their voices blend together. While the crew argued about monsters and crashing, I found the floor. I crawled along beside the galley table's bench seat, grumbling, "I hate things with wings . . ."

I heard the hangar bay hatch clang open, but from down here I couldn't see much. I stretched one hand toward the deckbox under the far end of the bench, the box with my travel gear inside. To the chippering of the wild and woolly creature in the air, I forced my fingers into the box and felt around, found my holster, pulled it out, and unclipped it. The high-powered plasma pistol fell into my hand. It was the best money could buy for licensed private enforcement. A badge of honor in its way, folks said. The gel-formed grip fell perfectly into my left hand and was instantly warm, a trademark of the manufacturer, specially made for left-handers.

"Clark," I announced, "I've got my plaz. I can shoot that thing." I forced myself not to shout. Adrenaline would wreck my aim.

"Don't shoot it!" he called back.

Holding the pistol in both hands, I rolled over onto my back and tried to follow the ugly duckling in the air. The thing had no flight pattern at all. It flapped out an erratic tracery and kept doubling back on itself. Every few seconds I caught a glimpse of two huge, shiny, ghoulish black eyes, repugnant little white teeth. It took all my training to remember how to aim at a moving object. Mostly instinct, but y'know. It's not like I'd ever seen anything quite *this* ghoulish before, being a city boy. I'd seen other kinds of ghouls.

The shadow of the first mate, Theo, crossed between me and the monster gargoyle as he made a dive to throw a blanket over it, but he missed. When the shadow cleared, I shimmied out into the middle of the deck.

"Oh, *please* let me shoot it—" I begged.

Clark's voice cut through the confusion. "Don't shoot, Rory. I'm serious!"

"Aw, come on . . . " I hugged the plasma gun to my chest and put my free arm over my hair just in time to duck.

The ship kicked and took a sudden surge forward, then sputtered and dropped under us, taking our stomachs with it. I recognized the sensations—riding the rapids. The *Vinza* was a heavy vessel, old, tested, and steady. Landing usually went like clockwork. Not today. The wingie thingie had screwed us up by scaring the wits out of our pilot before he had a chance to fire the landing engines. Now we were plunging in without steerage power. And we were still being strafed by a banshee.

"This is pretty damned demoralizing," I grumbled.

Sometimes a switch goes off in my head telling me to put an end to whatever's being dished out at me. After the switch flips, if I don't get control, whatever happens after that is my own fault. So I forced myself to get over the shock of seeing what I was seeing, stood up straight, and fixed my eyes on the screaming meemie in the air. My neck was sore in seconds. I shimmied out of my favorite jacket, custom-made in a fudge-brown leather and exactly the color of my hair. Okay, so it was custom-made for the guy who'd left it at the thrift store where one of my girlfriends found it for pennies on the dollar. So what? I got no pride.

I held the jacket in front of me like a bullfighter's cape and kept my eyes fixed on the flapper. Fast little freak! It flew along the lower wall supporting the pilot station, turning so its wings spread floor to rail on the wall. With its body flattened to the wall and its nose raised to show the way, its black eyes peered at me from the top of its skull in a horrifying stare. It knew I had become the one to watch—*it knew*.

Suddenly squeamish, I took a tentative step backward. My spine bumped the edge of the open bay hatch. It felt like someone pushing a weapon into my back and goading me to move forward. The thing was coming. It veered off the corner where the pilot deck wall met the galley wall and tilted its wings just slightly to come straight at me. Around me, Clark and Gaylord, Theo, and Pocket ducked and jumped in their attempt to do their jobs while fearing for their skins. Above us, Barry hunched over his helm, hoping not to get snagged by the hair.

Clark was a brawny guy, tall enough that his enviable auburn thatch barely cleared the headspace of his own ship. He had a semi-permanent bruise from the one strake just outside his own cabin that beaned him in the forehead every time he came out groggy. Now his height betrayed him as the brushfire-beast made a spiral around his head. He lost his cool, flayed fanatically, and somehow shrunk to half his size. "Little mugger!" he blurted.

A stripe of blood appeared on his nose—he'd been raked by a claw. The gargoyle seemed to have the claws pointed at anybody it was flying toward. My head began to swim. The creature was flying fast, but I was moving in slow motion, unable to comply with the erratic flight plan. I was three years old again, trapped in my bedroom in the new house, out of place, unfamiliar, dodging those other creatures circling my room, my bed—

For the first time I wasn't sleeping in my mother's room. My first real bed. My first room. Only to find I shared it with a nest of birds. They were only stupid sparrows, but to me, at three— so I still hate things that fly.

I held my ground. Would it attack? Claw my face? I raised the jacket up to my nose, held my breath, waited for the strike. The creature's body disappeared below my line of vision, which almost stopped my heart.

I felt the furry body brush the jacket. I saw a stretch of black webbing. Summoning power over my disgust, I snapped my arms closed.

A substantial ball of muscle writhed against my sleeves. A leathery wing formed itself to the left side of my head tight as a mask. A claw sunk into my scalp. Revulsion streaked from my scalp to my legs. I choked out my unintelligible opinion and held my face away. Against my body the monster twisted and fought, chittering its protest like a tap dancer's shoes. I dropped back against the galley wall behind the bay hatch door, trapped between the wall and the thing. "I've got it! Land the ship!"

"Thank you, thank you, thank you, thank you!" Gaylord percolated at me as he launched his large body to the ladder to the pilot balcony, where Barry battled the forces of nature. Engines that were normally almost silent now howled so loudly that we all had to shout to be heard. What the hell was I doing here? How did Clark Sparren always manage to get the better of my common sense? I was supposed to have a lot of common sense! Training! Judgment! Where was it when I needed it?

Controlling his voice, Clark thundered up the short ladder to the helm balcony. "Is the valve blown?"

"Valve's blown!" Barry reported.

"Gaylord, get Barry some electrical support. Theo, run out the wings."

"Wings, aye!"

"Gaylord, full flush in ten seconds," Clark called out. "Theo, get those wings out!"

"They're answering."

A drumming airy *shhhhhhtk* announced the deployment of the retractable wings, fins, and stabilizers. The roaring and shuddering of the ship's body began to level off.

"Ignition in five seconds!" Clark called out. "Five . . . four . . . "

From the helm, Barry ducked at a flash of light and squawked, "Where's that thing?"

"Steer the ship!" Clark ordered. "Two! . . . One! Ignition!"

The vibrations under my feet grew to a steady quick pulse like a snare drummer increasing the marching pace. The mechanical whining eased down to a loud but consistent buzz. Atmospheric engines working, wings out—what else could go wrong to ruin our good save?

Trapped with my own disgusting problem, I sucked air through gritted teeth and held the creature tightly in my jacket, hoping it wasn't crapping on my shoes or biting through to my skin. Clark snapped out orders, keeping his voice down to the absolute volume needed to communicate without causing any more stress. The ship's terrified whine settled to an almost musical hum. The deck found a nearly level footing, still at a slight tilt, and began to feel like a deck with support under it . . . air. All that was left of our near-miss was a faint high-pitched whistle from deep within the engine noise, and in a moment that too was gone. Flashing lights of warning began one by one to wink off.

"Stable," Theo finally reported. "Altitude, eight thousand fifty."

"Shit, we're low!" Gaylord gasped.

"Trimming," Barry huffed out, still shaken. The activity didn't exactly settle down, but became suddenly organized, deliberate as each crewman found his nerves and went after his own job.

"Altitude five thousand," Theo chanted out. "Four thousand . . . thirty-five . . ."

At the same time, Clark ordered, "Run out the stands and levelers. Hurry up."

I felt the creature's body heat through the fabric, only a layer or two away from my own skin. Would it bite through? Was it rabid?

"Keep holding it, Rory," Clark called. "Barry, is that landing vector still good? You still getting beacons or do we have to eyeball it?"

The pilot's voice was shaky, nerve-racked. He hunched over his controls. "Beacons are still in place." As if he didn't quite believe it, Barry paused and repeated, "Reading landing coordinates. Jesus, that was close."

"Cue the piloting computer and auto-thrusters for centerline adjustment. Let her take herself in."

"A hundred to one!" Pocket called out.

"Not now, hammerhead!" Clark snapped.

It seemed to me that auto-thrust would be an automatic thing, but I'd learned that sometimes even the simplest changes had to be approved by the command officer.

"Auto-thrusters green," Barry said, finally calmer.

"Set your lock-downs at three-two-three," Clark went on procedurally, though from here I could see he was sweating a fountain.

"LDs . . . three-twenty-three," Barry responded.

"Put the list sensors on auto."

"Listing sensors on."

"Secure from manual override."

"Shutting down MO."

"Secure plasma reactors and put 'em on standby. All hands, prepare for landing."

"Clark," I called. "Pardon me—"

"You're doing fine, Rory. You got 'im right where you want him."

"I want him in your shorts!"

If only I'd known *what* I had trapped against my ribs. All I knew right now was that it had teeth and wings. My two evil geniuses. For a few seconds it went suddenly still, which was almost more frightening than when it was squirming—then the squirming started again and slipped lower. I tilted my elbow downward to catch it, expecting a claw to sink into my leg.

Clark artfully ignored me. "Reduce speed one quarter. Cue magnetic bearings and couplers."

From where he stood on the pilot balcony, he had a full view of the sky and atmosphere we were rushing through at what seemed to be too-high speed. The crew didn't seem panicked anymore, so I took their cue and tried to stay calm.

It was crock. My heart hammered the animal pressed against

my sternum. I couldn't hide my agitation from it anymore than it could hide its quivering tension from me. It wasn't relaxing. Its struggles hadn't calmed. With every breath I took, the creature flinched and pushed outward against my arms in every possible direction.

"Fire verticals," Clark directed. We were coming in for our landing.

This was the worst moment of landing. I'd only experienced it four times in my life and hated it every time. It was the moment between forward thrust and hovering thrust, a complete change in engineering that had to go flawlessly, or the ship could literally fall out of the sky. The ship gave us that sickening dropping sensation again, as if there weren't enough air to hold it up, but it was just an illusion. We broke to a hover as the high-volume thrusters fired, the most powerful engines in the arsenal of aerospace. Their tremendous roar drowned out Clark's staccato orders, but somehow the crew knew what he was saying and one by one delivered the goods to get the massive ship on the ground. It was a fast process, scary fast, not like docking a big ocean vessel, because there were only so much power and fuel to hold the bulky ship in the air. Less hovering, less waste of energy.

I sank against the bulkhead, crammed my eyes shut, and clutched my ghastly package, hoping to live and wishing to die.

There was a sharp, loud gush. The ship dropped another five feet out from under me, and I fell to meet it. Then a hard stop . . .

I waited for someone—Clark or Theo—to shout some order. Nothing happened, except the ship landed itself. Solid ground scratched under us. I felt the texture of the surface rumble through the ship and into my feet. Then I realized the final landing process must all be automatic, to keep the thrusters from trying to drive into solid ground or blowing the ship over on its side. Sensors could react a thousand times faster than human hands.

"We're down," Barry confirmed. He sounded whipped. Beside him up there, Gaylord's round, brown face peeked over the railing.

Theo didn't wait around, but spun twice to scan everything around us, then disappeared into the cargo bay, probably to check on damage. He never stayed in one place for long, I'd noticed. A first mate was a jack-of-all-trades, and Theo's face, with its goatee and tight brown eyes, popped up everywhere high and low. He had the air of English aristocracy, but he worked like a yeoman. Pocket had told me Theo even had a title, and somewhere an estate, that his father had been knighted, but his family fortune had dwindled and the estate was being used as a hotel for whatever income it could generate. Everybody had a hard-luck story. At least, everybody aboard this ship seemed to.

On the deck, on his knees not far from me, Pocket had both hands clawed into the metal barrier grid that supported the pilot station. He peered at me through wayward strands of straw-colored hair that had pulled out of the thick ponytail. "Hundred to one," he murmured.

"Good job, everybody," Clark said with a sigh. "Let's not do that anymore for the rest of our lives, eh?"

The crew rewarded him with grunts and nods.

"Let's hear it for Rory!" Pocket panted out.

Applause broke out with a little weak cheering. "Yay, Rory!" Gaylord wheezed.

"Nice going," Theo said, and at the same time, Barry offered, "Touchdown, man."

"Yeah, good going," Clark said. "You got it."

"I've got it," I gagged. "Now . . . will somebody please tell me *what* I've got?"

"Just stay there a second."

"Somehow this is *your* fault."

"Let's do the housekeeping," he went on to his crew. "Where's Theo? Wasn't he here?"

"He went into the bay," I choked.

"Okay, everybody, do your lock-downs and secure from motive power. Check the throttle bearings and flat-line the Cobb-coils. Tell Theo to down-flow the inhibitors and assign somebody to check for crazing. I don't want any hairline breaks causing stresses when we launch. Have Gary and Mark look at the zinc disks and the loading transmission. Tell Kip to secure the galley. Gaylord, do a complete magnetological diagnostic on all systems. Barry, re-set the relief valves, and Pocket, check the cargo for damage and deployability. Get somebody to lube the king posts, safety winches, and lifting gear. I'll give you till thirteen-thirty to get me reports of stability and readiness. And somebody go see how badly we shook up the Marines."

"Hope we didn't scare 'em," Pocket commented as he got to his feet.

For the first time in several minutes, Clark's eyes fell on me. Pretty soon they were all looking at me and my . . . package.

Here I was, sucking air in little gulps, lips curling, both legs braced, knees bent, and my spine pressed against the hatch. I held perfectly still with my arms clamped and knees tight around the squirming package inside my coat.

From my left periphery, the ship's medical intern slipped toward me. She was a short, round girl with shoulder-length blonde hair and manly features, but enormous sweet blue eyes. She always seemed to be interested in talking to me during the awake parts of the trip.

"Something you need to tell us, Bonnie?" I asked through my teeth.

She raised her hands, but didn't touch me or my jacket yet. "Don't smother her, okay? Let her have some air?"

"What is digging its way through my undershirt on its way to my chest hair?"

She turned pink in the face. "Can I just take her?"

"'Her'?"

She gathered the squirming bundle out of my arms and coiled her own arms around it. "Thanks," she murmured. "See ya."

"Bonnie!" Clark snapped.

"Bye." She tried to push behind me toward the hatch with her bundle.

Clark dropped down the short ladder and only had to make a half turn to end up blocking her way. "Is that yours?"

"Well . . ."

"Why do you have a steroidal mouse aboard this ship?"

The girl hid behind a hank of blonde hair that had fallen in her face. "You always encourage us to bring creature comforts with us—"

"Not *actual* creatures, you idiot. Is this where my papayas have been disappearing to?"

Bonnie shifted from foot to foot. "Um . . . we ran out of apples. You know, you didn't have to panic. She was just looking for a place to land. She's hand-raised by humans, and if somebody had just stuck your arm straight out like this, she'd have just landed on you perfectly."

"Not on me," I grumbled.

We flinched as the creature jolted in Bonnie's arms and its head popped out of the folds of my jacket. A triangular head, big black eyes and a little nose, ruffled fur and little tiny black hands trying to pull it out of the jacket. Damned if it didn't look like a Pomeranian.

Keeping my newly claimed distance, I asked, "What *is* that?"

"Haven't you ever seen a flying fox?" she asked.

"That's no fox."

"Isn't it obviously a . . . "

Clark growled, "A flipping giant *bat.*"

He suddenly noticed that everybody was standing around us, peering at the critter, and nobody was jumping to do all those lock-ups and coil-things and up-downs.

"Hey, is this a show?" he said. "Get cracking!"

Like ripples in a pond, they dispersed. Bonnie would've gone too, except Clark blocked her way intentionally.

"A bat . . . " I found my feet and put a step between me and Bonnie's bundle. "What's it doing out in space with us?"

"Good question." Clark zeroed in on Bonnie. "Well?"

She blushed. "Well . . . who could I get to take him while I'm in space for so long? Isn't it pretty good that he never gets out of my cabin?"

"He never gets out?" he mocked. "Where'd you get that thing?"

"Remember that cute guy who hitched from the Doyle-Gray system on the last voyage? I fused his broken wrist?"

"That greasy-haired punk who liked you?"

"He has a lot of exotic animals, y'know, that he rescued from stupid people who think they make good pets? He had this baby flying fox, and it was too young and all, and what was I supposed to do?"

"Are you telling me you're this bat's mama?"

"She's kinda cute, isn't she?"

"Girl, blow this thing out the airlock!"

"You don't really want to kill her! Did she really do anything so wrong? Does she take up that much space?"

"Give or take the five-foot wingspan," I commented.

"Four fee—hee—hee—"" Bonnie started to cry and in seconds was sobbing inconsolably. She was such a studious and competent medic, hardly making a peep most of the time, that it seemed odd to find out she was really a girl. She hugged her bat, which put its little curiously human black hand on her cheek as if to comfort her.

"It's not a Chihuahua," Clark told her. "Girl, do you have to be such a turkey? Was that creepy thing in the cryotube with you?"

She nodded.

The fox bat squirmed again and this time flopped out an entire wing—a long segmented black leathery membrane that hugged my jacket's folds as Bonnie tried to keep control. I noticed her big blue eyes—Bonnie's, not the bat's—ranging to meet mine whenever she wasn't obliged to be looking at her captain's.

"Do you want your coat back?" she offered tentatively, and started to pick at her bundle.

I protested, "Uh . . . maybe you should just keep it . . . "

"Don't worry. Butterball doesn't have fleas or anything."

"Fleas . . . " My stomach churned as she disengaged the fox bat from my jacket, claw by claw and fold by fold.

"No, no, she's been completely decontaminated, just like everything aboard. I did it myself."

"You'd have to. 'Butterball'?"

Gaylord and Pocket appeared on either side of Clark to have a look at the monster we'd just conquered. With Gaylord hiding behind him, Pocket screwed up his face. "What's this? How'd it get into the salon?"

Bonnie shot back, "I asked you not to go in my cabin, Pocket!"

"You didn't inform me your cabin was Pandora's box! We log the magnetic coil readouts before we can land. They're in your cabin!"

Gaylord piped up with, "I had a stroke when this came flying out!"

She spun to glare at him. "Next time, stay *out*."

"I guess you guys should ask first before you go in the infirmary," Clark supported.

"Who's gonna check the feeds?" Gaylord asked.

Clark shrugged. "I'll check 'em."

"You're the captain!" Pocket protested. "If you do our jobs, who's gonna do your job?"

"Rory here'll do it."

"Yeah. Rory. Right." Annoyed and exhausted, Pocket slipped through the main hatch to get back to doing what should've been the work of a normal landing sequence. Gaylord punished Bonnie with one more disturbed glare before he too stepped out into the main bay.

I barely managed to keep my pistol down as Bonnie dropped my jacket and the fox-faced bat flipped over to hang from her arm as if she were a tree branch. It seemed content to hang from Bonnie's wrist with its bony hind claws firmly gripping the neoprene of her service tunic's protective sleeves. In the air it had spread its wings wider than the mess table was long. Now it coiled those wings around its body, just like the vampires in the stories, and stared at me and Clark with its doggie eyes.

Clark glowered at it, then again at Bonnie. "Take it away. Put it away. Lock it up. I don't want to see it again. From now on and for the rest of its life, you find some wicked witch to babysit that thing."

"I promise," Bonnie said. She raised her arm, straining from the not-inconsiderable weight of the bat. "She's friendly. She's not wild at all. See?"

She offered me a chance to—what, pet the thing?

I shrank back. "I hate things that fly."

"What? Like bluebirds and butterflies?"

"If they fly and they bite, I hate 'em."

"But she's cute just hanging here, isn't she? Admit it."

"Yeah, she's adorable," Clark interrupted. "I don't want to see one drop of guano on this ship, you got that?"

Without another word, Bonnie ducked through the aft hatch, heading toward the area where our bunks were laid out in little one-person compartments. Clark drew a long breath and took a moment to check his palm-link unit to the ship's systems. Things must be okay now despite the close call, because he squinted, nodded, and pocketed the device in his vest pocket. Then he looked at me, burying a hint of embarrassment.

I slumped back to sit on the edge of the mess table. "Long, quiet break in space, you said. Milk run, you said."

"Clam up, I said." He stepped past me to a comptech panel, one of many throughout the ship that allowed for almost total instant access to the ship's systems. He'd told me once before that, if necessary, one person could run the whole ship. Not maintain it, but run it for a while.

He spoke into the panel. "Official log access, code X1. Specialty Spacefaring Container Vessel *Vinza*, PlanCom Contract Seven-seven-four. Planet Rosamond 6 achieved, July 14, thirteen hundred hours, ten minutes, ah . . . four seconds. Safe landing on predetermined coordinates, no incidents. Clark Sparren, Master, authorization SP405. Log, secure, and send."

"*Log secure*," the computer responded. "*Sending voyage report now. Reporting to Nebula Habitation Division, PlanCom, Incorporated, Cincinnati, Ohio. Thank you and have a pleasant watch.*"

"Thanks." Clark punched a pattern on the control panel, then said, "Theo, put up all the scanners and scout the landscape. We'll have a look around before we go out."

"*On it*," Theo answered from somewhere in the ship.

"I love getting to this moment," Clark commented. "Didn't expect it to be so weird, though."

"'No incidents,'" I echoed.

"Quit repeating what I say."

"That was the most hideous thing I've ever seen, and I'm old."

"You're twenty-eight, Moses."

"Old enough to know what I want and young enough to get it." I wiped the sweat off my cheek. At least, I hoped it was just sweat. "Why wouldn't you let me shoot it?"

"Because we don't need a hole in the ship. You were aiming at an outer wall."

Now that he said it, I felt stupid for not thinking of that.

Clark heaved a clearing sigh and shrugged off the morning's unsavory action. "Nice way to start the day. Atmosphere scratch and a wild bat chase, all before breakfast. We get a pass for the rest of the month. Everything easy from now on."

I eyed him in a way we both recognized. "You don't know my mother. This isn't Maid Marian we're talking about."

He waved a hand. "Like it or not, tomorrow we'll be on our way back to Earth, with your mom and all her people tucked safely away in our ride-alongs."

"Give her a hobby. Put the bat in with her."

"Come with me."

He led the way through the bay hatch into the ship's wide-mouthed hangar bay. The bay—I'd been told on my orientation tour—was an open area built to carry shipping containers of almost any configuration. The ship was thick-bodied, massive, and utilitarian, with length almost proportional to its height. Folding bulkheads could be arranged to accommodate different kinds of cargo. I'd seen it done, and what a sight it was to watch a bay the size of a football field suddenly reconfigure itself at the push of a button.

There was no artistry in the bay, as in some passenger parts of the ship that indulged the aesthetics. Nothing here appealed to the eye, except to the trained industrial eye which might appreciate it. I think the crew appreciated it plenty. Everything was black, gray, and white, metallic colors, except for brightly painted rotating gantry cranes which were encoded red, yellow, green, blue, or purple for quick identification. Those looked like a kids' swingset. During the two months before cryo, I'd mostly followed Pocket around the ship and helped him, just to keep busy and not give anybody the idea that I was just watching. At first I'd followed Clark around while he did his captain stuff, but I always felt like an odd sock. When I followed Pocket, there were things I could do. I'm a great stooge. Bosuns always needed stooges. I could hold the ends of things, flip switches, ratchet something up, drive something, carry the other end, open hatches and close boxes, run and get things, and watch in admiration. Pocket and I seemed to be mutually useful; he was a loner who didn't like to ask for help but was glad to have it. We didn't chit-chat, yet we communicated great. I had a knack for anticipating what he needed, and I knew when to "stand by." When other crewmen came past us, doing their crewy work or driving the body-hugging loaders, I would be "working" too—either actually doing, holding, or ratcheting, or I would be "standing by" for Pocket. What the hell, half of success is identity, right?

Wishing I could be with Pocket instead, I followed Clark along the centerline bulkhead, a wall that ran the whole length of the bay. Around us the crew climbed, crawled, and rappelled around the stacked cargo containers. Clark hurried through without a glance at his crew. Perhaps that was a practiced habit, to keep them concentrating on their work and not on his watching them do their work.

We hurried along in the man-made pathway between stacked yellow containers, each as big as a garage and marked with the PlanCom logo, the silhouette of a cowboy on his mustang, lassoing a planet. I almost had to jog to keep up with him. He was serious about keeping to that tight schedule. His boots made a deliberate *skup-skup-skup* sound on the deck coated with recycled hard rubber, all the way to the engine room, where he finally stopped. The engine room housed the magnetic field propulsion units and the plasma reaction chambers. I only remembered that because the door said, "MAG FIELD PROP/ P.R. CHAMBER—CREW ONLY" and I had to walk past it to get to the aft head. I wasn't crew, so I never went in there.

Never? Sounded like I'd been aboard a year. Actually, I'd spent a whole two months awake and fifteen months asleep.

Clark gazed up at the massive containers. "These boxes make me nervous just walking by. The idea of malfunctions and all. Nobody's perfect—and no automated system is foolproof. If the containment's security system went bad, we'd all be eradicated in about eighty seconds."

Plumbing for reassurance, I commented, "Well, sometimes you just have to put your life in somebody else's hands, right?"

He didn't respond. He drew a breath and sighed it out, then stepped to the nearest giant green container, gazed the fourteen feet up to the top, then back to the high-security lock patch. First, both his thumbs were required for a print scan. At first the small screen showed a red light of activation and warning. Any further tampering could result in a sharp electrical stun if the patch didn't recognize the person doing the decoding of its program.

I sidled back, hoping I was out of range, but not far enough to let him know I was nervous. At least he'd had the guts to admit he was scared. Kinda made me ashamed.

The red light turned orange, with a green chevron in the middle. Clark leaned forward and presented his left eye for a retinal identification. The light turned yellow. The green chevron remained. Clark pulled out the MRI remote and pressed it to his left temple. A brain scan completed the security code.

The yellow lights went away and the green chevron began to flash, overlaid with the word CAUTION.

Caution . . . caution . . . caution . . .

The giant loading door panels on the container began to re-peal themselves, panel by panel, starting in the middle. The container was opening. Now nothing stood between the two of us and the nightmare inside.

I took another step back.

CHAPTER TWO

The massive door panels clunked one under the other, like curtain blinds moving slowly apart to reveal the sunrise. I bumped backward against the container behind me and spread my arms. "God a'mighty . . ."

There was no sunrise inside the giant container. Nothing so encouraging. We stood together, Clark a little taller and bulkier than myself, yet we were both suddenly very small. My chest tightened, my heart thudding as I looked up at a gleaming phalanx of robots. Like the Confederate line at Seminary Ridge, the mechanized regiment bristled with spines and explosive-tipped barbs, thousand-eyed sensors and all the things any human kid recognizes as "do not touch." Each of dozens just in this box alone, was shaped like a bullet cartridge with a round helmet. The helmet was embedded with spines, barbs, and feelers. There was no front, back, or sides, and each had six folded legs, usable in any combination. They could move in any direction. And they fired those poison-filled darts by sensors. The darts were supersonic. Once targeted, there was no getting out of the way. I'd seen smaller versions for urban warfare, but nothing this bulky and over-armed. Even standing there in repose, the machines broadcast aggression. They were scary as hell.

"They're something, aren't they?" Clark scanned the dangerous rank. The lights of the cargo bay reflected from the gleaming bodies of the robot soldiers, fell back upon his all-too-human face and changed his eyes to metallic disks. "Every one of them could kill a small town. They're loaded with sensors programmed to seek out any life form whose DNA doesn't match the planet. Those barbs are actually percussion hypodermics. Their bodies are canisters loaded with poison deadly to anything that's not native here. All you have to do is get too close, and *jab*. If I don't do this right, we'll kill ourselves and all those geeks out there. The poison-packers only have two targets—the aliens that have hijacked this planet, and us. Everything else on the planet will be spared."

I dredged up my voice. "How . . . how . . . many . . . "

Lost it again.

Clark also was subdued. "There are five hundred in every container, and I've got ninety containers."

His voice was laden with awe and responsibility. This was the most important thing Clark had ever done, or would ever do in his life, and it showed in his expression. His features, normally smooth, rosy, and carefree, were lined, hardened, and gray. We stood together in a profound hush.

My whole body snapped when something moved beside me. The first mate, Theo, had come up on me from the side. The kind of person who doesn't miss much and spends his life chasing details while understanding big pictures, Theo stared up at the poison-packers.

"Damn us all," he murmured. "So that's what they look like . . . "

Only then did I realize they hadn't surveyed their cargo before this. Probably the containers had been delivered fully loaded and secure from the security company contracted by PlanCom. Made sense—what if there were some kind of mistake? Something as simple as a bat loose on the planet had almost caused a crash. Had imaginings of deadly errors chiseled away at the crew's consciences? Or were they just doing a job? I didn't really know them well enough to say. I knew Clark would have found some way to justify the progress, to take this super-technology and put it to use he saw as good. Bonnie might worry about little animals that got in the way. Gaylord would probably hide till it was over.

For me, I was just intimidated. Seemed smart at the moment.

"It's okay," Clark said. "They're deactivated right now. I have to arm them."

He tapped a "warm up" code into the panel, which would start the download program, which was communicable to all the other containers.

"What activates them?" I choked out.

"I do," Clark said. "There's a series of fail-safes. Theo and I are the only ones who can deploy them. I know all the codes, Theo knows half. If I'm incapacitated, Theo has to activate his own series of fail-safes on the eyes-only computer in my cabin, then get the deployment fail-safes. It's not like pushing a button."

He pushed a button and the first bank of robots began to light and flash, their whirring scanners drawing energy. I stepped back more, and realized as I did that stepped back wouldn't matter a whit to these things. They'd follow, they'd hunt, and they'd never give up.

"Once they're deployed and out of the containers, there's no turning back," Clark said. "They can't be recalled till they completely exhaust themselves and account for every square inch of the planet. They even go under water. Can you imagine the ocean floor haunted by these things?"

"Good day for a swim," I managed. "What happens if you're both incapacitated?"

"It gets harder after that," Clark admitted. He shook himself free of the hypnotic effect. "Okay—let's close this up for now. I don't want the whole crew standing here staring like sheep at a corn show."

He activated the controls and in a few moments the accordion doors were grinding shut one after the other, until they came together in the middle of the huge container. Finally the last two doors met, clacked, locked, and fell hauntingly silent. The poison-packers were locked away in their box once again, but we held in our minds the picture of their helmeted blue-gray bodies, standing there like twitching draft horses, waiting for the bell to summon them to pull their enormous load.

Clark caught sight of his first mate checking the auto-diagnostics of each container, and ordered, "Theo, call all hands."

Theo clicked the shipwide com system on his personal comptech. "All hands, muster amidships." His call echoed slightly through the big bay.

One by one, the crew began to appear through hatches in the deck and bulkheads, and on walkways above.

There was the pilot, Barry, and the coxun, Mark, who was also a mechanic of a fairly technical order. Gaylord, the magnetologist, and Wade, an electrical specialist. Clark, of course, and Bonnie, the medic. Soon Axell, the squirrely computer guy, appeared with Pocket, who was in charge of generally keeping the inside of the ship in order and the cargo secure. Loading and unloading, that sort of thing. And there was Theo, the first mate, who was also an engineer.

Finally Kip Singleton ducked his completely hairless head through the galley hatch. He was the cook who talked to himself and who practically ran the place. He shaved his head every day, because he had a paranoia about getting hair into the food. The crew liked to tease him about his eyebrows, and Pocket was taking bets about how soon it would get to Kip and the cook would shave them off.

I didn't know them well and probably never would. We'd been fifteen months in cryosleep together, which gets you stiff legs and bizarre dreams, but nobody to stand at your wedding. Mostly I hung around Clark or Pocket and sometimes Bonnie, who liked to talk to me about my least favorite subject: my famous mother. I didn't like that topic of conversation, but Bonnie was sweet and star-struck and I didn't have the heart to brush her off. Or tell her the truth about my mother.

Everyone visibly stiffened when the Colonial Marine squad joined us. There were four men and one woman, specially trained for space missions, and they cut quite a swath through the mismatched ship's crew. The soldiers wore crisp matching field uniforms with special body-hugging padding in a head-to-toe brick-red color. Red wasn't the kind of color soldiers usually wore for field work on Earth, so they looked alien in their own way. Then again, they were entering an alien environment. This was my first clue that the planet's surface out there must be red.

Soon they were all here, and Bonnie was the last to arrive, *sans* her moonstruck mouse.

The whole mission was only going to take a matter of hours, not days, then another fifteen months in cryo to get back to Earth. By the time we got back, babies would be toddlers, stocks would have surged and plunged, and the multiple-murder case I'd pursued for three years would've become history, along with me. The precinct had given me the time off and counted it only as two weeks vacation.

This wasn't the kind of place where anybody in his right mind wanted to stay more than a few hours, and only if necessary. I'd seen the reports of the creatures we were here to destroy. I'd read the account, what few existed. Somehow these animals managed to take perfectly secure operations and skilled field personnel and turn them into shredded wheat in remarkably short time.

"Okay, this is the drill," Clark began, falling easily into "captain" mode. He was a long-distance hauler and the long calm ride was his nature as well as his job. "We are now on the planet's surface. Nobody leaves the ship without permission, you all know that. Permission can only be given by myself or Theo. Can I have a screen?"

Theo tapped his hand-held link to the ship's systems, and a screen whined right down out of a slot in the structure of the walkway above us. I guess they were all over the place on a ship like this.

I hunched my shoulders, ready to see a dark and ugly landscape overrun by wickedness, creatures more malignancy than life, a whole new kind of black plague.

The screen activated, giving us a picture of the immediate area around the ship, outside on this remote planet called Rosamond. The ship's scanners moved slowly across the land.

I squinted, looking for hazards and horrors.

Instead, around us was a peaceful alien landscape, with settled black pathways running between red pillars of various diameter that might be a forest, or might be a cathedral. Where was the pestilence? Where was the befoulment?

Clark stepped to the screen, which was as wide as his arm was long and gave us all a good view of whatever the *Vinza's* visual trackers could see, based on line-of-sight.

"The scientists' camp is inside the ship's automatic protection perimeter. Here you can see it just down about a half-kilometer from where we've landed."

He stood to the side of the screen and pointed at a humpy little village of pre-fab protective living quarters, the kind that deployed themselves, drilled themselves into the ground for anchorage, and had been tested in every possible land environment on Earth, including the Gobi desert and the Antarctic shelf. Shaped like upside-down bowls and ribbed with hyperflexion scissor-arches, they were as close to impervious to outside forces as was humanly possible to construct with current science. Once locked down, if the users were careful, no known animal could break in, including humans.

There was no one walking around out there, nobody coming out of the hyperflex huts to meet us. Pretty strange, after so many months in isolation. I'd have expected a welcoming committee. Not a soul came forward. "I don't see any movement," Theo commented. "No aliens . . . "

"No anybody, it looks like," Clark confirmed. "If there were aliens, the ship's auto-defense would be firing right now. So we can assume it's safe out there for an initial scouting."

I noticed that the settlement huts were colored the same as the landscape—my anticipated brick-red with black and yellow horizontal streaks. So somebody had been thinking ahead, because all the huts were pre-fabricated on Earth.

"Our orders are, first, to remove and, second, to destroy," Clark went on. "We stabilize our primary site, which means the ship and the immediate hundred yards in any direction, we do *not* have any more surprises—" The crew chuckled and rolled their eyes, still nerve-racked. "We probe out with our pre-assigned landing party, you know who you are, we collect these science geeks, Rory counts heads, and we secure them inside the *Vinza*. Rory has mug shots and I.D. codings for all these people and it'll be up to us to help him account for them. The whole operation shouldn't take more than maybe ten hours. Then we deploy the automated platoon of poison-packers and we fly back home while they do their job for the next eleven and a half months, but that's somebody else's problem, which makes me real happy."

"Question," Gaylord interrupted. "Are there forty-two or fifty-two of these people? I'm getting conflicting reports."

"Rory, why don't you answer that."

I straightened up. I hadn't expected any questions directed at me. "There are fifty-two of them, if they're all still alive. They're all science-oriented, specialists and interns, students, all hand-picked by my mother for this mission. They shouldn't give us any resistance."

"How can we evac fifty-two people and all their gear in ten hours?"

"Because we're not taking their gear," I said. "We're just taking them and the clothes they're wearing and any babies they might've had while they were here. Which, if they're smart, will be none."

"Will they go for this?" Bonnie asked.

"They'll have to," Clark said. "After the planet's sterilized, their gear and all their data will be retrieved in a calm manner, on a clean planet which will be under perfect control."

"What if they don't want to leave their stuff here?"

"Nobody asked them."

Silence fell, at least for a few long moments.

Finally Theo broke the tension. "How much do we know about these bug-things?"

Clark shrugged. "Big, ugly, gooey, fast, mean, aggressive, and sneaky."

"Lawyers," I grumbled.

An unexpected ripple of laughter made me suddenly self-conscious. I was a stranger here. Their reaction surprised me, made me uneasy. I froze in place, not wanting to blow it. I didn't need them to like me. I needed them to accept me for the duration.

"We're not sticking around to get fleeced," Clark went on. "The whole evac-deploy shouldn't extend past midnight. This

seems real simple and it should be. We're going down in daylight just after dawn, which is the safest time. Have all of you
done your homework on these aliens we're going to be *scrupu-*
lously avoiding?"

Everybody nodded. I watched them, their twitches, their eye
movements, the sulky postures. They hadn't all reviewed the
tapes like they were supposed to. Everyone one of their faces
looked like a mug shot.

"We have the Marines to take care of us," Clark went on,
"and Rory to help corral his mother, who runs this camp down
here. You've all heard of Jocasta Malvaux. Real powerful scientist, hobnobs in high circles. Once she complies, they'll all fall
into place. After that, we deploy the poison-packers and split.
Colonel MacCormac, you got anything to add?"

The Marine commander, a cylinder with no hair and powder-
blue eyes like an Alaskan dog, stepped forward. His voice was
fairly high for a man, and had a surprising gentility about it,
but that was the only soft thing about him and I didn't buy it
for a cover. "Contamination resistance is number one," he said.
"This ship and the surrounding area remains under heavy guard
and twelve-point automatic surveillance the whole time. The
ship's auto-defense will protect us if we don't make any mistakes. Nothing sneaks aboard. One egg can destroy a ship. It's
happened before. That's why we're evacuating and leaving the
robotic poison-packers to hunt down every last one of these
bastards."

"Do we know what they eat?" Bonnie asked. "I mean, do
they eat . . . us?"

"There's no record that they eat humans," Clark said. "We
don't know what they consume. Maybe nothing."

"Um . . . "

Everyone waited, but Bonnie suddenly got shy.

"Go ahead, girl," Clark said. "Speak up."

She flushed in the cheeks, but met the challenge. "Creatures that big and active have to consume something. They're too thin and bony to store much."

"Sounds fragile," Gaylord commented.

"I wouldn't bet on that," MacCormac warned. "Making assumptions like that is what got a whole squad of Colonial Marines slaughtered."

I looked at the thick-necked, strong, bull-like man and at his other seven human tanks, trying to imagine what could get past them. I was suddenly glad none of them had been in the galley when the fox bat broke free, given that shoot-through-the-ship thing and all. I could only guess that was why they weren't allowed to carry projectile weapons while the ship was in space. Not that they weren't armed anyway, with nerve neutralizers and shockers and just plain blades.

Suddenly I felt foolish for pulling my plasma pistol out of storage and forgetting why it was put away in the first place. I'd lost my cool. In hindsight, I was embarrassed about that.

MacCormac unclipped an unassuming blue cylinder from his belt and held it up. "This is a canister of base. Anybody who's ever worked in a kitchen knows that dumping baking soda on acid will neutralize the acid. These animals have been known to spit or spray acid if their bodies get ruptured. Everybody in the landing party will carry a canister of base. If any acid gets on you or the person next to you, spray this on him. It'll cut the effect till we can get medical treatment. Miss Bardolf here has been trained for treating acid burns."

Bonnie didn't look anywhere near as confident in her skills as MacCormac wanted us to believe. Her wide blue eyes batted around uneasily at us as if she were hoping nobody quizzed her.

Before those thoughts solidified too much, Clark asked, "Colonel, would you please give us a test firing of the auto-protection system?"

"Yes, sir." MacCormac did a sharp right turn to a fancy-ass control station with about a thousand little touch-plates, stations of which I happened to know there were only six on the entire ship. Executed in a bright, polished, yellow metallic, these "gold cores" were total-system access, and those who knew the right things could do almost anything from them. If the helm area or any other critical area ended up contaminated or depressurized, the ship could even be launched, steered, landed, loaded, and unloaded from any of the gold cores. Now MacCormac used the system to cause a deep rumbling in the body of the ship. Energy flowed from the otherwise recumbent magnetic reaction chambers and popped out some kind of deployment array high over our heads, on the outer shell of the *Vinza*.

On the screen, the view of the landscape and the camp huts turned a sharp, disturbing blue-green. An electronic buzz sent us all grabbing for our ears, then ended in a hard *snap*. Then the blue-green color faded back to the natural golden crunch of the planet.

"That's a field of bubble pellets carrying charged waves," MacCormac said. "It won't kill humans, but you'll be plenty bruised after that kind of punch. If you get caught in a volley, move *toward* the ship. The charges are most powerful at the widest perimeter."

"It won't kill humans?" Bonnie asked.

"But it's DNA-coded to cook anything that isn't human over the weight of five pounds," the colonel said. "Hopefully we won't be here long enough to charbroil any native herds of cattle or whatever lives here."

Bonnie looked worried. "Five pounds . . . you mean ordinary innocent animals can just wander in and get killed?"

"Yes, ma'am, that's right. We had to set the weight limit to account for certain growth levels of the creatures we're avoiding.

We won't be here long enough to do much damage. As long as we don't dump anything that attracts the local fauna—"

"We're not going to be down there long enough for any engagements," Clark said before anybody got the same thoughts Bonnie was having. "We'll go down in broad daylight. We're going to keep as tightly to our schedule as possible. We'll be gone before dusk, and the alien infestation'll be neutralized before any other human being ever sets foot back on the planet. These critters adapt fast, so I've got the latest formulation of the pesticide aboard, loaded onto the PPs, programmed to go after any species that's not DNA matched to the planet, leaving every other species alone. Dead aliens, healthy planet." He glanced around, making eye contact with each of the crew, then nodded. "Deploy, y'all."

As the crew moved away from Clark, I moved toward him and in a moment we were as good as alone in the middle of the bay and its cargo of enormous rectangular green containers.

"My mother's not going to go along with this," I said.

His expression didn't change, but his eyes got a little twinkle of trouble. "Then we'd better not tell her we used her research to come up with the current formulation."

"Yeah . . . let's not tell her that," I agreed.

"PlanCom should've sent synthetics in to do this research instead of a bunch of overeducated dweebs."

I shook my head. "Mother's the Dweeb Queen. Dweebs flock to her. PlanCom couldn't get the rights without giving my mother and her team the chance to study here. They wanted to go. She's influential. She wouldn't make the mission happen unless she and her little parade of sycophants were approved for infiltration." I got a chill and squeezed my shoulders.

"What's wrong?" Clark asked.

I looked him square in the eyes. "You keep talking about how easy this is going to be."

"Well, that's my job. A captain's supposed to be able to sound confident even if his shorts are on fire."

"Know anything about this planet? What kind of terrain is out there past what we can see?"

"In this region, rocky, semi-desert part of the year, fairly dry, hot, some plant growth. Livable, breathable, could be better and hopefully will be some day." He paused, musing. "This planet is one in about eight million, Rory. A livable, breathable planet with two oceans, that won't even need much terraforming . . . hell, another decade of atmospheric modification, and humans can move right in. We can actually live on it now, if we don't run marathons. We won't even have to destroy any indigenous species. You know how rare that is in the reachable galaxy?"

"I really don't." Translation: *I really don't care.*

"Get out of Milwaukee once in a while," he said. "A planet the right size, the right distance from a sun, with an atmosphere and a moon . . . hell, it's worth hundreds of trillions just in the arable land. That's not even starting with the mineral rights, the oceanographic advantages, the value in alien botanicals and native fauna for medical advancement . . . it makes you dizzy, all the things we can do with a place like this. Hell, we've found a living planet that won't be hurt at all if we live on it! We can have a second Earth up and running, and not in a hundred years after fortunes are spent on it, either. I'm talking ten, twelve years, if this crew does its job right this week. We got paradise here, except for this infestation we're here to stamp out. We come, we kill, we claim."

"How does this hunter-killer, poison-packer part stay inside the Alien Species Act?" I asked. "My mother and fifteen senators hammered that out. It's even got a subsection called the 'Malvaux Amendment.' It sure doesn't allow for killing off entire species just to get a claim on a planet."

"*Indigenous* species," he corrected. "Read the fine print. These things aren't from here. They're aliens."

"So are we."

He smiled and nodded. "Guess so. You never heard of a range war?"

"Has anybody ever found out where they come from? What they're doing here?"

"Nobody knows. They're cosmic hitchhikers."

I don't like mysteries. Maybe that's what drove me to get into law enforcement. We'd tried to do our homework—me included—but there wasn't much homework to be done. Not much was known about these animals we were here to exterminate. Of course, that was why my mother and her team were doing their dangerous work—to find out the things nobody knew about these aliens.

Clark shifted on his feet. "If this works out, it'll be my last mission. I'm sub-contracted for an estimated percentage of the mineral rights in advance. And they estimated high. The crew gets huge bonuses, and I get that, plus a cut of the profits. If it goes lower, I keep my percentage. If it goes higher, I get further dividends. Pal, if this planet works out, I'm set for life. Hey, how often do you get to be a hero and get rich? I can quit peddling bulk for a living, finally make good on that plantation."

"You and your plantation."

"Hey, we can do a lot worse than sit in the beautiful southwestern desert and grow guayule and sunflowers, then leave the land to our kids."

I broke out a little laugh. "What is this 'we' shit? We don't have kids."

"You need some. A nice chubby wife, and kids."

"Kids—I can't handle a bat! Kids."

I watched him for a moment, and tipped my head critically.

"I don't see you in a Panama hat, sucking on a big cigar and watching your fields grow."

"Well, you're gonna, bud. Get used to it."

"What is it you want to grow? Wahoo?"

"Guayule," he said, getting the "ee" on the end. "Naturally hypoallergenic latex. Medical applications, space industry, military, transportation, colonization . . . and you've always wanted to quit schlepping bad guys and come live with Nancy and me on our rubber farm and help me raise my kids. This is your dream . . . repeat after me. I, Rory Malvaux, dream of rippling fields of latex plants . . . "

"And you, Clark Sparren, are hallucinating."

He smiled. Caught up in his mental picture, I smiled too. No more Milwaukee-to-Chicago crime corridor? No more dirty streets, crime scenes, and outlines of dead guys? Was I ready to say goodbye to my whole identity? Clark thought I was. Of course, Clark thought I should never have said hello. He liked being in control. Nobody could control the streets.

I thought about these alien animals which would be the hair in our pudding on this trip. "How long have 'they' been on this planet?"

"Sometime between the first scouting androids, about eight years ago, and three years ago when the PlanCom returned to stake its claim. Sixty-two advance scouts and settlers were killed before they figured out these were the same monsters we've run into before on one of the mining spacelanes. That's when your mom was brought in to analyze the situation and decided she wanted a stab at research. She's had her chance, and now we're calling it quits and taking over. We think we know all we need to know about them for our purposes. We're not zoologists, y'know."

Why was I still sweating? I wiped my face with the leather jacket, then remembered it had just had a bat wrapped in it. I needed a few more seconds to get past that.

Clark glanced around to make sure we were out of earshot, or at least interest, of the crew, who were bustling around us the whole time. "I want you to deal with your mother for us. Don't waste a lot of time discussing her opinion. Discussions give people the wrong idea. No sense opening a carton we know is sour. Just tell her what's happening and strongly advise her to comply without a fuss."

"She hates being told what's happening unless she's doing the telling."

He rubbed his shoulder where the bat had driven him into the wall. "Maybe try to appeal to her motherly qualities?"

"She has no motherly qualities."

He grimaced. "You serious?"

"She protected her cubs until I was old enough to pour my own milk. After that, raising myself and my sister were my job. Mother became famous and I became screwed."

"Geez. Sorry."

"Nah."

"There has to be some way to get to her."

Annoyed at the load he was putting on my shoulders, and at myself for allowing him to convince me to come in the first place, I tried to turn away. He caught my sleeve.

He fell quiet for a moment of thought. "How about the leadership instinct? Her people will panic or get scared or confused, y'know, crushed, if she doesn't deliver a positive experience—"

"She's not a Girl Scout, Clark."

"Tough nut to crack, huh?"

"Accent on 'nut.'"

"Yikes. Okay . . . go do like we taught you to suit up and we'll go ahead out there. This won't take long. There's only one ending."

The conversation was over. He was already working his palmtech to do captain things. I was already out of his thoughts, his attention fixed on whatever the little screen was telling him as he cradled it in the palm of his hand and did a thousand things at once. We'd known each other for almost fifteen years and I knew the posture.

He'd done both of us favors by asking me to come along. He needed a legal officer, and I needed a break. I'd just wrapped up a murder investigation, the revenge murder of a fellow officer, his wife, three kids, and their two dogs. I'd jumped from street cop to plainclothes detective just to pursue the violent snake who'd slaughtered them slowly, starting with the dogs. For three years I chased the bastard across two continents. The idea was to bring him to justice. Instead, I cut his arms off and let him bleed to death. Oops.

The department covered it up. The official story was that the guy's arms were sliced off when he tried to escape across a farm co-op and got caught in a shredder. Nobody had any problem keeping that secret. I'd always been a loner, but the whole department stuck up for me anyway. Go figure. I'd have let me hang for it.

Clark took me out of the media storm by bringing me along on this mission. The P.D. was glad of it—they'd shoved me out the door. The idea was, I guess, that by the time we came back from forty-odd months in space, I'd be yesterday's news. Whether I wanted to be here or not, I had to be, for the good of everybody else.

I watched Clark, standing there in his blue flight suit with the lapel pin of a cloisonné bluebird which his wife had made for him in art class. He kind of looked like a big blue bird with a red crest. I appreciated him for his ability to live a utilitarian life of routine and practicality while still hanging on to universal visions. I couldn't do it. My visions never went past my shoes.

"This might not go the way you want it to," I warned.

He looked at me. "It will."

I stepped closer, to make sure none of the bustling crew around us could hear. "You can have this planet any time you want, but you and your crew don't get your big bonuses without my official certification that's it's clear of human life. If we can't account for every one of those researchers, dead or alive, then I don't sign off on the deployment of your poison platoon. I'm not here to do you a favor. If I don't certify, you don't collect."

I felt like a ghoul, silhouetted from behind by the brighter lights of the loading area, which now was bustling with active crew as Gaylord and Theo directed their preparation for what would come over the next few hours.

Clark squinted in mental discomfort and clearly some disappointment. Maybe he had expected me to bend to the occasion in his favor. If you want rules bent, ask a friend.

"Okay, Sherlock," he accepted. In the hangar bay light, his blue eyes matched the bluebird pin. "As long as you understand that I'll do anything I have to do to save this planet for humanity."

Several bad seconds passed. For this brief period, we didn't understand each other at all.

I started to turn away while he was still looking at me. After a few steps, though, I turned again and asked, "What did my mother say when PlanCom first told her about the evacuation?"

As if I'd asked him something complicated, he shifted to his other foot. Finally he pressed his lips flat and kind of shrugged.

"Oh . . . not much."

CHAPTER THREE

Moonset. A strange word for morning.

In the mist-veiled sky, a single green moon was too large for poetry. This planet's idea of daylight was grim. The greenish-yellow sun shone with an angry glaze, offering no comfort the way Earth's sun did. The environment was almost urban. There were so many tall blood-red pillars ranging to the horizon that we might as well have been in a city center with skyscrapers so close together that sunlight couldn't shine in unless the sun were directly overhead. Gauzy white topgrowth coiled and draped from pillar to pillar, high up at the tops, creating a rain forest effect and a world of patchy permanent shadows beneath. It looked something like the decorations I'd seen in a church during a wedding, as if human hands had carefully placed them, then forgotten them to become shredded and stale with time.

Corners, passages, holes, gullies, caves with no visible ends . . . it was a gory red world, redder than a barn, redder than the Grand Canyon, but not the color of blood. Not that kind of red. This landscape of towers, all diameters imaginable from pencil-thin to big as buildings, were a strange glossy red. When my space-dizziness faded a little and I could blink a clear field of vision, I realized that the columns were not stone at all in the usual sense. In fact they were translucent enough to see through all but the biggest ones. They were like rubies or art glass. The planet was the ultimate in rose-colored glasses.

White veils and red glass towers. No signs of anything alive.

"Where are they?" Pocket asked.

"They're not answering any hails."

"They could be hunkered down. Or maybe their comm quit working."

"They should've still heard the ship land, for Christ's sake."

"Yeah . . . "

While Clark and Gaylord spoke to each other in front of me, I couldn't find it in myself to speak up in this cathedral of red columns. The environment seemed almost holy in its imposing size and oddness.

We were only about ten feet from the ship, and had paused to take some readings and put out some feelers. Despite knowing that the ship would protect us within a certain perimeter, I couldn't settle my stomach. Imagine being on a whole different planet than Earth. I was the living inheritor of a stunning scientific advancement. My nerves danced with appreciation.

"Rory, you coming?"

Clark's imposing form was flanked on one side by MacCormac and on the other by a compact bundle of muscle named Sergeant Berooz. I noted that Clark's red hair disappeared into the red stone pillar behind him, making him appear to have a face without a head on top.

I felt the path floor with my shoe sole. It was spongy moisture underneath but not on top. I stooped down and brought up a handful of the planet.

"Rory, what's up?" Clark appeared over me. "We can't move ahead without you."

I offered him the sample. "Look at this stuff."

"Gravel. So what?"

"It's not gravel. It's billions of little skeletons."

He leaned closer to study the remains of some kind of small creature, desiccated to its elements, broken by time and . . . by trampling? What had trampled them?

"It's the consistency of tree bark mulch," I said, "but it's all skeletons."

"Skulch," he dubbed. "Yucky."

"Dead's dead," I commented.

He looked around. The surface of the land, everywhere we looked, was frosted with the remains of uncountable trillions of these tiny dead creatures. "Well, don't take it personally. Earth beach sand is basically the same thing, y'know. Little broken up shells and all."

I stood up and dropped the handful, then brushed my hand clean. "Yeah, let's keep telling ourselves that."

He laughed, but not very convincingly.

I reached out and touched one of the glass pillars. It was so narrow that my fingernails touched the heel of my hand, yet the pillar reached up to the same height as those with the girths of office buildings, and I could see a reflection of myself in its polished face. Too bad I wasn't more to reflect. I was the average of averages. Nothing special. Lost in a crowd of two. There was not and never had been anything the slightest bit interesting or striking about me. I had an Everyman face and a shadow of a beard I'd never really been able to grow into anything but a shadow. For a while, I'd tried to have a mustache, just to set myself apart, but it came in wimpy and I gave up when my fellow officers started calling me "Fuzz." If anybody was going to call me "Fuzz," it would be me, and for the right reasons, dang it.

Oh, well, I guess everybody can't be Clark Gable. Or Clark Sparren, for that matter. Besides, being the average guy, somebody who could get lost in a crowd of three, had helped me quite a bit during my undercover days.

Fifty-odd feet in the air, the skinny, glossy wand reached as high as the others and provided a support for the hat of gauze. I felt as if I were trapped at the bottom of a pencil box. The sun didn't shine very well down into the pillared landscape, but was always at some angle, creating a constant prism effect of banded light. There were no corners. Everything was curvy and round, bending down or upward, dipping and swirling in every direction. No angles, except the bands of sunlight stabbing through and being refracted.

"What a place . . . "

"It's a PlanCom kind of place. Dust bowls, glaciers, deserts, moons—you name it, we'll tame it."

"But you're right . . . it could be a paradise."

"Ain't I, though? You okay? Got legs?"

"I got rags with iron balls on the ends."

"Welcome to space travel," he said, and helped me to my feet.

"Hope I don't have to run."

Run . . . where? From here I saw about a dozen holes in the bottoms of the thicker glass columns, like cave mouths except that they opened up on other mouths. Then, up against the biggest of the columns were pathways shaped like half-tubes, like endless waterslides rolling senselessly as the eye could follow through the forest of glass.

"What carves a landscape like this?" I asked.

"Water," Clark said. "Lots of it, about twelve million years ago. Pretty much gone now, except for some subterranean flows. They can only be accessed with sophisticated drilling and plumbing, and the flows have to be purified for human consumption. PlanCom's subcontracting the job out to a cousin of mine."

Bottling our nerves, we came down the *Vinza's* ramp and the ramp dutifully closed behind us as soon as the last foot was off. They weren't kidding about security.

I followed the two lead Marines and Clark in that order, and the stocky Polynesian magnetologist, Gaylord, then the bosun, Pocket, right in front of me like usual. Gaylord didn't seem outwardly smart, but he had to be. He was responsible for all the zillion jobs done by magnets aboard the *Vinza*, including those pertaining to her complex propulsion system. In front of me bobbed Pocket's ropy blond ponytail. Pocket was detail-oriented and in a constant state of re-organization, and give or take compulsive gambling, was bright and in charge of his universe. He was also in charge of the details of this evacuation. Didn't seem like a bad job, all in all, being a bosun. If I'd had the brains, maybe I'd have liked his job. I like jobs that have beginnings, middles, and ends.

As we passed between two very large columns that were very close together, we had to squeeze to single file through a quite claustrophobic passage. When I came out, Sergeant Berooz stood escort for the first half of the line. He dipped his shoulder to make eye contact with the rearguard, a movement which caused me to bend sideways out of his way. My right foot skidded off balance and I started to slide down a dropoff. At the point of almost no return, Berooz caught my arm and put me back in place as if I were a doll falling off a shelf. I laced my hand into his field vest and clung gratefully for a few seconds.

Only when I regained balance did I look down into the grade and discover that I couldn't see a bottom. "Go down and get my stomach."

"Don't want to lose you," he said. "Looks like some kind of a sinkhole."

"Thanks . . ."

"No problem. Payback for when you found my lucky bandanna." He tilted his weapon so I could see the yellow cowboy bandanna with white swirls, which he had snugly tied around his wrist. "That was great how you helped me to think my way back to it."

"It had to be somewhere," I said. "All we had to do was eliminate everywhere else in the universe."

"Neat trick. You answered my prayer."

"I thought that was God's job."

He grinned and fell in beside me as we moved after the others, more cautiously now.

Behind me came Axell and Mark, the computer specialist and one of the mechanics. Axell was a misplaced forty-year-old egghead with an overbite, who could dismantle half the ship and put it back together without losing a single microbolt, but had trouble using a fork at dinner. Mark was a tousled-haired kid who'd run away from home and joined the space fleet. He delighted in sending communiqués home to his parents and crowing about not having to live with them anymore. Despite a punky, immature attitude, he had a mechanical aptitude that earned him a place on this fairly exclusive ship. At first, I'd rolled my eyes at them, but after watching them work for a while, I quit doing that. Between them, the odd couple knew more technical wizardry than most hundred other people put together.

After them came Bonnie with her medical pack, and two more Marines, Private Carmichael and Corporal Edney. Carmichael seemed out of place to me. He looked as if he'd just entered high school and was wearing the Marine uniform and sensor helmet for Halloween. Even next to Edney, a steroidal female bodybuilder, Carmichael seemed frail. Still, he was a Marine in this elite unit, so there had to be something about him that was qualified for combat.

Their sensor helmets were more caps than helmets, very scaled-down and easier to wear than a full-sized helmet. They weren't hard hats, but made of strong webbing, only slightly bulkier than baseball caps, with a sun-shading brim over the eyes, and embedded with nano-technology for communication, warning, and surveillance. I had one myself back home; most cops did, but not as fancy as the ones these commandoes wore. In fact, these Marines' caps were new issue, colored in the red-black stripes of the landscape around here, as were their uniforms. As they walked ahead of us, weapons poised, they melted into the panorama of columns and caves.

The rest of the crew would stay inside the *Vinza*, guarded at all times by the other Marines, also bristling with weapons. I envied them. I'd hoped for some nice bright sunlight and maybe a fresh cool breeze, but here I was with indirect light, no breeze at all, dry heat, and the smell of stale bananas. Not a bit of green. Not a leaf, not a spore.

I looked up at the hanging white gauze at the fading green-banded moon.

"What's the moon got to do with it, Clark?" I asked.

A pace ahead of me, Clark scanned the interior of a suspicious tunnel. "With what?"

"You said something about a planet with a moon. How rare it is."

"Didn't know you were listening. Having a moon stabilizes the rotation of a planet. If there's no moon, a planet wobbles on its axis and the weather goes nutzo. Tides, storms, polar changes . . . real wreck. Life would have a hell of a time surviving. We've tried to put colonies on some of those, but it makes for a miserable existence. All kinds of limitations on agriculture, livability, you name it. It's so hard to live that no progress can be made, so there's no point trying." He pointed up at the sky. "Gotta have that moon going for you. Gaylord, how close did we get to our mark?"

"The location of the original drop-off was forty meters north, just through those thicker spires," Gaylord said. "Good landing, considering."

"Nice job, Barry," Clark spoke into his wristcom. "You put us on the dot. Stand by."

"*Standing by, oh Great Red Leader.*"

Clark held up a hand. Everybody except the Marine vanguard froze in place, including me, instinctively. "Freeze" I can do. The Marines in front fanned out, their enormous weapons first, clearing the way. Their boots made a *crush-crush* noise on the slippery footing of dead critters.

"*Sparren*, Vinza. *Any sign of them?*" Theo radioed.

"Not so much as a food canister," Clark reported. "We can see the huts, but there's no movement. Try them again on the big com."

"*I've been trying. No response continent-wide. Dead air.*"

"No beacons? Locators? Auto-feeds?"

"*Just yours.*"

As I moved up behind Clark, he knew I was there. "Why don't we just go up and knock?" I asked.

"We will, but I just want to do this slowly and carefully, is all."

"Why aren't they answering?"

"Maybe they moved," he said. "Over the mountains or someplace else."

I didn't fall for it. "They should still be able to hear us."

He raised his com unit and spoke into it again. "Attention, Malvaux Research Team. This is Captain Clark Sparren. Anybody picking this up?"

The com emitted a soft buzz, but no voices. There was a sense of a signal's going out, reaching down through these many slides, into the empty distance.

"They're dead," Gaylord murmured very quietly. "This is bad." Fear glowed from his dark eyes and gave a pasty grayness to his bronze island complexion.

He glanced at me, then purposefully averted his eyes.

Clark digested that comment. "Jury's still out."

I don't know whether he was speaking for my benefit or not. Gaylord had just proclaimed the likely death of the only relatives I had. I think it bothered him more than it bothered me.

Clark stepped away. I reached out, caught his sleeve, and pulled.

"Tell the truth," I demanded. "When was the last time anybody contacted this outpost? When's the last time anybody heard my mother's voice?"

He licked his lips. "Been a while."

"How long?"

"This isn't the time for this, Rory. We're here. They're not. We have to find them. We have to confirm their status and evac anybody who's not—"

My face heated up and so did my tone. "Is that why we're really here? To confirm they're dead?"

"Nobody said anything like that."

"It's the *not* saying, Clark."

"Would I have brought you here if I thought they were dead? I could've taken anybody with a badge to be the legal officer. I asked for you, remember?"

I had no good answer. During the pause, he pulled away and crunched down the path of skeletal mulch, and I followed. The Marines and crew fell into formation again around us. The Marines carried some kind of new weapon I hadn't seen before, compact personal firing units with carefully balanced power packs. These things weren't exactly guns in the conventional sense. I was hoping to see a demonstration eventually.

From here, at the top of a sloping path between the forest of red columns of all imaginable diameters, we could see the humpy bowl shaped huts which to all but human eyes— the designers hoped—blended fluidly into the environment. Actually, except for the shape, they did. They were the only round things in sight, which was all that set them apart. The color pattern, though, went against the bowl shape and actually mimicked the horizontal stripes of black and yellow on the natural columns. Somebody had done a pretty good job.

"I don't see anybody," Bonnie said, her voice very tentative.

"They're not answering hails," Pocket confirmed. "I been broadcasting right along."

Gaylord somehow made his large body smaller as we carefully moved down the slope. "Maybe their coms are down."

Pocket made an unforgiving huff. "They still should've heard the ship land. I'm for blowing this burgh. If we can't find them electronically, we can't find them."

"I'm for that," Mark echoed. "We should split. We can't be Superman for everybody." Mark always wanted to do the least work he could get away with. He had a roadhouse singing voice and entertained the crew with his folk songs, but that was the only thing he was enthusiastic about. Everything else, he did exactly what he had to do and not a lick more. He was out here with us because Clark wanted to make him perform.

"We still have to account for them," Clark said. "Or satisfy Rory that they're no longer alive."

"This place is creepy," Bonnie said, voicing what we were all feeling.

"It's only the silence that's creepy," I suggested.

"Don't worry, ma'am," MacCormac said to her. "We're still well inside the ship's protection grid."

Despite his assurances, I sensed that nobody felt secure.

I wasn't that sure what we were facing. Clark and the Marines hadn't exactly been forthcoming about details, and I suspected that was because there wasn't much positive and they didn't want to be negative. Confidence was a tool. I, for one, believe in full disclosure.

"Sure is hot." Gaylord wiped the sweat out of his eyes.

Pocket kept his eyes fixed on his hand-held scanners. "Hundred four in the shade. I'll take bets on how cold it gets in the caves."

"No you won't," Clark warned.

We fell to silence again as we entered the camp of half-round huts, each big enough to house up to five people in fair comfort. For a moment we paused at the outskirts, just looking. The Marines scouted and Pocket scanned, but there was no sign of anything living. No movement, no readings.

The camp was in permanent shadows, overcast by the gauze hanging above. Four of the nine huts carried veils of fallen gauze, which was dissolving slowly as if melting over the shapes of the huts. To say there was no sign of life might be inaccurate . . . now I could see the evidence of bad housekeeping, if nothing more. Scattered clothing items, long abandoned, evidence of a fire long gone cold, and a pile of food containers.

As we cautiously entered the closet thing to a common center to the camp, I spotted four—no, five large lumps of the fallen gauze from above lying on the ground. What attracted me was that they were all shaped like bread dough, in seemingly tidy loafs.

"Look at the doors," Pocket pointed out. "They all look the same."

Every hut's sliding door was open about seven or eight inches, and obviously locked from the outside with clamps fixed to the scissor-arches.

"I don't like that," Clark said. "Big enough to look through, but not enough to enter or exit."

"Stay back, everyone," MacCormac ordered. "Berooz, recon that hut."

Sergeant Berooz thumped forward, leaving fat, booty foot-

prints in the skulch. I admired him for his forwardness. He
didn't peek inside, he didn't hesitate. He strode up aggressively,
shoved his weapon's muzzle into the eight-inch opening, and
clicked on the light beam to illuminate the inside. He watched
the little screen that saved him from having to actually stick his
face in there. As if it would fit.

"Sir, I got bodies," Berooz reported. "No life signs. No heat
signatures. All cold."

"What kind of bodies?"

"Seem to be human, sir, by the skull shapes."

"How many?" MacCormac asked.

"At least six."

"Oh, God," Bonnie murmured.

Clark glanced at me. "Let's get it open."

Berooz let his weapon pivot down on his harness, a smart device that let a soldier work with his hands without putting his
weapon on the ground or handing it over to someone else.
"Jaws," he requested.

Pocket pulled a portable hydraulic device from his backpack,
took a shallow breath, and did his duty by stepping through to
Berooz. Together they fitted the device, with its two pliers-like
jaws into the unwelcoming opening in the door panel, turned
the device on, and stepped back.

The jaws hummed for two seconds, then began to separate.
The squawl of protesting metal soon had us wincing, but not
for long. Five seconds, and the locks cracked. The doors were
free. Berooz moved in and slammed the panels aside.

The Marines went in first, Berooz and Edney together. It
didn't take long.

When they came back out, Berooz fought to control his expression and simply said. "It's clear. Four bodies, all human, all
dead, sir."

Clark looked a little sick, but he said, "I'll have a look."

I pushed between the others and caught his arm. "I'll do it."

"But they could be," he began, "your . . . "

"I'm a homicide detective. I've seen bodies before."

"Yeah, but they . . . " He stopped trying. "I'm real sorry about this. I didn't think it'd be this way."

"Didn't you?" Steeled with my own sense of reality, I forced myself to act as if I had no hesitation.

Tears of empathy ran down Bonnie's face as I passed her. Her face carried all the pain I was burying.

Or should've been.

I should've been feeling something, shouldn't I?

Much easier to keep moving. I didn't even pause at the door, but stepped all the way inside the hut. Berooz held his weapon so that the light source bounced off the far wall and cast a band of light on the contents of the pre-fab house. No, not a house . . . in its last use by humans, the hut had been something else.

My skin shrank as I entered the dim circular space. There was a stench, but in this dry heat the smell of decomposition was naturally diminished. Still, I recognized the odor of dead human flesh. There was no other scent like it. This hut would never be livable again.

Along the rim of the inner wall lay two human corpses directly in front of me, shrouded in a milky spun-cotton material. I steeled myself and started toward them. Something bumped my forehead. I jolted back and looked up, my hands pressed back against the wall of the hut.

I'd been bumped by a naked human foot. In the middle of the hut, suspended from a construction ring, hung a dead woman dangling by the neck. She had no clothing except panties and bra. Her face was mummified, like the rest of her, yet there was still a clear expression of desperate sadness in the set of the jaw, even though the jaw was twisted askew by the rope.

No, it wasn't a rope . . . it was the braided shreds of her clothing.

I reach up and stopped her from swinging. She'd swung enough for one millennium. "Sorry," I whispered.

The nearest body on the ground was wrapped loosely in that odd grayish shroud, like the forms outside. I knelt beside it and scooped the gray stuff away. It pulled like cotton candy, with only a pause for resistance, and it was slightly sticky and clung to my hand. It pulled against the partly decomposed body of a mutilated man. His skull and chest were large, bones bulky and obviously masculine. And there was a hole in the chest the size of a bowling ball.

My heart started to thump. The sternum was completely gone, along with about half his ribcage. On second look, some of the ribs were still here, but broken outward and hanging on only by filaments. I knew an explosion when I saw one. Something was in, and it came out on its own terms.

A tiny movement in my periphery made me blink and look at my own arm. The white-gray stuff was crawling up my sleeve.

"What—!" Instinctively I drew back. The gauze fibers snapped and recoiled. Embedded in the fibers were dark stringy items that I had mistaken for more fibers. They weren't. They were long ropy weevils with definite heads and tails if I looked closely. That was what made the gray haze in what was otherwise white fibrous material. They moved very slowly, but they moved.

I paused to think. After a few seconds, I went ahead and kept picking at the cotton, cord-weevils and all.

"Rory?" Clark called. "You okay in there?"

"Come on in, but be prepared."

Once he got past his initial reaction, I said, "They're all the same. Chests exploded. Except this woman up hanging here.

I think she hanged herself to avoid what happened to the others."

"What are they doing in here?" he asked. "It's the same out there. Two other huts have bodies. They couldn't get out, and nobody else could get in. Is it possible they locked themselves in?"

This was too weird. Had they locked themselves in or locked something else out? The locks were attached from the outside—were they bait? Was this punishment? Prison? Had the scientists gone crazy and had some kind of feud?

"How many bodies are in the other huts?"

"Four in one and three in the other."

I gazed up at him. "You know what happened to them, don't you?"

"Yeah."

"But there are also five outside the huts, wrapped in that gauzy stuff."

"It's not gauze. It's this planet's idea of maggots."

"Jesus . . . "

I moved to the next two bodies in the hut. They huddled together like the victims of Pompeii, braced against the side of the hut, one in the arms of the other, shrouded with thick gauze and only a few thin black weevils. Both had their chests bombed out. The one had held the other until his own time came. They had accepted their fates, unlike the woman hanging above. These were both men. Their faces still had flesh enough to see their features. They were broad-browed and handsome, with strands of straight raven-black hair. They each wore bright orange T-shirts that looked to me like sports team shirts. The torn fronts had white letters, but there was no way to read them now. Brothers? Was I witness here to a family tragedy?

"Wait a minute—" I stood up and looked at the woman who had hanged herself. "How'd she get up there?"

Clark looked around. "Nothing to climb on . . . "

I turned the woman's body like a bell. Her shrunken arms hung stiff, but her chest was unbroken and there were no weevils on her. They probably couldn't reach her up there. Her body had simply dried up.

"Do you think Bonnie could tell me how long this woman's been hanging here?"

"Probably. She must've worked on cadavers before. Bonnie! Brace yourself and come here."

There was a crunch of footsteps. Bonnie came in and made a terrible gasp at the sight. She clapped both hands to her mouth. "Oh—God—God—what—what happened to them! What—happened—to—them!"

"Shh!" Clark grabbed her by both arms. "Steady up! You know what happened."

"Oh—God—why—why are they in here like this? Who put them in here?"

Clark drew her to the middle of the hut. "Can you tell us how long this woman's been dead?"

I held the hanging woman still while Bonnie fought to compose herself, tears running down her face now. "It's okay," I reassured. "Her troubles are over. Let's get her down."

Grisly work, for sure. We cut the woman down, and had to be careful in handling her—she was ready to fall apart. This wasn't Clark's kind of work. He seemed very uneasy at the disrespect we had to show this woman as we lowered her stiffened corpse to the floor of the hut.

"Okay, Bonnie," I began. "I'm sorry to tell you this, but I need you to cut her open."

"Cut her open? Oh . . . you mean . . . " She made a motion on her own chest.

I nodded. "I need to know what's in there."

She grimaced in misery and opened her pack to expose a small surgical set.

While she worked, I crunched to the fourth body, this one very much alone, both arms and both legs twisted backward in the agony of a final throe. This one was a man, judging by its size and big hands, and seemed to be the most decayed. I pulled back the white gauze, which confirmed my guess by being completely free of black weevils. They had obviously finished with this one long ago and they were gone. Maybe they moved to other bodies, or maybe they went on their lives' way.

Bonnie's sniffs tapered off as she involved herself in her work. I tried to hover back from the work area, trying not to make her self-conscious as she did the ugly work I had asked of her.

Then, a silver flicker winked in Berooz's muzzle light, a flicker on the hanged woman's hand. It almost called to me. Moving slowly, not to disturb Bonnie, I turned the dead woman's bony hand over. The flicker was a brushed-satin platinum ring, very expensive, with a large marquis diamond and swirly black etchings around the band . . . a wedding ring. The bride's ring.

The hand fell apart, leaving the ring in my palm.

"Thanks," I responded quietly. "I'll take care of it." I put the ring in my breast pocket before anyone else could see.

As if she understood, the woman's contorted arm went slack and sank to the hut floor. So she was finally resting.

Tears still ran from Bonnie's eyes, but she was sternly doing her work. "About a year," she said.

I peeked at what she was doing. "What about . . . "

"It's there," she said, and pointed inside the woman's now-open chest cavity, at a shriveled and dried mass shaped like a carrot. "She killed herself before it matured."

"Jeez . . . " Clark murmured.

Bonnie looked up at him. "There's something else . . . she was pregnant."

The depths of sorrow that must have been played out in this

hut now communicated themselves to us as if they were fresh and immediate.

Bonnie started to cry, unable to hold it in anymore. "She didn't want to give birth to that thing before giving birth to her own child. Two things growing inside her . . . so sad . . . "

Somewhat coldly, I said, "Even sadder that she was here in the first place."

"How'd she get up there?" Clark asked again.

I looked at the ceiling.

"There's only one way," I said. "Somebody in here helped her."

Driven by sheer nerves, we took only nineteen minutes to catalogue the other bodies. The crew and Marines let me investigate first, before their boots and reactions disturbed any evidence. Bonnie followed me around, taking DNA samples for later, that is, after she got over her introduction to the black maggoty things. I looked for other details. A man with a pocket full of pictures of antique cars. Another man with military dog tags and cloisonné teeth—a fad from about twelve years ago. A woman with a diabetic maintenance armband. She wore a flight suit with a name tag: Sgt. Lorna Claver. All but two of them had something in common—they wore wristbands or anklets of white and red macramé cord, with black beads. Somebody had a hobby.

In fact, the two who didn't have these macramé bands were the two who had been dead the longest.

Every detail spoke to me. They were my best friends. All these dead people were my best friends. Live people . . . they come and go.

Finally, the last body, this one outside of the hut, lying in a cocoon. I pulled away at the wormy gauze to bear the mummy inside. Their stories would be much different in a moist environment.

"This is the most recent one," I said as Bonnie knelt beside me.

"How recent, do you think?"

"Not very . . . probably months, not weeks. It's a man. He walked with a limp from a leg injury. He also ate a lot of canned sliced carrots."

"How do you know that?"

"Because he threw up right over there."

"Oh . . . yes, he did, didn't he?" Bonnie's shoulders involuntarily hunched. "I admire that you can do this . . . put your hands into dead things and not be flustered."

"I'm a homicide detective. I have to be callous or I couldn't even sleep. I'd always be lying there thinking, 'Gee, I could be out there helping somebody.' There's always somebody to help. You run out of strength, you run out of pity . . . you never run out of helpless people."

Bonnie looked at me and studied my face until I wished she would turn away. I didn't like the spotlight.

"I really do admire you," she said. "You must be a lot like your mother. Strong, alert . . . perceptive, always seeing details other people miss."

"It's the training," I said sharply.

She retreated a little, and went back to looking at the decayed body in its cotton bedroll. "This was always my worst thing in medical school, and we always had clean, controlled environments. I guess maybe I went into the wrong field."

"Just because death bothers you? I like doctors who are bothered by death. Me, I look at dead guys all the time. If it's dead, it can't hurt you."

She looked up at the tops of the cathedral of pillars. "This must be the pupal stage of these . . . "

"Weevils," I supplied, so she didn't have to say maggots.

"Or maybe the adult stage," she went on, avoiding the word altogether. "The gauze in the sky must have some kind of microbes or eggs in it, waiting for their time. It's pure white up there, but down here it turns grayish because the parasites grow, and they're black. They must reproduce up there, on the tops of the columns. When the gauze falls, it turns into a natural protective cocoon and the young feed on whatever it falls on."

"If it falls on something dead."

"Or alive and they kill it."

"We know they feed on dead things," I said. "Things that feed on dead flesh don't eat live tissue."

"On *our* planet," she pointed out. "You're good at analyzing. Did your mom teach you?"

"I might've picked up a thing or two around the mansion."

She squeezed her shoulders with a rush of excitement. "It must've been just so stimulating to grow up with Jocasta Malvaux as your guiding force. She's so brilliant—she's made so many discoveries, and she's articulate enough to explain them to the public in all those books and articles and vids . . . I just love her way of describing strange wonders. It's true poetry."

"Uh-huh. Glad you enjoy it."

"Why didn't you become a researcher like your mom and your sister?"

"I wasn't born with the silver spoon of science in my mouth."

Behind us, the Marines kept changing position, checking out the location and keeping their eyes on the outskirts of the camp. I took a message from their posture. I'd seen SWAT teams and rangers, Special Forces and colonial security teams, but there was something different today. These Marines were twitchy and scared. I'd seen Clark's info-video of the animals we were avoiding, the things they did to humans and other animals, implanting the bodies of others with their young, then the young burst out . . . in damned little time, I noted. In just a few hours, the implanted seed managed to gain weight and develop into a head and tail with teeth, possessing the power of a shotgun. With that power, it would break out. In those huts, we had the result. Dead humans with bombed-out chest cavities.

And of course I'd seen the shadowy security recordings of the adult animals. The pictures weren't good—legs, arms, claws, whip-like tails, and flashes of a head shaped like a zucchini. There was a record—or was it just a theory—that humans did better against them if we weren't surprised by them, and if we faced them down properly, with the proper weapons. They could be killed, we knew that.

Beside me, Bonnie was beginning to shiver. The air was hot, so she was shaking with fear, not cold.

To distract her, I asked, "What about you? What are you doing out here among all these hard-boiled assholes? Shouldn't you be working in a quiet little petting zoo? Petting something?"

She smiled, softening her otherwise boyish features. "My education was privately funded by PlanCom. They put me through medical school. When I'm done in January, I'm indentured to the company fifteen years. It's working out great for me. At the end of it, I'll be a fully fledged family physician and I'll be able to open a private practice and already have the whole company as my patients."

"Save a bat, save the planet, huh?"

"Why not? Your mother would agree. Butterball's a beautiful little showpiece for the success of intervention."

"From what I saw on the ship, Butterball can take care of herself," I said. "I hate things that fly."

"Oh, you don't mean that."

"Yeah? Fly at me some time."

"You'll put your hand in decaying flesh, but you don't like birds and butterflies?"

"I don't like flying shit that bites. You can't keep your eye on 'em."

She sniffed and wiped her nose with the back of her hand, because her fingers and palm were caked with the remains of those who should never have been here in the first place. I'd insulted her in some way, I could tell.

Looking pale and unhappy, Clark came up to us and broke our need for further talk. "Well? Any conclusions before we stop pretending it's going the way we expected?"

I spared Bonnie the burden of going first. "All the bodies in the huts had their chests burst, except for the one woman. The bodies outside were killed by other means. One had some kind of segmented garrote around his neck. He was strangled. Two were speared through the body."

"By what?"

"I don't know yet. No sign of weapons. I don't know if the researchers went crazy and killed each other, or those aliens you're avoiding speared them."

"What about the other three?"

I glanced at the rest of the team over there, the twitchy Marines and the spooked ship's crewmen who were waiting unhappily in the dim midst of this death ring. I lowered my voice.

"They were pretty much ripped apart. One of them's in three pieces."

"How long ago?" Clark asked, burying a shudder.

"Different times," Bonnie spoke up. "In this arid environment, protected by the cocoons, the black parasites may have the luxury of taking their time. I'll have to let the medical computer analyze the tissue before we'll know for sure."

"I don't think we need to know," Clark said. "This doesn't look good for sticking around. They didn't last very long, did they? Rory, I hope you agree with me when I say that."

I shrugged. "There's a lot of violence here."

He leaned closer. "Are any of them . . . uh . . . "

"My mother or my sister? No. I've got three women here. One wore a wedding ring. One had dark red hair, and the third is too tall."

"I'm sorry to drag you into this."

"Quit apologizing. It's just business."

"Okay. You're lying, but okay."

"Captain! Over here!"

The call came from MacCormac. We knotted up into a group—mostly because nobody wanted to be alone—and Clark led the way down the hill and just out of the camp, into a grotto of red glass and dark black crispy mulch. On a quick look, I figured the sudden change from sand-colored skeletal mulch to this black stuff meant a lot of those black parasites tended to die in this area. At least, that was the uneducated conclusion. Actually, the black crunch could've come from any other source. What did I know about it?

"Stop!" Pocket called.

We piled into each other as we skid to a stop.

"We're about to leave the ship's protection grid." He showed us the screen on his palm-tech. "Not the brightest idea, right?"

"Should we do that?" Bonnie asked.

Clark looked bewildered and didn't have an answer. He hadn't expected to leave the grid at all, never mind so soon.

At the bottom of the slope, MacCormac appeared. "Come on down! It's safe! Be careful of the slope. It's slippery as hell."

The slope was indeed slippery, made of what must be millions of years of collected mini-skeletons crushed to a fine consistency and creating a dune-like slide. We helped each other down, but Carmichael stayed at the top when MacCormac signaled him to do so. I got the idea from the way he looked down here that he was perfectly happy staying up there. I only went halfway down myself, and was content to stay just far down enough to see what was going on.

At the bottom was a dimly lit grotto of mulch and glass that was like walking into the neck of a bottle and coming out inside. In front of us, Colonel MacCormac, Sergeant Berooz, and Corporal Edney stood around a nest of oval pods the size of beachballs. There were more than a dozen, each with its meaty top popped like a zit, triangular petals folded back and dried up. The Marines had their weapons pointed at the empty pods, and they were visibly nervous.

"Oh, crap!" Clark blurted.

He threw his arms out at his sides and stopped us all in our tracks. Bonnie and I bunched up behind him. "Oh, crap, crap," he boiled over.

"It's safe," MacCormac assured. "They're all expended. All hatched. They must've been the ones that . . . got a grip on those people in the huts. Y'know what I mean . . . "

"What are they doing here?" Bonnie asked, breathing in little gulps. "Aren't they supposed to be in some secluded incubation chamber? Isn't that what the reports say? This isn't like *any* of the reports. Why are they out here by themselves?"

Her confusion came out in fear. Information she had depended on was already falling apart, and we weren't an hour into the mission.

"It looks like there must've been an attack," Clark guessed. "Several of the researchers got pinched by the hatched stage of those creatures. The fingery, ugly, y'know . . . those. The researchers might have all died defending themselves."

Oh, boy, here it came. Did I have to tell them?

Yes.

"They wouldn't have defended themselves," I said.

Clark gawked at me for shooting down his theory.

"They wouldn't have had weapons," I confirmed when I saw his expression.

"Excuse me?" Colonel MacCormac stepped closer, his square face screwed up in military complaint.

"No weapons. My mother wouldn't allow it. You don't come into the wolf's territory, then shoot the wolf when it attacks you. You don't swim with sharks, then get mad when one bites you. If you're stupid enough to get killed, too bad."

"No defense?" MacCormac contributed.

Edney hissed, "Now, *that's* stupid."

I congratulated her with a glower. "Welcome to how Jocasta Malvaux thinks. She may not have allowed them to harm these—these 'animals.'"

"Why in the devil not?" MacCormac asked. He wasn't being rhetorical. He wanted clarification.

"Because my mother has a little religious colony going here," I supplied, "complete with martyrs. I've seen it before."

At the crest of the slope, Private Carmichael, his voice much more timid than his weapon-bristling appearance, asked, "Every living thing fights for its life, right?"

I snapped him a harsh look. "Not brainwashed sacrificial lambs young enough to think that after you die, you wake back up and then you're famous. Anybody who came on this trip because you wanted my mother's autograph should've gotten it a year ago in some nice bookstore. If she got herself killed, that's fine. I'm just sorry she took my sister and all those innocent starry-eyed chumps with her."

In the stultified second after my words obviously stunned everybody into a whole new scare, I felt bad that I'd had to tell them the unvarnished truth.

Not enough to coddle them, though. "Besides," I added, "notice that there aren't any dead aliens lying around. The researchers didn't fight."

There was no way to ignore the fact that something else happened than we had first assumed. Nobody reviled my declarations more than I did. Nobody wanted to turn around and get out of here more. I'd believed Clark's descriptions of an easy mission, quick on, quick off, drinks all around. I'd actually believed my mother might be the only problem and that we could handle her. I'd made the mistake of concentrating on that and letting somebody else worry about other things.

"Screw this shit to the wall." Colonel MacCormac shook his head in frustration and clumsy attempts to sound in control. "I gotta take a piss."

He crunched around to the other side of the nearest pillar, while the rest of us waited and had nothing to do but avoid meeting each other's eyes. True to Marine practice, Corporal Edney marched to the best place to keep an eye on us and also on MacCormac. Nobody was to be left alone, not even for an instant. Line of sight was to be scrupulously respected.

"*Sparren,* Vinza." Theo's voice came fairly clear over the speaker, so crisply that it was startling.

Clark cleared his throat to find his voice. "Yeah, Sparren here. What's up, Theo?"

"*I don't know. Something's going on outside. The guards are gone.*"

Everyone turned to Clark, holding breaths. He brought the com up to his lips and turned away from us, trying to have a private conversation.

"Gone? Like—"

"*Like gone. I can't see 'em, I can't raise 'em. You want me to go out there and look around?*"

"Negative. Stay inside the ship. Nobody goes out. They're probably just looking around the perimeter."

"*Why aren't they answering? It's not like they can walk out of range.*"

Clark crunched around and gave up trying to hide what was going on back at the ship. "MacCormac!"

"Yes, sir?" MacCormac appeared from the other side of the pillar, putting his pants back together after nature's call.

"Donahue and Brand aren't at their post at the ramp. They're not answering hails."

MacCormac's face flushed. His brows came down as he hit his own com unit. "Donahue, Brand, signal in immediately. This is MacCormac. Speak up!"

"What happened to them?" I asked.

"Nothing *can* happen to them," he assured. "They're in the ship's protection sphere and they're well-armed."

"Would they have left the protection sphere?"

"No. Not without orders."

"Because this is such a controlled environment?"

"Mind your own business, detective, will ya?"

I ignored him and demanded, "Has any of this protection equipment ever actually been tested on an alien planet?"

Clark's expression as he glanced at MacCormac, and the Marine's as he glanced back, gave me my answer. "Let's get back."

That was all Pocket, Axell, and Mark needed. The three of them scrambled back up the grade so fast that they lay a spray of black skulch on the rest of us.

Clark shouted, "Stay together! Hold your horses! Hey!"

As his three crewmen passed Carmichael at the top of the slope, Clark leaned forward to scratch his way up the grade, grasping Bonnie by the arm as he went and drawing her with him. "Come on! Come on, let's stay together! Rory, come on!"

"Let's move!" MacCormac snapped to his Marines.

Moving on the slope was like climbing around inside a bowl of cereal. Every step pushed more skulch downward. For every step, we slid two.

That was when Berooz slipped. His left foot went straight out sideways and he went down on his right knee. His weapon slammed into a pillar, splattering bits of hard material. The bits flew into my eyes, causing me to stumble for a crucial instant. Berooz twisted to recover, but the slippery grade shifted under him and he went over backward, his weapon flailing above his head. I made a wild reach for him, caught the tie on the bandanna on his wrist, and received a yank that almost pulled my shoulder out of joint. I couldn't hold him. The bandanna slipped out of my grip. Berooz pitched backward and head first, his back arched and his knees bent.

For just an instant I thought he'd be all right because all he had to fall on was expended egg pods and the skulchy mulch on the grotto floor. He landed on his back with his head bumping down inside an egg pod, which collapsed under his weight with a disgusting *splush*.

We all scratched to a stop and stared down. Berooz looked shocked, but blinked and lay there for a moment as if gathering himself to get up. In that pause, Edney uttered an aggravated, "Shit, jackass . . . "

Berooz grinned, embarrassed. Edney reached out to pull him up. As soon as his hand clasped hers, everything changed. Berooz's expression changed to blinks of bewilderment, then he began to twitch—his whole body from the spine, as if he were being given electrical shocks.

"Get him out of there!" Clark shouted.

Before anyone could move, Berooz began belching horrible broken yowps of agony and surprise. The back of his sensor cap was smoking, billowing with green stenchy tendrils, and suddenly liquid began to splash from behind his ears and neck. The screams became high-pitched with panic.

Edney recoiled for crucial seconds, then found her courage and met MacCormac at their comrade's sides. They pulled

Berooz to his feet. He was stiff as stone, his eyes wild, hands splayed and wagging aimlessly. Edney yanked off Berooz's sensor cap, and that in itself was a mistake. She stared at her own hand as it began to sizzle. Her glove dissolved in an instant, and her skin was next. She shrieked and fell backward into Clark.

"Acid!" I gasped.

I clawed for the blue cylinder on my belt and skidded toward Edney. I fell to my knees twice, which caused me to hold back after what I'd just seen happen to Berooz. Damning myself for hesitating, I tried to get to her. Heaving out short breaths, she stared at her hand as it fried like an egg.

MacCormac grabbed for his own and tried to spray it on the back of Berooz's head, but he fumbled and lost precious seconds. Berooz made one long howl of agony that seemed endless, stretching out until the last breath left his lungs. He dropped to a sitting position on the skulch, with MacCormac holding one arm, the other dropping flat at his side, palm up. The screaming stopped and changed to a prolonged wheeze.

MacCormac held him with one hand and sprayed the neutralizer base with the other, coating the back of Berooz's head until the canister hissed dry, empty. The wheezing of Berooz and the gasping of Edney. I pushed Edney up against a pillar and grasped her by the wrist, pushing her hand flat against the red glass. She gritted her teeth, lips peeling back, and hissed out her pain as I sprayed her hand with the base. The bubbling flesh began to settle down in a final thread of steam.

Only then did I turn to look at the nightmare playing out beside us.

Berooz's head was haloed in stinking smoke. His legs were twisted unnaturally under him. He pitched over sideways away from MacCormac, to land once again on his back, eyes glazed. What a stink . . .

MacCormac clung to him with both hands. "Help me get him up!" he shouted.

Clark and I were the closest. I pushed Edney, still in terrible pain, toward Bonnie. At the top of the slope, Pocket, Axell, and Mark had come back to look down at us, their faces pasted with confusion. Private Carmichael was on his way down the slope to help Bonnie with Edney.

To this audience the next horror played out. As Clark and I helped MacCormac take Berooz's arms and lift him again to a sitting position, the poor young man went instantly from alive to dead. When we picked him up, the back of his head stayed on the ground. His brain tumbled out, rolled down his back, and slumped into the puddle of white neutralizer.

And there it lay.

Clark stumbled backward, petrified. MacCormac stared at the empty braincase of his comrade, and down at the disembodied brain lying in a vomitous gout of bubbles.

Me, I just crouched there holding the dead man's other arm, once again gripping his bandanna-wrapped wrist. Berooz's body stiffened in place. He never did go limp. I'd heard of that. Corpses on battlefields, still holding their guns up, still aiming.

Above me, I heard Edney's pained gasps and Bonnie's sobs as she tried to hold it in, but couldn't.

I had to force myself not to pick up the brain and stuff it back into Berooz's head to wake him up. Only minutes ago he'd saved my life from the same kind of misstep. I hadn't caught him.

I hadn't caught him . . .

What good was I here? What good could I possibly do here? I couldn't save the life of a man standing next to me. What was I doing here?

What if that had been Clark?

Instantly I felt terrible for comparing a man I knew well to one I'd just met. Berooz was a simple guy, easy to make happy. And apparently just as easy to make dead.

"Bring him," MacCormac rasped. He threw Berooz's weapon over his shoulder, beside his own weapon. "Help me bring him . . . help me carry him . . . "

"It'd be better to leave him—" I began.

"We're taking him! I'm not leaving him here!"

MacCormac was either falling apart, or exhibiting exactly what we all needed. Since I didn't have the people sense to know which was which, I just clammed up and helped him carry Berooz to the middle of the grade, where Pocket and Mark solemnly met us and took his legs. We struggled to the top of the grainy slope.

As we reached the top, Clark appeared beside us, carrying Berooz's brain in the Marine's discarded and half-dissolved cap.

Clark's features were sallow and drawn as he met my eyes. "A man deserves to be buried whole."

I looked at Berooz's face as we held him suspended between us. The back of his head still dripped. His eyes peered up at me imploringly.

MacCormac's face worked and twitched with emotion as if he had a mouthful of glue. He was enraged and mourning, fighting for acceptance, for control, so he could continue to lead. I knew that look. It was the cold bottle of a cop's life, trying to get the job done without breaking down, to find answers without giving up the inner information that would chisel away our objectivity.

Clark started walking off his torment, leading in his own way. Carmichael moved to one side, Axell to the other, and Clark passed through them, heading back the way we had come, to walk through that sad camp to our ship, and then to leave this planet. It was all in their posture. We'd come too late, and botched the simple plan.

I would go with them, all the time wishing I'd never come to this pesthole. I was done too.

MacCormac, Pocket, and Mark and I carried Berooz. Carmichael bravely led the vanguard, though his steps were mechanical and halting. Axell waited until we passed, then helped Bonnie with the wounded Corporal Edney.

We were halfway between the grotto and the camp when Pocket's scanner started flashing red on its screen and beeping in broad tones. We all stopped while Pocket held Berooz's foot with one hand and picked up the scanner on its shoulder strap with the other. He looked at the screen, then looked up at the tightly packed columns and unwelcoming channels in the land-scape behind us.

"Uh . . . guys . . . " he murmured. At once he dropped Berooz's leg, clasped the scanner in both hands, and stared up at the long trenchlike gulley extending onward past the grotto's mouth and around a bend. "Something's coming! A lot of somethings!"

"People?" Clark asked.

"Not unless they've shrunken to the size of squids!"

"How many?"

"Sixty . . . seventy . . . seventy-five . . . Mother Mary!"

"Drop him!" I shouted to MacCormac and Axell.

"No!" MacCormac kicked at me as I let go of Berooz's arm and his body crunched to the ground. "You pick him back up! Pick him up!"

The argument was already history. At the end of the visible corridor appeared a single creature. It looked like a scorpion with extra-long legs—or a human hand gone mutant. No eyes, no head, yet it was taking a bead on us from fifty yards away. Behind it whipped a long segmented tail, waving in the air, snapping back, forth, back, forth in a manner of threat.

MacCormac dropped Berooz and grabbed for his weapon, somehow managing to disentangle it from Berooz's, which was also strapped to him. He cleared the muzzle, aimed, and fired without pausing.

The spidery ghoul exploded into uncountable pieces. Bits of it bounced off two pillars on the sides of the corridor, and I swore it squealed as it died.

"Not enough!" Pocket warned. "Nowhere near enough! There they are!"

As we stood stupefied in that one instant that everybody hates, when you can't move and you know you should, suddenly dozens of the craven creatures showed themselves at the gulley's bend.

They came around the pillars—on the pillars, crawling around the glass pillar the way squirrels do around trees, and they jumped from column to column, crossing wide spaces in instants, closer and closer by the leap. They crowded along the gulley floor, their fingery appendages clicking staccato on the skulch. Behind them came a second wave, fundamental as scorpions, tails high and snapping, racing toward us on their spindles.

"Face-huggers!" Clark shouted. "Think with your legs!"

CHAPTER FOUR

Berooz's mutilated body struck the path floor. His empty skull made a *pok* on the skulch. In an instant everyone was running. I drew my plasma pistol and fired on the run. A bolt of compact plasma streaked back and splattered two scorpions, but the others closed in and skittered over the exploded remains without the slightest disruption.

"Run, run!" Pocket called out with each of his own pounding paces. "Run, run, run, run, run!"

Impossible. A glance over my shoulder told me we might as well have been trying to run under water. The hyperkinetic face-hugger platoon covered the yards between us like brushfire.

"Marines!" MacCormac saw the same thing. He skidded around to face the hair-raising sight.

Despite every instinct of self-preservation instilled in Humanity since the dawn of time, he and Carmichael scraped to stops on either side of me. Even Edney, wounded as she was, shook off the support from Bonnie and Clark and ordered, "Keep going!"

Clark pushed Bonnie, Axell, and Mark in front of him. "Faster!"

"Formation!" MacCormac bellowed.

Corporal Edney cranked around, using her acid-burned right hand to support her weapon, and brought it to her shoulder to be fired by her left hand. I saw the pain reaming her face and admired her tremendously.

The three Marines came to meet each other and adjusted their stance to put all of us behind them and themselves in a perfect line, ten feet abreast of each other. I didn't understand why until an instant later, when the chittering fingers of the face-huggers became maddeningly close, rushing along the ground and jumping from pillar to pillar, covering ground shockingly fast. The whipping assault was almost upon us. I couldn't shoot over my shoulder, or I'd hit one of the Marines, so I stopped and braced to take aim. I never got the chance to fire.

"Ready!" MacCormac shouted. With the courage of training and of spirit, the Marines set their weapons on their targets and somehow waited for their commander's order.

"Volley!" MacCormac called.

The Marines engaged their enormous guns.

FOOOOM—crack!

Three arched waves of electrical energy in a blinding neon-orange blew from the Marines' weapons and shocked the flank of face-huggers. The wave actually rolled back a few feet. They were frying in place!

"Volley!" MacCormac shouted again.

FOOOOM—crack!

"Volley! Double!"

FOOOOM—crack crack!

With each volley the blinding orange energy wave drove the face-huggers back another fifty feet, buying us time to run. We made it back to the middle of the camp, jumping over the swaddled corpses and zagging between the huts toward the ship. The chittering sound faded back, then began to surge behind us again. After the third volley, the Marines broke formation and ran with us until they too were at the camp, where they again stopped and formed up, facing the nightmare. MacCormac's voice was the steadying force in the chaos.

"Flames! Fire at will!"

They uniformly clacked their weapons to another setting and opened up with streams of gas-fed flame, broiling the rolling ranks of creatures including the ones that were jumping from pillar to pillar. The creatures fell on each other, shrieking and raving, and began to tangle up and lose ground.

"Cease fire! Retreat and recharge!"

I stuffed my plaz back into my vest pocket and skidded against a pillar. "MacCormac!" I called. "Weapon!"

As the Marines caught up, the colonel instinctively tossed me Berooz's heavy weapon. It rolled once in the air and with a long reach I caught it. The weight, despite excellent balance, almost took me down. Like theirs, it was a military-issue combination explosive-tipped percussion rifle, flamethrower, and electrical field dispersal cannon and a dozen other exclusive features for sensing and accuracy. I hoped on the soul of my favorite person on Earth, if I had one, that I could figure it out in time.

The others were ahead of us now, gaining at least some ground. We turned again to stand our ground, this time with me and Berooz's weapon added to the rank.

"Volley!" MacCormac's command energized us all.

I pulled the trigger. Out came a shuddering bolt of flame instead of the energy wave, while the others all managed to actually work the weapon properly and get the shocker component. I stopped, lowered the weapon into a thin band of sunlight, and found the control pad so I could reset it for the shock wave.

"Volley!"

This time I got it right. *FOOOOM—crack!*

The mad alien squall blew into a wide roll of acid and flesh.
"Volley!"

Again we fired, each time driving the creatures back, but
they weren't stopping. Unaffected by fear or thought, they simply replenished their dead with more from behind, but we were
managing to slow them down and gain ground. Every volley
force decimated the front line of the aliens and tangled those
behind it as they stumbled into each other's fingers and tails.
Their physical momentum caused them to knot up with each
other's bodies and their long bones to snap in such numbers
that we could actually hear the crackle.

"Retreat!" MacCormac ordered at the right instant, just when
I would've done the same thing, just as the alien scorpions rolled
backward, stumbling into knots, fouling their advance.

The four of us scratched into a full run. We could see the
ship—the ramp—Theo at the top of the ramp waving us in.
My legs burned with the effort of running on the unforgiving
skulch that brushed away under every step.

Somebody hit me . . . something tripped me . . . what happened—I was on the ground. What happened? Something
rammed into my chest, drove me down, left me gasping, aching—

The Marine weapon was still in my arms. I clung to it and
tried to get to my knees. Why was I down? What had hit
me? I couldn't think . . . had MacCormac kicked me in the
stomach?

"Keep moving! Get up!"

It was Axell. Geeky and clumsy as he was, he'd come back for
me. He knotted his fists into my vests and twisted me to my
feet. I looked back just as I gained footing. The alien wave of
lariat tails and spindle fingers were coiled in bundles on the
ground between the camp and the ship. They squealed and
tumbled, trying to find their feet. Some staggered, then stumbled. Their bodies spat tendrils of smoke and tissue.

Ahead of me, Pocket and Mark were staggering to their own feet. Had they tripped?

Then it happened again—the big gut-punch. This time I saw the flash of green energy. The ship's protection system! At least now I knew what was knocking us down and I could fight it. This time I stumbled back into a pillar the diameter of my wrist and it shattered with the impact. Fragments of glass, broken into pieces the size of pop cans, collapsed onto my head and shoulders and on Axell as he ducked beside me.

"This is so unfair!" he complained.

Colonel MacCormac reached us and pushed Axell out of the raining shards. "Carmichael, volley!"

The two of them formed up and fired another volley. They were running on sheer training and determination. I knew they'd been punched hard just the same as I, and everybody. Between me and the ship, Pocket and Bonnie were dragging themselves and Edney up the ramp.

I planted my feet under me in the detritus of the fallen pillar and tried to take aim, but never got the chance. Two face-huggers blew past me, racing toward the ramp. Maybe they didn't sense me there in my cloud of rubble—I don't know—but one of them launched itself into the air and slammed into Axell's face.

I saw his face, his eyes and gaping mouth at the last instant. He saw the thing shoot itself directly at him, saw it close on his face, the reaching fingers and whipping tail crowding out the landscape. He made a gushing noise of insult just before it hit him.

Spinning, I aimed my weapon at it, but what could I do? His head was in there!

Axell clawed at the creature as it snaked its lariat tail around his throat and took an anchorage. Stumbling, now blind, the sorry little man grasped at the bony limbs clamped around his head.

I took the weight of the Marine weapon in my left hand and coiled my right arm around Axell's waist. He wasn't limp—he was still staggering. I steered him toward the ramp just as another deployment of the ship's weapon turned the air green around me. This time it didn't knock me down. I felt the tingle on my flesh and grimaced at the burning sensation, but I was apparently close enough to the ship that it let me come in while still striking the non-human animals with its hard charge. The charge must be heavier farther out, like the ocean ripple that would eventually build into a tidal wave.

I dragged Axell as he began to lose the power of his own legs. I wrapped both arms around him, trapping him and the Marine weapon inside, and could barely close my arms around both. We shuffled toward the ship in a weird kind of sidestep dance. The scent of the scorpion-like animal clasping his face turned my stomach. Its knuckles brushed my cheek as I tried to bend away, and there was a squishing noise as it tightened its tail and its fingers around his head. So tight was the grip the pink flesh of Axell's neck and his scalp swelled up between the fingers. He went even more limp just as my foot touched the ramp and another hammering of energy blasted from the ship's spine above us, blanketing the curving rank of face-huggers with another paralyzing strike. They curled into frying masses, and finally those who hadn't yet come into range gave up, rolled into tumbleweed, and unrolled running in the other direction. Finally, finally we had turned them back.

Axell collapsed in my arms and went completely limp, unconscious, without the slightest muscle tone. I lost my grip on him halfway up the ramp, but by then MacCormac and Carmichael were there to take over.

I turned and fired one more orange volley at the retreating scarecrows and crawled up the ramp. Theo cupped my elbow and pivoted me all the way inside, then hit the ramp controls and the ground disappeared beneath me. The huge metal ramp clacked shut and locked itself with a musical *chang*.

The landing party gasped and rolled in agony around me, still hammered by the protection bolt and just plain horrification. I fell to my knees beside Axell, then recoiled at the nearness of the face-hugger still clinging to him. Bonnie and the others, even the Marines drew back, away from the awful sight. Axell lay on his back, arms straight out, limp. The thing on his face was very much alive, tightening its noose around his throat and tensing its fingers around his head, as if it knew we were here and would challenge its catch.

Panting hard, MacCormac pushed himself off the ramp gears he was leaning on. He swung his weapon around from behind his leg and put the muzzle squarely on the spine of the face-hugger.

"No!" I shouted, but the weapon discharged a percussion blast that exploded on contact.

The face-hugger, and Axell's head, were blown to soup. In all my years of homicide investigations, I never saw that much blood. It sprayed out in a flat red streak along the entire walkway back to the bay hatch, and took with it the green acidic fluid and tissue that an instant ago had been a victorious little cockfighter.

"God!" Bonnie screamed.

Clark belched "Jesus, MacCormac! Jesus! That was slaughter!"

"It was mercy!" MacCormac spat back firmly. "This is the standard procedure! We will terminate anybody who gets wrapped by one of these things. There's no cure. No other course."

"You can't do this on my ship!" Clark protested.

MacCormac lowered his voice very deliberately. "I'll do it anywhere and everywhere, Captain." He lowered his weapon and wiped his face on his sleeve. "Anywhere and everywhere."

Clark trembled as if MacCormac had actually physically slapped the sense into him.

We all stared at the remains of Axell's detonated head and the stringy remains of the creature that had doomed him. Torn tubular parts of it were still moving, still searching, probing along the cold metal deck.

In that red streak of blood and skull fragments and brain tissue lay huge volumes of information about the ship's computers and all its intertwined systems, and the memories of a reliable shipmate who didn't say much, but could do much. The loss was alarming on many levels. I stared at the gory remains of yet another person who had saved my life today, whose life I then had failed to save. Twice in one day.

Clark shook his head, paced away, then paced back and almost fell over when he spun too quickly. "Theo," he choked. "Scope, will ya?"

Theo, whose calm English voice I kind of wanted to hear right now, said nothing. He engaged a viewer just as the ship belched another bolt of its protective green broad-band. We watched as a few determined scorpio-wigglers broiled in place while the last of those at the edge of the defense perimeter disappeared in retreat.

MacCormac grabbed Theo by the collar. "Where are Donahue and Brand? Did they report back? Are they in the ship?"

Theo braced against the Marine's big fist. "No—no answer."

"God damn it!" The commander threw Theo backward catching him on the ramp railing. "God damn it!"

"This . . . this . . . this . . . this is awful," Clark mourned. "It's clear we've got to get out of here. We're in over our heads. Those people must've had tragic ends . . . either they were implanted with the things that break out of the chests, or they were dragged away." He shook his head again, trying to think, to compose himself. "I don't want to add to the body count. Let's secure and prepare for launch as soon as we can deploy the poison-packers. Let's just . . . just get out of here. Let's just go."

"Wait a minute—wait!" I stood up and braced myself to stay standing. "The researchers are still out there. Maybe as many as forty people!"

"Aren't you watching?" Pocket demanded.

"We barely got back to the ship," Clark countered to me. "You said yourself they wouldn't have defended themselves and didn't have weaponry. We've got Marines, for God's sake, and we—we—" He waved his hand at the twitching corpses of Axell and the creature.

"They didn't die in that camp," I said. "They could still be alive."

"Add it up, detective!" MacCormac's anger came out in a string of spittle down his chin. "They're not even answering the hails. If you were stuck in this nightmare, wouldn't you *rush* to a possible rescue?"

"You don't know my mother."

Clark flapped his arms. "Nobody is the pathological nut you're describing!"

"Everybody is," I corrected. "You're here. I'm here. And somewhere out there, *they're* here. My mother can cultivate a martyr from raw material in about two weeks flat. I don't know how she spots 'em. Perfume, maybe."

He leveled a finger at my chest. "They're here because they were dragged away by those—"

"They weren't dragged away. They went on their own power."

"How can you be sure of that kind of statement?"

"The huts are empty. The camp is empty."

"Because they're dead! They got dragged away by aliens!"

"Did the aliens also drag away all their equipment?"

Sudden silence broke between us. In their minds they saw pictures of what I was describing. I saw in all their faces—in

Pocket's squinty eyes, in Bonnie's sorrow, in Gaylord's fear, in Clark's desperation, the Marines' desire to go home heroes—that I had struck them hard.

"The survivors went somewhere," I pushed, probably too hard. I should've kept my mouth shut.

Clark pressed his lips tightly together, so tightly that his whole face screwed into a grimace. "They went somewhere . . . and died."

"You don't know that."

"They're not answering, Rory."

"You don't know my mother."

"This, again. You said yourself they probably didn't even defend themselves. They just let themselves get killed!"

"But they might've found a way to survive. They were all survivors by specialty. They spent all their time in jungles and deserts and arctic shelves and in wildernesses where nobody in his right mind goes on purpose. You were too confident about being able to pull these people out quickly. You came unprepared."

"That's not a fair assessment at all."

"Yes, it is."

"You're not the expert here, Rory. You need to declare these people legally dead and let us get on with our mission to secure this planet for the good of Humanity."

"I don't care about Humanity. I care about this." I pulled out the wedding ring I'd hidden in my pocket. I held it up for him, and everyone, to see.

"Jewelry?" MacCormac scoffed.

"A wedding ring. I took it off the woman who hanged herself to keep from what was about to happen to her. If you don't know what that is, you're an idiot. I wish to hell I could ignore all this, but this ring is burning a hole in my pocket. I care about one person at a time. I don't ignore clues."

"Clue?" Pocket challenged. "What clue?"

"Like where's the dead woman's husband?"

Bonnie dared say, "Back on Earth, I hope."

"Where we'd like to be," Gaylord said.

"Except for one thing," I said. "She was pregnant."

Bonnie blinked. "Oh, that's right . . . oh, dear . . . "

"He's here, but he's dead somewhere," Pocket insisted. His ponytail bounced in emphasis.

I looked at him. "Maybe. But I want more reason to believe that. I want to find the second encampment. That's the condition. If we find a second installation and it looks like this one, then I'll sign off on all human life. But not without one more try. You get paid for accomplishing something, not for dumping and running. Without my okay, all you get is your standard ferry pay. No big pay-offs. You go home poor."

I raised my voice enough for the whole crew to hear, all the people who had planned on this all-or-nothing get-rich-quick scheme. All of outer space was a get-rich-quick scheme, much to the disappointment of the adventurers and dreamers. Space had turned out to be an exclusive and expensive Old West dust bowl, and, lo, there wasn't gold in every stream. This was only my second time in space. Most people stayed on Earth. Some worlds were being terraformed, but it would take decades, if not centuries before those worlds would support flowering populations of any but the hardiest. The jury was still out on how successful the attempts would be. I knew that was why Clark was so charged up about being the one who landed the big fish—the golden planet we could move into without retooling.

And these people around me were the sad hopefuls of space. The do-gooders like Bonnie, the work-a-day guys with one bright chance like Clark, the compulsive gamblers with big debts like Pocket, the guys who couldn't use their skills anywhere else, like Gaylord. When it was your only shot, a long shot was a good shot. They were the crab fishermen of the space age, those who could go out for a few months, and make a fortune if things went well. If things didn't go well, then at least their families would collect if they died. The contract was also life insurance. But they only got the big bonus if the mission succeeded in its primary goals. Success, or at least its cruelest definition, this time depended on me. Damn it.

I let the silence work for a few seconds as they contemplated our situation in all its prismatics. If only it could be somebody other than me doing the talking. If only somebody else would take over my thoughts so I could just go hide.

And there was the other angle. None of them really wanted to abandon other people in this contaminated pit. I saw that behind their terror. I saw it as they blinked down at the hideous mess that used to be their weird little computer genius. How long had they worked with Axell? Who took care of him when he was sick, and who played cribbage with him during the long, boring, hours in space? Who among them had shared jokes with him and found a way to make the awkward fellow laugh and be at ease? Who had he helped when they needed a favor?

And there he was, smeared to hell. To some of them he might be saying, "*Get out of here while you can.*" To others—like me—he said, "*Don't let this happen to anybody else.*"

I turned to Clark as if we were alone. "You want me to sign off so you can release those automated killers to exterminate everything that's not native to this planet? There's no goddamn way, Clark. I can't keep you from leaving, but you're not releasing those robots. If you do, friend or no friend, I'll file charges against you when we get back. I'm not just here for a family reunion, you know. I've been hired. I'm the company cop. PlanCom doesn't want human lives on their consciences. It's a good company made up of a lot of hardworking people with families. They deserve not to have blood on their hands. I respect that. I like it, for a change in my life. It's why I took a job I didn't want or need. Personally, I wouldn't risk the clippings off my fingernails for my mother or my sister. I'm here for other reasons. I'm legally responsible. I'm gonna tell 'em you released the robots and if those researchers weren't dead, they sure are now. It's murder. That's the charge."

Pocket rewarded me with a disappointed glower. He ended his part of the discussion by pulling a tarp out of a locker and spreading it over Axell. Gaylord was slow to move, but took the edges of the tarp and helped. Private Carmichael took Edney's arm and he and Bonnie disappeared into the ship, headed for the infirmary. Mark followed them. After a moment, Pocket and Gaylord also stiffly moved away. They, unlike my big mouth, couldn't find any words for this moment.

MacCormac remained a few moments longer, looking from me to Clark, me, then Clark again. I knew he was thinking about his own missing men out there. His face limned with bitterness, he snatched Berooz's big weapon from where it hung on my shoulder, and he too thumped into the depths of the ship.

Clark alone remained to scour me with resentment.

He stepped past me, on his way to the next few minutes and whatever they would bring.

"Guess you don't care if it's *our* murder."

"What are you doing?"

"Going out after my men. Find my live ones and retrieve my dead one."

MacCormac hadn't taken long to decide his next course of action. In fact, I think he knew what he was going to do before he even left the ramp.

Nobody wanted to lay eyes on me right now, so I was avoiding everyone. Hard to do on a ship, especially when I knew something had to happen, and fast if there was to be any hope for the two missing Marines.

I found the colonel in the mess area, where the guests' lockers and weapons racks were kept. He was loading up. Grenades, shock sticks, flamethrowers, bloodhound sensor helmet, the works. I'd been aboard with this guy for weeks before the cryo sleep, and a period after, and far as I could tell he had no personality at all. He spoke in a series of short descriptions or orders. Otherwise his dialogue consisted of single syllables whenever possible. He never socialized with the crew. But neither did I, so . . . *hmm*.

He packed armor onto his body with angry slaps and tugs, taking out his frustrations on preparation. I didn't close in on him, in fact stayed as far away as the narrow cabin would allow. He didn't look as if he could take much proximity right now. He also didn't radiate any desire for condolences, even though I was pretty sure he could've used them.

"Don't you think we should send out some remote drones first?" I asked. "Scout the area?"

"We don't have the right kind aboard. We didn't expect to have to search."

"Hindsight is so you can see what an ass you've been," I said. "If we lose you, we're screwed to the wall. Edney's wounded and Carmichael's a kid."

"He's a Marine. Don't underestimate him."

"I saw him stop from a full run and turn into the face of those things. He stood his ground and still managed to wait for the order to fire. I won't be underestimating him."

"He's supposed to stand his ground."

"What we're supposed to do and what we do when we feel the fire on our faces are two different things."

He snapped on a very serious looking cartridge belt with some kind of armaments I hadn't seen before. "You did it too."

"Only after I saw him do it. And you. Even Edney, wounded—"

"Go away, detective. I don't want to talk to you."

"Yeah, I know. Who's going out with you?"

"You volunteering?"

"I'd rather not." Good question—what was I probing for, exactly?

"Yeah?" He slammed the locker shut and thumped around to face me, peering at me from inside the perfectly fitted helmet. "Well, you'd better. You're the one who wants to do the snooping around. If you don't go out there, you'll never know for sure. Seems to me, after that performance at the ramp, you better have the guts to find out."

A clunking sound behind me almost scared the skin off my neck.

It was Carmichael, in full combat gear. "Ready, sir."

He had a little boy voice and little boy eyes peeking out from that helmet. Made me sick.

"You're taking this boy out there?"

MacCormac's eyes turned to angry slits. "He's a *Marine*."

My eyes shifted between him and Carmichael. I would've said more, except what choice did he have? Berooz was dead, Edney was in the infirmary, and Donahue and Brand were missing.

Missing . . . how could they just be missing? The ship's defensive shock weapon worked—we knew that. No living creature with DNA other than human DNA could get inside the perimeter. All the Marines would've had to do was run back up the ramp. Theo was standing right there to open it and close it after them. Constant presence in the ship was mandatory.

I thought back to Theo's call to the landing party. He had said something was going on, the Marines were missing, but he said nothing about the ship's defense lighting off or any other outward sign of trouble. He'd have mentioned that, wouldn't he?

"I know I'm going out," I told him. "I'll do my own dirty work. I need some protective gear. Can I have . . ."

My gesture toward his red body-armor suit was less than decisive.

He just stared at me as if I'd asked to wear his personal jock strap.

"Got any spare issue?" I requested.

Inwardly smoldering—well, actually outwardly too—he bit his lower lip to bottle his fury and kicked a locker. When he was done abusing it, he opened it and pulled out a red padded combat suit. "Put this on. Take Berooz's HPB. You already know how to use it . . . what the hell."

I fumbled some, but finally found the way to get into the suit. I had to take off everything but my underwear first—it was body-tight and formfitted, almost like an exoskeleton, lightweight, but strong. Strong enough against acid?

"They should've sent synthetics or robotics into this situation . . . urban environment, canyons . . . grottos . . . like a hollowed-out hive . . . Whose bright idea was it to send human researchers? Nah—never mind. I just answered my own question."

"How are we going to avoid another stampede by those scorpion things?"

"I don't know." He buckled and belted, snapped and booted himself into additional protective and assault gear. "Maybe by going out right now, after they've been stung, I guess, I don't know."

"How far will we go?"

"Wherever it takes to get to that second disaster you want to confirm. You set up the rules, not me. Hope you like 'em in action, pal."

"Don't know what I'll like," I said. "Not here to like anything."

One of the Marines stomped into the locker area, and only when he cast a mighty large shadow did I realize it couldn't be Edney or Carmichael. It was Clark, dressed up in one of those protective suits.

He said nothing to me, but that didn't stop me from whirling around and catching him by the elbow.

"What are you doing?" I asked. "Why are you wearing that?"

"What do you think?" His voice was raspy and worn.

"You're not going out there again—"

"What do you think, Rory? I have to go. I have to earn my 'big bonus,' remember? Pal?"

"I didn't mean anything like that."

"Doesn't matter what you meant, does it?"

"Why don't you let the Marines and me handle this? We'll go out after the other Marines and I'll—"

"Why you? You're just along for the ride."

"Come on. I'm the legal officer. I'm also a cop. It's my job to take risks for somebody else."

"This isn't Milwaukee or Chicago," he said. "You're not a cop here."

"Believe me, don't I wish."

"Well, then take a nap or something."

Aware of MacCormac over there putting things on himself and checking his suit, I didn't want to embarrass Clark or diminish his authority. Still . . . I didn't have time to train him in urban warfare, either.

"It's a bad idea for you to go, Clark," I said, flat-out.

"You're a real catalogue of bad ideas today, aren't you?"

"The ship needs you," I pointed out. "We can't lose the captain."

"We can't lose anybody else," he insisted. "I'm not stupid. I made sure everything can happen without me. Theo, Gaylord,

Barry, and Mark are all capable of launching and getting the ship back to Earth. If a ship can't function without its captain, the captain isn't very good."

Knowing I was bound to lose this round, I pressed anyway. "Why don't you just let me do what I know how to do? If you go out there with us, I'm going to be concentrating on protecting you, whether either of us likes it or not. I don't want to concentrate on you. I only have these two eyes."

"So don't go out."

He knew what I was talking about. The details didn't need saying and the point didn't need repeating. I'd bullied him, I'd guilted him, I'd shamed him, and now he was paying me back.

"Fine," I said. I turned back to the locker, yanked off my jacket, and tried to figure out the red body armor.

Clark kept going out into the bay.

MacCormac snapped a buckle very loudly. He was shaking his head in annoyance and disgust.

No time like the present. I dropped my trousers and pulled on the tougher, tighter pants of the Marine suit. "Colonel, how are you at taking advice?"

"Like what?" he grunted.

"The retrieval. Give it up."

His narrowed eyes scraped me. "What?"

"Leave Berooz where he is. He belongs to this planet now. If you lose more people trying to retrieve a body, you'll never forgive yourself, any more than they'll ever forgive me now."

His glare was utterly cheerless. The blue eyes were pure ice. Other than a slight twitching of his compressed lips, his thoughts were completely masked.

When he spoke, I think he surprised us both. Me, anyway.

"Yeah . . . all right."

It was a big step, agreeing to leave the fallen behind. Some of us—field officers, soldiers, cops—we just didn't like giving the bad guys the satisfaction. And we wanted something to bury. For the mothers, y'know. For the kids, so they could see that we care.

I admired him for giving it up. Sentimentality is hard to abandon when it's all you have. Here he was, in a situation he was supposed to be controlling, and he'd already had one of his troops killed, two missing, and one wounded. He'd kicked the locker, but he wanted to kick himself. Or me.

We dressed in silence. Then he checked my weapon, checked his, and I followed him into the bay. The land of glass was waiting.

We circled the ship. Its big boxy body was completely out of place in this world of rose glass. It was dull, black, marked with logos and graffiti, painted with murals and silly pictures by crewmen who had victoriously returned to Earth. It was their reward. Their mark. And in space, it wasn't like anyone was actually seeing the ship.

Kinda sad, really. As I circled the big dazzle-painted body, I sort of wanted other people to see it and witness the graffiti of her many crews over the years. Big old ship . . . dependable and purposeful. She'd kept us alive in the universe's most hostile environment—space—only to have our lives suddenly at immediate risk down here. I thought back to the moment of landing and what a relief it had seemed to be to touch solid ground again.

I followed MacCormac, with Clark behind me and young Carmichael once again bringing up the rear guard. We moved in a curve around the ship, and spiraled outward, moving between the glass pillars, trying to keep our eyes on each other, which quickly became very difficult in the bands of prismatic light and shadows. I tried to keep track of them by the sounds of their footsteps on the skulch. Soon that, too, was almost impossible.

Only a ten minute search proved that the two missing Marines, Donahue and Brand, were not in the inner areas of the ship's protection grid. We had no choice but to spiral outward toward the limits. Back at the ship, Theo once again stood waiting at the switch, ready to drop the ramp that had been tightly closed behind us. We'd heard of instances when these alien creatures had sneaked aboard ships. That wasn't going to happen to us.

Soon I was as good as alone in the glass forest. The red pillars with their gauzy hats laughed at daylight. I might as well have been in a basement with one lost light bulb trying to show my way.

I turned one of the many non-corners and felt even more isolated. With the Marine weapon pulled tight to my body, I tried to calm myself by running through the process for shifting it from projectile shot to flamethrowing to energy burst. That didn't last long. What invaded my mind instead was the vision of those spider-scorpion things rushing on their extended fingers toward us in a wide, flat stampede.

I hadn't come here to die. Who had? My stomach was inside out, all my muscles twitching with strain of tension. Better be careful—if one of our team came around the wrong way at me, I'd easily have sheered his head off before even noticing that I'd fired the HPB. I slid my shoulder along the trunk of one of the larger glass pillars, wider than an old oak tree on Earth. The glass radiated heat against me just from the way it caught the sun's light. No—that couldn't be right . . . this one wasn't in any direct light.

I twisted to look up. The sun wasn't touching this pillar at all. Could the glass somehow be holding heat? Maybe it wasn't glass at all?

Daring to take one hand off the HPB, I pressed my palm to the ruby pillar. Heat . . . there was heat inside. More than in the air. So they did hold heat somehow. They weren't ord-inary glass.

As I felt the glass, I took another step. The long darker stria-tions deep inside the pillar suddenly came together into a single form through the prism effect.

I froze. There was someone on the other side of this pillar. Some thing?

The red glass cast a distorted form through itself. Elongated and thin as if seen in a funhouse mirror, the shape was taller than I was. My heart came up into my throat.

Above the stumpy shoulders, there seemed to be a head. Round like a human, not elongated like a zucchini. But was I seeing from the correct angle? If the head turned, would it elon-gate? Was it a trick of reflection?

My hands turned suddenly cold and trembled all the way to the elbow. I wanted to call out, to see if the being answered with Clark's voice or one of the Marines. Years of experience in city streets held me silent. Calling out to your partner could get one of you killed. Never give away your advantage. Especially if all you have is the one.

In an instant of dread, I realized I was leaning back on the glass column, putting my weight against it. Bad—if I had to move—

And my boots were in the crunchy ground litter. I tried to shift my weight forward, to stop leaning, without moving my feet. The trillions of broken-up skeletons was to the enemy's ad-vantage. My own boots would give me away, and I couldn't think of any way around that.

The dark form wasn't moving—or was it? The light kept changing, the shape flickering.

Think . . .

My lungs hurt. Jackass! I was holding my breath!

It was the worst thing I could be doing! Now there was no

way to avoid a noisy draw through my nose or mouth to start breathing again!

I formed my lips into an "O" and very slowly drew as silent a breath as possible. Let it out . . . take another . . . my lungs started working again, but it took half my concentration.

The dark, thin form on the other side shifted in flickers of interacting light and shadow.

"Stay in sight, Carmichael." MacCormac's voice from over a hill nearly cracked my brain in half. They were somewhere up the grade. "Where's Malvaux?"

I didn't speak up. I hoped they didn't call out or come down here looking.

MacCormac was being smart. He kept his voice down, barely enough to hear. "Captain Sparren, your location?"

"Over here." Clark's voice was nowhere near the others, but seemed closer to me.

That terrorized me. He could be walking into a trap.

Adding to the terror was another simple fact. The form on the other side of my pillar wasn't any of them.

"Detective Malvaux, sound off." MacCormac kept his voice down, but if I answered we'd both be compromised.

Petrified, I had to either move or get the shadow to move. If I didn't act, Clark or one of the Marines could come stomping down here in to a trap.

Slowly I unstuck my left hand from the weapon and scooted my butt down the glass pillar, down more, bending my legs without shifting my feet. With my clammy hand I scooped up a handful of the skulch.

I took three short breaths. One, two, three—and threw the skulch at the next pillar, across the body of the dark form. When the broken skeleton bits rattled against the glass, drawing attention away from me and across the path, I jumped out under cover of the rattle and took aim.

The dark form didn't move. I fell back against the other pillar, shouldered my weapon, and choked, "Oh—Christ! *Christ!*"

In front of me was the wretched sight of Marine Private Donahue, propped up against the pillar, pinned to it by the throat. Embedded in the poor man's neck was a gray-brown spike, driven through his throat and into the glass pillar. The young man's wide face was paste-white, eyes beseeching the sky for help. One hand hung on the spike. His last few seconds had played out trying to pull the offender out.

The spike was sharply pointed, then grew wider into a series of leathery spinal segments. It sloped down to a disembodied wound of its own. It had been cut off nine or ten segments down. It was a tail.

"Aw, no . . . " Clark came around the pillar at the same time MacCormac and Carmichael showed up.

Carmichael took one glance and wheeled away, nauseated.

"Aw . . . this is despicable." Clark shook his head and said, "Aw," four more times before he ran out of energy.

MacCormac grasped the atrocious tail section with both hands, put his foot against the pillar, and yanked the spike free. Donahue's body jerked almost as if he felt the change, and he collapsed to the ground. With a heave of anger, MacCormac sent the tail section spinning off down a gulley. We heard a faint crunch as it landed somewhere out of sight.

"Looks like he . . . got a shot off." Sucking air through his teeth, MacCormac checked the weapon fallen at Donahue's feet. "Must've cut this off just as it hit him."

"Can we get out of here now?" Clark moaned.

"What about Brand?" I asked.

"We can't keep collecting corpses, Rory, please . . . "

"Clark, I wish you'd go back to the ship."

"Let's all go back. Please."

"No," MacCormac said. "We keep searching . . . a little longer."

The poor man was shattered. The image of the heartless soldier wasn't being honored here. He didn't have much personality, but he sure felt his losses.

"Everybody stay together from now on." The colonel didn't really seem to know what else to do, or what more to do. He fell back on his training, as I did. He turned away from the body of Donahue, to keep his eye on Carmichael, over there, shattered.

"Why didn't the protection blast go off?" I asked. "If he was killed while we were still down at the camp or the pod nest, why didn't it light off when he was attacked?"

MacCormac looked anguished. "Guess we're just at the edge . . . "

"It might be the landscape and all the reflections," Clark suggested unhappily. "The ship might not be able to read . . . aw, hell . . . we're in over our heads . . . "

"Give me that com unit!"

Quaking with fury, I snatched the link out of his hand before he even had a chance to extend it to me. I thumbed the wideband and shouted into the link, much louder than was safe.

"Mother, this is Rory. This isn't right for you to do to us. We came to help. Speak up!"

Truth be told, I didn't expect to hear anything. I was ready not to. If nothing had come, I would've given Clark the confirmation he wanted. We were seconds from that.

The com unit began to hum and its indicator light panel flickered, signs that a signal was being broadcast and being received.

Another crackle, and then we heard a human voice. My mother's voice. The angel of doom and the angel of salvation, all rolled into one phantom.

"Turn due north of your position. Come two hundred meters down the flume, then take the west fork another sixty meters. Hurry. They're moving toward you."

CHAPTER FIVE

You know how, every once in a while in your life, you get the feeling that life really is alive and it has a sick sense of humor? When I accepted this job, the general mission statement was straightforward and seemed to solve a bunch of problems. I had to get away from a few things for the good of the department, let things cool off, Clark needed a legal officer for the mission because somebody had to sign off on the condition of the research team before the poison-packers could legally be released to cleanse the planet of all alien DNA, and Clark personally wanted my help dealing with my mother and my sister, who were not the two most compliant women in history. My presence on the *Vinza* seemed to be a good thing all around, and when I agreed to come along, the mission didn't seem as if it would disturb my life much. We'd be in cryo a large portion of the time, then a quick in and out, and more sleep to get back home. By the time I came out of the months-long hideaway, the storms of my actions would have blown over.

Not that there was so much to disturb. No girlfriend, a job but not a career, taking every day as it came. The best part of my life had been the three bitter, frustrating years tracking the murderer of my fellow officer and finally catching the guy. Of course, that was when my real troubles had begun. Everybody was on my side except the law.

What could I do? Fight that which I'd spent my life defending? I didn't want to fight. I was guilty and I liked it. Some things need doing. I tried to be remorseful, but it was like trying to make yourself throw up when you just don't need to.

So I didn't bother. I said I was guilty, I wanted to take the lumps, but the department wanted to stick up for me. For that, the air had to be cleared and the lightning rod was better gone for a while.

Here I was, wandering an alien land, lost as a baby chick. I'd come around a pillar and between two more, and now I couldn't find Clark or the Marines.

We'd heard my mother's warning and followed it, moving down the flume, but MacCormac had done his job and made us move with controlled retreat instead of rushing panic. We'd spaced ourselves out, with the Marines going first to sweep the area in case we ran into anything dangerous, then Clark after, then me in the rearguard. After two turns, I realized I was in trouble. I'd lost the sight of others in front of me.

And I heard something. A constant crunching noise. I crept down a gritty slope, hoping not to fall or skid out of control. The skulch was dangerously slippery on anything but flat ground, as poor Berooz had found out the hard way. Somehow I had ended up alone, which was the main thing we had been trying to avoid. I assumed it was my fault. I'd sneaked off after another shadow in the red glass.

"*Go to your right, Rory. Five feet. There's a hiding place.*"

"Where are you?" I asked, keeping my voice dow.

"*You turned down the wrong path. You have to hide. Get down on the ground. There's a slab you can crawl under. And don't speak anymore.*"

The com unit buzzed slightly. How could she know what was happening? They'd planted observation devices, obviously, but I didn't see anything mounted anywhere. That told me something—that the researchers had some idea the aliens might recognize a camera unit. There was indeed a slab, and I'd almost missed it. I dropped to the ground, discovering a flat dugout under the slab which didn't fit the rest of the path's floor. It had been dug by humans and formed perfectly to fit my entire length. I shimmied in, weapon and all, making sure to pull the weapon all the way inside with me and leave no clue. What about my footprints and the scratchings as I'd crawled in? I had to hope for the best.

The crunching noise was louder now, and steadier. I stayed still and flat. I had to force myself not to shift or readjust, to press my toes into the skulch, keep my arms right where they were, despite the sharp ground pressing into me. My heart pounded downward into the planet.

At my eye level, only four or five inches over the ground, there was a separation under the glass slab, through which I could see the path I'd just come down. The path crossed my hiding place and went off to my right, on down to unknown destinations. To the left was the way back to the abandoned camp and the ship. They seemed a thousand miles away right now. Too far to do any good, like Earth.

I heard sounds loud enough now that I knew the source was within a few feet of me. Not footsteps, but the constant crunching noise, steady, but somehow varied. Many of the same type of sound. I recognized it after a few seconds—tires on gravel. Did the researchers have vehicles here?

The crunching noise came around the pillars and up the path. Black forms rolled past. Each roll left a residue of mucus behind to pull up in strings behind it. The silvery strings stretched longer and longer, until the next roller came along and snapped them. I caught a glimpse of shiny armor and quivering lips not quite closed over silver teeth.

Aliens . . . big ones. Adults.

They moved only inches from my hiding place. I tried to keep my sanity by counting them. Three . . . seven . . . ten . . . twelve— I couldn't keep up. Couldn't concentrate past the slamming of my heart as it tried to dig underground and hide.

They made a noise, these aliens, a noise other than the crunching sounds as they rolled. They made a soft hiss, uneven, overlapping. Respiration? Exertion? Or some kind of warning system to foolish beings who might be in their path?

Like tank treads the aliens' flexible bodies rolled past me. Through my four-inch-tall slit I saw their long, armored tails curled around in the shape of pneumatic tires, and how their zucchini heads fit into the slots of that bodily curve. I wished I could roll away too.

Then a black foot came down only inches from my face, heavily cabled with long brown Dracula claws and a spike out behind the heel. It ground into the skulch, then moved on, sucking bits of skeletal gravel, then dropping them to bounce into my eyes. The one walking wasn't dragging his tail, the lower curve of which swished up close and bumped the glass stone which cloaked me.

Dinosaurs . . .

"You're not very observant, are you, Rory?"

"Not as much as you, I guess."

"M'am."

"M'am . . . "

"Look at the difference. There was a time during early television and movies when dinosaurs were portrayed dragging their tails on the ground behind them. The hordes accepted the vision without question. That's what hordes do. Then, one day, an astute scientist looked at fossilized dinosaur tracks, I believe brontosaurs, and he

asked the question any four-year-old should've been able to see clearly, 'Where's the mark made by the tail?' Since that moment, all images of dragging tails were wiped out. Dinosaurs were never again portrayed as sweeping great thick tails along the ground. We realized the tails were for balance and were never dragged. On that single day, all of science changed. All the perceptions of an entire ancient species changed in that one moment. Science always bends. Remember to bend."

"Yes, M'am."

During this brief expedition into the crazed fear-reaction of a human mind, the last of the aliens rolled by and suddenly I was alone. Where were they on the move? What did beings like that travel after? Was there migration going on? Had they run out of food in one area and were looking for more somewhere else? Were they moving for food or for breeding purposes?

Where did this put them on the evolutionary line? I wished I were a scientist and could think of answers.

Being alone was a hundred times worse. For a terrible moment I wished the aliens would come back so I would at least know where they were. If I stood up, tried to move on, would I run flush into them? Would I turn the curve of a pillar and run into Clark's corpse the way I had run into Donahue's? Would my mother speak to me again over the com unit? Or would she change her mind and abandon me to my own devices? I honestly couldn't predict.

In the worst case, I'd be alone out here. Clark and the Marines would be gone, discovered, dead. I tried to mentally pace my way back to the ship, the shortest way, and horribly realized I didn't really know the way. I'd followed MacCormac and forgotten to read the street signs. I thought I remembered the way back . . . two bends, a long stretch of downward slope, a bend to the right . . . or was it two bends, one left, then right?

And weren't there tracks around at least three columns the sizes of buildings?

God, I couldn't remember. If I went down the wrong track, made the wrong turn—

Thinking of myself again. What about Clark and the Marines? If they were only a few yards away, also hiding, would I be leaving them behind? Even worse, if I skulked away, they might do what we were doing—waste time looking for me.

I felt like a fool, like a jerk, taken in by a sense of honor that had never paid off once in my life. I'd had a chance to get the ship and its crew out of this mess and blown the gift of escape. There were too many ways to die down here, for sure.

But there were survivors too. I'd heard my mother's voice. They were here somewhere, cloaked. Somehow I didn't feel all that vindicated.

The silence almost drove me to screaming. I bit my lip to keep from calling out and running madly away in any direction until I dropped of exhaustion, to be covered by gauze and eaten by weevils. I physically fought to get a grip on myself and only partly succeeded. Five minutes passed—or was it twenty? Eight—or thirty? I had no idea how long I lay there in paralyzing terror. Seconds, maybe. Panic isn't a good judge of time.

No matter how I played with time, the aliens didn't come back. They were headed in some direction for their own purposes, not just roaming around looking for me. Still, I had no way to know their behavior. Maybe they had rearguards. Maybe I'd still be caught.

Finally I found the nerve to shimmy backward out of my flat hiding place. When my head cleared, I almost dove back in, but managed to force myself to my feet.

Maybe heroes get scared. I don't know. Don't care.

"Where are you?" I hissed, caught between wanting to yell

out and wanting not to make a sound at all. "Answer me . . . somebody speak up, please, this isn't funny . . . "

No answer. I didn't dare raise my voice.

I looked for footprints, but the black skulch revealed nothing but the telltale scratching of the aliens as they had rolled past.

" *Sssst.* "

At the sound, which came from behind me, I spun and brandished my weapon, only to find there was nothing at which I could fire. Nothing but glass and skulch. But I knew I'd heard something. I *knew.*

The prospect of being stalked shot through me like electricity and that pounding heart darned near stopped. The wall of pillars, almost a solid wall before me, rippled and shimmered with such vigor that I was sure my vision was leaving me.

The planetscape before me turned flat, turned two-dimensional, and began to separate from itself, coming apart as if it were being unzipping from the top. My eyes were blinded by a sudden blue light, completely uncharacteristic for the land and sky here, obviously artificial and harsh. I wanted to stumble back, but my legs froze and now I couldn't even see.

I made another mistake—took one hand off my weapon to shield my eyes from the blue light. In that shameful instant the weapon flew out of my grip and I was defenseless. Forces grabbed me from both sides, both arms, and I was propelled forward into a sudden coolness. The sheet of sweat on my face turned abruptly chilly and I fell forward, knocked flat by the forces at my sides. Twisting over onto my back, I lashed out with both feet and nearly panicked when my weapon was yanked out of my hands.

"It's okay, Rory! Rory, stop! Stop! Knock it off!"

Clark's voice. He sounded okay, in some control.

My eyes cramped at the blue light and the sudden dimness

around me. Somebody hauled me to my feet. Clark leaned on me from the right, and total strangers from the left. I shook them off.

"We're secure, Rory," Clark told me. "We're in a blind of some kind, hidden. We're completely masked."

"Did you—see those—things that went by?" I shook my head, as if that would help my eyesight. "They weren't five feet away!"

"I saw 'em. Big suckers, aren't they?"

"Where are the Marines?"

"We have them in our south blind, down the hill," one of the strangers said. "Hi . . . I'm Neil, the camp director."

I blinked, and focused on a bald head, bushy blond eyebrows, and thin lips. Camp Director?

"What is this thing?" I asked. "What are we inside of?"

"It's a specialty cloaking hideaway," Neil said. "Our secondary camp site. The drapings of the camp are made up of thousands of micro-projectors that broadcast constant video of the landscape. It also masks sound and light. It's a good thing you moved close enough for us to pull you in. We don't want to give our position away."

"Who's 'we'?" I asked.

I pushed Clark aside to look, as well as I could manage, at the people who had until now been mysteriously absent. The researchers of the Malvaux Special Observation Expedition Team.

And there they were, seven . . . eight of them, standing before me. Like toddlers or gorillas, they gawked at me without the slightest social restriction. The rangy gaggle of researchers were all dressed in worn khakis, torn red rags in the shape of ponchos, or some kind of neon blue jumpsuit that I didn't recognize as field gear. How anybody could skulk around on a red glass planet in a blazing blue suit, I had no idea. Several of them wore those bracelets and anklets made of the glass-beaded macramé I'd seen on the body in the hut.

And here they were, bearded, scruffy, beaded, hair grown out, no combs in sight, faces pale from lack of exposure. Like missionaries living in a remote jungle tribe, they'd gone native.

And right in the middle of them, as if standing a post, was my sister. For a second I didn't recognize her. Her hair was twice as long as the last time I'd seen her, and braided in three long strands, one hanging over each shoulder, and, as she turned to glance deep into a man-made corridor to her left, another braid down her back. Rebecca of Scarybrook Farm.

"Gracie," I said. "Hey."

She scoured me with cold eyes. "You're out of your mind to come here."

"You too. Where's M'am?"

"She's on her way from the south entrance, with your clunky asshole clubfooted triggerhappy military hit-men whose lives we just had to save at our own expense."

I sighed in relief. "They're not dead? How many?"

"Two. And they should be, along with you and your klutzy pal, here." She gestured at Clark, who dipped his head in embarrassment.

Only two. There were three Marines out—MacCormac, Carmichael, and Brand.

"Where are they?"

"Right here, sir!" Private Carmichael's voice drew my attention to a man-sized opening in the blind's back wall. This whole room, which seemed like a central gathering area, was maybe twenty feet by twenty, probably made to fit a natural opening in the cave formation. My mother was always good at making use of existing land features. There were three tunnel openings, leading off who-knows-where. The place didn't seem all that secure, shielded from the dangerous outside by basically a high-tech curtain, but then survivalists learn to be comfortable with flimsy cloaks.

Carmichael came out first, grinning with fascination at our surroundings, then MacCormac, and right beside MacCormac's big over-dressed bulk was the diminutive and yet dominating form of my mother, the elegant and attention-commanding luminary Jocasta Malvaux.

She was smaller than I remembered. Growing up with her, she'd always seemed about six feet ten. One day as a teenager I overtook her, and discovered that she just acted tall. Walked tall. Made people believe she was tall. She had golden hair done like an old-time movie star, shoulder-length and off the brow. She was one of those people whose bone structure and complexion, the set of her lips and brows were classic enough that she could step out of a sauna, half melted, and look stunning. Everyone in the room became very still, as if royalty had entered, and she played off that. Being the center of attention was her best thing. Her glamorous and gracile elegance came out in a magical charisma that made people want to be near her and "yes" her and somehow chip a word of approval from her. Even unadorned in this wilderness environment, she was striking. Face to face with her, I was suddenly eight years old again.

"You wanted him," Gracie said to her. "Here he is. Now how do we get rid of him?"

Our mother never took her eyes off me. Her expression was complex, a combination of nostalgia and dismay. She spoke in that scholarly and slightly removed Quebec accent that was almost not there at all, but just present enough to punctuate her words with a *francaise* patina.

"Graciella," she lubricated, "be more welcoming to your only brother."

Gracie shrugged. "Yes, M'am."

Our mother created a special zone for herself as she moved forward through the gaggle of researchers, to approach—but not too close—me.

"Rory," she began. "Are you well, dear?"

"M'am," I greeted flatly. "Why didn't you answer our hails when we first arrived?"

She tipped her head. "Anger at first sight."

"We've lost people already. They'd still be alive if you'd spoken up."

"We don't run the wide-range transceivers unless we have to. We've been in seclusion for months. Why waste the energy?"

"And nobody heard or felt the ship land?"

"Actually, no. We were napping."

I sensed Clark and the two Marines as they measured every nuance, and decided I couldn't win. She'd have an answer for everything.

"Well, roll everybody out of bed and give me a head count," I said, "because we're leaving now."

"We have to launch soon, Mrs. Malvaux," Clark instructed without embellishment. "Every additional minute on this planet is risky."

"The sooner, the better," she agreed. "But you won't be making any actions outside the blind yet. The Xenos are on the move. You have to wait until after sunset, when they go underground for the ambient radiation during the cool night. Then, we'll be happy to accommodate your hurry. Your appearance here has compromised our work."

"How's that?"

"Your clumsy arrival has risked our carefully constructed veil of secrecy and stirred up the local population of animal life. We've been in ideal seclusion for many months, Captain. Time and great care have been taken to retreat into the environment so efficiently that the Xenos have forgotten we're here at all.

Unable to find us, they ultimately went back to their natural behavior and we've been able to study them interacting with each other instead of int—"

"How many of your team were killed," I interrupted, "before those creatures 'ultimately' went back to nature?"

My mother's sophisticated eyes narrowed slightly, as if scolding me. The look was too familiar. "Your ship's landing and your crass actions have tipped them off to our presence here. You've disrupted months of exacting behavior on our parts. We've learned to completely disguise our presence h—"

"I want to know, and right now, how many out of the original fifty-two are still alive. Tell me now, M'am. This isn't a visit."

She paused. "You'll interpret the information negatively."

"You're avoiding the inevitable."

"It's my responsibility to avoid misunderstanding of our work here. There are always casualties."

"How . . . many . . . are dead?"

"M'am," Gracie uttered.

I couldn't tell whether she meant to encourage or to warn.

"Nine," my mother said. "We've lost nine."

"The same nine we found at the camp? That nine?"

Her cheeks flushed, but only a little. I thought I might have caught her in a lie, and watched the others as a barometer. Nobody else flinched. I scanned them quickly, looking for bad poker faces.

"Nine," she said.

"How did they die? We saw what happened to the bodies inside the huts. How did they get caught so quickly? And what happened to the ones outside?"

"They made mistakes," she told me openly. "This environment takes getting used to."

"What kinds of mistakes? We need to know right now, so we don't make them."

My direct questions bothered everybody, I could tell. This wasn't the socially approved norm, where you walk in and take a while to get to know what's going on and gradually inquire about a few things at a time. Her followers were shocked by my grilling of this iconic woman whom they so completely respected and whom they asked for permission to ask a question before asking it.

My mother kept her cool, though I could sense the seething fury below the surface, only by experience.

"Our chemist, Amelia Forbish, went out without her scent masking. Donald Kent and Richard Hochleitner went out after her without checking the area first for stalkers. Several weeks later, Samantha North tried to make an impression upon us by setting up more video feeds than she had been assigned. She was always too bold. Niko Refinado went out alone after we made a policy of a buddy system. He never respected them enough. He made mistakes. Then he made one too many. It goes on like that. I will give you all the information you need for your records. You have no cause to cross examine before there has been an examination."

She was good. I couldn't think of a response. It's hard to grill a person who is seeming to cooperate.

"The arrival of your ship has compromised our work," she went on. "Hiding will be much harder now that you've tipped them off. We made hiding an art. A way of life. If you'd kept away, we could've gone on for years. Now we have to deal with this setback. Unfortunately, we do have something of yours." She turned to a very large bearded gentleman with a decidedly Bigfoot countenance, "Zaviero, show them."

Bigfoot glanced at Clark, at me, then MacCormac and Carmichael. "You sure they won't get mad?"

"Well, of course they'll get mad, dear," Ma'm said soothingly, but logically. "Go ahead. They won't be mad at you."

Could this prehistoric lox actually be a scientist of some kind? Or was he just the bouncer?

"Just don't want anybody to be mad." Zaviero stomped to a storage area with several tote-able containers with the same footprint, many covered with black tarps. He pulled back one of the tarps with a swish, like a magician's assistant making a dramatic reveal.

There, on top of a group of unevenly stacked containers, lay Marine Private Brand, dumped there on his side. His eyes were closed and his mouth slightly open, as if he were sleeping. He wasn't. Around his throat was a long, segmented, whiplike cord, very familiar since we'd just had a few hundred of them whipping at us during the crawler stampede. At the end of the garrote hung a dead face-hugger, its fingers hopelessly broken in several places so that they splayed out in every unlikely direction.

Clark moaned. "Another one . . . "

"How did this happen?" MacCormac demanded, boiling with rage. "Did this thing kill him?"

"We think they killed each other," my mother explained. "He must have been a very good soldier to break all its limbs while it was strangling him. You should be proud."

MacCormac grimaced in bitter dismay. He seemed tragically helpless.

I stepped closer, but Zaviero suddenly moved to block me from getting too close to the body. He seemed to want to protect the dead man from disrespect or disturbance.

"Where was he found? Inside or outside the ship's protection grid?"

"We know nothing about your ship's blasters," my mother denied. "He was found at the bottom of a gradient. He seems to have fallen while fighting for his life. He almost tumbled right into one of our holographic projectors. It would've been a disaster for the rest of us if he had. He could've compromised our entire southern blind system. Gracie, it's time for dinner. Oliver, make sure we have enough for our guests and that they have a chance to clean up. I'm sorry there's neither water nor is there hot food, but we can offer cleansing methods and sustenance. We eat only indigenous plant fibers and curds. We take protein supplements, but there's no cooking because of the chance of compromising our scent masks."

Clearly disturbed and out of his element, Clark fell back on his responsibility as the flight captain of this mission. I felt for him as he cleared his throat and forced himself to speak. "Mrs. Malvaux, I have a court order—"

"Please," she said sharply. "No discussions yet. We must eat dinner. You must understand, Captain, that we keep our sanity through our human social rites. We eat, we pray, we retain our humanity. You cannot go back to your ship until there is quiet in the countryside. Until then, please try to relax and mourn your loss. He will be disposed of in our way, appropriately, and in a sanitary manner that attracts no attention. Oliver is our chef and will be serving dinner in forty-five minutes."

A little spooked at my mother's ability to speak so fluidly of dead people and dinner in the same breath, Clark shifted on his feet. "Well . . . I'll have to notify my chief mate about what's going on."

"You may not make any communication," my mother told him. "The Xenos have methods of wave detection. We must not take that risk. Our lives depend upon silence. Your crew in the ship will not venture out on their own, correct?"

"They're not supposed to . . ."

Clark eyed me. I made a little warning scowl. I knew he expected me to ask her about the people in the huts, why they were locked inside. I didn't want to play that hand yet. There was too much emotion involved—the image of watching each other go through the abomination of being used as an incubator for the ulcerous little alien larvae, or whatever they were, watching your friends' bodies blown open and the pests scurrying out to freedom. It was a wonder they hadn't all hanged themselves.

"Then, fine. They'll wait." She made some nods and motions to her staff which I couldn't interpret. Some people stayed, while others disappeared through the three passages that linked this chamber to whatever else they'd built. I felt like I was inside a stomach. The dim place, lit by blue and white lanterns, was particularly unwelcoming. They seemed to settle down, but weren't comfortable with our presence. One by one they found some way to occupy themselves with whatever they did here to pass time, or work, or whatever.

MacCormac and Carmichael stood side by side, looking at their dead comrade. Brand lay there on his side, guarded by Zaviero, in death with his assailant, looking horrendously like a child curled up with a favorite toy.

"One more for your count," Clark rasped at me. "Hope you're keeping track."

The chef, Oliver, and two or three others began to set up a dining table made out of boxes and panels. I found it a little Jocasta-esque that they had a "chef" and not just a "cook." She had an odd talent for glorifying the menial. I think it was a way to elevate people in their own eyes, make them think *she* thought they were more valued by her than they actually were.

They obviously did this every night, like a ritual. There wasn't much chit-chat, but that might have been because we were here. MacCormac and Carmichael settled down in desolation and waited out whatever would come next.

I watched all this for a few minutes, and decided to work the room. I started with a sad-sack character with a bad left eye. His right eye did the looking, and his left one kind of went off on its own, but that wasn't what had drawn me to him. He was dressed in the red rags with some kind of glittering dust on them, which I assumed was some kind of crude camouflage, not exactly the height of technology. Probably one of the first things they developed, and now it had become fashion. Or just comfort, like a bathrobe.

The sad man just stood there uneasily as I approached him, and I flashed back to my days as a superskyway cop. Like somebody who didn't know why he'd been stopped, he seemed both guilty and bewildered.

"Hi," I said, as friendly as possible. "I'm Rory Malvaux. What's your name?"

He hesitated, moving his mouth some, as if he weren't sure it was okay to speak to strangers. "Diego . . . bacteriology and virology."

"Funny last name." When he didn't smile, or even react, I ignored my own joke and let him off the hook. "Sorry about your wife."

He blinked, first surprised, then perplexed, and soon looked the way you'd expect him to look.

I pulled the wedding ring from my belt pack. "You probably want this."

He stared at the ring, but didn't take it. I had to reach out, nudge him, and place the ring in his hand. He simply stood there, looking down at it.

"Amelia dreamed of having an adventure for a honeymoon," he admitted. "Starting our lives by doing something like . . . something . . . historic."

"You did," I told him. "You had the guts to live your dream."

One shoulder went up, then sank again. "She died of dreams."

"Most dreams are dangerous," I said. "You're not the first."

He gazed at the ring until finally his fingers closed over it.

"Thanks for bringing it to me. I thought about going for it. I couldn't make myself go in there."

"Now you don't have to."

I left him with his memories and went around a tall set of packed shelves to the next person. This aging bibliophile looked as if she lived in books and didn't know how not to. She was thin and flat, like a cut-out. I could've broken her by tripping those spindly legs. Yet, here she was, chosen for some reason of value to my mother's discerning eye, and she'd actually come all the way out here. I wondered whether she—or any of them—really comprehended the kind of life they'd been offered, and were living out here. Had she talked to them about heroism and groundbreaking glory? About being the pioneers of science? No doubt.

Something told me my mother had left out the inglamorous bits, like having to bury your own excrement and peeing into special containers for re-purification later, then having to drink it.

Then again, maybe she'd been completely honest and they were just jerks.

"Hi, there. What's your name?" I asked.

She was afraid to answer, so she didn't. Probably hadn't spoken to anyone she didn't know for years.

"Go ahead, tell me," I prodded. "I have to check you off the list. I'll get in trouble if I don't. Help me out, huh?"

"I'm . . . Yuki. Tech and data specialist."

Anybody sensing a pattern? They each gave me a name, only one, and a specialty.

"Those are nice bracelets and the other beaded things there," I bridged. "How long have you been making those, Yuki?"

"Beading? I was eleven and a half. My aunt and uncle were hucksters. They had booths. Carnivals, shows, festivals . . . When I was bored my aunt showed me how to string beads. I guess I was talented, guided by spirits, just had a touch. Because my hands always pick the rights things . . . glass and stone . . . hemp . . . How did you know it was me who made them?"

"Your fingers are stained pink with the glass dust."

"That's really good." She smiled, showing little white pointy teeth. "Observant. You're really good.“

"Have you been making much progress in this outpost?"

"With the beading?"

"Actually with the aliens."

"The Xenos?"

"What do you do concerning them? I mean, you're not here to make bracelets, are you?"

"No!" she laughed a little birdy laugh. "No, no! I mostly catalogue the new data. Dates and information, numbers, microdata analysis, complex applications . . . I process it all with programming . . . do comparisons . . . log results . . . crunch numbers . . . ”

"Keeping you busy, huh?"

"Oh, yes, very."

"So do you get out much? Go outside?"

"Oh, never. Never. I never go out."

"Really? Why not?"

"I'd get killed. They won't let me go out."

"Protecting you, huh?"

"Sure. The other tech specialist is gone."

"Gone . . . ”

"Long time ago."

"I see . . . so they need you."

"I'm very important."

"Bet you are. I might want to talk to you later. Would that be okay?"

"Talk about what?"

"Maybe you could show me some of what you do here."

"Oh. I don't know if I should do that. ”

"Well, we'll see. Okay?"

I left her, more disturbed than before. The idea that my mother would bring somebody like this woman out of the relative safety of Earth and lock her up in this bizarre clinic . . . I felt all my buttons pushing themselves.

By the time I came around to a chubby, large-eyed black man whose age was indeterminate because of his porky face and body, which tended to distort a good judgment of age, he was already expecting to be next. He was slightly overweight, but I could tell he had been more overweight before and now had sallow, hanging jowls and wide but sallow eyes. He was tapping information into a computer module, but mostly he was watching me.

I sat down next to him on a makeshift bench.

"Hi. I'm Rory."

"You're Jocasta's son," he said. He had a very friendly tone. "When I first heard of you, I thought it would be stimulating to be her son."

"You probably are, more than I am. What's your name?"

"Ethan. Crowd and traffic dynamics."

"Hey, that's great. I'm a cop, so I'm always grateful for good traffic management. What do you do here?"

"I'm a traffic control technician. I analyze and predict crowd flow. Large numbers of individual components and how they move . . . stadiums . . . highways, airways, pedestrians, traffic . . . crowds . . . "

"Why would you be here, though? There's no traffic, is there? No crowds?"

"I count things. I keep track of things."

"Like those scorpion finger-runner aliens?"

"How . . . do you know about . . . "

"We were almost overrun by a stampede of them."

He pushed back in his chair, both hands fixed on the edge of the table. "You were? How many?"

"Not sure . . . hundreds."

"How wide was the channel?"

"I guess about twenty-five feet . . . why?"

He tapped his keyboard furiously, using nine fingers, because his middle finger on the right hand was missing at the knuckle. The stump had no bandage and was pink, but not red, so the wound wasn't recent. On the screen was a display of a twenty-five-foot-wide simulated canal. He must've had hundreds of such visuals programmed in, and without my telling him specifically where we had been when the crawlers assaulted us, he still pulled up a display of the right place. At least, it looked the same. Might've been my memory playing tricks, but I didn't usually get things like that wrong.

He tapped more, and suddenly the simulation was peppered with hundreds of little pencil drawings of the crawlers, once more racing at me. When the crawlers in front came through, the program automatically filled in more behind them.

"Did it look like this?" he asked.

"It sure did . . ."

He looked at me with some emotion stirring. "I've never seen them do that before."

"How many are there in your simulation?"

"If it looked like this, about seven hundred to fill the passage and bottle up at that point. You can see on the simulation that they're not slowing down and bottlenecking, but actually climbing up the walls and pillars to keep the same pace constantly flowing. They're working together, even though only one or two of them had a chance of implantation."

"Is that a sophisticated behavior, do you think?"

"Very sophisticated. I'm going to write a paper on it."

"Do they always behave that way?"

"I actually don't know. I've never seen them do this before."

I looked at him. "This is the first stampede?"

"The very first."

"Really . . . Listen, thanks for telling me this, and I'd love to see more of your research when we get the chance."

He shrugged and seemed proud. "If Jocasta clears it."

"Oh, of course. No problem."

He shrugged, jogged his shoulders, nodded. "You *are* her son. I guess I can show you some things."

"I'd love to see what you do." Actually, I got the idea he was dying to show me his work. Isolated as they were, these people never got to show off. And there was that little added factor which I didn't fail to pick up—being Jocasta's son just might work to my advantage. Ethan was having trouble saying no to me, and had quickly decided to say yes.

One by one I made my way through them. Oliver, the chef. Tad, stealth tech. Sushil, microbiology. Neil, the camp director. Rusty, a chemist with a Cromwell haircut. Paul, the meteorologist and planetary geologist. Dixie, biology. It went like that. One person, one specialty, not much conversation. They either didn't want to chit-chat, or didn't remember how to. Or something else. Zaviero, it turned out, was some kind of entomologist savant. Bugs. He couldn't spell his own name, but he was an encyclopedia on insects and arachnids, larvae and worms and their behavior—kind of like weevils and scorpions, right?

The people I talked to were all in the nearest chambers, which apparently was two layers outside of the larger chamber where I'd been pulled in, and separated tunnel from tunnel by very exacting methods of lockdown. Not a sound would penetrate into the outer world, not a flicker of light, not a scent. Survival depended on very specific behavior, and generally the researchers didn't tend to move about any more than absolutely necessary. They'd perfected the method of sitting around without being fidgety. Rusty, the round-haired chemist, told me that they practiced yoga in order to gain calmness and resist shuffling about. Except for the immediate chance of death, this was like a weird spa or a Zen retreat. He was among the friendly ones, anxious to be around us, but hesitant to talk much.

My mother had given us forty-five minutes before dinner—slightly bizarre behavior, given the day's activities so far, but okay, maybe they had to normalize quickly in order to not go nuts here. I was determined to use every possible minute. I zeroed in on a sprightly Oriental girl, or maybe Filipino, about twenty years old, with a China-doll haircut and the figure of a boy.

"You're . . . Chantal."

"Yes—hi."

"Zoology, right?"

"And veterinary medicine." She forced a smile, then dropped it. "I'm so sorry about your soldier friends. It's such a tragedy."

"Yeah, our captain's pretty shook up. So you're a veterinarian?"

"Will be some day. I'm here to learn."

"What kinds of things are you learning?"

"It's just amazing. We've been anatomically analyzing the Xenos and studying them physiologically. I do most of the measurements and weights."

"How do you study them without exposing yourselves to them?"

"Oh, we have specimens."

"You meant you've captured some of them? Alive?"

"Well, we get parts sometimes. You want to see our collection?"

"I'd love to." I started to follow her, then noticed that Tad, the stealth technologist who until now had pointedly ignored me, was also following me into the passage. I paused. "Got a problem?"

Half-hidden in long stringy brown bangs, Tad's eyes worked at being expressionless. "No problem. Just going along."

I thought he might be there to protect Chantal, playing the role of a big brother or a bodyguard. What the hell, didn't bother me any. I wasn't about to touch her.

Chantal led the way through a bizarre maze of pre-fab tubular tunnels. They branched off from each other into a sophisticated anthill complex, some going upward, others down and others into curves. Sophisticated, yet still rough and spare. I was right about their following the natural cave structure. I had to be. There was no other way to set up something so complicated by digging all the tunnels themselves in a hostile area. This wasn't an engineering crew. They didn't have the expertise, the time, or the kind of environment where building would go unnoticed by the other residents, if you get my drift. The tunnels were oval-shaped, sectioned with ribs and connected by tough, flexible, and ultra-thin VyFlex, fancy new stuff just developed a couple of years ago for space and inhospitable environs. The whole tunnel, all fifty or so yards of it by the time we came to another chamber, packed in vacuum-sealed envelopes could probably fold up into about a square foot. These on-site living and work areas, impervious to weather extremes, moisture-proof, and easily rearranged, could be shipped in a single standard shipping container and still house hundreds of people. This team had probably packed their entire living complex into one duffel bag.

Didn't do much for claustrophobia, though, I'd have to say. By the time Chantal led me out of the tunnel, I was glad to be out, and glad to not have Tad pacing me from two feet behind, either. I'd had enough bad experiences in alleys that they weren't my favorite places.

And then we came all the way out, and I wished I were back in. I snatched at my plasma pistol.

Before me was a full-sized adult Xenomorph. Arms flared, jaws open, it towered over us more than seven feet tall, its sausage-shaped skull turned sideways so the full profile showed itself. Long arms were down at its sides, slightly flared, its gracile feet spread for balance.

"Don't worry," Chantal said. "It's stuffed. I'm also the taxidermist." She smiled in a pixie-ish way. "I'm really proud of it. I've never done anything as big as this."

"'Zat right . . . "

Overwhelmed by cold creeps, I slowly moved to the right, away from Tad, who paused there and stood like a castle guard. Not interested in him anymore, I circled the quite shocking presence towering in the middle of the chamber. As if the alien were the pivot at the center of an old-time vinyl music record and I were the edge, I moved around it, keeping as far to the circular wall as the limits of the chamber allowed. I wanted nothing to do with being near the monster.

Yet, there it was, free for the touching, the looking, from its raptor claws to its coiled cable-like tail. In fact, the whole creature was a construction of exterior cables and armor. Its ribcage was on the outside too, as were two huge shoulder fins which looked like they might have evolved to protect the sides of that long, long head. Its back was mounted with several snorkel-like extensions that didn't look as if they were for breathing, but hardly seemed as if they would be for anything else.

"Does it swim?" I asked.

"It could if it wanted to," Chantal said, gazing with adoration at her trophy. "There's not much fatty tissue, so it might actually have trouble staying afloat. That is, unless its native planet has heavily salinated water that helps with buoyancy."

"I don't see any eyes."

"The visual mechanisms are inside its helmet. It doesn't have eyes as we know them, but it does sense visually."

"How well does it see?"

"Compared to us? We're not sure yet," she said. "All other visually oriented beings from fish to higher predators have binocular vision. These have a kind of band that goes from where its ears would be if it were us, around the nose area and back again. At least, so far that's what we *think* they see with."

I gripped my plasma pistol as if it were a security blanket and gazed up at the monumental iron-black creature. "Well, that's . . . that's just . . . huge . . . "

The creature's enormously long skull was actually translucent on the top and I could see right through to a complex row of arched inner segments that didn't look like brain tissue, but like more skull.

Ultimately the laws of circles worked to bring me all the way around to where the creature's mouth was turned to meet me. The pointed lower jaw was dropped to show a set of piranha teeth the length of my fingers, and showing inside them was some kind of square contraption.

"Is that a . . . tongue?" I asked.

"That's not a tongue," Tad said, almost as if he were warning me. "It's a second set of jaws."

"Really . . . What do you suppose it would need a thing like that for?"

"We don't know."

Seemed to be a pattern here. Considering they'd been here a long time and doing all this studying, I'd heard more we-don't-knows than answers.

"How does it survive on this planet?" I asked.

Chantal seemed briefly confused. "Survive? What do you mean?"

I thought about Bonnie. "What do they eat? They have to consume, right, because they're energetic? The young have to gain mass in ratio to their growth somehow . . . and they use human bodies for reproduction, we were told, so if there aren't enough humans, then what do they do? That's how they spread, isn't it? With those face-hugger things—their young?"

"Those aren't actually the 'young,'" Chantal eagerly explained. She seemed happy to be able to teach. "They're the . . . more like sperm. They aren't the seed, but they carry the seed. They're receptacles for seed."

I laughed, mostly to let off the tension of being so close to . . . that.

"Are you saying they're fruit?"

She smiled. "Yes, I guess so! Once they implant the seeds, they die off. It's their only purpose."

"So they carry life," I said, "but they don't live a life."

She nodded, this time in silent thoughtfulness about what I had just said.

"So they'll use other animals," I went on, trying not to push her. "Not just humans."

"Yes, they use the indigenous population of hosts. They impregnate a creature large enough to incubate one of their young. The smallest we've ever recorded was twenty-eight pounds—"

"That's just a rumor," Tad quickly said. "It's not confirmed."

"Other animals?" I asked for clarification.

"Oh, yes!" Chantal bubbled. "This planet is loaded with life forms. Haven't you seen them yet?"

"We've seen the weevily things, but we haven't run into anything except the, uh—" I made a crawly motion with my hand.

"That's because the Xenos are on the move. Some of the native life has learned about them and clustered in the valley. We've noted a buffalo-sized animal moving in herds, and several types of homeothermic life and flightless birds, as well as a possible pre-mammal up to twenty-eight pounds—"

"We're not sure they're pre-mammals," Tad corrected. "We

haven't done much analysis. We've spent most of our time perfecting hiding techniques. We want to do the zoological research over the next year."

"Since you have this stuffed one," I began, "does this mean you were able to dissect one?"

Chantal tried again to speak. "We did what we ca—"

"We can't dissect them," Tad cut her off again and took over the explanation. "This one died in an unusual circumstance. It was impaled on a glass spike when it fell off a cliff. Its body drained of the acid blood and its internal cavities were excavated by the blackies long afterward. We managed to clean and retrieve the exoskeleton. Chantal pieced it together with some other parts we had lying around." His eyes flipped to Chantal and he added, "We just got lucky."

Chantal stared back at him for longer than was necessary. "I pieced it together."

Pretty soon she'd just be repeating whatever he said.

I wished I could talk to her alone. "Then you didn't have much chance to really have a look at its internal organs?"

"We'd have trouble with that," Tad said. "Their blood, once it's exposed to the outside elements, turns acidic. There's hardly any implement we can use to touch it that doesn't dissolve. It's just one of the things we haven't figured out yet."

"Still," I prodded, "You've been here a long time. Don't they eventually die of natural causes? Sooner or later you find road kill, don't you?"

Chantal opened her mouth to speak, but Tad cut her off again.

"We haven't found the Secret Xeno Burial Ground yet."

I pretended not to notice the discomfort between them.

"Well, it'll be in the same place as the lost hangers and safety pins."

After several minutes I was finally able to take my eyes off the astonishing presence of the stuffed alien, and my skin crawled when I did. I still had the idea it would come back to life. I had to force myself to look around the chamber. The whole room wasn't much taller than the alien trophy, and only about ten by ten feet, shaped in a pentagon, with five interlocked pre-fab walls. It was also a museum of alienhood. Much of the wall area was devoted to racks of file boxes, probably full of specimens of things I'd seen and things I hadn't yet. This was a scientific archive. I recognized it because we'd had three rooms like this in our house while I was growing up. We only had six rooms, and three of them were this.

Except in our house we didn't have parts of deadly creatures mounted on the walls. Almost as astonishing as the giant stuffed creature was the extended disembodied tail of another of its kind, cut off at a point that must've been very close to the body. The tail hung suspended near the low ceiling, extending all the way across one wall segment and halfway across the next. Its blunt end was mangled, but its serrated tip still intact and quite horrifying. Mounted on other parts of the wall were three alien hands, a foot, and an impressive collection of claws. There were also four siphon tubes, the snorkel things on their backs, the back part of a head, and two long squared-off . . . I reacted with a flinch when I realized those were two sets of the inner jaws, somehow cleaved from inside the throats of two aliens.

"We don't want to examine dead ones," Tad said bluntly, determined to get me off that track, ironic considering the macabre collection. "Before our expedition here, human experience with Xenos has been limited to the way they interact with humans. On this planet, we've been able to observe how they interact with other life forms."

"Where did you get all this stuff?" I asked.

"Road kill," Tad said. Was he making a joke?

I decided to leave that one alone and go after the other angle.

"Do they do something different with other life forms than they do with us?"

"No," Chantal perked up. "They have the same kind of reproductive imperative—"

"Chantal," Tad warned. "This isn't your field of expertise."

"Sorry . . . "

I glanced from one to the other. "So this is like spending years and millions of dollars to do a study to tell us that girls are different from boys. Anybody with kids can tell you that." Moving as far away as the chamber allowed from the alien trophy, I tried to steer the conversation my way. "Well, this is all damned impressive, I have to say . . . Chantal, maybe you know this. I was going to ask my mother, but I forgot. What happened to the people in the huts back at that camp? Why were they inside there? We couldn't figure out whether they were hiding and just got caught by the face things, or, y'know, what they would've been doing inside with the door panels just open a few inches. Were they in there for protection? Or maybe they were hiding from those things. I mean, who wouldn't hide? First they scare you to death, then they finish the job."

I gestured up at the enormous stuffed adult alien and implied I was making some kind of joke, to see if there were any takers.

Chantal blinked, but that was all the body language Tad's glower allowed her. "We . . . we . . . "

"She doesn't know," Tad said. "It's not her area."

I dropped the routine and turned to face him. "Is it yours?"

Tad bristled. "Jocasta warned us about you. She said you don't understand scientific research at all and that we shouldn't even address the issue with you."

"Yeah? What 'issues' would those be?"

I moved closer to him. Intimidation is an art form.

"In about two hours," I said slowly, "I've seen some pretty

horrible deaths, as deaths go. This planet is a slaughter field. And no matter how many heads I count, the number comes up short. That's *my* kind of scientific research. I admit it's simple, but in it the questions can be almost as important as the answers. You're the stealth specialist, aren't you?"

"I sure am."

"You'll have to give me a tour of the technology you use to hide. I'd really like to see that. I guess the only way not to be their target is if they don't know you're here."

He paused for a spell, measuring me, measuring Chantal and the intrusion on their private territory that I represented.

"I don't think you'll be around long enough for tours," he said.

Probably a big mistake, but I cut to the chase and cornered my sister next.

I listened around, then followed her voice when I heard it, and tracked her through one of the shorter corridors to a cramped chamber where she was giving instructions to Neil. Odd, because I thought Neil was the camp director and Gracie would be taking orders, not giving them. Then, being a Malvaux carried some weight here for her too.

My sister was an odd combination of a follower and a leader. She was a prime follower *of* a leader, willing to keep everybody around her in line behind the leader. She had the spark of science in her mind and her talents, but had always been over-shadowed by our mother, always assumed to have gotten the degree or the job or whatever because she was Jocasta Malvaux's daughter. All her life, and all mine, we had been known not as Rory and Graciella Malvaux, but as "Jocasta Malvaux's son" or "Jocasta Malvaux's daughter." We each coped in our own way, Gracie by embracing the role, and I by rejecting it.

I didn't fit into my mother's world of research, awards, expeditions, more awards, discoveries, and even more awards. In fact, I'd always found it kind of distasteful. Gracie always said it was because I was never the one getting the awards and I was bitter. On some level she was probably right. But on my own level, I'd always found the spectacle gauche and pretentious, especially the way our mother enjoyed the glow of the spotlight. I always had the idea she was making history so she could get another fix of that glow.

Maybe I was wrong. There certainly wasn't much of a glow way out here in the hindquarters of space. And she'd have to go a long way back to get it.

"Gracie," I began. "Can I have a word?"

She glowered at me, then nodded to Neil to leave us alone. He seemed glad to do it, and disappeared down a corridor I hadn't even seen, a short one that went off upward and that he actually had to climb to use.

When the scrapings of Neil's escape faded away and I thought we were probably alone—although I had no idea what kind of surveillance they used or how paranoid my mother was—I tried to modify my tone to be non-confrontational, although I did cut to the subject without any frills.

"You've lost weight," I mentioned.

"It's hard to stay fat on rations."

"Or is it from running?"

"We don't run. We hide."

"Yeah, that's what I hear. What are those things, Gracie? What kind of environment creates beasts like that?"

"A complex one, that's what. So what? You don't care."

"We don't know where they come from, do we?"

"No."

"Clark says they hitchhike around from place to place. Apparently our own space ships have given them a couple of free rides."

"I don't know, Rory. They're here. That's all that counts."

I leaned against a thick case of processed, flash-dried foodstuffs. "Not very curious, for a scientist. Come on, tell me something."

She poured herself a tin cup full of iced coffee—iced, so there was no aroma—and tapped artificial sweetener into it. "They're somewhere between instinct and intellect."

"Where?" I asked. "Like dogs or like dolphins?"

"We don't know where they are on the line. We know they communicate, and we know they learn. And we know they forget. After five months of perfect hiding, they finally forgot about us and stopped looking. They went back to their genetic imperatives. But it took five months. That's a lot longer than any animal on Earth. They're smart."

"And this genetic imperative is to spread out? And continue sucking up the life forms on this planet?"

"The planet will adjust."

"How many people have you lost?"

The question set her even more on edge than she was, but she tried to control her answer. "We lost some right away, before we learned to cope."

"You mean, when you found out that camp of huts wasn't going to protect you from those monsters?"

Her green eyes flashed at me the way they had when we were children and she felt slighted by being the younger child. "Yes, then, all right? Things don't always go right. This is a wilderness compound. We had a few accidents and then we got control. Just like you and the people you brought here today. You should all have known better than to come into an unstable environment without specialists."

"Maybe," I allowed. I didn't want to waste time arguing the wrong points. "Where'd you find these people?"

"They applied," she said. "You know that."

"So did thousands of others." I folded my arms and fought off a shiver. They kept it too cool in here. Probably as a precaution, to avoid putting off heat signatures. "I mean, people like Yuki and Ethan and Zaviero. Do you really think they had a perception of the brutality of this environment?"

"I wasn't in the screening process. You're talking to the wrong person."

"I know. I should be talking to M'am, but I don't think I could get an honest assessment out of her."

"Actually, we don't have to talk to you at all. It's not your business to 'assess' us or our expedition."

"I'm the only one who can," I stated bluntly. "Most people get goggled-eyed around M'am. She casts some kind of superstar spell on them. I'm just wondering whether she didn't take advantage of that to surround herself with people she could control. As scientists go, they're all pretty young. Nobody old enough that M'am couldn't be his mother. It's how she keeps authority, isn't it? She also has twenty years more experience than anybody here."

"That's good, isn't it?" she snapped.

"Unless you're the inexperienced one."

She spoke through set teeth. "These are qualified professional scientists and interns with specialties of use to this mission. They willingly came. They knew what they were getting into."

I moved closer to her, and leaned in such a way that she couldn't avoid looking directly at me. "Did you?"

She took a gulp of her iced coffee and made a throaty sound of disgust. When she swallowed, taking her time to do it, she shook her head in frustration. "Nobody wants you here."

"Maybe, but that's not my problem."

"What is your problem, Rory? Because, damn . . . "

"Maybe that I've only counted thirteen people here," I

pointed out. "M'am says you've lost nine. Where are the other thirty people, Gracie?"

"They're out," she said instantly. "On remote expeditions."

"When's the last time you heard from them?"

"I don't know . . . few weeks."

"You don't know?"

Gracie started moving around the little room, picking up bundles of the neon-blue suit I'd seen some of the researchers wearing. If I counted right, there were at least enough for everybody. She gathered them into a bundle in her arms, which got bigger with each suit she rolled into it. "Why should I know? It's not my job. We'd go crazy if we tried to watch over each other too much."

"I don't buy it. This is a dangerous environment where people live intimate lives. They get to know everything about each other and every bit of information is absorbed voraciously."

"When did you become a psychologist?" She snatched up another blue suit from a hook on the side of a shelf unit.

"You're lying and I want to know the truth," I said. "Where, precisely, are the other thirty people?"

She pushed me away and made room for herself to slip toward the tunnel.

"Get away from us, Rory. Go away. Go home. Go—get fried or get laid or dig a hole or live your own life, but get off our backs." She dumped the pile of blue suits into a sterilizer unit and cranked the controls to turn on the microwaves that would do the sterilizing. "It's time for dinner. And you'd better be respectful. We don't discuss business at dinner."

"Dinner" was happening, near as I could figure, around what would normally be lunch for the rest of the universe. I didn't question it. I had other questions, and maybe they called it this because it was the main meal of the day and they wanted to normalize at least one parcel of each day. Why they couldn't do it in the evening, I had no guesses.

In the twenty-foot-wide chamber which was apparently the central clearinghouse, the same chamber where I'd been pulled into the blind, they had set up a makeshift table made up of wall components on a trestle of long, narrow containers. They'd moved some shelves, making the chamber more like twenty by twenty-five, to make room for the extra people, and the table just got longer the more containers and components used. There were containers all over the place, each with markings and scratches and handles. Used for toting and storage, they were also used for furniture.

Another interesting feature—the projector curtain which had saved my life and which separated us flimsily from the dangerous outside world, was no longer transparent. While I had been able to see through it to the landscape before, it was now on some kind of "rest" mode, looking pretty much like a big metallic bathroom shower curtain with little squared cells in the fabric. Those must be the projectors. They could project an image on the outside, and project back into this area whatever was on the outside. Very fancy, as one-way mirrors go. Darkened as it was now, it created a neo-designer sensation to the basement-like chamber and made things feel more intimate, probably in deference to "dinner."

The campers had lit a line of electrical votives along the center of the table, simulating candlelight. Real candles would've created a scent. They'd managed to create a little living environment here despite strict restrictions on behavior, sound, and function. I looked at the fabric-like wall of special sheeting that masked the hideaway. It looked almost like a clear curtain from this side, except for a faint bluish tint, but I knew it wasn't see-through at all. We could look out, but no one could look in. I found it disconcerting to be standing here in front of what appeared to be a big open garage door, and I had to discipline myself to the idea that I wasn't visible from out there.

Nope . . . couldn't relax yet. The curtain had no lock-down, but just hung there, slightly weighted at the bottom. Anything could walk through—if it knew where to walk.

I stayed away from the long table as the campers went about their routine of setting up dinner. They didn't speak, except to point out what was needed, and set out sealable storage containers of various types of—I guess it was food. From here, most of the food appeared processed, dried, or distilled to an essence. Other than the colors—green, tan, reddish—I couldn't identify the food. They were all native edibles, to make sure that all bodily discharges didn't smell different from the environment. These things were no surprise. My mother had always embraced survivalism and guerrilla tactics, one of which was to eat only indigenous food, so body odor and discharges all smelled natural to an area. Soldiers had long practiced the trick to mask their presence. Of course, that meant the whole crew of the *Vinza* and the Marines and me smelled all wrong. I probably should've thought of this and told Clark well ahead of time. But then, we hadn't expected to take up residence.

Still, I should've warned him. I'd been too casual, too much of an outsider. I should've embraced the mission and done everything in my power to warn him, to inform him, make him understand what he was really dealing with.

Should I speak up now? Be seen whispering to him in a corner? Or would that do more harm than good? We were already getting suspicious looks and touchy glances and cold shoulders.

"Hi." Neil, the camp "director," and I would've like to know what kind of directing he did, came around a stack of drum containers. "Can I show you around?"

Okay, maybe I'm too suspicious, but I wondered if he'd been

sent by my mother to keep his eye on us. Would he show us everything or was there a tacit list of things he was *allowed* to show us?

Yeah, yeah, paranoid. Maybe. I'd lived with Jocasta Malvaux a lot longer than any of these folks had.

"Sure," Clark took up the offer. "We're just standing around."

"What I'd like to know," I asked, "is how you knew where we were when you gave us directions to come down the flume."

"Oh, that's easy." Neil seemed relieved by the question. I couldn't interpret that. Not yet, anyway. "The displays are right over here."

He led us through a maze of stacked containers, stacked higher than I was tall. Inside a quartered-off cubby which could be seen from the dinner area but not from the projector curtain, was a seating area of three inflatable chairs arranged around a shimmering scaffold of viewing monitors. I counted twenty-six monitors, each the size of a lady's evening bag, each showing a different location on the landscape out there. The quality of the pictures wasn't very good, often tending to flicker or become grainy. The equipment might not be holding up to the environment, but that was just a guess. One screen showed the nose section of the *Vinza* where she sat in her parking place. Another showed one of her stabilizer wings and part of her tail section. A third showed the camp huts where we'd found the dead people. So they'd been able to see us all along. A shiver ran across my shoulders, knowing that they had seen us and not spoken up. Rather than make trouble about it now, I kept my mouth shut. A glance from Clark made me wonder if he wasn't thinking the same thing.

Other screens showed various locations I didn't recognize, pathways, entrances to caves, views from inside caves out onto the red land, views from halfway up pillars that looked down upon tracts of land. Some showed different kinds of terrain than I'd seen so far—more lush areas with brushy yellow grasses, high red and blue ferns, and stick structures that looked like trees in winter, except they were white, not brown. There was an unrestricted quality to these places, like children's drawings of places they'd never seen.

"How are you getting these pictures?"

"We've been gradually installing video equipment throughout the terrain, one or two at a time. They're curious, but after a while they start to ignore the new installations."

I made a sound of admiration. "Must be dangerous to secure cameras in some of those places."

"Oh, it's dangerous. We lost six people just setting up the cameras."

"Six, huh . . . "

I might've pursued that, but something else caught my eye and stiffened my limbs. On four or five of the monitors, there were adult aliens moving along through a slight mist rising to their shoulders. They moved mostly in shadow, and in single file. Some rolled, some walked.

"Wow, look at 'em," Clark murmured.

"How close are they?" I asked

Neil sighed. "They're still in the vicinity, but moving way. That's the tribe that walked past you while you were under the slab. It's a good thing you hit the ground when you did. If they'd seen you, I bet they'd have found our opening here. Usually they don't pass this close."

"Are they migrating or what?" Clark asked. "Hunting?"

"We're not sure why they're moving around so much. Usually they don't move much during the day. Lately they've been . . . hey . . . who's that?"

We followed his gaze to the upper right corner of screens. Two screens in the top corner showed movement. Humans . . . three of them, dressed in standard gear except for the single Marine. It was Edney.

With her was Pocket, the bosun, loaded down with a medical backpack, and leading the way was the last person in the universe that I had wanted to come out of that ship again.

"Bonnie!"

While we stood there frozen in shock that they had dared to leave the ship again and were outside the protective area, our horrors were confirmed as we saw, as we hid here in our protective nest, a single face-hugger crawl up around the trunk of a pillar. After it, came two more. Then two more. The spider-legged fingers moved one at a time, a sight somehow even more ghastly than when they moved quickly.

I grabbed Clark by the sleeve. "They're being stalked!"

CHAPTER SIX

"Get out of my way!"

I shoved Neil aside, drew my plasma pistol, and veered through the stacked containers toward the projector curtain. Through it I could just see Bonnie step into the vicinity some thirty feet out from the entrance, on the other side of the slab with its low-lying hiding place that had saved my life.

"Stop!" Neil called, but he couldn't hold Clark and I was already dodging for the projector screen.

"I see 'em, I see 'em!" Tad came shooting through the east tunnel and slammed right into me. His neon-blue suit made him look like a cartoon superhero. With strong purpose he knocked me back. "Stay here!

"T'hell with you!" I found my feet and followed him out the projector curtain.

Behind me I heard Clark battle with Zaviero and Neil, who were managing to stop him from following. I heard him shout my name—or part of it—before someone muffled his mouth.

As I passed through the stealth curtain, there was somebody at my side—young Carmichael, the baby Marine, with his big ballistic weapon.

There must be twenty things wrong with what I was doing,

but I didn't take the time to analyze. I plowed out into the black drifty skulch and ran up the grade behind Tad. Carmichael was so close to me that my heels kicked the cereal-like skulch up into his face. He held his weapon in one hand and used the other hand to claw his way up the flume and keep up with me. I wanted to shout a warning—should I dare? Would noise turn a stalking into an attack?

During those moments between watching the monitor and gaining the crest of the flume, I almost had a coronary with panic. I couldn't see whether Bonnie and Pocket and the brave but wounded Edney had been hit yet and the suspense practically pulled my skin off. All I could see in my mind was MacCormac as he blew poor Axell's head off, along with the face-hugger that had clamped onto him. The idea that Bonnie—that Pocket—

I ran harder, afraid that just our frantic scramble was trumpet enough to set off an attack. In my periphery I saw Tad pull a blue neon hood over his head, then all the way down over his face until he looked like a big blue posable artist's mannequin. That's when we heard the FOOM-*crack* of Edney's weapon being fired over the hill. It had started.

I ran so hard that he and I crested the hill together despite his head start, with Carmichael, in the flower of almost teenaged strength, right behind us.

Only ten feet from us, Bonnie and Pocket were huddled against the trunk of a tree-sized pillar, while Edney fired away, round after round, tightly firing but each ballistic shot carefully and instantly considered. Four face-huggers lay writhing on the ground, two of them blown in half, while maybe a dozen others had appeared and seemed to know their cover was blown and were trying to rush the victims. Carmichael skidded to Edney's side and together they began volleying the energy beam.

I fired my plasma gun, adding my short, popping blasts to

theirs. I almost missed every other time because the face-huggers were covering the distance now by jumping from pillar to pillar. Edney and Carmichael shifted back to ballistics and blasted away at the crawlers who got too close.

Too close! Hell, they were all too close!

"Run!" Tad bellowed as he tore right toward them.

Because he was now in our line of fire, the three of us shooting had to pause. "Get down!" I ordered to him, but he kept running right for them, pushing buttons on some kind of wristband on a pair of gauntlets he'd pulled on somehow between the blind and here. Head to toe, his blue suit began to glow like the sign on a cheap motel. Sparks flew from the suit. Each spark let off a second spark just as it hit its fizzle-point. Tad snapped, crackled, and popped his way right into the center of the hugger phalanx. Just as he reached them, he tossed a grenade of some kind over his shoulder, which landed near us and exploded into a huge—and I mean *huge*—ball of white stenchy smoke.

There was a squeal, several squeals, which to my untrained ear sounded a whole lot more like anger than surprise. I didn't want to wait around to see how angry those things could get.

"Retreat!" Edney called.

Carmichael grabbed Bonnie and I grabbed Pocket.

Bonnie tried to pull away. "The ship! It's that way—"

"No ship! Come on!"

Pocket gulped, "Where—"

"Don't argue!" I took hold of his ponytail and cranked his head in the direction I wanted him to go, then put a knee in his butt to encourage him along.

I cast a quick look behind us at the slowly dissipating cloud of stink and saw the huggers turn and flock after Tad, who disappeared down a gulley. The face-huggers were after him now.

Should I help? I shoved Pocket after Carmichael, Edney, and

Bonnie, and stumbled for a moment at the edge of the stink cloud. Where had Tad gone? They were all after him—those god-awful things.

"Rory, let's go, man!" Pocket called as Carmichael hooked his arm and pulled him away.

"Right . . ." Reluctantly I turned and ran back toward the blind.

"Bonnie! What the devil in a bowl of spice are you doing here!"

Clark's voice boomed in the otherwise quiet hideout.

The blind felt cold now compared to the outside, and it seemed dark to my stinging eyes. I stumbled in after Carmichael, to find Clark already confronting Bonnie.

Pocket collapsed onto a box and sat there sucking air mechanically, while Bonnie, pasty pale with fear, blinked up at Clark. Neil and Zaviero made sure the projector veil was closed behind us.

"Tad's still out there!" I gasped.

"He'll be okay," Neil said. "He's cloaked."

"What 'cloaked'? He was running!"

"It's a distracting technique. Here, look."

He led us like a gaggle of baby ducks to the wall of screens and pointed at a screen in the middle, which showed Tad in his totally blue glowing suit, now standing perfectly still in a grotto. He stood in the open, and around him a dozen huggers clawed and scratched at the ground, hunting and snooping, but finding nothing. Or at least, seeing nothing. Did they have eyes? Sensing nothing?

"Can they see?" Clark asked.

"Somehow, they do," Neil said. "It's more than just sensing, because they've been known to jump at people from behind glass, which means they see."

"Why aren't they seeing him?"

"It's the suit."

"But he's standing right there," Clark pointed out.

"Somehow they can't see past the blue glow. We tested a whole bunch of spectral combinations. There are two they can't see. As long as he stands perfectly still and the projectors on the suit don't flicker, they'll lose interest."

Bonnie shivered and hugged her medical pack. "I can't believe he's standing so still!"

"It takes practice," Zaviero said from way up there at the top of his body. "Tad's talented."

I fought to calm my aching lungs. "What were the sparks?"

"Those, they can see," Neil said. "The sparking creates a movement, and they don't like the stink bomb, so sometimes we can get them to run in a particular direction."

"Sometimes?"

Neil wobbled his head. "Yes . . . most of the time. Sometimes."

"Okay, okay," Clark began, and turned to Bonnie and Pocket. "Okay, I'm calm. Now, what are you doing here and why did you leave the ship against orders?"

Pocket glanced at Bonnie, then back to Clark. "What do you mean, what are we doing here?"

"Should I say it in Spanish?"

"We got your message to come out," Bonnie said. "A distress call."

"What distress call? We didn't send any."

Bonnie blinked and faltered. "Y—yes, you did. Somebody did . . . Theo picked it up in the scrambler. When we unscrambled it, we got a signal of distress with flash for rescue."

Clark shifted his weight and hung his hands on his hips. "We didn't send anything."

Pocket, Bonnie, and Edney were mystified.

"We're not stupid," Pocket said. "We got a signal."

"By voice?"

"Yeah, but garbled. We couldn't tell whose voice it was."

"Male or female?" I asked.

Pocket rubbed the back of his neck. "Huh?"

"I'm gonna get to the bottom of that," Clark huffed angrily. He started to go toward the table, to ask around, but I pulled him back with a move so sharp that it drew attention. I waited a second, until that attention faded back.

"Don't say anything about it," I instructed.

He frowned. "Why in hell not?"

"Just don't. Something's going on here and I'd like the chance to figure out what it is."

"Aw, there's just some screw up and I'm gonna kill it."

"Does it hurt to shut up for a while?"

He paused, partly to calm down and partly to consider the fact that I was asking him to do something completely illogical. He trusted me and in that moment I felt gratified. "I don't know," he said. "Does it?"

"Somebody's playing with us," I warned.

"Come on, Rory, you're looking for trouble. There's some screw up or a malfunction. I need to make sure it doesn't happen again."

Baldly sarcastic, I chided, "I think we've been in some trouble so far, Clark."

"Those were just terrible accidents. Don't make more of it than it is."

"Just keep quiet. I want to hear what M'am volunteers about it, if anything. Later you can tell me I was wrong. Deal?"

He drilled me with a glare, during which I think he was remembering that I'd been right about the researchers' still being here and alive. He fought to control his frustration. "Mmm . . . well, deal, for now."

He shook his head and wandered away to watch Tad stand absolutely still on the bank of screens. There were now only two huggers lurching around Tad's glowing blue suit. The others had moved on their way, possibly still looking for us.

"You come with me," he said to Pocket. They went around the other side of the stacked containers for some kind of captain-to-crew lecture.

Corporal Edney turned to Carmichael. "Let's find the colonel and make a report."

"Yes, ma'am," the kid said, and followed her away. Neil stayed to monitor Tad's statue imitation. Zaviero lost interest and wandered somewhere.

I turned to Bonnie, who looked confused and ashamed. "That was pretty brave," I told her. "Brave, and nuts."

"This whole thing is nuts," she said with a sigh. "I kept thinking of what might happen to you and the captain out here, how you turned right around after we were attacked and you came right back out here . . . what would I think of myself if I didn't do my part? I couldn't go back to Earth and report to PlanCom that I hadn't even tried to participate. When the distress call came in, I guess I . . . thought . . . providence had kicked in."

"Like I said. Pretty brave."

Embarrassed by the compliment, she looked kind of cute and sweet there, with her blond dirty hair all wild and her blue eyes rolling at her own risky behavior.

There was a commotion near the table, and we discovered that my mother and several of her team had come into the chamber with MacCormac and the Marines, and everyone was clamoring about the episode we'd just barely survived—again.

"Why did you rush out?" M'am demanded as soon as she saw me. When she spoke, everybody else fell silent.

I shrugged. "They were in trouble."

"We'll handle the trouble from now on. You did it again—attracting attention to the wrong area. Now Tad's having to stand-pet out there to distract them."

"Stand-pet?"

"Petrified," she clarified. "It's a skill. You don't have it."

"Sorry," I said, just to get it over with fast.

"Sure you are," my sister commented. I hadn't even seen her come in.

Our mother made a mighty show of controlling herself. "You must let us handle these things. This place is like a hospital. Things are done in exacting ways for good reason. First and foremost, you may not leave the blind without escort."

"Tad was with us," I wryly noted. Okay, so I was just being snotty.

"For the good of us all," she said firmly, "while you live in our house, you follow our rules. All of you." She turned to make eye contact with Clark, Pocket, and the Marines. "Is that clear?"

The Marines looked at MacCormac to speak for them.

After a moment, he did. "We'll make every effort to comply, ma'am."

M'am looked at Clark.

He nodded. "Okay, my crew will comply. But I need to contact the ship to confirm that they are not to exit under any conditions."

"Graciella will help you do that without causing incorrect signals. Everyone, please clean your hands for dinner, using the dry cleaner which Neil will give to you."

She motioned the gathering toward Neil, who waved everybody to the far end of the dinner table.

Then she turned to me and Bonnie. "Rory, will you introduce us, please?"

Bonnie was busy beaming and trying to mash down her insane hair.

"Oh, sure," I said. "Bonnie Bardolf, this is my mother, Jocasta Malvaux."

"Miss Bardolf. Pleasure to meet you."

"Oh—me too!" Bonnie bubbled. "I'm *such* an admirer . . . I've read your books and watched your videos and I was hooked when you addressed Congress to push the Alien Species Act through!"

"Thank you most sincerely," my mother said milkily. "You're very sweet and devoted, I can tell. A medical specialist?"

"Yes, I'm a resident physician. Not quite there yet!"

"I'm sure you'll be marvelous. What will you do after your residency?"

"I'm indentured to PlanCom for fifteen years."

"Ah. Let me know if you ever want to get out of it. I have some influence."

For the first time, a shadow of something less than hero-worship crossed Bonnie's face. "Oh . . . thanks, but I'm very comfortable right now. PlanCom's been very good for me."

"Of course." My mother's gentle smile was as practiced as a professional model's. "You'll join us for our meal. You can sit next to me."

Bonnie fell for it. She bounced on her toes with excitement at meeting her idol. M'am took her by the arm and escorted her to the table, around which the mismatched gaggle of humans was beginning to form. They sat on little uneven benches made of boards and more crates.

Before we joined them, Clark leaned toward me and whispered, "Do you call her 'Ma'am' all the time?"

I nodded. "I was almost eleven before I figured out it isn't exactly the same as 'Mom.'"

He sighed. "She seems real sweet, Rory. You sure you're not just imagining this because you don't like her?"

"Maybe you better ask *why* I don't like her before you write me off."

He lowered his voice even more, which only gave me the idea that there wasn't surveillance inside as well as outside. Clark didn't suspect that—but I started to.

"You may not realize it," he said, "but you have control over something huge and important for all mankind. What you say goes, as far as releasing the PPs. Aren't you kind of intimidated? I know I am."

"It doesn't intimidate me all that much," I told him. "Unless I think about it or some jerk reminds me."

We joined the others and found places to sit. The so-called food sat in serving containers put on the table by Oliver, the "chef." There were bowls of grains, several kinds of dried fruit, dried, rolled tortilla things stuffed with something green, and spiky vegetables, also dried. I assumed the drying was to eliminate the aroma of fresh growth.

Nobody took anything. I got the idea it was the same as when Gracie and I were children—nobody touched the food till the queen was ready.

M'am took her seat at the far end of the table, in what was obviously the place of central attention and honor. "Attention, team, my dear friends, and children. Captain Sparren and my son Rory, and their Marine friends will be leaving soon and launching their ship off the planet. They know they've compromised months of work by coming here and we know it was an honest mistake. They've promised to leave as soon as the area can be cleared and we can deliver them back to their ship. We are sad to note the deaths of some people today who came to our planet without knowing how to live safely here, and we are crushed to lose them for no good reason. We would like to note their courage today and to mourn their loss. They did not come here to die, but to rescue us. They didn't know we don't need rescue. And to our new friends, Miss Bonnie and Mr. Pocket, and Marine Edney, we would like to note your courage as well for answering the distress call."

"What do you know about that call?" I asked, dashing her dramatic monologue. I didn't want to let it go by, and I didn't think Clark would ask.

My mother's eyes focused firmly on me and she paused long enough to make a dramatic effect. "The only possibility is that your Marine tried to send one before he passed away during his battle with the primal stage."

She made it sound romantic, as if Brand had "passed away" in his sleep during some moral quest.

It was a better answer than I expected. I suppose it was the best answer. Some of my suspicions began to calm down. I was probably more on edge about her than I needed to be.

When I didn't forward any arguments to her logic, my mother continued addressing the entire table. "Whatever things are now, they are. When we decide, we will deliver you back to your ship and you may be on your way. We'll enjoy our meal, and then I will take my son and Captain Sparren on a tour of our most beautiful area. It will be relatively safe by then."

Before we had a chance to mull over the term "relatively," I poked Clark and said, "'Scuse me."

He looked as if he'd eaten a bad olive. "Yeah?"

"Tell them, please."

His head wagged a little from side to side, then huffed out a breath and seemed to accept that there was no point in continuing the misconception. "Yeah," he uttered unhappily. "I'm sorry, but . . . Mrs. Malvaux, I'm afraid you got the wrong idea here."

My mother sniffed through a napkin. "Pardon?"

I knew that inflection. The one that pretended she didn't know exactly what he was going to say when really she did. I'd heard it before. Kids tune in to these kinds of things with their parents, then later nobody believes them.

Clark pulled a computer slide out of his pocket. He held it between his thumb and forefinger to show the official seal. "This planet has been declared a dying planet with a fatal disease. The aliens are classified BioHazard One, a plague that will destroy the planet's biosystem by wrecking the food chain. They'll consume every animal over twenty pounds and the food chain will collapse."

My mother counted off a dramatic pause before speaking. "How do you dare to say this? Where do you get such information?"

"From you," I spoke up. "It's all your own research, deep-spaced back to Earth for analysis."

"You're using our own reports against us?"

"Not *against* you, Mrs. Malvaux," Clark said. "For your own good. For the good of this planet."

Accustomed to arguing her point before committees, companies, boards of directors, and Congress, she kept her cool but spoke with a very firm and decisive method. "This is not "our good" at all. We will not be leaving our work behind before we barely get started."

Clark avoided the eyes of everybody else on the team and just tried to face down my mother. "Our ship is loaded with robotic hunter-killers filled with coded poison to neutralize these aliens. We call them 'PPs'. Poison-packers. We have orders to sterilize the planet of all non-native DNA."

"But *we* have non-native DNA!" Gracie argued.

He looked at her. "It's not aimed at you. Everybody in this outpost will have to be evacuated back to Earth until the poison-packers have completely scoured the planet, which we figure might take a year. It's aimed at the alien species you're here to study."

"But we're not finished!" my sister continued. "It took us half this time to set up this outpost! We just mounted the last two cameras yesterday! We've barely begun the real observation!"

"Nothing will happen to the outpost," Clark explained, faltering some. "It'll still be here and usable after the planet is cleansed and we have a good planet for colonization, right in a spacelace. You can return here in a year and take over right where you left off—"

Gracie slapped her hand flat on the table. "After you've killed off the subjects of our research!"

"You can't do it," our mother said. "No, you can't." She remained calm, but she was starting to twitch around the eyes, brows, and lips, and her hands were pressed knuckle-down onto the table. "These actions are in violation of the Alien Species Act."

Clark drew courage from a little glance at me, and went on with his obviously rehearsed statement. "This planet's been declared an exception to the ASA. The aliens are regarded as more dangerous to other innocent forms of native life populating this planet. We have your reports of the ecosystem's population of—"

"There is much native life here, yes! The Xenos are part of that life! They show intelligence enough that the ASA applies!"

"There's no point to arguing points," I said, as quietly as possible and still firm. "This planet has to be evacuated. The aliens need to be wiped out before they wipe out everything else."

"You have no right to destroy them on a planetary scale!" my mother said angrily. "You want to exterminate a healthy species for profit!"

We'd hit a nerve.

Knowing it would make her crazy, maybe break down her control, I leaned an elbow on the table and casually said, "Everybody does everything for profit, M'am. You courted billions so you could fund your expedition."

"That's not profit!" Gracie exploded. "This isn't just some decadent vacation!"

"Oh, like hell it isn't. You took somebody else's money and spent it the way you wanted it spent. What do you think 'profiting' is? You can profit for your purposes, but somebody else who spends the money on his own family is 'decadent.' What makes your choices more moral than anybody else's?"

"We don't spend our money on eccentricities!"

"Then what are you doing here?"

"Advancing science!"

"What've you learned? How they breed? How they kill? We already know that."

"I hate you."

"They have a right to be here," our mother said, breaking into our argument as she had so many times in our lives.

"No more than we do," Clark took over again. "They're as alien to this planet as humans. They'll destroy it. We won't. If you want to cherish the planet, this is the way."

"I will defend this helpless species, Captain."

"They're a disease, Mother," I said. "According to your own reports, they sweep through an area, consuming or implanting every species that accommodates them, then they move on to the next group. If you do the math, this planet won't have any of its native species left after another year of this invasion."

Gracie turned another shade of red. "That's a lie!"

"No, it's not. I read your reports. They're consuming their way through every native species big enough to host their larvae. A whole planet's health trumps one invading species."

Our mother pressed her arms straight and leaned on the table. "I refuse to allow you to use my own data against me to your evil purpose."

Sweating visibly now, Clark stood his ground. "'Fraid you have no choice. Your research hasn't given us any reason to be hopeful that this species would be, like you say, subordinated in time to save the planet's food chain. The Alien Species Act makes an exception when 'kill or be killed' is the rule."

"You're lying," she said with a twisted smile. "This is a lie. You're simply lying. There's no such clause in the Alien Species Act."

Clark shrugged in a kind of apology that wasn't really one. "I'm sorry to tell you the amendment was added after you left on this mission. A lot of people were nervous that it was so inflexible, given what we know about the, uh, Xenomorphics."

"This planet will *adapt*. It is adapting. I'll be able to prove it. I *will* prove it."

"Can you prove it now?" I dared. "This species is like small-pox. It's a kill-or-be-killed species. There's no living with them, there's no way to reason with them, and they don't respect other species' territory. I've heard you talk about things like this before, M'am. I learned this from you. This planet has a death sentence on it. You're enamored of a disease and you actually want the disease to win. Ask your . . . your virologist here how a virus works."

Diego, the virologist, looked as if he'd been fingered in a line-up. He seemed terrified that M'am would actually ask him something. That was the moment when I noticed that nobody beside M'am and Gracie were speaking up. These people were either worshipful, or they were just plain cowed.

"Ask Bonnie here," I added, gesturing at my uncomfortable shipmate. "She's a doctor. If a bear breaks into your house, you can kill the bear."

Bonnie seemed very uneasy at being asked to challenge her idol's work, but when you've got a weapon, you need to use it. I needed some leverage right now.

My mother's arms quivered with effort. She drew a few long breaths to steady herself. "This is not 'our' house. They have a right to be here. They are beautiful and intelligent. We will not be leaving. So you might as well turn around and go away from here."

The cold food somehow seemed even colder. Nobody had taken a single bite.

"Tell her, Clark," I said through my teeth.

He cast me a desperate gaze.

"Clark," I insisted, "tell her."

Under the prickling glares of the entire research team, whose dreams he was about to trample, he found himself compelled by responsibility and the pressures of his title.

He pulled a small leather pouch from his vest pocket and opened it, showing a legal envelope, stamped with a seal, and the corresponding computer disk with the identical information.

"I have a court order."

The whole group of researchers gawked, gasped, and looked at each other in astonishment. Had my mother finally been subdued? They couldn't imagine it.

"Why do you come here with a court order?" my mother demanded.

"Because I told him to," I admitted. "I knew you'd resist."

A moment of uneasy silence twisted the recycled air.

"This is human arrogance at work," my mother proclaimed. "Mankind has gone through changing moralities. Slavery. Dictators. Kings. We have rejected them. This is the age of cutting edge decisions. This is the age when we stop looking at other species as if they have no rights."

She drew another breath to continue her soliloquy, but I stopped her before she got rolling and everybody ended up in tears to her favor.

"Rights are something specific," I said. "Rights are given to human beings through the Constitution. Animals don't have rights, or we lose the definition of the word."

"Humans are just animals," Gracie challenged. "The Xenos are intelligent. They communicate. They figure things out.

They'll be the dominant species. The same thing has happened all through history. Species move in and out—"

"And we're going to help this one move out. This planet is in the process of being overrun by these things."

"It's a dying planet," Clark attempted. "They'll destroy everything."

If my mother had ever loved me for an instant, that instant was eradicated right here and now as she glared at us. "This planet is adapting. It's about to strike back and battle the Xenomorphs to a level of integration. Nature is bigger than any species. It will subordinate them. The environment is changing and the planet belongs to the species that are here."

"Humans are here," Clark pointed out. I gave him a lot of credit for speaking up that way. He really must believe all that stuff he told me on the ship.

My mother somehow seemed to get taller. I wished we could bottle that trick.

She grew strangely calm in a projection of having regained control. I wondered if she hadn't "lost her temper" on purpose, to demonstrate her passion, and now would re-establish her authority through purposeful dignity. She's actually taken seminars on how to control situations, so I didn't think I was imagining this.

Very calmly, she began again. "This decision is premature. Even if we could have evacuated, now you have ensured we never can. We must stay to protect this species. They are beautiful and vibrant. They learn. They change. You can't get back to your ship without us, and we will not take you until we are ready to do it under our conditions. We will not go voluntarily. Will you and your soldiers attempt to drag us through this land? With all the noise and commotion, you might get forty feet. We came an amazing distance to do the research of a thousand lifetimes, and now we will stay to protect them from you and

your small universal view. As long as we remain here, you cannot release your genocidal machines."

She stepped away from the table and had to move behind
those of us sitting on the outer bench. As she passed behind me,
I felt the knife of her mind sink into my spine.

She paused, and looked down at me. "I'm certain you have
told him that. Being the law."

Coming around to the other end of the table, making it clear
she had no intention now of sitting down to dinner with us—
dinner was probably over before it had even started—she addressed the uneasy group once again.

"However, in fairness," she went on, "there's only this one
opportunity and I want to make sure it isn't missed. Is there any
one among you, and I'm speaking to my own children now,
who would like to give up our work here and go with them?"

I sat still and watched them. The campers sat still too, with
just their eyes shifting as they watched each other. Their chins
were down and each seemed to want to draw as little attention
as possible.

"This is your chance," M'am went on after a pause to see if
there were takers. "No other ship will come here for many
months. Probably years."

Another few moments of silence. Somebody coughed.
Nobody spoke up.

"Please," my mother continued. "Please listen to me, my
dears. This is my life's work. I will not abandon it. I would like
to encourage you, each of you in your own heart, to think
clearly about leaving now that there is a chance to go. I admit
freely that this is a difficult environment, more unforgiving,
more bleak than I ever imagined. I may have misled you. You
may have imagined something better. You may be disillu-
sioned. We have lost friends here. We have lost lovers. I have
no right to ask you to stay and every passion to bless you to

leave. Please . . . if you want to go, speak now. No one will think ill of you."

Clark's eyes were big as baseballs. He stared at my mother, then, without blinking, shifted his eyes to me in helpless panic. Should he speak up again, or was he hoping I would?

My mother beamed at her own team members. Ultimately the beam of love turned into a humble smile. "I knew I had picked the best people out of all of Humanity. I knew when I saw your faces in the crowd that you were each so very special . . . to be this dedicated . . . so . . . " She broke off into an episode of fighting back tears. "I'm so very honored," she murmured through her hand pressed to her mouth.

Nobody jumped up to comfort her. They just looked down at their excuse for food.

"Um . . . "

The sound was almost a squeak.

All eyes flashed to the chemist with the bowl haircut.

M'am's eyes zeroed in on him. "Yes, Rusty?"

Rusty shifted in his seat, suddenly the center of attention. "I . . . might . . . "

"Go ahead," M'am pressed.

"I might . . . like to go with them."

His tiny voice boomed in the silence.

"Well," M'am said, "I don't blame you. You're young. This is no place to spend one's early youth when you should be at parties and dating young girls. We will all miss you, darling, very much. We will have your excellent work to remember you by. Everyone, we must wish Rusty the very best and be happy for his choice. Today, when I go out with the captain and my son, you'll go with me for a final walk through our adventure. It will be your swan song. Would you like that?"

In some kind of creepy cult thing, they all started halfheartedly applauding Rusty. He blushed and looked both relieved and . . . something else.

"You see? Life will go on," my mother continued. "The planet will adapt to the Xenomorphs. They are becoming part of the living biosphere. I'm on the edge of proving that. I need more time. I can prove it, I know I can. I have a sense for them. They have a sense for me."

She raised her perfectly appointed chin and gazed above all our heads to the dream she saw in her own mind. She stepped back from the table and, unless I was imagining it, struck a pose.

"Someday," she proclaimed, "I will walk among them."

Clark and I, Bonnie, and the Marines sat wide-eyed with the boldness of the statement. Admittedly it was so bold, so wild, as to have a certain poetic shock value. She was an influential woman, the leader of a notable socio-political and scientific movement, and she was taken with her own press clippings. Maybe she had a right to be. I don't know. Her own people, my sister and the other misfits, were transfixed with worship. She had a nice little coven going here.

Or was their silence and awe really disguising another emotion?

I never had the chance to find out.

M'am took four calculated steps to the projector curtain. Her eyes narrowed in a mischievous way as she held her finger to her lips. "Shhh," she uttered.

She put her hand to a control panel and touch-padded a code.

The projector curtain beside her began to ripple, then to grow transparent once again. There, not more than a few steps away from the spot where my mother stood, and backdropped by the pink glow of the afternoon sun, were two of the monstrous adult aliens. One was back several feet, casually picking at its own tail the way a cat grooms itself.

The nearer alien was only steps from us, gazing upward at the glassy mountain which coifed our hiding place. The underside of its chin was a perfect triangle, fringed with gray-white teeth and a string of drool.

Everyone at the table froze in apprehension. Beside me, MacCormac made a slight shift of his hand toward his sidearm. I pressed my hand to his wrist and stopped him. Like frightened quail in the underbrush, we held perfectly still. Clearly, she was right—we couldn't leave the blind. Not yet. They were all around us.

My mother gazed in adoration at the creature which didn't know she was so near, near enough to slaughter with a sweep of its clawed hand, which hung in repose dangerously near the curtain. It saw only a projection of the landscape around it. If it drew any nearer, its breath might ripple the curtain and give us away. Or our mother's breath could do the same from inside.

She moved her hand very carefully from the control panel toward the curtain. She raised her fingers and moved her palm along the curtain to the level of the alien's hand. There she stood, in commune with the devil, truly in love with what she saw.

Her eyes glowed and she tilted her head in admiration and love. Her lips moved, and there was only the barest of whispering.

"*Some day . . .* "

CHAPTER SEVEN

"How does it work?"

"Light refraction, nanochips, electrical pulse, specialty scent masking, microvid units that assimilate the environment and replicate what's behind you . . . lots of things. They also stop the natural sloughing of skin cells that happens naturally to people when we just walk around."

Tad, the stealth guy who had somehow returned in one piece from his close encounter with the scorpio-huggeroids, picked and poked the suit I was wearing. I'd never worn blue in my life.

And this wasn't just "blue." This was bleeooooo. Electric blue. Las Vegas blue. This one was a superhero costume, all glowy and satiny, as if lit from within. It wasn't unforgivingly body-hugging, luckily, but had some room to it, but was so weightlessly constructed as to be flexible and not baggy. In the front parts of the thigh sections, the part of the body less likely to bump or be fallen on, were the computer components that ran the smart elements of the suit. When I bent my arms or legs, the suit emitted a faint crinkling noise from the millions of emitter smart-fibers in the inner and outer mesh layers and signal-channeling conduction foam sandwiched between them.

"If you stand absolutely still," Tad said, "the suit masks itself from their senses. There are certain wavelengths that they have trouble sensing. They probably won't notice you."

"It's the 'probably' that bothers me," I mumbled.

"You have to control yourself. It's hard," Tad warned. "Every molecule in your body says 'run,' but if you run, they'll see you."

"Like quail hiding in the brush? You have to hold your nerves?"

"And they're the devil to outrun, so don't think you can do that. You can't just put on a suit and go walk among them. You have to stand still and hope they don't bump into you."

I glanced at Clark, who was being fitted into his suit beside me. "Permission to beat ass, sir."

"Permission denied," Clark said as the chemist Rusty taught him how to pull the hood over his face. "I went diving a couple of times at Little Africa reef off the Dry Tortugas. This feels like that wet suit, only lighter."

"The elastomers are basically the same," Rusty said, "but they're embedded with sensors and emitters. They draw information and conduct emission from all the other layers. They even have a chemical element so we can make them broadcast certain aromas. I was in on the development of the formula range. Each suit is worth about fourteen million."

"How did you test the reaction of the Xenomorphs?" I asked.

Tad shrugged. "We hung up a suit and monitored their reaction to different emissions."

"Lost six suits," Rusty added.

Tad flashed him a cautionary glance, which I caught. "We're also working on holographics," he said quickly, "and anti-Xeno cages that are acid-proof and caked with countermeasures and cloaking chips."

My mother came in, wearing a blue supersuit that made her

look like a space opera diva. She surveyed us with way too much joy. "Are you ready for your tour?"

"Yes, ma'am," Clark said. "I have to tell you, I'm nervous about this. I don't like going out without the Marines."

"Your Marines would create more chances for trouble. The fewer people, the more we can control any chance of mistakes. You have been given your instructions on behavior? You must strictly obey them, or we cannot go."

"We'll comply," I said. I didn't want her to be watching me the whole time. "What about weapons? Defense?"

"We don't use them," she said. "Any energy discharge disrupts the field emitted by the suit. All you have to do is stand perfectly still. Even if you are seen moving, you can stand still and become lost in the panorama. In all likelihood, we'll not encounter any Xenos at all."

"How do you know?"

"Because we know where they are. We always scan the landscape on our visuals and heat-seekers before we leave the blinds. We might see them at a distance, but we observe them this way often."

"Hope I don't crap in your fancy suit," Clark admitted.

I made a face. "Couldn't mask that odor, could we?"

"All right," Tad concluded. "You're all on line. Put your boots on."

Rusty provided us with surprisingly comfortable and supportive blue boots with calf-high stovepipe uppers. Which was where I hid my plasma pistol.

Yeah, I know.

The four of us—M'am, Rusty, Clark, and I—moved out of the blind under the careful supervision of Tad at the entrance. This was some kind of mixed ceremony, a chance for my mother to show us things that would make her case, and Rusty's "last walk" before leaving the planet with the *Vinza*. I watched Rusty and had to admit he seemed comfortable with going out on this walk, despite my nasty hopes that he would be nervous or frightened. I had it in my head that M'am was setting us up, maybe to get rid of us, but the barometer of Rusty didn't bear that out. He had no hesitation about getting the suits and helping us with the picky donning process. Was it an honor to go out on this kind of "walk"? Did it show something I hadn't expected about my mother—that she wasn't holding a grudge?

Or did she just want to keep her enemies close?

Behind us, MacCormac and the other two Marines, Bonnie, and a handful of campers watched us with mixed emotions. Bonnie came to the perimeter at the last moment, and Tad pushed her back. The curtain closed over them, and all we saw after that was a near-perfect image of the canyonscape. The hiding techniques seemed artistic and modern, yet also seemed to be veils, not forts. If the veil were ever accidentally discovered, the aliens would just walk in with nothing to stop them.

Walking through the landscape of planet Rosamond 6 was both dream and nightmare. We followed my mother on unmarked paths which she clearly knew well, through the forest of glass columns and out onto an escarpment of plant growth of the kind only an artist's imagination or nature's wild wish list could conjure up. Pink vines draped hundreds of feet, stippled with fleshy cherry-like nodules, each with a tiny black fan sticking out of it.

"What are these?" I asked.

Rusty touched one of the little fans, and it happily fluttered. "That's its idea of a flower."

As we walked our trail, a strange sense of calmness came over me. My mother moved with such confidence at the head of the line that her demeanor was reassuring. She walked along without her blue hood, but we all did have gloves on.

I felt like a bad boy, having the plasma pistol hidden in my boot, but if I had to use it, I figured the cover would have already been blown. Can't break old habits quite this abruptly. Some people carried rabbit feet. Some people had lucky nickels. I had my plaz. Sue me.

The environment had gone from stark prismy red glass and black skulch to a lush gold and blue forest, and just when I started to get alien-planet overload, puffs of green fernlike growth started to line the path and declare that green was not just an Earth color. In fact, it was seriously green, bright green. Green that made Envy jealous.

"You can see," my mother began, "that there is wonderful growth here and many forms of life. There is algaeic life, microbial life, insect life, flightless birds, all the way up to premammals. We think we may have seen mammals, but we are still researching. You see how beautiful it is here, and we have managed to live in this environment."

"How many outposts do you have?" I asked.

She looked back at me. "What?"

"Outposts. How many? The blind back there was the main one, right? You have others? Where other researchers are working?"

She continued walking. After what might have been barely too long, she finally said, "Yes, sometimes we have remote outposts. They're isolated for specific observations."

"Can we see one?"

"This is as far as we can go today." M'am motioned us to her sides, and we discovered she was standing on a ridge. "Behold . . . the Blue Valley."

And it was. Below us flowed a magnificent vista that could only be compared to a god-sized single peacock's feather, with a dark eye at the bottom and waves radiating outward in shimmering circles of metallic blue and green, separated by rings of platinum and shot with strands of gold. The sun, now thinking about setting, shone through the red glass spires behind us and cast soft shafts of colored light into the Blue Valley.

And there was indeed life. Herds of large grazers with some sort of quills or stiff hair. Flocks of those flightless semi-ostriches with short necks and tall feathery coronets. Clouds of glitter-winged flitters. The pastoral scene was almost quaint. It was certainly hypnotic, the kind of thing that causes people to build hilltop mansions and get Adirondack chairs and tumblers of iced tea.

That might happen here, if Clark's vision came true.

I looked to my right. He stood on the other side of my mother, gazing over the Blue Valley vista, thinking of the wonders of his simple mission, of how many people would find paradise here while he retired to his wahoo fields. I envied him his easy dreams. They were the kind that came true.

And Jocasta Malvaux gazed too. She was as proud of the Valley as if she had painted it on a canvas and it had come to life. This was her dream too, this planet and its creatures. She knew, and so did I, and Clark and all of us, what efforts were cast by eternity to come up with a planet like this, a living and breathing world finding its way to fruitfulness in a barren galaxy. I turned my gaze to the sky—yes, there it was, the all-important moon, with its green stripes and lazy glow. Now that the sun was leaning its shoulder down, the moon opened its single petal.

"You see?" M'am said. "Here is a living environment, un-afraid and adjusting. There is no cowering, no fear. No panic or confusion. They live their lives, and the Xenos are becoming part of the beautiful quilt. They serve their purpose, hunting the weak and the slow, leaving the swift and strong to reproduce and flourish. To interfere is immoral now. They have settled in. They are the splendid dogs of Anubis, handsome adapters who will melt into this environment and become one of nature's controllers. That they are sharks, that they are cobras, that they are wolves, raptors, and all this is both relevant and irrelevant. If predators reign, we must let them. There are limits. Nature knows the limits. They cannot destroy a planet. When the easy prey for them is gone, you'll see the Xenos die back to a balance. They will be out-performed by animals that are fleeter of foot, that can fly . . . other strategies which will rein them in. I will remain here with my loyal few, to watch the history of the galaxy unfold, and bring the story home to Humanity. Someday I will walk with them and they will accept me."

Clark looked at me right over her head—he was tall enough and she was petite enough. I shook my head quickly and lowered my brows. *Don't say anything.*

"All I have to do," M'am went on, almost as though she were talking to herself, "is find out what triggers their higher senses. Whatever is necessary, I will learn to live among them and they will accept me as one of them."

Clark, on the other side of M'am, and Rusty here beside me, were either hypnotized or just freaked. I was particularly aware of Rusty.

"You cannot terraform a planet," she went on, "which has potential intelligent life, Captain. Not legally, not morally. Primarily, there are very few of those. If this planet adapts, then you have no right. The Xenos are now indigenous. The Xenomorphs are potentially intelligent, if they are not already intelligent. They are already quick and smart, and they communicate. That overrides terraforming rights. You will not wipe out this excellent, successful species so humans can have this planet. We humans have had enough of that in our history . . . wiping out each other, wiping out whatever is in our way . . . and I will not have my own son becoming the next Stalin."

I eyed Clark, and he shrugged at me in mute desperation. Did she have a point? Legally?

"To put humans here would ruin this paradise," she continued. "Humans are the lice, the wreckers, the egos. If we try to have a war with them, we will lose. You and your poison robots . . . the Xenos will out-think you, out-wait you, out-evolve you. You want to take over the planet in a few months, but they will find ways to wait a century, if they must. You say the Xenos are BioHazard One? The impatience of Humanity is the true plague, Captain. These things take time, much time. Some people in my field of science have actually inherited their work from their parents and grandparents. My daughter will inherit this outpost from me. The only hope for your colony, your settlement, Captain, is to let me continue my work. We can't live in spite of them. Someday, when my work is done and I have discovered the Xenos' secrets, humans will be able to live *with* them."

Her words brushed by and were carried on a breeze that had a faint scent of perfume. Had I been wrong about her?

I tried to maintain the level of cynicism I had forged about her, but today I had to admit there was a sliver of doubt. I hadn't spoken to my mother or my sister in about five years. People can change, can't they? The one thing I'd really been consistently good at in my life was not lying to myself.

So now I asked myself—why was I the only person on two worlds who didn't respect Jocasta Malvaux? If she was right and I was wrong, or if I bore any doubts—which at this moment I did—then we couldn't release the PPs. My friendship with Clark and the whole crew would be ruined. Everybody on Earth would be mad at me for denying them this second Earth.

But if she was right and this world could adapt, could flex a muscle and bring the Xenomorphs in thrall to the overarching controls of the environment, who was I to dispute a current and effective law? The Alien Species Act had been argued before

Congress by people a lot smarter than I was. My mother could never have pushed such a thing through on her own. Somebody else had to consider the points. We were still on the cusp of its authority, of all this interaction with life not of Earth. The ASA was created in anticipation of alien life, not based on experience with it. It had also helped to boost exploration in space, which otherwise was a pretty hard sell. It caused dreamers to dream. This planet might actually be a researcher's heaven, on the edge of evolutionary leaps that could be witnessed in action and not just studied in fossil form.

If I weren't her son, would I think of her the way I did?

I should never have taken this assignment. The possibility that I might be too jaded, too close to the emotional core to see clearly over it. She was right—this was a living, breathing planet, with a beautiful biosphere just minutes from where the aliens stalked.

"We will retire now." M'am nodded in agreement with herself and led the way back down the same trail.

"Are we going in?" I asked. "We haven't had a chance to use our suits."

"You don't want that chance," Rusty said.

M'am looked at him and said, "I suppose it's good that you're leaving, then."

Her tone was sweet, but her eyes were chilling.

Was it just me?

We fell into a single-file line again and didn't speak. Silence, unless broken by M'am, was part of the rules.

I had no problem complying, except for the occasional urge to mutter some remark to Clark. I had a lot of questions for Rusty, though. Why was he leaving? Was he lonely, tired, or afraid? And what was the core of his fear?

The way I see it, anybody who *wasn't* afraid in this place was loopy. I don't mind adventure, but nobody in his right mind wants to live his life in the middle of a spider's web, trying to avoid the spider. You'd never get anything else done.

Good point . . . what kind of research could they possibly accomplish in an environment where most of the time they were fighting for their lives? Maybe that was why there were so many "I don't knows" when we asked questions.

Gracie had said they were just beginning to do the research after finally setting up their camp and surveillance and other things. How long had they been here? The better part of two years? And they were just getting started?

All the way back to the blind, my skin was clammy with dread under the supersuit. Going into the alley was one thing, and turning around and walking out was another. I had always felt that knife between my shoulder blades, the one the thug sticks in your back after you think you've checked all the shadows.

I wished we'd been able to look around safely without the tour guide. How could I get back out there without my mother?

Seeing the projector curtain being held open by Neil, with Bonnie standing behind it and watching us approach—that was a good moment. We slipped inside, and the curtain was positioned artfully after us.

"It was beautiful, yes?" M'am asked.

"Can't deny that," Clark said.

She turned and said, "Rusty, if you would come with me for a moment?"

He nodded and followed her into one of the tunnels. The dinner table had already been taken down. The meal had been strained and quick. Nobody much wanted to talk after what they'd heard from Clark and me, and the party had broken up like a bad family reunion. "If you'll come this way, Mr. Malvaux," Neil said to me, "I'll help you get out of the suit.

We have to remove them and store them carefully so they don't get damaged."

"You can call me Rory."

"Okay, thanks."

I almost took a step to go with him, then got a flash of an idea. "Listen, why don't you take Clark first? Captain's privilege, and all."

Clark smirked at me. "Privilege? I sleep last, I eat last, I get a shower last—"

I clapped him on the shoulder. "So this time you get to go first."

"Can I have this moment bronzed?"

"This way, Captain." Neil gestured to Clark, and they went off together, leaving Bonnie and me in relative privacy.

"What was it like out there?" Bonnie asked quietly.

"Breathtaking," I admitted. "In a good way, I mean. Lots of native life, flora, growth, wilderness . . . real pretty and sort of sparkly."

"Do you think I could see it? Tomorrow?"

I shrugged. "Think you'd look good in blue?"

She smiled in a clunky, awkward way. "You do."

"Oh, yeah?" I twirled once and modeled the contraption.

"I'd love to see what you saw," she went on mistily. "I love the diversity of life. What life is and why things are alive . . . space fascinates me because it has a chance for totally new life."

"What do you think of the environment that created the aliens?" I asked.

She paused and thought about it. "Well, it must be incredibly complex, with a long food chain. If you look at them evolutionarily, they're not all that different from us."

"What?" I blurted on a laugh. "You're crazy. Look at them!"

"Right, look at them," she persisted. "Relatively comparable in size to humans, within a few feet of height and not that different weight-wise . . . they have the heads on top and the feet on the bottom, arms with fingers, and we still have our tail bones, you know. In comparison to, say, even an elephant or a sparrow, they're much closer to us."

"I guess. My sister says we're just more animals."

She offered another little smile, this one less convincing, but I think that was only because she was insecure about herself, while not at all about what she was saying. She shrugged, almost apologetically, and suggested, "We're the only animals that care about other animals. Human life is the best thing evolution ever came up with. Humanity is what nature was heading for all along."

She was an insecure person, or maybe just shy, and yet I found her so attractive right now that she represented all that was best about people. I'd grown up in a world of eco-heads, who thought people were just about the worst disease ever to strike the universe. I'd never believed it—I was the odd kid out—and my mother never approved of my approval of mankind. It was like coming from a religious family and just never seeing the logic in religions. I couldn't help it. I was born that way. I always saw the underside of the plate that was put in front of me.

And here was Bonnie, in this goofed out nest of vipers and their herders, the only one with the universe completely in order.

"What are you looking at?" She broke out in a nervous giggle.

I pressed my lips together in appreciation. "Know what you are?"

"What?"

"You're my mother if she were nice."

We were interrupted when M'am and Gracie appeared on the other side of the stacked containers which created a maze of little semi-separate areas in this central chamber. I held my hand up to quiet Bonnie. I knew an opportunity to eavesdrop when I saw one. Had my stalling actually paid off?

"Send Rusty," M'am said. "He still has his suit on. Put this recharged power pack in. We want no trouble in that sector."

"Oh, I'll send him, all right," Gracie responded. "I'd like to send him down some deep hole somewhere."

"As we have found, nothing stays the same. Better to shed the detritus than try to glue it on."

"He makes me sick."

"Send him immediately. And remember to have him code his suit to the new charge frequency."

"Fine."

They split up, and Bonnie started to speak, but I motioned her silent, and in a few seconds Gracie reappeared with Rusty.

"Just get it done. Replace the third and fourth broadbands and clean the lens."

"Isn't it kind of late in the day for Sector Nine?" Rusty asked. "Another hour, it'll be dark."

"Then I guess you had better move your useless ass, shouldn't you?"

"Aw, Gracie . . . "

"Turn around, traitor."

"Why?"

"Fresh power pack."

"Oh . . . thanks."

"Screw you."

I saw the point of her shoulder and a flick of long braid as she exited through the tunnel just opposite from where we were standing. I put a finger to my lips, signaling Bonnie to be quiet and stay here. Then I slipped out of our seclusion and caught Rusty at the projector curtain.

"Rusty, where're you going?"

He glanced around, not expecting that anyone else was still lingering around here. "Huh? Oh—I have to go do some maintenance in Sector Nine. It's my last official duty. I've done it before . . . just never alone."

"Is it a good idea to go alone?"

He seemed dejected. "I, uh, no, we usually go in pairs, but I've got the suit on already, so—"

"How about if I go with you?" I suggested. "I'm all dressed."

Rusty palmed his roundhead haircut and hesitated. "Doesn't sound like a good idea . . . I don't know, we've never had visitors. I don't know what the policy is. Maybe we should ask Jocasta first."

"I think I'm old enough to go out without asking my mommy. I'll behave. I'll be your rearguard. How about it?"

"I do have some fears about my rear," he allowed. "Guess it's okay."

Then he paused, and a strange thing happened. His eyes brightened and he pressed his lips flat, and said, "Yes! Good idea! Come on!"

Well, that was an odd change . . .

On the way out, I cast a glance back at Bonnie. She bit her lip and crossed her fingers in silent well-wishing. I put my finger to my lips again. *Don't tell anybody.*

She nodded.

Sector Nine was in the other direction from the way we'd gone with M'am. Rusty and I turned left instead of right out of the blind's curtained opening, and within just a few minutes the story began to change from the rosy glory my mother had wanted me to believe. This area had no lush beauty to boast, but soon turned decidedly less attractive.

And that wasn't just the landscape. Not more than seven or eight minutes out, Rusty cast me a glance at just the moment when a gassy odor struck me full in the face. I stopped walking, and sniffed. Rusty paused, his eyes wide.

I nodded at him. "I smell it."

He didn't say anything, as if wanting me to come to my own conclusion.

"As different as this planet is," I said, "the one constant in the galaxy is the smell of death."

Rusty closed his eyes for a moment of relief. He motioned me forward.

Within only a short distance, Rusty was leading me through a bone yard, the telltale leavings of assault. Skeletons and desiccated remains of fairly large beasts, maybe the size of adult pigs, littered the land, so prevalent we had to zigzag through them.

"What's this all about?" I asked.

"The Xenos killed them," he said. "It's a whole herd, wiped out in less than four days. Hundreds of them. Even what they don't consume, they slaughter. We don't know why. They destroy just to destroy."

"So much for the pretty picture," I said outright.

"Jocasta just sees the pretty part," he told me. "Keep your voice down."

"Sorry."

"Keep your eyes open."

"Any my mouth shut. Right."

"Yeah, mostly."

The carcasses around us were grotesque, with their ribcages exploded or their heads torn off, limbs separated from bodies while still on the run, or spines pulled out from the bodies with shocking ease. They told a story of gratuitous violence that most animals didn't engage in.

That was it—I'd never thought about it that way before . . . these aliens were violent for the sake of violence, for the joy and pleasure of it. I was sure my sister would tell me humans had been engaging in that hobby for eons, and that was probably true, but other humans policed the violence and were disgusted by it. This killing field around me spoke of a unified delight and unrestrained purpose that was species-wide. The Xeno-morphs had no self-restraint, no moral guardrails, and no sher-iffs among them. There was no controlling factor. They just killed to kill.

We moved with dispatch through the field of slaughter, and by the time we moved on to the next area, I was disgusted be-yond measure. We moved into a narrow passage flanked by what appeared to be very thin trees almost like fringe.

"Rusty, why do you want to leave?" I asked. I sensed he was afraid I'd want to know this, but also that he wasn't surprised to be asked.

"Just done my time here, is all. Ready for something differ-ent. Watch out for this web. Don't step in it."

I sidled away from the wide complex web he pointed to, which was spread across almost the whole path.

"Thanks. Look, I need a break, okay? I don't have all the time in the world. Can I get a couple of straight answers?"

"Like what?"

"Those people in the huts," I ventured, "were they locked in? Those huts were prisons, weren't they?"

He didn't answer right away. His hesitation stiffened my sus-picions that things were darker than my mother wanted por-trayed.

Rusty met my eyes as we came abreast of each other and picked our way through more bodies of animals, this time a flock of the flightless birds.

"You won't say I told."

"What is this, a Boy Scout troop?" Sarcasm didn't help. I chided myself with a glower and said, "Sorry. I won't tell."

He didn't seem reassured, and even lowered his voice, as if anybody could hear us out here. "They were incubation chambers. We took care of them the best we could. Jocasta said it was as kind as possible. Watch out for this crevice. Don't get your foot caught."

"So they were implanted with the . . . what do you call them, larvae? You shoved them into the hut and left the doors open to put food in?"

He blushed with humiliation. "We didn't feed them. It would've been—"

He cut himself off.

"What?" I demanded. "A waste of food?"

Ashamed, he nodded. We came around to a pathway that was actually a ledge. With a motion he warned me of the cliff we were now standing on. Rusty stopped and pointed.

Cliff . . . that was a crystal clear accuracy. The drop was shear and straight. We stood on the precipice of a two-thousand-foot ravine. Across the ravine, which was another thousand feet wide, was the floor of the Blue Valley. We were now level with the lush blue-green space, with its population of undisturbed herds and flocks, and from here I could see that the Blue Valley was actually a shelf. This ravine prevented access to it.

My mother had deceived me and Clark on purpose. The Blue Valley wasn't pristine or undisturbed by the Xenos . . . they just hadn't reached it yet. It was protected only by the huge protective gap now open before Rusty and me.

Rusty's eyes shifted to mine, and we understood each other. Postponing the inevitable didn't make it any less inevitable. He wanted me to see this.

"In a month," he said, "they'll be over there too."

He moved on, only another twenty feet to a sensor/transmitter array that had been drilled into the edge of the cliff, supported on a tripod. Rusty got down on his knees to reach the array and began to service it after rolling out a small set of very surgical tools. All I could do was watch.

"Why were the huts' doors open?" I pursued. "To hear their screams?"

"No . . . no. Even with the creatures in us, we were told we had no right to make our end swift and easy . . . no right to kill what was inside us. The infected people were locked in and the door was left ajar for the young to get out." He hung his head briefly. "Jocasta kept them inside so the rest of us wouldn't see the torture. Wouldn't see the young Xenos burst out of their chests or the blood . . . she treats us like children. She ritualizes the bad things and makes them holy. Like the Catholic Church celebrates the torture and mutilation of Christ, makes it into some kind of nice holiday with little bunnies and pictures of sunshine. If you sanitize something enough, people will embrace it."

The grimness of the moment betrayed many other dark truths about this place and the way of life the scientists had discovered here.

"I'm sorry, Rory," Rusty quietly said. "I shouldn't talk this way about your mother. I wasn't brought up that way."

I knelt beside him. "That's probably the best description I've ever heard, from anybody."

The compliment seemed to do him some good as he went on with his work.

Scanning the Blue Valley, way over there and seeming now like an oasis in a deadly desert, I asked, "I'll bet the doors were left open because she wanted the little gargoyles to live. Right?"

"She doesn't believe we have a right to kill them," he confirmed. "I don't blame her for that."

"Don't you?"

"We always knew that. She didn't hide that part."

"It'll be good to go home, won't it?"

He rolling his eyes and communicated a thousand fears and fatigues in that one moment.

I had a golden opportunity here. Like those times interrogating a witness, sometimes you have to know just how far to push—and when to take a leap.

"How many people have you lost, Rusty?" I asked, careful with my tone. "They're not in other outposts, alive somewhere, are they?"

Slowly he shook his head. His mouth worked as if he were about to throw up.

Again, I prodded, "How many are dead?"

"God, I really shouldn't be telling you this."

"I'll find out anyway. There's no more hiding about things like that. How many of the original fifty-two are dead?"

Like a valve releasing, he said, "Thirty-six." He turned to me in desperation. "We can't live here. We can't research here. They found every one of the other outposts. They never give up. They understand psychological warfare."

"My sister said you waited them out. That it took five months for them to forget."

Once again he shook his head, but not as if Gracie were wrong. It was as if Gracie knew the truth and had lied to me.

"They don't forget," he said. "It's impossible for us to wait them out."

"Then what is my mother up to?" I murmured, almost to myself. "If she knows you're all doomed if you stay, what's she trying to prove?"

He flopped back, knees folded under him, and stared down into the deep ravine. "She really seems to love them." He sighed a couple of times, then suddenly perked up. "Let's go back to your ship! Let's go right now, okay? Why go back to the blind? We can launch tomorrow, right? Can we leave tomorrow?"

His desperation and excitement about the chance to leave

confirmed what I had suspected—no matter what my mother said, these people needed rescuing.

I reached over and pressed his arm, hoping to keep the conversation on an informative track. There was no telling when I'd get another chance for clarity. "Who else wants to leave, Rusty? Who else is afraid to speak up?"

He parted his lips, and wasn't I surprised when the sound was a steady electrical chittering noise, fast and frantic. Rusty jumped to his feet without even using his hands to push off, and yanked his blue hood over his head and all the way down over his face.

Surprised, I bolted to my own feet. "What—what—"

"Stand up! Back up against the wall! Over here, over here! Stand still! Stand perfectly still!"

"Do I have to—do I turn it on?" Panic shot through me. "What do I do?"

"It's automatic! Pull your hood on!"

He reached for the back of my neck and for a horrifying few seconds we were both tangled up in trying to get my hood over my face. When we finally got it down, I was illogically confused by the fact that the hood seemed almost clear from inside, even though I could no longer see Rusty's face through his. More one-way-mirror fabric.

"Stand still!" He shoved me backward against the wickery of spindly growth, which felt like a wicker fence. "And be quiet!"

"Oh, shit!"

"And don't shit!"

How was I supposed to be still with my lungs heaving and my limbs quaking with panic? With monumental physical effort I flattened against the wicker and nearly suffocated trying not to pant or heave. I never worked so hard in my life.

Rusty, because he had to tend to me, ended up having to position himself right at the edge of the ravine, between the array tripod and a jagged finger of black rock standing straight up on the cliff's lip. The rock was almost as tall as Rusty, and he pressed sideways against it to have something to brace against. With almost military poise, he came to attention and froze in place.

I fixed my gaze on him in pure admiration and wished like hell I could get halfway that still. His suit began to glow softly, emitting something—sound, scent, I had no idea what—that would send some message or other to whatever was coming.

Where were they? How close? Did we have enough time to run back the way we'd come, or was that the direction they were coming from?

My mind flashed on the destruction I'd seen, on the punched-out ribcages and the acid-dissolved flesh, the impaled throats and dismembered limbs. So far I'd only witnessed the creatures' power by proxy. What the hell was I doing here?

This was one of those moments when every attraction for coming on this voyage suddenly dissolved and became microscopic. All I wanted to be was back home, being chased down a blind alley by some drug-crazed gang of Satan worshippers. That I could handle.

That noise . . . there it was . . . the rolling, crunching slow approach.

The noise was faint, purposeful. My feet turned hot and itchy. This path wasn't covered with the cereal-like skulch, but was shear weather-shaved rock. The approaching noise was soft and hinting. In my head it turned loud, deafening, enough to set my ears to drumming.

I was still panting! How could I stop? I fought to breathe evenly.

Overcome by fear, I dared to whisper, "Am I glowing?"

Rusty's hand flinched. "Yes. Shh!"

Suddenly a huge black form leaped out of the unseen area

around the bend. With a whump it landed between me and Rusty, arms up in a dare, knees bent, ready to leap again, and there it hunched, looking, sensing . . .

It had heard us. I'd tipped it off.

I wanted to kick myself—to run, to draw attention away from Rusty since I'd stupidly drawn it to him.

The alien was huge, bigger than the one Chantal had stuffed and mounted. Its elongated head was at least two feet above mine. Inside the smoked-glass skull rippled rows of cerebral sensors. The long anaconda tail drifted elegantly, held high and curled. Its outer jaws separated, drawing strings of saliva, and the creature began to sizzle in its throat.

The alien's shoulders rose, its knees bent more, long feet and claws scratching at the rock slab. The second set of jaws, the small square jaws, extended on their bony stick and made one decisive *snap*.

I knew a challenge when I saw one.

Dare you . . . Show yourself

Know you're here

It was a scout. Its job was to tease out whatever was in the path of the others. There could be a dozen behind it, or a hundred. Did they swarm or herd? There was a difference.

Rusty and I were only about seven feet apart. The alien stood almost perfectly between us. If it pivoted, that tail could hit either of us.

Rusty held his ground right at the edge of the cliff. His blue suit glowed softly, emitting a pale silvery corona all around his body. He was masterful in his stillness and I envied his self-control. I wasn't managing so well.

The alien hissed and threatened, turning its long tubular head as if it were listening for clues. All its senses were being scrambled or confused by the supersuits and somehow it couldn't tell we were here. I had to give a nod of approval to my mother's research team. They'd done it—they'd found out what *didn't* trigger the alien's senses.

I breathed a *wow*.

The alien's head snapped around to face me. I sensed it knew I was here—probably the same deep instinct that told it I was nearby.

We sensed each other. Now the sheer terror helped me to freeze in place, the kind of reaction I'd spent my professional life avoiding.

Rusty, a silvery man-shape a few feet away, made a scrape with his toe. Very short, very deliberate.

The alien snapped around. So it could hear, for sure.

Its spiny back twisted at my eye-level. Its tail floated past my face so close that I had to raise my chin to keep the spike from touching my noise.

Rusty stood absolutely still in his silvery corona. The alien hunched its spiny back, its snorkels fanning outward as it moved in small serpentine motions, never quite still, not quite moving. The huge head came down as if to run its teeth along the glow of Rusty's arm. If it pushed, nudged—it would find him.

Could I scrape my toe and distract it the way he had done for me?

But he was the expert here, the one who knew how to move among the grizzlies. If I took him into the crime district of a major metropolitan area, I'd expect him to let me make the moves.

My upper arms twitched, aching. My thighs trembled. The alien's tail whipped past my face again. I had no doubt that spike could take off my head.

Then, just when I felt as if my legs were breaking from tension, the alien relaxed its shoulders and turned its face away from Rusty. The second set of jaws, on their cartilaginous extension rod, drew back into the elongated main teeth, and those teeth closed into their relaxed position. The tail fell lower and stopped whipping, instead moving in gentle balancing motions to the shifting of the body. The creature took on a poised grace, that cobra beauty my mother saw when she looked at them. At this moment of near-death, I saw it too. She was right—they were the dogs of Anubis.

The supersuits were working. We had a chance to live. Our trust in technology was fulfilled.

Turning its body again to the path, the alien changed its posture, bringing its snorkels parallel with each other again, and it began to move past us.

I saw a flicker across the path. Heard something too. A crackle of electric surge. The silver corona around Rusty's suit began to sizzle and change color from silver to a sick yellow. Rusty's head moved, as if to look down at himself. In that deep place in a human mind that recognizes another human's body language after a lifetime of practice, I knew from that small change that he was in trouble. From the other side of the path, I watched with the terrible realization that his suit was malfunctioning.

CHAPTER EIGHT

The alien's bullet-shaped face snapped around toward Rusty. Its lips peeled back on a warning hiss. Again the shoulders came up, the knees bent to spring and the tail whipped.

Rusty's hands twitched as he tried to decide whether to grab for his power pack or the controls in the thighs of the suit. With each movement he destroyed the finely constructed field of disguise. What the alien saw, I don't know—ripples, flickers—but it saw something and it crouched into a threat position.

My mind raced. What should I do? Distract it? Make myself the target? There was no jumping on it—that was suicide.

Rusty shifted in burgeoning panic. His suit chattered and failed entirely with a weak final *szzz*. He ripped back the hood, and in that second the terror in his face was heartbreaking. I don't know why he pulled the hood off—something about looking death in the face?

"Oh, my dear Lord," he murmured at the creature, as if it understood.

The alien responded with a punctuated roar that separated its main set of teeth into a wide-open spiked weapon. This time the second set of teeth stayed in, but made a sharp snap at Rusty.

It leaped at him. Rusty let out a single yelp as the animal sprang. Its long limbs made quick work of the few steps between them. As Rusty yanked backward, the alien's teeth clapped shut on the flopping blue hood instead of his head, but its long fingers and claws cupped his head and sank into his shoulder. His arms came up in defense and the two bent into a wicked embrace.

A bird in the claws of a young cat, Rusty bellowed in agony and terror. Even in the middle of his desperation, he found the empathy to shout, "Run! Run, Rory!"

And he began to scream that bone-breaking high-pitched scream that can't be faked.

Moving was almost a relief. But I didn't run. I pushed off the wall and grabbed the alien by the tail. My hands, in the blue gauntlets, fitted into the spine-like segments and I put all my weight into pulling backward. The animal had Rusty by the hood with its mouth, and its hands had him by the ribs. When I dropped backward, almost dipping my butt to the ground, it parted its teeth, dropped the blue hood, and growled at me.

And I almost crapped my trousers. That was some sight. The dead one in the blind had been hideous enough, and now this.

I tucked the animal's tail under my left arm and clamped my arm down so I could use my right arm to go after my plasma pistol. I drew on it and fired instinctively. The plasma blast blew a hole in the alien's braincase a little forward of the middle, splattering acid on Rusty, who threw his arms up to shield his face. Acid droplets began to eat away at his sleeves, causing streams of green smoke to rise from the fabric. He made an awful gasping noise and writhed back toward the cliff's edge, and one foot went over the side. He toppled over like a bottle knocked off a table.

His weight took the alien with him. I would've fired again,

except the first shot caused my supersuit to fritz and spark. Damn! The energy flush must be disrupted by the plasma bolt!

A jolt of shame struck as I realized there really had been good reasons for telling us not to take weapons along.

As the alien's tail whipped powerfully in my arms, coiling around the back of me, I dropped the plasma pistol. It fell between me and the cliff's edge. Now bearing the weight of Rusty and half of the alien's body, I fell to the ground and used my heels to dig in. That wasn't going to last—the physics weren't there.

Over the cliff, Rusty gasped and cried out in panic, still in the grip of the alien, and the damned thing wasn't dead yet. As their weight dragged me to the edge, I braced my left foot on the embedded housing for the video unit, clamped my left arm down as tightly as possible, and grabbed outward for my plasma pistol with my right hand—and caught it.

I brought it up shooting. Three bolts flew wild, arching down into the ravine two-thousand feet below us in what would've been a real pretty display if only somebody had been around to appreciate it. Rusty and I, we were busy.

Just as my legs started to inch over the cliff's edge, I gritted my teeth and aimed, and fired.

This bolt went right into the back of the alien's long head and powered through to the front, then took out it's entire excuse for a face. The skull case broke in half the long way and fell to the sides in two unevenly cut pieces. In a final convulsion it dropped Rusty.

With one long pitiful howl, Rusty tumbled into the ravine, his arms flapping and legs pumping. I dropped the animal's big tail, and it went over too. Together they spun into the depths. I twisted around and looked over in time to lose them both in the toupee of overgrowth below. Another second, and Rusty's cry abruptly stopped.

Not only had I lost a good man, I'd now lost the only other person who knew this was no paradise about to be born. Would anyone else believe me?

And then, I heard the crunching sound. The rolling sound. The advance scout was dead, but his roars had been heard.

I got up and ran. Somehow I still had my plasma pistol in my right hand, but my left gauntlet was missing, probably over the cliff, caught in the alien's tail. My suit stopped fritzing because I wasn't shooting. I ran down the grade, hearing the clicks and hisses of aliens—no idea how many—behind me all the way. I tried to tell myself it was my imagination, that I was just spooked, overwrought, scared—but, no, they were there, coming for me.

At the bottom of the grade I skidded to a halt and, lungs heaving, tried to stand-pet again, to stand perfectly still and let the suit reboot itself and begin the masking technique it was developed for. If it fooled one of them, it could fool several. A whole herd. Right?

I tried to stand still. Maybe I didn't do it right. The suit began to glow and make that faint hum, only to fritz and crackle just when it got going. I'd wrecked it! I'd ruined the effect by shooting my plaz! The electromagnetic pulse had completely fried my only hope.

I had to live through this hour. I had to save these people. If there were more like Rusty, but afraid to speak up—and I had to save Clark and Bonnie, so close to falling under my mother's spell. The message of the slaughter fields had to be delivered.

At the top of the grade, in the last vestige of the setting sunlight, I saw them. They were black silhouettes against the crest of the hill and the evening horizon, a solid line of undulating heads and tails, hands and snorkels, as if dozens of aliens were being melted into a black stew.

The suit fritzed again, as if to say, "*Go!*"

I fired twice over my shoulder as I ran. Shrieks rewarded my shots, but also howls of anger. The suit crackled one final time, overwhelmed by the energy flush from the pistol. It was all done.

I rounded a bend, went through the stick-like field, jumped and dodged the seemingly endless carpet of corpses in all their many stages of decay, racing the best I could in the fading light through the killing field that would soon describe the whole planet, if these creatures had their way. If I survived, what could I say to the others? Were there more like Rusty, but afraid to speak up? His suit had failed—that was no coincidence. Fresh power pack, sure! It didn't take a forensic team to add that up, did it? This was what my mother meant by "a last walk."

They were on me the whole way back. I didn't know whether they could outrun me or whether they had the inclination to and wasn't interested in clocking them, but I'll bet I set a record or two that I could wave under the noses of a few high school acquaintances. I traveled down two slides on my ass, which shaved off seconds and put a whole new definition to thinking with my legs, like Clark said.

When I hit familiar territory I was rewarded with a surge of victory, like maybe I'd actually get out of this alive. Only then, when I caught sight of the patch of landscape which I knew was the projector drapery, did I skid to an insane halt and catch myself on a glassy stump.

I couldn't go in there! I couldn't blow everybody else's cover! If just one alien saw me run through the opening, every person inside was doomed.

With a sinking stomach I veered away from the hiding place. I hoped I'd turned in the direction of the ship, like possibly I could make it back there and hope somebody would open the ramp for me, hope they were on their toes, because I had no idea how to make the ramp open from the outside. Nobody had ever taught me that—who'd have thought I'd need to know it?

Before I even made it up the flume, while still in sight of the projector curtain, they rounded the bend and closed on me. They swept past the hiding place and up the flume toward me. I fired again with my plasma pistol, repeating the shots, hoping to discourage them. My plaz was beginning to weaken, almost out of power. It was never meant to be an assault weapon, fired more than eight or ten times. It was just for self-defense.

Self-defense—what a joke!

The rank of Xenos were behind me, and now two of them appeared in front of me. They'd headed me off.

Skidding to a halt, with nowhere to run, flanked by glass columns and trapped on every side, I shouted wildly in that last moment when all I could do to save my life was shout, even knowing it wouldn't work. And they were on me.

One of them came out of the circle as they closed on me, possibly a leader or just the one that got to me first. I threw my drained plaz at its head. The gun made a silly *pok* on the creature's skull and bounced to the skulch. The animal looked down at the gun, and at that moment I leaned back on a broken glass stump and brought my foot around in the best kick of my life.

I knocked out some of its teeth. Good for points, but it had no effect except to make the creature mad at me.

"Come on!" I screamed. "Come on!"

It tilted its head at me and hissed. The jaws parted and the second set made a quick series of snaps at me. The other aliens closed around us, making an unbreachable fortress for my demise. My pounding heart slowed and I could suddenly breathe again as I accepted my fate.

"Make it fast," I said.

The creature stiffened before me, hunkering into a threat position. Its claws clicked inches from my face.

A soft, long noise began on a finger of wind. It came from over the rocks, through the glass spires, from far away, like thunder.

No, not thunder . . . this sound was like the low hum of a brass instrument, a baritone or trombone, or two together making a chord. I thought at first it was the sound of my blood running cold. Then I knew it was real sound and I was really hearing it.

The alien before me raised its head and turned the great long skull as if trying to hear the location of the trombone call. Its companions did the same, each turning its head in the same direction.

Was I still alive? For a few seconds, I honestly wasn't sure.

The long moaning call grew in intensity over the land. The aliens around me straightened to their full heights and extended their tails horizontal with the ground. Inside the smoke-glass tops of their skulls, the flesh of their brains—or whatever that was—began to ripple and buzz in answer. The buzz increased and became the same low, moaning, brassy call.

The alien in front of me stepped back. It lowered its hands and tail, shoulders and snorkels. I recognized the passive stance. For creatures I hadn't wanted to be anywhere near, never thought I would get to know, I recognized a lot all of a sudden.

Through the long moaning call, I head the shouts of human voices. At the crest of the flume, Colonel MacCormac appeared with Clark, flanked by Carmichael, Edney, Pocket, Bonnie, and Tad, and in the middle of them, oddly out of place, appeared my mother. She was yanking MacCormac's arm just as he raised his weapon, and Edney had to kick at Tad to get him to leave her alone with her weapon raised. I got the idea they'd charged out of the blind against her orders, and she and Tad had been sucked out with them, trying to stop them. Carmichael and Edney raised theirs also and prepared for MacCormac's order to volley.

I raised my hand in a signal to them. *Stop.*

MacCormac, ever alert, caught the motion and held fire. The other Marines, well-drilled, did the same.

The fluttering inside the alien's braincases became softer, all at once. It was as if they were all singing in a choir, being directed by some conductor in the sky. They lowered their heads and drew up their tails, let their arms down and became sordidly calm, reminding me of black storm clouds.

I motioned again to the others to stand still, not break the sorcery. What were we seeing?

The alien right in front of me, the one who had been about to take my head off, relaxed suddenly. The deep sound of horns tapered off and echoed into nothing. The land was once again still in the last vestige of sunset. The last ray of the sun lay on the head of this alien.

I pushed myself up off the stump and braced my legs, standing before the animal in a truly eerie equality. This was like being haunted.

Armored by the heady drug of having accepted my death, I was emboldened to reach out. I slapped the animal in the head.

Its head tipped sideways, then came back straight. It made no moves to retaliate. It didn't want the fight I was trying to pick. Didn't want—or wasn't allowed. I didn't know which.

I took off my right gauntlet and slammed the creature right in the mouth.

It shook that great head almost the way a horse shakes its withers. But it wouldn't attack me.

"Well, dang," I grumped.

I wanted, strangely enough, to ask my mother what she thought of this. Maybe she knew.

As if called by a mental signal, M'am moved forward from the others, leaving MacCormac and the Marines, Bonnie, Clark, Pocket, and Tad stood poised to run, shocked by the stillness. My mother came closer, daring to step between two aliens, who simply turned their eyeless faces toward her and stepped back to let her pass.

"What's happening?" I choked. "What . . . what is this?"

M'am's petite body, in khakis and still build like the ballet dancer she had been in her youth, turned in a delicate pirouette of study.

"I'll tell you what's happening," she murmured. "This is a giant leap forward."

As my chest ached with plain old terror, she came to the center of the circle of aliens. She raised her wrist to her lips, and touched the communication link strapped to it.

"All of you, come out. It's safe to come out. Graciella, bring everyone out. This is history. You must see this."

In mere moments, the other researchers, led by my astonished sister, appeared in the line of humans at the crest of the flume. My sister stared, poised for something she couldn't predict, and with her came Diego, Zaviero, Chantal, Dixie, Neil, Oliver, and the others. Amazing, really. They had all actually come out at my mother's call, without the slightest question. Were they more afraid of her than of the aliens? Could that actually be true?

And there she was, arms raised in honor of the creatures standing here in the small area with us. You must see this, she had said. What she really meant was, you must see *me*.

"Come," she said to the audience. "Come, witness all of you . . . and you who were ready to exterminate them . . . you, who can now go home. Witness this evolutionary leap! I told you it would happen. Nature is controlling them." A necromancer performing her danse macabre, she raised her graceful hands. "We can walk among them!"

I don't believe in my life or any time in history I've heard of a more fulfilled human being than my mother at this arcane moment of transcendence. For her, this was a religious experience. The gods had opened the doors and invited her in.

She was allowing us to see, to be her witnesses, not exactly to walk in with her.

We all stood stupefied, waiting for the spell to be broken and chaos to erupt. For a while it didn't. Then, it did.

Just as we were beginning to believe that we might be safe through some bizarre favor of providence, a chittering noise broke the enchantment. I heard Bonnie gasp. She clapped her hands to her mouth. MacCormac spun to his right, then left. Carmichael and Edney brandished their weapons.

Suddenly, leaping from glass pillar to glass pillar, came a squall line of face-huggers on the attack. Pocket grabbed Bonnie and shoved her toward me, toward the middle of the circle of Xenos. Tad and Gracie came together into what might very well be a final embrace. The huggers moved with breathtaking speed, sensing that several of them could fulfill their genetic goal today, to impregnate a creature with their seeds of doom down some poor sap's throat. And here we were, sitting ducks.

"Oh, God," Gracie croaked. "A trap . . ."

Our mother twirled again, looking now at the horrid position we were all in. Thanks to her, we were all in it together. She'd brought everyone out to witness the wonder.

MacCormac shouldered his weapon in a quick movement, but at the same instant the parasites began to leap—all at once. No volley could get them all without also killing all of us. All he could hope to do was take ballistic shots and maybe bring down a few of them before they overwhelmed—

For the third time today I prepared my self to die, and again I got a shock. The aliens flanking my mother turned and snatched the face-huggers out of the air by their fingers, by their tails, by the body like lobsters snatched from nets. More and more face-huggers attacked, only to be snatched out of the air by their own adult soldiers. High-pitched shrieking drove us to cover our ears and writhe toward the ground while the adult Xenos ripped into the huggers, whipping them like toys, smashing them into rocks, tearing their limbs off and casting them away to flop in desperation on the ground. Acid spurted and bones snapped as loudly as firecrackers as the butchery gained momentum. What moments ago had been an unspoiled clearing now became a slaughter zone. Face-huggers tried to leap to reach us, and I saw Bonnie, then MacCormac pointedly rescued at the last moment by the adult aliens. It was sheer deliberate butchery.

Instead of attacking us, they were attacking their own.

CHAPTER NINE

"Come on!" MacCormac waved the direction back toward the blind, then snatched my mother by the wrist and dragged her out of a tornado of aliens slaughtering their own offspring. I dodged between two slashing tails and scrambled in the same direction just as a parasite was swung through the air by its tail, eight fingers scrambling, and was splattered on a glass pillar like a bug hitting a window. I dodged sideways into a jet of spittle from one of the adults as it sprinted to catch a face-hugger just as the grabby little bastard would've clamped onto my head. The hugger squealed and was dragged back into the cockfight.

We out-of-place humans dodged toward each other, trying to get out of the middle of the maelstrom. MacCormac took a few shots and blew away one or two huggers, as the other Marines quickly coordinated an escape through the catfight of aliens.

Pocket was there to pull me over the crest. "What'd you do?" he yelped, his ponytail bouncing between his shoulderblades.

"Pissed 'em off somehow! Move!"

Tad dragged Gracie, Clark pushed Bonnie, MacCormac hauled M'am, the other Marines led the way, and we ran for our silly little lives from the deliberate extermination of seeds by the very tree that had borne them.

I knew a window of opportunity when I saw it, as did we all. For the first time since leaving Earth, everybody on this planet was of one mind. We flew back the way we'd come, to the curtained entrance to the blind, and I guess we just hoped none of the aliens was watching to see where we went. Sometimes you just have to make the dive and hope for the best.

I was the last one in. I pulled the delicate curtain closed, remembering only at the last moment that it was actually delicate, and took a last look over the crest of the flume. No aliens appeared to see our hideaway. Still, I could hear them. The noise of the holocaust going on over the hill was accompanied by a smothering odor of acid and oil.

"Shut it, shut it!" Clark panted at my side. He pushed the curtain closed. "You haven't seen enough?"

"I wish I knew what I just saw! Where's my mother? M'am!"

"Yes. Here." She was lost in the crowd of taller people. "Keep your voice down."

With Herculean effort, I dialed down the volume as I pushed between Tad and Gracie to face her down. "What did we just see? What was that all about?"

Gracie edged between me and our mother. "Don't speak to her in that tone."

"Tone? What did we just witness out there? Why would the adults rip their own young to shreds?"

M'am began to pace quietly. "Their priorities have shifted, obviously."

"We have to test this," Gracie said anxiously. "Make experiments . . . design trials . . . compare—"

I growled, "How about if we evacuate and worry about comparisons a long time from now?"

Our mother snapped her fingers at us. "Be quiet, I told you. You could risk all our lives with your noise."

"Aw, I wouldn't want to do *that!* Admit that you've lost control of this situation, if you ever had it."

She raised her green eyes to me. "Not at all."

"What's going on, M'am?" I demanded. "They not only didn't kill us, but they refused to fight with us. What makes consummate predators suddenly sublime?"

"It was like a feeding frenzy," Bonnie pointed out, "except with their own kind. In a frenzy, anything is fair game. They were very particular about what they killed. One of them deliberately pulled a spider-thing off my leg and broke it in half." She showed the torn trouser near her ankle.

I nodded and pointed at Bonnie's leg. "That's right. Why did they kill their own kind? Why did they protect us?"

Clark, now sitting exhausted on a crate, raised his head. "They *did* protect us, didn't they?"

Bonnie parted her lips to speak, then held back, no doubt intimidated by my mother and sister, who were such experienced scientists while Bonnie felt she was just starting.

"Say it," I charged her.

She flinched. "Oh . . . I . . . "

"Go ahead."

She floundered briefly under the scrutiny of these experts. "Aggressive predators only protect three things . . . their young, their territory, and their prey."

"Oh, that's helpful," Gracie snarled. "As informative as an afterschool special." She waved her hand at me. "This is the kind of experts you bring along and you have the gall to question us?"

"Are you even going to ask about Rusty?"

M'am faced me with a bitter glare. "Rusty was incautious. He took too much time. Because of you, no doubt."

My mother continued her pacing, with her arms folded and one hand pressed to her lips. "This is new," she admitted.

"Behavioral changes like this are scientific gold. There's no record of any such behavior *en masse*. Life is fighting back." She paused in front of Clark and faced him. "You must take your ship and go. My team can't leave now. This could go on for months. Years. I can study them. Catalogue unimagined volumes of information. We've stumbled upon a treasure. Every thing is different. They've accepted us."

Bonnie's eyes got big with recognition as the fantasy began to flag and she finally saw my mother for the obsessed phantom she was. I didn't like seeing the illusion die, but was glad to have Bonnie entirely on my side.

"Whatever happens," my mother went on, "no one must leave the blind until the area is completely clear. We have no way to define this behavior—"

"Oh, wrong," I said. "If we can walk through them, then this is the *perfect* time to leave."

"This is the time to *stay*," M'am countered. "Nature has given us a doorway. This shift in focus could go on for months. Years! We can study them and they will even protect us!"

"A team of synthetics can do this work!" I said, matching her tone. "It's time to cash in our chips and honor the people who have died here and move out. All of us should head straight for the ship and get the bejeebers out of here. Tonight."

"Seconded!" Pocket supported.

"Sounds firm to me," MacCormac chimed.

Gracie rounded on him. "Great, coming from a man who led them into this mess without knowing what he was facing. Why don't you just plan the next picnic too?"

"You can leave," our mother said, unmasking some of the bitterness she held toward me. "But in the morning, when things are calmer. This area is dangerous now, you foolish boys. This is not the time to listen to my son's juvenile defiance."

"I thought you said they go underground where they pick up

ambient something at night, so night is better for moving around. Do you know these creatures or not?"

"I agree with Mr. Malvaux," the Colonel said. "We're going to bug out as soon as possible and all the researchers are going to be compelled to come with us. The situation's too volatile to leave anybody here."

M'am's eyes narrowed and shifted to him, but she said nothing. Behind her Gracie wrinkled her nose in contempt. Tad slipped his hand onto her shoulder, but he also said nothing.

"I need a chance to think this through," Clark uttered. "We sure can't go out there right now. They could just as easily turn on us again."

"You will wait until they move on," my mother said. "Decisions about your ship can be made in the morning. In a compound such as this, you learn to be patient and wait things out." She sought out the crowd of confused and spooked people. "Neil—dear, be sure all the video feeds are recording. We'll want to have records of this new behavior. Chantal and Ethan, be sure to process all the data as soon as possible. If there are large flocks moving, we must know the dynamics and behavioral subtleties. Paul, we will need readings of atmospheric changes, if any. Diego, Dixie, all of you . . . don't be so overwhelmed that we miss opportunities. Monitor your posts. Gather data. Find answers."

Neil, pale and shaken, glanced around self-consciously and acted as if he couldn't believe he was being asked to do something so mundane at this monumental moment. He went off into the maze of chambers, followed by Chantal and Ethan. After a few seconds, Paul, the weather and rock guy, went off into another tunnel. Diego, the bacteria guy, lingered a little, then he too went somewhere. Zaviero looked uneasy, then trundled off to do something about bugs. Before long, only Bonnie, Clark, Pocket, and the Marines were left here with me, my mother, my sister, and Tad. The smaller group seemed more intimate, more manageable.

I stalked away, knowing that I needed to get control and think clearly. My mother always brought out the worst in me, even when she wasn't trying.

"Hey—Rory," Clark called. He got up and came to me, took me by the arm and turned me so he could look at the side of my leg. "You're bleeding."

I twisted around to look at the back of my right thigh. Yeah, ripped supersuit and blood. "Okay, thanks."

"You want attention?" Bonnie asked. "I have—I have my kit—somewhere . . . "

I gazed down at my bloody thigh. Clark held my arm, and we paused there, each thinking about different things. During that moment of calm, a little oasis of time during which my wildly ranging thoughts began to coalesce, I suddenly fell silent and just stared at my leg. Predators . . . prey . . . territory . . . prey . . . prey . . .

But nobody knew whether the aliens ate humans. We just knew they *used* humans. We might not be prey. We were something else. Not prey, not their young, not their territory . . . what were we to them? In the big scheme, why would they protect us?

"You okay?" Clark asked.

I blinked at him. His honest face and tousled red hair, pure concern for me in the middle of possibly losing his dream and ending up maybe dead . . . this was one pure and simple guy.

"Simple," I murmured. "There has to be a simple answer."

They all watched me. I felt like an egg about to hatch.

"Like what?" Clark asked.

Just as the pain finally hit me and my leg started to throb, I uttered, "I don't know yet. But what if they snap out of it?"

The answer seemed to float just outside my reach.

"Graciella," my mother spoke up, "and Tad, please, check the perimeters. Do a heat-seek check. Secure all the openings and post watchers. I think we're safe for now. This behavior could continue indefinitely. We have a new chapter, and we must take the responsibility of careful data keeping. Nothing will happen until morning, and then we will escort these intruders back to their ship." She looked at Clark, then at me. "They cannot legally terraform a planet with potentially intelligent life. The problem is over. They will leave us in peace."

"I wouldn't bet on that," I warned. No sense letting her fantasize any more.

After a calculated pause for flare, she turned and led Gracie and Tad out of the chamber.

We were alone. Us intruders.

"Sit here, Rory." Bonnie opened a folding chair that Pocket handed her. "I'll bandage that."

"Strip out of that suit," Pocket told me.

Like a gang of personal assistants, they plucked and pulled until the supersuit was a lump on the floor, with its sensitive science and its torn leg. I pulled on a T-shirt and sweatpants that Pocket conjured up—now, that was a good bosun, able to come up with merchandise in a completely foreign environment. He had a touch, for sure. Suddenly I was a lot more comfortable and for some reason felt very vulnerable.

Clark stuffed me into the folding chair—I hadn't even noticed that they had chairs at all—and I hung my arm over the back and sat sideways so Bonnie to could clean up my leg. I had no idea when the injury had happened, no idea whether it was from a tail slash or a shard of red glass. Didn't care.

Clark sat down nearby. MacCormac and his two Marines tried to get comfortable without exactly relaxing.

"She didn't ask," I uttered.

"Who didn't ask what?" Pocket knelt beside Bonnie and helped her clean my wounded thigh.

"My mother," I said. "She didn't even ask what happened to Rusty. She just said he wasn't cautious enough. She wasn't interested in what actually happened to get him killed."

"You think she doesn't care?"

"I think she already knew."

MacCormac leaned closer, suddenly interested. He waved back the two younger Marines, who were clearly spooked and out of their element.

Clark shook his head. "Don't get paranoid on us, Rory. You know they can see a lot with those installations of video feeds. She probably already knew because it was fed through on a camera. Keep your head."

"Keep my head? I'm trapped here with a bunch of eco-terrorist bug-huggers. This is her dream? To be out there in the middle of those things? My mother actually thinks that if she learns enough, she can live among those things? This isn't an expedition! It's a cult!"

"Bonnie, what do you think?" Clark asked. "You're a doctor and you know a lot about animals . . . have you ever heard of something like what we saw out there?"

We all looked at her, which caused Bonnie to flush with self-consciousness. "I'm not the expert . . . Mrs. Malvaux might be right . . . but . . . "

"Go ahead," I said. "You're as smart as she is."

She smiled in a small way. "Oh, wow . . . thanks."

"Was she right?" Clark prodded. "Could this period of change, whatever the change is, when they leave us alone and go after each other, could it last for years?"

"Are you asking me about precedents in nature?"

"Whatever you think."

She dabbed antiseptic on my wound, which I have to say was finally waking up and starting to hurt, and took her time formulating an answer. "It might last," she finally ventured, "but violent behavior within the same species doesn't usually represent a norm. Doesn't usually last protracted lengths of time."

"In other words," Pocket finished, "we're not all that safe."

"We're not safe at all," I told them. "Clark, you have to stick to your original mission. Evac this planet and release the PPs to eradicate the aliens. We have to save these people. There must be more like Rusty, who want to go home but are afraid to speak up. You have to take charge, you and the colonel here. She's got this Kum-Bah-Ya thing going with these people she pretends to care about, but whenever they die, somehow it's their fault. It's never her fault or the fact that they're here, and it's certainly never the aliens' fault. These laws don't fit the situation anymore. You have to make a decision, Clark, maybe one that's beyond the letter of the law. You have to be a captain and not just one of the drones."

"Sucks," Pocket commented. "No mission, no bonuses."

"Oh, there'll be bonuses," MacCormac spoke up. "For the next ship."

"What next ship?" Bonnie asked.

"The one that comes after we go home, and releases the PPs that we didn't release. You don't think this is a done deal, do you?"

Clark twisted to look up at the colonel.

"That's right!" Pocket exclaimed. "It'll get done anyway, and nobody'll ever trust the *Vinza* crew for another mission! We'll be space dust!"

"You'll retire, all right, Clark," I said, "and some other guy'll come out here and do to those aliens what they do to everything in their way."

Clark put his hand out to calm the storm. "I'm not releasing a hundred thousand robotic hunter killers until I think this out, bonus or no bonus, retire or not. I don't want to break the law."

"This is bigger than the law," I said. "The Alien Species Act is fiction. It was made up before any of the details were known, before anybody really knew anything. There was one rumor of one ship fifty-odd years ago, and one expedition from which I don't think anybody survived. It's based on nothing. On my mother's imagination. A rosy picture, I might add, and with money and influence she pushed it through. Let me ask you this—can you believe that, after we get back and tell this story, that the Alien Species Act won't see a lot of amendments and refinements?"

Clark shrugged. "True . . . "

"Then how can you suffer over obeying it? It's a hollow law, Clark."

"Yeah . . . " He seemed to be accepting my argument. I knew his only real doubts were about himself, and not really about what I was saying. Being the captain, he wanted to make sure he wasn't being influenced by friendship. If I'd had the time, I'd have respected that. "I just want the time to think for a few minutes."

"Well, think fast," I said, "because somebody around here is working against us. And I don't mean spreading rumors."

Clark moaned and mumbled, "Don't jump to conclusions."

I twisted around, pulling my leg out of Pocket's grip and messing up the bandaging process. Turning to face them all, I motioned Bonnie to leave my leg alone for now. "Conclusions? Let me give you some meat for conclusions. What happened to Donahue and Brand? How did they get killed by aliens if they were inside the ship's protection grid?"

"We found Donahue on the edge of the grid," MacCormac reminded. "I can't be sure he wasn't over the line."

"Or maybe he was killed inside the line and dumped at the edge, so you wouldn't be sure."

Clark parted his lips to argue, then paused and waited to hear me out.

"And when we found him," I went on, "there was no acid anywhere around him. Not on his uniform, not on the ground, his hands weren't burned . . . the tail spike that killed him would've been full of acid if he'd blown it off the animal himself. Maybe you haven't had the tour in here. Just a few steps away is a museum of alien parts, all cleaned out and mounted."

"Rory . . . " Clark murmured. "Tail spikes used as weapons? Come on . . . who'd think of that?"

"I just did. I wouldn't put it past a few blood relations to think of it too. Or passionate cultists. They thought of a few other creative things, like using those huts as incubation chambers. Can you imagine those poor people? Able to see out, watching each other's chests explode and the little larvae racing out, knowing what was coming to them? No wonder Diego's wife hanged herself before it happened."

Bonnie shuddered and let out a gush of sorrow. "Horrible . . . "

"What about Brand?" MacCormac asked. "You don't think they used those . . . "

"That maybe he was strangled by one of those parasites that was already dead?" I said. "Yeah, I might be enticed to entertain that idea, Colonel, since there were no scratches on his hands or face." I allowed a pause while they all traveled back in their minds to see that I was right about that. "There are a handful of us on the planet and the first ones to die are our Colonial Marines? Think about military tactics. The first advantages you want to take away from your enemy are his guards."

"Your mother, that little woman?" Clark wondered. "She overwhelmed three Marines?"

"Or Tad, or somebody in her thrall."

"You'd better make the direct charge," MacCormac said, "if you're going to. I need to know exactly what you're saying."

With a wince at the freshening pain in my leg, I fixed my gaze on him and gave him what he wanted.

"Monsters do exist," I told him. "But they're human."

CHAPTER TEN

Life goes on day by day in the universe, and every once in a millennium pauses for the truly surreal.

All the rest of us shrank back into the blind, unable to read the situation, knowing things were changing too fast to predict. Scientists want to be able to predict everything. It's their lives' work. They were uneasy, I could tell.

What made us even more uneasy was my mother's behavior. Not only was she Jocasta Malvaux, but she was "into" being Jocasta Malvaux, as if it were a title and not just an identity. She proved this to us in the most poetic illustration possible . . . she went out of the blind alone.

We huddled inside, watching through the projector curtain as she walked out farther and farther, as far as she could and still be seen. Being seen was important.

There were adult aliens all around us now, though they hadn't been tipped off to the location of the blind. Even my mother wasn't quite that enraptured yet, to give away our only hiding place.

"What's she doing?" Clark asked as we stood side by side, with Pocket and MacCormac. Around us were a few researchers—Paul, the microbiologist, Chantal, the vet, Neil, the camp director, and Ethan, the crowd dynamics guy. Their presence made me wonder where the others were, and why they weren't here watching the "show."

It was nearly dark, but the big green-striped moon provided a conveniently bright glow across the landscape and we were able to make out everything. The moon was big, bigger than Earth's moon, or closer or something, so the glow was luminous and the shadows sharp.

I motioned Clark to silence, and we watched as my mother walked out to meet the aliens. Of those which were wandering by in seeming aimlessness—not like before, when they had moved in one direction with purpose—two noticed my mother. Then, a third.

"They've got her," MacCormac announced. I think he was warning me that my mother was very likely to die right now, before my eyes, in case I wanted to look away.

I didn't. In fact, I disgusted myself by wondering if that wouldn't make things a lot simpler for all of us. She was a lightning rod. Without her, the club would crumble. Would it help if the aliens took the struggle away?

My own mother . . . what was I thinking? What had I turned into?

My soul was saved by a strong desire to rush out there and drag her back. I was stopped by the fascinating sight as she raised her hands to them the way she might to beloved horses in a stable.

Morbid curiosity took over as the three aliens undulated closer to her. They were snakelike in their movements, never quite still, though not quite advancing. Even standing over her, touching her with their tail tips and moving their toothy jaws along her sides and upraised arm, they continually shifted and coiled, uncoiled and flexed. One by one they lowered their snouts into her palms as if she were feeding them by hand. This was her dream, her quest, to walk among them.

I knew the other researchers were somewhere in the complex, eyes fixed to monitor screens, watching the prophecy come true. This could only make things worse. These people had to be evacuated before the spell was broken.

I bit my lip and shook my head. "I swear she's scarier than those things."

I sat by myself in the museum chamber, mostly twitching and trying to think clearly. Sudden decisions could have tragic consequences and I had to make sure we were acting with good sense and not just acting. The hardest part would be figuring out who among the campers was working with us and who was working against us, whom we would have to drag, and who would happily run to the ship once they were freed from the spell of the Wicked Jocasta of the West.

The museum chamber seemed to be my favorite place, with its giant creature staring—or whatever it did—down at me. In here, I was able to look my enemy in the face, if not the eyes, and try to measure him up. And there wasn't usually anybody else in here, so the chance to be alone was a factor.

Which was why I flinched when somebody came into the chamber. I looked up and discovered the visitor was Carmichael, the boy Marine.

"Hello, sir. Sorry if I disturbed you."

He had a slight squeak in his voice, as if puberty weren't quite finished.

"Private," I greeted. "Resting up?"

"Patrol, sir. Interior."

"Guarding something from coming in here or us from going out?"

"Don't really know, sir." He sniffed and muttered, "Sure wish I did."

"You've been pretty quiet this whole mission."

"Not much to say, sir. Gonna have a lot of stories to tell,

though, assuming I get back, that is. Wait till my folks hear about all this."

"Where are your parents?"

"Waukesha, Wisconsin."

"Hey, I'm from Milwaukee."

"That's what I heard, sir."

"Have a seat."

"I . . . I don't think I should."

"You deserve it." I patted the folding chair next to mine.

He sat down beside me, but kept his pulse rifle right against his chest.

"How old are you?" I asked.

"Twenty-two, sir."

"You can call me Rory. I'm not much into the 'sir' thing. What's your first name?"

He made a face. "Mike."

"Mike?"

"Yeah."

"Michael Carmichael?"

"Yeah . . . "

I rewarded him with a cranky laugh. "Mothers can be such turkeys."

"Yeah!"

"What would you rather have had?" I asked. "If you could choose your own name."

"I . . . I always . . . my grandfather's always been great to me. He was a war veteran, like. He's why I joined the Corps. I always admired him. He's got this real strong first name . . . "

"Go ahead."

"Aw, no. It's dumb."

"Nah, go ahead. What is it?"

"Kensington. Shit, I shouldn't have said it! Sounds so dumb . . . "

"Kensington Carmichael?"

"No—his name is O'Keefe. His last name."

"Kensington O'Keefe," I tested. "I like that. You're right, it's great sounding. Has a lot of character."

"Yeah, yeah, it sure does. Sure does."

I slapped my knees. "Well, let's just do it."

"Do what?"

"Change your name."

"Come on . . ."

"People do it all the time."

"No kidding? Just like that?"

"Yup. On your feet."

He bounded to his feet and twitched with anticipation, adjusting his uniform, and finally shouldered his weapon.

I stood up too and squared off in front of him. "Ready?"

He whipped his hat off. "Ready."

I looked around and picked up a drinking straw left behind on a desk, and tapped him on the shoulder. "I, Detective Rory Theodore Malvaux, Duke of Earl, do dub thee Private Kensington Carmichael, Colonial Marine Corps, Esquire."

Carmichael beamed and gasped, "Oh, man!"

We shook hands vigorously, enjoying the moment.

"Can I call you 'Ken'?" I asked.

His grin could've lit up Broadway. "Ken . . . Thanks!"

I offered a sort of goofy salute, and he responded.

"Better get on with your patrol," I said. "You're a whole new man now."

"Yeah, thanks!"

When he left, I didn't sit down again. Somehow the conversation with him had relaxed my brain and given me some focus. I knew what I had to do.

I went looking for my sister again. She was fanatical and devoted, but there had to be some line of communication that would work. We'd protected each other a lot when we were kids. She'd grown up knowing our mother wasn't exactly like the other girls' mothers, or anybody's for that matter, and I'd grown up knowing I didn't count for much. There had to be some of that lingering inside her hardened survivalist exterior. Right?

What the heck, I was desperate. Clinging to delusions actually helped somehow. Or at least maybe I would eliminate some dead ends.

The chambers were mostly darkened, lit only by tiny red lights that allowed us to move around without stumbling, but caused no glow or sharp shadows. Like a ship's bridge in red alert, we could function almost in the dark.

I passed by several people, hunched over screens, watching the delirious scene of my mother in communion with her subjects. Others muttered to each other and tried to distill the tons of new information they'd picked up. To me, it was one or two interesting episodes. To them, it was a flood of data. Scientists who looked at things in micro-slivers were pulling apart the fabric of our day and trying to reassemble it into something they could sift for patterns. People who devoted their entire lives to translating one page of manuscript had stumbled upon a whole library.

The hideout was really an ant colony of pockets joined by tunnels. Until now, I'd only been in a few of the chambers, but now I toured quietly, by myself, deliberately not disturbing anyone else, whether they were working or trying to sleep. The darkness helped.

When I heard Gracie's voice in one of the lab chambers, I stayed in the tunnel without coming out into the chamber. She was talking to someone. This wasn't the voice of the shrill sycophant nor the gruff defender of science I'd heard earlier. This was much softer, more fearful, fraught with passion and urgency. I couldn't make out the words, but the emotions were there. I'd heard enough impassioned whispering in jail cells and interrogation rooms.

I peeked into the chamber, taking a chance. There they were—in silhouette against a bank of working screens that showed the activities of the day, aliens and huggers, replays of my adventures and Bonnie's, speed-takes of MacCormac and the Marines in action, like flashes of bad dreams. The pictures glowed behind the forms of my sister and the stealth guy, Tad, locked in an embrace and whispering to each other.

I tried to hear what they were saying. No good. They were too good at being quiet and still getting their messages across. They probably lived like this all the time, sneaking kisses, murmuring in corners, no privacy, no future.

What could I overhear, anyway? Lovers' promises?

I backed up into the tunnel, then made a big deal out of stomping my way into the chamber. When I unfolded myself and coughed to make sure they'd heard me, they were on two sides of the chamber, with Gracie seated at the monitor bank. Tad did a poorer job of disguising their tryst.

"Hi," I said amiably. "Hope I didn't wake you."

"We're awake," Tad said coldly. He looked at Gracie. "I'm gonna go."

"Okay," she agreed.

"You want me to stay?" He looked at me, but he was talking to her.

She glanced at me. "No, I can handle him."

He would rather have stayed, but didn't. I gave him ten seconds to get way down the corridor and watched to make sure he wasn't lurking around as I had.

I tugged a bulk food crate up to the monitor bank and sat down on it. "Gracie, I need your help. No fireworks, okay?"

Her face was patched with moving lights from the screens, and she self-consciously checked the snaps on her shirt to make sure they were closed all the way to her collar. "Oh, I'll jump right up, then."

I tried to calm her by using a very even tone. "This isn't sibling rivalry. This is official business. I need your help getting these people off the planet. You can influence M'am."

"Think so?"

"You have to evacuate. Everybody. All we want is for you to evacuate without a fight."

"That's all," she lilted sarcastically. "Gosh, why didn't you say so? Until you showed up in that carnival wagon, with all your calliopes chiming, we were successfully hiding and observing a hive of Xenos in their natural environment—"

"Cut the toe-dancing," I said more sharply. "This isn't their natural environment. They came here as aliens, same as us. They're on a slaughter mission, same as us. Has anybody studied them? Did you do autopsies? Analyses? Did any of you try to figure out how to fight them?"

"We don't want to fight them. We want to live with them."

"That only works if they agree. They're closing in. You're all doomed if you stay. That means I can't allow you to stay."

"We've been successfully hidden for months. They didn't know we were here until you—"

"They knew you were here all along. They've spent those months closing the noose. Haven't you looked at Ethan's crowd control data?"

"They don't know to close any nooses. You're making that up." She hunched her shoulders and tapped at her keyboard, communicating that the work was far more important than anything I had to say. "You're just uncomfortable because you're not the top of the food chain anymore. You think they're ugly because they're a different kind of parasite than humans are. If we can grow beyond our parasitic ways, who's to say another species can't grow beyond theirs? They're beautiful animals and they're here living their lives, unless we gum it all up for them. You and your genocidal robots—"

"Why is it any animal, all the time? Why don't humans ever come first?"

"Because they don't deserve to."

"'They'? What are you, a corn flake? You never give Humanity credit for doing anything good."

"Oh, like what?"

Bless me, I actually had the answer. "Like cherishing culture while embracing change."

"Oh, sure, we embrace a lot," she spat, rewarding me with a cold glower. "What have we got to show for ourselves in the galaxy? We've wiped out entire cultures of our own kind, killed ancient languages—Gaelic, Sanskrit, Assyrian—"

"Or," I punctuated, "maybe they just played themselves out and weren't needed anymore. Did you ever think of that? Maybe the unification of language is the great victory of cultural Oneness you always wish for. Or you say you do. You hate when it really happens. Maybe the fading away of ancient cultures means we're finally getting together. People are always sentimental about the wrong things!"

"Don't yell. Hold your voice down. You never had any self-control." She went back to poking at the keyboard and adjusting the screen, which showed several windows of data that could've been critical or could've been nonsense. No idea which.

I had to admit she was right about that. If I'd had any self-control, I'd have turned down this mission in favor of an enforcement officer who could be dispassionate about my mother, my sister, and the dubious sides of their work.

"I came here to get as far from Humanity as I could," she

continued, almost musing. "Humanity is the only species that wipes out other species."

"Gracie, that's eco-head crap." I was even quieter this time. "How jaded can you get? You sound like M'am on meth. Species have been getting wiped out for millions of years without Humanity's help. It's the natural cycle. Thousands of species lived for eons and died natural deaths before Humanity ever appeared. Who can say that's not a success?"

"I can say it."

"And I say keeping them going artificially is a travesty. It can't be done. You can only keep that sort of thing going for so long. Remember the Chinese panda? The millions of dollars poured into the futile effort to save them? Never was there a species more determined to go extinct. They couldn't breed, they only ate one thing—"

"Why don't you write an article or go on a concert tour?"

"You can waste your life protecting a tree, but eventually it'll die its own death in its own time and you can't stop it. And you shouldn't. Maybe our being here, Clark with his payload, maybe we are the natural chain of events playing out. Maybe we're the hand of nature this time. Have you ever thought of that?"

"You're not the hand of nature, Rory. You're just another passionate murderer." She twisted in her chair to face me and leaned forward to make her point. "We know what you did, you know. M'am and I. We know how you did it. Mr. Law Enforcement, Mr. Detective, Mr. Defender of the People. When push came to shove, you abandoned the law. You cut that man's arms off and let his life bleed out. No trial, no due process, you just took the law into your hands and carried out a sentence. And wasn't it brutal, too. Wasn't it ugly and cruel. Wasn't it savage. You're the real monster. Not them. Not us."

How far could I get with this barricade between us? She was

bitter and angry on a deep level, deeper than the things she was saying. This fury went back to our childhoods.

Determined to keep the issue in the moment, I shifted gears—a little. "Okay, I'm a monster. As long as we're monster-building here, maybe you can tell me what happened to Rusty's stealth suit."

Her eyes narrowed and her brows came down. She paused. "What about his suit?"

"It stopped working at a critical moment. Right when the alien was standing in front of him, it stopped masking. That's interesting timing, to me."

"Of course it is, yeah, malfunctions never just 'happen' in Rory Malvaux's world of order. We've had lots of them here in the real world."

I hesitated. "How many?"

She retreated from that line of questioning. "Some."

I watched her for a moment, trying to get something out of that odd expression. "M'am ordered a fresh power pack just before he went out. The suit ran out of power. Take the blinders off, Gracie. She doesn't care about anybody around here. Don't you notice that with her it's always 'I' am doing this, 'I' will be recognized? When's the last time she used the word 'we' or talked about 'our' work? She doesn't even know you or these other disciples are here except to provide her with information and do the dishes. She'll go back to Earth some day and take credit for all—"

"And she'll deserve it!" The passion in my sister's expression almost knocked me off my crate. She poked me in the chest with a finger that I'm pretty sure she'd rather were a dagger. "Our mother is the Dian Fossey, the Jane Goodall, the Charles Darwin of this age. You don't see it because you've always re-sented her. You've spent your whole life avoiding things that make demands or warrant loyalty."

"Loyalty is for people who think of others first." My voice grew rough, and I forced myself to hold it down. I had to find something that would work on her, appeal to her common sense, if she had any left. I knew she did. Gracie's common sense was always fighting with her idealism—she'd always been like that. I just had to tap it. "Do you actually believe that if you just learn enough, you can actually live among them? Live real lives? Have families? Grow? Do anything other than hide or die?"

We fell silent for a moment, just glaring at each other. I was sorry I'd tipped my hand about Rusty's suit. I'd hoped to release that information with a little more finesse. Now I'd lost that trump card.

Gracie's face was flushed and hot, shiny with perspiration in the red glow of the night lights. She looked overworked, exhausted, deeply stressed, and ready to fall apart, yet somehow was holding herself together and fighting for stability. She didn't have our mother's coolness. She's never had it.

"She's walking among them," my sister vowed. "You were wrong and she was right."

"Okay, she might be right," I accepted. "I don't know. I'm not a scientist. But I can tell you other things that might happen. Some day, tomorrow or fifty or a hundred years from now, some innocent ship from some innocent race will land here, not knowing what's waiting for them. The cosmic hitchhikers will take advantage of that and find their way to space again. Maybe to Earth. Maybe to some other innocent civilization. Then those things will start killing again. You want an image of genocide? Try that one. These aliens are acting differently from anything anybody seems to know about them. I think you should tell me right now the full scope of the pile we've stepped in."

The bald demand disarmed her. She had no pre-recorded sarcastic response this time.

I don't know which part got to her. I felt as if I'd spilled my pebbles to have told her about the suit. Had I shocked her?

Then, something worse occurred to me. Because she didn't look so shocked.

I flashed on Pocket's face during our last card game—which he won, as usual. "*No poker face at all, Malvaux, my man. Hand it over and let's go again.*"

"Please leave me alone," my sister requested. She seemed weakened and wasted. Was she thinking about her own future, about possibly someday having a life, kids, a home, maybe with Tad?

Was she thinking there was no future for her?

"Okay," I said miserably.

Should I slap the cuffs on now or later?

After pushing the food crate back where I'd found it, I left her alone in her cubicle to pretend to keep working.

Played out and empty, I slunk back through the tunnel, moving more slowly than necessary, trying to think. With all the weird activity outside, even Pocket couldn't run odds on whether any of us would survive. The scientists were clearly befuddled, and when experts are befuddled, the rest of us are just plain lost.

I was lost. Clumsy. I'd blown my one advantage, and now didn't even know whether I was on the right track. My instincts were all clogged up. Sentiment and memories were clouding my brain. Was I ever the wrong man for this job.

The next chamber was the place where Chantal had taken me to see her "collection." There, I stopped.

Before me, the stuffed Xenomorph stood in elegant repose, positioned for the edification of human eyes, its outer teeth held open to emit the distended inner jaws. It would probably stand there forever, or until this fortress were breached. Its own kind would find it someday, perhaps soon, and circle it in a confusion of wonder. Would they pick at it and feel its cables and armor, sniff and poke it the way elephants did to the bones of their own dead? Would they try to make it move and come back to life? Or would they know somehow that it was a trophy?

How intelligent were they . . . really?

"It's beautiful in its way."

I spun around and almost knocked into the creature. "Bonnie!" Bonnie sat on the foam floor with her legs folded, tucked back into a nook. She clapped her hand to her lips. "Oh! I scared you!"

"Scared me?" My own hand was on my chest, nursing the coronary. "Just a mild infarction."

With a guilty smile she said, "I guess this isn't the place where you should surprise anybody."

"What are you doing in here?"

"Just thinking."

"With this thing?" I gestured at the big alien.

"It's amazing to be able to just look at one."

I sat down next to her and stretched my legs out, leaning back against the pressed-plastic wall. "According to my mother, you can just go outside and introduce yourself."

"No thanks!" Despite sitting quietly and seeming in control, she picked at her fingernails.

"Any luck with your sister?"

I sighed demonstratively. "Total titanium wall. The second generation is always worse than the first."

She didn't seem to like the way I talked about my family.

"Sorry," I offered. "I know this pops the Jocasta bubble for you. Every silver lining has a cloud, y'know."

"That's not very nice to say," she scolded mildly. "She *is* your mother. Hasn't she ever given you anything worth valuing?"

"Like what? Life? Yeah, she gave me that. I was a . . . mistake."

"Mistake? You mean she didn't want to get pregnant?"

"Oh, yes, she wanted to. She was trying to have a girl. I was in-vitro. They thought I was a girl, but somebody screwed up in the lab."

"Oh, Rory . . . that can't be true."

I shrugged. "It's okay, I accepted it a long time ago. She never hid it from me."

"Sounds like the kind of thing you'd *want* to hide from your child." Her empathy was charming.

"It can't be hidden in my family," I explained. "All the wealth in my family comes down through the women. Our great-great grandmother had one daughter, our great-grandmother had two daughters, each of those had two daughters, and my mother, quite unintentionally, had a son. She never wanted any kids, but the family fortune had to be protected. She takes her obligations seriously. When I was born, she took one look and decided to try again as soon as she could. She had to have a daughter to leave the kingdom to. The queendom, really."

Bonnie's face took on all the pain I'd avoided about this issue. I didn't like making her feel so bad, when I really didn't.

"Are you sure you're not reading this through a jaundiced eye?" she asked. "You're diminishing your personhood so much!"

"No, not really. We're more than how we're conceived."

She paused and thought back over what she'd just heard. "You mean, out of your mother's incredible fortune and all her investments and holdings, you don't . . . "

"Right. I don't get anything. Gracie gets it all. That's why I can never get married."

"Why can't you marry?"

"Because the wife gets my inheritance. Womanhood trumps everything. I would never know for sure why anybody was marrying me. Technically, she could stay married to me for a year, ditch me, and keep the fortune. There's no protection against that in our inheritance. No pre-nuptuals, no nothing. It's some kind of bastardized protectionism for women as a 'species.'"

Bonnie's eyes widened with amazement at the concept. "My goodness, that sounds . . . "

"Warped. I know. You'd have to know the women in my family. They're kinda sick in the head."

"Rory, I'm so sorry . . . "

"It's okay. Right now I wish it were all that's twisted between my sister and me."

"You mean, that 'second generation' thing?"

I nodded. "Lenin was bad. Stalin was worse. . . . Alexander the Great stood on the empire created by Philip of Macedon and really pushed too far. The French botched their own revolution and Napoleon was there to take advantage."

She tipped her head into my periphery. "What are you really talking about, really?"

I didn't want to voice my suspicions. They'd hardly had a chance to simmer. Bonnie's sensitivity prodded me gently to think out loud, and somehow it was helping.

"My mother's obsessions have always been out in front," I said. "She's never thought she was wrong, so she never had to sneak around. As for Gracie . . . she can be heartless and single-minded. She takes seriously her role as the custodian of greatness, never believing she could ever be great herself. My mother always insisted on being the great one, and Gracie's always bought into that. Nobody's more ferocious than a child defending a parent."

"You mean a parent defending a child."

"No . . . I mean a child defending a parent. I've seen it before in my line of work. Horribly abused children will clam up and refuse to indict their own parents, and sometimes even defend the parents' actions. It's one of the little ways humans are different from other animals. The blindest of devotion. Gracie has it."

Bonnie was a simple person, definitely a lot smarter than she let on, or than she believed. I could tell she got the message I was trying hard not to say outright.

"Are you telling me," she attempted, "you think your sister has been . . . doing something wrong?"

I nodded. "I was so focused on my mother, so wrapped up in my own resentments, that I quit thinking like an investigator and just believed what I wanted to believe. I think I might be completely off track. Rusty's power pack—my mother ordered it replaced just before we went out, but it was Gracie who replaced it. My mother could never overpower Marines the way Donahue and Brand were overpowered, but I just saw Gracie and Tad romancing it up. Gracie has a man at her beck and call. A man devoted to the compound. A stealth expert."

She shivered. "Oh, my goodness—this is terrible . . . what are you going to do? Can you . . . arrest them?"

"I actually can. On suspicion. How about that? A bazillion miles from Earth, and I actually have jurisdiction. Can you believe it?" I reached into my pocket and pulled out my shield. "See? Badge and everything."

"My goodness . . . when will you make your decision?"

"I don't know, exactly. Is she really a murderer? If so, I have to act before anybody else gets killed. Somebody's doing the killing, I know that. Some human. Usually I just bring 'em in and the system takes over. I have backup."

"You have the captain. And the Marines." She smiled. "And me."

I looked at her. "I love having you for my backup."

"Even if it's just to bandage your leg?"

"Especially for that. Imagine how distracted I'd be, hobbling around with an infected leg!"

Again she laughed a little, nervously, in her cute schoolgirl way. "I can definitely stop that from happening. I can even stop the scar."

"Hey, I kinda like having the scar. Makes me surly. Gorilla-like. Attractive to ladies of ill-repute."

She blushed and wiggled her shoulders. Tonight she seemed a lot less boyish than she always had before, despite her not-particularly-petite build and her goofy manners and the fact that she didn't seem to understand how smart she was. Despite the fact that she was on the fast track to becoming a doctor—a no-dummics-allowed profession—she wasn't quite aware of her own value. Actually, I found her shyness endearing.

I nudged her shoulder with mine. "So how's your reputation?"

She laughed again, brightening the dim room and my spirits. Her blushing cheeks glowed and her smile flickered in the red light. She covered her mouth coquettishly—and she was really lousy at being coquettish—but I knew she was covering because the red light made us both look as if we'd just eaten a crate of tomatoes. Not exactly dinner in candlelight.

I wished I could give her that. Treat her like a girl for once. We hadn't treated her much like a girl on the ship. Maybe that was why she needed little animals around.

Logging away that I owed her a nice evening out, I asked, "What time is it?"

"Almost midnight."

"Did my mother ever come in?"

"She did. It was amazing, seeing her out there, with them . . . "

"I couldn't look after a while," I admitted. "Is anybody still scanning outside?"

"They've been scanning all night. Here. I'll show you."

She picked up a remote and clicked it. A bank of screens, six of them, flickered to life above the head of the stuffed alien. The creature suddenly looked as if it were appearing on stage.

"Wow—I didn't even see those up there," I commented.

"Well, the room has its distractions."

"Sure as hell does."

We settled back to watch the pictures of the landscape. Dreamy pictures of aliens moving around . . . just moving, squabbling amongst themselves, stalking the universe in their way . . . and other scenes where other kinds of animals sniffed and lurked. I hadn't been able to pay much attention to the panoply of other life on the planet. For Bonnie's sake, I wished we could just take a walk out there, maybe get a pair of binoculars and go critter watching. I thought she would like that, and deserved it. Instead we were the animals, trapped in our hole.

There had to be a way to get out, to entice the researchers to escort us back to the ship, and then to actually get on. That would be the ugly scene—forcing them to comply. And dangerous too. Those moments would be crucial and leave us vulnerable. They had to be planned, with Clark, with the Marines, and if possible with Theo back aboard the ship. If I'd done my job better, I'd have a clearer idea of just who would work with us when push came to shove, and who was too devoted to my mother to do anything but fight us. Gracie and Tad were definitely over there in the fight camp. How would Neil react? Diego, who'd lost his wife and unborn child? Zaviero? Couldn't exactly muscle him around, could we? I'd feel bad doing it too. What else—take the time to explain to him what we were trying to accomplish?

Beside me, Bonnie rubbed her arms and shivered. "They keep it cold in here, don't they?"

"Something about not expelling heat signatures. They've developed some fancy ways to hide. Most of them as combat basic, though, if I read it right. Most of hiding is what you *don't* do, not what you do. Keeping quiet, not moving around much, not expelling heat or gas, odor, that kind of thing. They've taken it to other levels, though, with holographics and these smart suits and all."

"You have to give them credit, don't you?"

"Oh, I do. It's the motivations that worry me, not the tactics."

I leaned back against a stack of drums and put my head back, closed my eyes for a moment. My exhausted brain started swimming and seeing colors in spite of my eyes' being closed.

"You're tired," Bonnie mentioned. "How about getting a nap?"

"Is that an offer?" I opened my eyes and poked her in the side. "Hmm? Cinderella?"

She giggled. "Cinderella . . . what's that mean?"

"I don't know. You look different in this light. Kinda . . . sporty."

Palming her unruly blond hair, she tried to finger it back. "Every girl's dream to look 'sporty' to a guy."

I smiled and pulled a few strands back where it had been before. "Don't change your hair. I like it. It's honest."

"Honest hair . . . "

"Oh—God, I'm stupid!" I thumped myself in the head. "You said, 'It's cold,' and like an idiot I actually commented on why! That's not the right reaction!"

"Huh?"

"What a fool, what a goof! I couldn't get a message if the bottle hit me over the head! Here's the *right* reaction."

I raised my arm and tucked her under it, pulling her close and rubbing her arm and shoulder to make her warm.

"See? That's the right—"

A movement on one of the screens caught my eye. Something about it was different from the movements of the aliens or the other creatures moving slowly in the photographable distance.

On the second screen from the left, there was a picture of the area just outside this blind, the place where I'd hidden under the slab, where the aliens had lumbered past me and I first saw them in person. In that area was a broken glass pillar, with craggy remains sticking up as if a tree had been cracked by lightning. And from one of those crags there now hung a flapping creature whose movements I recognized. Black leathery wings, twitchy flitting motions, finally settling down to an elongated upside-down triangle. Even on the grainy screen, I could make out two black eyes looking toward the camera.

I shoved Bonnie aside and scrambled to my feet. "Holy God!"

Bonnie jumped up. "What? What's wrong?"

But I was already gone, running down the corridor toward the main chamber.

"Clark!" I shouted, forgetting all about keeping my voice down. My shout boomed in the otherwise quiet compound.

A half-dozen people flinched and jumped up, shaken, including Clark, who had found a moment to doze off.

"Huh! What?" he gasped. "What's wrong?"

"Get up! The ship's been breached!"

CHAPTER ELEVEN

"Look!"

I stepped over Pocket, who was asleep on the floor, and tapped the controls on the panel which I had previously seen my mother use to turn on the projectors in the stealth curtain.

As the crowd increased around me, everyone reacting to my trumpeting, the projector curtain also woke up and gave us a picture of the landscape on its other side. There, hanging on the glass spire, blinking her eyes at us, was Buttercup the fox bat.

"Oh! Buttercup!" Bonnie blurted, and stepped past me toward the curtain.

"Don't go out there!" I seized her by the shoulders which I had hugged gently only moments ago, and dragged her back.

"The ship!" Clark pushed Pocket and me out of his way and crashed through to the main bank of monitor screens.

Everybody followed him, and in this moment my mother appeared.

"What's this noise?" she asked.

"The ship's been breached," I said, pointing at the screen that showed the right angle. "The ramp is down!"

"I see," she responded. "More mistakes?"

We crowded to the monitor bank and Clark leaned close to

the three screens which showed parts of the *Vinza*, parked at its landing site. Sure enough, the ship's ramp was down. At the bottom of the ramp were four Xenomorphs, dead or dying. And moving down the ramp on frighteningly proficient segmented legs, were five metallic-hooded shapes.

"The poison-packers! Shit me blind!" Clark gulped. "Somebody activated them! What the hell! What the hell!" He jumped up. "I have to contact the ship!"

"You must not, Captain," my mother said bluntly. "Any disturbance in wave use could trigger another behavioral change. We simply do not know enough yet. "

Colonel MacCormac made a noise of contempt and growled, "Well, that's that. Squad!"

I spun around to him. "Are you going out?"

"That's right."

"You know those robotics will target you as well as the aliens—"

"That's why we're going out. We have to neutralize them before they find their way in here. You don't give up your only bivouac. Captain, how can we neutralize them? Do you know?"

"Theo was the only one who could've activated them!" Clark exclaimed, shaken. "Him and me—we're it! He must've had a reason!"

"I think the reason is clear." MacCormac pointed at the screen. "The aliens got inside the grid and somehow inside the ship, and your first mate didn't know how else to fight them."

"How could they get inside the grid?"

"Don't care."

"Yeah, but I care." I couldn't help an all-too-human glance at my sister and Tad. Tad caught the glare and returned it with a twist of his mouth. Not a good sign, as body language goes, but a helpful one.

"What are those helmets made of?" MacCormac asked.

"Quadra-fold TGX," Clark said.

MacCormac turned to Carmichael and Edney. "Grenades only. Load up. Take sidearms in case the bugs give us trouble."

"You want an extra hand?" I offered. Was I crazy or just stupid?

"No," he said sharply. "Everybody else stays inside. I don't want to have to worry about anybody but my own squad. This is now a military operation. Is that perfectly clear?"

Heads bobbed like daisies all around.

While he and the other two Marines loaded up with grenades and sidearms—down to two, stoic, brave, silent—MacCormac turned to Clark. "How many do you think there are, Captain?"

Clark was deeply disturbed, frustrated that he had to be here. "A hundred to a container, five pallets, twenty to a pallet. They have to be activated in bulk, a pallet at a time, so the least you'll face is twenty. Look, it's my ship—I want to go with you. My crew—"

"Out of the question. We'll see to your crew." MacCormac slung a whole belt full of grenades over his shoulder. "If there are any left."

"Don't let them see you first," Clark warned. "The darts are hypersonic."

"Understood."

The Marines moved out, leaving the rest of us feeling as if we were baby birds left in the nest. The flurry they caused at the projector curtail startled the fox bat, and she spread her huge wings and flew off over our heads.

"Oh, no!" Bonnie cried. "Buttercup!"

"Stay here, stay here," I ordered, holding her by the arm so tightly that she winced. "Pocket, where are you?"

"Here." He stepped between Tad and the chef, Oliver.

"All right, how could that have happened? How could the ship's security blaster be turned off?"

"You mean, other than we turn it off inside?"

"Obviously!"

He paused to think. "Maybe a targeted frequency pulse. But that's a fancy procedure. The frequency would have to be diagnosed first, then rolled down to a tight beam."

"Like stealth technology?" I faced Tad in full accusatory mode.

"Somebody did this on purpose to make sure we didn't launch tomorrow. It fits."

"Back off, man," Tad fumed.

Clark grimaced and shook his head. "I hate that it fits."

"You're paranoid!" Gracie accused. "You're trying to turn us against each other!"

"Graciella, remain calm," our mother instructed, leading by example. "From their point of view, I understand."

I rubbed my face, feeling the fatigue race through my fingers into my eyes at her smooth performance. "Uh, cripes . . . All right, everybody quiet down and don't move around. Those robots are programmed to kill anything that's not native DNA to the planet, and that means us. Let the Colonel do his job and don't attract any attention."

"Aren't you afraid we'll escape?" my mother snidely said, letting out more emotion, I'm sure, than she intended.

"You want to escape?" I spread my hands and gestured toward the outside world. "Go ahead. Go on out there. Make my job a hell of a lot easier."

The uneasy crowd dissipated into groups of two or three, but nobody was talking much. We now had two kinds of creatures on this planet gunning for us, and I knew that was because the *Vinza* had come here loaded for bear. Now what?

"Please," Bonnie spoke up, "let me go out and get Buttercup!

She's so lost out there . . . she's all by herself. She's just out the door!"

"Have you looked outside?" I chided. "There's a jungle. She'll fit right in."

"She was raised by humans! She's looking for us! All I have to do is put out my—"

"Bonnie, forget it," I snapped. "I think you're smart. Don't prove me wrong."

"But what if those things catch her?"

"She can fly. They can't. She'll be okay."

"I can get her to come to me. I'll use some of that dried fruit—"

"No! Just . . . no."

Bonnie broke down into a spate of angry sobbing, during which I realized I was being unfair to her.

I coiled my arm around her. "Sorry . . . okay, okay . . . I'm sorry. Look, Bonnie, she's probably a lot better off out there than we are. There are a zillion insects, according to Zaviero, and lots of fruit or whatever she eats. She'll live."

"We can't just abandon her," she moaned. "You'll help me, won't you?"

"Me? Honey, I'm not going out there again for anything. Nothing and nobody. I'm done. Anybody who goes out is crazy."

"Oh, please . . . "

"The only thing that'll get me outside again is to go back to the *Vinza* and launch off this sin of planet. We'll go first thing in the morning, all of us, whether these idiots know it or not."

"And just leave her on this planet by herself?"

"She's a *bat*."

Tears broke out again.

What was the big deal? It wasn't as if we were leaving a child out there. Or even an Irish setter.

A bat, for pity's sake.

"Hey, look at this!" Pocket called. He drew our attention to one of the screens, on which we could see a poison-packer moving on two of its six legs down a gully ridge.

We crowded around the screen, desperately wishing we could see the events unfold in person, knowing that we'd be dead if we did. The poison-packers had no genetic imperatives or behavioral changes. They just hunted relentlessly any life form not native to this planet. There would be no walking among them.

"Look at how it walks," Pocket appreciated.

"They have six legs," Clark said, "for any kind of terrain. If they lose one, they just use the others and keep going. You can't outrun them. All you can do is hope they don't catch you on their senses. They're programmed to examine every inch of the planet. If our first wave is successful, the plan is to deploy another ten million of them from subsequent ships."

We watched, unable to participate, as the poison-packer's supertechnical helmet glowed with special sensors and dart ports. An adult alien was approaching it with a strange innocent curiosity. The aliens didn't care about machines, didn't know about them—at least, we assumed they didn't.

On sight, the poison-packer zeroed in on the alien and fired one of its darts. We never even saw the dart, it happened so quickly. The alien jolted physically, let out a bawling howl, and clawed at its ribcage, where the dart had struck it dead-center. The poison-packer simply trundled on past the alien and went on its way, seeking the next one.

The alien began to claw at its body. It wagged its huge head, then tipped its head sideways and bit furiously at its right arm, tearing ligaments and cables, chewing furiously, and then the left arm. It stomped its legs, finally dropping to the ground and snapping its second set of jaws at its thighs. As the DNA-specific poison coursed through its body, the alien was helping to rip itself to shreds. The long clawed hands tore at its open wounds, opening them further, spurting acid all over itself and over the ground, creating a sizzling, smoldering puddle for the creature to die in.

Within seconds, the process was finished. The alien lay twitching and sizzling in its own remains.

"Genocide," my mother commentated. "Who thinks of such things?"

Drained and overwhelmed, Clark turned to her and spoke in an honest way. "Mrs. Malvaux, I'm just the delivery man. This picture is way bigger than any of us."

"Lies," she accused. "You believe what you're doing is right. You shouldn't be here. You're destroying, and they're fighting back, and you and my son have the temerity to be angry about it. What's happening here is natural and we have no right to interfere."

"If we don't interfere," I argued, "we're all dead and I'm not ready for that. This is not an endangered species."

Her eyes drilled into mine. "But you mean to endanger it."

I nodded in annoyance. "Well, you've got me there!"

"Yes, I have you," she caustically agreed. "They have a natural controlling factor. We're witnessing it. There are no evil species. Nature doesn't create destruction."

"Nature creates almost nothing *but* destruction," I disclaimed.

That was when we heard the sound of more grenades, distant muffled booms rumbling along the landscape.

"Nobody goes out," I said. "We'll wait for the Marines."

I felt dangerously alone. I'd much rather have actually *been* alone. Instead I sat here and stewed, watching the monitors and trying to figure out how to get everybody back to the ship and fly off this rock without losing anybody else.

This wasn't my best thing. Clark was theoretically the one who should be calling the shots, but he was, as he admitted, a freighter captain and not an adventurer, not a soldier, untrained in this kind of maneuver. Colonel MacCormac was probably the best one to make decisions, but I didn't want to say that kind of thing out in the open, because he could so easily become a target. Somebody was working against us, and as an investigator I was supposed to be able to tease out that identity. Most investigations took weeks, months, maybe years. I had minutes.

As I sat alone, the bank of screens had turned strangely calm. The calm was worse than action, I think. My legs quaked and wouldn't settle down. I was a bag of nerves.

One of the screens showed the flume between us and the camp of huts. That was a dangerous road now. It had probably seen more traffic in the past twelve hours than it had . . . well, ever. Parasites flicked around, full-sized aliens trod the area. Being out there was like wading a swamp in the Amazon—no telling what manner of horror would leap up and snap you down to your death. Nature could sure be creative in a bad way.

I squinted my tired eyes. There, hanging on a drape of gauze between two skinny spires, was the bat.

There it was, with its big soggy eyes and its Chihuahua face, hanging out on the gauze.

"What are you doing, Buttercup?" I murmured. "Why don't you fly away while you can?"

The bat flexed one wing as if it had heard my thoughts, then coiled the wing back around itself like the cape in the old Dracula movies, and just waited there.

What was it waiting for? For us to come and get it?

"Is that it?" I asked the caped image on the screen. "All the way out here in space, you know somehow which group is yours? You know you're an Earthling?"

My head pounded with exhaustion. I leaned back and rested it on the stark black wall. No chance for sleep.

The bat rearranged its feet and continued looking at me. Somehow it was even looking in the right direction, toward the camera, and thus we were eye to eye. She was. Bonnie said the bat was a girl.

I wondered if there were girl aliens and boy aliens.

We paused for a moment of silence as we processed the information and what we thought was a pretty good theory about the things we'd seen. During that pause I found myself looking at Chantal, the pixie-ish veterinarian, which made me think of something else. I looked around the table, then past it to the tunnel opening,

"What's wrong with you?" Pocket asked.

I scanned the group again, just to be sure. "Where's Bonnie?"

They glanced around, just realizing she wasn't here.

Clark darkly confirmed, "I haven't seen her . . . "

I reached for the control panel as I'd seen the researchers do when they wanted to speak to each other inside the blind's tunnel system. We weren't really supposed to use it, but I didn't care. "Bonnie? Bonnie, where are you? Are you in the compound? Wake up and talk if you're in here. Bonnie, come in, Bonnie, Bonnie."

The mellow communications system, on a constant low-volume, made my voice seem soft and distant.

There was no answer.

Then it dawned on me *why* there was no answer.

"Oh, crap . . . " I scratched past the table and the people on the bench and ducked into the area with the stacked video monitors and scanned them. I missed a lot the first time over, and then saw the terrible sight I knew was out there. On the bottom left screen, almost behind a stack of foam coffee cups, was Bonnie. She was lurking between two pillars, and in her hand she held two lumps of dried fruit.

"What the hell's she doing?" Clark demanded.

"Trolling for bats!" I burst past him. "I'll get her! Everybody stay here!"

I ran out into the forest of glass. I hoped I was going in the direction where I'd seen the fox bat lingering. If the monitors showed a circular area around the blind, and the bat had been on the monitor to the left, I reasoned that I had to go left.

Only when I got outside and discovered that looking at the land on the monitors and looking at the actual land were two completely different things. Getting my bearings took too long, and I still wasn't sure.

"Bonnie!" I dared to yell. My own voice startled me—we'd tried so hard to remain quiet that speaking up was a shock.

I ran around the rocky terrain which seemed to be the house for the caves in which my mother and her people had built their anthill. From here I could see that it wasn't a solid lump of rock with caves inside—it also had dozens of openings that clearly showed on the outside. The rock was Swiss cheese, offering only the basic of scaffolds for the blind. The walls and tunnel material of the blind were the only real separation between those inside and the outside world.

The land was still pocked with shadows and the moon, now having arched almost all the way across the sky, still shone fairly brightly, enough that I could navigate.

But I'd lost my way. This wasn't looking like the place where the bat had been. There was no hanging gauze here. Where was I supposed to go? Where would Bonnie have gone to reclaim her pet?

"Bonnie!" I called again—and skidded to a clumsy stop.

I'd run into an open plain, almost a meadow, of black and white spiky growth no taller than ten inches, and now I stood like a single turkey at a shoot. Flanking the entire northern ridge of the meadow were aliens. Hundreds of them. They turned in a single file and looked at me, heads bobbing and claws fanned. Their lips peeled back—greenish lips with phosphorescent drooling liquid running in strings to the ground.

"Aw, thank you, providence," I murmured. There was no hiding. They all saw me.

I thought I was dead. Except that they didn't move on me. Standing out here alone in the moonlight, looking at them, them looking at me, I felt like the lone conductor of a really big orchestra. With one flick of the baton, I could destroy the perfect pause.

"Rory?"

The voice came from my right. I pivoted only enough to see Bonnie sitting in the black and white furze, as if she were sitting at a campfire.

Moving in slow sidesteps, I closed the gap between us. "What are you doing?"

"I followed Buttercup," Bonnie said, trembling violently. "I didn't see them till I was all the way here."

"Neither did I." Extending my hand, I said, "Stand up *very* slowly and get behind me."

She unfolded her legs and took my hand. I pulled her to her feet.

"Getting behind won't matter." She raised her trembling hand and pointed over her shoulder.

Behind us, less than a hundred yards away, was the other edge of the meadow. To our right and extending the width of the available space, was a squall line of aliens. They flexed and threatened, hissed, rolled, and stalked with a physical message of singular purpose.

And they were moving toward us.

With awful deliberation the two lines were closing on each

other. Because of the angle of the land, they'd meet first in the place where we'd come from—our escape route back to the blind.

"We're cut off," I said unhappily.

"Why are they divided up this way?" Bonnie squeaked, her voice barely working.

I drew her close against me and began to move laterally across the meadow.

That's when I saw the Marines. The three of them stood enraptured by the sight of the two lines of aliens closing like pincers on the body of the meadow.

There was no sign of anyone but the three Marines. Had they made it to the ship? Was everybody at the ship dead?

MacCormac had his sidearm raised. As we approached the Marines and they came into the meadow to meet us, I called, "MacCormac, don't . . . shoot."

"Say that again?"

We finally came together two-thirds of the way across the meadow.

"Don't antagonize them," I said. "They're leaving us alone. Don't trigger any other kind of behavior."

Not being an idiot, he did as I instructed and waved his two Marines to hold fire. Never thought the day would come when I'd be giving tactical instructions to a Colonel in the Colonial Marines.

"What happened at the ship?" I asked. "Is everybody dead?"

"No, they're in the hold, locked up," the colonel said quickly. "Your first mate left a com link on the ground outside, with a code to talk directly to him in the hold. We destroyed six of the PPs with grenades to get to the link. Aliens got aboard somehow, and Theo didn't know what to do except release a pallet of PPs. He threw the com link out the ramp, hoping we'd find it. We couldn't get in. There were still PPs in the cargo area."

"It's the 'somehow' that bothers me," I grumbled.

We hunkered together, trapped, as the astonishing tableau unrolled around us. From the south came the longer phalanx of the dogs of Anubis. They bobbed the curves of their hammer-shaped heads, holding their faces low to show the curved transparent shells of their skulls in some kind of species-specific signal. Distending their main jaws, they expelled and flexed their second sets, glistening with silvery saliva and sticky drainage. All in all, they were a disgusting display.

"We're cut off," I croaked.

MacCormac crouched on the other side of Bonnie, with Carmichael and Edney huddled at my side. "We could try flanking them," the Colonel said. "Lay down suppressing fire—"

"Too many," I told him. "No chance."

"I'm going down shooting!" Corporal Edney swore, and caressed her pistol, which seemed very small right now.

"There are other ways to fight," I told her. "Like not drawing attention to yourself."

"He's right," MacCormac said. "Make a circle around these civilians and hold fire!"

The three brave Marines, taking their roles seriously, arranged themselves flat to the ground around Bonnie and me. Then came the terrible moments of watching without being able to do anything else. The aliens moved in two concentrated waves toward each other, bundling into tighter units as they closed the gap between them. I felt as though I were watching one of those old-time Biblical epic movies with waves of extras creating endless throngs to showcase the power of the pharaohs. They came up through the spillways and out of the ditches, across volcanic lakes and down flumes. Each army was a juggernaut, moving toward us as if two vault doors were closing to lock us in. The hair-raising sight made us feel tiny and tortured, about to be killed by inches.

My skin came up in prickles. I coiled my arms around Bonnie and we made ourselves small.

Then the doors closed. The two squall lines of aliens came together around us, leaping over us to get to each other. Then the slashing and tearing began.

"Duck!" I dragged Bonnie down and pushed Carmichael sideways. He rolled away as two aliens landed between us, going at each other like cats.

The noise was mind-blowing. The world around us erupted into an atrocious and craven battle. The aliens leaped at each other and instantly tangled up into balls of two and three, after which others would leap onto the balls and create globes of five, ten, more, all tearing and biting at each other. Tails whipped out and stabbed back into the balls, spraying acid and glowing bodily juices around each battle ball. Parts of the aliens' brittle bones splintered past us as they tore each other apart, rolling in their huge balls and leaving tire tracks of body parts and acid sizzling on the writhing bodies of the not-quite-dead who were left behind. The aliens paid no attention to those of their own who were wounded or trampled. The fallen became launch pads for others to stage their own grisly barbarism.

"Move!" MacCormac shouted, and led the way.

We crawled on all fours, almost down to our stomachs. Carmichael couldn't stand the pressure and opened fire twice before following us. Edney shouted something unintelligible, and Carmichael responded with another round, which struck home on one of the creatures and sent a firework of acid spraying past us on our left.

"Come on, Ken!" I called. "Don't bother!"

"Too many of 'em!" Carmichael confirmed, and gave up trying to use his weapon. He might as well have been spitting at a tornado.

Corporal Edney doubled back to avoid the twisting body of a dying Xeno, a critical mistake that put her in the path of a massive battle ball. I started to shout a warning, but never got the chance. The battle ball of ripping, thrashing aliens rolled over Edney and when it came up off the ground, she was inside it.

She screamed—we heard the terrible sound of shock and defiance—and then we heard the ballistics of pistol fire inside the tumbleweed of aliens. Tail sections and an alien hand came blowing out of the ball, and we caught the sight of Edney's tanned face showing between a pair of alien legs. Her mouth was open in horror, one eye nothing but a bloody socket. Her hand came out of the ball, still shooting wildly.

Then Edney's entire arm fell free of the ball and dropped to the ground, pistol, hand, and all. Her screams drained away. The battle ball rolled on, and she was gone with it.

"Shit, shit, shit!" MacCormac stopped crawling and rolled backward into me and Bonnie as we bumped up against a low-lying outcropping of silver stone.

Crumpled on the ground, we looked up at the sight that now completely blocked our way.

Three aliens, enough to kill a suburb, scowled down at us with their gracile bodies splayed in threat. They were hell's dragons, so frightful that even the Marines froze and just stared. We could have shot them, but there would be three more, then thirty more after them, then three hundred. I think in those seconds we established a silent pact to let ourselves die now, be over with it.

The trio of aliens stretched their arms and necks, rolled their heads back, and cried to the heavens with their glass-breaking shrieks. The uproar almost cracked our skulls. Bonnie dug her face into my shoulder, having seen enough, finally. MacCormac gritted his teeth and peeled back his lips in a mockery of the aliens, and Carmichael took his hat off to welcome death uncovered.

A scratching sound behind us alerted me and I dropped Bonnie and cranked around. More aliens—four of them, rose over the rock I was leaning against.

"MacCormac!" I warned. "Get out of the way!"

The colonel spun around as the three dragons launched themselves at other four. He was trapped!

The aliens clawed at each other and amazingly pushed MacCormac out of the way. It wasn't a mistake—they deliberately pushed him away! The seven aliens rolled into a weird ball, limbs and tails and heads all curved into each other, and actually rolled across the land in a nasty fighting mass.

I grabbed him and pulled him into the pile of us. "Get up and run!"

We scrambled out of the boiling pot, not even bothering to try to hide anymore. The riot went on, aliens slashing and biting at aliens by the hundreds, while we ran right through the middle of it, trying to avoid being splashed by acid or just rolled over by tumbling masses of aliens locked together in battle. Rolling around in every direction until they smashed into pillars or rocks or each other, the battle balls tumbled aimlessly as those aliens locked in them used their tails to whip outward and punch back in, spearing madly and leaving trails of dead fighters behind them like tire tracks on a demolition-derby field. The field now had a ghastly smell about it—acid, oil, saliva, a gaudy stink of flesh and befoulment. More butchery for this sad planet.

Our legs pumping against the unwelcoming ground, we crested a mound of glass that was the remains of a crumbled pillar. The mound was hard to climb since we didn't dare use our hands on the crushed glass. I pulled Bonnie, and she pulled Carmichael. Behind us, Edney and MacCormac scrambled awkwardly up the talus spread by the rest of us. When we hit the top of the mound, I took one look at the landscape and shouted, "Back!"

Right in front of us were two poison-packing robots, spewing hypersonic darts from their hoods, taking out aliens left, right, and around. The poisoned aliens forgot about each other and began biting and ripping at themselves, biting their own arms off and trying to claw out the poison spreading inside them. If a sight can be more horrible than what we had already seen, this was it. The poison made them actually help in the killing process.

I fell on Bonnie, and lashed out a foot to trip Carmichael. "Down, down! Keep your head down!" I landed on my back and swept my arms out to hold Bonnie, then strapped Carmichael down with the leg that had tripped him.

MacCormac dropped on his side. "That's all we need!"

"Maybe the aliens won't kill us," I said, "but those robots sure will."

Trapped between the two approaching poison packers, we could almost feel our DNA screaming for attention. The poison packers were proximity weapons, not predisposed to operate at a distance, but the proximity was closing fast. In seconds, if we showed ourselves, they'd pick us up just as they were picking up the aliens, and they'd start shooting those darts at us.

"Stay here!" I shouted, and pushed Bonnie flat.

"Rory!" She didn't want to leave me in the open.

I dropped and rolled as if my clothing were on fire, toward the corpse of one of the dead aliens—or the half of it that was left. Expecting to be burned by the acidic remains, I reached for the mass and came up with two disembodied snorkels and the sinews that once held them onto the creature's back. With an instinctive heave, I threw the first mass like a hatchet at the nearest poison packer, then whirled and threw the second at the other PP. I dropped behind a stump just as its ultrasonic darts began to fire. Darts splattered on the stump above me.

Suddenly more darts came from the other direction, and then from both directions in rapid succession. Through the red glass stump, I watched the two PPs approach each other, their casings smeared with dripping alien remains. Picking up the DNA signatures or the remains, they fired madly at each other, punching darts into each other's shells until their delicate innards were sparking and shattered. The one on the right lost its imperative and tipped sideways, crashing its helmet into a spear-shaped spire. Less than a second later, the other one tipped all the way over on its head, twirled madly, and thrashed its legs in a futile effort to stay upright, an effort that failed. It landed head-down in a pool of smoldering acid.

"Wow!" Carmichael appreciated. "That was smart!"

"Your hands!" Bonnie grasped my wrists.

"It's okay, I grabbed the outside ends."

"Nice going," MacCormac said. "Follow me, people."

"Gladly."

While the turbulence of the two alien crowds fighting continued around us, we scurried under cover of insanity back toward the blind. MacCormac seemed to know the way better than I did, so I was glad to let him lead. The Marines had the sense to know when weapons wouldn't do the trick and no longer tried to shoot at the aliens which seemed so effectively distracted and deliberately parted to let us pass—and if that weren't weird enough, actually seemed to protect us from each other. Just as we came around a bend in the flume, a mass of them rolled past us, but suddenly dissolved their battle ball when they almost hit us. They gawked at us briefly, and us at them, and off they went again in another direction, pointedly avoiding us.

"Keep going!" MacCormac shouted.

We got right up and ran harum-scarum again. I could tell by the way MacCormac checked every turn that he was looking for PPs. As for aliens, we just dodged between them and they let us go.

I wouldn't delude myself. They were still horrendously dangerous and we were walking some kind of tightrope. I didn't know what kind yet, but we certainly weren't safe among them, as my mother fantasized that we were. Bonnie said nothing like this ever lasted long in the animal world, and I believed her. Whatever the trigger was, it could be tripped any time and we'd be back in the soup.

"Hold!" MacCormac spat, and struck me in the chest with his arm.

We fell up against a sheer wall. He peeked around the edge of the wall.

"C'mere," he hissed, and drew me closer. He whispered, "Look."

I ducked down and peeked around his thick body.

Only twenty or so feet away were seven face-huggers sitting together on a rock, standing up on their eight fingers and quivering like bachelors in a dance line. Their tails were straight out behind them, but not flaccid or hanging on the rock. I held onto MacCormac's belt and we watched.

Slowly, trying not to draw attention, he pulled a grenade from his belt, right near my nose. In slow motion I watched the small and powerful casing rise out of the cartridge holder between his fingers. That grenade could take out everything within fifty feet, including us. But it was also the only way we could possibly get by seven of those parasites. We could only hope that the rock which was now hiding us would also give us some kind of protection. I knew that the concussion wave would probably knock us silly for several minutes, during which we'd be even more vulnerable than we were now. I didn't like the odds. I thought about stopping him.

He held the grenade in both hands, judging the distance. Just as his thumb went to the detonator and was about to come down, I saw something and grasped his elbow.

The face-huggers were up on their fingertips, making tent-shapes of their bodies. The flank lobes with which they grasped the faces of their victims were up high in a gull-winged fashion instead of down in the usual position. I couldn't believe what I saw next . . . the huggers, all together, began to puff their bodies—*puff, puff, puff*—and the flank lobes began to grow into rings with membranes in the mid-dles. The membranes spread wider and wider, thinner and thinner, the way balloons open up and get thinner as they're filled with air, except these membranes were flat and getting broader with every puff. The huggers, one by one, began to fan their membranes, flapping more energetically by the second, and there was a whirring sound, almost the way a hum-mingbird's wings make that constant buzz.

Then, in a true flocking manner, all seven face-huggers crouched on their fingertips and launched themselves into the air. They stretched their tails out behind them for balance and flew right over our rock and on into the sky over the field of rolling battle balls and dead and dying aliens.

As we watched, dumbfounded, the fliers were joined by other flying parasites. They flocked briefly in the sky, and buzzed off into a swarm, joined by still others. The swarm whirled to the left, then the right, then found a direction they liked and flew off into the distant sky over the glass spires, to-ward the Blue Valley.

We stared after them, slowly digesting the full gravity of the mess we were now in.

MacCormac blinked, still holding the uncharged grenade in both hands. "I'll be damned . . . they can fly."

CHAPTER TWELVE

"Theo released a pallet of poison packers. Somehow the ramp got open—he has no idea how. He saw some aliens, a dozen or more of them, coming up the ramp and he didn't know what else to do. He shoved the crew down into the provisions hold and triggered one pallet—twenty PPs—hoping they'd take the aliens out and then just venture out into the landscape and go on their way. He figured we were probably dead, and even if we weren't, we'd never live if the ship were taken."

MacCormac paced away his bottled fury at the useless death of Corporal Edney, stalking back and forth in front of the deceptively calm main stealth curtain. He paused only to drop the communicator link into Clark's hand. "He said he tried to contact us, but the frequencies were all jammed. He threw this out the ramp just before triggering the PPs. I was able to contact him, and he explained what had happened. He also told me the PPs instantly fired their darts on the aliens, and the aliens went crazy from the poison. He says the dying aliens attacked the PPs. Get that—even though they won't attack us, they'll still attack the PPs! Can you imagine that? So the PPs shot 'em, and then the dying aliens jumped *on top of* the PPs and clung there until their bodies fell apart and the acid burned through the PPs helmets! I'll bet nobody back at tactical ever though of *that!*"

We once again huddled in the main chamber, trying to think things through. Most of the campers were in other chambers. Only my mother, Gracie and Tad, and Neil were in here with Clark, MacCormac, Bonnie, Carmichael, Pocket, and me.

"So they're safe?" Clark asked hopefully. "My crew's safe in the provisions hold? Theo's okay? They're alive?"

MacCormac wiped the spittle from his mouth. "I think so."

"If they stay down there, they're safe," Pocket reassured. "Those robots aren't programmed to decode our locking system."

"If they come up," MacCormac said, "the PPs will take them out if there are any robots left in the ship. The aliens took out five PPs with their acid trick. The remaining PPs probably killed off the other aliens that were in the ship and then ventured on down the ramp and are now running wild in the landscape. We took out seven of them with grenades, then Rory took out another two. That means we still have six of them wandering the landscape which we have to avoid."

He fitfully kicked a crate and sent it crashing across the chamber. Full of silverware and dishes, it crashed so loudly that it left us all shaking. I didn't want to say what I was thinking—that the aliens had figured out the PPs already and maybe the assumption that we could save this planet at all was mistaken. This would be a real war, with Humanity sending more and more PPs in waves, then synthetics, then entire armies. The story was just beginning.

"I'm sorry about your young lady Marine," my mother told him. "They didn't mean to kill her. She just got in the way."

"And that's supposed to make me feel better?" MacCormac spat.

I turned to her. "It's never their fault, is it, M'am?" I turned to Gracie and Tad. "How did the ramp get opened?"

Tad closed his eyes in misery. Gracie just stared at me.

They stared at me. It was like a party, only without the cheer. I guess that would be a funeral.

"Your mechanical troubles are your own problems," my mother said.

"What's happening to them?" I demanded. "Why are they fighting each other?"

Gracie, standing halfway between my mother and me, seemed truly in the middle. "They've stopped foraging and we think the queen has stopped producing. They're putting all their energy into defense."

"That wasn't defense," I corrected.

"What is it, then?" Clark asked.

"It was more than defense. They're not hunkering down. They're going out to meet an enemy and fight. This isn't a castle under siege. It's a battlefield. They're not interested in us because they're putting all their energy into fighting each other." Still wanting some kind of direction, I persisted, "But *why* would they fight each other?"

Gracie thought about the question, and her answer wasn't what I expected. "Because the one thing ants never tolerate is other ants."

"Are you saying they're *not* fighting each other? They're fighting a whole other hive? Another colony?"

"Yes, they're different!" Bonnie spoke up. "When I was out there, at first I just thought it was the light shining through the glass, but it wasn't. The one hive, our hive, they're all black. The other hive, they've got some green and blue on them! I thought I was imagining it!"

"Green where and blue where?" Gracie asked.

"Blue between the ribs. Green inside the mouth and under the arms." Pocket made a low whistle and said, "That's subtle."

"But it bears up the theory of two hives," Clark said. "How

can there be two hives? Didn't they all start with one 'hitch-hiker' or just a few?"

"This could be their evolutionary strategy," Gracie supplied. "They diversify into several hives, develop new queens, and when they come upon each other they pause in their impera-tives and fight in elimination rounds, working down to the mightiest hive. They can potentially evolve faster on the time-line of evolution. Very much faster."

"And this flying part?" Clark asked. "It's temporary?"

Gracie half-nodded, half-shrugged. "Like carpenter ants, they fly, they take over an area, they kill everything, and start a new colony. Then they don't fly anymore for a while."

"No bets on how long, right?" Pocket commented.

I waved him away from his compulsion. "Then when they expand enough and bump into each other, they stop everything and engage in this bug war. And the winners get the spoils."

"The spoils?" Bonnie wondered.

I forced myself to look at Gracie and Tad, Pocket and Clark.

"It's not just a bug war," I told them. "This is a war to see whose genetics get to spread all over the planet. We're not being protected. We're being stored for the winners to use. It's a DNA war."

"This is it," I announced. "I've made my decision. I want to save this planet. I want to save the Blue Valley. We're getting out. Clark, you were right from the start. These things need to be wiped out. There's no more discussion of the ASA. These things are a plague and we're going to smallpox 'em. With these animals here, this planet doesn't represent any kind of life." I turned to face my sister again. "Get everybody together. We're all leaving, if we have to stun every last one of you and carry you,"

Tad hung his hand on Gracie's shoulder as my sister stood

there, arms crossed tight to her body, glaring at me. When her eyes shifted to my mother, I saw the first play of doubt.

M'am nodded. "If that is the verdict," she said, "gather everyone."

Gracie, fighting tears, didn't obey. She turned to me. "Is this the only way that works for you?"

I fixed my eyes on hers. "For you, too. We're releasing the payload. Anybody who stays will be hunted down and killed by the robots. That means Tad, too. And it means you. If the ship leaves without you, that's the end of your chance for a future together with him, with children . . . a future as somebody other than Jocasta Malvaux's daughter. If you care about him and yourself and these people, you'll bring them here right now. Because we're all leaving."

Fighting her own emotions, she nodded. She tried to speak, but couldn't. With a soulful look at Tad, she led him out of the tunnel.

My mother watched them go. Her self-control was admirable, I have to say.

"So you have won," she said quietly to me. "You've taken my daughter away from me."

All eyes were on me as my mother slipped away.

"Ken," I said to Carmichael, "Go with them and make sure they don't pull any fast ones."

Carmichael pushed off toward the tunnel. "Yes, sir!"

MacCormac forced himself to think clearly. "If we can avoid the PPs, we can get everybody back. If the PPs Theo released on the ship have rolled down the ramp and are out of there, then the ship should be clear."

"We can scan with infrareds," Clark said. "The PPs show up on those scanners."

"We'll have to keep our heads low," the colonel went on. "If the PPs pick up our DNA signatures, we can't avoid those goddamned darts. Humans were never supposed to be on the planet with those robots. This is a complete screw-over."

"If Theo only released one pallet and there are only six left to avoid," Clark computed, "then we have a fair—"

"They're gone! They're gone! Mr. Malvaux! Rory!"

Private Carmichael came barreling out of the tunnel, all worked up.

"They're gone!" he gasped again.

"Who's gone, son?" Clark asked.

I caught Carmichael's arm. "You were watching them!"

He shook his head. "They were right in front of me, and then somehow they just weren't there anymore! Turned out I was following holographs! I can't find any of them!"

Pocket pushed through to the monitor bank and did his bosun thing at the keyboard. Dozens of pictures popped up of the interior of various chambers and the exterior of the compound. No longer were there any people milling around, sleeping or working or eating. The chambers were completely unpopulated, except for the one museum chamber and its stuffed trophy.

"Oh, glory, we'll never find them," Clark groaned. "We'll never find them in a thousand years! They're too good at this!"

"We'll flush them out," MacCormac swore. "Goddamn it, I'll grenade the whole mountain if I have to!"

"Listen!" Bonnie's urgent warning came from the projector curtain, where she stood watching the picture of the dim glass forest. "Listen—"

A low moan began in the distance and grew more intense, deeper, until the whole landscape and the cave and all the sky was humming. With its underlying vibrato, the trombone call set the ground beneath us to quivering.

Clark stared out at the projected land. Pocket's face swiveled as he twitched in fear. The Marines were still and tense.

The *hoooing* noise rolled through the valleys and grottos, down the flumes and up the grades, traveling farther and farther across the land. It lasted ten . . . twelve . . . fifteen seconds. Maybe more.

When it began finally to draw back and fade away, we were all as spooked as anybody ever had been in history.

Bonnie turned to look at me. "It's over."

CHAPTER THIRTEEN

The DNA war was over. One side had won. They'd be coming for us, to present us to their parasites for impregnation. We were back on the losing side. The period of grace had ended.

With one confrontation comes all of them.

I shook my head, sighed, and let my anger lead the way.

"Mother!" I shouted. "Where are you!"

MacCormac made a noise of disgust. "Who are you kidding?"

"Rory . . . " Clark began at the same time, steeped in doubt.

"Oh, she can hear us," I told him contemptively. "You don't think she lets anybody do anything in here without her knowing about it, do you? She thinks she's a god. Gods are always watching."

Over the blind's muffled sound system came my mother's voice, velvety and superior.

"*We are in hiding. You will never find us. So you might as well leave. You are here without invitation and you have worn out your welcome. Go on your way and leave us in peace. Go home.*"

"I'll be damned," Clark murmured.

"Fine!" Pocket snarled, pushing to his feet. "If that's the way they want it! To hell with 'em! Let's get out and save our own skins! They want to be stupid? Fine! I'm all for suicide, as long as it's somebody else's! Let's get out and leave these morons to their own fate!"

"Here, here," MacCormac chimed.

"Fine," I said, "except for one thing."

"What thing?" Clark asked. "What one more thing can possibly matter anymore?"

I turned to him. "How many of them feel the way Rusty did? How many really want to leave, but they're so duty-bound to my mother that they're afraid to defy her? We can't just walk out on them."

"I can," Pocket said.

"Well, I can't!" I shouted, and kept going, shouting at the air. "I'm out for humans, Mother! We have a right to exist. We're in our own DNA war with these things. This is the next big evolutionary test for humanity!"

"*The stronger should prevail.*"

"We're the stronger."

For a few seconds, silence fell. My words actually echoed. Maybe it was just in my head.

Then my mother's voice came again, somehow even more calm than before.

"*If you are so strong, my son, and your friends are so strong, then you can live or die on your own. I withdraw my protection from you.*"

For a moment we didn't know what that meant. Then things started to shut down. The bank of monitors was first, falling dark all at once with a single bright flash before the power died. Immediately after, the projector curtain faded to black, then unhitched itself from its delicate conduit-loaded rod, and dropped to the ground in a glittery puff. Before us spread the outside world, bathed in a dangerous dawn.

The fabric of the tunnels suddenly began to snap and repeal, collapsing on themselves and returning to their original super-thin folded form. Light from holes in the rock above began to punch through the darkened anthill, as if giants were shining flashlights in at us from dozens of portals. The full dynamic of the stealth technology hiding us revealed itself as it died.

The fabric walls of the main chamber now fell around us, collapsing into thin rolls, leaving us standing in a bright rocky hole, open to the world outside.

We blinked in freakish morning light. With no place left to hide, we were being forced out.

MacCormac seized his pulse rifle, but the expression on his face was near-panic. Knowing that two Marines with rifles could never protect all of us from the multiple terrors out there, he handed me Berooz's pulse rifle, then handed Clark and Pocket each a pistol.

"We've got to run," MacCormac ordered. "Stay quiet and keep your heads down. I'll take the lead. Carmichael, take up a position in the middle and watch our flanks!"

I pushed Clark and Pocket toward the wide-open flume, looked to make sure Bonnie was behind me, and caressed the pulse rifle.

"All right, Mother, we're leaving," I announced. "Hell of a way to win."

"*I hope I never see you again,*" she said over the sound system, which now had a hollow quality in the open air.

"Yeah," I muttered, "but I think you're the one who's weak." I raised my voice, just in case any of the others could still hear me. They deserved to know. "Did you tell these people the truth before you brought them here?"

There was a pause. Not the good kind.

I thought she might speak, but she didn't. By now, Clark and Bonnie, Pocket, MacCormac, and Carmichael were all waiting for her to speak. Instead, I was the one who spoke.

"Were you strong enough to be honest?" I demanded. "Did you tell them they were coming here to die glorious deaths in your holy service? Did you tell them you brought them here to be martyrs? That you never intended for them to leave this outpost alive? Did you tell them what their lives mean to you?"

I pushed a fresh cartridge into the pulse rifle and slapped it into place.

"I know I forced your hand," I finished. "Now you be sure to tell those people that you're taking sides with the aliens."

With that, standing out in virtually the open, I signaled to MacCormac. "No reason to stay, Colonel."

"Single file!" he ordered, and jogged toward the flume. The rest of us went out behind him, never to return to this manmade haven which had fallen away under us.

We broke out into the open and ran, but not too fast, not so fast that we became clumsy, that somebody fell or got hurt. MacCormac paced us from the front of the line.

Even though it was trying to be morning, much of the land was still skirted in darkness. We could barely see the path in front of us to keep good footing. As I ran, I thought about the Blue Valley, probably the only remaining pristine area on this continent. Who knew how far-flung the infestation was? Was it worldwide? Was the damage already done and could it ever be reversed? Was this planet doomed, extermination efforts or not?

That was for smarter people to decide. I had one thing on my mind, and that was launching off this cursed red mirror.

The huts! There they were—we were almost to the abandoned camp.

MacCormac slowed us down before entering the camp, leading with his pulse rifle like an urban Special Forces leader. I recognized the stance and took it myself, not knowing what we were looking for, afraid of what we'd find.

"Looks clear!" the colonel called. "Carmichael?"

"Clear right, sir!" the boy called from a few paces behind and to the right of me.

Suddenly the sound of ripping paper escorted a flap of wings from over the top of a hut—just that fast—a skitter of knuckles, the whip of a tail, and Colonel MacCormac was struck in the face.

"Oh, God!" Bonnie shrieked, and ducked back.

MacCormac went down hard, clawing at the thing on his face. The parasite's tail lashed around his throat and tied itself tight.

I turned the muzzle of my rifle on MacCormac's head, but that wouldn't work! I threw my rifle to Clark and tore into the animal on MacCormac's face with my bare hands. The strength of the eight elongated fingers was unbelievable! I couldn't budge so much as one claw.

"No!" I cried wildly, and dug my fingernails into its pulpy flesh. Its wings began to shrink, returning to that rounded state in which they were a set of clamps on the victim's cheeks. I dug my nails into one of the wings, popped through the membrane, and ripped the wing off. I felt the sting of acid burns on my hands, but rage drove me to ignore it. I swore at the creature something unintelligible, and went after the other wing.

MacCormac struggled briefly, then went limp. His hands released the creature on his face and he fell into my arms with the malignancy locked onto his head, settling down to its wicked, pitiless work.

I let him fall to the ground and rearranged myself on my knees beside him and pulled his service knife from his belt. Damn it, I'd slice the noxious thing off layer by layer!

There was a loud boom next to my ear. My hands and the knife turned red, wet, and hot. MacCormac lay at my knees, now a body without a head, missing its left shoulder too. The remains of his head and the face-hugger were soaking into the skulch a foot away from me.

I looked up.

Private Carmichael gazed down in that awful moment after. His face was a plate of misery and resolution. I knew he had followed orders, but his expression betrayed more.

He shook himself and turned his weapon on the tops of the huts, in case any more huggers were flitting around on the wing.

Clark pulled me to my feet. "Come on, Rory."

He kept the pulse rifle, but handed me the plasma pistol he'd been carrying. Shaken, startled, numb, and hardly knowing he was talking to me, I let him pull me along. Poor MacCormac—all he'd wanted to do was just the best thing at every step.

"Keep moving!" Pocket called from the far end of the camp. He was almost through. "It's clear! Don't lag!"

That was when something jumped out at him.

Emotionally exhausted, I just paused and watched, ready for anything.

Okay, anything but this.

"Rusty!" I yanked free of Clark's grip and rushed toward Pocket, who was helping to his feet the last person I expected ever to see again on this planet.

Rusty was a bruised and cut-up mess, his hair all natty and his blue suit in rags, but he was here, alive.

Knotting my fists into his collar, I dragged him all the way to his feet. "You're alive!"

"I'm alive . . . I lived . . . "

"How?"

He pounded my shoulder in victory and said, "Survived the fall somehow. I woke up on the floor of the ravine next to that Xeno you killed! I've been climbing for hours! I was so scared you'd leave without me! Can I still go with you?"

"Can you? *Can* you!" I threw my arms around him and whooped with joy. Finally something to go right!

"I don't want to stay here with Jocasta any more!" he babbled, looking at me and Clark with pleading eyes. "She doesn't care about us! She only cares about those things . . . I'm so sorry I didn't fess up right when you first landed! Those people in the huts—" He pointed at the makeshift tombs around us. "She set them up! They were the ones who didn't like it here, who wanted to call Earth and have a ship sent for us. One by one, she arranged for them to get caught by the huggers or for their stealth tech to break down. I was the only one who knew about it, because I pretended to agree with her. Jesus, it feels good to spill the beans!" He huffed out a breath and looked around. "Where is everybody? All my friends—are they all going with you? Are they already at the ship?"

How could I tell him he was the only one who would be freed of this planet?

"No, we're right here," a voice said from nowhere.

It was my sister's voice. Between two of the huts the fabric of the air began to ripple. Forms appeared, then solidified, two by two, into the missing researchers. They were hiding right here all along, in a clutch of personal blinds, probably among the first developed before they moved into the big blind.

My sister walked toward me, her face red and plastered with tears. Behind her, Tad came up close.

"It was Jocasta all along," Tad said. "I've been trying to get Gracie to leave here for months. Gracie's been protecting me from your mother. She knew Jocasta would kill anybody who betrayed her."

I reached out to shake his hand. "You're not betraying her by wanting your own life."

My sister blinked at me, holding back sobs, but I could tell that for the first time in years, she was with me. And I was with her.

I touched her face and gave her a little smile. Right here in the middle of hell.

"Come on," I said. "Let's go home."

Private Carmichael—Ken, Esquire—took charge in a manner that would've made MacCormac proud. He led the way as the gaggle of us fell in behind him. In tight formation we struck out through the glass forest that separated us from the landing area. Finally—seemed like years—we saw the ship.

The *Vinza* was as we had left it, but now the magnetic field propulsion units were on, whirring and hot from the plasma being directed through its reaction chambers. Theo had fired the ship up, anticipating that we were coming. Good!

As we approached, the loading ramp began to lower in true mechanical fashion. Clark dashed aboard first, brewing with purpose, and was instantly yelling orders inside.

"Couplers on max! Prepare for launch and deploy! Theo! Barry! Where's Gaylord!" He kept shouting, but I didn't care.

I stepped aside and Carmichael went to the other side of the ramp, and together we funneled the remaining researchers into the ship, every one of them more than glad to pile in.

Rusty put his foot on the ramp and turned to me, clasping my hand again. "I don't know what to say! You came just in time!"

I grinned at him and clapped my hand to his arm in gratification. "That's my job. To come in the nick of time."

"I heard this horrible noise, like a factory whistle that just went on and on—and I kept running. I thought it might be your ship trying to take off without me, so I ran right through a whole swarm of Xenos! They just looked at me and left me alone! I figured it was a miracle!"

"Yeah," I agreed. "You say you ran through them *after* you heard the noise?"

"I really ran as fast as I could. My legs hurt! My chest hurts! I can't believe I made it!"

If I'd ever been sick to my stomach in my life, this was the worst. No matter how I added it up,

"Rusty . . . "

"Yeah?"

I drew my pistol upward and aimed it at his chest. "I'm sorry, I'm so sorry . . . I don't think I can let you get on the ship."

"Huh?" He reacted, then laughed. "Oh—funny!"

That's when the convulsion started. Rusty coughed, gagged, and pressed a hand to his chest.

"Oh, no—" I choked. "goddamned squalid bastards!"

Horror erupted in Rusty's eyes. He grabbed my shirt and dropped to his knees, shuddering and heaving, then pitched over backward onto the ramp. A mound appeared under his blue suit as if a bony fist were trying to punch through from inside.

Rusty pulled me down with him and snatched at the pistol. His eyes beseeched the worst favor of me. As my own lips peeled back with disgust and empathy, I drew the pistol around, pushed it against the bulge in his chest, and did the only thing I could do to ease his horrific plight. Unshrinking, I pulled the trigger.

Rusty died at my feet, along with his tormenter, still holding my arm.

"Sir, I'm so sorry," Carmichael uttered.

With Rusty's blood soaking into my trouser legs, I gently rolled the body off the ramp, wishing there was time to bury him decently in this indecent place.

"Get aboard," I said.

I looked around to make sure there was no one else still waiting to board.

More than ready to leave, I put my foot on the ramp and

took hold of the scissor strakes which would pull it up after I came aboard.

"Rory."

My shoulders hunched at the sound of that voice. I turned and looked.

At the base of two large red pillars, with the morning light kissing from behind and causing a faint aurora, stood my mother—holding Bonnie by the arm. Against Bonnie's throat my mother held a disembodied alien tail spike, sharp and strong enough to take Bonnie's head off with a thrust.

M'am waited until she was sure I saw clearly what was going on. She held Bonnie by the arm with her bony white hand, and Bonnie stiffly complied, with the spike pressing against her jugular so firmly that I could see the grazed red welt rising.

"She belongs to me now," M'am said. "I need her now, more than you do. As long as I have her, you will not release your poison robots. She'll be safe here, Rory. I will take care of her. Launch your ship and go. Leave me and my new daughter here."

They were almost beautiful there, bathed in pink light, backdropped by drapings of gray gauze. As if to punctuate the sonnet, I saw Bonnie's pet bat hanging in the gauze behind them, confused and not knowing what to do. The little Earthling had followed us.

And so had others. In the depths of the glass forward, I saw the haunting movements of aliens moving closer. They shifted in their craven fluid way, coming in our direction, looking like dragons moving through a medieval passion play.

I stepped off the ramp and moved a few steps out into the open. I didn't dare try to shoot. Even with the pistol's fair accuracy, the refracted morning light through the pillars created a prism effect and ruined my aim. I could easily hit Bonnie. And as hard as my heart felt right now, I wasn't sure I could actually shoot my own mother. I didn't trust myself.

Instead, I put the pistol down on the black skulch. When I straightened up again, I raised my arm, holding my elbow straight. Carefully, I lowered my chin once, then raised it, and lowered my arm.

Once again, I raised my arm, but just slightly this time, with my fist knotted.

Bonnie balled her left fist, the one my mother couldn't see. Slowly, she began to raise her arm, straight out at her side.

In the background, Butterball the bat unfolded her raincoat-like wings, flexed one, then the other. The wide strutted membranes took on a Gothic grace. She dropped her grip on the gauze and was instantly flying in that neurotic nut-case batty way, right toward the two women.

"Bonnie, down!" I blared.

She dropped like a sack of sand.

The bat veered toward the now-empty spot where Bonnie's arm had been, but there was no place to land except my mother's head.

The bat's enormous wings closed around M'am's hair and folded tight around her face. She screamed inside the leather hood and beat her face with her little hands. Bonnie scrambled to her feet and ran to me.

"Get aboard." My voice was strangely calm as I shoved her up the ramp.

Behind my mother, the ghouls drew closer.

"Rory!" Bonnie called from the top of the ramp.

"Coming," I said.

I stretched my arm out straight to my side and raised it high, with my fist in a ball.

As my mother squealed in her panic, Buttercup disengaged her big wide wings and managed to launch from my mother's head. My mother was on her knees now, shocked and off-balance.

Whirling once in the air, Buttercup landed on my forearm and took an experienced purchase there. She let her giant wings go limp and hang almost to the ground, adjusted her grip on my wrist, then politely folded her wings around herself like a girl at a prom adjusting her wrap.

My mother and I met gazes for a last few seconds, and for the first time in our lives I think we understood each other. She drew herself to her feet and regained her poise, just as the aliens came around the pillars to surround her.

The interior of the ship was warm and buzzing with energy. Bonnie and Clark met me in the bay as the ramp whirred and clanked closed behind me.

I stroked the bat hanging from my arm and took the piece of fruit Bonnie offered, and fed it to the little doggie face. Buttercup happily took the fruit in her batty hands and began to eat. With my other arm, I pulled Bonnie against me and gave her the kiss I'd been saving up for the right moment. "How would you like to be a really wealthy woman?"

"Rory, it's your call," Clark said, as he had always promised. "Do we deploy or not?"

I looked at the cargo bay, where Pocket and Gaylord, Theo, and the deckhands stood poised beside the belly cranes and huge roller hatches that would drop the containers full of poison packers onto the planet as we safely rose into the sky, never to look back.

"Deploy," I told him. "Nothing down there but monsters."

ABOUT THE AUTHOR

DIANE CAREY is a best-selling science fiction writer with more than forty-five novels to her credit, including nine *New York Times* bestsellers for her Star Trek work and several number one chain bestsellers. She holds the distinction of having written many of the episode-to-novel adaptations of seminal Star Trek episodes, including the novelizations of the finale for *Star Trek: Deep Space Nine* and the premiere of *Star Trek Enterprise* and has gained a reputation for her care and attention in expanding and extending the rich backstories of the characters she works on. An avid sailor of historic tall ships, Carey lives in Michigan with her husband, writer and computer programmer Greg Brodeur and children Lydia, Gordon and Ben.

The Big Lie

If I kept a journal, I would have recorded that fifteen, the year things were supposed to get better, was the year I uncovered the Big Lie. Big Lies are myths made up by grown-ups. Peel away the soft, fluffy outer shell of these myths and you find a hard grain of truth.

The first Big Lie I unmasked was about love, that even if you love someone, there's no guarantee he will love you back. The second Big Lie concerned the old adage that when you have your tonsils removed, you can have all the ice cream you want.

**Other Apple Paperbacks
you will enjoy:**

Thirteen
    by Candice F. Ransom

Fourteen and Holding
    by Candice F. Ransom

The Rah Rah Girl
    by Caroline B. Cooney

Almost Like a Sister
    by M.L. Kennedy

With You and Without You
    by Ann M. Martin

Jeanne, Up and Down
    by Jane Claypool Miner

FIFTEEN AT LAST

Candice F. Ransom

AN
APPLE
PAPERBACK

SCHOLASTIC INC.
New York Toronto London Auckland Sydney

*For Pat, whose fifteenth year was
certainly a lot more exciting than mine.*

ISBN 0-590-40849-6

12 11 10 9 8 7 6 5 4 3 2 1   7 8 9/8 0 1 2/9

Printed in the U.S.A.   01

First Scholastic printing, November 1987

Chapter 1

I guess it was just fate that I received the science book with the message in it.

My life is like that. I have been known to break open fortune cookies and find a blank piece of paper. Once a dog ran past a whole line of people to bite *me* on the ankle. My friend Gretchen said the dog probably didn't like my socks.

The science book with the message in it could have been handed to Gretchen, who was sitting next to me, or the kid behind me, or anyone, for that matter. But no, Mr. Chapman gave the book to me. As I said, all part of the design.

We were given our physical science textbooks a week after school started. The science books were used, but that was the only thing about Oakton High School that wasn't brand-new.

As soon as I got my book, I wrote my

name on the inside cover in the handwriting I had been practicing all summer. *Kobie Roberts*. The capital *K* and *R* were three times bigger than the rest of the letters in my name. It was a signature befitting an up-and-coming artist whose career was held back only because she had to finish the last three years of high school.

Actually it was kind of nice being a sophomore (anything was better than groveling at the bottom of the heap as a freshman), and nicer still to be going to Oakton High. Compared to Woodson, the school I went to last year, Oakton was like Disneyland. Woodson was crowded, beat up, swarming with seniors, and dangerous to kids who weighed ninety-five pounds, like me.

Oakton was so new, the freshly painted white walls glared off the banks of shiny metal lockers, and you could see your reflection in the polished floors. Even better, there were no seniors. Since Oakton's student body was made up entirely of kids transferred from existing schools, seniors were allowed to graduate from their old schools. Instead of being next to the bottom of the heap, sophomores were in the middle, closest in line to the juniors, who would rule Oakton.

Nothing will go wrong this year, I thought, *now that my best friend is sitting beside me.* If that doesn't sound like any great feat, let me tell you that the two years Gretchen and I were separated were the worst I'd ever had. Woodson is still buzzing over the day a crackpot freshman practically got herself murdered. If Gretchen had been there, none of those awful things would have happened, and anyway, I'm not *really* a crackpot.

Gretchen Farris has been my best friend since second grade. We shared classes at Centreville Elementary, and seventh grade at Robert Frost Intermediate, and life was peachy-keen. But in our eighth grade year at Frost, life became inky-stinky. Gretchen was rushed into the "in-crowd," while her unpopular best friend withered on the sidelines. Then Gretchen was in an automobile accident that kept her out of school most of the year. She had a head injury and a terrible scar that was later fixed with plastic surgery. But because Gretchen had lost so much time, she had to repeat the eighth grade and I went on to Woodson High to suffer my freshman year. Through summer school and a lot of hard work, Gretchen managed to catch up. Now we were in tenth grade, in the same school, and even in some of the same classes, where we belonged.

And I was fifteen, at last. Last year, when I was having such a terrible time, my mother promised me things would definitely get better after I turned fifteen.

This *would* be the best year ever, I decided. But that was before I opened my science book.

Gretchen leaned over and whispered. "What do you think of orange and black and tigers?"

I looked at the mimeographed sheet she pushed across the table at me. Oakton High was like a volcanic island that had sprung up in the ocean overnight, without history or traditions. We were supposed to choose our own school colors and the school mascot.

"They do go together," I said. "But orange and black make me think of Halloween."

"What did you put?"

I hauled out a grubby paper from my notebook. "I was tempted to put turquoise and lime-green." Those were my favorite colors. "But turquoise and lime-green might be too distracting on the football field. So I picked royal blue and gold. And an alligator for a mascot."

"An alligator!" Gretchen exclaimed. "Why an alligator?"

"Well, they're ferocious and mean if you get too close to them around dinnertime. What's wrong with an alligator mascot?"

"Kobie, alligators live down south, in

Florida. We live in *Virginia,* northern Virginia, at that. The mascot should be an animal we can identify with."

"And how many tigers do you see prowling around Fairfax?" I countered.

"You know what I mean." Gretchen flipped her strawberry-blonde hair over one shoulder. She had let her hair grow over the summer and it fell in soft waves halfway down her back.

After a disastrous session with the scissors last year, in an attempt to give myself a Vidal Sassoon geometric haircut, I wound up instead with a half inch of hair that looked singed. My hair was now down to my chin, a respectable but boring length. All the girls in Oakton had long, long hair.

"I'll change my mascot if you change yours," Gretchen said, doubtful over her choice.

"Okay." I erased "alligator" and wrote in "skunk." "How's this? It's an animal native to our region."

Gretchen started giggling. I snatched up my physical science book and buried my face in it to keep from laughing. Mr. Chapman had let us pair off as lab partners, and I didn't want to risk our position by messing around in class too soon.

The page that I randomly opened to, a bunch of chemical equations, had been defaced with a big red heart inside which "I love Mike" had been scrawled. That was the trouble with used books. In the English book issued to me last year, some kid had underlined all the words beginning with "t" and drawn eyes in every double "o." I found myself stressing words beginning with "t," even when I talked, and coming across "boot" or "look" made me feel as if I were being watched.

I turned the page. "I love Mike" was blazoned across the end of the chapter questions and on the first page of the next chapter. I riffled the pages impatiently. On *every single page* some dippy girl had proclaimed her devotion to Mike. It was like snooping in somebody's diary.

I was about to raise my hand and request another book when I saw it. On page 289. *I love Mike still as in forever till there is no end.*

But on the page following that heartfelt vow, "Mike" had been ruthlessly crossed out and "Wayne" written under his name. Throughout the rest of the book, Wayne substituted for Mike, somehow canceling the declaration of undying love on page 289.

I had been thinking a lot about love lately. When I signed up for physical science, I hoped the class would clear up some of my questions. Judging from the book, physical science appeared to be a numbing combination of biology, physics, and chemistry, with absolutely nothing about love, unless you counted the previous bookowner's fickle vows.

What was love *really* like? Was it so powerful it caused a person to announce her feelings on every page of a textbook? And if love was so strong (as in *forever till there is no end*), then how could that girl have switched from one boy to another?

I nudged Gretchen to show her my book. She ignored the jab. Her round blue eyes were focused on a guy four tables over. Doug McNeil. He wasn't the cutest guy in class, but he had intense gray eyes and a slouchy, I-don't-care, James Dean kind of attitude. Gretchen was obviously attracted to him, and from the looks Doug was zinging back at her, the feeling was mutual.

"Gretch," I whispered. "Your chair is on fire."

No response.

"Gretch, a white mouse just ran over your foot. Didn't you feel his tail?"

Blue eyes continued to lock with gray.

I settled back in my seat with a sigh. That Gretchen had snared the interest of a boy was hardly earth-shattering. She had a great figure and a certain perkiness that most guys couldn't resist. Even as far back as eighth grade, Gretchen had boys falling over themselves. Last year, she'd been too self-conscious over her scar and too swamped with catch-up work to pay much attention to boys, but I could tell she was planning to make up for lost time.

As for me, there were no guys on the horizon.

The bell rang, snapping Gretchen out of her trance.

"See you later." She gathered her books in a hurry.

I caught her arm. "Gretch, what's with you and Doug McNeil?"

"Nothing," she said evasively. "I don't even know him."

"Maybe you ought to introduce yourselves before you stare holes through each other."

"Kobie, your imagination is working overtime again." But she held back just enough to walk out the door with Doug McNeil, leaving me to walk to French by myself. I felt a tremor in the air between us, like one of those unexplained ripples on the surface of a perfectly calm pond.

French class was just down the hall. As soon as I walked in the door a husky voice cried, "Kobie!"

"Stuart!" I shrieked back. Stuart and I always greeted each other like people reunited after twenty years on separate continents.

"Sit here, Kobie," Stuart insisted, patting the desk next to his and even dusting it off.

"Stuart, I've been sitting in that same chair a whole week now." I sat down.

"I want to make sure you don't *change* your seat."

Stuart Buckley and I had what novels called a "tumultuous relationship." I was friends with Stuart only because it was foolhardy to have him as an enemy. Stuart burst into my life like the stars you see when you are conked on the head. He was very short, wore thick glasses, and had a chip on his shoulder. Stuart resented his height and the fact that his new stepmother hated him. Even after his grandmother got custody of him (an act of great courage), he didn't settle down.

Mrs. Hildebrandt took attendance and then began writing on the board. As this was second-year French, I knew we would have our lessons conducted entirely in the language.

Stuart tipped his chair back on two legs and grinned at me. Mrs. Hildebrandt, who apparently had eyes in the back of her head, swiveled around and caught him. Stuart's chair hit the floor with a resounding *clunk*.

Dropping the chalk, the teacher said, *"Class, attention, s'il vous plait."*

"Ici," Stuart said, in an accent straight

out of an old Charles Boyer movie. We all knew *ici* means "here." He extended his palm, as if offering Mrs. Hildebrandt an invisible bar of soap.

The other kids broke up. Mrs. Hildebrandt looked as if she wished she had gone to work in a torpedo factory instead of teaching.

I had never had Stuart in one of my classes before. He had been a locker neighbor, a lunch partner, someone to bump into in the halls — encounters highlighted by slamming, stealing, and bumming money, in that order. Now I understood why Stuart's teachers were reportedly seen gulping Tums and looking at the retirement schedule posted in the main office.

I wondered why Stuart felt it necessary to be so disruptive. Was he always this bad or was there a special reason for his showing off? And then I saw the reason.

Her name was Rosemary Swan.

Rosemary was smiling back at Stuart and he was blushing forty shades of red. My heart plummeted to the soles of my imitation Bass Weejuns. Rosemary Swan, a gorgeous girl with glossy black hair, snapping black eyes, and a shape that made me seethe with envy, was way out of Stuart's league. For one thing, she was nearly six feet tall. I knew, because Rosemary was in my gym class and we had all been weighed and measured last week. Stuart only came up to my shoulder and I barely stood five three.

"That girl up there," Stuart said, for once lowering his voice a decibel. "She thinks I'm funny. I bet she thinks I'm the funniest guy she's ever seen."

"Maybe," I conceded. "What do you care what she thinks?"

"Oh, I care," he said. The hope glowing on Stuart's face made me feel a little sick. First Gretchen and now Stuart!

This love business was getting more complicated by the minute. I was fifteen, not a kid anymore, yet already I felt years behind everyone else.

At home, I started to toss my books on the chair by the front door.

"In your room," my mother yelled from the kitchen. The woman has X-ray vision.

"Hello to you, too," I said.

"Hello," she added. "Don't forget to hang up your clothes, Kobie."

As if I could. In her determination to make her only daughter into a neater person, my mother had instituted an anti-slob campaign, directed at me. It was *hang up your clothes, don't throw your books around, pick up those papers* the second I opened my eyes in the morning, until I wearily closed them again at night.

I went into my room and took off my school outfit. This year, at least, I wasn't saddled with the ugliest clothes in the world. For my birthday this summer I got three skirts with matching blouses and sweaters, the Weejun lookalikes, and a genuine leather ring belt. If you didn't check the labels in my clothes, you'd never know I wasn't one of the cool "in" girls.

I hung up my skirt and blouse, which were too good to stuff in the pile of uglies I kept beside my dresser. From the pile, which my mother had been nagging me to get rid of for two years, I yanked out old corduroy jeans and a sweat shirt.

My room was actually shaping up okay, compared to the way it was last year. After pestering my mother to let me get a purple carpet, I finally convinced her that lime-green and turquoise were the best accent colors. We painted my filing cabinet turquoise and it really set the room off. Mom bought a fabric remnant in a turquoise and lime-green print and sewed new curtains. I still had my old, half-bald chenille bedspread, but it was hard to find bedspreads in turquoise.

Right before school started, Gretchen and I went shopping with our birthday cash (our birthdays are seven weeks apart) at the new mall at Tyson's Corner. I bought a turquoise and lime-green owl mobile, a set of felt pens, a record album by Bob Dylan, the folk singer, and a five-gallon aquarium.

The aquarium really made my room look cool. Sitting on top of my filing cabinet, it had turquoise foil on the back side, turquoise and lime-green mingled gravel in the bottom, a treasure chest that opened and closed with the action of the aerator, plastic plants, a diver, a ceramic castle, and a ceramic mermaid. My mother claimed the fish barely had room to wiggle through all that junk, but what did she know about marine life? We must have really crummy water because the four ungrateful fish I bought at Woolworth's all died within a week. Rather than invest in more fish, I just let the aquarium run empty.

My mother came into my room without knocking, a bad habit I was trying to get her to break.

"Mo-other!" I accused. "What if I'd been changing?"

"Oh, excuse me," she said with exaggerated politeness. "It isn't like I haven't seen you unclothed before. I used to change your diapers, remember." Only a mother would bring up another person's disgusting pre-toilet-trained days.

"Let's not talk about that," I said.

"Why not?" Mom lounged in the doorway and folded her arms. "You used to be such a cute little girl, Kobie. You had curly hair and fat, dimpled little legs . . . whenever I came to get you out of the crib you were so happy to see me."

The implication that I was no longer cute (the truth since my dimpled knees were now knobby and I Scotch-taped my hair to make it lie flat) made me testy. "Who wouldn't be happy? How would you like to be stuck in a crib until you're five years old? No wonder I'm underdeveloped."

"I couldn't trust you in a regular bed. You kept falling out on your head — "

"And that's what's wrong with me today," I finished for her.

"What's wrong with you today has nothing to do with your falling out of the crib," she said ominously.

"I know, I know. I'm a terrible, horrible, gruesome adolescent, and you wish I still had dimpled legs and dribbled Pablum all over the place." The trouble with mothers was that they couldn't face facts and let go of the past. I was fifteen, an *adult*.

"What do you want?" I asked.

"Nothing. Can't I come in to see you without a reason? How was school?"

"Okay."

"You act like you want to tell me something," she said. "What is it?"

I was dying to ask somebody knowledgeable about this love business but figured my own mother would be a bad candidate for two reasons: (a) she would automatically jump to the conclusion that I was carrying on in school instead of paying attention to my lessons, and (b) whatever she once knew about love had happened so long ago it would be like asking Rip Van Winkle what he did when he wasn't napping.

"Do we have any Ding Dongs left?" I said instead.

"You ate the last one yesterday and I haven't been to the store."

"How come whenever we run out of something dumb like coffee or milk you run up to the store in your bedroom slippers, but if I run out of goodies, I have to wait till next grocery day?"

"I do *not* go to the store in my bedroom slippers." As usual, my mother selected the least important part of my complaint to comment on. "You know, Kobie, Ding Dongs are not a right but a privilege. And privileges can be taken away."

I wanted to argue my rights, but it would have been self-defeating for an almost-adult, fifteen-year-old to take a strong stand over Ding Dongs.

"I'll fix you some peanut butter crackers," Mom said, letting me off the hook. "Are you going to draw?"

"Maybe later."

Stored in the turquoise filing cabinet was my latest art project, illustrations from the Walt Disney movie *Lady and the Tramp*. My ambition was to be an animator for Walt Disney Studios in Burbank, California. In the evenings after my homework was done, I would sketch scenes from a Golden Book version of the movie in India ink, and color them in with my new felt pens. I was very diligent about this project. By the time I graduated from Oakton, my portfolio would be so good, I'd be hired on the spot as an animator.

But today I wasn't in the mood for drawing. I flicked on my record player.

My mother immediately yelled from the hall, "You're not going to play that awful record, are you?" For some reason, my mother despised my new album. I played it every day. You'd think she'd be used to it.

I put the album on the spindle.

"Kobie, don't play that record!"

The tone arm settled into the grooves and the first song twanged out of the speaker. Down the hall, my mother slammed a door.

I opened my physical science book to the "Mike" message. I had a lot to think about.

Chapter 2

Right Things I Have:
1. *Three new outfits (A-line skirts, blouses, and matching cardigans)*
2. *Imitation Bass Weejun loafers*
3. *Genuine leather ring belt*
4. *Makeup: blush-on, mascara, eyeliner, lipgloss, "Iced Espresso" eyeshadow*

Right Things to Get:
1. *Real leather purse (lost cause)*
2. *Long hair (let grow)*
3. *Long fingernails (stop biting!)*

One morning in late September, I skimmed my "Right Things" list before leaving for school. Gretchen and I started a "Right Things" list last year, so we would know what things to buy or do in order to be popular. Gretchen didn't really need a list — she usually had the right things, and people just naturally liked her anyway.

17

Even if I had been born wearing a designer diaper, I'd have been snubbed in the sandbox by the popular babies.

But this year all that would change, I realized as I tallied both columns. On the plus side, I had the same clothes the other girls were wearing, and my mother, after a heated debate, had consented to let me wear makeup. Those two items were the most important.

I didn't have a real leather purse, it was true. My mother said she refused to mortgage the house to pay for one pocketbook. And my hair was definitely too short. I tossed my head to see if my hair was long enough to swirl the way Gretchen's did. Then I remembered to pull off the row of Scotch tape I had wound around the ends to keep my hair from curling. My fingernails were the worst, bitten past the quick and bristling with hangnails. Every year *Stop biting nails* was number one among my New Year's resolutions, but I couldn't quit for more than a day before I'd get a terrible nail-biting attack.

Still, the positive side of the list outweighed the minus side. One item on the plus side I hadn't included was Gretchen's influence. She would pull me into the popular crowd with her. Armed with the "right" things, all I had to do was wait for Barb Levister or Patty Binninger, two popular girls around whom cliques seemed to be forming, to ask me to sit with them at a pep rally or something. Maybe when I got on the bus today, Gretchen would announce that we had been invited to sit at Barb's library table during study hall.

"Bus in five minutes!" my mother called, rapping her spoon on the wall.

I pounded the wall back to let her know I was almost ready.

My bedroom was located next to the kitchen. Instead of getting up from the table and coming all the way in here to wake me up or to tell me to hurry, my mother merely leans over and raps on the wall with a butter knife or her coffee spoon. *Crackcrackcrack!* It certainly does the trick.

After slapping a handful of Ambush cologne on my neck, I clicked off my radio and grabbed my books. My mother was stationed by the front door to give me my lunch money and/or inspect me.

"Whew! Don't you think that cologne's a little strong for this early in the morning?"

"Oh, Mother! *Everybody* wears Ambush!"

"The boys, too?"

"Of course not. Boys wear Hai Karate or English Leather."

"Then I pity your poor teachers, facing

a whole reeking classroom every morning." She frowned and I knew what was coming next. "What's that stuff around your eyes?"

"Eyeliner. Mom, why do you start these discussions right before the bus? You told me *ages* ago I could wear makeup."

"Just because I said you could wear it doesn't mean I approve of your going to school looking like a raccoon with insomnia."

We stared at each other, the old mother-daughter-eyeball battle. I blinked first. The four coats of mascara I had applied in an effort to lengthen my stubby lashes until "they swept the floor" were making my eyes water. My mother must have thought I was going to cry, because she kissed my cheek and told me to run catch the bus.

Gretchen had saved our special seat, third from the front on the left. We had been sitting in that same seat for years.

"Boy, Mom was really on my case today," I told Gretchen. "According to her, I have on too much eyeliner and too much — "

"Kobie, guess what! You're not going to believe this!" Gretchen squealed before I was finished griping.

Excitement shivered down my spine. My dream was about to come true! After years of waiting to get into the popular crowd, I was about to hear we were now part of either Barb's or Patty's group. At last!

"Hurry and tell me! I'm dying!"

"Doug McNeil called last night and asked me out! This Friday — tomorrow! Kobie, isn't it the greatest?" Her blue eyes were shining.

"How did he get your phone number?" I asked, pulling my mother's annoying trick of picking the least important part of a shocking statement to comment on.

"He asked me for it in homeroom yesterday."

Gretchen and I were in three classes together: typing, gym, and physical science, the class where she and Doug made goo-goo eyes at each other. Clearly, things had progressed beyond the staring stage, and it had evidently happened in homeroom.

I pretended to be miffed. "How come you didn't tell me on the phone last night?"

"He called after we hung up. I would have called you right back, honest, Kobie, but it was late. You know how your mother is about phone calls after nine." She clutched my arm and gave it a joyful squeeze. "I can't wait till tomorrow! What do you think I should wear?"

"Are you allowed to date so soon?" I asked, trying not to let disappointment show in my voice. This sounded serious.

Gretchen had gone out with guys before, but only on a casual basis, like meeting them at a party or something. As for me, my mother's opinion about dating at fifteen was the same as getting phone calls after nine. In words of one syllable, *no!*

"Sure, I can go out," Gretchen replied breezily. "Kobie, you'll have to talk your mother into letting you date before sixteen. You'll find a guy and then the four of us can double."

Gretchen didn't seem to realize that I had wheedled my mother about as far as I could. I had talked her into letting me wear short skirts, stockings, makeup, buy a purple carpet she had no intention of buying, and keep a fish tank, even though there weren't any fish in it. But mothers are like mules; they can only be pushed to a point and then they balk.

"You'd better forget about doubling for a while," I said. "With me, anyway. Besides, you haven't even gone out once with Doug. You might hate him after Friday night."

"No, I won't." Gretchen looked at me with a new grown-up confidence, and I wondered how the seven weeks between our birthdays could make such a difference. "Kobie, I think this is *it*. Doug is the one."

"The one what?"

She poked me in the ribs. "The *one*. *The* one. You know."

"Oh, yeah. The one." *As in forever till there is no end.* "Gretch, how do you *know* Doug's the one?"

"I just do." She smiled slyly. "When it happens to you, Kobie, you'll know, too."

Easy for her to say. Unless I became skilled with a lasso, there was no chance of my getting near a boy long enough to find out if he was *it* or not. Why did Gretchen have to stir up this boy stuff before I was ready? Why couldn't she have been satisfied with buying the "right" things and hanging out with the "right" crowd? She always had to be a jump ahead of me.

I had another item to add to my "Right Things to Get" list: *Number four. A boyfriend.*

Thanks to Sandy Robertson, I was the only person in the history of W.T. Woodson High School — maybe even the state of Virginia — to have almost been murdered in the parking lot during D lunch shift. Separated from Gretchen, I had let myself fall into the wrong company last year. It wasn't hard.

Robertson comes from right after Roberts and this Robertson in particular turned up like a bad penny in three of my alphabetically organized classes. Sandy and I shared a locker and nearly shared a jail cell before the first semester was over.

Sandy had green eyes, a cute smile, taffy-blonde hair, and a slight limp because she'd had polio when she was very young and refused to wear the built-up orthopedic shoe that corrected her hip displacement. She also attracted trouble like a lightning rod.

It was Sandy who angered Jeanette Adams, but it was *me* Jeanette threatened to murder in the parking lot. Obviously Jeanette Adams did not kill me, but one crazy afternoon, during which I ran to the police and was then brought back to school in a squad car while Sandy hunted for my crumpled body under the cars and my mother sobbed in my guidance counselor's office, was enough to permanently stamp me as "weirdo" at Woodson.

My reputation at Woodson was in tatters, but I stood a better-than-fair chance at Oakton, where everyone was new and reputations, even weird ones, had been left behind. Unfortunately, Sandy Robertson had *not* been left behind.

Sandy wasn't a bad kid, really. She meant well and she was actually fun to be around, if you had nerves of flint. Last summer I introduced Sandy and Gretchen, hoping they would hit it off since it appeared I would be burdened with Sandy as long as there were "R"s in the alphabet. Just as I had hoped, they got along fine. Gretchen had a soothing influence on Sandy, but whenever it was just me and Sandy, Sandy tended to go out of bounds. This year Sandy was in my "dummy" math class, as well as English, gym, and the same lunch shift.

By lunchtime, I was in no mood for Sandy or Stuart or anybody. In first period typing, all Gretchen did was rhapsodize over Doug. Doug this. Doug that. How gorgeous she thought Doug was.

Between English and gym, I saw Gretchen and Doug lingering by her locker. She never even heard me when I yelled hello. As I trudged through the food line, I had a not-very-nice-but-typical-Kobie thought: Maybe Gretchen would have a rotten time with Doug and then we could go back to our original goal — getting into the right group.

Sandy had saved me a seat in the cafeteria. "I bet I did terrible on that English quiz," she said, as I sat down with my tray.

"Me, too." Miss Boyes was turning out to be one of those teachers who felt obligated to pop a quiz every other day.

"Not you. You probably got an A, like always."

Sandy had a short memory. Last year, I flat-out flunked — as in *failed* — home ec and gym, the two classes I had with Sandy and Jeanette Adams, the gangster who masqueraded as a freshman. I usually did okay in most subjects, as long as no one was gunning for me.

The spiral notebook Sandy used for English had the name "Cassandra Robertson" on the cover.

"I didn't know you name is really Cassandra," I said.

"It isn't. I don't like Sandy anymore. It's so ordinary." She pointed to my notebook. "I'm practicing to write my name fancy like you do. Your signature looks so neat. I wish I had a 'K' in my name." Grubbing for a pencil in her purse, she scrawled, *Kassandra Robertson.* "What do you think?"

"I think it's dumb. What's wrong with Sandy?"

"Fingernail check," Sandy announced.

I held out my hands, splaying my fingers so she could examine my nails. "You don't need to squint so. They haven't grown any."

"I think they have. I can almost feel the edge of your thumbnail."

"That's the one I chewed in English this morning."

She wouldn't give up. "You only chewed

it a little. It definitely looks longer than it did yesterday."

The thing about Sandy was that she wanted to be just like me. *Exactly* like me. When I told her I wanted to grow my nails, she gnawed off all her own fingernails — *perfectly good* fingernails — so we could grow our nails together. She followed me around like a cocker spaniel, imitating every aspect of my mostly dull life, forever telling me how smart I was, how well I could draw, how good I looked.

Next to Sandy, I did look pretty good, not because I thought I should be Miss America, but because Sandy always looked like she lived in a bus terminal.

Gretchen and I were alike in lots of ways, but we didn't want to be Siamese twins. Sandy was more an appendage than a friend. I learned long ago that it was easier to remove flypaper welded to the sole of my shoe than get rid of Sandy.

Today, though, Sandy's attentions were welcome, after Gretchen's unending fascination with Doug McNeil.

"Are you having corned beef hash and canned peas for supper tomorrow night?" Sandy asked.

My parents ate a late supper on Fridays, so my mother fixed me whatever I wanted on that night. When Sandy found out I ate corned beef hash and canned peas every single Friday night, she made her mother fix that, too. I'm sure the Robertsons are sick of corned beef hash and peas.

"I don't have hash and peas anymore," I said. "Now it's homemade pizza with bacon, an RC, and a pack of Suzy-Q's." My mother, I knew, was hoping that this Friday night obsession would fade. She grumbled every week about the chore of rolling out pizza dough *extra-thin* and frying up bacon *extra-crispy* to suit my picky tastes.

Sandy dropped her fork with an indignant clatter. "You didn't tell me!" she cried, outraged. "You didn't tell me you changed the menu! What kind of pizza mix? In a round pan or a square one?"

I responded to her questions, thinking that Mrs. Robertson would soon have her hands in sticky pizza dough, hands she would rather wrap around my neck. "Sandy, you don't have to eat the same thing I do," I told her. "Come up with your own Friday night supper."

"I like doing what you do," Sandy said. "You do everything just right, Kobie. Anyway, if we eat the same thing, it's kind of like being together on Friday nights, isn't it?"

All this talk about Friday night reminded me of Gretchen's upcoming date with Doug. "We shouldn't be sitting home eating pizza," I said. "We ought to be going out. On real dates. Are you allowed to date yet?"

"Sure," Sandy replied, surprising me. I thought her mother was as behind the times as mine was. "If anybody asks me out, I can go."

"Your mother would let you?"

Sandy shrugged. "She doesn't care. After raising three girls, she's used to dating." Sandy had three older sisters, all married. "Linda, my oldest sister, says Mom got more easygoing with each of us. Now that there's just me, she's practically putty in my hands."

The day my mother becomes putty will be the day the earth orbits too close to the sun. Even if I'd had an army of older sisters, my mother would still be plaster-of-paris stubborn when it came to letting me date.

"Has some guy asked you out?"

"No." I tasted the bread pudding, then pushed the dish away. "And no one will, either."

"How can you say that? You're really cute, Kobie. You're always putting yourself down."

"I'm too skinny," I said. "Boys don't like skinny girls. That's why I eat all that junk on Fridays. To gain weight."

"What about that boy down there? He's

been staring at you ever since you sat down. I bet *he* likes you. He must, to keep looking at you that way."

I followed her gaze. A chunky boy in a blue sweater was sitting at the end of our table, all by himself. His English book was open before him, but he was staring at me. When he caught me looking back, he smiled shyly.

"He does like you!" Sandy cried. "He's crazy about you, anybody can see it! That boy really likes you!"

"That's no boy," I said dismally. "That's Eddie Showalter."

"What do you mean, that's no boy?"

"I mean, it's Eddie Showalter. He doesn't count."

He didn't, believe me. At least not in the pool of boys I would consider dating. I knew Eddie Showalter from ninth grade geography. Eddie was noted for wearing the same sweater every day, no matter what the weather, and for drawing cartoons of the White House and jet airplanes in the margins of his textbook. Despite the color change in his sweater today and a nice kind of pudginess, Eddie Showalter had not vastly improved over the summer. There wasn't anything terribly *wrong* with Eddie, but there wasn't anything quite *right* about him, either.

"I think he's cute," Sandy said. "He's

got big brown eyes like yours. You both look like Lassie."

"Maybe we should get married and start a kennel," I said dryly.

Gretchen's date tomorrow night with Doug McNeil was only the beginning, I sensed. After all, Gretchen claimed Doug was *it*. *It* also described Eddie Showalter and Stuart Buckley, the only boys I knew, but the two situations couldn't be compared in the same breath. If I didn't want Gretchen to get too far ahead of me, I would have to get myself a boyfriend, one who didn't mind that I was skinny, couldn't talk on the phone after nine o'clock, and would be content with an at-school relationship.

Glancing over at Eddie, I rejected the possibility of going out with either him or Stuart. And since all the other boys in Oakton — who were more interested in types like Rosemary Swan — had already rejected *me*, I would have to look elsewhere.

Chapter 3

"And while we were eating French fries in the Pot O'Gold, he asked me if I'd be his girl. I said yes. I didn't even have to think about it, Kobie. I've known all along I wanted to be Doug's girl. Then he took off this ring and gave it to me. He said, 'Now that you're my girl, I want you to wear this. Promise me you'll be mine, always.' Isn't that the most *romantic* thing you ever heard?"

"Mmmmm," I replied vaguely. Gretchen told her story without missing a beat on her typing exercise, but I had just discovered that my right pinky finger did not reach the backspace key like it was supposed to.

"Isn't it a beautiful ring?" Gretchen asked. She stopped typing long enough to flourish the gold ring with the onyx stone she was wearing on a chain around her neck. "When we order our class rings later this year, I'm ordering what Doug wants and he's ordering what I want, since we'll exchange rings as soon as we get them."

I thought that arrangement was like two people building a house before they were formally engaged, but I said nothing. It was hard to get a word in edgewise. Gretchen had never been so talkative, so full of herself. Since Sunday night I had heard her saga — a love story to rival Cleopatra and Marc Antony — five times, and it was only first period Monday morning.

She called me Saturday morning before anyone in my house had gotten out of bed to report, in breathless detail, how wonderful her date Friday night had been with Mr. Magnificent. So wonderful that Doug was taking her to the mall on Sunday afternoon. Sunday night she called with the news that Doug had asked her to be his girl and had given her his ring. Then she called later, after she had talked to Doug to say *he* had called, and then she called me a *third* time to tell me the story *again*. I listened to her again on the bus this morning, my eyes glazing over, and once more in typing. I fully expected to look in the mirror and see the account of Gretchen's date etched across my forehead.

"Gretchen, are you sure you aren't rushing into things?" I asked, finally figuring out that I would have to raise my right hand off the keyboard in order to backspace. According to Mrs. Antle, our teacher, this method of typing had been designed so that a person's fingers would never have to leave the keyboard. I needed to find a method that compensated for midget fingers.

"I mean, you've only had two dates," I went on. "Before you start singing 'Oh Promise Me,' shouldn't you get to know Doug better?"

Gretchen stared at me. "Kobie, I *do* know Doug. How many dates we have doesn't matter. We both knew from the beginning that we were made for each other."

I lifted my eyes from my copy stand to look at her. If ever a person was in love it was Gretchen. She positively radiated happiness. As for me, I had a splitting headache, caused by either thirty clattering typewriters or the knowledge that Gretchen had taken another giant step away from me.

Ever since we both turned thirteen, I had been running to keep up with her. Gretchen was allowed to wear stockings before I was, and have her ears pierced, and stuff like that, but her pulling away from me was more than just getting grown-up things. I pictured entering adult-hood as passing through a haze-shrouded doorway. I could see the door but my feet were dragging. Gretchen was halfway through to the other side. Pretty soon she'd be out of my sight.

"Eyes on your work, girls," Mrs. Antle said, making one of her frequent circuits behind our chairs to watch us.

Gretchen looked away first and resumed typing. I noticed her pinky finger had no trouble at all reaching the backspace key.

By lunchtime my headache was worse and my throat felt scratchy besides. I took my tray over to our regular table. Sandy Robertson wasn't holding a seat for me, but Eddie Showalter was.

He smiled as I sat down. "Hi, Kobie."

"Hi." I searched the area for Sandy, thinking maybe she had switched tables. She wasn't anywhere to be seen. I un-zipped my straw wrapper and stabbed it into my milk carton. "Aren't you eating?" I asked Eddie.

He shook his head. "Naw. I never eat lunch." He must have made up for it at dinner, since he was on the chunky side.

Still, I felt guilty eating in front of him. "Are you sure you don't want a bite? Part of my macaroni or something?"

"No, thanks. I got your note. What did you want?"

I nearly choked on a spoonful of applesauce. "What note?"

"The note you sent me."

I had not, under any circumstances, sent a note to Eddie Showalter. I had nothing to say to Eddie Showalter, either verbally or in written form. There must be some mistake. "I sent you a note?"

"Don't you remember?" Eddie's thick, wiggly eyebrows shot upward. "I found it in my locker right before third. And it was definitely from you."

I rubbed my forehead, which felt hot and dry.

"Are you okay, Kobie?" Eddie sounded concerned.

No, I was not. Gretchen was going steady, which meant I could forget about her helping me get into the in-crowd, my little finger was at least an inch too short, and I had apparently written a note to a boy I didn't particularly like, asking him who-knew-what.

"You might as well know the truth, Eddie. I have this — condition. It's called . . . note amnesia."

"Note amnesia?" He didn't sound the least bit convinced, but I plunged ahead anyway.

"Yeah. See, sometimes I write notes to people, but I forget about it as soon as I've delivered the note. It's sort of like when people sleepwalk and do things that later they don't remember doing? Well, when I write notes, it's instantly zapped from my memory. Just exactly what did I *say* in my note?"

"I've got it right here." Eddie produced a much-crumpled sheet of notebook paper.

Dear Eddie, the note said in an experimental backslanted handwriting I immediately recognized as belonging to a certain green-eyed blonde who would have to learn to write with her other hand by the time I got done with her. *Please meet me at lunch at the end of the table I saw you sitting at the other day. I have something to ask you.*

"Do you remember what you wanted to ask me?" Eddie asked in a careful tone.

"Yes," I said before I could think properly. "It's about that homework assignment we got today. I don't understand it."

"What homework assignment?"

"You know, in the class we have together." I knew Eddie and I shared a class but I was too rattled to remember which one.

"Kobie, we're in *homeroom* together."

"Oh. Well, that was some roll-call Mrs. Wade gave today, wasn't it?"

Mercifully he changed the subject, rescuing me from a poor recovery. "How do you like Oakton?"

"After Woodson? It's great. But weren't we supposed to get a students' lounge with Coke machines?"

"I heard that same rumor, but only the teachers have a lounge. We do have a planetarium," he added, as if he'd been elected a one-man Oakton High School Chamber of Commerce.

"We had a planetarium at Woodson," I said. "A lot of good it did us. Only little kids on field trips got to use it."

Eddie nodded. "I went to the planetarium when I was in seventh grade."

"Me, too. When I was at Frost. Did you go to Lanier?" Sandy Robertson had gone to Sidney Lanier Intermediate. I was wondering how she was connected with Eddie. Also how I'd keep from choking her when I saw her again.

"No, I went to Poe," Eddie replied.

What an exciting conversation. Planetariums and old intermediate schools. Next thing, we'd be talking about who we pushed on the swings. How had Gretchen managed to advance beyond idiot remarks like these to an onyx ring around her neck? Then I remembered the way she and Doug stared at each other in science class. Love had nothing to do with *talking*, it was all in the *eyes*. I looked into Eddie's, then glanced away, embarrassed. His eyes were brown, like mine. Looking at him was too much like gazing into a mirror.

Whatever had happened to Gretchen and Doug would never happen to Eddie Showalter and me. No meaningful looks passed between us, no electricity sparked the air over my half-eaten macaroni and cheese.

My last class was "dummy" math, actually Algebra I, Part II. Because my feeble brain couldn't take first-year algebra in a single dose, I opted for the two-year watered-down version. The class was held in the industrial arts wing, where kids took shop and mechanical drawing and the math dummies wouldn't contaminate the smart kids.

Sandy Robertson was in algebra with me. I was most anxious to see her, despite the fact that I was feeling awful. Sandy's lunchtime matchmaking scheme was fairly mild compared to the escapades she got me into last year, but I suspected this little thing with Eddie was just a warm-up exercise.

Though the late bell had rung, my math teacher was outside the classroom, deep in conversation with another teacher. Sandy was standing boldly on the other side of the doorway, waiting for me.

"How did it go with you and Eddie?" she asked.

"How did you think it went?" I replied. "What possessed you to write that note? I felt like a fool when he asked me what I wanted."

Sandy was unconcerned. "I knew you'd come up with something. You always do. At least you and Eddie were alone together, thanks to me. He really likes you, Kobie."

"Thanks to you, he probably thinks I'm crazy. Anyway, even if he does like me, I'm not so sure I like *him*."

"Yes, you do," she persisted. "You just don't know it. If I tell you your fortune, will you believe it then?"

"Only if it is written in the stars that a certain nosy girl will butt out." I rubbed my eyes again. My face felt taut and shiny, like the skin on an eggplant. Every time I swallowed, my throat hurt. Maybe I was coming down with the flu . . . or a virus. I wanted to go home, but I had one more class.

"Let's go inside," I said. Mr. Bell was still talking to the other teacher. The second teacher had his back to us, which meant that Mr. Bell could look over and spot us any minute.

And he did. He called over the other teacher's shoulder. "Girls. You belong inside."

The teacher he had been talking to turned around to see who had interrupted their conversation.

I gulped. The other teacher was young and drop-dead gorgeous. He had light brown hair, cut very short, as if he played a lot of sports and didn't want to mess with long hair in the shower; and blue eyes, the bluest eyes I had ever seen. No, not ordinary blue, *turquoise!*

He stared at me with his beautiful turquoise eyes. I couldn't tear my own eyes away. Electricity sizzled between us. We could have lit up the whole county with the energy we were generating.

My face was on fire, my throat like a branding iron. But it wasn't the flu or a virus at all . . . I had fallen in love!

Chapter 4

"Tonsillitis," the doctor diagnosed, retrieving what felt like a two-foot-long tongue depresser from my mouth.

"Does that mean she has bad tonsils?" my mother asked.

"They're pretty rotten, all right," the doctor replied cheerfully, scribbling on a prescription pad.

I wasn't even insulted. My throat hurt, but I hardly noticed, my thoughts were so full of the Man with the Turquoise Eyes. One minute I was stunned by this man in the hall outside my math class, the next I was in Dr. Wampler's office undergoing an examination. How could a person fall in love and get tonsillitis at the same time?

"They'll have to come out," the doctor said. With a shudder I realized he meant my tonsils.

"It's so early in the school year," my

mother murmured. "Can it wait until summer?"

Dr. Wampler had red hair and freckles. He was young, for a doctor, and he winked at me as he tore off the prescription and gave it to my mother. "Okay, ladies, here's the scoop. Kobie's tonsillitis isn't serious, but it's probably going to be chronic until she has those tonsils removed. This antibiotic will clear up her infection in a few days, but every time she gets run down or has a cold, you can expect another seige."

My mother looked distraught but not half as distraught as *I* must have looked. After all, they were talking about *my* tonsils, not hers.

"If she has the operation, will she miss much school?" My mother gets totally upset if I miss more than five minutes per semester per grade, afraid I'll turn out to be a dumb bunny or a juvenile delinquent or both.

"Kobie is fifteen, by medical standards, an adult." I sat up straighter, delighted to be recognized as an adult at last, if only by a surgeon who couldn't wait to operate on me. Dr. Wampler continued, "She'll only be in the hospital overnight, barring complications, but her recuperation period at home could vary. It's difficult to say how much time she'd lose."

"We'll wait," my mother decided. "It would be better for her to have the operation in the summer."

It wasn't until I was tucked in bed with a new issue of *Tiger Beat* and a big glass of juice on my nightstand that the impact of Dr. Wampler's diagnosis hit home. Tonsillitis! I had *tonsillitis*, a disease only *children* got. Tonsillitis was for *babies*. How could I, a fifteen-year-old *adult*, come down with such a degrading condition? This was as bad as getting measles or chicken pox. Why couldn't I have something respectable, like mono?

One good thing about staying home sick was that Gretchen would miss me at school. She'd call the second she got off the bus, in a lather of worry over me. I lay back on my pillows, making little hurty sounds every time I swallowed (this was for the benefit of my mother, who fluttered around my door because I was missing one whole day of school) and thought about Turquoise Eyes.

He had to be the handsomest man at Oakton High, maybe even the world. It was no coincidence that his eyes were my favorite color. As Sandy would say, it was Fate. He had been lightning-struck, too, that was apparent. Something had definitely happened between us those few powerful seconds we stared at each other.

"Feeling better?" my mother asked for the two hundredth time that afternoon, intent on saving me from possible ruin by sending me back to school as soon as I lumbered to my feet, like an old workhorse.

I almost told her "no," but actually the medicine was making me feel better, and anyway, I had to get back and see Turquoise Eyes again. "I think I'm okay. I can probably go to school tomorow," I said, amazing my mother.

"We don't want to rush things," she said, contrarily. "Maybe you ought to stay in another day."

I flopped on the mattress, sweaty and petulant. "I *have* to go to school tomorrow. I have a big French test." I had no such thing but I couldn't stand the thought of being away from Turquoise Eyes another twenty-four hours.

My mother narrowed her eyes. "We'll see. You can make up the test. Your teacher will understand if you're sick." She left to make me creamed potato soup for supper.

Four o'clock came and went and Gretchen did not call. At four-thirty I got up and padded out to the phone. Gretchen's line was busy. It was busy at four thirty-seven and still busy at four forty-nine. She was probably yakking to Doug when she should have been inquiring after my health . . . I dialed her number the umpteenth time. This time it rang.

Gretchen's mother answered. "I'm sorry, Kobie, Gretchen isn't here. Charles picked her and Doug up after school and took them to that new miniature golf place in Annandale."

Dating during the school week yet! Why didn't Gretchen and Doug just announce their engagement and get it over with? She knew I wasn't in school and yet she hadn't even bothered to call! There was something indecent about a person out with a boy, hitting a little white ball through a fake windmill, while her best friend tottered at death's door.

The phone rang before I got back into bed. It was Sandy.

"You weren't in school today!" She nearly pierced my eardrum. "What's wrong?"

"I'm sick," I whined. At last, *somebody* cared.

"Poor Kobie! What've you got? The flu?"

"No, it's — " I stopped myself just in time. No way would I reveal to the general public that I had a little kid's disease. If I told Sandy I had tonsillitis, I might as well print it on the front page of the *Washington Post.* "It's nothing," I amended. "Just a sore throat."

"Those can be real awful. Anything I

can do for you while you're out?"

Having a second-best friend, even one as questionable as Sandy, had its merits. At least *she* wasn't whooping it up on a miniature golf course. "I'll probably be back day after tomorrow. But there is one thing you can do for me."

"Name it."

"You know that teacher Mr. Bell was talking to yesterday? When we were out in the hall? Find out who he is."

Gretchen did call later, but I was asleep. My mother kept me home the next day, overriding my loud protests that I was well enough to go to school. My temperature was down, but she claimed I might have a relapse or something. Now if I hadn't *wanted* to go to school, she would have propped me up at the bus stop on crutches, forcing me to adhere to the Virginia state law that every child shall receive an education.

I was grumpy by late afternoon when my mother told me Gretchen was on the phone.

"Talk an hour," she said, clearly at her wit's end. "Talk all night if you want. Be sure and tell her what a big baby you've been the past two days."

"You'll be sorry when I'm gone," I said, taking the receiver. "Gretchen?" I made my voice faint and scratchy, like my father's old 78 records.

"Kobie?" Gretchen said anxiously. "What's wrong? I called you last night but you were already in bed."

"That's because *some* people are too sick to stay up waiting for *other* people to get back from a date. How's your golf game these days?"

"I knew you'd be mad. Sorry I didn't call earlier. When Doug asked me to play miniature golf, I only had time to make arrangements with my mother and Charles." Charles, her older brother, had a car and was often pressed into service to taxi Gretchen around. "Kobie, what *is* the matter? I've been worried."

"You have?" Despite her recent thoughtlessness because of a mere boy, Gretchen Farris was still my best friend. "I've got tonsillitis. I have to have my tonsils out next summer. Don't you dare laugh! Gretch, promise you won't tell anybody?"

"Not even Doug?"

"Doug! Why would he care whether my tonsils were rotten or not?"

"We don't have any secrets. I tell Doug everything."

"You mean, you blab stuff that happened to you and me?" I could imagine their date the other day.

"Well, not so much about you," she admitted reluctantly. "We haven't gotten to that stage yet."

"What stage?" Gretchen's love life was, if nothing else, a great way to forget about a sore throat. Plus, I needed all this information. Sooner or later — maybe tomorrow! — Turquoise Eyes would declare his feelings for me and I had to be prepared for all the stages that come after that.

"See, we're still finding out about each other. We talk about personal stuff. Our childhoods, things like that. Doug wants to know every detail about when I was a little girl. When we're done with our pasts, we'll start in on our friends."

"Oh, really? And which chapter in your autobiography do I come in?" I didn't know how Gretchen could spend three entire dates with a guy talking about herself and never once mentioning me, her best friend.

Gretchen giggled. "Kobie, you're so funny."

"Yeah, that's me. Funny old Kobie." Time I quit clowning and let Gretchen know I had caught up to her, almost. She wasn't the only sophomore girl in Oakton to fall in love. "Listen, Gretch, I've got something really important to tell you on the bus tomorrow."

"Why not now?"

"The pho-ne," I said, singsonging the word to let her know my mother was hovering in the vicinity.

The next morning it was pouring. My mother drove me to school so I wouldn't have to wait for the bus in the rain. I didn't see Gretchen until first-period typing.

"What is this important thing you have to tell me?" she asked, adjusting Doug's ring so it wouldn't clank against the metal edge of her typewriter.

"I'm in love," I blurted. "Just like you."

"In love!" Gretchen gasped. "With who? Anybody I know?"

"I don't think so. He's new here this year."

"We're *all* new at Oakton," Gretchen pointed out.

"I mean, he's not anybody you'd know from our old schools." I fiddled with the carriage return lever.

"Kobie, will you spit it out? What's he look like? What's his name?"

"His name is — well, I call him Turquoise Eyes. T.E., for short." I liked the idea of my true love having a nickname.

"Turquoise Eyes? What kind of a name is that?" She frowned, probably thinking I was making him up.

"I don't know his real name yet," I said in a rush. "I'm still working on that. But he's absolutely gorgeous! Tall, light brown hair, and the bluest eyes you've ever seen. Not blue like yours, but turquoise. That's why I call him T.E."

"How come you don't know his name? Is he a junior?"

"Not exactly," I hedged. "But he *is* older than me." As soon as she found out T.E. was a teacher, she'd really tease me.

Gretchen thought out loud. "If he's not a junior and he's not a sophomore, he sure wouldn't be a freshman. He can't be a senior because there aren't any. That only leaves — " She stared at me. "Kobie, you're not talking about a *teacher*, are you?"

"Yes, but it's not what you think. He's interested in me, too. We had one of those stages you and Doug went through — you know, with the eyes? When we looked at each other, it was just like you described. I knew he was *it*. This isn't one of those dopey teacher-crush deals. This is *real*."

"But, Kobie, a teacher!" She shook her head. "Does *he* know this is it?"

"He must! Gretch, when our eyes met, it was — like lightning! He'd have to know." In my excitement to recreate the moment for her, I forgot my typing drill. "The walls and floors disappeared and there was nothing but him and me . . . and electricity! The air practically crackled between us. We just kept staring at each other. That was *it*, all right."

Gretchen was still doubtful. "You don't even know his name — he doesn't know *your* name."

Her doubtfulness was wearing thin. Simply because she had Doug's ring around her neck didn't mean that my relationship — such as it was at this point — was any less sincere.

"I told you I'm working on that. I bet he's down at the office this very minute tearing through the files." I deepened my voice. " 'That girl — that girl! I've got to find out who she is!' "

"Kobie, the man's probably married. Why bother liking somebody that old?"

"He's not that old," I said defensively. "And he can't be married. We wouldn't have looked at each other that way if he was. You know how boring married people are." I embroidered the dream that had been spinning in my head the last two days.

"Older men are more dependable than boys. T.E. and I will be the perfect couple. We'll go steady, just like you and Doug. He'll give me his college ring — " I especially liked that touch, a college ring was a lot classier than an onyx ring any day. "I'll meet his friends and he'll meet mine. We could even double-date, me and T.E. and you and Doug."

Gretchen snorted. "Double-date with a teacher! Kobie, what's in that gum you're chewing? Your mother won't even let you go to the movies with a boy until you're sixteen, much less date a grown man!"

"So I haven't ironed out all the wrinkles yet. The course of true love never runs smoothly," I quoted. "A little trouble makes it more romantic."

Mrs. Antle patrolled behind our chairs. "Kobie, Gretchen, get busy. I'm going to separate you girls if you can't stop chattering."

"Yes, Mrs. Antle." Obediently Gretchen placed her hands on the keys, her fingernails, painted a pretty shade of pink, curving over the row. I was *so* envious of those fingernails. Her nails had grown long and feminine since she started going with Doug McNeil.

Mrs. Antle also noticed Gretchen's nails. "Cut those claws, Gretchen. A good typist keeps her nails clipped short."

I looked down at my own ragged nails. Love affected people in the strangest ways. It made one girl write in her science book. It made Gretchen's nails grow long, like drinking gelatin every day. But love hadn't seemed to affect me yet.

Of course, I had only fallen in love with T.E. last week. In another week or so, after T.E. and I were going steady, my fingernails would be as long as Gretchen's. Maybe longer.

Chapter 5

His name, Sandy found out from one of his students, was Mr. Brown. Rather dull and disappointing, considering the color of his eyes, but I was sure T.E. had a grand *first* name, like Montgomery or Andrew. He taught freshman shop and was good friends with my algebra teacher, Mr. Bell.

For some strange reason, he didn't notice me after I returned to school. I couldn't understand it, because I knew he must have been as jolted as I was the Day Our Eyes Met. Sandy thought maybe he was more like shell-shocked, afraid to let his feelings for me show.

"I have a plan," Sandy said one day in October. Ordinarily, to hear her utter those four words would be enough to send me running for cover. "I know how to get T.E. to notice you," she added enticingly.

It was all Gretchen's fault I had to rely

on somebody as unreliable as Sandy Robertson. If Gretchen had been behaving like the best friend she was supposed to be, I wouldn't even have listened to Sandy.

I couldn't talk to Gretchen anymore. Excuse me, not Gretchen, but *Gretchen-and-Doug*. You see, Gretchen was no longer an individual person. She and Doug McNeil were an item around Oakton. They were going steady, which evidently meant exchanging rings, not eating lunch, pledging to be with each other as many hours a day as possible, and ignoring best friends and the rest of the world in general.

To be truthful, Gretchen-and-Doug made me more than a little sick. You never saw one without the other attached at the hand, hip, or lip. They floated down the halls, lost in their private fog, either holding hands, or with their arms wound around each other's waists, or kissing. Kissing on school grounds was strictly forbidden, one of those rules that was impossible to enforce, like not cutting in line.

Gretchen-and-Doug even lingered by her locker, which Doug now used so forty seconds of togetherness wouldn't be wasted while he got his books out of his own locker, heads nearly touching, murmuring what appeared to be endearments. I boldly eavesdropped once and heard Gretchen coo to Doug, "Do you have that test in geometry today?" to which Doug softly replied, "Yeah, but I forgot to study."

Doug materialized outside Gretchen's classes like smoke from a genie's lamp, whether the class let out early or late, to escort her to her next one. He carried her books hooked under his right arm in order to hold her hand.

Hand-holding was a position that could not be broken, like a sorcerer's spell. One time I met Gretchen-and-Doug in the corridor between the gym and science wings. A janitor's mop and bucket barricaded one side of the hall, leaving the narrowest of passageways. Gretchen-and-Doug were joined at the wrist that day and, even though it was obvious that I could not get by unless they split up or I polevaulted over them, the three of us danced and dodged the bucket until I managed to slither past.

"You *do* come unlinked, don't you?" I asked, hanging my foot in the wet strands of the soapy mop. "What do you do when it's time to go home?" I pictured Gretchen-and-Doug disentangling at the bus stop every afternoon, parting with a *pop* sound, like a suction cup pried from a tile wall.

Sickening. Yet the sight of them made me feverish with jealousy. I yearned to be one of those hyphenated couples, to be paired off with a boy. But not just any boy. I longed to be the other half of Kobie-and-T.E., if he'd ever notice me.

I tried to talk to Gretchen about my problem on the bus, one of the rare occasions that Gretchen was Doug-less, only because Doug McNeil lived in another section of the school district. I wondered why Gretchen-and-Doug didn't fix that by making the superintendent rezone the boundaries in order to be on the same bus route, or beg their parents to move so they could live next door to each other.

But even when I was alone with Gretchen, she wasn't really there. "Gretch," I said. "I have to talk to you about T.E. It isn't working out quite like I thought. He doesn't seem to know I'm alive."

"Mmmmm." Gretchen was dreamily writing *Mrs. Douglas McNeil* just beneath *Gretchen Farris McNeil* on a scrap of typing paper.

"Gretch, did you hear me? I need some advice."

"About what?"

"About *T.E.*" Honestly, she was deaf as a stone these days.

"I don't know," she finally replied. "I have to ask Doug and see what he thinks."

"I don't want Doug to know I'm in love with a teacher!" I yelled, practically spilling my secret to everybody on the bus. "What do *you* think?"

"I have to ask Doug."

Was it any wonder I turned to Sandy Robertson?

"I should *follow* him?" I repeated, when Sandy unveiled her latest harebrained scheme. "Where?"

"Everywhere," Sandy said. "Whenever you see him in the hall, follow him. But don't walk behind him. Sort of walk beside him, so he'll see you."

"I don't know." I sounded as vague as Gretchen. "He might not like it."

As she spoke, the object of my desire sauntered down the hall, innocently heading toward the industrial arts wing. He looked taller today, his turquoise eyes brightly offset by his yellow shirt. My heart swelled like a puffy satin Valentine. How I loved him!

"There he goes," I said, tracking his progress down the hall.

"He *is* cute," Sandy agreed. "I was thinking about falling in love with a teacher myself, just like you did, but you've already picked the cutest teacher in the school."

T.E. passed without even a glance in my direction. "He never even saw me," I said forlornly.

"He will." Sandy stuck her pencil behind one ear, suddenly businesslike. If I had been operating on all cylinders, I would have sensed the reversal in our roles at that moment. Sandy was about to take control of my life — at least the romance part of it — and I, too lovesick to realize what was happening, let her.

Thus I began a dual life. There was the outwardly normal Kobie Roberts who wore heather-toned skirts and matching sweaters and worried over math and archery practice like any other sophomore girl. Then there was the *other* Kobie Roberts, the one who slinked around Oakton, following the unsuspecting Mr. Brown, alias T.E.

When T.E. failed to notice the small, pointy-faced eager-eyed girl jouncing alongside of him as he strode to the teacher's lounge or to the cafeteria, Sandy increased her intelligence-gathering tactics.

"After third, he usually goes out to his car to get a thermos," she reported, consulting the clipboard on which she plotted T.E.'s every move in minute detail. "Walk out with him and say something like, 'Isn't it a nice day?' "

" 'Isn't it a nice day!' " I scoffed. "It's pouring for the twenty-seventh day in a row. Sandy, T.E. *knows* I'm there, but he's deliberately ignoring me."

"That's because he's afraid of his feelings. What you want to do is get him to look at you like he did that day outside math class. Get in front of him. Bump into him accidentally-on-purpose. Make him see you."

"But he never *does*. I might as well go around with a bag over my head." To emphasize my point, I pulled my sweater up over my shoulders, wrapped it around my head, covering my face, and tied the sleeves in a tight knot under my chin. "You think he'd notice me any better like this?" I asked, my voice muffled through the cloth.

"The plan will work. Stick with it," Sandy urged. "Don't let up for a single minute."

Just then she clutched my arm in a death grip. "Here he comes! Now's your chance, Kobie!"

"My chance to do *what*?" I couldn't see with the stupid sweater over my face. "Get me out of this thing!" I pawed frantically at the knot, but it held fast.

"No time!" Sandy shoved me sideways, the sweater still snugly turbaned around my head.

"Not like this!" But it was too late. I was already moving, a prime example of that famous law of physics: an object in motion tends to remain in motion until she has made a complete fool of herself. Spinning across the hall, I ricocheted off the lockers, then bumbled back again, blindly grabbing at other people's coats and jackets.

"Sandy, where are you?" I cried.

Laughter echoed up and down the hall. "Boy, somebody sure pulled the wool over her eyes," some kid quipped, and the others groaned at his terrible joke.

"Will somebody *help* me?" I demanded, before tripping over a rather large shoe.

Two strong hands gripped me above the elbows and lifted me to my feet.

"Young lady," said an amused voice, "you ought to watch where you're going." He steered me out of the stream of traffic and stood me up against the wall, the way you would position a dummy in a department store window.

"Need some help getting that off?" he asked.

"No, thanks," I replied nonchalantly through the left sleeve, as if having a sweater tied over my head was an everyday occurrence. "I'm fine. Really."

"Well, if you're sure — "

"You'd better hurry or you'll miss your class," I insisted.

The amusement level in his voice heightened. "I certainly don't want to do that."

He must have left because the next thing I heard was Sandy's voice chirping, "Kobie, are you okay? Are you okay?"

"Sandy, I'm the laughingstock of Oakton and I'm suffocating in this sweater, but other than that, I couldn't be better. There's one teensy little thing, though."

"What's that?"

"*Get me out of this sweater so I can kill you!*"

She ripped the sweater off me the hard way, naturally, jamming the buttons up my nose and nearly severing an ear in the process.

"Tell me that the nice man who brought me over here was not T.E. Tell me I did not make an idiot of myself in front of the very man I want to impress so he'll love me back. Tell me that didn't happen, Sandy Robertson."

Sandy wasn't even contrite. She flashed me that green-eyed grin. "At least he noticed you."

"But he didn't know who I was! With my head covered up, he couldn't tell me apart from any other dumb girl in this school, though I ought to be thankful for that."

She pursed her lips. "You wanted T.E. to notice you, and when he does, you get mad at me. There's just no satisfying some people."

A day distinguished by blundering into my true love with a sweater over my head couldn't possibly get worse. But that was before Stuart Buckley nailed me in French class.

"Hey, Kobie, you're a girl — " Stuart shouted as soon as I walked in the door.

I sat down, feeling at least a hundred and twelve. Sandy's schemes were aging me prematurely. "Really, Stuart. You shouldn't be so generous with compliments."

"No, wait." For once, he seemed genuinely upset. "You have to help me."

"With what?"

"It's about — I need to know what girls think of me," he stammered.

My heart hardened. "What *girls* think of you or what *one* girl in particular thinks of you." I had a sneaky suspicion where this discussion was leading.

"One girl . . . two girls . . ." He wiggled his fingers. "What's the difference? Since you're a girl — "

"We've already established that fact."

" — you should know all about these things."

"*What* things?" Why did he talk in riddles all of a sudden?

"About what girls like in boys." He leaned so far into the aisle, he nearly fell out of his desk. "Take Rosemary Swan, for instance — "

I groaned. "Are you still crazy about her?"

"Would she go for a guy like me, you know, who's a little shorter than her, do you think?"

"A little shorter! You're at least a foot — " I stopped when I saw the earnest, pinched look on his face. He really wanted to know if I thought his height, or lack of it, would be an obstacle in dating Rosemary. I decided to break it to him gently. "Stuart, why don't you set your sights a little lower? I'm sure there are lots of shorter girls in this school, just as pretty as Rosemary and maybe a whole lot nicer, who'd be dying to go out with you."

His upper lip stiffened and I realized I had injured his finer side, though to be truthful, I didn't know Stuart even *had* a finer side.

"You're just jealous," he said bitterly. "You'd probably like to have me all to yourself, wouldn't you, Kobie?"

"Jealous! Me? Well, that's gratitude." Where did that little shrimp get off thinking I was losing sleep over *him*. "Why did you ask my advice if you weren't going to take it?"

"Because I thought you'd tell me something better than that," he said, huffily opening his French book, a gesture that spoke of his contempt for me, since Stuart never studied. "I should have known you'd let me down."

He refused to speak to me the rest of the period.

The next day Stuart stalked into class late, confidently stumping past Rosemary Swan's desk. He was definitely taller, but he hadn't *grown* any, certainly not overnight.

When he sat down at his own desk, he tossed me a smirk of triumph. Rosemary Swan had noticed him, all right.

"What did you do?" I asked him. "Sleep on a rack?"

"It's my shoes," Stuart replied. "I put blocks of wood in them. Pretty neat, eh? Did you see her face when I walked by?"

Wood blocks in his shoes yet! The lengths we went to to be noticed by the ones we loved.

Chapter 6

Just as Dr. Wampler predicted, I caught a cold in November that developed into tonsillitis. I stayed home one day, taking medicine until my temperature dropped, and then it was back to the old grind.

"My throat hurts," I complained to my mother as she heartlessly packed me a little "survival" sack containing my pills, lemon throat lozenges, and a pack of tissues.

"I know," she said. "But it'll be better in a few days. As long as you don't have a temperature, you can go to school."

"But I feel awful! It hurts to swallow and I ache all over."

"Kobie, you're going to have to put up with it. You can't miss a week of school every time you get tonsillitis. You're in high school now and your grades are important. If you feel worse, call me and I'll come get you."

I shuffled despondently to the front door. "You'd send me to school in an iron lung. A person has to produce a death certificate in this house to stay home. You don't love me."

"Don't push me, not after yesterday." She hugged me. "Stop dramatizing. You're not dying."

Not that she'd care if I was. Still, I had her promise. If I dragged myself off to school the next day with no argument, she'd let me have Gretchen and Sandy over to spend the night.

"Night-spending!" she exclaimed yesterday, as if I had requested something outrageous. "That's all you kids think about, spending the night at somebody else's house."

" 'Night-spending?' " I repeated. "Mother, must you sound so nineteenth century? It's a *slumber* party."

"When I was growing up," she began in that mother tone that brought to mind hoop skirts and buggy whips and one-room schoolhouses, "I never thought of spending the night at my friend's house. In my day, you went to sleep in your own bed."

"In your day, you slept in the same room with two of your sisters. In the same bed with Aunt Lil. You had a slumber party every night."

"Some party," she said scornfully. "Lil kicking me and hogging the covers."

Now, as I shrugged into my stadium coat, I reminded her of the promise. "I'm asking Gretchen and Sandy if they can come *this weekend.*"

"Only if you're better."

"If I'm well enough to go to school, I'm well enough to have my friends over Saturday. Aren't I?" I asked.

Mother handed me my muffler with a sharp glance. "You're getting too smart, Kobie." But she said it in such a way I knew I had won.

Some victory. I really and truly felt yucky. Because I had the chills, I kept my muffler wound around my neck, even in gym. The scarf was striped burgundy and gold, the school colors the committee finally settled on, and I figured people would think I was displaying school spirit by wearing the colors all the time. Unfortunately, a long striped muffler did not go well with my gym suit or any of my outfits. Instead of hiding my condition, I attracted unwanted stares and comments. Once again I had my old Woodson reputation, the one I had tried so hard to bury. People thought I was weird.

Except for Gretchen, no one knew my sordid secret. Even letting people think I was weird was a notch better than letting them know I had tonsillitis, a sickness only little kids got.

"You just dipped your scarf in your gravy," Eddie Showalter said at lunch later that week.

"Thanks." I wiped gravy from the tasseled ends of my muffler. The thing was really a nuisance, forever falling in my food and getting caught on the handle of my locker.

"Are you cold?"

"Of course not. What makes you think I'm cold?" I fanned my napkin furiously, pretending to be hot to erase his impression that there might be something wrong with me. "I wish they'd turn the heat down in this cafeteria. I'm burning up."

"It *is* a little stuffy in here," he agreed amiably.

Eddie Showalter had camped at my lunch table ever since the note-amnesia episode. Like a puppy dumped on a doorstep, Eddie just sort of stayed. Sandy conveniently disappeared during lunch about four days out of five, leaving me and Eddie alone.

Eddie was usually at our table when I sat down with my tray, his science book or Spanish book in front of him. He never turned the page and he never ate.

He was pleasant to be around. He never bugged me like Stuart did, instead asking how my drawing was coming along, and sometimes showing me his own sketches, chiefly of the White House and jet airplanes. His ninth-grade obsession to be both a pilot *and* president had not cooled.

"The only way you'll get in the White House," I told him, examining a tiny crosshatched view of the East Wing, "is with a ticket like the rest of us."

"Anyone can aspire to the top office," Eddie said. "Everyone has the same chance in this country."

"I think you've been watching too many corn flakes commercials."

He changed the subject. "Are you going to the game?" Our school was playing Marshall High. "They might bring the real mascot."

In addition to choosing burgundy and gold as the school colors, we voted to have a cougar as mascot. A local farmer who had raised a pair of cougars from cubs offered to lend our school one of the cats, chained and caged, for halftime at big games. A goat would fill in for the rest of the games.

"After watching our team at the pep rally last Friday, they might as well bring the goat," I said.

Oakton had only a junior varsity team and a pretty pathetic one at that. Witnessing our pitiful team stumble out onto the field to the manic cheers of our equally stumbling cheerleaders and the off-key music of our band did little to instill hope we would beat Marshall, or even Oakton Elementary in a game of kickball.

"I'm probably going," Eddie said, suddenly glancing down at his science book. His eyelashes were long, longer than mine no matter how many coats of mascara I put on. "I thought I might see you there."

My throat tightened, a reaction that had nothing to do with tonsillitis. Was Eddie asking me, in a roundabout way, if I'd go to the game with him? "Well, actually, I'm busy Friday."

"Oh. You're going out, then."

"Not exactly." Why didn't I tell him Sandy and Gretchen were coming over? Why lead him to believe I had a date, an event as unlikely as striking oil in my backyard.

"I should have guessed you'd be busy," Eddie said. "You're probably booked up weeks ahead."

"Months," I said airily, although anybody who spent more than three minutes in my company knew my social calendar was free until the end of the century.

Stuart would have guffawed over the notion that I was popular enough to actually be busy on a Friday night, but Eddie accepted my greatly exaggerated status as one of the "right" people.

Sandy leaped at my invitation to a mini-slumber party, but Gretchen was a lot tougher to persuade. She couldn't bear to be away from Doug on one of their regular date nights, she said. You could always call him, I argued. It wasn't the same thing, she said. At last I convinced her it was entirely possible for her to have a good time at my house even *without* Doug. When she relented, I felt exhausted.

Friday night the three of us went to see *Romeo and Juliet.* By the time we got back from the movies, my mother had set up a camp cot and an old chaise lounge in my room. There wasn't an inch of space to walk in, but that didn't matter since all we did was loll first in one bed and then the other, playing records, leafing through magazines, and listening to Gretchen sigh.

Gretchen was turning into a real party-pooper. She drooped around like a moulting chicken.

"Stop mourning," I told her. "Doug didn't go off to war."

"I know. But I *miss* him." And she let loose another gusty sigh, like the wind caught high in the treetops. Most annoying.

By eleven-thirty we had annihilated a bacon pizza, three packs of Ho-Ho's, five RCs, a bowl of Fritos, a pan of brownies, plus all that junk at the movies, and we were wondering when my mother was going to bring us some *real* food when

Sandy suddenly cried, "Here's your answer, Kobie! Here's how to get T.E. to notice you!"

"What is it?" I struggled over to my bed where Sandy was stretched out reading Gretchen's *Seventeen*.

"Right here." Sandy held up the glossy advertisement so I could see it. "Just like in the movie. It's perfect for you, Kobie."

In the ad, a beautiful girl modeled an updated Juliet gown with deep lace sleeves dripping over her wrists, to illustrate the girl's pearly pink nails. *The romantic look is always in*, the ad proclaimed, praising a brand of lipstick and nail polish.

"You buy this stuff," Sandy said, "and you get a soft pretty dress and T.E. will fall for you just like Romeo fell for Juliet."

"I'd look awful in an Empire-waist dress," I said. "I haven't got any bust as it is — that style will make me look even flatter."

Sandy scrutinized my figure, which of course did not show to advantage in the rumpled pajamas I was wearing. "Well, maybe not a dress exactly like this one. But something pretty. You're good at drawing. Why don't you draw your own?"

"You mean, design my own dress?"

"Yeah. And maybe fix your hair different. That girl's hair isn't any longer than yours — you could curl it and put a ribbon in it. And stop carrying your books on your hip."

"How do you want me to carry them? On my head? What does that have to do with looking romantic for T.E.?"

"Hold your books like this." She cradled the magazine to her chest. "*You* carry them on your hip, like the boys do."

I actually considered her suggestions, demonstrating the depths of my hopelessness over T.E. Heeding beauty tips offered by Sandy Robertson was like asking Dracula where he went to the dentist.

One day last summer, Sandy, Gretchen, and I all bought the same makeup and practiced putting it on. Gretchen was a natural and could sub as an Avon Lady. Because I could draw well, my hand was the steadiest with the eyeliner brush. But Sandy! Her blush-on was like tire treads, her mascara tipped her lashes in little globules, and her eyeliner was thick and crooked.

Even with these facts uppermost in my mind, I heard myself say, "So you really think the romantic look will attract T.E.? You know, if I didn't tape my hair, it would be curly like that model's." I minced around the camp cot. "Am I walking like Rosemary Swan?"

"Swing to the right. That's it," Sandy coached. "Don't you think Kobie will make a great Juliet?" she asked Gretchen.

Gretchen, who was moping over not being able to call Doug any more that night, sighed so hard she nearly blew the sheets off the beds.

"She left with no forwarding address," I said to Sandy. "Anyway, she doesn't believe I should waste my time over a teacher. Do you, Gretchen?" I yelled in her face.

"No," she replied absentmindedly. Then, injecting a little strength into her voice, "Kobie, this whole business with the shop teacher is stupid. The man is probably married."

"He doesn't wear a ring," Sandy put in.

"That doesn't prove anything. Neither does my father. He's allergic to gold," Gretchen said.

Sandy asked thoughtfully, "Why doesn't he wear a silver ring?"

Gretchen threw her a dark look. "Will you grow up? The point is that Kobie is going to make a fool of herself over this teacher and for what? She's only fifteen. Her mother isn't going to let her date a man that old — "

"Shhhhhh! Do you want her to *hear*?" I knew if my mother thought I was interested in a teacher, she'd have me in reform school until I was thirty.

"There isn't *that* much difference in their ages," Sandy defended. "My father is older than my mother and he says the age gap closes the older they get."

"Fifteen is too young for a grown man," Gretchen said primly, sounding like our old fourth-grade teacher. "What would he see in a girl like Kobie? To him, she's just a kid."

"I am not! According to my doctor, I'm an adult. We're all adults in this room. Mostly," I added with a glance at Sandy.

The remark sailed right over Sandy's head. "We start driver's ed next week. Pretty soon we'll get our licenses."

"*Classroom* driver's ed," Gretchen corrected. "We won't be allowed to get behind the wheel until next summer."

I didn't expect to get behind the wheel until I was old enough to buy my own car. My mother had only learned to drive the year before, sufficiently frightening my father, who decreed he would never teach anyone to drive ever again. Gretchen would get her learner's permit before me, naturally, and she'd zoom off into the sunset with Doug, leaving me stranded and dateless.

Our party mood hit a snag. Gretchen resumed her sighing and pining. Sandy wondered when my mother was going to bring fresh rations. I sat on the chaise lounge and imagined the beautiful dress I would design, the one that would make T.E. fall to his knees when he saw me.

Chapter 7

Saturday evening I decided to get my homework out of the way. Algebra problems, an English paper, French, the usual stuff. But inside my physical science notebook was a reminder: *bring slug to school.*

I had forgotten all about that stupid assignment! The last thing Mr. Chapman had called out as the bell rang was for each of us to bring a *slug* to class for some weird biology experiment. I couldn't imagine a lesson involving thirty-five slugs.

My parents were having a snack at the kitchen table and discussing the necessity of having our septic tank pumped in the spring, a topic that went nicely with coffee and oatmeal cookies, when I interrupted.

"Where are your old boots?" I asked my father. "I have to go out in the garden and look for a slug for school."

"You can't go out in the damp and look for slugs until you're over your sore throat," my mother said, never turning a hair at the silliness of such an assignment. My mother seldom questioned anything I did for school; she firmly believed my teachers knew what they were doing.

"It rains every day. I can't wait until it stops," I protested, more to be argumentative than anything. I wasn't really that enthusiastic about hunting for a slug.

My father finished his cookie in one bite. "Never saw such a wet fall. If it snows as much as it's rained, we'll be snowbound till July." He drank the rest of his coffee. "I'll get you a slug, Kobie."

"I need it for Monday," I said, relieved. Digging through a bunch of dead wet leaves for an icky, slimy slug was hardly something I was eager to do. My father wouldn't have much luck finding one either, since slugs probably inched south for the winter. I looked up slugs in my encyclopedia, in case Mr. Chapman popped a quiz, and learned they are actually pulmonate gastropods. I had gone fifteen years thinking they were just snails too poor to afford a little house to carry around on their backs.

The next day I was designing romantic dresses when my father called me from the back porch. I went out to see what he wanted.

Holding a five-gallon bucket by the handle, he grinned proudly. "I bet none of the other kids will have beauties like these." He tipped the bucket forward so I could see inside.

If I hadn't been raised in the country, I probably would have fainted at the sight of the two huge leopard-spotted slugs wiggling on the bed of moss at the bottom of the bucket. At the very least I would have screamed.

Instead I asked, "Where did you get such big ones? Not out of our garden?" If he had, I wasn't setting foot off the porch as long as I lived here.

"In the woods," he replied, and I saw his pants were soaked to the knees. "Under a rotted log. You have to know where to look. What'll your teacher think when you show him?"

My heart fell somewhere around my heels as I realized I would have to take those huge prehistoric slugs to *school*. Despair was followed by a rash of guilt. Once before I complained to my mother about the way my father always went around in his green school-board uniform. "So he doesn't get dressed up in a suit," my mother had snapped at me. "He works hard to earn us a decent living. You should be ashamed, making fun of him."

Even without my mother to accuse me, I felt ashamed again. Here my father had slogged through the rainy woods and lifted countless logs to get me the biggest and best slugs any kid ever took to school, and I didn't want them. I wanted ordinary garden-variety slugs that wouldn't cause people to stampede.

"Maybe my teacher will be scared of them," I said hopefully. "I wouldn't want to give Mr. Chapman a heart attack. He's only expecting us to bring in little bitty slugs." Certainly not Godzilla and his brother.

"Those little bitty things the other kids'll have will look sick next to these fine specimens," my father said. Actually, I thought it might be the other way around.

"I only have a small glass jar," I said, grasping at any excuse now. "They won't fit in it."

"We'll fix up something," my father reassured me. "Don't worry."

Monday morning, I let my hair curl naturally, put on a pale pink blouse with a lace collar, and was all set to conquer T.E. with my new romantic look when my mother handed me an enormous Tupperware box along with my lunch money.

"Don't forget your science project," she said.

Gingerly I piled the box on top of my books. "This looks like a bread box."

"It is." She pried open one corner of the

hole-punched lid. "Your father put wet moss inside, so the slugs will rest comfortably." She closed the lid quickly. "Awful-looking, aren't they? You ought to get an A."

Like my father, my mother thought size was related to good marks. "Mom, I can't take these horrible things to school! I'm wearing a pink blouse!"

"What does that have to do with your project?"

Nothing I could make her understand without revealing my campaign. "Tupperware clashes with pink," I said weakly.

Her patience suddenly frayed, like an old rope. "You take this box to school and stop acting like such a brat, Kobie Roberts. Your father tramped half the day Sunday, his only day off, to find you those slugs. You should be grateful."

"I am! I'm grateful to be carrying the biggest, grossest slugs in the history of the world to school on the day when I want to look pretty! I'm also late." I pulled on my coat and left without kissing my mother good-bye. I didn't know what had gotten into her. Instead of our fighting occasionally, say, once a day, it was just one long fight with her lately.

Gretchen was writing Doug a note when I sat down beside her on the bus.

"Good grief," I exclaimed, glimpsing the

mushy greeting. "You're going to see him in about forty minutes."

"I know, but this is for him to read in first period. Then he'll answer me back and I'll read it in second period and so on. That way we can talk to each other all day."

"Honestly, Gretchen, why don't you two just elope?"

She looked up from her tablet. "What's eating you?"

"You are! You haven't said one word about my hair. Why go to all the trouble of wearing it different if nobody's going to notice?" I shifted the books in my lap, jiggling the Tupperware box.

"You hair looks very nice," Gretchen said dutifully. "What's in the box?"

"Our science assignment. Remember? Mr. Chapman asked us to bring in a slug. Where's yours?" I didn't see any evidence of a jar or box.

"I think Doug is bringing one for each of us."

"You mean you don't absolutely know for sure what Doug McNeil is doing this second? Did your walkie-talkies break down? No, wait — I've got it. He's going to surprise you with a slug set in gold and onyx so you can wear it around your neck."

"Boy, somebody got up on the wrong side of the bed."

"You'd be grouchy, too, if you had to lug around this stupid bread box." I tapped the lid angrily.

"Why didn't you use something smaller?" For the first time in ages, Gretchen's curiosity was roused. "What *have* you got in there? Let me see."

"You don't really want to do that." I didn't want to be blamed for her heart attack.

"Oh, come on," she pleaded. "Just let me peek."

"All right, you asked for it." I yanked the lid off, exposing my pulmonate gastropods in all their slimy leopard-spotted splendor.

"AAAAAAAACK!" Gretchen reeled backward, scattering books and papers and Doug's letter in a panicky wake. "Kobie, you — you! Why didn't you *warn* me?"

"I tried."

"You're perfectly horrid, Kobie Roberts! I'm not sitting with you!" She flew down the aisle to find another seat.

Guilt engulfed me for the second time in two days. It *was* mean to spring those dinosaurs on Gretchen like that. I guess I was tired of her smugness over Doug, as if she were rubbing my face in the fact that she had a boyfriend and I didn't.

You wouldn't think an entire school

would go ape over a couple of meatloaf-sized slugs in a Tupperware bread box, but that's what happened. Rumor that I had two slugs with glandular problems spread like a brush fire, and before I knew it, every guy in the tenth grade crowded around me to see what I had in the box. I couldn't have been more popular if I had given away tickets to the Superbowl. Or more embarrassed.

If I hadn't been such a tenderhearted person, I would have chucked those monsters in the nearest trash can. But I felt responsible for them; after all, they had been minding their own business when my father ripped them from their happy home under the rotten log. My conscience wouldn't let me leave the box in my locker, so I was stuck with the blob twins until fourth period.

Mr. Chapman greeted me with a smile. "I've been hearing about your prize gastropods all day." As he lifted the lid, he turned an interesting shade of green but bravely put his hand inside and brought out Godzilla I and II.

"Do you think your father could get me three or four?" Sandy asked as we raced to math in the industrial arts wing. "They're great for attracting boys."

"Did you check your IQ at the door?

How would you like to go around all day with slug juice on your sleeve?" The girl's elevator clearly did not go to the top.

Sandy stepped on my foot, crushing my big toe in her haste to back up. "Look, there's T.E.! Too bad you don't have your little friends with you."

I shoved her off my bruised foot. "Wouldn't that have been romantic? I'm glad he didn't see me before now. It was awful enough I had to run into him with a sweater over my head." I patted my hair, making sure it was still curly. "At least now he knows I have pretty hair."

T.E. didn't look up until he was in front of me. His beautiful turquoise eyes met mine in startled recognition. Then he whirled around as if he suddenly remembered a previous appointment and hurried in the other direction.

"Why did he turn and run?" I cried, dismayed. "Do I look that bad?"

T.E. didn't act the slightest bit gallant and suave, the way he'd been the day he'd helped me across the traffic-clogged hall. Was he only nice to girls with sweaters over their heads? Or had he heard about my mega-gastropods and was afraid I'd sic them on him?

I sniffed my armpit. "I bet my deodorant failed. Sandy, he hates me!"

"No, he doesn't. He *likes* you. Can't you

see — he's afraid to let you know how much he likes you."

Of course. It made perfect sense. In novels men were forever denying their feelings for the women they loved.

"I told you this new plan would work," she said. "Romance gets 'em every time."

"Not quite. How do I get him to run in *my* direction, not the other way?" What would I have to do to attract him? Send up flares?

"The dress," Sandy stated. "You need a beautiful dress, like Juliet's."

Designing a romantic dress wasn't that easy. It required intense concentration, lots of paper, plenty of Twinkies, and the right mood. In order to put myself into a romantic mood, I played my new album over and over, a lot of love-gone-wrong songs that my mother said sounded like funeral dirges.

"Kobie," she barked from the hall. "If you play that ghastly record one more time, I'm leaving home!"

"There's nothing wrong with this record," I yelled back. "Plug your ears if you don't like it."

"Why don't you play *real* music? Anything would be better than that awful racket. I'd rather listen to . . . Elvis Presley!" she concluded in desperation.

"*El*-vis *Pres*-ley! Mom, you are so out of it." I selected a gray felt-tip pen to color in the chinchilla cuffs of the Russian-style coatdress I had created.

My mother hung around my door. "I may be out of it, but at least I know good music when I hear it."

"Mother, I like this record and I'm going to keep playing it."

"You might come home and find a big scratch across it," she said menacingly.

"Then I'll buy another one."

"What do those songs *mean*? About the jewels and binoculars on moose antlers. What's that supposed to mean?"

I wouldn't get any peace by ignoring her. "It doesn't mean *anything*. It just *is*. I don't try to analyze it — I just listen to the words and let the pictures flow through my mind."

"But the pictures are all *weird*."

"I know. That's why I like it."

She went away then, shaking her head over the decline of my generation and how she dreaded placing her future in the hands of people who grew up listening to such drivel.

I colored my Russian coatdress with the silver felt-tip pen, thinking of the futility of parents and teenagers trying to communicate.

Chapter 8

"What's that?" Stuart asked, reaching for a paper poking out of my notebook.

We were in French, writing an essay about these mountain climbers lost in the Alps. At least, *I* was writing; Stuart was angling to copy off mine.

I swatted his grubby little fingers. "Hands off."

"Why can't I see? It's one of those Mickey Mouse pictures, isn't it? How come you never show me your drawings? You let everybody else see them but not me. You don't like me anymore."

Now I understood the principle of the Chinese water torture — just keep at somebody, drop by drop, until she caves in.

The drawing Stuart tried to steal from my notebook was not one of my Disney cartoons, but the dress I had designed, the one that would topple T.E. I didn't want Stuart to see it. I didn't want anyone to see it, not Stuart or Sandy or even Gretchen.

Designing this dress had been an almost mystical experience. For weeks, I had crumpled up dozens of designs that were either too impractical to make, like the Persian lamb and chinchilla coatdress, or just didn't do anything for my particular figure type (Classic Bed Slat). But yesterday my pen started sketching with a life of its own, and suddenly, there it was. *The* dress.

Tiers of gathered white lace attached to a white satin underskirt, the lacy ruffles falling from an emerald velvet yoke to just above the knee. Flowing chiffon sleeves cuffed with pearl buttons, a green velvet bow tied at the neckline, the ends of the ribbon drifting over the wedding-cake lace. Juliet would have sold her Capulet name for a dress like this.

The dress was so breathtakingly beautiful, I couldn't believe it came out of my head. Half afraid the design would evaporate, I brought it to school and checked every so often to make sure the paper hadn't gone blank. Every time I saw the sketch, I felt all trembly inside — that dress was going to change my life. I wasn't ready to share my creation with the world. Not yet.

But Stuart was still badgering me. "You never let me see your dumb old drawings. What kind of a friend are you?"

"Stuart, the last time I showed you my drawings, you made fun of them."

"That was years ago. We were little kids then."

It was only *two* years ago and one of us still qualified as little. Fortunately, I could shut him up because I also had with me one of the preliminary sketches from the *Lady and the Tramp* series I was working on before fashion design consumed my spare time.

"Here," I said, flinging a torn piece of sketch paper at him. "No smart remarks."

The drawing was from the scene in the movie where Tramp and Lady share a romantic spaghetti dinner behind an Italian restaurant. The two dogs are eating the same strand of spaghetti, not knowing that they are going to wind up in a kiss. The expression of sweet canine innocence in their eyes, especially in Lady's, was difficult to achieve and I wasn't sure I had it. I brought the drawing with me to get a new perspective.

"This is great! You really are a terrific artist! Such talent," Stuart gushed. If I'd been wearing false teeth, I would have dropped them on the floor.

"What do you want?" I asked, instantly

alert. "If you're buttering me up to let you copy my essay, forget it — "

"I don't want anything," he said, astonished that such an outlandish thought had crossed my mind. "Except maybe this."

"My drawing? You want my picture? What on earth for?"

"Gretchen has a whole bunch of your pictures. Why not me?" he said. "I'd really like to own a Kobie Roberts original. Some day when you're famous I can say I knew you when."

"When you were driving me crazy, you mean." Yet I was flattered by his request. Could it be that Stuart was interested in me? No, the idea was too unbelievable. Playing the part of the terrific and terribly talented artist, I said, "It's yours. Let me have it back and I'll sign it."

"No, no." Stuart hung onto the drawing. "It'll be worth more this way. If you sign it, it'll be like you knew you were going to be famous and that kind of ruins it. People expect artists to starve and struggle for years and give away their work for nothing."

"Is that so? Now that you've got my future all mapped out, what are *you* going to be doing while I'm starving and struggling?" In the two years I had known Stuart he'd never indicated what he wanted to do beyond squirming out of as much work as he possibly could and still remain in school. Amazingly, he made fairly decent grades.

"I have no idea," he replied.

"What about acting?" I remembered how good he had been as the Artful Dodger in our eighth-grade production of *Oliver!*

"Nah. I don't know what I want to do. I guess I just want to live and have a great time." His sharp gray eyes zeroed in on Rosemary Swan. "And get that girl," he added, almost to himself.

"Good luck."

Stuart had stopped wearing blocks in his shoes to appear taller — the rough chunks of wood gave him blisters, he said. I wondered what course of action he planned to take next to win Rosemary. Too bad he didn't have a scheme as foolproof as mine.

My mother stared at the sketch, then the materials I had listed in one corner.

"You want me to make you this dress," she said finally. "without a pattern, without measurements, without anything to go by except this picture you drew."

I hopped up and down on one foot. "Mom, it's not as hard as it looks. I'll help you."

"Some help you'll be. If you recall, you ruined your sewing project in eighth-grade home ec and *I* had to fix it. Not to mention failing home ec last year." She was never going to let that rest — it would probably be inscribed on my tombstone: *She failed home ec and broke her mother's heart.*

"Mom, I *have* to have this dress. I'll just *die* if I don't have this dress."

"Where are you going that's so important you have to have such a fancy dress?" she demanded.

I couldn't tell her the truth, that I intended to wear the dress to wring an admission of love from T.E. If she knew *that*, she'd lock me in my room and throw the key down the well.

"I — it's for a party," I improvised. "Gretchen's having a big New Year's Eve party and I want to wear it then."

"Clare hasn't said anything about a party." My mother and Gretchen's mother were good friends and frequently exchanged spy reports about me and Gretchen.

"She doesn't know about it yet," I said. "Gretchen and her boyfriend want to get every detail just right before they ask her."

My mother laid my sketch down, momentarily distracted. "That girl is entirely too young to be going steady. I don't believe in dating too soon. There's plenty of time for boys."

When? I'd been fifteen for six whole months — soon I'd be over the hill. But I had to get her back on the subject at hand.

"Mom, I really really need this dress. Can you make it for me?"

She regarded me with that fierce, steely look geared to get a daughter to confess she spilled the nail polish on the tablecloth and ate the dessert meant for company. "Why do you need this dress so badly? Why *this* dress? Why not buy a pretty dress?"

How could I explain that *this* dress was totally unique, that no one else in the world would have a dress like this, that it would make me *special*. While it was important to have the same clothes as the other girls at school, it was suddenly more important to have a dress that was *different*.

"I just want this dress," I whispered, without attempting to put my hazy desires into words.

Something in my tone must have registered with my mother because she said, "All right. I can't promise you it'll turn out just like your picture, but I'll try. *On one condition.*"

"What?" I asked, afraid she would demand an unreasonable favor in return, like washing the dishes every night or scrubbing the basement floor.

"Promise you won't play that infernal record. My nerves can't take it any more."

"Deal." A few weeks without my album was a small sacrifice.

We went to Manassas that weekend. The

stores were decorated with plastic holly and styrofoam reindeer, reminders that Christmas was bearing down on us. In Sew Forth, my mother purchased heavy bridal satin for the underskirt of my dress, tulle to attach the lace to, emerald velvet for the bodice, and a half a yard of chiffon for the sleeves. The pre-gathered lace was the hardest to find. We found a spool of it in Woolworth's and lavishly bought ten yards. It was horribly expensive, even for Woolworth's, but my mother never said a word as she handed the girl at the cash register a twenty-dollar bill.

After such an extravagant spree, I expected to go home for lunch, probably birdseed and distilled water drained out of the steam iron, but my mother headed for the luncheonette counter.

I love eating in Woolworth's. I twirled on my red leather stool, getting swimmy-headed until my mother smacked my knee.

"How old are you?" she asked.

The reprimand didn't bother me. I had the fabric for my beautiful dress and a willing, if somewhat snippish, seamstress to sew it. The world was rosy.

I read the menu carefully, and said, "I want a hot turkey sandwich and a large Coke."

My mother ordered the grilled cheese special. "I can't believe how much money we spent on material today. I must have been delirious to let you talk me into making that dress."

The waitress brought our drinks, spilling them so the sides of the glasses would be sticky. I unwrapped my straw and took a long pull of my Coke.

"I've got an old pattern of yours I can use for the yoke and the length of the dress. The rest I'll have to do without a pattern. Sewing that lace on the tulle will be the worst part."

"You can do it," I said confidently. "If you could fix that shirtwaist dress I made in eighth grade, you can do anything."

"That was a job and a half," she agreed. "Have you thought about Christmas shopping?"

"I have thirty dollars saved. Enough to buy presents for you, Dad, Gretchen, and Sandy. Charles is supposed to take me and Gretchen to the mall next weekend. That is, if she can unglue herself from Doug McNeil."

Bringing up Gretchen's dating situation was a grave mistake. Mom was off.

"Fifteen is too young to be hanging around one boy all the time," she declared as our food arrived. "In fact, fifteen is too young to even be thinking about boys, much less going steady."

"Too young to be thinking about boys!

Mom, what am I supposed to do, shut off my brain? You can't tell me you weren't interested in boys when you were my age."

She bit into her grilled cheese. "My mother wouldn't put up with such foolishness. She'd have tanned my hide if I so much as looked at a boy before I was eighteen. No boys until then, that was the rule."

"What a stupid rule." I never really knew my grandmother; she passed away long ago. "Mom, you told me last year that *this* year, when I was fifteen, things would be better. In fact, you *promised* me. But if I can't date, I might as well still be fourteen."

"I never said any such thing. I said your life would get *easier* — you wouldn't have to fight so, the way you've been the last couple of years. And you aren't. You're more grown up. You've got nice friends, pretty new clothes, a brand-new school to go to — " My mother felt I should be thrilled over Oakton's modern facilities, unable to realize that *no school* was preferable to *new school*.

Whenever we ate in Woolworth's I always ordered the hot turkey sandwich. Usually I'd pile the mashed potatoes on top of the turkey and sprinkle the whole mess with peas and the little cup of cranberry sauce. Today, however, I cut a tiny sliver of the sandwich with my knife and fork and ate it with dignity, hoping to convince my mother I was an adult now, just like her, only not as stodgy.

"If I'm more grown up," I said, daintily wiping cranberry sauce off my mouth, "I ought to be able to go out with a boy."

"What boy?" she demanded, her eyes drilling into mine. "Have you been chasing after some boy, when your father and I told you you can't date until you're sixteen?"

"I haven't been chasing after any boy," I replied truthfully. T.E. couldn't really be classified as a boy and she didn't say anything about chasing after a *teacher*. "But if one did ask me out, what am I supposed to tell him? I'm sorry, but you'll have to wait a year, until I'm sixteen?"

"If he respects you, he'll wait."

"You don't understand. Boys don't care about respect! They just want to go out and have fun. And so do I! Honestly, Mother, you make it sound like a boy has to come to the house and request my hand in marriage before we can go have a slice of pizza."

She rubbed her forehead, as if she had just gotten a terrific headache. "Kobie, I don't want to argue with you about this anymore. No dating till you're sixteen and that's that. If you bring it up again, I'll move it to seventeen. Eat your lunch. I want to get out of he.

I didn't speak to her
instead, I stared out the
stockyard and the Dairy
muddy Bull Run river and w
my mother and I could find
ground. Sure, she'd relented
me expensive material to m .e my fancy
party dress, but she *refused* to bend when
it came to dating. I couldn't make her see
how wrong she was. Our relationship was
like some kind of a dance. One step forward, two steps backward.

Chapter 9

I threw the last of my cinnamon roll into the wire-enclosed aviary, ignoring the sign forbidding people to feed the birds. The finches flitted down from their perches and skittered over to investigate. Gretchen was still eating her bun, chewing slowly, her eyes focused on the bubbling drink machine at the Orange Bowl, where we had bought our midmorning snacks.

"Where to first?" I asked, prodding her out of her reverie. "Spencer's?"

"I guess. I want to buy Doug something funny and something serious. Spencer's is a good place to get a gag gift."

Gretchen had managed to insert Doug's name in every other sentence, no matter how trivial, since her brother Charles had let us off in front of Tyson's Corner mall. Ecstatic since we had nearly a whole day to shop together, *alone,* I decided not to complain, figuring she was sure to purge Doug from her system. After an hour or thereabouts, her Doug mania should taper off.

I wadded my napkin. "Let's get started then."

The mall was decorated to the hilt, swags of evergreens scalloped the storefronts and clusters of mechanical elves bowed and gyrated in the center of the mall. The whole place smelled like a giant candy cane. Christmas was in the air.

I had thirty dollars to spend on presents for my parents, Sandy, and Gretchen. I planned to buy Gretchen's gift while she was elsewhere, hunting for the perfect present for Doug, which, from all outward signs, would take the whole shopping trip.

In Spencer's, Gretchen debated over a rack of fake Snoopy trophies. "Do you think he'd like this one? 'World's Greatest Golfer'? As a souvenir of our third date?" She put the trophy back on the shelf. "No, he might get the wrong idea. The time we played miniature golf was very special — I shouldn't make light of it."

I tried to be helpful, if only to speed things along. "Gretchen, if you like the trophy, get it. It's cute. Anyway, it was only a *date*, not a state funeral."

"You don't understand," she said, forgetting she had asked my advice. "You're not going steady."

Not yet, but I would be very soon. My mother was nearly finished with my dress. As soon as she sewed the last stitch, I'd be able to dazzle T.E. with my ravishing Juliet-like beauty. The man didn't stand a chance.

I bought Sandy a mirrored makeup case before we left Spencer's. It was green plastic, with a mirror in the lid and compartments to hold her lipgloss and eyeshadow. Sandy would love it.

We went on to Hecht's department store, where Gretchen hovered over a selection of men's sweaters.

"What do you think? This one — " she held up a gray and maroon argyle vest " — or this one?" Her second choice was a navy and white crew neck. "Which one do you think he'd look the best in?"

At this point, I thought Doug McNeil would look just fine in a hand-knit strait jacket with a matching muzzle.

"The gray one," I said, wondering when we'd ever get around to buying *my* presents. "It'll go great with his eyes. The other one would make him look like a referee."

"You're right, Kobie. There's just a hint of blue in the weave, the same shade as his eyes. Have you ever really looked at Doug's eyes? I mean really *looked*. They're an incredible color, a deep gray, like the ocean after a storm."

My stomach heaved, either in rebellion over the yeasty cinnamon bun or Gretchen's poetic description. "I can't say I've really noticed Doug's eyes," I replied, "since they're always fastened on you. All I've seen is the back of his head. By the way, did you know his hair is thinning at the crown? He'll probably be bald by the time he's twenty."

"He will not! Doug has nice, thick hair!" she cried indignantly.

Gretchen did not buy the sweater. Our fun day rapidly went downhill as I traipsed after her from one store to the next, unable to resist making nasty little suggestions. ("How about a hammer, Gretch? He could probably use a new one. Here's a pair of G.I. Joe pajamas. I bet he'd love those.")

"Gretchen, don't you have *other* presents besides Doug's to buy?" I asked in Becker's. "Charles, your parents . . . you know, those people who live in the same house with you. Not to mention best friends."

"Shhhh. You're breaking my concentration," she muttered, sweating with indecision over a display of men's jewelry boxes. "This is very important, what I buy Doug. It's our first Christmas together."

"Do you think he's agonizing over what he's getting you? He'll probably zip into People's Drug Store on Christmas Eve five minutes before they close, sniff a couple of colognes, and buy you a bottle of Wind Song or something." I was positive that Edward the Eighth hadn't spent half as much time deliberating over what engagement ring to give Wallis Simpson and *he* had been about to forfeit an entire kingdom.

After two and a half hours, I discovered that mall-shopping was tough on the feet and that a best friend's quest for the Perfect Gift for her steady was taxing on the nerves.

"I quit," I announced in Hoffritz's Cutlery, right in the middle of a Swiss army knife demonstration. "I'm going to get something to eat. You coming or are you going to stay here and count blades?"

Gretchen reluctantly surrendered a nifty forty-nine-dollar job to the clerk. "I know he'd love the one with the can opener and corkscrew, but I don't have enough money," she said sadly.

Observing Gretchen's crazed behavior, I decided that having a boyfriend wasn't worth the trouble and was glad I didn't have one. But then I noticed the way the store lights illuminated the gold and onyx ring hanging around Gertchen's neck.

Whatever Doug put her through, either real or imagined, she wore his ring and the whole world knew she was loved.

I dragged her away from Hoffritz's before she began foaming at the mouth. "Gretchen, this is crazy. It's almost two o'clock and we haven't even eaten lunch yet. Charles will be back to get us at four and I've only bought one piddly present!"

My pep talk must have hit her like a faceful of snow. "I'll go back to Hecht's and buy Doug the gray sweater," she said, and I foolishly believed her. "And then I'll get the little trophy at Spencer's. Then we can go eat."

But we didn't. The sweater still wasn't *quite* what she was looking for. She was certain the perfect present lurked around there *some*place.

What happened next I attribute to the temporary leave of senses one has when deprived of food too long. We staggered past Piercing Pagoda, a little stall in the middle of the fashion court where you can get your ears pierced or just buy earrings. Residue from the sweet roll I had eaten hours ago sent a sugar rush to my brain, causing me to lose control.

I said, "I'm going to get my ears pierced!" Now normally I don't make such hasty decisions, but three hours of watching Gretchen waver over one rotten present had turned me into a rash person.

"Get your ears pierced?" Gretchen repeated. "Do you think you should? Your mother will be furious." Last year when Gretchen had her ears pierced, I pitched a fit to have mine done, too, but naturally my mother wouldn't hear of it.

"I'll worry about that later. Maybe I can hide it from her." I pulled Gretchen into the booth with me.

I picked out a pair of fourteen-karat gold studs and, while the lady prepared the gun that would blast the earrings I had chosen through my lobes, I sat in the chair with the same it's-out-of-my-hands-now feeling I once had when I was buckled into the first car on a roller coaster.

"Sure this won't hurt?" I asked Gretchen anxiously.

She shook her head. "Mine didn't hurt, much."

"The device works so fast you won't feel a thing," the lady assured me.

I closed my eyes. *Whomp!* The impact of the ear piercing gun was like being skewered with a hot wire. "Ow! You lied! I thought you said it wouldn't hurt!"

The lady looked concerned. "You're not going to faint, are you?"

Gretchen prevented me from leaping out of the chair. "Kobie, you can't leave now. She's not finished."

"Yes, she is!" My ear throbbed like a toothache.

"My dear, you can't go away with one ear pierced," the lady soothed. "Your lobes must be a little on the thick side. After you've rested a bit, we'll do the other one."

"Great," I groaned. "First, I've got rotten tonsils. Now I have fat earlobes. Okay, I guess I'm ready." I braced myself. *Whomp!* The second blow nearly drove me through the wall of the booth. Now both ears were killing me.

The lady collected the remainder of my Christmas money. "Come back in an hour. I'll see if there's any bleeding."

Numbly I wobbled out of the stall, my ears feeling as if they were clamped in a vise.

"Kobie, your ears are red as a beet," Gretchen remarked unnecessarily. Every dram of blood in my body must have been flooding my ears. "You'll never hide this from your mother."

"My whole head is busting! All I wanted was pretty gold earrings like Juliet. Instead I feel like I've got spikes jammed in the center of my brain. Plus all my Christmas money is gone, every last penny!" I wailed. "I don't know what came over me. Yes, I do! It's your fault, Gretchen Farris."

"My fault!"

"If we had eaten when we were supposed to, I wouldn't have given in to the temptation. What am I going to *do*?"

Of course, there was no answer to that question. The deed was done. My ears were pierced and there was no way I could unpierce them.

Impending doom (mine) apparently pushed Gretchen into action. While waiting for my last hour on earth to be up, she bought the gray sweater and the Snoopy golf trophy for Doug. Despite my pain, I came close to bopping her over the head with a blunt object. If she had bought those stupid presents when she first saw them, I wouldn't have blown my Christmas savings on pierced ears and earrings and would have more than a few hours to live.

Back at the Piercing Pagoda, the lady instructed me to turn my earrings and to swab the holes with alcohol until they were healed.

"I'll send you a postcard from reform school," I told Gretchen.

"Come on, Kobie. It's not that bad." For her it wasn't. After all, *her* mother had encouraged her to get pierced ears.

"Are you kidding? I bet she's getting my suitcase down from the attic right now."

"Look, there's one of those photograph booths," Gretchen exclaimed. "I've got exactly one dollar left. I'm going to have pictures of myself made for Doug."

Gretchen primped like a movie star preparing for a press conference. "Do I look okay?"

"Gorgeous. Hurry up. Your brother will be here any minute."

The orange curtain fluttered behind her. I studied the sample photos pasted on either side of the doorway. Where did they get such dorky pictures? And how come nobody cut up in them the way Gretchen and I used to when we took them on the boardwalk at Ocean City?

The light flashed for Gretchen's first picture, making me feel nostalgic for those wonderful days on the beach. Our families hadn't rented the beach house last July, the first summer we'd missed in years, because Gretchen had summer school. The second light flashed. I thought of how much we had changed. Sure, we were still best friends, but there seemed to be a gap between us, a chasm that was getting wider and wider. I was never very good at the broad jump. If Gretchen didn't look back soon and give me a hand across, I'd be left behind forever.

Gretchen's third picture was over. Suddenly I had an urge to recapture a little of our carefree past, bring back those long summers at the beach.

I stormed through the curtain. Gretchen

squealed, "Kobie, what are you doing?"

"What does it look like? Move over," I said, squeezing beside her on the bench. I had forgotten how little those booths were inside. Either that or we had gotten a lot bigger.

I grimaced at the hidden camera. "Come on, Gretch. Ham it up. This is the last shot." We always mugged on the final shot.

Giggling, Gretchen pushed up her nose and pulled down her bottom eyelids with one hand, her old standby Pekingese face. I twisted my mouth, stuck out my tongue, and crossed my eyes just as the flash went off.

When the processed strip dropped into the basket, still damp, Gretchen snatched it out. "Oh, Kobie, look at us!" We both screamed with laughter.

"That's our best gross picture yet!" I said. "Somebody ought to elect this to the Horrible Picture Hall of Fame. We look just like we did a few years ago."

"Yes, we do, don't we?" Gretchen agreed. Then she frowned at the studio-perfect poses of herself alone. "Which one should I have framed for Doug? The first one — no, maybe the third. My ring shows up better in that one, don't you think?"

She put the picture strip in her purse and we walked back to the aviary court to wait for her brother.

Chapter 10

"I asked my mother if I could get my ears pierced and she said no," Sandy remarked at lunch one day. "We don't have the money, she said."

"That's my mother's answer for anything I want," I replied. "Even if I want something that's *free* she claims we don't have the money. Of course, you can't believe them. Grown-ups work. They get a paycheck. But they think we still fall for that old line. Can I have your bread?"

Sandy was generously dividing her lunch with me. Half her Salisbury steak, half the potatoes, half the corn which she was laboriously counting kernel by kernel to make sure she wouldn't cheat me. I couldn't afford to buy my lunch this week or next week either. Since I had squandered my Christmas savings at the Piercing Pagoda, I was hoarding my lunch money to buy my mother and father a Christmas present. I was forced to rely on the kindness of strangers or starve.

Sandy pushed a gravy-soaked napkin over to me. "If you want more, just take it off my plate, but it should be even."

"It couldn't be more even if you had used a computer." But I ate hungrily.

"I'm dying to have pierced ears," Sandy said wistfully. "Then I'll be just like you."

"Do you want a prison uniform and a number around your neck just like me, too?"

"Your mother didn't get that upset."

Actually, she didn't. And my mother's basic reaction to my little adventures was well-known; it would have made the six o'clock news. When I came home from the mall with inflamed ears, new gold earrings, and guilt blazoned across my face, my mother did not rant and scream and lecture as I expected.

Instead she froze me with an icy stare and said only, "I'm disappointed in you, Kobie," before launching into a chilly description of the effects of blood poisoning, evidently the direct result of disobeying your mother and spending your Christmas money on yourself.

"I don't know why you girls are so anxious to get holes in your earlobes," Eddie Showalter said, shading the wings of a DC-9 he was drawing in the margin of his science book. Then, with a quick apologetic glance at me, he added, "Except your earrings look nice, Kobie."

"Thanks, but I'm paying for them dearly." I gobbled my half of Sandy's lunch so I could get to work. Because of my cash flow problem, I was drawing sketches from *Lady and the Tramp* to give as Christmas presents. For my mother, the spaghetti dinner scene I let Stuart have; and for my father, a scene outside Tony's restaurant, where the two dogs go for their date, both pictures duplicated from my portfolio. At the end of two lunchless weeks, I thought I'd have enough money to buy picture frames.

Eddie admired the Tony's restaurant sketch. "This is really good. The way you've got the light from the windows falling into the street."

"I must have done that over a hundred times," I confessed. "Lighting is so hard to do."

"Did you hear about Gretchen?" Sandy asked before Eddie and I lapsed into artist's talk.

"If you mean Patty Binninger's party, I've heard more about it than I want to." The story I had given my mother about Gretchen having a New Year's Eve party had come true, sort of. Gretchen wasn't having a party, but she and Doug had been *invited* to one at Patty Binninger's house, leaving you-know-who to stay at home wearing emerald velvet and lace ruffles.

"Maybe you'll get your invitation today," Eddie said. "Patty's in my science class. She's still asking people."

"And maybe the Queen of England is really my cousin," I said sadly. "Patty is only asking *couples* to her party, *popular* couples."

"Kobie's right," Sandy agreed. "Patty is awful stuck-up. In gym the other day I was trying to fix my hair and she butt right in front of me, like I wasn't even there."

"That's the way it is with those girls. We don't exist, according to them." I fished a piece of Aspergum, cleverly disguised in a regular chewing gum wrapper, from my purse. To add to my other woes, I had tonsillitis again. I hadn't told my mother yet, figuring she'd blame this new attack on my stupid ears.

"Can I have some?" Sandy held out her hand.

I could hardly refuse her, not after she'd donated half her lunch to Feed Kobie Roberts Week. She unwrapped the gum and popped it in her mouth. Aspergum wouldn't hurt her, just make her throat a little numb. I waited for Eddie to ask for a piece too, but when he didn't, I put the pack in by purse, hoping he wouldn't think I was stingy. I really needed the stuff for my throat.

"New Year's Eve isn't everything," he said, still locked in the old conversation. Sometimes Eddie was slow. "My folks just stay home and watch that special TV program until midnight."

"So do mine," Sandy said.

Mine didn't even do that. "It's just a night like any other night," my father always said before going to bed at his regular time. I was probably the only living soul in the United States who has never seen the celebration in Times Square.

"We throw a big eggnog party — " I started to lie when Sandy grabbed my arm.

"Look! Isn't that Stuart? And *Rosemary Swan?* What are *they* doing together?"

I blinked twice. Stuart Buckley and Rosemary Swan, big as life at the next table. Stuart was actually helping Rosemary sit down without yanking the chair out from under her, the way he did to me one time. He hovered around her like a head waiter, unloading her tray, unfolding her napkin. I was surprised he didn't taste her food or open her milk carton.

"What a disgusting spectacle." I made vomiting motions. "Stuart's gone over the edge."

"What's he see in her?" Sandy wanted to know.

"What's she see in *him*, you mean." I wondered how Stuart managed to snag fickle Rosemary. He was certainly having better success with her than I was with T.E. My true love avoided me. At first I couldn't believe it, that a teacher would actually run away from a student, but he changed course whenever he saw me coming. Sandy said his love for me was evident and the look on his face was one of anguished torment. His facial expression looked more like irritation to me, but you never could tell with this love business.

"Stuart must be a riot," Sandy said. Rosemary was laughing so hard she could barely eat.

I watched them glumly, faintly aware of a strange emotion — could it be *jealousy?* Ever since Stuart asked me for my drawing, I kind of thought he might be interested in *me*. Not that I would consider going out with him for a minute. Yet all those questions he pestered me about — what girls like in boys and what did I think of him — he could have been pretending to like Rosemary as a trick to find out how *I* felt about him. At least, that's what I thought.

"Cheer up," Eddie said. "Christmas is coming."

As it turned out, I had little reason to be cheerful, Christmas or no Christmas. I went back to the doctor for my tonsillitis, which was so bad this time, swallowing brought new levels in pain. Dr. Wampler told my mother that my infections might get worse if my rotten tonsils didn't come out soon, but he agreed with my mother that we could wait a while longer before making a decision. For a second there, I thought he was going to take them out right in his office.

My mother mellowed again, fixing me custards and soups, the pierced ear incident apparently forgiven. Christmas Eve was a real bummer. I was too sick to decorate the tree. From the couch, I directed my mother in the correct placement of the ornaments, but she didn't follow orders very well and kept wanting to put my grandmother's star-shaped bulb near the bottom of the tree instead of near the top where it belonged, and drape the tinsel strand by strand rather than flinging it over the branches. As a result, our tree had an overdone, lopsided appearance.

When my father came home, he pronounced our tree lots nicer than the national Christmas tree and handed me a sack of my favorite old-fashioned peppermint sticks. I couldn't eat the candy, which depressed me so much I refused to join my parents in our Christmas Eve ritual of opening one gift each. Instead I sulked in the glow of the twinkling lights, feeling extremely sorry for myself and positive I was the only sick person on the planet. Fifteen, at last, and I was having the rottenest year imaginable.

Christmas Day was even worse. My parents had their traditional oyster stew for breakfast. Sitting across from those disgusting gray lumps bobbing in milk at seven in the morning was hard enough to take in good health. My mother also served French toast, which was too tough for me to swallow, so I had that most festive of all Christmas dishes, oatmeal.

Usually I wolf down breakfast so I can descend on the pile of presents heaped under the tree, but this year I shambled into the living room, coughing, and pulling my bathrobe around me. Listlessly, I opened my presents. My mother got me black patent leather pumps and a matching purse, plus white lacy stockings to wear with my fancy dress.

"I thought you were going to Gretchen's party," she said. "But Clare tells me she isn't having a party. Doug is taking her to some girl's house in Annandale."

"Patty Binninger's," I sniffed. "She's having the party, not Gretchen. And I wasn't invited."

"You're too sick to think about going out next week anyway."

My father's gift was a real surprise: a leather-cased manicure set. I stared at the gleaming implements neatly tucked into elastic straps.

"This is great! I love it. And it goes with Sandy's present." Sandy had given me the pale pink lipgloss and nail polish from the *Seventeen* ad, the one that inaugurated my ruffles-and-ribbons campaign to win T.E.

My father was unwrapping his present from me, a package that had the same suspicious shape as my mother's from me. "You're growing up more every day. I thought you could use something to make your fingernails pretty."

My fingernails were hopelessly stubby and, unless the kit contained a magic growth potion, they would remain that way despite my arsenal of cuticle pushers and nail buffers. But I kissed my father and told him again how much I adored his present.

Both he and my mother acted pleased with their framed sketches, my mother going so far as to take down the Spanish dancer prints on either side of the fireplace and hang up my pictures. Still, I felt shabby. I had received wonderful, grown-up presents, yet I had resorted to giving dowdy homemade gifts, because I had greedily spent my Christmas money on myself.

"Homemade presents are the best kind," my father said.

"Anybody can run out and buy something," my mother put in, "but making something takes time and thought."

I shuffled back to my couch, unable to eke out the teeniest feeling of goodwill from my shriveled, un-Christmasy heart.

Gretchen breezed by on her way to have Christmas dinner at Doug's. She burst into our too-warm living room, wreathed in a new mohair muffler and bringing in draughts of crisp, cold air. After wishing my parents a happy holiday and giving my mother a fruitcake from her mother, she handed me a tiny white box.

By then I had dissolved into a jellied mass of self-pity. Two frail tears trickled down my cheeks.

"Gretchen," I whispered, though I talked normally and even yelled at my mother up to the instant Gretchen had walked in, "I didn't get you anything. I didn't have any money. It was all I could do to scrape together enough to buy picture frames."

"So I'm one up on you," she said. "Now I'm ahead of you for the first time since second grade. Open it!"

Inside, anchored to a puff of cotton, was a pair of tiny silver hoops.

"They're beautiful! Where did you get them?"

She grinned at my pleasure. "International Bazaar. Doug helped me pick them out. See what he gave me?" She lifted her leg to display a delicate silver chain clasped around her stockinged ankle. "An ankle bracelet. Isn't it neat?"

The sight of such an intimate gift made me choke with envy. When I could speak, I said something crummy. "A *slave* bracelet. That's what they call those. He's your master and you're his slave."

"Kobie! What's the matter with you? It's an ankle bracelet, that's all."

"I'm sorry," I said, and meant it. "It's very pretty. Did Doug like his sweater?"

"He's supposed to be wearing it today."

"Oh, that's right. You're going to his house for dinner. Well, I hope you have a nice time."

"Doug says his folks are dying to meet me. Gotta run. Charles is waiting." She said good-bye to my folks and dashed back out again.

By New Year's Eve I was better, but my fate had already been decided. "Make the best of it," my mother suggested.

I spent the evening alone in my room, working on the final sketch for my Lady and the Tramp portfolio, a background scene of a Victorian house, elaborate with carving and towers, steeped in snow. It was the most ambitious picture in my whole portfolio, the showcase picture that would land me a job when I arrived in Burbank, California, two years from now.

Listening to the radio countdown of the Top 100 songs of the year helped pass the time. I wrote them down in my notebook as the dj announced each song, and made a private bet with myself which song would be number one. My fancy dress, starched and pressed, hung from the doorframe of my closet, the new patent leather pumps positioned beneath.

As the evening dragged on, it grew darker outside and I quit drawing because I didn't feel like switching on the lamp. Crouched in the dim light of the radio dial, I thought about Gretchen and Doug at Patty Binninger's. My white lace dress glowed eerily in the half-light, like the ghost of a young girl who had missed a long-ago New Year's Eve party.

Chapter 11

I was informed of Stuart's deceit during our first week of driver's ed.

"Rosemary was showing everybody that card in homeroom," Sandy announced, keeping a watchful eye out for the teacher. "I accidently kicked my pen under Rosemary's desk so I could get a better look. It was two dogs eating spaghetti, just like the picture you were drawing for your mother. Stuart had made it like a card with a poem inside and signed his name. I couldn't read the poem, but that was his signature, all right."

Now I knew why Stuart hadn't wanted me to sign my drawing. "Worth more," indeed. The little rat planned to pass off my picture as his own the whole time.

"What are you going to do?" Sandy asked.

"I don't know yet. Boil him in oil,

maybe. No, that's too fast. The end ought to be slow and excruciating."

"Girls!" Miss Barlow glared at me and Sandy. "Are you paying attention? We're going to have a test and I expect you both to make A's."

Miss Barlow was expecting a lot. Despite a burning desire to learn how to drive, neither Sandy nor I were getting much out of classroom driver's training. So far we had both flunked a quiz based on state driving laws. We studied the pamphlet backward and forward, but all those regulations eluded us. Questions like, "When you are making a left turn, do you (a) signal, look in the mirror, then move over to the left of the center line when traffic allows, (b) signal and get over as quickly as possible, or (c) throw up your hands and hope that your car will somehow manage to drift into the left lane."

Sandy poked me with her pencil. "How many feet in a car length?"

"You're asking me? My driving information is mixed up with my mother's hysteria when she learned to drive last year. All I know is when you back out of a Seven-Eleven lot, you do *not* hit the sheriff, who might be walking behind your car just then."

"Your mother did that?"

I nodded. "Luckily, the sheriff jumped

out of the way or he would have been a goner. He could have had her permit revoked, but I guess he felt sorry for her. He told Mom when she got her license to let him know and he'd stay off the road the days she was out."

Gretchen was using the simulator. We all had to practice braking. From my seat in the back, I could see Gretchen's right foot pouncing from the gas to the brake pedals as she stared at the "windshield," actually a projection screen playing a movie. The movie made it seem like you were driving down a real street, passing houses and stuff, when all of sudden a child's ball would appear and you were supposed to stop.

I was so bad that I hated to think how many rubber balls I hit and innocent kids I nearly ran down.

Gretchen braked correctly every time, the silver ankle chain winking in the sun as she pumped first one pedal and then the other.

"Very good, Gretchen," Miss Barlow commented. High praise from a teacher who inscribed "Try to do better next time" on papers with perfect marks.

Gretchen returned to her seat in front of me, her face flushed from the compliment. "Boy, this driving is harder than I thought."

"At least you didn't come away with a record like I did."

"You'll catch on, Kobie," she said, confident because she had done so well.

Beside me, Sandy ripped a page from her driver's ed notebook, labeled "Sondra K. Robertson," and wrote, *I know how to get T.E.'s home address. Interested?*

I wrote back, *Does the sun rise in the east?*

Meet me at the main office before sixth, she replied.

Three periods from now. Fine with me. I still had a score to settle with a creepy little art swindler.

Stuart ambled into French, whistling. Rosemary towered over him. They made a comical couple, like Mutt and Jeff. After repeated reprimands from Mrs. Hildebrandt, he finally tore himself away from Rosemary's side.

He plopped down in his own desk and sighed happily. "Great day, isn't it, Kobie?"

I didn't answer.

"The crocuses are coming up in the courtyard," he rattled on. "Rosemary and I went out to see them at lunchtime. The juniors put benches out there. It'll be strictly a senior courtyard next year so you ought to go while you can."

I stared stonily at my French book.

He tugged a lock of my hair, trying to tease me into a smile. "Ko-bee. Are you in there? Look at your old friend Stuart. Come on."

Turning my head, I glowered at him so hard my eyes hurt.

He withdrew his hand swiftly, frightened I might bite him. "What a face! Better watch out, it could freeze that way."

I compressed my vision into twin lasers, riveting Stuart to the spot. I hoped to vaporize the little weasel into a confession.

"Quit staring at me like that. What's bugging you?"

"I think you know."

"I *don't* know."

"Don't play dumb, Stuart. I know why you asked for my drawing, unsigned. You made it into a card for Rosemary and she thinks *you* drew the picture."

He shrugged. "Yeah, so what?"

"So *what?*" Was there no limit to Stuart's nerve? Next he'd be forging my name on checks. "You told me you wanted one of my drawings as a keepsake. You didn't say anything about giving it to the Amazon Queen. That was a dirty, underhanded, double-dealing trick and I have a good mind to tell Rosemary the truth."

Stuart actually appeared jittery. "You're not, are you, Kobie? You wouldn't do that to me? Rosemary has just started to like me. You wouldn't ruin it for me by squealing, would you?"

"No," I said after a minute. "I won't say a word, Stuart."

"Great! You're just terrific, Kobie. I always knew you were!"

What Stuart didn't know was that Just Terrific Kobie wasn't going to say a word to *him* again. He had really hurt me with this betrayal and I wanted nothing to do with Stuart Buckley as long as I lived.

Sandy was waiting for me outside the main office. "You stay here," she said. "I'll only be a sec." She disappeared into the office, leaving me to hang around the bulletin board.

I felt T.E.'s presence before I actually saw him. His back was to me as he studied the basketball schedule. I feasted my eyes on him, shamelessly drinking in every detail, the blond highlights in his hair, the softness of his powder-blue sweater, the way his slacks broke over the instep of his loafers, just so. How could anyone that gorgeous breathe and walk around like the rest of us mortals?

Then, as if sensing me, he turned around. His expression went from uncertainty to concern as he recognized me. Without so much as a nod, he stepped into the office, practically running into Sandy, who was coming out.

"I got it!" She waved a slip of paper. "Did you see T.E.'s face just now? He's weakening, Kobie. He'll soon be yours."

I wasn't so sure about that.

"I also got his first name," Sandy said. "Want to hear it? Harold!"

"Harold? Harold Brown? Are you sure that's *my* Mr. Brown?" Harold wasn't at all manly, like Andrew or Montgomery. Harold wasn't a name that went with turquoise eyes. Still, T.E. couldn't help what his parents named him.

"There's only one Mr. Brown who teaches ninth-grade shop," Sandy said. "And he lives at 415 Sycamore in Fairfax."

Four-fifteen Sycamore, an elegant-sounding address, even if his name *was* Harold. I had to see T.E.'s house. Just knowing where he lived would bring him closer to me.

It took every ounce of my powers, but I lured Gretchen away from Doug Saturday morning with a trumped-up excuse that we *had* to go to the library. Charles drove us.

I had diligently studied my father's map the night before to pinpoint the exact location of T.E.'s street. Halfway there I told Charles, "I know a shortcut. Take a right here and we'll wind up in back of the library."

"But this road goes *away* from the library," Charles protested, turning right anyway. Gretchen's brother was neat. If I had to choose an older brother, it would be somebody like Charles. Although he took classes at NOVA, the community college, he had a wonderful tolerance for the whims of sophomore girls.

"This street," I said, pointing. "Turn here, on Sycamore."

Gretchen flashed me her fishy eye. I hadn't filled her in on my scheme, but I think she figured what I was up to. We'd been friends too long not to understand how each other's brains worked.

"You sure this comes out at the library?" Charles coasted down the residential lane.

I was busy looking at the house numbers. Then I spied *his* house, a brick bungalow with green awnings. His station wagon was parked in the driveway, a couple of metal garbage cans were stacked just outside the front gate. How domestic and cozy. It was even better than elegant. Any second T.E. could come out and pick up his newspaper and he'd see me . . . *riding* down his street. Suddenly, it was vital that I *drive* past his house. When he came out, I didn't want to be slumped in the backseat like a little kid.

"Charles!" I screeched, startling him so he nearly ran up on the sidewalk. "Let me drive!"

"What? Are you nuts? You don't know how to drive."

"Yes, I do!" Never mind that Miss Barlow had tagged me Menace of the Highway. "You give Gretchen steering lessons. Won't you give me one? My parents won't let me use their precious old car." That was true. Whenever I mentioned taking a ride to show off my new skills, my father made noises about not having enough insurance.

Charles sighed, weakening. "Kobie, if anything happens to you and Gretchen I'm responsible — " I knew why he was leery. Two years ago he was driving on a rain-slicked road when the car hit a tree and caused Gretchen to hurl through the windshield. Gretchen said even now Charles sweated bullets when he gave her steering lessons in their driveway.

"Nothing will happen," I said. "I'm just going to drive to that stop sign. Just that short distance. That's all."

"All right," Charles relented. He put the car in park but left the engine running while we switched places. Gretchen climbed into the backseat. She didn't say a word, but I could feel disapproval radiating from her.

I gripped the wheel like a life preserver while Charles adjusted my seat so I could reach the floor controls. I still had trouble seeing over the dash. If I didn't grow and *soon*, my driving days would be confined to go-carts and tricycles.

"Put your foot on the clutch," Charles instructed, "put it into first, then let the clutch out slowly as you accelerate."

"Could you run that by me again?"

"I thought you said you practiced this."

"Oh, I have," I replied, indicating I had been driving straight-stick since infancy. With my left foot, I fumbled with the pedals on the floor, struggling to remember if our classroom simulator even had a clutch pedal.

"That's the brake," Charles said.

"I know! I'm just making sure it works. Uh, which way is first?"

He leaned over and pushed the gearshift lever over and down a notch. "Kobie, I think you'd better forget this today."

"No! I'm okay. This car is different from my — from the one I'm used to, is all."

"Gearboxes are the *same* in cars with manual transmissions. You're in first. Put the clutch to the floor and let it out slow — "

I jammed the pedal to the floor and let it out with a jerk. The car idled forward about a centimeter, then stalled. Scared out of my wits, I screamed, "What'll I do?"

Charles rolled his eyes skyward. "Start the engine and try again."

I turned the key too far and the engine made a horrible grinding sound. Charles looked as if he might cry and I didn't blame him. His car was his pride and joy.

"Sorry." This time when I let out the clutch and the car coughed, preparing to stall, I pounded the clutch to the floor again, preventing the engine from dying.

"The gas!" Charles yelled. "Give it some gas. Let off the clutch!"

I *couldn't* let off the clutch. My foot had developed a will of its own, jackhammering the clutch to the floor, then jerking back like a piston, slamming, jerking, until the car bucked like a bee-stung bronco.

Finally the car panted to a halt, undoubtedly exhausted. We had progressed a grand total of twelve inches. I felt like I had just spent a month in a blender.

Charles was opening the passenger door. "Kobie, let's do this some other time. You really aren't — "

I bobbed up and down in the driver's seat. "Please, Charles! Let me try again. I think I have it now. Please, give me another chance!"

"Come on, Charles." Gretchen loyally came to my defense. "Let her try again. I haven't had this much fun since the county fair last summer."

Charles closed the door. "Three strikes and you're out, Kobie. We'll try it once more. Get your foot on the *gas*. That's what makes a car go."

This time I would drive smoothly past

T.E.'s house, showing the love of my life my professional technique. "He just has to see me," I muttered to myself.

"It's February," Gretchen said, linked to my train of thought as always. "Why would he be outdoors?"

"Then maybe he'll see me from the window."

"Eyes on the road!" Charles shouted. "Clutch to the floor, Kobie, ease it out at the same time giving it some gas."

I squashed the pedal to the floor but as I started to let it out, the car trembled, wanting to cut off again. Whipping my foot off the clutch, I hit the gas so hard the wheels spun and laid a strip of smoking rubber. The car bounded forward with a bone-jarring lurch. The three of us sat terrified as we bore down on 415 Sycamore with the speed of a runaway locomotive. All I could think was that the love of my life would certainly get a good look at me as we plowed into his living room.

The car steamrolled over something crunchy, as if the grill were being chewed in a meat grinder. Charles reached over and shut off the ignition.

"We just demolished that man's trash cans," he reported gloomily. "Not to mention the tires and drive shaft of my car. When you strike out, Kobie Roberts, you *really* strike out."

Chapter 12

"Stuart tells me you're not speaking to him," Gretchen said a few days later in typing. She shifted the carriage to check the letter Mrs. Antle had just dictated to us at machine-gun velocity.

"That's right, I'm not," I said. "Why should I, after what he did?"

"I know what he did was terrible, but aren't you carrying this revenge thing too far? That was ages ago."

"A true friend doesn't betray another friend," I said loftily. "I can stand anything but dishonesty."

"I never realized you were so hard-nosed, Kobie. I always thought you were easygoing."

"Not any more." I cranked the platen of my typewriter to look over my own letter. *dearmrjones*, I had typed. *thisisinresponsetoyourtelephonecalloflastfriday* —

Mrs. Antle had dictated so fast, I didn't have time to capitalize or put in spaces. I could almost see the glee on Mrs. Antle's face as she scratched a big fat D- on my paper.

"Darn." Gretchen frowned. "I transposed twice. Typos count ten points."

I mentally revised my D- into a graphline that dived off the chart. My mother had suggested that I take business courses. "You can always be a secretary," she said last summer when we were planning my classes. "I know my little girl has her heart set on going to college, but we simply can't afford it, Kobie, unless you win a scholarship."

Actually, her little girl's heart was set on going to Walt Disney Studios in Burbank, California, approximately twelve seconds after graduation. I went along with my mother, believing I could get a job for a few weeks as a secretary until I earned enough to buy an airplane ticket to California. Now, adding up the jillions of typos in my letter, I realized my job opportunities would be severely restricted to bosses who didn't speak English, began every letter with "This is in response to your telephone call of last Friday," and were, in addition, a little soft in the head.

Gretchen glanced over at my paper. "Your space bar get stuck or what?"

136

I didn't answer. Today, despite my troubles in typing, I felt very self-contained. I knew exactly what I was doing. I wasn't bothered by Stuart's feeble attempts to talk me into making up. I didn't even care that Gretchen hardly ever called me anymore; I had finally accepted her as more or less a permanent attachment to Doug McNeil.

My newfound peace was due to a secret plan. By second period tomorrow, T.E. would pledge his love to me. I was banking on it.

"Absolutely not," my mother said the next morning. "You are not going to school wearing a skimpy party dress!"

"But, Mom, I *have* to. We're having Paris day in French and I'm supposed to be one of those runway models like they have in Paris fashion shows." The fib, concocted in bed last night, rolled out with practiced ease. I had chosen this day very carefully. It was February 14, Valentine's Day. The date, along with my party dress, were important parts of my plan.

"Well, you can be a Paris runway model in your red blouse and a skirt. You're not wearing that party dress to school and that's final, Kobie." She stalked off to reheat my breakfast.

All was not lost. I had too much at stake

to let a minor obstacle like my mother block my way. Humming, I brushed more "Iced Espresso" eyeshadow on my eyelids until my eyes looked sultry.

The lace dress skimmed over my head as I slipped it on. It felt deliciously light and cool, after I had been encased in layers of wool for so many weeks. From my pile of uglies next to my bureau I plucked out an awful button-down-the-front number and put it on over my party dress. The effect was lumpy, but I would get past my mother. I stuffed my white lace stockings in my purse, then dropped my black patent leather pumps in the deep pockets of my stadium coat.

"No time for breakfast," I told my mother.

"Kobie, what have you got on? That dress needs ironing."

"It needs dynamiting," I replied tartly. "If I can't wear my party dress to school, then I'm going looking as dowdy as possible. I hope you realize this means I can't be in the fashion show." I stomped out the door without saying good-bye.

The monkey wrench my mother tried to throw in my plan caused barely a ripple. Phase One had been accomplished with only a slight hitch. On the bus the second fib tripped off my tongue.

"I have an appointment with my counselor during first," I said to Gretchen, who clasped an enormous red cardboard heart on top of her books. Doug's Valentine, undoubtably. "Tell Mrs. Antle I'll bring her a note tomorrow." That is, if I was still in town. T.E. might impulsively swoop me off to the Caribbean.

I didn't reveal my plan to Gretchen. She probably wouldn't have cared. Sandy would have been avidly interested, but I hadn't told her, either, for a different reason. Sandy was a blabbermouth and my plan hinged on the element of surprise.

As soon as the bus hesitated by the curb, I catapulted myself into the school like a guided missile, aiming for the nearest girls' room. Locked in a stall, I unbuttoned the dress, stashed it behind the toilet, stripped off my regular hose and put on the lacy white stockings, traded my loafers for the patent leather pumps. Phase Two completed.

The image in the mirror over the sinks astonished me. A vision in white emerged from the stall, a living Valentine with a halo of curly hair, long coltish legs, big dark eyes. Plain old Kobie Roberts was transformed into the new, improved, and utterly romantic Kobie Roberts. T.E. was a sure goner. On to Phase Three.

I stayed in the bathroom until the late bell for first period rang. When I was certain classes had started, I walked to the industrial arts wing, my stomach fizzy with anticipation.

Someone had left open the big double doors that led to the outside unloading platform. A stiff winter breeze billowed the wispy sleeves of my dress. Chiffon, I discovered, was about as warm as cheesecloth, but even an arctic wind couldn't dent my sense of purpose. I marched to T.E.'s classroom with my head high, picturing his expression when he saw me. His turquoise eyes would bulge with disbelief, then fill with true love as he realized he couldn't deny it another instant. He might even propose without further delay.

Skilsaws whirred from behind the closed doors of T.E.'s shop class. I knocked, but evidently no one heard me over the racket. I knocked louder and a boy wearing safety goggles came to the door.

"Yeah?" he asked, unimpressed with my angelic finery.

"I have a message for T — I mean, Mr. Brown," I stammered.

"He's busy. What is it? I'll give it to him."

"No! I have to do it! I — it's personal." My throat suddenly felt lined in cotton.

The kid yelled, "Mr. Brown! Some girl here to see you!"

"Don't cut off any fingers until I get

back," a man's voice said. The door opened wider and there he was. "Can I help you?"

My heart stopped. Just stopped cold, like a conked-out battery. I had no idea what I was going to say. With all my detailed scheming, I had never planned what I would say to *him*. It ought to be something devastating, to go with my devastating outfit. Instead, I opened and closed my mouth like a fish out of water.

T.E.'s turquoise eyes did not bulge in amazement but the veins on his neck did. His face got redder than Gretchen's Valentine card. At first I thought he was blushing but then it occurred to me he was closer to having a stroke.

"You — !" he accused and I quaked, thinking he had recognized me as the culprit who ran over his garbage cans. "I just can't — " Abruptly he pushed past me, striding down the hall away from his class, and students in danger of slicing off their fingers, away from me.

I stood rooted to the floor.

"Boy," said the goggle-eyed kid. "That must have been some message."

His taunting words jarred me. I fled down the corridor to the open doors and out onto the delivery platform. In a flurry of flying lace, I leaped from the concrete dock to the grassy area between a parked milk truck and the building. Curled up against the bricks, my knees pressed to my chest, I let the sobs go.

What was the matter with T.E.? Why did he run like that? He acted as if the sight of me in my beautiful white dress was the straw that broke the camel's back. He was supposed to fall madly in love with me, as in forever till there is no end, not run away.

I cried until no more tears were left and my makeup was thoroughly smeared. I was half-frozen, but I didn't care. If only I could stay there the rest of the day. The rest of my life, even. How could I go back inside, knowing I had made such a fool of myself?

Practicality won. By the time the second-period bell shrilled, my teeth were clacking like castenets from my shivering. I considered faking a tonsillitis attack and calling my mother to come get me, but then she would see me in the very dress she'd expressly forbidden me to wear to school. No, I would have to return to my classes. Much as I wanted, I couldn't run away like T.E. had and I couldn't sit outside all day.

Feeling worse than the time last year when I was hauled back to school in a squad car, I brushed dirt off the tiers of ruffled lace and went back in. The old button-down-the-front dress I had stuffed behind the toilet in the girls' room was still there. I put it on over my party dress, splashed cold water on my face to rinse away the mascara streaks, then walked slowly to English.

I moved through my classes like a robot, ignoring barbs about my sack dress, refusing to participate in discussions, never volunteering answers. I skipped lunch and got a pass for the library instead, where I skulked behind the stacks. I didn't want to see anybody I knew, especially Sandy. After all, she had masterminded this whole romance business.

A ball of hate formed in the spot vacated by the warm feelings I'd had for T.E. I hated Sandy for getting me in trouble, and Stuart for being such a sneak, and my mother for her rules about dating, and Gretchen-and-Doug for being so much in love, and T.E. for destroying my dreams. Deep down inside, like a worm buried in an apple, I also hated myself.

A day already tainted by a rejection from my true love could not possibly get worse. Or so I thought.

I walked into math. I had dreaded this class most of all. T.E.'s shop class was just around the corner. Frequently, my algebra teacher and T.E. would be chatting in the hall.

Today, though, I didn't see either T.E. or my math teacher. The kids were antsy, wondering where Mr. Bell was. Sandy jabbed me in the back with the eraser end of her pencil.

"What's with you? You look terrible." I knew she meant the awful dress I had on over my party dress but was too tactful to come right out and say so.

"That's my natural state," I replied.

"How come you didn't show up for lunch? Eddie was worried about you."

"*Eddie* was worried? What about you? Weren't you worried?"

"Yeah, I was. You didn't speak to me or Gretchen in driver's ed. We've hardly seen you all day. What's up?"

"Nothing's up. In fact, it's all over. Between me and T.E. Your dumb idea didn't work. I don't know why I bothered listening to you."

"What are you talking about?" She poked me with her pencil eraser again, but I didn't respond.

Mr. Bell came in. "Sorry I'm late," he said. "I've been helping a friend with a problem." He picked up the attendance book, then slammed it back on his desk, obviously upset.

Mr. Bell was the kind of teacher who liked to share whatever was on his mind. On Mondays, he often told us what he did over the weekend. If he read an article in the *Post* that disturbed him, he confided his views to us.

Now he paced in front of the blackboard, as if wrestling over whether to tell us what was bothering him. A prickly sensation crawled along my arms. Suddenly I knew what he was going to say.

He sucked in a deep breath. The class was absolutely silent.

"This friend of mine is a teacher here in his first year of teaching," he began. "Nice young fella. For the longest time, this teacher has been chased by a young girl, a student. *Tormenting* him, for weeks. My friend isn't used to dealing with a situation like this. Today, something happened that really got to him. I've been in the lounge, advising him on how to handle the problem next time."

My whole body felt hot. That was *me* Mr. Bell was talking about. *I* was the young girl tormenting his friend. T.E. must have told Mr. Bell that the girl bothering him was in his sixth-period math class. Even if T.E. hadn't told him, all Mr. Bell had to do was look over and see guilt branded across my face!

"Who's the girl?" a boy asked.

"Who she is doesn't matter," Mr. Bell said, warming up to his subject. "What is important is this teacher's feelings. That girl didn't consider his feelings when she followed him around." What about *my* feelings? "I don't think you people realize how difficult it is for teachers —"

Sick to my stomach, I blotted out his speech. Sandy nudged me with her pencil, sharp persistent punches. I didn't turn around.

"That's you!" she whispered. "He's talking about *you*, isn't he?"

"Be quiet!"

"Kobie, I feel awful! I only wanted to fix you up with T.E. I never meant to get you in trouble."

"Forget it," I said out of the corner of my mouth.

"But you're mad at me."

"No, I'm not." I really wasn't, I decided. What happened today wasn't her fault. She didn't make me go to T.E.'s class dressed in white.

Mr. Bell's lecture about how sometimes students were inconsiderate to teachers droned on and on. I hunched my shoulder blades against his tirade, mortified to the core. I couldn't have been more humiliated if I had been put in stocks in the public square and flogged.

Chapter 13

If I kept a journal, I would have recorded that fifteen, the year things were supposed to get better, was the year I uncovered the Big Lie. Big Lies are myths made up by grown-ups. Peel away the soft, fluffy outer shell of these myths and you find a hard grain of truth.

The first Big Lie I unmasked was about love, that even if you love someone, there's no guarantee he will love you back. The second Big Lie concerned the old adage that when you have your tonsils removed, you can have all the ice cream you want. I had plenty of time to contemplate lies and truths, especially the ice cream one, from my bed in Prince William Hospital.

Thanks to the escapade on Valentine's Day, I came down with the worst case of tonsillitis ever, prompting Dr. Wampler to recommend surgery. My mother wanted to wait until Spring Break, but that was almost a month away. So this morning I was operated on and woke up, groggy and tonsil-less, about an hour ago, furious at being betrayed by an adult for the second time in a week.

"I don't *want* any," I whined in a cracked voice to my mother, who was trying to force-feed strawberry ice cream down my throat. "I can't swallow!"

"You can swallow this," she insisted. "It's soft and cool. It'll glide right down."

I had already tried some and hadn't liked it. Petulantly, I shoved the spoon aside. "I'm hungry. I want real food. I want a hamburger."

"Forget the hamburger." My mother set the ice cream dish on my over-the-bed tray with a clatter. "You can only have soft foods for a while, like custard and cereal. And nothing but ice cream today. Doctor's orders."

I flung myself back on the pillows. My throat felt raw and incredibly sore, but did I get any sympathy? No. Just somebody poking a bunch of dumb ice cream in my face and telling me I had to live on oatmeal the rest of my life. I wished I was dead. Then I looked over in the next bed and wished my roommate was dead.

When Dr. Wampler scheduled my operation, I dampened my panic with thoughts of rooming with a girl my age, someone who knew how tough it was being fifteen, grown-up but not allowed to do anything yet. I imagined the two of us sympathizing over our illnesses, cementing friendship over thermometers, the way Gretchen had made friends when she was in the hospital after her accident and during her plastic surgeries.

What I got was so far from what I had dreamed it wasn't funny. When I swam up from the thick, opaque ether sleep, the first thing I saw was a little girl with long sausage curls lying on the next bed, coloring in a coloring book. Then my eyes took in the television set suspended overhead, tuned to a cartoon program.

The girl stared at me. "She's awake," she said to other people in the room I hadn't noticed. She scooted across the bed, holding out an orange crayon. "Want to color? I'll let you do the Huckleberry Hound page. I saved it for you."

I turned to the wall and gagged.

"She's sick," I heard my mother say.

A nurse swished to my side and held a kidney-shaped pan under my chin. "It's the ether, honey," she reassured me. "What they used to put you to sleep. It sometimes upsets the tummy."

I wasn't nauseated from the anesthetic but from the sight of that girl offering me her Huckleberry Hound page. So much for sympathy.

"This is Beth Ann," my mother said. "She likes to be called Bethie."

What else? "What's she in here for?" I croaked. "She looks fine to me." Except for a terminal case of nerdiness.

"I'm having some tests. Now you're awake," Beth Ann chirped, "we can play."

I groaned, but not with pain.

Two facts I learned about Beth Ann: one, she was twelve years old, though she looked and acted about six; and two, my mother was infatuated with her. My mother had a fondness for nice little girls with long sausage curls.

Beth Ann's taste in television ran to Bugs Bunny and Daffy Duck and she laughed at everything including commercials. When she wasn't coloring for my mother, Beth Ann charmed her with tearjerking stories about how she was an only child and had always wanted an older sister just like me.

Of course, the contrast between Beth Ann and me as patients was like night and day, with Beth Ann falling into the ideal patient category and rewarded by nurses and her roommate's mother fawning all over her. I was regarded as "difficult" and was taken care of grudgingly.

"Why can't you be sweet like Bethie?"

my mother chided after I pushed away the strawberry ice cream with such violence the dish skidded to the floor.

"I'd like to see how sweet you'd be after you had *your* tonsils out!" Hospitals and twelve-year-old girls with long curls made me grumpy.

"Everybody's mean to me," I whimpered. "The nurses don't like me."

"They do like you. It's just that they've never seen such a big baby before," my mother said. "Kobie, if you don't straighten up, I'm not staying here tonight."

She had arranged to have a cot brought in the room. Dr. Wampler told her it wasn't necessary for her to stay overnight, but she was scared I might choke or something and nobody would hear me. Given the attitude of the nurses, who were probably hoping I'd meet an untimely end, maybe it was best a relative spend the night with me. But I didn't want her to know that.

"Don't stay," I snapped. "I don't care."

"Kobie, you shouldn't talk to your mother like that," put in Pollyanna.

"Bethie has more sense than you do," my mother said.

"Will everybody leave me alone?" I threw the sheet over my head and tried to shut out the world.

The worst moment came at dinnertime. An orderly wheeled in a cart bearing two trays topped with metal covers. The wonderful aroma of spaghetti persuaded me to come out of my cocoon. I hadn't had solid food in years, it seemed. My mother propped up my bed so I could eat and rolled the over-the-bed tray closer.

Beth Ann sampled the entree with her pinkie finger. "Mmmmmm. Spaghetti! My favorite!"

I snatched the cover off my tray, but instead of tantalizing spaghetti and tomato sauce like Beth Ann's, I had a dish of glop, something pale green and half-melted, like a bar of soap scooped up from the bathtub drain. "What is *this*?"

My mother was digging the spoon into the gummy substance, preparing to feed me. "Lime Jell-O. I asked the doctor if you could have anything besides ice cream."

"What's *wrong* with it? It's runny."

"They let it soften a little," she replied. "Even regular Jell-O would be too hard for you to swallow. Now open up."

I wasn't opening up for anything green. "I want spaghetti!" I said, straining my vocal cords and my mother's patience to the limit.

"Stop it!" my mother hissed. "If you don't behave, I'm going home!"

I pushed the bowl off the tray, where it flipped over on my bed. Disgusted, my mother rang for the nurse, who cleaned up the mess with a tight-lipped if-that-was-*my*-kid-I-know-what-I'd-do-to-her look.

"Kobie's tired from her operation," Beth Ann said.

I despised Miss Goody-Two-Shoes making excuses for me. My throat throbbed, but my heart hurt worse. Dr. Wampler was able to snip out my rotten tonsils, but there wasn't any cure for a shattered heart.

Visiting hours began as the supper trays were being collected. I expected Pollyanna to have an endless stream of grandmotherly types ooh and aah over her, but surprisingly, the first visitor was for me.

Gretchen came in, bringing me a stuffed dog that looked like Tramp. My mother, relieved to escape from me, left us alone.

"I didn't expect to have company," I said, after thanking her for the dog.

Gretchen sat down in the visitor's chair. "I know how it is to be in a hospital, remember? I thought you could use cheering up. What pretty flowers."

The carnations and mums were from my father, delivered right after supper, but I found myself casually lying, "They're from T.E."

"Who? Oh, that teacher." Gretchen gave me her fishy eye. "Come on, Kobie. No teacher sent you those flowers."

"He did! He knew I was going in the hospital and he sent them!"

"If you say so. Before I forget, this is from Stuart." She handed me an envelope from her purse.

"What is it, a poison pen letter?" I held the envelope between two fingers, as if it might explode. "How did he know I was in here, anyway? Did you blab?"

Gretchen shook her head. "He doesn't know you're in the hospital. I just told him you were out sick."

The envelope contained a homemade card, a crude amateurish version of my *Lady and the Tramp* dinner scene. Inside was a poem: *Roses are red, Violets are dumb, Sorry I acted, Like such a crumb.*

"He didn't sign it," Gretchen said, reading over my shoulder.

I leaned the card against the water pitcher where I could see it. "It's worth more unsigned." This was the best get-well message I could have received. Stuart and I were friends again.

Gretchen rambled on about school, but seemed subdued.

"What is it?" I asked her.

For an answer, she drew the chain from underneath her sweater. Her precious gold and onyx ring was gone.

"You lost your ring?"

"No," she said. "Doug and I broke up."

I couldn't have been more thunderstruck if she told me she had enlisted in the Navy. "Broke up? But *why?*"

"We were seeing so much of each other. In school, out of school, phone calls every hour when we weren't together. I felt like — like he owned me." The image of her silver slave bracelet flashed through my brain. "I guess I missed hanging around with my friends, with you. Doing stuff in school. Doug was taking up my whole life."

"But you *loved* him. Doug was *the one.*"

"I don't know if he was or not, now." She paused. "I think I was more in love with the *idea* of being in love."

She wasn't the only one guilty of being in love with the idea of love. Maybe, just *maybe*, I manufactured the bolt of lightning in the background the first time I saw T.E. Even if I had been infatuated with him and not really in love, I still felt scarred.

"Does it hurt, since you gave Doug back his ring?"

Her blue eyes reflected a misty sadness. "Yeah. It does." She gathered up her purse. "I'd better go. Charles is waiting in the lobby. He said hi. You know how he is about hospitals. He hardly came to see me after my accident." Her wallet tumbled out on my bed.

I picked it up for her. In the plastic

window where a driver's license was supposed to go Gretchen had slipped in the goofy photo-booth picture of us, taken the day we went Christmas shopping. Something caught in my throat when I saw it. Such an honest, loyal gesture demanded equal honesty from me.

"Those flowers," I confessed. "My dad sent them."

"I know." She clasped my hand briefly and I realized there had never been any gap between us. We had different interests because we were individuals, but we were still best friends and probably would be forever.

About a half an hour after Gretchen left, my mother declared there was *a boy* to see me.

"A boy?" I sat up, wishing I was wearing something more glamorous than a hospital gown. My mother told whoever it was to come in, then went down to the nurse's station, confident that Beth Ann was more than capable as a chaperone.

Eddie Showalter entered the room, smiling shyly. "Hi, Kobie." One arm was hidden behind his back.

"Eddie! What are *you* doing here?"

"I came to see you." He presented me with a wilted bouquet of daisies. "These got a little limp. I guess they need water."

Cardiac resuscitation couldn't have revived those flowers.

"The florist was closed," he explained. "And so was the Giant supermarket. But out back they had a whole bunch of stuff they were throwing out. Out of all the flowers in the Dumpster, these were the best."

What, no dented canned goods? I started to ask, then bit back the remark. It was really very nice of Eddie to visit me in the hospital. "Thanks. I'll have the nurse put them in water," I said grandly, aware the nurses would rather assist Dracula than come near me. "How did you know I was in here?"

Eddie perched uncomfortably on the edge of the visitor's chair. "I asked Gretchen and she told me."

"She wasn't supposed to."

"Kobie, I knew you were sick. You'd come to school with your neck wrapped up in that scarf and were always chewing Aspergum . . . I had tonsillitis when I was eight. I remember like it was yesterday."

"Did you have your tonsils out?"

He nodded. "They said I could have all the ice cream I wanted but ice cream was so cold, it made my throat hurt worse."

"That's what I tried to tell my mother!" It was wonderful having someone who really *understood*. "If you knew I had tonsillitis, how come you kept quiet?"

"It was obvious you didn't want anyone to find out," he replied with a shrug. "I figured you had your reasons for coming to school sick and it wasn't my place to give you away."

Why hadn't I noticed how wide-set and sincere Eddie's brown eyes were? T.E.'s — *Harold's* — were too close together and a bit shifty besides.

A nurse announced that visiting hours were almost over. Eddie stood up so quickly, he banged into Beth Ann's tray-table. "I'll see you in school when you get back," he said.

"Okay. And thanks again for the flowers."

Eddie stuffed his hands in his pockets and gazed at the lamp over my bed. "Kobie — uh, maybe you and me could go out sometime? When you're all better?"

If I hadn't been lying down already, I would have swooned. "Gee, Eddie, I — " For once, words failed the Smartmouth. Then I recalled my mother's ironclad edict about dating. "I'd like to go out. Do you mind waiting five or six months?"

"Is it going to take you that long to get well?"

"No. I'm not allowed to date till I'm six-teen." I felt unbelievably infantile telling him that. He left, probably wondering if I was old enough to cross the street by myself.

Beth Ann had been silent during Eddie's visit. When my mother came back, twitching with curiosity and ready to question me, Beth Ann piped, "That was a real nice boy, Mrs. Roberts. He asked Kobie out after she got better. I think you should let her."

Beth Ann's unsolicited opinion took the wind out of my mother's sails. "We'll see," was all she said.

I turned over, signaling I wanted to go to sleep. I had a lot to think about — Gretchen's startling news and Eddie's visit. My infatuation with T.E. But mostly I lay there thinking how the biggest lies are the ones we tell ourselves.

Chapter 14

I was out of school three weeks and then it was Spring Break, which meant I had an extra week to recuperate from my operation. My throat healed slowly and I lost eight pounds because it hurt so much to swallow. Now I didn't even resemble a coatrack.

"Dr. Wampler said it's natural to lose a few pounds," my mother assured me, mixing up yet another calorie-laden milk shake. "I know your throat is sore, but you have to eat."

"I'm just not hungry," I told her, day after day, meal after meal. And I wasn't.

I spent a lot of time in my room, listening to the hum of my empty fish tank and doing the homework assignments Sandy and Gretchen called in to me. My mind spun free, like a bicycle wheel, and when I closed my eyes to rest I saw nothing but white space behind my eyelids.

One afternoon, I lay on my bed watching the first robins dotting our backyard. I wondered if the birds had returned after a winter vacation or if they led two separate lives, one in the north, the other in the south, with no ties to either place. Most of the robins were paired off. How did the birds find their mates? Was there an even number of male robins and female robins born each year? Somehow I doubted it — life was seldom that fair.

I picked up my physical science book, but I knew the answer: There were leftover birds just as there were leftover people, and I was one of them. I didn't fit in anywhere.

My mother came in with a tray. She'd become a regular Florence Nightingale since my surgery. "What's wrong?" she asked, looking at my face. "Are you sick?"

No more than usual, I felt like replying. I showed her the page in my science book where the girl had written, *I love Mike still as in forever till there is no end.*

"Will I ever feel this way about anybody? Will anybody feel this way about *me?*"

My mother sat down on my bed and brushed my bangs off my forehead. "Someday someone will. Falling in love is a wonderful experience."

Falling in love with T.E. had been anything but wonderful. I was tempted to tell her about my crush on the shop teacher, but decided the wound was too raw.

"But it won't happen this year or in your junior year or probably not even in high school," she continued. "You have to be emotionally ready to fall in love and you're too young right now."

But not too young to be hurt. I twisted the bedcovers around my ring finger.

"Kobie, why are you moping around so?" my mother said. "You sit in this room all the time . . . you don't even play that awful record anymore. Having your tonsils out isn't the end of the world. What's bothering you?"

I sighed. "I thought this was going to be such a good year, that things would really get better. But they haven't. The year is practically over and I'm still not popular. I didn't learn to drive. I got sick. I'm not having any *fun*."

"Life isn't always fun, but it *is* what you make it."

My mother could always be depended on to produce one of her mottos. *You made your bed, now you lie in it* was one that had nothing to do with cleaning my room. *Life is what you make it* was trotted out whenever I was at my lowest, like now, as if my misery was my own doing.

"Life *isn't* what you make it," I argued. "I tried to make things happen, like learning to drive and getting in the popular crowd, but it didn't work. Nothing ever goes right for me. I don't even know why I'm here."

Mom smiled. "Because your father and I wanted you, that's why. I don't like to see my little girl unhappy. What would you like to do? Go shopping? Have the girls over for another slumber party?"

"I want to go out on a date," I blurted. "With Eddie Showalter. He's already asked me to see *Fantasia*, this old Walt Disney movie that's an animated classic. Can I go?"

The strangest expression came into my mother's eyes, as if she realized the ground we had gained so precariously these last few weeks was shifting again.

It was her turn to sigh. "You know the rule, Kobie, and you won't be sixteen until July." Before I opened my mouth to protest, she went on. "Remember I told you how my mother wouldn't let me date until I was eighteen? I thought my mother was terribly unfair. All my friends were going to church socials with boys and I had to stay home. I loved my mother, but I resented her rule."

"Just like *I* resent your rule." I had lost before the battle began.

"Resent the rule, but don't resent me. I'm only doing what I think is best for you. But rules aren't set in concrete, which is why — " and here the earth stood still " — if it's okay with your father, I'm going to allow you to go out *this once*."

"I can go!" I shrieked. "I can really go!"

"Yes, you can go — but *only* according to my rules."

My movie date with Eddie was contingent upon so many restrictive clauses, I felt like a prisoner let out on good behavior. *Only* the early show on Saturday was acceptable and we could stay out afterward *only* an hour to get a snack and that was *only* if we were accompanied by a responsible adult. Eddie had to come in when he picked me up and meet my parents formally and probably sign an affadavit that he would have me back no later than six-thirty. Eddie's father volunteered to be the responsible adult.

Friday, the day before the Big Event, my mother came back from the store with a bag from Robert Hall.

"None of your clothes fit anymore," she said, "so I bought you this to wear tomorrow."

The new dress, a tiny purple and brown checked fabric, had a dropped waist and a short flounced skirt. The high neckline and elbow-length sleeves hid my jutting collarbone and skinny arms. I twirled in front of the mirror. With my lacy stockings and new black pumps I would look — well, not like Juliet, but not too bad.

"Will Eddie think I'm an enchanting creature?" I asked my mother. I always wanted to be called an enchanting creature. "Or will he think I'm just a creature?"

"You look cute," she replied. "That dress suits a thin person."

In addition to the new dress, I had — miracle of miracles — long fingernails! For some reason, I quit biting my nails when I was in the hospital. My nails had been growing for three whole weeks and were almost a quarter of an inch long.

"I didn't know you even liked Eddie," Gretchen said Saturday morning on the phone. She was home on weekends, now that she and Doug weren't seeing each other.

"He's always been sort of a friend. But when he came to visit me in the hospital and brought me those awful flowers — okay, so he's not gorgeous like T.E. — "

"Don't put him down, Kobie, like you're always doing yourself. Eddie is a nice guy. Have a great time this afternoon. Don't forget to call me as soon as you get back." I couldn't detect a shred of resentment in

Gretchen's tone. She was sitting home alone these days, but seemed genuinely glad for me.

Eddie and his father arrived at exactly two-thirty. They were so punctual I wondered if they had spent the night in the bushes outside the front door until it was time to knock. My mother talked to Mr. Showalter, a plumper, older edition of Eddie, while Eddie and I looked at the floor and out the window and finally at each other.

For the occasion, Eddie wore a white shirt under his inevitable blue sweater and had squeezed himself into a new pair of Levi's, at least a size too small. He seemed so uneasy I couldn't decide whether he was nervous about our date or suffering from acute waistband.

I was nervous enough for both of us. After my mother had extracted a promise from Mr. Showalter that they would have me back *by dark*, Eddie took me out to his father's car. Our hands grazed. My palms were so clammy he must have felt like he was touching a dead mackerel. We got in the backseat with Mr. Showalter in the driver's seat, like a chauffeur.

The matinee crowd at the movie theater consisted of hollering little kids with their parents and Eddie and me. Mr. Showalter discreetly sat on the other side of the theater, stoically eating popcorn, while toddlers raced up and down the aisles and poured grape soda on his shoes.

Eddie bought a box of popcorn the approximate dimensions of a laundry basket and set it on the armrest between us.

"I got extra butter," he said.

My first date was only about thirty-seven minutes old and already I had to register a complaint. "Eddie, I love popcorn, but I can't eat it." All I needed was to get a popcorn hull stuck in my stupid throat.

"Oh, that's right!" He smacked his forehead. "I forgot. Would you like something else? Jujubes or something?"

"No, I'm fine. Can you eat all that by yourself?" I worried he would feel compelled to gobble the whole box and make the waistband of his jeans even tighter.

Then the lights dimmed and I was consumed with a new panic. The theater was a place where a boy traditionally "made his move" on a girl. Which move would Eddie try? The old yawn-then-drape-the-arm-across-the-girl's-shoulder routine? Or the sly reach-for-the-popcorn-at-the-same-time-and-wind-up-holding-hands ploy?

I sat stiffly, staring straight ahead, every pore braced for the invasion. But then the feature started and, to my amazement, Eddie did nothing except watch the movie. After a few minutes, I relaxed and let myself enjoy the movie. *Fantasia* was so mesmerizing, our eyes never left the screen.

When the movie flickered to an end and the lights came up again, we walked out of the theater, jabbering excitedly about the great animation we had just seen. In fact, we forgot about Mr. Showalter completely until he came staggering out into daylight.

"Where to now?" he asked Eddie.

Eddie turned to me. "Is Dino's Den okay with you, Kobie?"

I had never eaten in Dino's Den, a restaurant in the basement of a nearby shopping center. Dino's Den was so dark, customers should have been supplied flashlights to find their tables. Eddie and I sat across from each other in a booth, while Mr. Showalter squinted at the menu at the only other available table, one right next to ours. He sat with his back to us to give us a little privacy, but his constant presence made me feel like we were being hounded by the Secret Service.

"I liked the 'Night on Bald Mountain' part the best," Eddie said, still discussing the movie.

"Me, too! Weren't those dancing trees neat? When I get home, I'm going to try to draw one," I said.

"Will you bring it to school when you're done?"

"Sure," I replied, flattered Eddie was so interested in my art projects. To muffle my confusion, I studied the menu.

"They've got terrific ice cream here."

I wrinkled my nose. "If I never see a dish of ice cream again, it'll be too soon."

"I keep forgetting. Well, have whatever you want," he offered.

"You know what I want?" For the first time in weeks I was *hungry*. "A hamburger! I'm starving for a hamburger!"

"Me, too." Eddie ordered us both cheeseburgers and onion rings to share. Beside us, Mr. Showalter had a cup of black coffee.

"I like your dress," Eddie said. "I like your other dress, too, but this one is prettier."

"What other dress?" Usually I wore skirts and blouses to school.

"The white one with all the lace."

So he had seen me on Valentine's Day, when I had foolishly tried to make Turquoise Eyes fall in love with me. I didn't say anything. Somehow I think Eddie knew about my crush on Mr. Brown, the way he had known of my tonsillitis.

Recalling the role I was playing that day, it dawned on me that I made a poor Juliet, mainly because I wasn't being myself. But weren't we all playing roles? Sandy, the romance coach, trying on different identities. Stuart, anxious to appear dashing for Rosemary Swan. Gretchen, eager to be half of a couple before she was a whole person. And me, wanting desperately to outdo Gretchen by landing an improbable boyfriend. Only Eddie Showalter played himself, wearing his blue sweater, doodling the White House and jets. Never pretending to be what he wasn't. Maybe Eddie knew where he fit in this world. I was starting to figure out what my part was.

We ate our hamburgers and talked some more about the movie and about art. I never had such a good time and I told Eddie as much when his father stopped the car in front of my house. I thanked his father and started to open the car door myself, but Eddie jumped out and sprinted around to my side.

"I'll walk you to the door," he said. I loved the attention. He made me feel special.

At my door, we stood awkwardly. I wondered if my mother had surveillance cameras installed while we were gone.

"I had a really nice time," I said again.

"So did I. You always make me laugh, just like at lunch. You know, Kobie, I think you're — " He paused, as if searching for the right words.

"Yes?" I said, ready to supply a dozen suggestions. You think I'm what? Enchanting? Ravishing? Bewitching?

" — swell," he finished on a note of triumph.

I weighed being called an "enchanting creature" in my daydreams against being called "swell" in real life and decided I'd settle for "swell" any day. "I guess I'd better go inside."

The Big Moment was here. Eddie hesitated a few seconds, glanced about nervously as if anticipating my mother to spring out of the rhododendrons, then kissed me, very fast, but definitely on the lips.

" 'Bye, Kobie," he said, reddening from the neck up, like mercury rising in a thermometer. "I'll call you."

I went into my house, my feet scarcely touching the floor.

My mother was reading and not hanging out the window, spying on us as I thought she'd be. "You look happy," she said.

I was supposed to call Gretchen immediately and fill her in on the details, but I wanted to relish my first date alone a while. I'd call her later.

"I am happy," I told my mother. And I was. Happy to be myself, at last.

About the Author

CANDICE F. RANSOM, who to this day is amazed she made it through her freshman year, lives in Centreville, Virginia, with her husband and black cat. She writes books for young people and enjoys going out to eat whenever she can. She is the author of *Thirteen* and *Fourteen and Holding*.

"You find those letters, Flip. Read them if you want, then give them to my niece. Give them to Lee."

"Don't you worry," I told the poor woman as the paramedics bundled her off, hooked up to God knows what, maple syrup for all I knew. "I'll get those letters right now, hand them safe and sound to Lee, and we'll meet you at the hospital. Everything's going to be fine."

Her face was a satisfaction to me, trusting and content, as if she'd slipped her house key into my apron pocket and run off on vacation. "Thank you, Flip." Her voice trailed away. "You take such care of us all."

I think back now to that moment. Those letters changed everything. Funny how something buried so deep in the past can suddenly break through this earth and grow tall, branches sweeping out to scrape one, offer shelter to another.

THE BELLES OF
SOLACE GLEN

Susan S. James

BERKLEY PRIME CRIME, NEW YORK

THE BELLES OF SOLACE GLEN

A Berkley Book / published by arrangement with
the author

PRINTING HISTORY
Berkley Prime Crime mass-market edition/ July 2004

For information address: The Berkley Publishing Group,
a division of Penguin Group (USA) Inc.,
375 Hudson Street, New York, New York 10014.

ISBN: 0-425-19713-1

Berkley Prime Crime Books are published by
The Berkley Publishing Group,
a division of Penguin Group (USA) Inc.,
375 Hudson Street, New York, New York 10014.
The name BERKLEY PRIME CRIME and the
BERKLEY PRIME CRIME design
are trademarks belonging to Penguin Group (USA) Inc.

PRINTED IN THE UNITED STATES OF AMERICA

10 9 8 7 6 5 4 3 2 1

To my husband, Jim,
Who made dreams of toys underfoot a reality,
Who made swimming with tropical fish in February happen,
Who gives generously, inspires unknowingly,
Supports without question, and loves without limits;
A husband, a lover, a father, a friend,
You make all things possible—even Solace Glen.

Acknowledgments

Boundless thanks to Mary Tahan, who first believed in the quirky little community known as Solace Glen, and her brilliant sidekick, Jena Anderson. To Christine Zika—you signed on the dotted line and made the dream come true. Deep thanks to my parents for giving me the best education they could, in all things, in every way. To the teachers in my life who believed I could—Tim McCorkle, Tommy Samaha, Elizabeth McColl, Elizabeth Keith, James Skirkey, Jonathan Holden, and most especially, Cecil Dawkins.

And a great big HA HA to the teachers who thought I couldn't (who shall remain nameless).

R. BELL/LUCY HANOVER BELL
(1755–1800) *(1760–1821)*
m. 1781

RICHARD/KAYE THOMAS
(1782–1842) *(1790–1836)*
m. 1812

FERRELL/SARA DODDIN
(1784–1845) *(1785–1852)*
m. 1808

LUCINDA/JOSEPH PACA
(1787–1850) *(1781–1843)*
m. 1817

HAROLD
(1813–23)
ANN
(1815–35)
JOSEPH
(1817–30)
RICHARD
(1820–22)

FERRELL/GRETAL STUBING
(1828–99) *(1830–1908)*
m. 1850

JOHN BELL
(1820–61)

LUCY BELL PACA TANNER/JASON TANNER
(1829–1912) *(1800–50)*
m. 1847

LUCINDA ANN TANNER
(1850–90)
( )

ROLAND/FLORENCE OPENHEIM
(1851–1908) *(1859–1929)*
m. 1878

ROLAND, JR./KATRINA T. CHAPELLE   FLORIE O. BELL
(1880–1945) *(1873–1940)*   *(1884–1939)*
m. 1898

ROLAND, III/PENELOPE HIGGINS
(1899–1971) *(1910–71)*
m. 1930

LEONA BELL JENNER/JAKE P. JENNER   ROLAND, IV/GARLAND DAY
(1931–) *(1915–86)*   *(1941–)* *(1944–)*
m. 1952   m. 1968

FERRELL T.   HILDA HIGGINS
(1977–)   *(1986–)*

PART ONE

✳

CHAPTER 1

※

THE LADYBUGS COME in September, right when the first chill sneaks in. They cluster together on the ceiling in the corner of the bathroom, little round faces turned into each other like a ladies' sewing circle. Occasionally, one wanders off as if she's stepping away for an iced tea. "Be back in a jiff," she might say to the others. That's when I make my move.

I pluck the wanderer off and, just as quick, throw her in the toilet. When you touch a ladybug, she gives off a smell, dry and woody, smoky, a candle just blown out. I don't have anything against ladybugs, mind you. I just don't want them taking over. Everything in life needs culling now and then.

I guess you could say that's what I do for a living. I cull. People in Solace Glen, Maryland, have called on me for more than twenty years to come pick through their houses, throw away the trash, put things right, scrub things down. They trust me completely to do the job neat and thorough. I can't stand a dusty baseboard, and they know it. I'll do windows for extra. I'm the only domestic help in this burg. If you want more than once a week, you have to import. Only one of my people ever did—Leona Bell Jenner. Brought in a teenager from Baltimore and she cleaned all right. Cleaned the Bell house out of half the silver and jewelry Leona was saving to give to her niece and namesake, Lee. I could have told her. Stick with who you know. Flip Paxton doesn't cheat people, anybody'd tell you that. I just want enough to pay the mortgage, splurge once or twice a year on something frivolous, and go to Ocean City in the summer to kick up my heels.

Leona apologized, though. "Flip," she said (nobody calls me Felicity and stays on my Christmas list), "you forgive an old woman for being silly, don't you?"

"Miss Leona," I answered, "if all we did was forgive each other for being silly, none of us would get a damn thing done sunup to sundown. I'll be at your place Thursday."

I had left her time slot open, sure she'd see the light, sure that all she'd tried to do was ease my mounting workload and didn't mean any insult or injury. A woman the caliber of Leona couldn't harm a flea. She'd always kept a watchful, protective eye on me almost as intently as she did her niece Lee. I counted her as one of my "mothers," one of the ladies in town who lovingly slipped into the empty shoes of my own mother who died in a car crash with my father when I was eighteen. Between Leona and other women like her in Solace Glen, the blank space my mother left was almost filled, and I couldn't have been more grateful. From the moment I raised my eyes from my parents' grave at the sound of the last "amen," a circle of women surrounded me, all dressed in black, all wearing faces of comfort. And suddenly, to me, Solace Glen became a town with one house, a house of mothers and sisters. When I started my cleaning business, each house I cleaned felt like the house before, each house a connecting room of a large home, a home where love and care wrapped around me whenever I walked through the door.

Two hours was all it took to clean the huge, old Bell house with only Leona to fill the rooms and a cat called Jeb, named after Major General J.E.B. Stuart, the Confederate cavalry hero. Leona said the general not only passed by, he stopped and stayed awhile, and there lay a story. She said she'd tell it to me sometime, and she did. While she was having her heart attack, she got part of it out.

"It makes this house important." She spoke in a raspy whisper, crumpled on the carpet like a leaf of tissue paper left out of the gift box. I had to lean into her face to get all the words. "It makes all of us important. You and me. Solace Glen."

"Solace Glen is already important, Miss Leona." I patted her hand till the ambulance arrived, hoping nobody else in town scheduled an emergency that day. "It's important for its people. Like you."

"Flip," she smiled, eyelids flickering, same as her life, "you are a treasure." She gripped my hand as if I were her last of kin and went on with the story. When the ambulance pulled up, she jumped to the part about the proof.

"You find those letters, Flip. Read them if you want, then give them to my niece. Give them to Lee."

The paramedic twins, Jesse and Jules Munford, went about their jobs and listened to Miss Leona at the same time, their bristly white blond hair shaved so close to their skulls they both looked like eggheads. People would say, "Are you Egghead One or Two?" Whichever one breathed first was Number One. He knew who he was, but nobody else in Solace Glen had a clue.

The Eggheads gossiped the same as they breathed, so I knew Miss Leona's half-told story would rush around town like a flash flood, swirling with incongruous details and wild conjecture.

"Don't you worry," I told that poor woman as they bundled her off, hooked up to God knows what, maple syrup for all I knew. "I'll get those letters right now, hand them safe and sound to Lee, and we'll meet you at the hospital. Everything's going to be fine."

Her face was a satisfaction to me, trusting and content, as if she'd slipped her house key into my apron pocket and run off on vacation. "Thank you, Flip." Her voice trailed away. "You take such care of us all."

I think back now to that moment. Things might have been so different if the Eggheads hadn't heard any part of Miss Leona's story. I would have found those letters, probably not read even one, and handed them over to Lee Jenner at the Historical Society, where nothing ever happens. As it was, I read all three letters so I would know the facts, something the Eggheads never had a grip on.

Those letters changed everything. Funny how something buried so deep in the past can suddenly break through this earth and grow tall, branches sweeping out to scrape one, offer shelter to another.

CHAPTER 2

✳

LEE JENNER LIVED on Center Street smack in the middle of downtown Solace Glen, though calling Solace Glen a town is stretching it. The rust red brick of her two story home, brick almost as old as Frederick County, Maryland, exhaled a fine crimson dust even on wet days, and the iron-lettered marker above the little green door let visitors know the house was built in 1794. A peeling picket fence outlined the square yard, and at the entrance gate hung a ten-year-old sign that read in faded green letters, "Solace Glen Historical Society. Contributions Welcome."

With nothing but time on her hands after college down the road at Hood, Lee took the old house her Uncle Jake left her and made it into a sort of tourist attraction, open whenever she felt like it, which wasn't often. She majored in history at Hood (an education I would have given an arm for) and liked the idea of taking that pile of crumbling brick and elevating it above its station in life, buying antiques in New Market, furnishing the downstairs the way it might have appeared two hundred years ago, years before J.E.B. Stuart even rode into town. But Lee also had a quirky, artsy style (she said it was "the Jenner-inner") that her poor Aunt Leona would fret about and Lee would laugh about. A prime example is when she paid a visionary artist from the Maryland Institute to create a make-believe early nineteenth-century woman and plopped her in a chair with a wooden bowl on her lap as if she was shelling butter beans.

Lee called the make-believe woman Plain Jane, but I never thought she was. Her hair rang out tomato red and her mouth wore a wicked tilt to it that made you wonder what those early American women had up their sleeve.

People got a lot of mileage out of Lee's big doll, and the public mention of Plain Jane's name gave Leona the vapors. Dancing to her own drum, Lee didn't care what people thought. She kept to herself more than most, earning a reputation (according mostly to Marlene Worthington) as "rude when approached," and "too smartie pants for her own good." But I loved Lee like a sister, sharing our "mother," Leona. We considered each other best friends. She was thirty-two, ten years younger than me, let me borrow books any time, always had coffee and Danish out when I came to clean, took seriously any advice I doled out, and had the most wonderful, vicious sense of humor.

"We need a name for Marlene," she said, just a week before Leona's heart attack. The first fall breeze of mid-September flowed through an open window. I flapped a dust rag around Plain Jane, wondering to myself how that visionary artist envisioned the doll's black eyes, which I only then realized were dyed condoms. What would Leona think?

Lee bit into a Danish and wiped a sticky finger across

her jeans. "Marlene Worthington. Marlene Worthington. Saint something." She mulled it over. "Our Lady of Vicks VapoRub."

"She does stink of it," I agreed, moving away from Plain Jane's soulless black eyes. "One time I saw her out in public with two wads under each nostril. Looked like she needed an operation. Her mother would have been mortified, dear woman."

Lee nodded. We both adored Louise Lamm, another of my "mothers," who languished away from cancer, losing a little bit more of herself every day. I felt even closer to Louise than Leona. She'd almost filled the roles of both mother and father to me ever since the car crash took my parents and I had to start up a business to support myself.

"Poor Louise," Lee sighed. "She's got enough to think about without having to wipe her daughter's big troll nose."

"You're right about that." I didn't want to get weepy, even in front of my best friend, so I picked up a can of cleanser and headed upstairs to Lee's midget bathroom. Everything in her house could be measured by the inch. Shoe box windows, cramped ceilings, rabbit hole doors. The people who lived back then must have come from Oz. Lee herself stood five foot five, no more than 110 pounds. She wore her long auburn hair swept up in one of those toothy, tortoise shell dime store clips. Her face claimed the name Jenner—jaw set in concrete, a wide, courageous mouth, nose straight as a paring knife, and hazel eyes that always carried a question in them, never satisfied with any answer.

"I like 'Our Lady of Vicks VapoRub,' " I called downstairs to her. "That's a good one."

"Take a book when you leave," she called back, and I heard the kitchen door open and close. She'd gone outside to the garden, I guessed, to work on the historical herb plot.

I scrubbed her munchkin tub. Maybe, instead of a regular scarecrow for the herb garden, she'd get a visionary nineteenth-century man to carry on with Plain Jane. Maybe his eyes could be IUDs.

I glowed at how artsy I'd become, and pictured Leona, dying of embarrassment. Little did I know that a week later, she'd simply be dying.

I KNOCKED ONCE on the door and went right in, as usual. It was Thursday morning, two days after Leona's funeral. Lee sat at the antique pine farm table on a painted chair beside Plain Jane. She sat so still, for a second I thought both were made-up women, that she'd gotten a bosom buddy for Plain Jane.

"Brought back that book I borrowed." I laid it gently on the table. "Thanks."

She cocked her head to view the title. "*Straight On Till Morning*. So what did you think of Beryl Markham?"

The hazel eyes held some luggage under them, a sign of traveling, no rest stops.

"I'd say she got around." I drew an old milking stool from under the table and planted myself at her feet. "How you been, Lee? Like I have to ask. You look awful."

"I feel awful." Lee never minced words. "I just lost my only remaining family. Leona was good to me. She was so good after Daddy, then Momma died."

Her voice choked on the last few words and she took a deep breath, prepared to dive low. I reached for her hand, conscious of the taint of disinfectant covering my fingers, and barely brushed her skin, the way I might dust one of Leona's dear little heirlooms. I almost said, "You've still got the Bell's," but fortunately I caught myself. Leona's brother, Roland Bell, and his twisted crew could hardly be called family. His was the one disconnected room in my house of Solace Glen; his home was the only place that didn't feel like home.

"Tom Scott says she left me almost everything. I'm supposed to meet with him in a few days to go over the will." The dip of Lee's mouth said it all. "Flip. What am I going to do with that big house and this one, too? It's not like I'm married and have a pack of kids. It's just me and cranky ole Jeb now."

The mention of Jeb, Leona's worthless cat, reminded me of my mission, a mission I hadn't accomplished as fast as I'd told Leona I would because Leona's own timing had left me shaken. I hadn't expected her to die before I could call Lee. I hadn't expected her to leave at all. "I've got something for you, Lee." I drew my rough, smelly hand away and pulled the velvet bag of letters from the carryall. "This was Leona's last request, though I didn't know it at the time. She told me where to find them, and now I'm handing them over to you."

"What is it?" She fingered the blue velvet. "A tiara?"

I took the yellowed pack from the bag. "Letters."

"What kind of letters?" She leaned back and studied the three envelopes tied with red ribbon, not touching, letting curiosity grow.

"Love letters."

The dip in her mouth turned up. "Leona and Uncle Jake?"

"No. . . ."

"No, paper's too old. Somebody in the family way back?"

"I don't know. Leona didn't tell me who the woman was."

"Well, you've read them, haven't you?"

"I read them. Leona gave me permission."

"Don't get nervous. I wasn't pointing a finger. You're just being so mysterious."

"So was Leona. Maybe she didn't know who the woman was in the letters. Maybe she did and wouldn't say. Could have been a cousin, a friend, a visitor staying in the Bell house. But Leona's mother told her the man who wrote the letters was J.E.B. Stuart, even though the signature on all three is K.G.S."

She reached her hands behind her head and pulled the clip out. The auburn hair fell long and glossy over one shoulder.

"Well?" I shoved the letters closer to her.

The hazel eyes questioned that stack of yellow paper like it might rear up on the table and give a speech.

"Why," she looked at me hard, "would Leona tell you to give me some antique letters as a 'last request'? What's so important about these pieces of paper?"

"Why don't you read them and tell me. You're the historian. I'll come back later to clean." I rose from the milk stool. "Leona said something else kind of curious. She said the letters were handed down only by the women in the family. From the beginning, the Bell men were kept in the dark."

When my hand gripped the brass doorknob of the front door, I turned and told her, "Leona had those hidden in a waterproof canister inside a plastic bag stuffed in the arm of an upholstered chair under a sheet in the corner of the attic. She wanted those letters hidden, but she didn't want them destroyed. The rest is up to you."

My fingers twisted the knob. "And Lee," I hated telling her this part, "the Eggheads heard enough of the story to make you miserable the rest of your life."

I could swear when I shut the door, even Plain Jane looked alarmed.

CHAPTER 3

✳

ROLAND BELL, LEONA'S miserable brother, owned the only restaurant in town where he peddled decent, home-cooked food and held the town patent on cheapness. You sat down at a table without any flourish from a menu-toting hostess. You picked up the list of specials, hand-written and photocopied that morning, right at the table. You made your choice and wrote it down with a pencil and a pad, also supplied at the table. You handed it to whoever passed by wearing a red Roland's Café and Grill T-shirt, and you didn't wait more than fifteen minutes for your steaming-hot meal to arrive.

Paper napkins, but real plates and flatware. The plastic flowers changed with the seasons, four times a year: white carnations, yellow tulips, orange mums, and red poinsettias. If you left a tip of more than fifteen percent, Roland, never one to squander a buck, thanked you in a prosecutorial

manner and might lecture you on the Great Depression
next time you walked in. I never got that lecture.

The Jenners and the Bells were kin only by marriage;
Leona Bell married Jake Jenner whose brother, Henry, was
Lee's father. But Lee never thought of the Bells as family,
except for her Aunt Leona, because Roland, his wife Garland, and their two children, Hilda and Ferrell T., stopped
acting like family. They acted more like she didn't exist,
which came to suit Lee just fine. When Leona and Roland's
parents died, the big house—the Bell house—was left to
Leona, not her younger brother; he got the money. Leona
and Jake moved out of the 1794 munchkin cottage and set
up digs. Roland nearly blew a gasket.

"I'm the only son! I should inherit the big house!" He'd
tell anybody who would listen how he'd been terribly mis-
treated, how Leona must have exerted undue influence,
gotten his parents drunk or read up on hypnotism so she
could snap her fingers from across a room and they'd start
signing legal documents by the truckload.

"Thank God he wasn't a twin," is what Leona used to
say behind his back. While Jake lived, he never spoke an
ugly word about his cheap, whiny brother-in-law. I don't
know how, though. The rest of the quirky, artsy Jenners could
hardly contain themselves. Lee's mother and father, Marie
and Henry, used to take turns imitating Roland and his
scaredy-cat wife, Garland.

Marie, who for too short a time was one of my "mothers," would hunker down behind a lamp and squeak, "Oh,
Roland. I'm so ashamed. I forgot to wash your socks by
hand in lavender water and gold dust the way you like."

And Henry would pounce up on an ottoman, hands on
his hips and sneer, "Woman. That's probably why my parents left Sister the Big House and we're stuck here in this
Victorian monstrosity of only fifteen rooms. If you'd done

what you were told and washed those socks, we wouldn't be in this fix."

I count Henry and Marie as my first customers. They did everything in their power to help get my business going. Called their friends, raved about my detail work. Slipped a fifty in my apron pocket that first New Year's Eve, which was a lot of money to an eighteen year old who'd suddenly found herself alone. "Have a happy," Marie whispered and kissed me on the temple, the way my mother used to do. Then Henry poured me my first glass of French champagne, and we had an early toast to Auld Lang Syne. He sang in a magnificent Welsh voice. A few months later, when he passed so quickly from pancreatic cancer, we knew Marie couldn't last long in this world. Never strong alone, she lived the next couple of years as though split in two, desperately longing for her missing half. She drank herself to death, leaving Lee, only ten years old, without parents, same as me—one reason we bonded so close. Lee, at least, had her Uncle Jake and Aunt Leona and went to live with them. I rejoiced at the good care they gave her, but harbored envy, too. The drunk driver who took my parents left no family in their empty place. Leona swept Lee under her wing and cared for her like another mother, not wild and crazy like Marie, but solid and sympathetic, which was what she needed.

As good as God made Leona, He still gave her a sufferance. Roland made Leona miserable all her life. Lee told me from the time she moved in with Jake and Leona, Roland would appear at least once a month to whine and pout about some piece of furniture or doodad. He'd pick up a china bunny and claim his daddy or momma told him he could have it after they passed. Sometimes he would burst into tears. Sometimes he would throw a temper tantrum. You never could predict Roland's reaction to anything, but you could always count on his greed. The will gave everything in the house to Leona, lock, stock, and barrel, but she felt a little guilty about getting all that stuff, so she played along and gave in to Roland's whining, going as far as to feel sorry for him. The visits increased after Jake died. Still, Leona never said no to her brother.

By the time her heart gave out, Leona had given more than half her belongings to Roland. His fifteen room Victorian overflowed with sofas, chairs, tables, rugs, porcelain, crystal, silver, art work, and linen—a lot to keep clean. I noticed, though, the Bells had little in the way of books and family photographs. As long as his house spilled over with impressive knickknacks, Roland could look down at the rest of us. That's how he measured himself against others—with a yardstick of touchables.

If he'd known how valuable the Bells' library was, though, he might have asked for the written word up front. As it happened, most of the books went with Lee when she moved to the 1794 house, and over the years, she added to the collection. Books gradually replaced walls in the little Historical Society, giving Plain Jane and her butter bean bowl an unexpected air of dignity. But to Roland, a book was something you kept your accounts in, tallying up at year's end. His fist closed tight around money and the stuff crammed in his house, but Roland's grasp around the important things in life went undetected. Under normal circumstances, Roland never would have wanted those letters I handed to Lee. Letters, books, family photos—that was just the worthless junk you threw in the trash at the end of the day.

The Eggheads, however, specialized in colorization of normal circumstances. Leona hadn't been buried two weeks, and they sat blabbing over lunch at Roland's Café and Grill about her last words to me, the story of the letters. You never heard such distortion of truth.

Roland got an earful, along with everybody else in town.

"She never told me about any letters," he said, casual, matter-of-fact.

Small hints give way to an awful truth. The trembling of a coffee cup, the touch of purple in a cloud, a faint dip in pressure, a few raindrops, creeping water. All little things that lead to people asking what if. What if the Eggheads had kept their mouths shut? What if the half-story Leona told hadn't filtered its way through every living soul who passed through Solace Glen?

Roland rang up a customer, slid a peppermint across the counter, wiped a cotton cloth over the cash register. "You're awful quiet, Flip."

My usual table hovered behind the cash register, out of the mainstream against a wall in the corner, a table most customers wouldn't want or even notice. The nicest table, of course, the one by the center window, invariably berthed the town cop, Officer Palmer Lukzay, who claimed the dubious honor of being Roland's only friend. He received all his meals on the house, the only person who ever did.

"What do you want me to say, Roland?" I turned my gaze toward Lukzay, then in the opposite direction where I could see the Eggheads straining in their seats, wanting to hear the parts they didn't know, but wouldn't admit to not knowing.

"I don't want you to say anything. I'm just curious if what Jesse and Jules say is right." A curiosity that sounded like an accusation.

"Right?" I dotted my mouth with a napkin, anxious to switch the subject. "Eggheads don't know right from left. Remember the time Pal nearly severed his left arm off chopping wood for Miss Fizzi? Eggheads came and got him, took him to the emergency room, found out they'd slapped the tourniquet on the wrong arm. Lucky he didn't die."

"Flip Paxton!" One of the Eggheads shot up, I don't

know which one, stabbing a fork in the air. "That was our first job, and there were extenuating circumstances the average layman wouldn't understand."

"Yeah," I said, "like how the two of you ever graduated from high school."

The other Egghead sprang up. "OK, Flip, Miss Smartie Ass, why don't you stop trying to change the subject and answer Roland about those letters. We were there. We heard it all. Don't you go acting like we're a couple of liars."

"Who said anything about lying?" I concentrated on my Swiss steak.

"You insinuated that what we said wasn't right."

"That's true, Flip, you did." Marlene Worthington, Our Lady of Vicks VapoRub, sashayed up to the cash register to pay her check. She handed Roland a ten and leaned both elbows on the counter as if she might camp out awhile, as curious about the letters as everybody else. But then, anything you could sell for money intrigued Marlene.

"This town is lucky to have you as a moral compass, Marlene. We all breathe easier with you around." I waved a hand in front of my nose.

Roland gave Marlene her change. "The gist of it is this, Flip. If Leona had some valuable letters, historic and all, then as her next-of-kin, I should get them."

He looked to Officer Lukzay for official confirmation. The cop nodded officiously enough, brushing cornbread crumbs off his bushy, gray mustache.

"How do you arrive at that? And, I might add, Officer Yes Man over there is no attorney-at-law."

Lukzay squinted sternly at his cornbread as if it owed him a juris doctorate.

I shoved my plate across the table, eager to make an exit. "Leona gave those letters to Lee while she was still alive. They're not part of the estate. Anyway, as far as I know, the will hasn't been read yet. Has it?" I couldn't believe I'd asked Roland such a blunt and personal thing. I scrambled to pick up my stuff.

Roland plopped a peppermint in Marlene's outstretched palm. "Not that it's any of *your* business, but Tom Scott's reading the will tomorrow. Guess I'm in it or he wouldn't have bothered to inform me."

I threw a five and two one's on the table. I couldn't reach the door fast enough to get out on the sidewalk. Roland was right. None of this was any of my business, and if Leona hadn't had her heart attack on my cleaning day, I wouldn't be worrying myself into a fever.

"Flip!"

I screeched to a halt, my clumsy plastic carryall banging against the well-toned thigh of the man in front of me. It was Tom Scott, followed by his ever-present black Lab, Eli.

"Flip," he removed his hat even though it was beginning to rain, a cool, late September rain. "I've been talking to your answering machine for two days."

"Oh, sorry." I set the carryall down. I loved Tom's low, husky voice. "Sometimes I forget I have that thing."

"Sometimes I wish I could forget I have one, too." His smile could grace the cover of any magazine, an off-center Harrison Ford grin. "We are reading Leona's will tomorrow at my office, around two. You should be there."

"Me? Why?" Maybe he wanted a dust-up after everybody left.

"Because you're in it," he said, putting his hat back on. "Don't be late."

I nodded, too shocked to protest that I am never late, thank you very much.

I picked up the carryall, shuffled down the street to my horrible diesel car, and climbed into the driver's seat. I turned on the ignition, punched at the radio, and sat there, stunned, listening to WFIB's Screamin' Larry announce the jazz lineup for later that evening. John Coltrane. Diana Washington. Ella Fitzgerald. Tim Weisberg.

I could only think of two things: I would have to reschedule Louise Lamm, and Roland Bell was going to have a fit when the woman who scrubbed his toilets showed up at Tom Scott's office.

Chapter 4

I TELEPHONED LOUISE Lamm around eight o'clock that night. When someone doesn't have long to live, you're never sure when is a good time to call. With some folks, no time is right, but with Louise, any time suited her fine. She appreciated the attention because her worthless daughter, Marlene, barely gave her a nod. Everybody in Solace Glen tried to make up for Marlene's deficiencies, bringing Louise little bouquets and casseroles, cutting the grass, painting her porch. The Circle Ladies at the Episcopal Church even pitched in and got her a VCR, rotating movies every week, and books, too.

"You see the local news?" Louise admitted to being a news addict. She would watch the Farm Report if that was the only thing on.

"Nope." I unloaded a bag of groceries consisting mostly of three pints of Ben & Jerry's Cherry Garcia and a vat of skin cream for my horrible hands. "Somebody's cat stuck up a tree? Or maybe Roland's Café burned to the ground, nothing saved but the plastic mums and a peppermint?"

"You're close. The Café got honorable mention, but the big story was the Eggheads blabbing to a TV reporter about secret Confederate spy letters turned over to the Historical Society, which will put Solace Glen on the map."

I didn't want to break any confidences, so I simply said, "Things must have really popped after I left the Café. Who else made the news?"

"They showed Screamin' Larry and Pal and Joey Sykes. Larry was eating, of course. Pal and Joey looked like they'd come straight out of the hood of a Ford at the Crown station. Those two were hanging on every ridiculous Egghead word, eyes the size of hubcaps poking through the oil and grease. Marlene's face made its television debut for about three seconds. She was sucking in her cheeks trying to look skinny."

"Yeah, well," I scooped into my ice cream, "hope springs eternal. Any Circle Ladies get their five seconds of fame?"

"Just Tina Graham, and she looked mortified. You know how TV always makes you look fatter than you are, and Tina's no condensed version. Poor thing doesn't need any more hard knocks to her terrible self-image."

I made a noise of agreement, cheeks filled with ice cream. Tina, a golden-hearted gift to the Circle Ladies, had battled the bulge all her fifty-eight years, attacking every fad diet in the book with true conviction that this would be the one to turn her into a Barbie doll. Over the years, she'd probably lost as much weight as she'd gained because the pounds always seemed to end up in the same place. She had a beautiful face, though, and could have been a Lane Bryant model if she'd ever wanted to.

We talked a little more, as we usually did two or three times a week, trading stories about the rich and famous and people we knew. We never considered our conversations gossip, just part and parcel of the national and local news, as Louise liked to say. For twenty-four years, talking to Louise was the closest thing I'd had to talking to my own mother. I rescheduled her cleaning so I could run over to Tom Scott's office the next day. Louise showed real interest in my surprise invitation to hear the will, and thought maybe Leona bequeathed me a piece of jewelry or a soup tureen, something she'd kept from Roland's greedy paws.

"Yeah. That'd be nice. I'd like something to look at and remember her by." I fixed myself a Working Girl's Martini—a lot of rocks, a lot of olives, a lot of cheap gin. "But whatever she left me, I'll tell you this, Louise, and mark my words." I took a swig. "Roland Bell will try to get it."

CHAPTER 5

※

A T TWO O'CLOCK the next day, on time as always, I
crept into Tom Scott's law office determined not to
look at Roland Bell if I could help it. I spotted Lee, crossed
over, and sat down beside her on Tom's nice leather couch.
As a rule, lawyers have better office furniture than doctors.

"Hey," I said, patting her hand, a little nervous. "Do we
have to sign in or anything? I've never been in here but to
clean."

I threw Ferrell T. a glance (the T. as much a mystery as
the name Ferrell). Tom, for reasons known only to himself
and God, hired Roland's useless son as his secretary. Most
men, like Tom, made my palms feel clammy, but Ferrell T.,
like the Eggheads, brought out some sassiness in me, since
none of them had hit thirty yet, and I felt I at least had more
brains than all three put together. Despite his lofty airs, so
much like his father, Ferrell T. couldn't intimidate me the

way Roland always had. There he sat, a lumbering hulk, looking like a circus bear behind a desk. He must have looked the same to his teachers back in high school. Margaret Henshaw, our ever-so-correct English teacher, told me as much one day when I was cleaning her house. I was fussing out loud to myself about how Tom could put up with a guy who twanged rubber bands at Eli's bad hip when he thought nobody was looking. Margaret chimed in that Ferrell T. had every appearance of a dolt, but whatever filled his head, ninety-nine percent of it was devious. She said every time she used to turn around, he was up to some no-good prank, like switching the smart girl's homework with his and setting cigarette fires in the bathroom trash cans. I guess Tom would have hired Ferrell T.'s sister, Hilda, but she was still in high school and a bigger idiot than her brother. Kind-hearted in her own fashion, the most she could do was wait tables at the Café. Even that taxed all her brain cells.

"Hey, Ferrell T.," I called, "we supposed to sign in?"

Ferrell T. pushed up his black-framed glasses, which were always slipping halfway down his greasy nose. You'd think somebody in his mid-twenties would have grown out of that bad skin, but Ferrell T. still struggled with the worst kind of zits. It didn't earn him any sympathy in my book; the bad skin merely enhanced a repulsive personality.

He shifted in his chair from one cheek to the other. "Of course not."

He launched the first volley so I shot back. "Don't speak to me in that tone of voice, like I'm stupid and you're God's gift to Mensa." I knew that'd confuse him. "Don't know what Mensa is? Ever pick up a book, Ferrell T.? Or is *Hustler* the closest thing to the ABC's you've ever seen?"

"Mensa?" He touched a finger to his bow tie. "Why would you come in here talking about female stuff? You're so weird."

Lee and I exchanged a look. The top of her lip quivered and she bent down to bury it in the heel of her hand. I reached for a magazine, *Forbes*, not something the average domestic subscribes to. I hid behind it and checked out who else got invited.

Roland and Garland sat in two matching armchairs, legs crossed in the same direction, ankles jiggling up and down in the same rhythm. I could feel Roland staring at me and Lee while Garland fussed with a tassel on her pocketbook.

I thought the five of us filled the room until a little whimper came from the corner behind the Bell's. I strained my neck and spotted Wilma Fizzi, head bowed, a lace hankie covering her nose. The sweetest, godliest, most well-respected example of senility in Solace Glen, Miss Fizzi never made a move in life without asking herself the question, What would Jesus do? Then she'd try to one-up him.

"Miss Fizzi?" I flopped the magazine on Tom's expensive looking coffee table and crossed the room, careful not to make eye contact with Roland. "You OK?"

She nodded, face still turned into her lap, and patted my hand when I placed it on her shoulder. It felt like touching a dress on a hanger, no flesh and blood beneath, only the outline of bone holding up a piece of fabric.

"Leona was one of my best friends." Her voice broke into the handkerchief, shoulders trembling.

I knew Leona had paid close attention to Miss Fizzi, making sure her heat stayed on in winter and that she had plenty of fresh garden vegetables in summer, as anyone might do for an elderly neighbor. But apparently their friendship ran deeper than I'd imagined.

I crooked a finger at Lee and she immediately moved toward us. I noticed she avoided eye contact with Roland, too.

Lee kneeled down in front of Miss Fizzi, reached up, and gripped their four hands together. "Miss Fizzi," she whispered, sincere and dignified, "Aunt Leona was like a mother to me, and I think you were like a mother to her. So I guess that means you've got a granddaughter." She kissed Miss Fizzi's wrinkled hands and buried her head in the old lady's lap, a thirty-two-year-old little girl. With that, the colors in the room changed.

Miss Fizzi's shoulders stopped shaking. She sat up straight and the bloodshot eyes rested on Lee kneeling at her feet. "Get up, child. You'll mess your pretty skirt. And I was really more like a big sister to Leona than a mother. Heavens, don't make me older than I am."

Lee tugged on Miss Fizzi's arm and said, "You come sit over here with us," and Miss Fizzi followed like a lamb.

For all my good Christian feeling about Lee and Miss Fizzi, I bristled when Roland spoke.

"Miss Fizzi," he couldn't hold it in, "you and Flip here on some business? Because if you are, Lee and us were here ahead of you. May be awhile."

Miss Fizzi drew a blank. For all she knew, she and I did have some business together.

"Ferrell T.," I said, using a tone you'd employ with a five-year-old, "why don't you tell your daddy what Miss Fizzi and I are here for."

Roland turned and glared at his numskull boy. "Well, boy?"

"They're in the will, Daddy."

"What will?" He still didn't get it.

"Leona's will, of course."

Roland's mouth dropped. "Leona? My sister, Leona? My dead sister, Leona, who just died two weeks ago?"

I fixed my eyes on the ceiling as Roland leaped out of the chair. "Why in hell would she leave anything to a crazy old lady and a goddamn maid, for God's sake!"

Miss Fizzi shrank into the sofa, assaulted by the obscenity. Lee and I wrapped an arm around her, in tune with each other.

"Oh, Roland, sit down," said Lee, tired.

Garland popped out of her chair, a little late following Roland's lead. She watched him, clutched her pocketbook, held her breath.

"I can't believe it," huffed Roland. "I just can't believe it. She must have been influenced. You must have gotten her drunk or drugged or both."

"Neither," I retorted, feeling brave with Lee beside me. "Miss Fizzi jumped on her back and I pulled a knife on her. Butcher's knife. About this long."

"Merciful heavens." Miss Fizzi's hand touched her heart.

I figured any second Roland would order Ferrell T. to phone the police, which could have meant trouble because Miss Fizzi would confess to anything. The pure in heart are always willing to take on the sins of the world—Jesus and Miss Fizzi two cases in point.

"I wouldn't put anything past you, Flip Paxton," Roland growled.

Garland curled her lip. She was doing a fine job of mimicking her unfortunate choice in husbands. "Uh-huh," she said, which was the most she said all day.

Roland moved a step closer to me. "I never trusted you," he hissed, voice growing louder. "I never trusted you with my sister's things, *my* things, and I flat out told her so many a time."

I focused on Roland's hands, dangerously close to making eye contact when the door swung open and Pal Sykes ambled in covered in axle grease. The big, white teeth shined, framed by blackened skin.

"Howdy, howdy," he croaked, happy as a cartoon character.

Roland twisted around. "What the hell are you doing here?"

Pal stopped in his tracks and beamed. "I'm in the will!" You'd have thought he'd won the Lotto.

"Oh, good God," moaned Roland, collapsing into the armchair. Garland dutifully wiggled backward and slowly lowered her bottom into the chair beside him.

"Well, congratulations!" I started laughing so hard, so relieved at the break in tension, that pretty soon Lee was laughing with me and Miss Fizzi, too, although she couldn't fathom what was so funny.

We wriggled around in this undignified manner until Tom poked his head around the corner and requested we all come in. Ferrell T. grabbed a yellow pad and herded us into a conference room that doubled as Tom's law library. I'd always thought the books made the room, spines of blue, red, and green lined up together with the gold lettering. Books like that inspire confidence, which I suppose is why lawyers have them.

Tom asked that we take a seat, and we formed into two opposing camps: Roland, Garland, and Ferrell T. on one side of the table, Miss Fizzi, Pal, Lee, and I on the other. Tom sat at the head with his faithful dog, Eli, stretched out at his feet. He opened a blue paper and spread it out—Leona's will. "I'll just get down to it and separate the chaff from the grain."

"Or the sheep from the goats," chirped Miss Fizzi, rolling with the Bible verses.

Roland mumbled something to himself and Garland chimed in with a responsive purr. Ferrell T. started scribbling notes on the yellow pad, a good little secretary.

"Lee," said Tom, "as you and I previously discussed, Leona left you everything but a small trust and a few personal property items that she devised to the people in this room. You and I have been over the exact provisions, and an appraisal of the personal property items has been rendered. Therefore, unless anyone cares to protest . . . ," he paused and glanced Roland's way, "those items may be disbursed immediately."

"You mean Lee gets the house?" Roland blurted, slamming his fist on the table. At the same moment, Ferrell T. stabbed a period on his legal pad so hard the pencil point cracked.

"Yes," said Tom, firm and quiet in a tone that hinted there better not be any more uncontrollable outbursts. Even Eli threw Roland a dirty look. "Lee inherits everything but the items we're about to discuss."

Roland snaked his arm back into his lap and shut up. Ferrell T. tossed the broken pencil aside and whipped a pen from his shirt pocket.

Tom turned to Lee and she nodded, expressionless.

"Now then," he said, and let out a big sigh as if sitting took a lot out of him. He flipped a couple of pages and started reading. " 'To my dear friend, Pal Sykes . . .' "

Pal's grease-streaked face lit up. "Whutn't she sweet?"

" 'I leave my 1972 Cadillac . . .' "

Pal gasped.

" '. . . because he has always admired it and I know he will take such fine care of it.' "

"Oh, my Lord." Pal clapped his charcoal hands together and wrung them out. "Whutn't she sweet? Whutn't she sweet? Wait'll I tell my little Joey!"

I smiled. Pal's half brother Joey, barely seventeen, towered over Pal by a good five inches. He had come to Solace Glen two years before, when their father went to jail down in Georgia. Because of that, and a seventeen-year age difference, Pal treated his half brother more like a son.

Tom slipped an envelope across the table. "There're the title and the keys, Pal. She's all yours."

"I'm happy for you, Pal," said Lee.

Roland snarled, "Well, isn't this just the damn *Wheel of Fortune*. All we need is some bimbo handing out the goods."

Ferrell T. snorted and smirked.

Tom snapped the pages of the will like a cracking whip.

Roland shut up again, and his useless son tried to imitate Tom's professional demeanor without success. " 'To my dear friend, Wilma Fizzi.' " He stopped, daring Roland to say something, anything, but all he got was silence. " 'I leave two thousand dollars a month to be taken out of the trust established in paragraph seven above and to be administered by my niece, Lee Jenner, as stated above. This monthly sum will continue for the lifetime of my dear friend, Wilma Fizzi, and will, I hope, grant her peace of mind regarding her mortgage, utilities, and groceries. Whatever is left, I hope she will take a nice trip every now and then and think of me.' "

Roland started gagging so hard he had to get up and hang out the window. Garland grabbed a paper cup of water Tom had thoughtfully put at each place and handed it to her husband.

"You OK, Daddy?" Ferrell T. turned and glared at Miss Fizzi as if she'd tried to physically catapult Roland out into the street.

I patted Miss Fizzi on one shoulder, Lee handled the other. "Your worries are over, Miss Fizzi," I said, happy as a clam.

"You deserve a nice retirement." Lee absolutely glowed.

"Whutn't she sweeeet!" Pal could hardly contain himself. This was the most excitement he'd seen that didn't involve transmission fluid.

"Damnation," coughed Roland. "Damnation."

Miss Fizzi sat awhile, letting the news sink in. Finally she said, "Leona was the kindest woman I ever knew, and I will do my best to make good use of her resources. With your help, dear." She grasped Lee's hand.

Tom cleared his throat and went on. " 'To my dear friend, my treasure of more than twenty years, Felicity Ann Paxton, . . .' "

I cringed.

"'. . . and I apologize to her for using her legal name, but this is a formal document and Tom says I have to for the first mention. To Flip, . . .'"

I relaxed again, settling my gaze on the green carpet.

"'. . . who was always there for me, always listened, always gave good, common sense advice, always gave comfort even in her own sorrow, and always lifted my spirits in times of darkness, I leave one of my most cherished possessions, . . .'"

I could feel Roland's eyes burning into me.

"'. . . one of my mother's most treasured possessions, . . .'"

My face flamed. I could not look at him.

"'. . . the Bell family Bible.'"

My pupils twanged from floor to ceiling to Tom Scott to Ferrell T. to Roland Bell. I watched as Roland's fist closed tight around the paper cup he held. It crumpled and dropped to the floor. Ferrell T. stopped writing.

"The Bell family Bible," Roland repeated, hoarse. "The family Bible?"

"Allow me to finish the paragraph, please," said Tom evenly. He continued. "'I leave this Bible in your care, Flip, knowing your deep appreciation of books, your love of this community and its history, and your own aloneness since the loss, so many years ago, of your family. May this old book, with its words of wisdom and inspiration, its pages filled with Bell family mementos, give you what I believe you long for most.'"

After trying so hard to avoid him, I could not tear my eyes off Roland, his gray face, gray hair, gray eyes.

"And what is it you long for most, Fe-lic-i-ty Paxton?" He swaggered to the conference table, anchored both hard hands on its surface and leaned toward me.

I sat, a lump on a stump.

"Well, I know," he whispered low and eerie. "I know

what you long for most." He reared back and boomed, "You want to steal what is mine! You want what is rightfully mine! Mine and my children's inheritance!" He flung a pointed finger in Ferrell T.'s direction.

Lee's hand reached for mine.

"Sit down, Roland," Tom Scott rattled the will slightly, moving one finger across the page, his free hand touching Eli on the head to stifle the rising snarl. "If you wish to legally contest any portion of this will, you better let me know. You're next on the list."

"You mean there's something left? For little ole me? Her own brother?" Roland flopped into his chair, a sulky teenager. Ferrell T. picked up his pen, aiming it at me like a javelin he wanted to throw.

" 'To my brother, Roland Bell, and his family, I leave the remaining Bell family portraits, the ones I still have in my house.' "

"Great," spat Roland. "I get stuck with a bunch of dingy paintings that aren't worth a plugged nickel."

Tom's jaw twitched. " 'I also leave the houseplants, Garland has such a green thumb, and the Bell sterling and china.' "

He quit reading and folded the will up.

Roland's narrow mouth leaned to one side, eyebrows crossed. "That's it?"

"That's it," replied Tom. "Lee, I suspect you can work out with Roland and Flip when to pick up these items. Miss Fizzi, we'll be in touch soon. Pal, the car is parked out back."

Pal took on the appearance of somebody miraculously healed. "Thank you," he said, backing out of the room. "Thank you, thank you, thank you, thank you."

"I'll see you later, dear," Miss Fizzi pecked Lee on the cheek. "I think I have a hair appointment." She nodded good-bye to me and Tom, avoided Roland and Garland altogether, and wafted out of the room.

"I guess I ought to be going." I spoke to Tom and Lee, my back to the Bell's. "Lee, I'll see you this week when I come clean and we can . . . you know, do the Bible thing."

"I'm really glad Leona left you the Bell family Bible," Lee squeezed my arm. "She showed it to me once. I only glanced through it. There's a lot of local history between those pages: pictures, letters, dried flowers, and little poems. The past really does come alive."

"Letters?" Roland jerked his chair back and stood up. "More letters, Lee? Like the ones you got from Flip right after my sister died?"

Lee's nostrils flared and she faced Roland head-on. "What of it?"

"Those letters are stolen property! They were stolen by her." He pointed a long finger at me. "And I intend to get them back and prosecute to the full extent of the law! Everybody get that? Ferrell T., you still writing stuff down? You get that?"

Ferrell T. nodded furiously and kept his head low.

"Prosecute your heart out, you greedy maniac. But I tell you this right now." Lee raised her own finger at Roland. The blood rushed to her face, and the temperature in the room rose with it. "You will not succeed. You will lose. You have taken all you are going to take. I will hand over to you exactly what Leona wanted you to have and no more, Roland. You hear me? No more! Don't even think of coming around the house every couple of weeks like you used to, pointing at this, that, and the other thing and carrying stuff away. Leona was too good. She should have told you to go to hell ages ago." She lowered her finger and held both hands at her sides, fists tight. "You come get the portraits and the sterling and the china on Friday. If you don't, I'll pack it all up and leave it out on the street. Is that clear?"

Roland appeared to hang in midair, measuring the weights on either side of him. Suddenly, his whole demeanor changed. The gray of his skin turned to a childlike pink. His shoulders relaxed and he slowly sank back into his chair, smaller, a beatific expression on his face. "I guess I owe everybody an apology," he said sheepishly. "I don't know what got into me. My dear Leona's death came as such a shock." He pointed at the will in Tom's hands. "These words are her last wishes on earth and she obviously meant to be generous to the ones she loved. Who am I to question that? I don't want to make trouble. Tom, Lee, I'm not going to contest the will. I may not agree with all of it," a momentary glint flashed in the placid eyes, "but lawsuits are nothing but a waste of time and money."

That was it, then. The cheap side of Roland won out over the insult of not inheriting everything.

"Flip," Lee spoke to me, voice even as a lead pipe, "if you stop by my house after work, I'll make sure you get the Bell family Bible tonight. OK?"

"No problem." I was ready to leave, for sure. I ducked down the hall, stopped, leaned against a door frame, and took a deep breath.

In the quiet of Tom's office, I heard Roland's voice, wheedling and whiny. "But there's room for a little negotiation, isn't there, Lee? Surely, you'd agree—I got my rights. What would you take for those letters, for instance? They're only paper. . . ."

CHAPTER 6

✹

THE NIGHT AFTER Lee handed it to me, I sat down with the Bell family Bible, publisher's date 1898, and took the first step down a road that would lead me to a place I had no idea existed. I'd decided to keep the Bible hidden way up on top of a kitchen cabinet, shoved against the wall inside a big basket, protected by plastic and covered with Spanish moss I'd bought at a garden shop. Better safe than sorry where Roland was concerned.

The damn thing must have weighed eight pounds. I studied the inside cover. A family tree stretched across the paper, spilling onto the next page. Years and years of prominent Bells, going back to R. Bell, the first to land in Maryland in 1778, during the Revolution. He found somebody named Lucy Hanover to marry him three years later, and they had their first child, a boy, the next year. Six more children followed that boy, four of them dead by the time they turned six, a common tragedy before the progress of medicine caught up with the progress of disease. The three who lived—Richard, Ferrell (mystery of the name solved), and Lucinda—all married, had children, survived into their sixties, and were buried here in Solace Glen.

The writing of the entire chart changed three or four times with the generations, though the same hand wrote all the early part of the family history. I could picture a little wife of a Bell sitting down in 1898 with her new Bible she got as a wedding present and painstakingly drawing her new family tree, maybe from the memory of her husband's relatives, maybe from an older Bible on its last legs. Something to leave her children so they'd know their roots.

I knew so little of my own. Grandparents on my father's side seemed but a dull memory; I only knew the names of my mother's Baltimore parents. Beyond that, the branches of my pitiful family tree hung bare and fruitless. If my parents had lived, I would have learned more of the Paxtons once I reached an age where such things intrigued me. But my parents didn't live; I would never know. I hated that the older I grew, the larger that void within me stretched, replacing the contentment I should have earned by now with a stifling restlessness and loneliness.

Leona knew how much I envied people with an orchard of family trees, so she gave me hers to tend. That must have been why she left me such an inheritance, why she chose me as the gardener.

I closed the Bible and lugged my grove of Bells back to the top of the kitchen cabinet, safe from one of their own, safe from Roland Bell.

By mid-October, the tension between Roland and those of us unfortunate enough to inherit from a Bell cooled to a steady simmer. Roland couldn't stand the thought of paying good money to the cleaning woman who'd cheated him out of the illustrious family Bible, so he dumped me, something of a relief given my state of anxiety. The note read: "Miss Paxton. Due to circumstance, your service is no longer required. R. and G. Bell." Not that Garland signed it herself. I imagined Roland told her she'd have to vacuum her own floors now, on top of her nonpaying job at the Café. No skin off Roland's back. He could brag about the money he'd saved.

Fall appeared without much fanfare. Foliage changed color in the blink of an eye. I'd drive down Center Street in the early morning and the sugar maples lining the sidewalks flashed by in the mid-October sun like a parade of bright orange school buses. The chilly air required a sweater at the start of the day, but by ten o'clock, I'd peel off the extra layer and do my business in shirtsleeves.

"What's Plain Jane going to be on Halloween?" It was Thursday, my regular cleaning day at the Historical Society.

Lee glanced up from her coffee mug, considered Plain Jane, and twisted her mouth. "A car mechanic or a prostitute. She can't decide."

I deposited my carryall on the floor and reached for a Danish. "Why not both?"

"That's an idea. I could dress her in a white jump suit zipped down to her navel with her name sewn on the shoulder in flame red, and she could wear black, vinyl stiletto boots." She dipped her nose into the coffee mug. "So, aren't you curious about what Roland wanted to do?"

"About what?"

"About the letters."

We hadn't discussed Roland's reaction to Leona's will until now, and I hadn't wanted to pry. I licked icing off my thumb. "Did he offer to buy them?"

Lee smirked. "Roland spend a nickel he doesn't have to? No, he wanted to trade."

Now it was my turn to smirk. "And what, pray tell, was his generous offer?"

"Half price meals at the Café. For forty-eight hours. Tuesday and Wednesday only."

We burst into gales of laughter, and it felt so good. I snorted, "He may as well have offered to steal them."

Lee drew a deep breath. "Yeah. Tom Scott told me to watch my back."

Behind my smile, a shiver iced my spine. Tom possessed both brains and common sense. If he'd told Lee to be careful, the rest of us had better mind our p's and q's. I pictured the Bell Bible on top of my kitchen cabinet and wondered if the hiding place was good enough.

"Where'd you put Leona's letters?" I glanced around the room for secret spots. "Somewhere safe, I hope."

"Don't you worry about them." Lee reached over to Plain Jane, unbuttoned her high neck collar a few inches and drew out the velvet bag of letters. "Jane's bosom buddy."

"Ooooo." I had to hand it to her. "Even Roland isn't weird enough to look there."

"That's what I thought. Anyway," she stood up and stretched, "I've been too busy dealing with renting the big house to worry about the letters."

"Renting the big house?" I blinked. "I didn't know you were looking for anybody. I thought you might change your mind and live there yourself."

"Oh, please. Abandon Plain Jane? Keep Jeb, the spoiled cat, in the manner to which he's grown accustomed? He'll just have to get used to the smaller things in life."

"Well, I can't say I blame you. I couldn't picture you anywhere but here. This house suits you."

I didn't say it suited her because she was single with no kids. She wouldn't have said such a thing to me, either. The difference between us was I'd almost accepted my lot in life, dusting the pictures of other women's children and picking up the dirty clothes of other women's husbands. In the back of my mind, on the smallest shelf, I still held onto the hope that there was somebody out there for me, but as the years passed, the hope faded. With my endless work schedule from age eighteen on, the most eligible men I met consisted of vacation drunks on the make in Ocean City. Any other single man I lucked upon turned out too old, too young, too stupid, or not single enough. So I dusted and cleaned and traded what wishes and dreams I had for the happy dreams of friends. Lee wanted the Cinderella dream, the whole enchilada, and she possessed the beauty and brains to snare a prince, but she was also old enough to understand we don't always get what we want.

"Yeah." She glanced around the room, so cozy and familiar to her. "It'd depress me to move right now. If I rent the big house, I can always change my mind at the end of a year's lease. A history professor from Hood's going to live there."

"You met her?" A new resident always tweaked my curiosity. The last newcomer we'd welcomed to Solace Glen was Miss Fizzi's awful grandnephew, Suggs Magill, who moved into her basement apartment three years ago. He proved himself so surly and antisocial, we'd snatched up the welcome mat before he could plant a dirty boot on it. No need to knock yourself out for somebody who's only going to spit in your eye.

"It's a him, and I haven't met the man. He came through a real estate agency in Frederick, but he's stopping by this morning to say hello to his new landlady. Moves in tomorrow."

"Where's he been living?"

"How should I know?"

I picked up a rag and started wiping down the pine table. I worried about Lee. "Well, what do you know about this man? He's going to be surrounded by a lot of nice family heirlooms. He could run off with everything for all you know."

"The agency checked him out, Flip." She batted the hazel eyes. "He's only a murderer and a serial rapist. Not a thief, thank God."

"All I know is what I read in the papers."

"Then you ought to read more optimistic papers." She stared out the back window. "I'm going to plant more rosemary this spring. Maybe some extra basil."

A thought struck me. "Who's going to tend to Leona's roses?" She'd spent half a lifetime mothering her flower garden.

"Oh, my gosh. I hadn't even thought about that." A knuckle rapped on the door and she jumped. "Damnit. I need a doorbell."

"You need a lot of things," I mumbled, wiping the table, keeping an eye on the door she opened wide to a stranger.

The man hesitated. "You are Mrs. . . . Miss . . . Ms. Lee Jenner?"

"Lee." She whipped a hand out. "I'm Lee Jenner. Come in."

He had more than six feet on him because he had to tilt his neck to one side in order to get through Lee's front door. He stepped into the house and stood, waiting for further instructions as a gentleman should. I stopped pretending to clean and took a good look.

Not movie star handsome, but his face might turn a few heads. Regular features; strong cheekbones; a firm, if slightly lopsided mouth; long, thin nose; deep-set eyes that looked like layers of blue scraped down to the barest color; brows straight as a shot across a high, intelligent forehead; rust-colored hair; a few wisps of gray combed back off his face. My guess—early forties. Good shape. Probably a runner.

Also, probably married, gay, or divorced with baggage.

He caught me inspecting him, nodded, and turned to Lee. "I'm Sam Gibbon," he introduced himself, voice deep and smooth with an accent I couldn't quite place. "But I expect you know that."

"She only knows what she reads in the papers." Good thing I was there to say that.

Lee flung me a dirty look, and I slapped the dust rag at Plain Jane a few times, arching an eyebrow at Sam Gibbon.

The high, intelligent forehead creased at the sight of Jane. "Are her eyes made out of . . . condoms?"

"Why, I'm not sure," said Lee, puzzled. "Flip, show the professor your eyes."

I gaped, fuming.

"You know, I believe they are. Are they Trojans, Flip?" She crossed her arms and one ankle as I grabbed the carryall and stomped upstairs. I could have killed her, embarrassing me like that.

"Former friend of yours?" I heard Sam Gibbon ask.

"That's Flip Paxton, our local caregiver. If you want," her voice carried upstairs, "she'll keep house for you."

He must have nodded because she called out, "Yeah! He'd like you to come by every . . . once a week? . . . every other week! Got that, Flip?"

"Mmmmm," I mooed downstairs, suddenly wishing I was the one who owned the Historical Society and Lee was the one who mopped floors.

"What day is good for you, Ms. Paxton?" he called up.

I remembered Roland's open space. "Friday mornings!"

"Done deal!" Lee sealed the contract and I heard Sam Gibbon wonder how expensive I might be.

"Oh, twice a month cleaning is part of the rent," she answered.

That's when I knew she liked him. And wanted me for eyes and ears.

CHAPTER 7

❋

SAM GIBBON WASN'T the only new face in town. The day after he moved into the Bell house, Solace Glen experienced a major storm—Hurricane C.C.

At the Crown station, where the sign above the door read, THE ONLY GAS IN TOWN YOU CAN PUT IN A CAR, Pal Sykes handed out Styrofoam cups of coffee with one hand and directed Joey how to pump gas with the other. His only help in this endeavor rested on the iron shoulders of Suggs Magill, Miss Fizzi's silent, surly, bullish nephew, a man the exact opposite of Pal in every way except mechanical skill. Pal handled the customer contact; Suggs rarely emerged from the garage.

The Crown stood kitty-corner between Center Street and Dorsey, perched on a triangular lot so if you drove up from the Center side, you had to exit onto Dorsey and vice versa. Unless you happened to be Cecile Crosswell.

The first time C.C. drove into the Crown and honked her silver BMW for Pal and Joey to come running and fix her up, we knew Solace Glen was in for some push and shove. I'd just pulled up to the diesel pump, so I saw the whole mess.

C.C. sat on her horn for a good sixty seconds until she couldn't take the terrible lack of service any more. The car door flung wide, and this creature emerged dressed to the nines and reeking of the perfume counter at Sak's.

"My God!" she exploded loud as a firecracker. "My Gaawwd!"

This religious exclamation enticed Pal out of the garage, wiping his oily paws and blinking like some forest animal that hadn't seen the light of day all winter. "Ma'am?" he chirped. "What can I do for ya? Didja want some gas? Joey! Where is that boy? Probably round back sittin' in the Cadillac again." Pal loped over to the BMW to check if it read "Unleaded Only."

"*If,*" C.C. flung her brunette coif around and clapped her hand across her bosom, "it would not be too much t-rou-ble." Then she hurled Pal an expression that could have drawn blood.

The moment C.C.'s car registered full on the gauge, she slapped a ten and a twenty in Pal's dirty palm and started to back onto Center like a bat out of hell. I watched all this thinking, that's none too smart, somebody's surely going to be coming the other way. Sure enough, somebody was. Screamin' Larry from WFIB 102.7, Frederick's Defiant Jazz station, drove up in his Big Orange Volkswagon Beetle with the Syracuse University sports logos plastered all over it—ten for basketball, fifteen for lacrosse, thirty for football, and who knows how many more. Never played a sport in his life, but the coaches used to beg him to come to games just to scream.

This is who C.C. nearly creamed in her pretty BMW.

After a horrific screech of tires from both sides, the dust cleared and the two vehicles sat nose to ass, with Screamin' Larry wiping a jelly doughnut off his face. C.C. sat ramrod straight and glared into her rearview mirror. Larry cleared a little jelly path for his nose to breathe and sized up the situation: brand new BMW, obviously a newcomer or a visitor unaware of Solace Glen road protocol, Northern Virginia, maybe, or worse, D.C. He didn't have to be at the station until nine p.m., six more hours.

He turned off the ignition, opened his dinner pail of KFC, and started the picnic.

C.C. tapped her manicured claws on the steering wheel. Finally, after a whole two minutes, she steamed out of the car, stationing herself by the driver's leather seat, arm draped across the top of the door like it was her best friend. "*Ex-cuse* me. I need to get out. Please back up."

She pronounced each word as if she'd found herself in a foreign country where none of the natives spoke English, especially obese men in orange Beetles. She bobbed her head in a take-no-prisoners fashion and slid back into the BMW.

Larry was having a fine time with his picnic. He'd gone through a breast and a cup of mashed potatoes.

Other motorists and pedestrians began to notice this roadside drama at the Crown. Marlene dawdled outside the cleaner's across the street. I caught a glimpse of the Eggheads and Officer Lukzay staring through the picture windows at Roland's Café and Grill. Lee coasted to a stop at the Center Street stop sign and idled, windows rolled down. Tina Graham and Margaret Henshaw, window shopping at Solace Glen's pitiful retail offerings, lingered in front of Connolly's Jewelry Store.

C.C. did not budge. Nobody in front of her, a clear exit.

But she came in Center Street and was hell bent on going out Center Street. End of story.

Screamin' Larry tossed a chicken bone out the window and helped himself to a biscuit.

C.C. reemerged from the BMW holding up typed directions with a map, same stance. "Ex-*cuse* me . . . sir. I have a very important appointment with my decorator. I drove in from that street and that is the direction I need to go. Now. My husband, Leonard—Leonard Crosswell? THE attorney? Well, he and I have just bought the O'Connell estate. . . ."

At this point, the audience snickered at her hoity-toity reference to that old barn as an "estate." But like any good actress worth her salt, C.C. let the reaction pass and moved on with her lines.

". . . and I am sure you would agree that it is in the community's best interest for you to back up and let me get started renovating an important local landmark, and then you can get on with whatever it is you do." She thumped her map, repeated the same sharp bob of the head and climbed in the BMW, her foot gunning the engine ever so slightly. Maybe she figured she'd get lost if her wheels touched any street except Center, but her head problem was now Larry's.

Screamin' Larry popped open a carton of coleslaw, amused by C.C.'s entire performance. His amusement tripled when a car pulled up behind him. He grinned at C.C., strands of coleslaw sticking out of his teeth, and pointed a finger behind him, shrugging his massive shoulders.

C.C.'s jaw dropped. "How many jackasses are there in this town?"

The jackass who pulled up behind Larry was none other than Wilma Fizzi.

Screamin' Larry doubled over, heaving. Miss Fizzi would wait in line for days, a good sheep, no complaints. He peered into his rearview mirror. Miss Fizzi smiled back at him and fluffed her hair up with a knitting needle, lighting his candle something fierce. This called for dessert.

The crowd, growing steadily, waited in anxious anticipation. C.C., our new neighbor, could make or break the welcome mat, have crab cakes and spiced shrimp on her doorstep next week or end up wondering why the Christmas carolers always skipped her house.

The BMW backed up, slowly, slowly, the rear fender barely kissing Larry's front bumper. No doubt C.C. thought this creeping adagio would intimidate the dumb local yokel into backing up. When he realized what C.C. was doing, however, Larry fired up the Big Orange. C.C. gradually applied the gas. Larry leaned forward, gripping the steering wheel, licking the last of the apple tart off his lips. The Beetle pushed against the BMW. After all those years of watching the action, Screamin' Larry had at last found his athletic niche.

The BMW, however, owned more horses, a fact not lost on C.C., who apparently could care less if her insurance company had to mend some scratches. Larry's Big Orange Beetle bumped into Miss Fizzi's Oldsmobile station wagon. The crowd moaned, "Awwww." Joey Sykes came running from somewhere behind the Crown station and screeched to a halt, bug-eyed at the excitement. Here and there, somebody called, "Hang in there, Larr!" "Give it the gas, boy!" Michael Connolly from the Jewelry Store yelled, "Miss Fizzi, wake up! Whatchoo think Jesus would do?"

The startled face gleamed pasty white as Larry's Big Orange Beetle again rolled into her wagon. Lips mouthing the Lord's Prayer, Miss Fizzi grabbed the gearshift, searching for reverse. Her corrective shoe stomped the gas pedal and the Oldsmobile lurched forward forcing Larry into a Beetle sandwich, squished in front, rocked from the rear.

C.C. floored it.

The Beetle shook so hard, it looked like a big, round

jackhammer pounding into Center Street. Screamin' Larry did his best to hold on, arms wrapped around the steering wheel, a crazy, murderous glint in his eye. I wouldn't want to be C.C., however this turned out.

Finally, Miss Fizzi had all she could handle. Her tiny hands grasped the air, pupils rattling wild around the whites of her eyes, settling on the two faces that stared out the window at Roland's Café. The Eggheads. She slapped her palms against the driver's window and mouthed the words, *Hellllp meee,* and the Eggheads leaped into action. Chairs turned over, plates bounced off the table, paper napkins tucked into their collars flapped like white flags as they raced out of Roland's leaving the immovable Lukzay in their dust.

The crowd yelped, "Hoorah!" A tourist, grabbing an oyster stew at Roland's, wriggled through the commotion and aimed his camcorder. At this point, even Suggs Magill emerged from the Crown garage, in time to see the Eggheads attempt to rescue his great-aunt. He could have at least helped but, true to form, Suggs stood stone still looking mad at the world and the Eggheads, in particular.

The Eggheads galloped to the wagon and halted, studying the situation. The Oldsmobile rocked back and forth, engine roaring, gear stuck. Miss Fizzi bammed on the window.

The Eggheads conferred, blond heads locked together. Suddenly one started pacing back and forth, waving his arms at Miss Fizzi, chanting, "OK, OK, OK," in an apparent effort to calm her down. The other one bolted off, pants on fire, into the Crown station. Within seconds he bolted out again carrying a tire iron, Pal skipping along behind him, calling, "Jesse/Jules, Jesse/Jules! Whatchoo doing with my iron? I was using that iron. That was my daddy's iron."

The Eggheads now had weaponry.

One yelled at Miss Fizzi to get out the way while the

other one raised the tire iron quarterback-style and made a play for the window full steam, leaving Miss Fizzi just enough time to dive for cover before the tire iron rammed through the Oldsmobile. The crowd murmured, "Oooooooo." Egghead No. 1 withdrew the weapon while Egghead No. 2 reached in, pulled up the lock, and opened the door. He dragged the shocked Miss Fizzi out of the car, flung her fragile little body over his shoulder, and took off running, the winning touchdown in the big game. The crowd roared. The tourist with the camcorder got it all.

Meanwhile, the Oldsmobile, without Miss Fizzi in it to occasionally stomp the gas pedal, no longer lent Larry the added force needed to defeat Cruella Deville in the BMW. The Big Orange edged back against the wagon, and the two cars gave way to C.C. With a smirk of red lips and no looking back, the newest addition to Solace Glen neatly shifted gears and sped away.

"I'll be." Marlene, eyes wide, grinned like the Cheshire cat. She and Larry always took delight in each other's misfortunes.

"Praise God no one was killed." Miss Fizzi wobbled around in front of Roland's while her surly nephew, Suggs, shrugged in her direction and retreated back into the garage. One Egghead fetched her an iced tea; the other one proudly inspected the smashed window of the Oldsmobile. Officer Lukzay, still seated at the window, sipped his free coffee.

Pal and Joey pulled Larry out of the Beetle. Larry stood up; chicken bones and biscuit crumbs tumbled off his chest and lap. They walked to the front of the Big Orange, shook heads, shuffled to the rear, shook heads. Larry glanced in the direction C.C. disappeared. His eyes narrowed as he stroked his overgrown beard.

"You gonna press charges, Larry?" Pal rubbed a finger across the new indentations in the tail of the Volkswagon. A Syracuse lacrosse sticker floated off.

"No," said Larry. "I'm gonna take care of this myself."

My eyebrows shot up. The last time Larry announced he was going to take care of something himself—involving a notorious slumlord—the town ended up having to pay for a whole new gas line. Nobody got hurt, and those who suspected Larry considered the act a civil service since the slumlord picked up and slithered elsewhere. (An astonishing fact, Larry held duel degrees in music and chemical engineering and would use either discipline to accomplish his streaks of revenge.)

I capped off the diesel and screwed the lid on my tank. The crowd dispersed. Pal and Joey swept up the glass by Miss Fizzi's car, Joey chattering excitedly in his high-pitched falsetto. Larry drove the Big Orange next to a pump and filled it up. Marlene hung some dry cleaning in her car and puttered off. Lee pulled away from the stop sign and headed home. Margaret and Tina resumed their stroll. Michael Connolly steered his wife, Melody, back into the store, both of them handed something to talk about the rest of the day besides the usual bad business complaints.

I climbed into the car and hurried to my next appointment. On the way, I turned on the radio, WFIB 102.7. Larry's prerecorded voice screamed a commercial. "The DEFIANT jazz station," the radio boomed, "that DEFIES country. DEFIES classical. DEFIES rap. DEFIES, most especially, bluck! the Oldies."

I wondered what Larry would play that night on his show. I'd bet anything the whole town would be listening.

CHAPTER 8

✻

Sam Gibbon knew about roses. He greeted me in the garden, intent on rewinding a hose around a rusty container, a pair of pruners dangling off a belt loop of his old jeans. He wore a faded red chamois shirt and weathered boat shoes with hole-ridden socks that used to be white. I studied his eyes, so watery blue, slightly crinkled—eyes I'd started to imagine lately in daydreams. He glanced up from the hose and smiled. I quickly looked away.

"I forgot you were coming today."

That pretty much summed me up. Forgettable. My hair, a nondescript brown, never got more interesting than a tight ponytail and hadn't seen a pair of scissors in six months. No make-up and a washed-out complexion probably appealed to him, too. At least I had flat mouse ears and a long neck, my only good features.

I hoisted the carryall, practically another limb on my

body, and headed for the front door. "It's been two weeks. Guess Lee forgot to remind you."

The words flew out so fast, he stumbled over them. "How well do you know Lee?"

I paused at the front door and wiped a rag across the brass knocker, hiding my frown but not my curiosity. "You two getting to be good friends?" Lee had become uncharacteristically close-mouthed on the subject of her new tenant. At her last cleaning, I couldn't pry a word out of her with the most obvious hints.

"Now that's a question my mother might have asked about a new buddy on the block."

"OK, I'll try to be more sophisticated." I spit at the doorbell and rubbed it clean. "Taken her to a pig roast yet?"

Sam rhythmically swung the hose, eyes dropping to his feet. "Garsh, Miz Flip. I haven't known her a month."

"You're absolutely right." So maybe they weren't an item yet and I had a chance. I squinted at the drab face reflected in the knocker. "I should never have asked such a sophisticated question." Then I shamed myself by lying, "I'm just looking out for Lee."

Sam slit his eyes at me and laughed. "I guess I should expect this sort of thing—probing, personal questions. Small town. Not that many singles under fifty. Any newcomer is suspect."

I swung the carryall onto my hip. "Yeah, not many singles around here under fifty. *We're* a definite minority."

I zipped inside to work on the house, worried I'd been too forward. When I finished a couple of hours later, Sam was attacking the yard with a rake.

"I didn't know history professors came out of their ivory towers long enough to do manual labor." I set the carryall at my feet and watched him rake. He appeared comfortable enough.

"Oh, we poke our poor, strained eyes out the tower door

occasionally on the chance a beautiful maid and her Rebel general might come riding by."

My eyes twitched. Which maid did he mean? "You been talking to Lee about those letters?"

"No," he quit raking and leaned against an oak tree. "She's been talking to me."

That really straightened my spine. "You? Why you?"

"I guess she figures I'm some sort of expert." He grinned a sexy, disarming grin that made me wonder if I was jealous of Lee or protective of her. "I haven't actually *seen* the letters, but she described the contents to me. Our friend J.E.B. got around."

I didn't return the grin. If he knew Leona had entrusted those letters to me while she was dying, then his little joke fell flat, but maybe he didn't know. "Well, *I've* seen the letters."

He snapped to attention. "You, Flip? I had no idea." He observed the serious frown I wore. "I'm sorry—I just realized Lee said they were her aunt's last request and . . . you delivered them, didn't you?"

I replaced Sam on my pedestal, but still worked my way through the conversation with a caution flag raised. It bothered me that Lee would discuss the Bell women's secret with a virtual stranger, but maybe it was her way of breaking the ice and getting to know him better. "Just what has Lee told you?"

"Not much." Was he lying? "She's mostly asked me questions, like somebody thinking out loud." That did sound like Lee. "She's wondering who to have look at them to check out their authenticity. If they're not by Stuart, why go farther? They could be written by anybody."

"But they refer to members of his family by name. . . ."

"Really? She didn't tell me that."

Should I have? I kept quiet, my protective instinct tuned high.

"Anyway, I told her I know somebody who can authenticate them."

I bet you do, and I bet *you'd* have to be the one to take them to your so-called expert.

"She can drive them down to D.C. or FedEx them. He's at the Smithsonian."

"Oh." Sounded plausible enough. "You're sure *nice* to take such an interest in our little slice of history."

Sam shrugged good-naturedly. "History's my bag, what can I say. Gives me a chance to get to know Lee."

That really set my antenna zooming. I picked up the carryall and slowly walked to the car. Sam fell in beside me. I quickly ran through an idea and cleared my throat. "If getting to know people around here is important to you, *sometimes . . .*"—like never—"Miss Fizzi throws a little Halloween tea party and some real nice people drop in. . . ."—like *me,* her cleaning lady—"and you'd get a chance to mingle." Or change the course of your entire future forever.

Sam nodded enthusiastically. "Great! I'd love it! Is there something I can bring? I'm not familiar with the local standards."

"Sam Gibbon." Flirting came as easy for me as nuclear physics. "You've lived here two whole weeks, you have all those big books stacked up in every room, you're a big college professor, and you can't look around and see how high our standards are?" I gave up, embarrassed at how stupid I sounded and tossed the carryall and mop in the car. "Wear a shirt that covers your chest, pants that cover your rear, and shoes that cover your feet. Exposed opinions are acceptable."

He stuck his chin on top of the rake. "So I should dress how I want and say what I will."

"Only if you wish to impress the ladies," I replied, sweet as a jonquil, giving it one last shot.

He watched me go, chin balanced on top of the tool. I glimpsed him in my rearview mirror, lost in thought, a tiny, faraway smile slowly spreading across his face.

Now what the hell was I going to tell Miss Fizzi?

CHAPTER 9

✳

Louise Lamm kept a picture of Marlene on her dress-ing table taken on Marlene's sixth birthday, around the time Mr. Lamm died. She posed in a stiff yellow crinoline dress, new white patent leather shoes, and an Easter bonnet that sprouted tiny pink and purple pansies. The color in the photograph had faded over the years, the same way Mar-lene's love for her mother had.

I hated dusting that picture. Louise kept dozens of other pictures, too, little monuments scattered all over her bed-room to the daughter she used to cater to. Baby pictures in sterling silver frames, buck-toothed elementary school pic-tures in brass, high school pictures of Marlene wearing red lipstick and white pearls, framed in floral fabrics. As if Marlene had only lived to age eighteen. No pictures of her beyond that time existed in Louise's home.

The story ran that when Marlene went off to college in

southern Virginia thirty years ago, she met a boy right off the bat and Louise hated him. She told Marlene the guy was nothing but a redneck out for only one thing, and it wasn't Marlene's winning personality. Louise refused to pay for Marlene to continue a second semester at that college unless she ditched the boyfriend. Marlene declined the offer.

Everybody thought that, without means, Marlene would slouch back to Solace Glen and sulk until she got that boy out of her system, but she suddenly grew a backbone and ran off with him. This happened in the early seventies, and Marlene imagined she was experiencing free love, but all she had really latched onto was a freeloader.

The boyfriend took every penny of her meager college savings and dumped her, leaving Marlene crying in Santa Somewhere, California. She had no choice but to call Louise and beg for travel money to fly east. Louise slapped her back in that woman's college fast as you could spit, and Marlene eventually graduated with a degree in Social Embarrassment. Their mother/daughter relationship never recovered, and Marlene's resentment gradually rivaled, then outdistanced, Louise's mortification. She returned to Solace Glen, lived with her mother only until she could afford to rent a place of her own (thanks to Louise who bought the local flower shop for her to run), and began to treat her mother with such disrespect and disdain, it made the whole community sick.

Sooner than later, Louise showed the strain of having her only child reject her. Before she got sick, before the cancer set in, she tried everything she could to make amends with her ungrateful daughter. She started buying things: a new car, landscaping for the ugly shack Marlene rented, expensive vacations, fancy clothes, jewelry. Anybody could have told Louise she was wasting her money. Marlene took and took and took; Louise gave and gave and gave.

There are people in life who are natural born takers, and no matter what you give them, no matter what you do for them, no matter how hard you try to win their affections, you are fighting a losing battle because all they really care about is numero uno. So much time and attention was lavished on the child Marlene that the girl thought the world owed her something and the woman knew for sure it did. Marlene grew from spoiled brat to snotty snit to obnoxious teenager to arrogant, cold-hearted bitch. And Louise watched wide-eyed, horrified, and disbelieving.

Finally, Louise realized nothing she did and nothing she bought could patch the holes that had erupted during Marlene's rebellious college years. So she simply stopped. She told me she would wait, she'd done enough; now Marlene would have to make her own move toward reconciliation.

I could have told her how that plot would play out. Zilch. Nada. All she wrote.

Marlene never called her mother on the telephone. Never visited. Never wrote a note. Never asked anybody to look in on Louise to check how she was getting along. She even married a man and didn't tell her mother. Nobody knew anything about Marlene's husband except his name was Worthington. They never lived together and divorced within a year. She probably paid some illegal English alien who jumped ship to marry her so she could ditch the Lamm name.

So Marlene and Louise lived in the same town, attended the same church, knew the same people, shopped in the same stores, ate at the same restaurant. Bloomed off the same family tree. Yet, the two barely made eye contact. Marlene lived her life; Louise lived hers. People came to appreciate the family dynamics, would ask one to a party, not the other. Next party, they'd switch off. If Louise and Marlene showed up at the same event, the room tended to split into two teams. I'd gravitate to Louise's side; the Fifth Commandment means something to me. It was Louise, two weeks after my parents died, who hemmed my graduation dress and saw to it that I carried a dozen red roses just like the other girls. In that sea of faces that ran together in the high school auditorium, hers was the only one I saw when they handed me my diploma.

Louise put down the book she was reading, *The Shell Seekers*, and stretched out her legs on the ottoman in front of the rocker. "So how are all Leona's heirs and heiresses this Monday morning?"

I slapped a dust rag at a Marlene exhibit, age ten. "Everybody's holding their own, including me."

We shot each other a knowing look.

Louise took a sip of orange juice. "Pal's car hasn't been vandalized?"

"Nope. Even if it were, he'd never believe anyone from his own hometown could be involved in hurting a beautiful old Cadillac."

"Miss Fizzi doing OK?"

"You mean except for the fact she's got Suggs as a nephew?" I forced a thirteen-year-old Marlene to face the wall, giving me the illusion of punishing her.

"Isn't he awful? I heard he didn't lift a finger to help her get out of the car with that mess between C.C. and Larry."

"Yep, it was a despicable thing to witness. You'd think he'd be more appreciative, a thirty-year-old man living rent free in her house the last three years. But, at best, he treats her like she doesn't exist and, at worst, acts like her kindness is unbearable punishment. Makes you wonder where he sprang from because he's nothing like Miss Fizzi."

"Nobody's like our Miss Fizzi." Louise took a possessive view of Solace Glen's residents. "And how are you? And Lee?"

I rolled my eyes. "We're big girls. I've got the Bell family Bible well hidden and Lee has those Civil War letters in a *very* safe place."

"Well," Louise sighed hard, "all I can say is you and Lee better . . ."

"Watch our backs?"

Louise nodded. "Exactly."

"That's what Tom Scott thinks, too." As soon as I said the words, I bit my tongue.

Louise dropped the book. "Tom said that? Tom's worried?"

"Oh, you're out of juice." I didn't want her blood pressure skyrocketing. "It was just talk. Matter of fact. Casual."

"But Flip," Louise slid her legs off the ottoman and straightened her back, "if Roland is serious about getting everything Leona gave away, he'll do anything. Anything. You can't trust him, and do not underestimate him. He's volatile, mercurial. Tom's right about him."

I gently pushed her back into the rocker and lifted her legs to the ottoman. "Read your nice book and quit worrying about that idiot Roland."

"He's not an idiot," she protested. "A greedy Scrooge, yes. An illiterate materialist, yes. But he's not an idiot. I repeat, don't you underestimate him."

I patted her shoulder, so thin and bony, knowing she spoke the truth. "I won't. I promise."

"Good." She breathed easier and caressed the jacket of the book in her lap. "Now tell me about Lee and this new young man in town."

"Sam Gibbon. I was just over there two days ago." I felt the red flood my cheeks. "Cleaning." People were already saying his name next to Lee's, even though those blue eyes had floated through my mind more than once.

"I'd like to meet him. So would Miss Fizzi."

Unknowingly, Louise had just solved my dilemma. "Miss Fizzi wants to meet him?"

Louise closed her eyes, drifting off. "This weekend, Flip. You arrange it. You're so good at arranging. You take such good care of everybody."

I took a mohair blanket from the foot of the bed and ballooned it over her outstretched legs, two matchsticks.

"Tea," she murmured. "Or lunch." Her head slowly drooped to one side. I could hardly catch the words. "I'm tired. You decide. You decide for me."

Before walking out the door, I leaned over and whispered in her ear, "I'll talk to Miss Fizzi about a tea on Halloween. Don't you worry. I'll take care of everything."

CHAPTER 10

❈

I NEVER UNDERSTOOD why Tom Scott hired anybody to clean his office; it was never the least bit dirty. The man was a housewife's dream. I'd never even stepped foot in his old, stone house outside of town where he lived with his younger brother, Charlie, who traveled the exotic places of the world as photojournalist. Tom always said it wasn't worth my time to clean his home, but I suspected he valued his privacy more than just about anything, except Eli. I also suspected he dust-busted his office before I arrived to clean because I never saw any evidence that Eli shed. Highly impossible for a black Lab. Nevertheless, every Wednesday, come hell or high water, I climbed the narrow oak steps to his second-story office above Marlene's Gift and Flower Shoppe, loaded down with scrub sponges and disinfectants, prepared to do combat with the dirt, grime, and filth of the twenty-first century.

He always said the same thing when he saw me, his voice as smooth as the red silk ties he wore. "Ah. Flip. My heroine."

As if I came galloping in on a white horse to sweep him and all his dustballs up and trot off into the sunset to Tahiti.

I always said the same thing back to Tom. "I'll start with the john, if you don't mind."

Tom hovered in his early fifties but looked younger. Despite the youthful good looks, he got a kick out of quoting eighteenth-century writers like Swift and Pope, and his jokes usually flew over everybody's head except Margaret Henshaw's. He made a good lawyer, but I pictured him more as a suave English professor in a distinguished old British college, peddling a rattling bike around campus in his gym shorts, black gown flapping in the breeze while the lusty coeds whistled at his legs. He stood a feather under six feet tall with graying coal hair, hawk ebony eyes that could spot a flea on a black dog, and a sharp nose able to savor a fine wine and smell a deal gone sour at the same time. When he smiled, ice melted two states away.

Tom was another one with an orchard of family trees. He counted two governors and a State Court of Appeals justice among the branches, but his was the last branch, and we'd all given up hope he or Charlie would pick a wife and continue the Scott name. Tom—because of his love of privacy, and Charlie—because he could never touch his feet to the ground long enough to make a footprint.

I always felt ill at ease with Tom. Inferior. He constantly asked questions, much worse when I was younger. Back then I didn't know any better than to answer. By the time I hit thirty, though, I started saying, "Mmmm," when he asked me something I considered none of his business. A smart guy, he took the hint.

I finished the bathroom, spotless before I cleaned, spotless after, and started on the conference room. Tom sat at the long table, poring over a pile of red books and looking sexy and scholarly at the same time. Eli raised his intelligent head when I entered, matching his master's scholarly expression.

Tom pulled his wire-rimmed reading glasses off, rubbed the bridge of his nose, and leaned back in the chair. "I hate custody cases," he moaned.

"Who doesn't?"

His mouth barely twitched into a grin and he shook his head. "How's it going with you, Flip? You enjoying the Bell family Bible?"

"Makes a good doorstop," I lied.

The hawk eyes flew at me, formed an evaluation, relaxed. "I'm sure you've put it in a safe place."

"He'll never find it. He'd have to burn the whole house down to destroy it."

Tom shifted in his chair and stared out the window. From that view, we could see Pal's newly shined Cadillac behind the gas station. Pal worked away, scrubbing hubcaps with a toothbrush and beaming at his brilliant reflection. Twice he had to shoo Joey away from the driver's door. No way was he letting a seventeen year old with a new driver's license behind the wheel. Suggs slouched against a soft drink machine, wiping a dirty rag over an engine part and shooting Pal sly, envious glances. It wasn't in his makeup to feel happy for anybody's good fortune, especially Pal's. Pal churned through each day with the energy of a four year old and expected the same from his employee—go, go, go, work, work, work. Too bad garage work formed Suggs's only employable skill. No doubt he pictured himself in quite different surroundings—the kingpin of a Las Vegas casino with glitzy showgirls draping each iron shoulder. But the road from here to there lay buried under reality.

Tom chewed on his lip. "I hope Pal's careful, and you . . ."

"I know, I know. Watch my back."

He stood up and did a couple of shoulder rolls. "To tell the truth, it's Lee I'm most worried about. Roland is . . . unpredictable. I wonder if *I* shouldn't act as custodian of those letters."

I rested my back against the windowsill, one question on my mind, one on my lips. "You think Roland would go after those letters Lee has?"

"He's curious enough about them."

"Aren't you?" That was the question on my mind.

Tom's eyes crinkled. "Jesse and Jules made it sound like they're worth a fortune. Something about J.E.B. Stuart and a woman?"

Lee obviously hadn't told him. "An expert needs to see them."

He eyed me and I could see the questions lining up in his brain, little soldiers ready for their marching orders. I zipped across the room and attacked a bookshelf with a dust rag while he stood by the window watching me, cradling his chin, scuffing the carpet with the toe of his shoe. A few minutes later, I announced the room was fit to do business in.

"Flip," he said, as I was sauntering out, "who is Sam Gibbon?"

"Sam Gibbon? Why?" The words squawked out of my mouth so high-pitched, he must have guessed who my daydreams centered on.

But Tom only answered my question with a question. "He's renting the house from Lee, isn't he?"

I lowered my voice and spoke slowly. "If you already knew, why'd you ask?"

He scratched his cheek. "Just wondered. I'd like to meet him."

"Oh. I see." A devious thought struck me. "You know, Miss Fizzi and Louise are having a tea Halloween afternoon to do just that. I arranged it." Thoughtful me. Unfortunately, my great idea had backfired in my face. When I

called Miss Fizzi to set up an intimate little tea for four—
her, Louise, Sam, and me—she'd started winding up like a
spin toy over what an incredible opportunity this would be
for her and Louise to find a husband for Lee before Christmas. So now Lee was the main event.

I studied Tom. "Why don't you drop by? Sam will be
offered up as the entertainment and Lee is going to serve
as the sacrificial lamb. Or maybe it's the other way around,
I forget."

He perked up. "Lee will be there, too?"

I studied him harder. "First you say you're worried about
Lee, mention Roland, and ask about Sam. Are you worried
about Lee and Roland or are you more worried about her
and Sam?"

The hawk eyes zoomed in on me. "What about her and
Sam?"

"Mmmmm," I lifted one eyebrow at him.

"*Is* there a Lee and Sam?"

"Mmmmmmm," I said, slow as melting butter, lifting
the other brow. "Gotta go."

So that's how it was. That's how it was.

LATER THAT NIGHT, I took down the Bible from its hiding place again, feeling guilty I'd neglected it for so long,
knowing these were Leona's people and she'd wanted me
to tend to each one. I made up my mind to do just that.

I reread the names of the first three Bells born in America who survived their childhood—Richard, Ferrell, and
Lucinda. The oldest son, Richard, married Kaye Thomas
in 1812, and by 1820, they had four children who, sadly, all
died before age twenty. Only one sibling lived long enough
to marry, in 1834, and she died within a year, probably
from childbirth fever. The child must not have survived,
either, because that whole branch of the family broke off,

nothing but blank space beneath the four names with their birth and death years.

I thought of Tom Scott and pictured his name, birth date, and date of death inscribed in the Scott family Bible. Underneath, the same blank space. It made me sad.

Somehow, I couldn't imagine my own name and the empty space beneath because I owned no Paxton family Bible, no special book handed down generation to generation. Granddaddy Paxton lay sleeping in the Presbyterian graveyard with my grandmother and parents; my mother's parents died by the time I turned two. So, whenever I pictured my own death, I saw only a few lines of print in the local newspaper—thin, crisp paper collected by the Boy Scouts, tied in bundles, and recycled.

The second Bell son, Ferrell, married Sara Doddin in 1808. They produced one offspring, another Ferrell, born twenty years later in 1828.

Think of waiting that long for a child. Poor Sara. She must have been knitting baby booties for other women, for her nieces and nephews, for twenty long, heart-wrenching years. She probably gave up hope and accepted the pity of those other mothers. Probably prayed a lot and listened when the family preacher told her it was God's will she live life barren. Maybe he even hinted she was being punished for some silly thing she carried out as a child: pulling her sister's hair or refusing to share an apple with her little brother. Nobody would have blamed her husband. Anything related to hearth and home fell squarely on the woman's shoulders.

Then one day, at age forty-three, the miracle happened. Out of the blue, God answered her prayers with a single nod of his head. He gave Sara a son in 1828, the year John Quincy Adams sat as president and Webster published the first *American Dictionary*.

I breathed a sigh of relief for Sara (my own mother gave

birth to me at age thirty-eight) and ran my finger parallel
across the page to discover what happened to the last sibling, Richard and Ferrell's sister, Lucinda.

Lucinda made her appearance in 1787 and married late,
at age thirty, in 1817. Her husband's name was Joseph
Paca. She bore him two children: a boy, John Bell, in 1820,
and a girl, Lucy, in 1829.

John Bell Paca never married and died in 1861, no doubt
a war casualty. I wondered which side he fought on, with
J.E.B. Stuart or against him. If you claimed Maryland as
your home state back then, the coin could land on either
side. I'd strolled around Gettysburg many a Sunday afternoon and the Maryland state monument tightened my chest
every time. Two wounded soldiers, one in ragged Yankee
blue, one wearing torn Rebel gray, helping each other, leaning on each other. Both wanting to go home. The words on
the statue read, "Brothers Again. Marylander's All."

Poor John Bell. One of many who didn't make it home
to his momma and daddy and little sister in 1861. No wife,
no children. A blank space beneath such sheared numbers.

CHAPTER 11

✼

A FEW DAYS before Halloween, I took my lunch break at the regular time at the Café. I nodded at Garland who twitched her nose like a rabbit on the run and dipped back into her hole, the kitchen.

Hilda traipsed over, red T-shirt tight as a tick. The high school proved lenient about letting her work during her own cafeteria time. I took a hard look at Hilda. She'd done an awful job of painting her face, as usual. The mascara hung off her lashes in black, spidery clumps. The sides of her round face and the heavy flesh of her lips looked like a child had dipped his thumb in ketchup and conducted an experiment across her. I couldn't help but think of the Bell family Bible and Hilda's illustrious background.

I handed her my order as she attempted to engage me in conversation.

"In gym class yesterday . . ."

"I can't remember. Do you graduate high school this year or is next year your time?"

"Next year," she answered quick and hustled lickety-split back to the kitchen.

Hilda's sensitivity on the subject of her two extra years in high school was common knowledge, a fact I counted on whenever small talk with her seemed too large a cross to bear. She struggled with math; she struggled with science; she struggled with gym class. And for what probably seemed an eternity to Hilda, she struggled with Margaret Henshaw. Whenever Margaret graced the Café, Hilda automatically sank into a deep slouch.

I drew my pocket atlas out of the carryall and settled in to contemplate New Mexico and Arizona. Each week, I'd plan a trip to a different part of the planet. Sometimes, the trip might include more than one place. I figured if I ever got the chance to see Arizona, I might as well throw in New Mexico, too. I pictured myself in Albuquerque, hanging out of a hot-air balloon swigging champagne and singing "We May Never Pass This Way Again" at the top of my lungs. These little imaginary vacations kept my hopes up that one day I might actually go someplace besides Ocean City, Maryland. I easily, if unrealistically, pictured myself the happy counterpart to Charlie Scott.

I was enjoying the hell out of myself when the front door of the Café swung open and Marlene Worthington swished in with who else but the already infamous Cecile Crosswell. For the past three weeks, Screamin' Larry's hint of coming catastrophe took the form of song dedications to "the red-lipped babe in the silver BMW," songs like "I'm Painting the Town Red." Not a good omen. It came as no surprise to me after the Battle of the Beetle that Marlene had sought out C.C. and now sported a new best friend.

I scrunched down behind the pocket atlas.

Marlene searched out a table by one of the picture

windows on either wing of Officer Lukzay's permanently reserved table, as chic as it gets at Roland's Café and Grill, and the two of them slithered into their seats for a power lunch. C.C. sported a lime-green suit with black piping while Marlene put on a pretty good show in a beige cashmere sweater Louise picked up for her one year in Bermuda. Her heavy black corduroy skirt hid a multitude of sins.

Hilda appeared with my liver and onions. Waiting on my table as often as she did, she'd learned that when the pocket atlas came out, a DO NOT DISTURB sign might as well be dangling around my neck. She quietly put the plate down, refilled my tea glass, and wandered off again, reminding me she did have a decent streak.

Five minutes hadn't passed when the Eggheads tramped in with Pal, disrupting the peace. Pal rarely left the Crown station for lunch, preferring to share a pitiful Spam sandwich and some chips with Joey, but every now and again he stepped out "for the sake of public relations," he said. The three feuded in a loud conversation with each other on the merits of Lawn Boy versus John Deere. They did this all the time. One would choose some particular consumer product and rant and rave about how great he thought it was, and the other two would get equally steamed up about a competitor's product. The problem was they watched too many commercials.

I sawed at the liver on my plate. Tom Scott and Ferrell T. strolled in while I downed the iced tea, Tom explaining in a patient tone something about trusts, Ferrell T., Mr. Paralegal-in-Training, nodding as if he understood every word. I gobbled a final bite, scraping the ittiest bit of onion up with the meat, and was about to leave when Lee popped in.

She glanced across the crowd and spotted me, raised a hand and skipped over, pretending not to see Roland at the cash register. Nearly two months of time had lapsed since Leona's funeral. When I'd stopped by to clean her house that morning, I'd noticed a definite change for the good in Lee. The peach in her cheeks reappeared, her hazel eyes sparkled, her auburn hair gleamed, the set of that Jenner jaw showed confidence and positive thinking.

"Hey, guess what?" she plopped into a chair.

"What? You get Plain Jane a playmate?"

"No," she picked up my empty tea glass and slid a piece of melting ice into her mouth. "I'm going to use Sam Gibbon's big, fat rent check to buy you a hair cut and some new clothes."

"Very funny." I slipped a stray strand of mousy hair behind an ear. "So . . . is it only business between you and Sam Gibbon?"

Mischief shined in the hazel eyes. She opened her mouth to speak. That's when the door swung open and Screamin' Larry bellowed, "After you, beautiful ladies, stealers of hearts!"

Louise Lamm, having a good day, and Miss Fizzi bustled into the Café, blushing and giggling into their kidskin gloves.

"Isn't he the cat's pajamas?" said Louise to Miss Fizzi, who nodded and mewed, "Mercy, yes."

Trotting right behind, Melody Connolly and Tina Graham gave their favorite radio personality huge grins.

Larry bowed and scraped the four of them to a table against the wall and proclaimed he hated to kiss and run. He pecked each one on the hand and lumbered across to his regular seat in the center of the room. Melody, never without an impeccable piece of jewelry from the family store, twisted her fingers around a dark necklace of jade beads and fondly watched Larry take his leave. Tina, too, basked in the light of his attention. Larry was probably the only man in the world to ever kiss her hand.

Larry's appearance offered the lunch crowd a whole new option of entertainment besides talking to themselves, and gradually the place grew quiet. For the first time, he and C.C. occupied the same air space since the Battle of the Beetle. His radio song dedications to "the red-lipped babe in the silver BMW" ran with such frequency, nobody could miss them.

So there Larry sat, not twenty feet from the object of his personal obsession.

The place bulged with customers yet nobody said a word, clinked a glass, or bent to retrieve a stray napkin. Larry, however, ran a finger over the menu, humming "Satin Doll," tapping at the food items he wanted, scratching away on his order pad. A demented Paul Prudhomme.

Everybody participated in Larry's lunch order. Every eye in the Cafe followed the movement of his hand as he wrote. Every ear attended the notes of "Satin Doll" as he hummed. Every face searched for Hilda to come snatch the order from Larry's fingers so the first scene of the drama could begin. Even Roland laid bony elbows on the counter and focused full attention on Larry.

After Hilda trotted off with Larry's order, nobody breathed. Any moment, he would glance up and see C.C., a sitting duck, in open view at the window.

C.C., as one might expect, wore the air of a woman bored out of her mind. Her lunch companion had clammed up when Larry blew in. Marlene's pop eyes bounced from Larry to C.C., C.C. to Larry, anxious for her to see him or him to see her and all hell to break loose.

C.C.'s idea of hell, however, was slow service. In a loud voice tailored especially for restaurant personnel, she squawked, "Does anybody work here? I'm famished!"

Marlene's mouth unhinged and she whispered loud enough for everybody to hear, "Why are you calling attention to yourself? Don't you know that's Larry sitting over there?"

Hearing his name, Larry glanced up from chomping his

fingernails and spotted Marlene. Then he saw C.C.

C.C. scowled at the room. "You mean that person who's been playing songs for me on the radio?"

Marlene pumped her head up and down.

"Which one is he?"

Larry stood, a towering man.

"Is that him?"

Marlene scooted her chair backward, prepared to leap out of harm's way. "Yep. That's the man you pushed your car into."

C.C. squinted at Larry. "He was in my way." She dipped red nails into a purse, pulled out a gold cigarette case, drew one long, skinny tobacco stick out, and lit it with a long, skinny sterling silver lighter.

I saw Roland open his mouth to recite the no-smoking speech, think better of it, and clamp his lips tight.

"You there," called C.C., spewing a thick, gray cloud that slowly drifted in Larry's direction.

Larry glimpsed over both shoulders, stuck a simper on his face, and pointed a finger at his chest.

"Yes, you," said C.C., irritated at his antics.

He took two steps forward.

You'd have thought he wore a holster with a .38 and growled, "Draw, cowboy." Chairs scraped the floor, women gasped, Roland ducked behind the cash register. Marlene reared back in such a panic, she toppled over and nobody cared.

C.C. exhaled more inconsiderate second-hand smoke. "If you find it funny to play those stalking songs on the radio to me, and we all know you mean me because I am the only one in this dump who owns a silver BMW—which had to be expensively fixed, thanks to you—then I can assure you, I do not find it funny, mildly amusing, or remotely clever." She tapped some ash on the floor. Roland gawked but kept quiet. "My husband, Leonard . . . Leonard

Crosswell? Perhaps you've heard of him if you read the *Post* or the *Times*? I'm assuming you can read. Well, Leonard is a very high-profile Washington attorney."

"Yikes," shuddered Larry and moved two steps closer.

"You could find yourself out of your little radio job if you continue to harass me in this manner. That is all I have to say to you." She swiveled her brunette hairdo around, completely finished with Larry and completely ignorant of the maniac she was dealing with. "Now, where is that waitress? I have an appointment." I hadn't seen a gleam like that in Larry's eye since the gas line blew up. He spoke three words and took three steps: Listen. Here. Babe.

The newest addition to Solace Glen was about to become its only homicide victim when a terrible crashing noise stopped Larry in his tracks and scared everybody out of their seats. "What the hell was that?" C.C. glared at Larry as if he bore responsibility.

Larry tore his eyes off her and stared out the picture window over Officer Lukzay's half-finished lunch. Everybody stared with him.

"Oh, mercy," whimpered Miss Fizzi. "I hope that nice young man isn't hurt."

The Eggheads took that as their cue to rush outside and lend expert assistance. Pal rose in his seat, curious.

"Who?" called Marlene from the floor. "Who is it?"

"Not so much who as what," announced Larry. He turned sly, gleeful eyes on C.C. "Pal's big . . . heavy . . . Cadillac. Looks like he lost control. I am so sorry, Mrs. Crosswell, on your recent loss." He peeked out the window again. "Your *total* loss."

Pal gasped. "But . . . but I'm here, Larry. That couldn't be my car. Unless . . ."

C.C. followed his gaze and started coughing and hacking and stomping out her cigarette and gathering her designer purse and clutching her throat. "That idiot!" she gagged. "Not again! That stupid boy! I just had that car fixed! Can't anybody do anything right in this hellhole?!"

She flew out of the Café, denying herself the pleasure of Roland's liver and onion special and us the pleasure of her company. The door of the Café banged open and everybody stood and strained their ears to hear the street-side drama. Pal raced after her.

With an attentive audience, C.C. lurched ahead of the Eggheads and screamed into the demolished Cadillac. "What-is-wrong-with-you?! Can't you drive?!" She got no answer and barely paused. "Don't you have anything to say for yourself? How could you manage to hit *my* parked car and nobody else's!"

Pal yelled explanations at the back of her head, complete bewilderment in his eyes. "I don't know, Miz Crosswell! I don't know! I'm telling you I just fixed the brakes! I don't know how this could happen! Joey! Are you OK?"

"Imbecile!" C.C. did an about-face, grabbed hold of Pal's shoulders, and shook him hard before crunching her high heel into his sneaker and whipping out a cell phone. She marched away.

The Eggheads guided a white-faced Pal to a sitting position on the curb and got busy attending to Joey, alive but covered in blood. I felt so bad for Pal, I wanted to cry.

Roland, however, displayed a different reaction, focused only on the Cadillac Pal inherited from Leona. His chuckle became a loud cackle as he bent over, pointing a long finger at Pal. "Perfect! Serves him right." He twisted around and looked Lee straight in the eye. "Isn't that just perfect! One down, Miss Jenner—and I didn't have to lift a finger."

CHAPTER 12

❈

ALTHOUGH NONE OF us had known Joey Sykes very well or for very long, we'd known Pal for almost as many years that made up Joey's precarious life. For days, the boy teetered on the edge, in a coma at Frederick Memorial Hospital. The Circle Ladies rallied around Pal in his shock and helplessness, making sure he received proper nourishment and rest during the vigil.

I put in my two bits around day four, sitting at Joey's bedside while Pal tried to grab a nap on the cot they'd brought in. He mumbled to himself all through the fitful sleep, "It's my fault. Car keys on my desk. Wasn't a good driver yet. Never checked the speedometer. All my fault."

I wondered. In his fluster at the scene of the "accident," Pal blurted out that he'd just fixed the brakes on the Cadillac. Did he do a bad job of it? Not likely for someone of Pal's skill and experience. Did someone tamper with the brakes? For what reason? Or maybe, like most people believed, Joey simply drove too fast and lost control.

At any rate, Officer Lukzay was conducting an "investigation" in between free meals at Roland's. I had little doubt he'd turn up nothing, if he even bothered to glance under the hood.

THE NEXT DAY, the day before Halloween, the doctors told Pal that Joey had slid out of the danger zone, but might be in the coma for days, weeks, or months. Pal breathed a sigh of relief and got back to work, content to visit his brother in the evenings until he finally woke up. So on Halloween morning, Pal reappeared at the gas pump, throwing himself into his work with the usual energy, vigor, and irrepressible good humor. I felt awful that now his only work companion was the uncompanionable Suggs Magill.

I edged my car past the Eggheads and sidled up to the diesel pump. They were at it again, arguing over which brand of motor oil could save the free world, Pennzoil or Quaker State.

"There is no comparison," one said to the other, and that one barked back, "You don't know what you're talking about."

Behind me, Pal, no doubt happy to engage in familiar and distracting conversation, dragged a third brand of oil into the mix. Just as I was about to add Oil of Olay as a fourth choice, a horn blew. I didn't need to turn around to know who it was.

"Coming, Miz Crosswell," Pal squeaked. A regular fire ant, he crawled over her second BMW, shining and polishing, doing what he could to make up for Joey's unforgivable driving. "This is a mighty fine car. This your husband's car? How's the house going?"

"Slow," she huffed. "Too damn slow. And yes, as if it's

any of your business, this is my husband's car. I hope your insurance company doesn't drag its feet."

I gaped. This woman really did take the cake. Pal merely nodded in response, never violating his standard of customer service.

"Patience, patience," drawled a man's voice. "Mr. Sykes fortunately uses a very reputable company. *You* won't suffer any loss over this."

I focused in on the black BMW. C.C. sat in the driver's seat, checking her lipstick out in the rearview mirror. Beside her, a man leafed through the *Wall Street Journal,* elbow stuck out the window so he'd have more room to turn pages, tortoise shell glasses perched on his long, fox snout, white hair smooth as silk thread, a cashmere camel coat, bright yellow and navy tie. Quite the dapper gentleman.

"I am devoid of patience, Leonard," she snapped. "At least that's what you always tell me."

"And I'm right," was all he said, deadpan. He never slid her a glance or cracked a smile, the way couples do when they share a little on-going, private joke.

Suggs appeared, a jumpsuited apparition, and eyed the two of them with the usual silent envy and anger he directed at everyone in his path. He held the familiar rag and piece of equipment in his dirty hands.

I topped off the diesel and started to open the car door.

"You there! Flip Paxton!"

I toyed with the notion of ignoring her, but tacked a polite smile on my face and strolled over, taking my time. "Ma'am?"

Before she could tell me what she wanted, Leonard fired a question. "Flip Paxton?" He hardly glanced up from his paper. "Isn't she one of those people Marlene was talking about? An inheritance, wasn't it? Valuable letters from the Civil War period?" Then he mumbled, "Might fit into my collection."

I bristled. "I doubt you'd fit into mine."

The fox snout rose out of the paper. Iron eyes strafed me over the tortoise shell frames.

"My schedule, of course. And I wasn't the one to inherit the letters. I received a family Bible."

He tipped his head, the only hint of interest. "Right, it was Lee Jenner. Miss Jenner owns the letters."

As if he were telling me astounding news I didn't already know.

He snapped his paper to the next page. "Old family Bibles have a small following." His eyes returned to the *Wall Street Journal*, but I could tell his mind lingered elsewhere.

I turned to face C.C. "You rang?"

She cocked her head and jutted her lower teeth, trying to get a fix on the attitude. "Yyyyyes, I heard from my good friend, Marlene Worthington, that you are the person to speak to about house management. Now, mind you," she rattled on, "we have a little ways to go before the house is finished, but my contractor assures us it will be in move-in condition before the end of the year."

I twisted my mouth. "That is fast."

"Maybe for some. Not for me." She patted a flat chest. "Leonard says I'm impatient as a flash flood. Anyway, I wanted to line you up as soon as possible, arrive at some understanding, so that when the property is finally done, we can have a smooth transition as far as cleaning and so forth."

God only knew what she defined as the "so forth" of life.

She suddenly jerked her head down and rooted around in her handbag, ripped a fifty out, captured Pal's filthy palm as he scurried by and plunked the bill into it. She pulled a linen hankie out of her Chanel suit jacket like a magic trick, wiped her hands off, and dropped the dirty cloth inside the Gucci purse.

"Well. Have to run. Leonard has a train to catch."

She brushed my arm with her fingertip, as if that gesture sealed the bargain.

I stood there, dumbfounded. I'd hardly said ten words, and the woman took it for granted I would work for her.

Pal appeared beside me, eyes large over the fifty-dollar bill. He waved as the Crosswells zipped away in their luxury vehicle. "She left me a tip. Must be her way of helping out with Joey. Itn't she sweeeet?"

I took a good, long look at Pal. He'd said the same thing about Leona at the will reading, a woman the polar opposite of C.C. To someone like C.C., a fifty-dollar bill zipped out of her purse as often as her lipstick—a mindless, insignificant habit.

Pal grinned, apologized, said he had work to do, excused himself, and skipped off into the garage, motioning Suggs to hop to it.

I recalled the Parable of Talents, the story preachers make constant use of to compel us to take advantage of the special gifts God gives each individual and not waste those gifts.

I decided then and there: Pal's special gift from God was the ability to see no evil.

CHAPTER 13

❋

BECAUSE OF THE usual Halloween hoopla, my workday ended earlier than usual. I drove past houses decorated with craggy mouthed pumpkins and paper witches. Sheets with ghostly faces flapped in the autumn trees. I decided to make a quick stop at Connolly's Jewelry Store and buy myself a pair of hoop earrings, something to set off my mouse ears at Miss Fizzi's tea party. Not that a couple of fake gold hoops would have Sam Gibbon swooning to his knees, but they might make me easier to look at.

Melody Connolly put down the glass cleaner that practically served as another limb and cheerfully gave me her full attention. A compact, spry woman with a boundless get-up-and-go attitude that could outmatch Pal's, Melody ran the Episcopal Ladies Circle with the common sense, efficiency, and community spirit of her Jewish heritage. Somewhere along the line, she'd drifted away from the religion of her birth, and marrying an Irish Catholic, she told us, had been the final straw for her staunchly Orthodox parents. Her family shunned her. I couldn't fathom parents cutting themselves off from a child, or a child— even an adult child—losing family when there's been no death. Melody had her orchard, but a NO TRESPASSING sign barred the way.

"I gave up a nice inheritance and much more for love," she'd tell any young couple shopping for engagement and wedding rings. Then she'd yell over to her husband, Michael, "For you! For love! For this!" And her hands would sweep across the jewelry store.

"Oy vey," Michael would chirp, and they'd both break into gales of laughter. They shared the same laugh—loud, infectious, pure from the heart.

Melody almost fit into my list of mothers, but she, like Tina Graham, hadn't hit sixty yet. They made my list of sisters, though.

"Flip! What brings you by?"

"She's getting engaged," called Michael from the back office.

Melody turned on me with openly astonished brown eyes. I didn't know whether to be insulted by her astonishment or flattered by her belief.

"Yeah, that's right." I plopped my ugly pocketbook on the shiny glass counter. "But I can't decide between Screamin' Larry or Mel Gibson."

"Mel's taken," Michael responded.

Melody's wide eyes drew narrow and she threw her husband a nasty look he no doubt could picture as he worked in the back room office.

"That man. What can I do for you, sweet pea?"

I smiled and shook my head. Melody's mantra—what can I do for you? When she wasn't fielding the Episcopalian flock's problems, she was delving into the needs of

Catholics, Methodists, and Presbyterians. For such a small package, she spread herself wide.

"Gold hoops," I answered. "Nothing too gold."

She nodded knowingly and went for the gold-fill case.

"So tell me," Melody and Michael loved to gossip even more than Louise, "who does this C.C. person think she is and what's this I hear about Lee having such important historical letters?"

"History belongs in museums so we can all stare at it." Michael could participate in any conversation from any point in the store.

"Don't interrupt, Mr. Gift-of-the-Gab. I should talk." Melody waited for me to answer both questions. Her curiosity never limited itself to one subject at a time.

Before I could open my mouth, the door opened and the October chill wrapped around my neck. Tina and Margaret walked in, both talking over each other. They made a funny pair, one so wide and the other long and straight as the pointer she rapped on her chalkboard.

Tina glanced around the store, checking that Michael worked in the back. She clutched both hands to her massive stomach and yanked up. "Damn pantyhose. They're about to cut off my circulation."

Margaret clicked her tongue in disapproval and scurried away from Tina. "Where are your social graces, for heaven's sake."

"I lost them in your class." The two had known each other all their lives, though Margaret had five or six years on Tina. The first year Margaret taught English at Solace Glen High, Tina sat in her senior class. Margaret handed her a C for her final grade, and Tina still held a grudge. She'd been a B student all her life. Lord, Lord, she'd cluck, how could her good friend Margaret have blackened her good name that way. They'd feuded good-naturedly ever since.

I, myself, held Margaret in high regard. I'd worked my

bottom off to earn an A in her class and still felt the need to work for her approval. Probably the reason she'd never made my list of "mothers" owed to the fact I did hold her in such high esteem. She seemed unapproachable, somehow, as if she'd sting my knuckles with her pointer if she didn't fancy how I dusted.

Margaret lingered over the pearl necklace display and called to Melody, "Go on and help Flip. We're just browsing."

"Speak for yourself, old woman, *I'm* not browsing." Tina smoothed her dress. "I'm going to buy myself something big and gaudy to wear in Florida when I go visit my parents."

Margaret's eyebrows tilted up but she kept her opinion to herself. From the back, Michael's voice could be heard. "Big and gaudy is nice."

Melody leaned forward. "So, Flip? You were saying about this C.C. person?"

Margaret and Tina moved closer in unison.

"Well," I started fiddling with the earrings in front of me, "you know what they say about first impressions."

"They're everything," Melody's index finger punctuated her statement.

"Everything," agreed Tina.

I held a pair of hoops against one ear. Too small. "All I know is, she's shown more compassion for her wrecked BMW than for poor Joey Sykes lying in a coma, *and* she's hired me to clean her new digs. I hardly got to say a word about it."

"Unbelievable," murmured Margaret. "Pushy."

"Charge an arm and a leg," advised the voice from the back.

I picked up a second pair of hoops, wondering if I should reveal my doubts about how "accidental" Joey's car crash was, but decided against it. I stuck to concrete gossip. "And . . ."

All three bent their heads closer.

"I met Mr. C.C. this morning at the gas station."

"You did!" Tina's blue eyes fluttered. "What's he like?" I could tell she wanted to hear the worst.

"Oh, I'd say they deserve each other. Pretty smooth. Sophisticated dresser. Looks like the sort who's raided a few hen houses."

"A ladies' man, is he?" Melody hated men who thought they were God's gift to women. Her own husband couldn't have been more humble in that department. "He didn't try anything with you, did he, darling?"

"Oh, yeah," I held the hoops to my ear. Too big. "I wowed him with my refined manner and movie star teeth. He especially lusted after my jug of Clorox."

"I've always admired it," Michael said.

"Is he as rude as C.C.?" Tina picked out a pair of earrings and handed them to me. When she wasn't doing secretarial work for Frederick County, she moonlighted at Sally Polk's Salon, selling and applying makeup. She'd always wanted to give me a makeover. Earrings were a start. "C.C.'s about the most bitchy person I've ever met in the world."

"Watch your language, you're in a public place," Margaret chided. "And given the fact all bitches are female, you could have condensed your sentence."

I held the earrings up to my ear. Perfect. "No, he's not rude like her. He's more . . . dismissive. But I'd bet anything he can turn on the charm when he wants something. I bet he turns it on full force for Lee."

"Lee?" Melody's forehead wrinkled, then the light dawned. "Oh! Does this have something to do with her historical letters?"

Tina and Margaret drew even closer to me. Michael appeared in the doorway, deft fingers polishing a silver bracelet, jade eyes glued to me. I really didn't like gossiping about Leona's letters, I considered them so private. But the cat was slowly creeping out of the bag. Anyway, I excused myself, the subject really centered on Leonard Crosswell.

"Yeah, in a way. Leonard—that's Mr. C.C.'s name—let it spill that he collects Civil War documents and that Lee's letters might fit into his collection."

"Presumptuous," huffed Margaret. "Lee would never give up to a stranger something Leona left her. Her morals are too high."

High morals can't pay the bills, I thought, *and Leonard probably had a ton of disposable income to throw at Lee.* But I responded, "You're right. I'll take this pair, Melody. Thanks for the help, Tina."

Tina glowed from any compliment. She busied herself searching for something big and gaudy with Michael's help while I paid for the hoops and said I had to hurry home and change for tea at Miss Fizzi's. They pressed for details, but I squirmed out of the store quickly and headed home.

Standing in front of my bathroom mirror, I found it impossible to attach the gold hoops to my ears. Thoughts of Sam Gibbon made my palms so sweaty and shaky, it took forever to do the simplest thing.

I appraised the final product in the mirror and frowned. The hoops did nothing for me; my lipstick covered everything but my lips; bobby pins stuck haphazardly out of my glamorous bun as if a satellite landed on my head.

Happy Halloween. Perfect day of the year for me.

Chapter 14

In Solace Glen, a guest at an afternoon tea party could arrive empty-handed and nobody would think a thing of it, but most people toted along a small tray or plate of something. I stepped out of the car and carefully lifted a tray of ham salad sandwiches from the back seat, balanced the tray with one hand, and smoothed down my dress with the other. I wore my usual autumn number, a navy blue corduroy jumper with navy pumps and a rust sweater trimmed in black. Not an outfit to either merit astonishment or get me thrown out of a public place, as Margaret might say.

"I didn't know you had legs."

Sam Gibbon strolled up smiling, swinging a small, Halloween-theme gift bag from the candy store.

I dipped my head involuntarily at my legs, mostly shrouded by blue corduroy, and realized he'd never seen me in anything but khaki work pants and an apron the size of Baltimore.

"Sure I've got legs." I stood staring at him with his perfect smile in his handsome tweed jacket. I'd never known a man to get better looking every time you saw him. Finally, I took a step toward Miss Fizzi's house and stumbled out of one navy pump.

Sam grabbed my arm and herded me toward the front porch. "After our talk last week," he spoke in a conspiratorial tone, "I've decided to make an indelible impression on the entire female population of this town, being a new single under fifty, you understand, and you could help immensely by pretending to be madly in love with me."

I jerked my arm away, open-mouthed, sure I'd been discovered.

"OK," he wasn't even looking at me, "then I'll pretend to be madly in love with you. That'll have the same effect."

I wrapped white knuckles around the tray of sandwiches. "Is this about me asking 'probing, personal questions'?"

"Something like that." He rapped gently at Miss Fizzi's front door. When we heard footsteps, Sam whipped an arm out and hugged me into his side. "Darling." The door opened and both Louise and Miss Fizzi stood there, fresh pink lipstick stretched into wide, welcoming smiles that iced on their faces when they saw Sam's long arm wrapped around me like a python.

"Hello, hello," chirped Sam, cheerful as a kindergarten teacher greeting his first class.

I could practically see the little film winding through their heads, The Story of Lee's Heartbreak, how a handsome, middle-aged college professor rode into town, won her affection, then dumped her for the town domestic who, sadly, was probably beyond her childbearing years, unlike the fertile Lee.

"Don't get all excited," I said, extracting myself from Sam. "He's fooling around. Doesn't mean anything."

I brushed past them and headed for Miss Fizzi's parlor, face on fire.

Sam called after me, "Babycakes, does this mean the elopement's off?"

My eyes popped. Poor Miss Fizzi would believe anything.

"It is a pleasure to meet you, Sam," she said, but it sounded more like a question.

"Come in, come in!" Louise started chattering about the weather, how it'd been warmer than usual this year.

"El Niño," replied Sam.

"Oh, you speak Spanish," twittered Miss Fizzi. "I used to know Spanish. Or was it Swedish? Started with an *s*."

They entered the parlor together, Sam towering over the two ladies on either side, the apex of an odd pyramid. I excused myself abruptly, mindful of the glance Sam hurled for leaving him with two women he'd never met but who'd already mapped out his future.

I waltzed into the kitchen and bumped into Lee drawing cookies from the oven.

"Those should impress him," I snipped, feeling a little miffed at her presence until I saw what she wore. I slapped a hand on my hip. "What are you doing dressed like that? Looks like you've been playing in the mud."

"What are you doing wearing a dress? Is the Queen coming?" She brushed a hand across the seat of her jeans. Caked mud fell off. Over her pants hung a plaid flannel shirt streaked with dirt and pocked with dead leaves. "Do I look that bad? I'd forgotten this thing, this *tea* was today and by the time I remembered, I rushed right over."

I snapped the collar of her shirt. Bits of dried marigold floated to the floor. "Have Miss Fizzi and Louise seen you?"

"No, I came in through the kitchen a minute ago." She

sighed and brushed hair off her face. "Well, too late. I'm not running all the way home to change. What's the big deal, anyway?"

I lit into her. "You know what the big deal is! Miss Fizzi and Louise want to marry you off to Sam Gibbon. They're going to throw a hissy fit when they get a load of you."

She took a step back. "What are you so hostile about? Maybe it's you they want to marry off, ever consider that?"

No, Lee, I wanted to say. *You're the golden girl, not me. Never me.*

Louise entered the kitchen with a festive grin, took one look at Lee and muffled a scream. "Lee! You look like a street urchin! And that nice young man dressed so sweetly in his tweed jacket, the perfect gentleman." She shot me a disapproving face, as if I'd been trying to seduce an innocent bystander right out there on the front stoop.

I shoved both hands in my sweater pockets and scrutinized the magnets on the refrigerator as if I might purchase one.

"Is Sam by himself in the parlor with Miss Fizzi?" Lee peeked over Louise's shoulder.

"Yes." Louise couldn't hide her displeasure. The Big Plan was about to blow up.

Lee turned to me, mouth twitching. "I wonder what they're talking about."

My mouth twitched back at her. "Calculus. Astrophysics. Sex."

Louise tapped her foot and spoke between clenched teeth. "Stop it. Both of you. You're talking like a couple of wild teenagers." She drew herself up, suddenly taller than her five feet three inches. "The two of you may serve tea. I will go into the parlor and await our other guests."

"What other guests?" Nobody'd told me about other guests. Then again, I hadn't mentioned my invitation to Tom.

"The other men, of course. Miss Fizzi felt Sam might be more interested if he believes he has some competition." She blew out of the kitchen.

Lee fell into a chair. "Oh, no," she groaned. "You *know* who she's talking about."

I nodded, grim-faced. The pickings were pretty slim.

When we somberly carried the tea finery out to the parlor, Louise and Miss Fizzi were howling as loud as tornadoes while Sam took over the room, acting out a story. He barely noticed us as he played a dozen parts. We set the trays on the coffee table and slid into our seats as silently and quickly as if we'd entered Carnegie Hall in the middle of a Horowitz concert. When he delivered the last line, we stomped our feet and applauded, and Lee and I gave him a standing ovation, a cup of tea, and a chicken salad sandwich.

"What an entertaining fellow you are," praised Miss Fizzi, wiping tears off her powdery cheeks. "You must be a wonderful teacher."

"I don't know about that." Sam stirred his tea. "That was my one and only parlor story. It's all downhill from here."

I studied Lee's face. She liked Sam. Liked him a lot. If she had felt any embarrassment about her clothes, you couldn't tell. Sam possessed an easy, natural manner that pulled us out of ourselves, as if we'd boarded a raft with Sam at the till and all we had to do was sit back while he steered us gently downstream, telling funny stories along the way.

I could see the good impression he made on Louise and Miss Fizzi. Miss Fizzi constantly threw a glance of approval at Louise who tossed one after another at me. And we all three slid eyes at Lee, measuring her interest. Especially me.

Sam had traveled a good bit, which easily kept my attention. I was enjoying his account of getting lost in Wadi Rumm when the doorbell rang.

"Oh, *Lee*," Miss Fizzi smiled like the cat with feathers in her mouth, "who could *that* be?"

"I'm afraid to guess." She chomped into a cookie.

I sat closest to the hall so I hopped up and opened the door.

Screamin' Larry bowed low, dressed elegantly in brown sandals, red sweatpants, and a matching WFIB 102.7 sweatshirt. "Flip."

"Larry."

He lay one hand across his heart. "I have answered the call."

I stepped aside and Larry tramped in, his huge frame filling half the entrance hall.

"I heard there was gonna be food."

"Naturally you'll be paid. In the parlor."

Larry dipped his head at me and headed straight for the coffee table, scooping up a fistful of sandwiches before addressing the others. "Thanks for inviting me," he mumbled and swallowed his fist. "I haven't eaten yet."

"You poor dear," clucked Miss Fizzi.

"He means in the past ten minutes," Lee sniped. "Hey, Larry."

"Lee."

Making Sam believe Larry's intentions lay anywhere beyond the spread on the coffee table would be a hard sell.

"Sam," Louise stepped up to the challenge, "I'd like to introduce you to a *special* friend of Lee's."

As Lee's eyeballs fell into her lap, Sam stepped forward, extending a hand for Larry to shake. Larry turned away from the food long enough to wave two greasy fingers in the air. Sam gave the fingers a firm, polite shaking and made a stab at normal conversation.

"Glad to meet you. I believe I've heard you on the radio."

"You BELIEVE?" Larry bellowed. "If you'd heard ME, you'd damn well know it!"

Sam retreated a few feet. "Now that you mention it, it was definitely you."

Larry stood proud and smiled wide, pink wads of ham salad decorating his teeth. I thought he might start singing or initiate name-that-tune to really show off, but thank God the doorbell rang again.

"Now, *Lee*," a look of incredulity covered Miss Fizzi's face as if Lee was pulling eligible bachelors out of the wood-work, "who could *that* be?"

"It's your party," sniffed Lee, already exhausted from so much male attention. "You ought to know."

I leaped up, the good domestic help, and opened the door to Pal, one Egghead on either wing. The Eggheads still sported their mint green work uniforms. Pal, I was heart-ened to see, wore a smile and a fresh brown garage shirt with his name stitched over one pocket and the Crown Petro-leum symbol patched across the other.

"Hi, Flip," they all chimed in their best party manner.

"Hi, boys. Welcome to the *Dating Game*. Chow's in the parlor."

The humor zipped over their shaved heads, and all three marched into the house single file, members of a band unit about to perform the half-time routine.

Miss Fizzi waved at them in gleeful schoolgirl fash-ion and beamed at Sam, certain the sheer quantity of Lee's suitors would impress him into an immediate proposal of marriage.

Louise again offered the introductions, emphasizing what *special* friends they all were of Lee's. The three man-aged to act proper for about ten seconds before descending on the food with Larry.

Miss Fizzi courteously inquired after Joey's health, and in between bites, Pal explained the unknown as best he could. "So they don't know when he'll wake up or what his . . . his 'mental state' will be like when he does. I can't figure for the life of me why he couldn't stop the car and why he'd be going so fast." His thin chest heaved. "I got a quick look at the Cadillac down at the garage yard where Officer Lukzay had it towed. It's totaled."

I made a mental note to ask dear Officer Lukzay the status of his "investigation" and noticed Sam edge away from the crowd to go stand by Lee.

"Praise God Joey wasn't totaled, too," said Miss Fizzi, putting an end to upsetting subjects. Then she batted her eyes at Sam, "Isn't this lovely?"—ecstatic at how well her plan was working.

I didn't think it was so lovely. Even in my best corduroy dress, I couldn't compare to Lee in her mud-caked jeans. Sam started up a quiet conversation while the ladies glittered, Lee's special friends devoured the coffee table, and I sulked.

Somehow, I don't know how, Suggs suddenly appeared. He must have stolen up from his basement apartment. For such a stocky man, Suggs possessed the unusual talent of wafting in and out of places. He hadn't gone to the trouble of changing clothes, that would be too social, but had at least managed to wash his hands. Without a sound, he moved to a chair in the corner with a napkin full of cheese biscuits and hunched down to feed himself.

Miss Fizzi eventually realized her nephew had joined the party—invited or not—and frowned at his attire. When Louise spied him, her face went sour. Neither lady introduced Suggs to Sam as a *special* friend of Lee's.

Not five minutes had passed when the doorbell rang again, but this time both Louise and Miss Fizzi wore only question marks. I got up and slouched to the door.

"Hello, Flip. I took you up on the kind invitation." Tom Scott stepped into the house to escape a light rain shower and suddenly wrinkled his forehead, staring at my dress. "Did you take the whole day off?"

"Halloween's a national holiday, isn't it? Welcome to the celebration."

"Tom? Is that you? You didn't bring that dog, did you?" Miss Fizzi called from the parlor. "Come in and join my little soiree."

"A soiree is an evening affair," corrected Louise. "This is an afternoon tea party, dear."

"Tom knows what I mean," said Miss Fizzi, tickled pink to add another man to the mix. She'd probably left him off the list in the first place because she considered him too serious to qualify as a *special* friend of Lee's. Everybody knows there's no fun in lawyering.

Tom motioned me to go ahead, ladies first, and followed me into the parlor. I slid back into my chair, a creaky Victorian upholstered in cranberry velvet. All the furniture in Miss Fizzi's house fell under the heavy Victorian variety, dwarfing her and most visitors.

Tom smiled politely at Miss Fizzi and Louise. "Eli's at home reading Shakespeare." He caught sight of Sam and crossed the room, arm extended. They shook hands and said each other's names. When he spotted Lee, his eyes softened like gelatin, a change so subtle I doubt anybody noticed but me.

"Ah. Lee. Good to see you." He nodded in a short, businesslike manner.

Miss Fizzi crooned, motioning Lee to pour a cup of tea. "We were just having a little get-together to meet Mr. Gibbon, and he's been entertaining us so. I can't remember a more enjoyable afternoon."

"Well, that's fine," said Tom, taking the cup from Lee a bit shakily, "that's fine. Are you from Maryland, Sam?"

Here come the questions, I thought. You may commence your cross-examination now, Mr. Scott.

"Eastern Shore." Sam gobbled down a sandwich no

bigger than his pinkie. Louise probably whipped those up. "Tilghman Island."

"Tilghman Island?" Pal had probably never heard of it. "That on the Eastern Shore?"

"Eastern Shore," croaked one Egghead with food in his mouth.

"Eastern Shore," the other Egghead bobbed his head up and down like a dashboard dog ornament.

Larry grunted and scarfed down a row of sugar cookies. Suggs slowly chewed on a biscuit. Exhibiting his normal horrible personality, he glared down at the carpet.

"Ah," said Tom, "lovely place. Some development going on down there, am I right?"

"Yes. The residents are more or less split in their opinions."

"Are you antidevelopment, then?"

"No. I'm anti–stupid development. My father was a waterman, owned his own skipjack. My mother taught high school history. They taught me to appreciate the wisdom of the past and the beauty of the present. I guess that means change is unsettling to me."

That speech constituted the most background information any of us had been able to wheedle out of Sam Gibbon. Lee crossed her legs and leaned forward, hugging a mud-caked knee and jiggling her ankle up and down.

The motion distracted Tom for a moment before he said, "Change isn't easy for any of us, past a certain age."

"Tom," Lee teased, "you self-conscious about your age?"

Before he could answer, I blurted, voice harder than intended, "You self-conscious about yours? Because you're the freshest chickadee here."

She frowned at me, eyes quizzical. "I mean, change is unsettling to me, too."

She looked straight at Sam, a little too bold for my taste.

He didn't utter a sound, but something passed between them that had a strange effect on me. For the first time in my life, I didn't want the best for Lee. I wanted the best for myself.

My cheeks burned and I had to turn away from the two of them. Tom abruptly stepped to the window and stared outside. His eyes squinted the way I'd seen them do when he'd been reading for hours. His mouth tightened as it sometimes did when he struggled with a difficult case, searching for issues and answers.

He told me once that the hardest part about being a lawyer is determining exactly what the right issues are. If I miss the heart of the case, he said, it doesn't matter what answers I find because I will have wasted so much time barking up the wrong tree. If I don't pose the central issue precisely, I lose and people suffer. I told him it sounded pretty simple to me and if being a lawyer boiled down to figuring out the right questions instead of the right answers, this was a screwier world than I thought.

I could only imagine the questions flying though Tom's mind as he stared out the window, and the one question he wouldn't want to ask: Have I waited too long?

Sam cleared his throat and jump-started us onto a new subject. "Lee was just telling me, speaking of the wisdom of the past, that you, Flip, inherited a family Bible from the aunt who left her the old letters."

This perked up the Eggheads. They stopped mowing through appetizers long enough to stammer, "Letters? Leona's letters?"

"Lee," Tom turned around, composed and courteous as ever, "are you going to have an expert evaluate them? I hear," he glanced at the two shaved heads hovering over the coffee table, "you might have a valuable piece of history on your hands. Flip might, too, for all we know."

Par for the course, I only warranted a footnote.

As soon as he said valuable, the Eggheads started to shake and shimmy. "See? See?" They nudged Pal and poked fingers into each other. "See what we told you?"

Larry snorted and reached an arm between them to get at the onion dip. Suggs quit chewing on his third biscuit and actually showed interest in the conversation.

Lee's forehead wrinkled and she huffed, "Thank you for bringing it up, Sam and Tom. I'm glad everybody's so engrossed in my business."

Nobody, apparently, cared about mine.

"So you gonna give 'em to an expert, Lee?" Pal never was one to take a hint.

Sam poured himself more tea. "I told Lee I know somebody at the Smithsonian who would love to take a gander at anything bearing J.E.B. Stuart's name."

"But the signature isn't . . ." I began, but Lee rattled her cup, tossing me such a scornful look, I immediately clamped down.

"It is J.E.B. Stuart! It is!" Cheese bits flew out of the mouth of one of the Eggheads. True to form, neither one could contain himself and started spouting a sermon of misinformation.

"Leona said so. Said he'd stayed in the house during a major campaign. Antietam, it was. Or was it Sharpsburg?"

"Same thing, moron. I believe she said General Lee was staying at the house, too, along with Longstreet and, and . . ."

"Grant. Didn't she say something about Grant?"

"Yeah, that's right. Her dying breath. It's all in the letters, all ten of 'em. And there was women."

"That's right! A network of spy women recruited from right here in Solace Glen. Right out of the Bell house by J.E.B. Stuart and General Lee and General Grant."

They twinkled at each other, thrilled with their combined version of impossible events.

Tom's jaw twitched. "Now that certainly is a history worthy of expert interpretation."

Nobody said much more after that. When the food ran out, so did Larry, Pal, and the Eggheads. Suggs had managed to evaporate into the atmosphere some time before without anyone noticing. They'd added nothing to the conversation or the gay social atmosphere Miss Fizzi and Louise had shot at and missed. Sam and Tom drifted out soon after with a promise to fish the Monocacy.

I folded plastic wrap on two lone celery sticks and stuck them in the refrigerator for Miss Fizzi to nibble on. Lee washed out the teapot, cups, and saucers; Louise dried. Miss Fizzi sipped a sherry.

"What an interesting character that Sam is," commented Louise. "So well traveled. So educated."

"So handsome. So polite," added Miss Fizzi. "Bilingual, too."

"What do *you* think, Lee?" Louise prodded her in the side with an elbow.

"Let's see," said Lee. "We have well traveled, good education, good-looking, good manners, and knows one Spanish word." With each item on the list, Louise and Miss Fizzi got more excited. "Yep." Lee popped the stopper out and the water slurped down the drain. "When's the wedding?"

"I don't know, dear," said Miss Fizzi. "Before or after he elopes with Flip, I suppose."

"Ohhhhh," Lee wiped her hands on a towel, checking me out. "So we're rivals?"

"Miss Fizzi is teasing." I pretended to be extremely busy opening and closing a drawer.

Miss Fizzi sipped away, ignoring me. "All I know is, you two girls need to work it out between yourselves."

"We could arm wrestle," I suggested.

Lee shrugged. "Or have a bathing suit contest."

"Or a wet T-shirt competition."

"Or a spitting tournament."

"Hush, both of you," Louise snapped. "You wear me out." Her tone contained enough edge in it to shut us up.

"It is getting late," said Lee. "I walked so I can't offer anybody a ride."

I offered Louise a lift right away, but she'd driven, too. "We'll talk later," she whispered in the hall, out of Lee's earshot.

Miss Fizzi escorted the three of us to the door and happily waved good-bye; in her mind, the little tea party a great success.

I drove home, listening to Larry's tape-recorded announcement of the Saturday night jazz lineup. George Winston. Earl Klugh. Billie Holiday. Diane Shurr. I couldn't wipe the scowl off my face.

Usually, Halloween launched me into a holiday mood that lasted straight through New Year's. My favorite part of the evening was flinging open that door, mouth wide, eyes round as pumpkins to spout, "Oooooo! Look at yoooooou! Aren't you the scariest bunch of Raggedy Ann's I ever saw! Here's a whole bag of chocolate bars and jelly beans!" That's the fun of Halloween. Like Christmas, it's an overload holiday, centering on children.

I pulled into the driveway and trudged to the front door, trying to work myself into the Halloween spirit before the trick-or-treaters arrived. The moment my fingers touched the knob, my stomach lurched. The door stood cracked. Someone had been inside my house.

I yelled through the screen, "Hello! Anybody in there?" Nothing but silence. I walked slowly in.

A tornado might have done more damage, but I doubt it. Tables and chairs lay overturned. Drawers gaped. Paper cluttered the floor. Books torn from shelves. Pillows strewn across the floor. Everything from eye level down blown apart. Whoever tore apart my house kept his focus low.

I froze, breathless, as if movement might animate the chaos. Gradually, my breath returned. My fists clenched and unclenched. This was no Halloween prank. I walked in angry, long strides through the living room into the kitchen, knowing exactly where I needed to go.

I flicked on the kitchen light and zoomed in on the kitchen cabinet. The basket still sat on the roof of the cabinet, undisturbed, shoved slightly toward the wall as I'd left it. I shimmied onto the counter, reached up and pulled it down. The Bell family Bible lay safe and sound hidden under the Spanish moss, a baby Moses in its cradle. I stroked the Bible and remembered who Moses was: God's own tool in His plot to restore an inheritance.

PART TWO

❄

CHAPTER 15

✳

THE MONDAY LUNCH crowd hadn't filtered in yet. I walked quickly to my table behind the cash register, picked up the daily menu, and scribbled out an order on the notepad, my heart pounding.

I hadn't slept the Saturday night before; the mess in my house took care of that. I even considered skipping Sunday morning services and opting for TV church, but that's like having a side dish instead of the main course. God knows, I tried like crazy to concentrate on those high Presbyterian ideals and not on the hate building, spreading, seeping from every pore as I sang "O Come, My People, to My Law" and glared at the back of Roland Bell's neck two pews away. Who else could have been so brazen to try to steal back an inheritance? I could still hear his bizarre cackle over Joey's mysterious "accident." Anger clouded my vision, and I could barely read the words on the page. *A*

*testimony and a law The Lord our God decreed, And bade
our fathers teach their sons, That they His ways might heed.*

The whole time Reverend McKnight conducted the
service, delivered the sermon, accepted our tithes, and bene-
dictioned us out the door, I simmered, plotted, and calculated. By the end of the service, as McKnight glided down
the aisle to the front door, I knew what I had to do.

Hilda finally showed up, busting out of her red T-shirt,
make-up the same old clown face. She'd decided to play it
safe and avoid conversation.

"Hilda," I gave her the notepaper that trembled in my
hand, "is your daddy in today?"

The slightest encouragement and she burbled.

"Oh, yes, he is. He'll be back at the register in a minute,
but would you like me to get him for you? I can look in the
kitchen, and if he's not there, I can go upstairs to the office.
He might be there if . . ."

"No, no. That's all right. I'll see him when I pay up." I
whipped the pocket atlas out.

Hilda's lips dutifully clamped and she left me alone.

A trip to the Caribbean was just what I needed. After the
house salad with blue cheese dressing and a pork chop
with baked apples and green beans, all of which I barely
touched, my trip measured out in the month-long range because I couldn't decide which islands to skip. *What would
the exotic Charlie Scott do,* I wondered.

By the time I'd neglected a full meal and traveled half
the Caribbean, the Café brimmed with customers, about a
dozen strangers plus the usual staff and patrons: Louise and
Miss Fizzi (Miss Fizzi proud to pay the bill herself), Tom
and Ferrell T., Garland floating ghostlike through the
kitchen, Hilda waiting tables, the Eggheads arguing over
brands of flashlight batteries, Marlene and C.C.—the Ladies
Who Lunch, Lee picking up a sandwich at the take-out

counter, Screamin' Larry, in a wonderful humor since C.C.'s BMW took a dive, and Tina with Melody, both admiring Tina's big, gaudy peacock brooch. The only ones missing were Pal, who practically worked nonstop now; Margaret, holding court at the high school; Michael, waiting for Melody to bring him back a plate of something; and Sam, disappearing Mondays through Thursdays to Frederick to teach American history to young, nubile, good-looking college girls. Suggs, of course, never stepped foot in the Café; that might require him to speak.

And there, walking through the door like he owned the place, was Officer Lukzay. Before I launched into Plan B, I'd have to give Plan A a stab. I waited for the beer-gutted old grouch to sink into his chair, took a deep breath, and walked over.

"Officer Lukzay, I have a crime to report. But first," I presumptuously sat down across from him, "I'd like to hear how your investigation of Joey Sykes' 'accident' is going."

The bushy eyebrows met and he crammed a napkin into his collar. "You say the word like you don't believe it was an accident. What's that expert opinion based on?"

"The fact that the brakes didn't work and Pal had just fixed them."

"How do you know that dumb, juvenile hick thought to apply the brakes? I saw him myself come speeding down the hill into town like a bat outta hell. Car's totaled."

"Look out the window. You see any skid marks? And none of us heard a terrible screeching, did we?"

Lukzay rubbed the ends of his mustache and chortled. "You're a regular Nancy Drew."

I leaned into the table. "Can't you do something as simple as have the brakes checked? Or are you trying to protect somebody?"

The chortle froze in his throat. "You watch your mouth,

missy. I'd be careful of who I accuse of what if I were you. Now why don't *you* do something simple like tell me what crime you have to report."

"My house was broken into Halloween night."

He snatched the menu Hilda handed him on the fly and opened it, creating a barrier between us. "Too bad. Kids these days do crazy things for fun."

"This wasn't a prank."

He huffed, "Another expert opinion from Miss Drew," and briefly lowered the menu. "I'll look into it. When I have the time."

Plan A dissolved in a heap. Officer "Look-away" went back to his menu—so much more important than any crime committed against the town maid—and I went back to my table to fetch my sweater. No sooner had I thrown it on than Roland reappeared behind the cash register to stand sentry over his kingdom. Routinely, I would pay the check at my table, sliding the meal dollars under the salt shaker and the tip money under the pepper. Not today. I filled my lungs with one long, deep breath and slowly exhaled. Time for Plan B.

Roland reached for the bill, smiling, more money in the bank, until he saw it was me at the register. He froze, scrawny fingers suspended in midair. The smile dried up.

I raised my head, screwed courage to the sticking place, and lightly touched one of his fingertips with the bill for $5.95.

"Not gonna grab it, Roland?" I snatched the bill away and turned up the volume so the whole audience could hear. "What's that? My meal is ON THE HOUSE?"

That was a conversation-stopper.

One of the Eggheads yelled out, "You giving Flip a free meal, Roland? What's the deal?"

Roland unhinged his jaws to bark but I jumped in first.

"He certainly is giving me a free meal!" I yelled back. I glared hard into Roland's shocked face, the vision of my wrecked house the only thing anchoring my feet to the floor. "He *owes* me. Don't you, Roland?"

"What the hell . . ."

Before he could finish, I called out, "Miss Fizzi, everything OK with you?"

"Yes, dear, fine." I'd thrown her a loop.

"Just wanted to make sure all your belongings are OK." I never took my eyes off Roland. "There's been a little trouble in the neighborhood lately."

"What kind of trouble?" One of the Eggheads wanted to know.

"A break-in."

"Who?" somebody asked.

"Me," I said. "Saturday night."

Roland snarled, "Tut, tut. What's that got to do with me?" He threw Lukzay a look as if to say, arrest her and her big mouth. Lukzay sneered back at me.

A knee buckled, but I called out loud and clear. "Lee, everything OK at your house?"

"So far," she replied, in sync with the situation.

I drew a bead on one of Roland's two pupils and aimed every syllable, willing my voice not to shake. "It had damn well better stay that way." I leaned across the counter and added for his ears alone, "And if anybody else's property gets torn up, totaled, or destroyed, anybody who happens to be in Leona's will, that is, we'll all know where to point a finger." I wadded up the bill and threw it at his feet.

Screamin' Larry burst into applause and pumped a fist in the air, always eager to encourage conflict, sports, or otherwise. "Yes! Bravo! Huzza, huzza!"

Roland glowered. "That'll *still* be $5.95, Miss Paxton!"

I ignored him and walked out, astonishing everybody,

even myself. I had publicly accused Roland Bell of breaking and entering, destruction of property, and being a damn liar without aid from our local police or giving Roland a case for slander.

My only thought was, *Had I gone too far?*

THAT NIGHT, NEEDING some comfort, I opened the Bell family Bible again. I ran my hands over the pages that contained Leona's family tree, touched the branches, slowly stroked the names of the people I'd thought about so far, wondered about, imagined what they looked like, how they talked, the clothes they wore.

Leona knew this comfort all her life, always knew the worth of her stock, knew the long ago names of the people she sprang from. Just as a living family is supposed to lend support and give you a sense of self-worth, a written history can do the job as well. Sometimes even better because a flesh-and-blood family can be tough to take at times, the way Roland bothered Leona all her life. Still, having a family history at all, written or walking like the Bell's, beat living alone with only a paltry photograph album. The fading pictures of my mother and father did nothing but emphasize my own fading. Leona probably expected the Bell family Bible to put some color back in my life, to help fill the empty spaces. In a strange way, she was right.

Sara and Ferrell's only child, another Ferrell, born in 1828 after twenty years of waiting, married a German girl, Gretal Stubing, in 1850 when he was twenty-two and she, twenty. The German influence in central and western Maryland runs high. Lots of German names—people, towns, landmarks, streets. As far as I could tell, Gretal counted as the first instance of Germanic breeding in the Bell family. They probably needed it. I pictured Gretal

Stubing Bell, a hard-working rural girl, hands hard as horse-shoes, nagging Ferrell to get out of bed and go milk those cows so she and baby Roland, born 1851, could have fresh milk over their oatmeal at breakfast. I bet he did what she said.

Ferrell lived seventy-one years, dying before the turn of the century in 1899. He was thirty-three when the Civil War started, thirty-seven when it ended, so he probably enlisted. Maybe he and his cousin, John Bell Paca, enlisted together. Maybe they fought on opposite sides. Maybe a bullet from Ferrell's gun ended up in John's heart or liver. Not probable or likely, but stranger things have happened. I wondered what life offered up to Gretal at home in Maryland with a ten-year-old boy during the war. That child grew up fast, no doubt, performing his daddy's chores.

Gretal died in 1908 at the age of seventy-eight. In that time, she witnessed twenty-two states enter the Union and lived through a war that nearly destroyed it. The year she was born, Sir Walter Scott wrote *Letters on Demonology and Witchcraft*; the year she died, H.G. Wells published *New Worlds for Old*.

Most of us don't appreciate the changes we live through. We can barely recall most historical events, things that occurred twenty years before, as if our memories were news magazines stacked high in a corner, never opened or referred to after that first, brief glimpse.

Gretal Stubing Bell and her generation might have been different. I don't know. She lived through a major war and the industrial revolution. Horse and buggy to Model T. On her deathbed, she might have lain back on the pillow and sighed, "O Lord, the sights I've seen! The sights my son will see!"

I'll never know, but I'd like to think she did. I touched her name lightly with one finger, then Ferrell's, then John Bell Paca's. Their names, scratched in ink so long ago, couldn't completely fill the empty spaces, replace the family I'd lost or become the family I'd given up hopes of ever having, but somehow those names, now in my keeping, did give a kind of comfort. That alone was more than I'd ever asked for or come to expect.

CHAPTER 16

✳

EVEN THOUGH LOUISE lay pale and listless, propped up against her bed pillows, she felt talkative.

"No need to change the sheets this morning, Flip. I actually had the energy to do it last night."

I quit fiddling with a dusty picture of Marlene, age twelve, braces in her mouth and jodhpurs on her bottom. "What are you doing wearing yourself out like that? You know I do it every Tuesday. Plus," I shook a finger at her, "you've been going out too much lately, gallivanting around with Miss Fizzi."

"Well." She examined her hands, so small and white, as if surprised they belonged to her. "I've a right to enjoy myself. But after lunch yesterday, I had a feeling I wouldn't want to get out of bed today, so I went ahead and did the sheets."

I frowned. "You been to the doctor lately?"

"Doctors don't help any more, Flip," she said wearily. "But I take comfort in knowing I can slip away peacefully in my own home. Now, tell me what gave you the courage to make such a scene at the Café yesterday. Everybody thinks you've gone plum crazy, including Roland."

"I must have because there's no other explanation for me getting in his face."

"You certainly got the town talking."

"Then I accomplished something." My face turned serious. "Roland's the one who's gone crazy, Louise, wrecking my house the way he did." I didn't tell her my suspicions about him tampering with the brakes in Pal's car.

"Are you *sure* it was Roland?" she whispered, as though somebody might be hiding under the bed, listening.

"If he didn't do it himself, he hired somebody. That would be just like him—pay a few bucks to some drug addict off the street in Baltimore to rip apart a woman's belongings. And for what? A Bible that normally he wouldn't shake a stick at. He's sure never read one."

"Flip," she pursed her lips a moment, "do you think he might go after Miss Fizzi? Or Lee?"

I chewed on my cheek awhile, not wanting to upset her, already sorry I'd conjured up images of rampaging drug addicts. "I can't for the life of me think what he could do to Miss Fizzi, the way things are set up, with a trust and all. He can't get at the trust. Lee . . . I don't know."

Honest enough words, but as soon as I said them, I wanted to rake them back in. Me and my big mouth. Louise started to whimper, wringing her hands, shaking her head.

"No, no," I tried to soothe her. "Don't misunderstand me. Lee is a strong, independent person. Don't go getting all upset over something that's not going to happen. And she's got plenty of good people watching out for her."

"Like who! She lives alone except for a big, weird doll and a useless cat, for God's sake!"

"Well, Sam, for one." I hated to admit it. "And Tom."

"Oh, Tom," Louise rolled her eyes and chuckled. "He's as good-looking and sophisticated as James Bond, but not exactly prone to kicking doors down."

Tom might surprise you one day, I thought. I swiped at a ladybug kissing Marlene's face, age fourteen.

"Sam, though." Louise smiled as sly as a coyote, obviously cheered by this particular theme. "Sam's a different story. You know he's been calling her on the phone."

"Oh, yes," I replied, too sharp, "and I'm sure he'd turn into Superman for Lee if he had to."

"Oooooo," she shook a finger at me. "I spy a green monkey on somebody's back."

"I don't have time for green monkeys." My shoulders drooped. "I'm tired. That's all. I've had a full three days."

Louise eyed me quietly. "You need some recreation, Flip. Why don't you take a day off and go to Baltimore? Get some nice seafood. Have your hair done while you're at it." She scowled and tilted her head, "And buy yourself a new wardrobe. We're all sick to death of seeing you in the same things."

"Gee, thanks." But suddenly, I wanted nothing more. "You're right." I jammed the dust rag in my carryall and hoisted it up. "If you don't mind, I'll clean your kitchen and be gone. I might even call and cancel my appointments for tomorrow."

"Good for you! Get the hell out of Dodge."

She was absolutely right. I needed to get the hell out of Dodge.

NOTHING INSPIRED MY mood like throwing on a dress, taking my one credit card out of the sock drawer, and heading for the big city. Admittedly, such an adventure didn't crop up every day. But once or twice a year, besides my normal vacation to Ocean City in July, I would go a little nuts and treat myself. If I made the one day special enough, it could feel like a long weekend holiday.

I lolled in an overstuffed chair in the safari bar at the Harbor Court Hotel, staring out of the huge picture window at the sunset water view. The *Clipper City* sat moored to a dock while motor boats and water taxis scurried behind her through the waters of Baltimore's Inner Harbor. Little lights began to twinkle in the twilight.

Checking into a fine hotel for one night with room service, maid service, dining service, and bar service could turn any maid-in-waiting into a pampered queen. I loved drinking champagne out of the tall flute glass, watching the tourist boats shuttle back and forth. I loved the bartender keeping a protective eye on me, sending the waitress over now and then to see what they could get for me. More cashews, ma'am? Is this bottle of Taittinger cold enough for you, ma'am? Would you like an appetizer with that? Caviar? Shrimp? Crab cocktail? Would you like a bellboy to take those expensive-looking shopping bags to your room?

I sat on the ugly, worn, black handbag I'd owned practically since high school, hiding it from view, the pocket atlas inside. When I felt looped enough, I'd take the atlas out and go to Brazil. In the meantime, Baltimore, Maryland, suited me just fine.

Even though I'd arrived in a nice enough dress, I decided to really splurge and buy something I'd never owned: a suit. I found something half price, a little designer number at the Gallery, and I couldn't stand not to wear it immediately. So there I sat in the safari bar showing off a sea green silk suit, short skirt, long jacket, a new shell-pink blouse underneath. I'd even bought a pair of pointy shoes and gotten my hair done, figuring Christmas tips would cover the difference. No handbag, though. I had to draw the line somewhere.

Of all the ridiculous things to pop into my head at that moment—swishing bubbles around in the glass, appreciating the color of light on the water, admiring the pointy toe of my new shoes—I thought about Roland's Café and whether I'd ever be able to eat there again. Half of me said yes, Roland couldn't turn away a dollar to save his life; half of me said no, he could not forgive what I did or said in front of all those people. With Roland, forgiveness never figured into the equation.

I shifted a hip to one side of the chair and slowly pulled at the old handbag. The strap stuck and I tugged harder.

"Flip? My goodness. It is you!"

My arm jerked at the sound of Tom's voice and the ugly purse flew like a startled crow, into his face. Tom reached to his bruised nose with one hand and retrieved my handbag with the other.

I sprang up. "Are you all right?"

He held the bag out for me, dabbing the space between his eyes. "Fine. Fine. Funny thing. Nothing to worry about."

He blinked a few times and focused.

"You sure your eyes are OK?" They fluttered uncontrollably.

"No," he said. "I'm not sure I see what I'm seeing. Flip, you are a vision. I mean, you are . . . stunning."

I reached for the handbag and maneuvered it discreetly behind my hip. "I clean up good as anybody."

"Much better, I'd say." He smiled that magazine smile. "Hope you've recovered from your break-in. That's an unsettling thing, even as a Halloween trick. Did you report it to Lukzay?"

I nodded mutely. Why spoil one of my rare evenings of luxury whining about lazy Officer Look-away? Stumped for conversation, I examined the bubbles in my glass.

Tom leaned forward and gently took my elbow. "And the blush is very becoming, too. Sit down, sit down."

The waitress must have thought we were together because she sprinted out of thin air in a flash. "An extra glass for the gentleman? Or would he prefer a cocktail?"

Tom appeared perfectly at ease. "He'll take the extra glass and, ah, another bottle of what the lady ordered." He plopped into the cushy chair opposite mine as though he belonged there and pulled the bottle from the ice. "Taittinger. You have excellent taste in champagne, Flip." The hawk eyes settled on me. "I wonder where you acquired it."

For once, he didn't ask a question outright, but he may as well have.

"That's a sneaky way to ask the town maid how she knows anything about the finer things in life. What champagne to drink, what nice hotel to stay in, the right kind of clothes to wear." I aimed the point of my new shoe at him accusingly. "I think maybe it's time I get to ask the questions."

The waitress sidled up to him with a flute glass and another ice bucket of champagne. She filled his glass from my bottle, inquired if we wanted the other one opened, and zipped away when Tom said, no, he preferred to pop the cork himself on this occasion. I wondered what sort of occasion he thought it was.

He held up the glass. "Fire away."

"What brings you to Baltimore?"

"I'm a lawyer. They have courtrooms here."

"What brings you to this hotel?"

"A meeting with an out-of-town client."

"Male or female?"

"Male. Unfortunately."

"What brings you to this bar?"

"I wanted to relax with a drink after a long day of jousting with a hostile court and an uncooperative client."

"Come here often?"

"Not often enough."

"Why haven't you ever asked Lee out?" The heart of the case. The Right Question.

He opened his mouth to speak, closed it, stared through the golden liquid in his glass and took a long swallow. "Only recently have I felt this attraction. I'm not sure how real it is or what to do about it."

I didn't know whether to laugh at him or pat his hand. How could a man with Tom's looks and abilities have the slightest struggle of indecision about a woman?

"Tom." I shook my head. "How old are you?"

"Older than you. Certainly older than Lee."

"Then don't be such a schoolboy." Now was my chance to salvage the best for myself. "Ask her to something that doesn't seem like a date."

His eyes rolled skyward. "A county bar meeting, perhaps."

He wasn't getting it. "It is rumored by drunks and thieves that lawyers *are* fun, but I doubt she'd see the humor."

"I'm overwhelmed by the compliment. What then, counselor? We don't even go to the same church."

The image of Tom and Lee sliding next to each other at a pancake prayer breakfast made my throat contract.

I drew the Taittinger out of the ice, finished it off, and stuck the bottle upside down in the bucket.

"My cue." He rubbed fingers together like a safe cracker and expertly pried open the cork in the second bottle.

All the time, my mind raced. What were Tom's hobbies? His interests? His sports? As the cork slipped out with a smooth, enticing hiss, I blurted, "Why don't you take her fishing?"

I expected to hear "Objection, Your Honor," but his face softened. "That may not be such a bad idea."

I worked up some enthusiasm. "It beats a bar meeting. Or a prayer breakfast. And it's not so romantic that she'd get suspicious."

Tom leaned back in the overstuffed chair, deftly loosened his silk tie, and beamed. "Flip. I toast you. You're a genius."

Genius. What a laugh. Devious, mean, back-stabbing—yes. And for what? For the minute chance I could get Sam interested in me instead of Lee.

"You still have to ask her out. And she still has to say yes. But I don't mind accepting a toast. I deserve it for other reasons."

With questions in Tom's searing, dark eyes, we both drank to me. Me in my pretty new suit, queen for the day. Me, the maid of Solace Glen, living the high life at the Harbor Court. Me, the caregiver, the peacekeeper, the listener. The good friend. The very good friend.

CHAPTER 17

✳

ROLAND WAS NOWHERE to be seen when I spied Lee sitting at my table behind the cash register finishing a meal. I took a deep breath and made a beeline for the chair beside her.

"So." I slid behind a menu, one eye on the lookout for Roland, one eye catching Officer Lukzay's grimace. "What's new with you?"

"Not much." She kept her nose in *The Sotweed Factor*. "I'm supposed to meet with Sam and his expert about the letters next Friday."

"Good." I scribbled an order. "You seem pretty matter-of-fact about it. Aren't you excited?"

She lay the book down and thought a moment. "I'm mostly curious, I guess. Curious to know if J.E.B. Stuart really wrote them. Curious who the woman was he wrote to because they're . . . they're so beautiful, aren't they, Flip?"

I nodded, remembering.

"And I'm curious about why the Bell women kept the letters such a closely guarded secret. I don't get it. And why only the women in the family?"

I thought about the Bible on my kitchen cabinet. "Beats me. The names on the family tree can't exactly talk."

We sat there, shaking our heads in puzzlement. Finally, I sighed. "So, what else is new?"

"I decided to get Jeb spayed."

"Always a good idea."

"I accepted Tom's invitation to go fishing Saturday."

"Gooood."

The hazel eyes bore into me. "What do you mean by that? Nice hair."

"What do *you* mean? Thanks."

"That 'good' had a little something extra on it."

"I'm sure I don't understand," I said primly. Then I added under my breath, a very loud breath, "Except Tom is becoming quite the ladies' man." There. I'd opened the door to the lie. Devious. Mean. Backstabbing.

"Whoa, whoa, whoa." Lee flung her book to the side. "Tom Scott, a ladies' man?"

"Uh-huh." I fooled with a pencil.

"Our Tom Scott? The legal eagle who probably wears a suit to bed?"

"Trust me. He has a way of loosening a tie that sends a tingle to your toes." I swallowed hard and fast. "I ran into him when I was having a drink in Baltimore at the Harbor Court."

"Whooo-eeee," she shook her wrist. "The Hawba Coort."

"Yes, it was very nice, thanks for asking. And Tom strolled into the bar with a really tall, good-looking model-type woman clamped on him tight as an oyster and she was laughing like crazy. He must be real funny when he's out of town."

"I can well imagine."

"And this woman, this girl-child, couldn't keep her hands off him. I mean, it was embarrassing."

Lee bought every word. "What was he doing?"

"Tom? Eating it up, of course. Having the *best* time. Bought a bottle of champagne. Was running his finger slooooowly up and down her leg. She had on a real short skirt, up to here. Was nipping at her neck. She had cleavage down to there." I jabbed my diaphragm with the pencil.

Lee's eyes popped wide, "Ohhh myyy Looord! Did he see you?"

"No, I was hiding behind a palm tree." Once I stuck my toe through the door, who was there to stop me? "But when she got up to go to the ladies' room, I followed her."

"You didn't!"

"Oh, yes. I wanted a close-up, you know. So there I was, standing at the mirror, pinching my cheeks, a regular Scarlett O'Hara, and she walks over to reapply her makeup."

"Did you talk to her?"

"Of course. Struck up quite the conversation. I said, 'Why, I used to have a blouse just like that.'"

Lee clapped a hand over her mouth, stifling a yelp.

"Said she got it at Neiman Marcus and that's where she met her date."

"Tom?" She slapped her thigh. "At Neiman Marcus?"

"In the lingerie department."

She slapped the other thigh. "Get out! What was he doing?"

"Buying panties for another woman. Asked her opinion, then asked her out."

"What a wolf!"

"That's not all. She said he ended up buying those panties for her and she was wearing them right then and had promised to model for him in their suite later on."

Lee beat the heel of her hand on the table. "NO!NO!NO! This is not our Tom Scott!"

"Keep it down." Tom walked in with Ferrell T. I slid my eyes sideways until Lee saw him, too. "I tell you, Lee," I hissed, "he's one of those Jekyll and Hyde types who goes out of town and turns into a sex maniac. And the women *love* him."

"I'll be damned," she said in a disbelieving voice, but believing every word. "Gaaaa, what should I wear on this fishing trip?"

"Something revealing," I suggested, such a big help. "You'll be out of town."

She peeped at Tom over one shoulder, nose wrinkled up like a bunny's. "I know. I'm excited."

I'll show you excited, I thought. Excited is what Tom's going to be if he ever finds out about this. He might even get excited enough to chop my head off.

Hilda swooped by and grabbed my order. While I was planning my funeral, Sam strolled in. Lee was too busy stealing glances at Tom and readjusting her image of him to notice. But I did.

Fingers flew to my hair and started fluffing. I couldn't quit wetting my lips. I pulled at a bra strap under my sweater, tugged my shirt down tighter, straightened my spine, lifted my chin. Smiled like I was running for Miss Maryland. If anyone had shown me a video of myself later, I'd have thrown up.

He didn't even look our way. Nodded politely at the Eggheads, Garland, Hilda, Reverend McKnight and Father Gower, made his way straight to Tom and Ferrell T., shook hands, and flopped into a chair.

"Is that Sam?" Lee twisted full around. "What's he doing here?"

"Must have a luncheon date with Tom." A different spin came to mind and I added suggestively, "Maybe there's something we don't know."

Lee snickered. "I don't know about Tom, but Sam's *definitely* more interested in bra straps than jock straps."

"Oh. Really." I glared at the back of her head. More than anything at that moment, I wished Lee was ugly. I imagined car wrecks, flying glass and terrible operations. Skin grafts and the immutable tracks of stitches crisscrossing flesh. Then I remembered Henry and Marie, Jake and Leona. That was all it took.

"Why don't you go over and say hello?"

The edges of Lee's lips curled. "Ooo, what a good suggestion." She oozed out of the chair and slithered across the room to where Tom and Sam sat unsuspecting, ankles boyishly crossed over their knees. Spanky and Alfalfa.

I must say, Henry and Marie would have been proud of their girl. I crouched in the chair, mesmerized, while the custodian of the Historical Society played two men against each other like the bookie at a cockfight. Ferrell T., of course, didn't figure into it, a sack of potatoes with a bow tie. His only reaction to Lee was annoyance at the interruption.

Chairs scraped and four eyes lit up. Two mouths tried to speak at once. Four hands grabbed a chair, pulling it tug-of-war for the golden girl to sit on. Four ears waited to hear the magic. Two egos pawed at the gate of the pen.

Lee ate it up, confidant of Sam's interest and believing my lie that other women pursued Tom. Both plots intrigued her.

Hilda dropped off my lunch, but I couldn't eat for watching the show. Lee barely glimpsed in Sam's direction, that territory already conquered. Instead, she aimed all weapons at Tom—the dazzling smile, the starry eyes, the flip of her auburn hair, the cock of her pretty chin. She even reached out at one point and touched his arm. I thought the man would blast out of his chair, toes flapping like propeller blades, steam pouring out of each ear. Frankly, the whole scene made me feel sort of sorry for Tom, even though Lee was delivering what I'd paid for. A jiggly ankle signaled the only give-away of Sam's jealousy.

When Lee stood to go, the Little Rascals popped out of their seats like jack-in-the-boxes, bowing and scraping. Her performance had been perfect and the exit would have been, too, but she backed straight into Roland coming the other way. The laughing face turned bitter.

"Ex*cuse* me, Mr. Bell." She shook him off as she would a nasty horsefly.

Roland possessed none of the basic social skills. He pointed at Sam. "That the man you got living in my family's house, isn't it? Sam Gibbon?"

"It's my house and it's none of your damn business." She started to go, but Roland clamped onto an elbow.

"I'm not finished with you yet. What're you doing about those letters?"

Lee wrestled her arm away from him. "What the hell is it to you, Roland?"

By this time, both Sam and Tom began closing the distance between them and Roland, flashing that protective warning sign men get in their eyes. Roland measured their interest and drew a few inches away from Lee. His tone mellowed instantly.

"Just curious, like everybody else in town. My offer to you still stands. After all, if it weren't for Flip, you wouldn't even have those letters. They'd be mine by right." He shifted his gaze from Lee to me, the brave soul hiding behind her iced tea. "Ain't that right, Flip?" The harsh tone returned.

Lee would have none of it. "Flip was nothing more than Leona's messenger and you know it, Roland, so don't you go attacking her." There I sat, Lee's Judas, intent on going after Sam, and she still came to my aid. I said nothing and let her do all the talking. "Anyway, those letters might amount to zilch. We'll know soon enough."

"What's that supposed to mean?"

I watched as the Eggheads rose from their seats, Roland's Greek chorus on the subject of the letters. "You getting that expert from the Smithsonian to look at 'em, Lee?" one sang. "That friend of Sam's?"

Garland stepped out of the kitchen, wiping her hands on a dishtowel, forehead creased.

"Oh, Sam Gibbon's involved in this thing now, is he?" spat Roland. "A perfect stranger! Get back in the kitchen, woman! This is none of your concern!"

Garland zipped through the swinging door and disappeared.

"Well hell, Lee, why not turn all the Bell property over to him right now?"

"Maybe I will." Lee stepped a foot closer and Roland matched the move.

Finally, somebody with some sense took over.

"Lee, go home." Tom edged between Roland and Lee with the ease of Fred Astaire and whisked her toward the door. To Roland, he smoothly suggested that the service appeared slow today and could he check on their table's orders in the kitchen. Then he escorted Lee through the door and out on the street where I saw him motion her to trot on home as he would a truant caught hanging around the candy store during school.

He walked back to his table, sat down, and calmly resumed his conversation with Sam, who plopped into his chair with a lop-sided grin, and Ferrell T., who had not risen an inch from his spot.

I twisted my watchband between nervous fingers. With Lee gone, I had no idea what tune Roland might play. I gobbled lunch, threw money at the plate and would have made a clean getaway, but for Reverend McKnight asking how I was getting along since the break-in. Roland came barging out of the kitchen. He made straight for me.

The whole of my scalp tingled, and the food I'd gulped so fast rose in my throat.

He hesitated when he recognized McKnight and stopped in his tracks the moment Sam stepped into his path.

"Flip, I've been meaning to ask you something." Sam picked up the carryall as if he always scooped it up, a boy carrying his girl's schoolbooks. He started walking, motioning me to slide along beside him. Side by side we bustled past Roland with his popping veins and flinty eyes.

I met Sam stride for stride until we were outside where I swallowed a mouthful of fresh air.

"Thank you, Sam." I took the carryall from his hand, eyes on the sidewalk. "That was very kind."

"Don't thank me." He skipped backward into the Café, relishing the game. "Tom thought you could use a friendly face."

My head jerked up. I stared at the closed door a moment, whipped around, and marched to my car, teeth gritted, ears ringing. It wasn't Sam. It wasn't Sam rescuing me at all. He'd only helped out because Tom Scott thought I could *use a friendly face*. Well, thanks a lot, Tom Scott! How very, very kind of you!

As I stepped into my horrible car, Sam's voice called out. I looked up to see him running down the street. "Oh, by the way, I really did have something to ask you!"

He pulled up a few feet from the car. "How about a fishing trip Saturday? You up to showing me the Monocacy?"

He was using me. Using me to spy on Tom and Lee. Using me to get Lee jealous. Did he think I didn't know?

"Sure!" I called out, bright as a Christmas star, summoning everything I had to cover the catch in my voice. "You got yourself a date!"

Not that Sam Gibbon considered me his date, but that could change. He was, after all, giving Judas her chance.

CHAPTER 18

❄

SALLY POLK, SOLACE Glen's barber and beautician *extraordinaire*, understood perfectly why I got my hair done once a year in Baltimore and once a year with her.

"I know that hell-out-of-Dodge feeling, honey," she'd drawl through her chewing gum. "I won the Hell-Out-of-Dodge pageant."

A year younger than me, Sally had lived a pretty packed life for a forty-one-year-old woman. Born in North Carolina, a speedway queen at seventeen, married to a NASCAR driver at eighteen, pregnant with twins at nineteen, divorced at twenty-one, remarried three times before thirty-five, now on husband number five and pregnant out to here.

"What are *you* doing here?" She popped her gum in my direction as she worked on Miss Fizzi.

"Don't you remember?" asked Miss Fizzi. "I'm having my hair done."

Sally threw her head back and almost choked on her Wrigley's. "No, Miss Fizzi. Flip just walked in. See?" She swiveled the chair around so Miss Fizzi could eyeball me. "She got her hair done in the big city. Her next appointment here isn't for six months. What's the deal, Flip? That break-in make you go crazy?"

I slipped into a chair next to Margaret who politely put aside her magazine for conversation. Melody waved one freshly polished hand at me while Tina worked on the other one. They all waited for a logical explanation to my bizarre behavior. I could tell they wanted to discuss the break-in, too.

"Maybe I've decided to get my hair done once a week like all of you."

"And maybe the Pope's Jewish," said Melody.

"Or maybe I've decided to pamper myself more often." They weren't buying it.

"Or?" asked Margaret, skeptically.

"Or," I pretended to search for a magazine, "maybe I have a date."

"A date!" Melody jumped in her chair, eyes large and mouth open, the same reaction as when she thought I was engaged—equally impossible announcements.

Tina yanked her hand down. "Melody, you'll smear." But she could hardly contain herself, either. "Who is he, Flip? Somebody you met in Baltimore? You can't date somebody from Baltimore without makeup. Oh, I hope that's why you came in!"

Poor Tina. We both knew she'd never get me in that makeup chair.

"No," I cut her off. "I had a little time and I thought maybe Sally could work me in at the end of her day for a touch up."

"Want that freshly made look, do ya?" Sally gleamed as she finished up Miss Fizzi's standard coiffure. "Who is the gentleman, pray tell?"

Miss Fizzi tried her hand at guessing. "Pal? Jesse? Jules?"

I was surprised she didn't say Suggs. With each guess, my nose wrinkled tighter.

"Oh, Miss Fizzi," Margaret sighed, "Flip has some taste. All those boys are too young for her."

As if I could only attract centenarians.

"You'll at least want a manicure," suggested Tina, desperate to do something, anything, to improve the pitiful town maid.

"Noooo," I said between clenched teeth. "Could you give me a wash and blow dry, Sally?"

"Only for you, hon. You're *finito*, Miss Fizzi. Hit the highway."

Both Margaret and Miss Fizzi knit their brows together. Miss Fizzi because she could not understand half of Sally's slang expressions, and Margaret because she thoroughly disapproved of the uncouth tone.

"You're up, Margaret." Sally took a long drink from a Mountain Dew while she waved Miss Fizzi out the door.

"You mean, 'You're next, Miss Henshaw,' or 'It is your turn now, Miss Henshaw.' "

Sally shrugged, a good-humored grin on her face. "Whatever, hon." She had not had the benefit of Margaret's grammar and public speaking class.

The subject turned to concern over my break-in and expressions of doubt whether Officer Lukzay would get off his lazy butt and investigate. None of them could imagine Roland taking the risk of criminal conviction for a Bible, of all things, and assured me the ransacking held all the marks of wild teenagers on a trick-or-treat rampage. I wasn't convinced.

Thankfully, the subject switched back to the topic on everyone's lips before I walked in—C.C. and Leonard. I joined in, hoping I could avoid the dating inquisition and keep my date's identity a secret. If things went as planned, my romance would be a nice surprise for everyone later on. If the whole thing fizzled, no need to embarrass myself further.

"What I don't get," said Tina, apparently picking up where she'd left off, "is why Solace Glen? Why do we have to be the town to get C.C. and Leonard? We usually have such nice people move here." Under her breath she added, "Except for Suggs, of course."

"Tell me about it," Melody took over. "That Leonard, that fox in Brooks Brothers clothing, he comes into the store and orders Michael around like he's a lowly office boy. Lemme see this. Lemme see that. I was thinking, OK, Mr. Tall and Handsome Big Bucks, show us the money, but nothing. Didn't buy a thing after all that ordering. Just questions, all the time questions."

"What sort of questions?" My ears perked up.

"Wanting to know about certain people."

"People with Civil War letters?"

Melody emphasized each syllable. "And others."

"What others?"

"Like you, for instance."

My cheeks burned and my stomach lurched. "Me? Why would Leonard Crosswell want to know about me?"

Everyone wore concerned faces. We all sensed a malevolent air about Leonard.

Melody went on with her story. "At first he made it sound like he simply wanted to check out your references before you came into his house. But then he mentioned your inheritance from Leona, as if old Bibles really knock his silk socks off, and wondered in an oh-so-innocent manner what else you got in the way of old publications. Then he had the nerve to ask, is it certain *all* Leona's old papers are accounted for? Does the man who lives in the house—Sam Gibbon—does he have any control over things or is it all Lee's?"

Margaret could not believe her ears. "Of all the gall! What is that man thinking?"

"He gives me the shivers." Tina's large body shuddered dramatically. "You better watch it, Flip."

A picture of my wrecked house came to mind and I began to wonder.

"If ya want my opinion . . ." Sally stopped combing Margaret's hair and tapped the comb against the sink to knock out the strands. "Lee's the real target. I mean, that Bible's not worth anything, is it, Flip?"

"To me it is."

She raised one shoulder. "Well, sure, but maybe Leonard knows something you don't. At any rate," she tilted the chair back and Margaret's head disappeared into the sink, "Lee's the one with the most goods. He'll go where the money is. That's his type."

I rubbed the back of my neck, suddenly tense and tight. "Yeah, that is his type. I better warn Lee about him."

The topic of conversation changed again, the usual comments about Marlene and how badly she treated Louise. The deteriorating health of Louise. Poor Joey Sykes and what in the world was he thinking driving so fast? Bets on what Larry would finally do to get back at C.C. Whether Charlie Scott would ever return to Solace Glen. Whether Marlene's mysterious ex-husband would ever show up and beg her to come back—that one always left us laughing.

My sense of humor evaporated, though, when I left Sally's and got back behind the wheel. WFIB played "I Get Along Without You Very Well."

One thing was sure. We could all get along very well without Leonard Crosswell.

Chapter 19

MID-NOVEMBER IN CENTRAL Maryland can catch your breath in the early morning. Frost strikes with predictability and dead leaves, no longer in the crisp and crunchy state, cover the ground, soaking up moisture, wet and black. Snow is a promise in the air, right around the corner of the breeze.

I knew exactly where Tom would take Lee—a boat landing just off Route 15. If they took two cars, they could cover more distance canoeing downstream, but I figured for this first time, he'd want to drive her; he'd have a captive audience.

Sam picked me up in his decrepit jeep. It stank of raw shrimp and vanilla air freshener. I named the boat landing and we took off, the sun peeping over bare hills and stripped cornfields outside of town. I cracked the window to let in sweet, crisp air and stared at the landscape flashing by. If

Sam wanted to use me to make Lee jealous, fine. I'd lead him to the object of his desire and make him compare. The slim chance did exist he'd find my company easier to take. To give myself a little head start, I'd packed a picnic that included a jug of red wine.

Sam and I had pulled the same things out of the drawer that morning: jeans, plaid flannel shirt, down vest, hiking boots, and heavy socks, but even with the same outfit, he looked L.L. Bean, I looked Kmart. At least my hair shone, and the gold hoops added a feminine touch to my drab appearance. I tugged at a thread on my sleeve and silently carried on a conversation. *You should have seen me in my silk suit at the Harbor Court. Boy, was I a hot property.*

"You and Tom good friends?"

The question took me by surprise. "Yes and no. It's only been the past ten years or so we've had any real conversation." I fiddled with the thread on my sleeve.

"Ten plus years is a long time for an answer like 'yes and no.' Seems you ought to know by now."

I jerked the thread and ripped a hole in the shirt.

"Well," he wouldn't let go, " is it more yes or more no?"

I rolled the sleeve up over the hole. "Tom makes me nervous. He's real smart and blue-blooded, so I feel like a poor, dumb relation most of the time."

My arms hugged my chest, the air blowing in from the window cold against my face. I didn't know what more to say.

Sam let the silence flow awhile then quietly commented, "Lee told me how much you like to read." I didn't respond so he continued, dropping all pretense of interest in my hobbies. "I've spent a lot of time on the telephone with her. I've asked her to a few things at the college. She doesn't seem interested. Then I run into her and we're on a totally different level, get along great. I get encouraged, call and ask her to something. She declines. I'm spinning in a circle with this woman and I want to break through, you know? I just want a normal *date*. Doesn't she date?"

"Sure." I got a little huffy. "She's out fishing with Tom this morning." My fingernail scratched at a dead leaf stuck in the window. "Same as we're out together."

He remained quiet a minute then said, "To be honest, I was hoping you could help me with Lee. Not that I don't think you're good company. I think you're great. . . ."

I turned and looked him right in the eye. No more shy glances or shuffling feet. He'd laid his cards on the table, so would I. "You asked me out because I'm Lee's best friend."

"Well, yeah." He took his eyes off the road long enough to toss me a helpless look, as if he knew I'm a sucker for that look every time.

"Mmm. I figured you were just trying to make her jealous, because I'm so stunning and everything, but I decided to come, anyway, because . . ." I hoped my voice wouldn't crack, "I think you're a really nice guy."

"Thank you. I mean that, Flip. And if you could give me any advice, I'd really appreciate it." He blew out a breath. "I thought for awhile she was playing hard to get. But she ain't playing."

So there it was. My bubble burst. Sam Gibbon harbored no more interest in me than the road sign we'd just passed. I could give information; I was a means to an end. At least he was nice about it, honest, and I could do with a day on the Monocacy with good company.

In the back of my mind, though, I couldn't help holding onto that thin sliver of hope that he still might pick me at the end of the day.

THE SCENERY PASSED by quickly. Church steeples on hilltops in the distance, clapboard farm houses with red barns and rusty silos, Canada geese blanketing the chopped brown fields. We took the Creagerstown exit off Route 15, arrived at the landing, unloaded Sam's canoe and all our gear at water's edge, and parked the jeep under some trees.

For a waterman's son, Sam didn't possess much in the way of fancy fishing equipment: one busted up, plastic tackle box crammed with lures, lines, and hooks and two disassembled reel poles that he spliced together before we climbed into the aluminum canoe.

"You sure there aren't any holes in this thing?" The canoe looked like something he'd scavenged at a flea market for fifty cents, the color of a thundercloud, dents and dings pocked each side. "Where are the life preservers?"

He pulled something out of a ragged duffel bag stamped U.S. ARMY.

"What's that?"

"A life preserver, what do you think?"

I punched two thumbs in the rust-colored vest. They sank into the crumbly insides without resistance. "What vintage?" Besides the normal fear of furry spiders, hooded snakes, and long-toothed rodents, I held a healthy respect for the power of running water.

"Not to worry." Sam delivered a tightlipped, reassuring teacher's smile, dealing with yet another pupil, scared how she'll do on an exam. "We'll stay close to shore."

One of the belts fell off in my hand. It couldn't save a Chihuahua. Nevertheless, I popped the moldy preserver over my head, gripped a paddle and climbed into the bow of the canoe. Sam pushed us into the river and jumped toward the stern, steering for the current.

The Monocacy runs slow and easy in mid-November, slightly up from the autumn rains, not fat and hurried as in the spring. The current, a small resolve against the press of a paddle, pulled gently beneath my knees.

"Go upstream," directed Sam, and we lined up our oars

parallel to the riverbank, easily pushing the boat northward. "Not too bad, is it?"

The fungus smell of the life preserver was dizzying. I tossed it behind me. "No. Not too bad. So far."

It was barely eight o'clock, and I hadn't eaten breakfast. We slid into a little cove. Slick, black tree branches stuck out of the water where they'd broken off from the trees that encircled the bend of the river. I reached into the picnic basket and grabbed a sandwich.

Sam helped himself to a bag of chips, idly fixing a neon yellow glowworm onto a hook. "Do much fishing?"

"Nope. I like my water in a tub or a glass."

He lightly flicked the rod backward and let go of the line on the downswing. The smooth *zing* of the reel and the plunk of the lure broke the monotonous gurgling of the river. "This is most pleasant," he sighed.

I had to admit, alone in a beautiful place with a handsome man—there were worse things in life. I nibbled the sandwich, content, watching the swirls in the river, the play of morning light, hoping Tom and Lee wouldn't show up.

"What's your favorite era in history?" The reel clicked as Sam wound in the line.

Good God, a test. "I thought men didn't like to talk when they fished."

"Oh, I've always associated fishing with deep, honest conversation. I used to ask my dad a million questions about fishing and life and death and sports and women. He listened. Told me what he knew about each painful subject."

I examined the pole at my feet. "Sounds like the two of you were close."

"Your mom and dad died when you were in high school, right?"

Lee must have told him my life story. "Yeah, young enough to be completely devastated. Old enough to fight to live on my own."

"You won the battle and lost the war?"

"I thought living alone at age eighteen would be a kind of paradise. Every teenager's dream. I craved independence, but what I ended up with was isolation. When I finally discovered the difference . . . well." I flicked the rod backward and forward. The pole flew out of my fist into the water.

"We'll continue this deep, honest conversation after we retrieve my fishing gear."

He plucked the pole out of the river. The tangled line shook in his hand. "Jeez. You might try sticking some bait on it next time."

He baited the hook with an ugly piece of plastic goop, picked up his own pole, and demonstrated the correct way to cast. With both our lines in the water, we settled down to the sluggish repetitions of fishing out of a drifting canoe: cast out, reel in, eat something, paddle upstream, cast out, reel in, on and on.

"The American Revolution," I said.

Sam pitched a crust of bread into the Monocacy. "That's what I thought you'd say."

AN HOUR LATER, we'd progressed beyond the American Revolution to history of a more personal nature. I dipped a finger in the river, the water cold as February. "So you arrived in Solace Glen and you're happy. Ever married?"

"No. I was too much of a cad and a bounder."

"But you've seen the error of your ways?"

He tilted his face into the sun, smiled like there was no place on earth he'd rather be. "I've seen the error of my ways. I've seen that my parents were right all along, horrible thought. And I'm at a place in my life where I'm ready."

"For what?"

"To share." He reeled the lure in and tossed it out again in the same smooth, lazy manner I'd watched for over an hour. "I cast selfishness away. Sharing is the watchword of this man from now on."

"And you've got your eye on Lee."

"Speaking of . . ." He pointed through the leafless trees on the opposite bank. Tom's car crept down the road to the boat landing. "You were right. Here they come."

We watched, camouflaged in the cove, as Tom parked the car and the two of them unloaded the canoe. They didn't notice Sam's jeep in the trees. The two of them climbed into the red canoe, spotless, dingless, and toting the proper form of life preserver, I noticed. A big picnic basket along with a cooler served as ballast in the middle of the boat.

Our sandwiches had disappeared, as had the chips and cookies, leaving only the jug of red wine. "Wonder what they brought to eat," I thought out loud, hungry again though it wasn't ten o'clock.

"Probably goose liver pâté, a fine round of French Brie, whole grain bread, assorted fruits, and champagne." He wiggled his pinkie finger.

My face went cross. Champagne. Probably Taittinger.

The red canoe hit the current and stroked upstream. I squirmed on the hard aluminum, knees stiff, and glared at the approaching boat, disappointed they'd shown up in the first place, but also brazenly curious.

"Sam?" Lee squinted as the canoe neared. "Flip?"

"Why, hello there." Sam blinked at her, creasing his forehead. "Are you following us?"

Tom drew the red canoe along side ours. "Why, no." He zeroed in on me. "But you might have told *us* of *your* plans."

"Yeah, Flip," Lee smiled with a question in her eyes, "I didn't realize you and Sam had plans. The two of you. Together."

Before I could open my mouth, Sam blurted, "Well, you know us. Spur of the moment. Wild and wacky." Eyes trained on Lee, he flung a hand out to pat my back and whacked my head. "Sorry, baby doll."

Tom laid his paddle across the canoe, sneered and mouthed the words *baby doll*?

"Catch anything?" Lee peered into our dingy canoe. "Where's your cooler for the fish?"

"We forgot it," I said. Catching fish wasn't the point of this game.

"But we remembered the vino, didn't we, hon?"

I screwed my head around to get a good view of Sam. He'd gone crazy and beamed like an Irish setter out for his first romp in the cow pies.

"Oh, yeah. We wouldn't forget the vino."

"Tom brought champagne," Lee twittered. She'd left the top three buttons of her chamois shirt undone, revealing a camisole's lace and a hint of cleavage.

Tom pulled a bottle out of the cooler and held it like a trophy over his head for me to admire. Taittinger.

"Tom has such good taste in champagne," I snipped.

Sam sat mesmerized by Lee, practically drooling. "You really look pretty today, Lee." All pretense crumbled into the water.

She smiled ear to ear, biting the tip of her tongue, hazel eyes sparkling.

"Time to fish!" Tom pushed away from us and dug a paddle into the current. "Paddle, Lee. I said paddle, Lee!"

They disappeared behind the bend.

"They'll be back." Sam shook a finger wisely in the air. "The river flows this way."

I slapped both hands on my knees. "*Ooooo, Miss Lee, you really look pretty today*. That was cool, I must say."

He leaned back on one elbow and clucked his tongue at me. "What about you? *Tom tastes so good in champagne*."

"Has good taste in champagne!"

"Whatever." He yawned and whizzed a line into the river.

We sat in silence a few minutes. Finally he said, "Lee did look pretty."

"I'm sure Tom thinks so, too."

"Yeah, but he probably hasn't said so. Too uptight, our old Tom."

"He's not that old."

"He's what, ten years older than we are? Good God, the man should be on oxygen."

I poked a lip out and zinged a line into the same spot I'd been splashing down in for what seemed like days. "There aren't any fish in this river and there's no food on this boat. I suggest inebriation."

"That's the frontier spirit." Sam popped the cork on the jug and filled two plastic cups. "It's women like you who made this country great."

We toasted. To women like me.

BY NOON THE jug lay empty. I hooked my fishing line on it and tossed it overboard. The jug bobbed cheerily down the current.

About that time, we heard laughter. Tom and Lee drifted toward us, but pulled into a basin of still water before rounding the curve. We could just make out the tops of their heads through the underbrush.

"What are they talking about, do you think—Medicare or Social Security?" Sam strained an ear. "Naw. That'd be too personal for old Tom."

I slumped into the bow and dangled my legs over the gunwale. "Ha! That man could beat you in the hundred yard dash, argue you into the ground, and deliver a heart-stirring eulogy at your funeral while sipping the perfect Merlot."

Sam snickered. "Probably regaling her with quotes from Nasdaq."

"Yeah, that'll get her so worked up he won't have any trouble making his move."

"What move?"

"You know. A move. A pass. A kiss."

Sam's face collapsed. "He is not going to try to kiss her!"

"Oh, yes, indeedy he is. Tom is quite the wolf. Quite the ladies' man."

At this point, Lee's laughter acquired a riotous edge to it.

"She's screaming!" Sam yelled. "Old Tom's attacking her!"

He plowed through the water, splashing me with freezing river water. I lay crunched in the bow, feet in the air, trying to reel in the jug. As we slid around the bend, Sam mumbled curses. I crooked my neck over the gunnel. First Lee, then Tom came into view. They faced each other in the red canoe, sitting Indian style with the picnic basket set up as a table between them. Flute glasses, a red and white checkered cloth, linen napkins, dessert plates with apples and pears, cheese and bread. Sam had pegged it.

I called out, "You two gonna eat all that?"

Lee turned around, eyes glassy, lips covering half her face. "I never knew I liked champagne." She let out a squeak and drained her glass.

"I might try one of those apples," I pointed at the largest one just as our canoe slammed into theirs. "With cheese, if you don't mind."

Lee whooped and broke into a giggle fit as Sam maneuvered the boat so she practically sat in his lap and Tom and I could arm wrestle if we wanted.

"Isn't this cozy now?" Sam glowed from the wine. "We ran out of food. Didn't we, sweetie pie?"

I reached into Tom's plate and plucked off half an apple and a hunk of Stilton.

Lee cradled her empty glass and turned flickering eyelashes on Sam. "You want some of my champagne?"

"I would love some of your champagne." He leaned into her.

Tom and I caught each other's eye; they weren't talking about the wine.

"Well, you can't have any," Tom snatched Lee's glass away. "It's mine."

"We can share," pouted Lee.

"No, we can't."

"That's not very adult of you."

"Call me an old-fashioned fool." Tom crammed a stopper in the bottle.

"Party pooper." She leaned back and propped two elbows across the canoe. Her shirt pulled open where the buttons were undone. "Where's that red wine you guys brought?"

I stopped eating and reeled in the empty jug.

"So what now?" asked Sam, staring intently at Lee's exposed cleavage.

"What do you mean 'what now'?" Tom growled. "We all came here to fish, didn't we?"

"We came, we saw, we fished," I munched at the apple. "Pass the Brie, please."

Tom slapped a slice of goo into the palm of my hand. "Then I suggest we all go home."

Lee put on a Mae West act. "Oooo. And sleep it off?"

"It wouldn't hurt you any."

"I have a better idea," chirped Sam. "Tom, you go home and sleep it off. I'll chauffeur the ladies around the river having deep, honest conversation for a couple of hours."

"I'm all for that!" Lee shot up and clambered into our canoe.

"I've had enough fun for one morning." I licked the last of the cheese off my fingers. "I'll go with Tom."

"Wait a minute!" Tom clutched the gunwale as Lee and I fell into each other's spots. "Lee!"

Sam pushed away the moment Lee landed safely in and

I thudded safely out. She peeked a sheepish eye over the edge of the canoe, saluting us as Sam whisked into the current paddling hard. He called over his shoulder, "Thanks for the picnic, Flip! Catch ya later!"

In an instant, they were gone. Tom shut his open jaw with a loud bite then turned on me. "You!" he roared. "You did this!"

"Did what? Pushed Lee out of your boat into Sam's arms?"

"You brought him here! You did it on purpose!" He jerked the stopper out of the champagne and searched for a glass. "Oh, hell." The bottle went into his mouth.

"You could at least be a gentleman and offer me some."

He glared sideways as he slurped, popped the bottle out of his mouth, and offered it to me, wiping tight lips with the back of his hand.

"No, thank you," I said primly. "I've had enough."

"I have, too." He took another swig. "I've had enough of this Lee and Sam thing."

"Then do something."

"I was trying to do something when you screwed it up!"

"My, aren't we touchy. When were you going to do something, when you took her home? A peck on the cheek?"

"No." He grew quiet. "I had it all planned. I was going to ply her with wit and champagne, fruit, bread and cheese, a box of Godiva," he drew out a small golden box for me to inspect, "then I was going to recite one of my favorite poems, Walt Whitman, 'Are You the New Person Drawn Toward Me?'"

The dark eyes looked right through me, focused on something far away.

"Are you the new person drawn toward me?
To begin with take warning, I am surely far different
from what you suppose;

Do you suppose you will find in me your ideal?
Do you think it so easy to have me become your lover?
Do you think the friendship of me would be unalloy'd
*   satisfaction?*
Do you think I am trusty and faithful?
Do you see no further than this facade, this smooth and
*   tolerant manner of me?*
Do you suppose yourself advancing on real ground to-
*   ward a real heroic man?*
Have you no thought O dreamer that it may be all maya,
*   illusion?"*

I felt my face flush and go red. "Oh."

Only the river spoke for awhile, sweetly, sadly.

Tom smirked at his reflection in the bottle. "Then I was going to slowly lean forward and gently kiss her. Lightly, but insistently, holding her face between my hands."

He kissed the reflection, sighed heavily, then wrapped one fist around the neck of the bottle and scraped it against the floor of the boat. "BUT. You . . . screwed . . . it . . . up." He tore open the Godiva and bit into a chocolate square.

"I think I will have a drink," I whispered.

We sat in the drifting red canoe, me sucking on the heavy green bottle, Tom stewing over his box of sweets. Both of us scheming how to get what we wanted, though I was no longer sure what that was.

CHAPTER 20

✻

A WEEK AFTER I'd last touched it, I reached for the Bell family Bible and again let my imagination supply the missing pieces.

Ferrell Bell, who'd married Gretal, the sturdy German girl, had two first cousins, both bearing the same middle name: John Bell Paca, who died during the war in 1861, and Lucy Bell Paca, his little sister, born in 1829. Their mother, Lucinda, must have been awfully proud of her maiden name, a pride of name that extended well into the twenty-first century.

Nine years stretched between Lucy and her brother. She must have looked up to him, that big brother who played games with her during the early 1830s. Then came the day he went away to school and she missed him. When he returned home, he was all grown up, tall and handsome. Lucy probably didn't know what to make of John Bell, but I bet he doted on her.

In the mid-1840s, she suddenly sprouted and became a magnet for all the county boys. I could just imagine her— medium height, reddish hair, green eyes like Leona's, lots of freckles, and an infectious laugh. Her brother must have advised her: *This boy's an arrogant son-of-a-gun, Lucy. This boy's from a trashy family, Lucy, for all his good looks and charm. This one's suitable, Lucy. Good family and a solid career in business.*

She quickly settled on one, and at age eighteen married a man named Jason Tanner, twenty-nine years her senior. What could she have had in common with a man forty-seven years old? Did she have affection for him, or was it purely a business deal, promoted by her brother now that her father was dead?

From father to brother to husband, Lucy had little chance to try her wings at an age when most modern girls already know all there is to know. So Lucy moved in with her older husband, and three years later, mid-century, her life took another turn. She had a baby girl and her husband died.

Maybe the shock of fatherhood at age fifty caused him to keel over. Maybe once she got pregnant she thought, *I've got what I want,* and she poisoned him. Maybe her brother shot him in a duel over a business venture gone bad. Or maybe he just took ill and passed away in a fever. However it happened, Lucy found herself a single mother with a sort of freedom she'd never known before.

At about this time, John Bell Paca started building the big house that Leona's parents left to her and Leona passed to Lee. John's name and the date 1855 are inscribed in a cornerstone. Even though her husband probably left behind a nice house and a good income, family ties would have prompted Lucy to move in with her bachelor brother. She never married again, but raised her daughter, Lucinda Ann Tanner, in her own way.

In 1861, the country went to war, with Lucy thirty-two years old raising an eleven-year-old child. She and Lucinda Ann might have helped sew uniforms or make bandages. They might have visited soldiers in the hospital. They were proud when John Bell Paca rode off to war and wept when he was lost to them so soon.

Lucy and Gretal must have commiserated together, two women alone with their two children during the long four years. Gretal, at least, had a husband coming back to her while Lucy had no one but her little daughter.

I contemplated the war in Maryland, how it reached out and touched even Solace Glen, especially in 1862. That was the year of South Mountain and Antietam. The year J.E.B. Stuart rode with his troops through our little region of Maryland. I thought of Leona's story and the letters Lee still held out of Roland's reach, safe now in the hands of Sam's Smithsonian expert. We would know something soon, Lee had told me, after a couple of tests.

How a woman like Lucy made it through the war, I could only guess, nor did I know how in 1912 she died, having outlived her parents, her only brother, her husband, her cousin and his wife, and her only child, Lucinda Ann.

Beneath Jason Tanner and Lucy's name was written, "Lucinda Ann Tanner (1850–1890)." But underneath Lucinda's name was something else—empty parentheses. As if somebody was missing, and they didn't even know who.

FERRELL T. JEERED when I walked into Tom's office to clean.

I smiled sweet as cinnamon sugar. "Ferrell T., you're so much like your daddy. Except for the lack of brains." I set the carryall down. "Why are you still here, anyway? You always manage to be gone when I show up."

"Mr. Scott has a motion that must be filed in Baltimore tomorrow. As if I owe you any explanation." His bad skin looked like he'd gone bobbing for apples in a mosquito pit.

"You don't owe me a thing, thank God, and I can't think of anything worse than being obligated to you. Where's Tom?"

He looked down his nose. "*Mr. Scott* is in the conference room with someone."

"Look here, Ferrell T." I didn't care if he was Roland's son; Tom's office felt more my territory than his. "You are Tom's young secretary/paralegal and are supposed to call him Mr. Scott. I am his independent contractor and only ten years younger than he is. Plus, I've known him all my life, as if I owe you any explanation. I can call him Tom, Tommy, Tom-Tom, or anything else I want and I don't need your permission. You got that?"

A familiar voice answered, "Got it." Sam swept in and pinched my waist.

You could have knocked me over with a pencil point. "What are you doing here?" I searched his face for bruises.

"Had a little business with Tom."

He looked fine enough. Very fine, in fact. "Is Tom still in the conference room?" Decked out on the floor, maybe?

"Yeah, I'm showing myself out. Just dropped by to apologize so I may as well ask your forgiveness, too. I was rude. I'm sorry."

"No harm done. I enjoyed myself. You and Lee have a nice evening?"

He actually blushed, leaned over, and kissed my cheek. "Thank you," he whispered. Then he was gone.

"Guess so," I said to the door as he walked out.

I lifted the carryall and crept down the hall to the conference room. The door stood ajar. Tom hovered at the window, hands in his pockets slowly jiggling loose change.

"I see you had a visitor," I said to announce myself.

He remained silent, dipping his head slightly.

"Oh." I entered the room and got to work. "You're still in a mood."

His eyelids shut tight and popped open again. "And what mood is that, pray tell?"

"A childish one." I dusted around his books and papers on the table. "A little-boy-who-didn't-get-his-way-having-a-long-pout kind of mood."

He whirled around, a broad grin on his face. "That is the first time you ever dressed me down. Please," he sat, swinging side to side in the swivel chair, "don't stop. I'm sure I deserve it."

"I haven't yet decided what you deserve." Nor could I decide what to make of this new Tom Scott.

"Whoa. She's on a roll now, boys. She draws back for the pass, she's looking, looking . . ."

"Isn't it strange when men don't know what to say, they fall back on sports analogies."

"Ho! She's sighted Tom Scott, she lets one loose and it hits him—POW!—in the chest!" He clutched his heart, doubled over and sprawled across the conference table. Eli showed some concern.

"Are you done?" He didn't move. "Are you?"

"Asked you first."

"Asked you second." My teeth chomped my bottom lip to keep from smiling.

Tom slid into the swivel chair while Eli shoved a cold nose under his hand to check the pulse. "Sam came to apologize for absconding with my date."

"I hope you were gracious."

"Yes, Mother, I was. Told him it worked out fine. More champagne for me."

"Quite the cavalier attitude we've adopted. If I recall,

you were a bit upset at the time. With all three of us."

"You at least got in the canoe with me. That's more than I can say for Lady Lee. Apparently, she couldn't wait to get out."

"Tom." Cards were laid on the table all around. "Lee is falling in love with Sam. And I know he is in love with her." My hand slapped the dust rag against a chair. "Don't think it gives me any pleasure to say so."

The dark eyes narrowed. "Why wouldn't it give you pleasure to say so? You have something against Sam? Or don't you want Lee to be happy?"

I sat down in the chair I'd slapped and faced him across the table, a client telling her side of the story. "I think Sam Gibbon is a very attractive man. He's someone any woman would find agreeable."

"Agreeable? What a nineteenth-century word."

"So I read a lot of Jane Austen, what of it?" He clamped his mouth and waved a hand for me to continue. "OK. Not just agreeable. Sexy. Smart. Funny. Handsome. A good companion. Easygoing."

"Fine, fine, fine." He started swiveling again. "I get the drift. He's perfect."

"No, not quite. I did have my doubts about him in the beginning, especially about his interest in Lee's letters. But I found myself attracted to him, anyway, knowing he was attracted to somebody else. One of my best friends. And I realized pretty quickly that Lee had feelings for him, too." While I spoke, my toe tapped against the base of the table.

"How quickly?"

"Ohhhh, the first five minutes they met."

Tom's eyes soared into his forehead. "Thanks for telling me."

"I didn't know you were interested until too late. Then I tried to help you and I was trying to help myself, then Sam, and I had Lee to deal with. Well, I did what everybody wanted, brought everybody together hoping the chips would fall," I exhaled, "and they did. Not where I wanted them to, but they did fall."

Tom stared into space a moment. "At least I never kissed her. I would have felt compelled to propose."

"Yeah," I mimicked the serious tone. "She would have been ruined for Sam."

"I bear a clear conscience on that score."

Tom displayed a ton of bravado for a man who'd been dumped before he even got started.

"I am sorry, Tom."

"Aw, that's all right. I'll survive." He ran ten fingers through his thick hair. "How about you?"

"Sam didn't ruin me for anybody else, if that's what you mean." I pouted.

"No surreptitious kisses on his yacht? A stolen embrace in the shadow of the trees?"

I shook my head sadly.

He returned a grim smile. "Then we're both saved."

"Yep. Pure as mud."

He propped an elbow on the table and tapped a fist lightly against his mouth, black eyes boring into me until my skin prickled.

"What?"

"I was just thinking." Long pause, all the while staring at me.

"What?" My patience snapped. "What are you thinking?"

"I was thinking of that lingerie model you saw me with in Baltimore." He leaned toward me. "What was her number?"

As a result of my big wipeout in the romance field, I hadn't had the chance to warn Lee about Leonard Crosswell's intentions—too busy licking my wounds. I still wanted to expose his character and relay other people's impressions of this snake in the grass. Sam's preference for Lee may have hurt my pride, but that didn't mean I'd stop looking out for her.

After I finished up at Tom's office, I drove over to the Historical Society, but waiting five days to expose the fox proved too late. Leonard's black BMW sat parked out front, a dark omen. I pulled up behind it and hurried to the front door.

The door stood slightly ajar and I paused to eavesdrop, more to confirm my suspicions than to arrive at any revelations. I knew the sort of man Leonard Crosswell was. If Lee needed backup, I could always burst in to the rescue.

Lee's laugh rang clear and sweet. Sure enough, the fox intended to charm the pants off the hen.

"That's a great story, Mr. Crosswell. I hadn't heard that one about General Longstreet."

"Call me Leonard," the fox said in a voice dripping with honey. "You and I shouldn't stand on formality."

"Oh? What should we stand on?" Lee's low purr had that Jenner edge to it. She remained friendly, but wary.

"Informality, of course. Generosity? Friendship?"

"Generosity." Lee jumped on it. "That's an interesting choice of words."

You tell him, Lee, I rooted.

"Yes, it is." Leonard obviously wanted to get right to the point along a sly, if charming route. "I think we could mutually benefit each other."

"How so, Mr. Crosswell?" She fell back on formality.

"*Please*—Leonard. I do want us to be good friends."

"What else do you want?"

"Hoho. Good looks and smart to boot. An enticing combination."

Compliments will get you nowhere with this woman, fox face, I sneered to myself. The wind picked up, and I wrapped my coat close but stayed put. Lee could obviously hold her own ground. She didn't need me charging in, a one horse cavalry.

Leonard wormed his way along. "I hear we have a mutual interest."

"What might that be?" But I could tell she'd guessed.

"I collect Civil War memorabilia, quite a substantial collection, if I say so myself. Books, military documents, *letters*." He let that settle in, as if she needed time for the light bulb to click on. "Do you see where I'm going with this, Lee?"

"Gee, Mr. Crosswell," I heard her pour two cups of coffee and the warm aroma drifted through the cracked door. "I'm only guessing, but I'd say you're about to make a monumental offer for the letters my Aunt Leona left me."

"Well," the fox chortled, "I don't know about 'monumental.' I don't even know if the letters have been authenticated yet."

Lee kept those cards close to her vest. "It doesn't matter one way or another. They're not for sale. Not now. Not ever."

The fox sat silent, cataloguing his options. At last he spoke. "You appear to have made up your mind. I won't try to change it."

Oh, no? I rubbed my freezing hands together, dying to ambush the coffee.

"But, Lee, take it from an old courtroom warrior, it's never wise to rule out something that could prove so helpful down the road."

"What do you mean?" Her spoon clanked impatiently against the coffee mug.

"If the letters are authentic, I'd like to see them. Once I see them, I know I'll want them. When I want something, I'll do anything and pay any price to obtain the object of my desire."

I didn't like the way he said those last five words.

Neither did Lee. "Sorry. They're not for sale. You wouldn't understand."

"Perhaps I'd understand better than you think. I can be a very understanding man. Your Aunt Leona would want the best for you, wouldn't she? The best house. The best car. The best life has to offer. I can help you."

I smirked. If only Margaret stood outside listening with me. She'd be appalled at Leonard spouting off about what Leona would want.

"Thanks." Lee dismissed him, employing a tone of voice Leonard was accustomed to using, not hearing. "I don't need your 'help.' And you have no idea what my Aunt Leona would want for me. So unless you have any other business, Mr. Crosswell, the Historical Society is closed."

The hen kicked the fox out.

I ran like wildfire to my car and started ambling toward the front door as if I'd just arrived.

"Why, good evening, Mr. Crosswell," I greeted him formally as he swooped by, buttoning his coat.

His head reared up momentarily and I almost fell backward from the look in his eyes. The charm had drained away; what remained sent a cold chill through my chest. He didn't return the greeting, only growled and hurried to his BMW.

I watched him drive away, the ominous black car an unshakable image. Even when Lee spotted me and announced she had an untouched cup of coffee, I couldn't shake the bad feeling Leonard left behind.

Tina's words popped into my head and I tossed them around. Why Solace Glen? Why us? Why did we all know in our hearts that Leonard Crosswell brought nothing but trouble?

CHAPTER 21

✳

"LATELY, IT SEEMS I have more bad days than good."
I helped Louise out of bed and into her rocking chair so I could change the sheets. "Have you had somebody over to help? You been eating right?"

"Haven't felt like eating. But yes, the Circle Ladies have been most helpful, and I've had more than enough attention. My refrigerator is packed full enough for a football team. Those Episcopal women tend to go overboard, you know, trying to outshine the rest."

I covered her legs with a throw blanket and got to work. Such a big bed for such a small body.

"How was your weekend?" Louise never stopped wanting to know about everybody else.

"Enlightening."

"Oh?" She let it pass. "And did you go into Baltimore last week for a good time?"

"Yes. That was enlightening, too."

"I'm happy to hear you're so well lit."

"I'm happy you're happy. That's all you'll get out of me." I stripped the mattress bare and threw on the fresh linen. "What have you been up to?" I expected to hear about her latest book.

"I went to see Marlene," she said.

My head whipped around. "Why would you do such a thing, feeling the way you do?"

"That's exactly right, Flip. Feeling the way I do." She swallowed, a simple reflex, but it seemed such an effort for her. "I know it won't be long, and I had to see my only child."

For some reason, I thought of Lucy and Lucinda Ann when she said that. The faceless names from the past were starting to people my present.

"Whatever you had to say to her, I'm sure it went straight over her head."

"Doesn't matter. I said what I had to say."

"What did you say?"

"That I would be dead before the year was out. That I was sorry for any mistakes I made with her, but I really couldn't think of many. That our relationship, or lack of one, was largely due to her own self-centeredness and cold heart. That I had tried my best, like any parent, but my attempts to love her were thwarted at every turn because she revels in bitterness, takes delight in it, wants me to grovel and pay homage to her, a mother to her child. I let her know that's not how God intended us to act. We owe our parents something, even bad parents, but I've been a good mother. I know I have in my heart. I've only wanted the best for her, and she has hurt me whenever the opportunity arose. Getting married and not even bothering to call. What kind of daughter treats her mother like that? She's lived half a mile from me for twenty-five years and has never asked me to dinner. Won't even cook a meal for me. Won't pick up a telephone to say hello, how are you feeling, what can I do for you? Because all she cares about is what the world can do for her. If you have nothing to offer—no money, no social position, no material gain—she cuts you off like a dead limb. I told her I felt sorry for her. That I prayed for her and always would. With my last breath, I will still be praying for her."

She buried her face in one hand, fingers spread temple to temple.

I dropped what I was doing and knelt beside her chair, hoping the right words would come. "Louise. Louise, look at me. I can't explain why a child ends up the way she does. I can't explain why some are born giving and some are born taking. God gave you a loving, giving spirit. You have not wasted that gift, ask anybody in this town. There's not a soul in this community who has not been touched by your generosity. It is a mystery to me, and a tragedy, that the one person you want so much to reach will not be reached. Don't fret about it, Louise. Don't let Marlene distort the truth of your whole life. She's been your cross to bear for many years. It's time to hand it over. It's time to let go. You took the first step when you confronted her and got all those feelings off your chest. Now let it go. Drop the burden and be free of it."

Her hand dropped from her face to her lap. Tears spilled across the pale cheeks, but she smiled. "Flip," she whispered hoarsely, and took my hand, "your friendship has meant the world to me. You know that, don't you? If I lost a daughter in Marlene, I gained a child in you. You don't give yourself enough credit. No self-confidence. But you possess the heart and the stamina to sustain us all. You," she squeezed my hand so slightly, "are a giver, too. A treasure, that's what Leona called you. Take a lesson from my life, sweetheart. Give the most to those worth giving to. Don't do what I did and throw all your seed on hard, unforgiving ground. Nothing grows, try as you will, nothing takes root. You deserve better than I got. Please. Promise me. Give to those worth giving to."

I nodded, again and again, as if I understood her meaning, but all the while I grappled with the problem—who? Who were the ones worth giving to? Nobody? Everybody? A select list that never changed or a list that changed daily? She'd handed me my own cross to bear, but I nodded because it gave her peace of mind, and if I could give Louise peace of mind, then I had fulfilled my promise to her at least once. A gift to one worth giving to. A mustard seed thrown on rich and fertile ground, soft, forgiving soil.

She fell asleep almost instantly. I finished my work, cleaned the room, changed the sheets. It was almost five o'clock. I half-lifted, half-sleepwalked her back to her bed and laid her gently down, wrapped between clean, white sheets.

I did not turn the light out when I left. I wanted it on so when she awoke, she could see all the familiar things in her room that had always given her comfort. The books and china doodads, the mohair throws and needlepoint pillows. The pictures of Marlene, the first-born, the only born, from birth to age eighteen.

BEFORE GOING HOME for the day, I made a last stop at Marlene's Gift and Flower Shoppe. Not a soul browsed in the Shoppe among Marlene's tacky "country" gifts—homemade pot holders with badly quilted images of dogs and cats, tiny glass animals with plastic black eyes, cardboard picture frames glued with hideous, cheap fabric, glopped with ribbons and fake lace.

Marlene busied herself sticking outrageous price tags on the new collection of Christmas ornaments. I'd never seen so many rubber figures on skis.

"Hello, Marlene." I picked up one of the rubber ornaments and scowled at it.

She struggled to conceal her natural aversion to me with polite shoptalk. "You looking for some tree ornaments, Flip?"

"If I were, I wouldn't buy any of these gross things."

She snatched the cow on skis out of my palm. "Then what do you want? Spit it out and quit wasting my time."

"Time is a valuable commodity, isn't it, Marlene?" Her eyes held no reflection, completely blank. "How much time do you suppose your mother has left?"

"That's up to God, not you," she sniffed. "It's none of your business."

"Why, Scrooge, don't you remember what season it is? 'Mankind was my business. The common welfare was my business. . . .' Your mother's health is this whole town's business, except for you. Her own daughter."

She tried to run off and hide in the storeroom, but I grabbed hold of her arm and wouldn't let go. The image of Louise, my mother and father for nearly twenty-five years, cleared everything else from my mind until all I could see was her worn out, cancer-ravaged body lying solitary and alone in a bed that swallowed her whole.

"Whoa now. You're going to listen to me. Everybody talks about you behind your back, but nobody has ever said to your face what a cold-hearted bitch you are. Please. Let me be the first. You cast souls into hell for the tiniest slight against you. Somebody doesn't do things your way, you act like that person no longer exists. There isn't one iota of compassion or forgiveness inside you. You care only about you, yourself, and the almighty dollar. How a woman such as Louise, so warm and full of goodness, mothered a robot like you, I cannot fathom. Ever since she disapproved of your terrible taste in boyfriends, you've done whatever you could to spite and hurt her. She's gone out of her way to put things right between you, but you love your hatred, don't you, Marlene? You've nurtured it so long, it's a part of you. So sad. Such a waste. All those years you could have enjoyed the sweet friendship of your mother, who would have done anything for you. Now she's dying and you haven't made peace with her. It would make all the difference in the world if you did. If you went over there and made her comfortable in her last days. Can you do that, Marlene? Do you have it in you to do such a small thing that would mean so very much?"

She jerked her arm away and leaped behind the counter. "Get out. If you're not buying anything, get out."

A face without remorse, no twinge of guilt. Just meanness and spite and flat, dull eyes.

"I am buying something," I said quietly. "I'd like to order a bouquet of Thanksgiving flowers. On the card write, 'Hope you are feeling better. We all love you.' Sign it, 'The Town of Solace Glen.' You know where to send it, don't you, Marlene? Don't you?"

Chapter 22

Wednesday found me working furiously on several houses—my usual ones, plus a couple of emergency treatments. Women with visiting in-laws. Husbands whose wives had gone out of town for a week and now whimpered like puppies, scared to death the little woman might notice the barbeque chips and cigar ash ground into the bedroom carpet.

I looked forward to the weekend and two whole days of time. Here it was, almost the end of the year, and I hadn't bought one Christmas present or picked out cards or figured what to bring to the Thanksgiving Day Picnic.

Solace Glen partied together as a community twice a year: Thanksgiving and the Fourth of July, two nondenominational holidays. The four town churches could commingle, sing the same songs, and pray the same Lord's Prayer without too much politicking, except our congregation always said "Forgive us our *debts*" instead of "Forgive us our *trespasses*" during the prayer. A minor point, maybe, but we relished the difference and put aside our usual Presbyterian dignity, shouting out "debts" and "debtors." I don't think God minded. I'd spent some time in the early morning before work poring over cookbooks, searching for a nice casserole recipe to whip up for the picnic. I chose something called Carolina oysters, a stewy mix of oysters, butter, cheese, and cracker crumbs sprinkled on top with parsley and more cheese. Anything with seafood the Thanksgiving crowd demolished in ten seconds. Anything with spinach or cauliflower found its way back into the refrigerator.

By the time I left the house, the morning hung heavy with gray clouds; autumn seemed gone already. Any moment now the first snow would fall and we would gasp and say, how beautiful, knowing in another month or two we'd be sick to death of it, longing for robins and baseball. By noon, the air blew frigid as I finished cleaning the third house. I gave in to a craving for Roland's oyster stew, the one thing in the world he did right.

I slipped into the Café. Rarely did I discover anybody sitting in my seat since the table melted into the back wall, out of the way, unsavory to most tourists, and the regulars knew my schedule. I glanced over the specials and wrote down oyster stew, hot tea, biscuits, and apple crumble.

Hilda showed up to take my order. She'd been experimenting with pink and green eye shadow. Her eyes looked like frogs draped in flamingo feathers.

"Hey," she said.

"Hey," I replied, prepared to pull out the atlas if she went on a gab streak.

"Somebody was asking about you."

"Who?"

"That lady with the BMW." She took the order and headed into the kitchen.

I made a face like I'd caught a whiff of something foul and cussed under my breath. In seconds the object herself appeared, dressed in a tight black jumpsuit that showed off the expensive gym work.

"Flip Paxton," she singsonged, "I've been looking for you." She invited herself to sit down. "I have good news."

"Oh?" *Leaving town?*

"I have been driving those stupid workmen to distraction, but it has paid off." She paused, waiting for the drum roll. "We can move in the weekend after Thanksgiving! A whole month ahead of schedule!"

I pictured C.C. wearing a lime green, monogrammed hard hat, standing on the necks of those poor construction men, screeching over the sound of electric drills and hammering. No wonder they finished the job early.

She babbled on about painters and cabinet people, the work on yellow pine walls and how gorgeous they'd turned out, the window people and how she designed those touches herself because the right lighting was crucial and she was a child of the light. Hilda dumped my lunch on the table and shoved off, probably wondering why I didn't flip open the atlas in C.C.'s face.

"Anyway," she finally sucked in a breath, "you can start Monday after Thanksgiving. How's that?"

"I'm full up Mondays."

"I'm sure you can work it in. It's the best day for me. I'll be home so the time isn't important. Seven o'clock at night for all I care. Leonard's home then and can show you his silly Civil War collection."

That *would* make my day, spending hours with him.

"Or seven in the morning." She bit a lip, worried. "But I'm not a morning person."

I couldn't imagine she was. Probably slept till noon then took two hours to apply her eyelashes. I opened my mouth to reemphasize a packed schedule when the door swung open and Screamin' Larry strolled in, larger than life in a fur-lined, red hooded parka and boots the size of Detroit.

"G'day all!" He glowed as bright as Santa Claus.

C.C. slit her eyes. The powdered face turned into a prune. "That man is a monumental nuisance. How does anybody put up with him?" She glared self-righteously at me until I answered the question.

"He's a damn good disc jockey. And a credit to the high school cheerleading department. Also," I leaned forward, "if your husband goes out of town a lot, Larry's available for . . . whatever." I wiggled my eyebrows and slapped an evil leer on my face, as though I'd enjoyed the fruits of Larry's labor myself. C.C. brought out the worst in me.

She turned up the self-righteousness full force, twisting her mouth in disgust. "I should have expected this from you. Nevertheless . . ." She scrambled to her feet, afraid to sit with me any longer as if something wicked might rub off. "I will look for you on Monday."

She hustled away. Unfortunately, the floor plan forced C.C. to pass by Larry's table. She reined up, studying the options. Finally, she jutted her chin as high as a thoroughbred and pranced ahead in long strides. Larry sat perusing the specials, apparently oblivious to C.C.'s moral dilemma, but when she swished by his table he reached out fast as a cobra and clamped onto her hand. He yanked it to his lips and planted a loud, wet smack across her knuckles.

"S'damn great to see you again, Mrs. Crosswell! How's the hubby?"

C.C. stared at him, horrified, and threw me a glance that said, "My Gawd, you're right!" She snatched her hand back, rubbing the spit off diamond and emerald rings.

"You are a sick man," she muttered between gritted teeth. "And I told you to stop playing those songs for me on the radio."

Larry clapped his hands and bounced in the chair. "Oh,

goodie! You're a listening fan! Would you like me to autograph something? A thigh, perhaps?" He scooped up a pencil and aimed it at her hip with a polite bat of the eye.

"Stay the hell away from me, you pervert." She stalked away, retrieved her purse, and stormed out of the premises. Several customers applauded the slammed door.

Larry yelped, amused as hell, and returned to the all-consuming task of writing down his lunch choices.

"You ain't through with her yet, are you, Larry?" One of the Eggheads chuckled.

"Far from it," answered Larry, not bothering to glance up and engage in conversation with one of the town idiots.

"You gonna sit with her at the picnic?" The other Egghead snorted into a paper napkin. "Serve her up a plate of arsenic crab balls?"

Larry smiled down at his lunch order, clearly delighted by the picture of that scene, and started humming, then broke into song. His voice, a truly beautiful gift, could charm the beak off a canary, but he refused to donate time to any church choir (against his personal religion, he said), so we rarely got the chance to enjoy his talent.

Don't sit under the apple tree with anyone else but me,
Anyone else but me, anyone else but me. No, no, no!

He rose to have more room to swing his hips and interrupted himself once to boom, "This goes out to everybody's favorite red-lipped babe in the brand-new BMW!"

As he sang, the Eggheads beat time against tea glasses and even Roland's kitchen staff crept out from their slave quarters to clap along. When the song ended, Larry leaped around the table taking bows in all directions, never shy in the limelight.

I could have departed the Café in a good humor after that, but I had to pass by Roland at the cash register. He didn't

speak and neither did I, but I read something in the depth of
his cold eyes that sent a shiver down my spine. A promise
of winter, sure to come. A promise of ice, the purest form of
treachery. A promise that he would have what he wanted.

THAT NIGHT, EXHAUSTED, anxious, pushing down a trou-
bling premonition that had haunted me all afternoon, I
opened the Bible.

Ferrell Bell/Gretal Stubing Bell. Lucy Bell Paca Tan-
ner/Jason Tanner.

Lucy and Ferrell, first cousins, represented the second
generation of Americans in the Bell family. I set out to
study the third generation on Ferrell's side.

Roland Bell was Ferrell and Gretal's only child, born
1851, died 1908. In 1878, he married a girl named Florence
Openheim, herself only nineteen.

Both Roland and Florence walked and breathed in two
centuries. Both played, ate, and slept as children during the
Civil War. Both witnessed incredible changes in their country and the world. Florence lived through a World War in
her middle age and died at the height of economic prosper-
ity in 1929. She saw skirts go from the floor to the knee.
Florence could count herself fortunate to have a husband
around while her two children, a boy and girl, entered young
adulthood. Still, she outlived her husband by twenty-one
years and rejoiced in the birth of a grandson who fathered,
unfortunately, Roland and, fortunately, Leona Bell Jenner.

Roland died the same year as his German-blood mother,
Gretal. I wondered at the coincidence of the two reaching
heaven the same year and puzzled over who went first. Was
he so dependent on Mother that her death drove him to suicide? Or was it the other way around?

With nothing but names and dates in front of me, I cast
dullness to the wind and turned my speculation into a

Hollywood production. Occasionally, a dried leaf or flower petal floated out from between the pages of the Bell Bible, and I carefully picked it up by a fragile edge and placed it safe in Psalms or Luke or wherever it fell from. I noticed scraps of paper and little envelopes stuck in the Bible, too, but decided to familiarize myself with the family tree before sorting through the poems or notes jammed helter-skelter among the pages.

So the first Roland and his wife, Florence, were born, grew up, lived, gave birth, and died here in Solace Glen. Florence helped found the Solace Glen Presbyterian Church in the late 1890s, joining forces with dissatisfied Methodists and Episcopalians. Both Roland and Florence's names were etched in a window shining down on the Bell aisle, shining down on Roland and Garland, Ferrell T. and Hilda.

I had worshipped beneath that window every Sunday of my life, and now I had a part of them, Roland and Florence, sitting on top of my kitchen cabinet, hidden in a basket under a mound of Spanish moss. The sad thing was, I was hiding that part of them from their own flesh and blood, their own great-grandson.

The thought occurred to me that maybe I should give the Bible to Roland. When I was through reading all the names and dates, all the poems and notes on yellowed scraps of paper, maybe I should hand it to Roland for his children and his children's children. Then he would leave me alone.

I closed the Bible and moved the tips of my fingers up and down the spine. Maybe that's what I'd do. But something nagged at me and wouldn't let go.

Why didn't Leona want Roland to have it? Why leave the Bell family Bible to me?

CHAPTER 23

❈

THURSDAY AFTERNOON, I worked on two small homes, then drove to Miss Fizzi's house sometime after four o'clock. I climbed the front steps and rang the doorbell, gave her a minute, then walked inside, yelling, "Hey, Miss Fizzi! It's Flip!"

The house smelled of freshly baked lemon chess pie.

Maybe she was in the powder room. "I'll start downstairs today!" I called. Downstairs didn't include the basement apartment. I wouldn't touch Suggs' lair with a ten-foot pole and Miss Fizzi knew it. No telling what crawled around down there. "That pie sure smells good!"

I hadn't spent fifteen minutes vacuuming and dusting the parlor when Lee burst through the front door.

She drew up, surprised. "What are you doing?"

"Earning a living. What's it look like?"

"Why aren't you at the clinic?" Solace Glen wasn't big

enough for a full-fledged hospital, but we supported a pretty good health clinic where a parade of residents cut their teeth delivering babies, listening to bad hearts, and sewing up victims of farm equipment.

"The clinic? I just walked through the door a few minutes ago."

"Miss Fizzi had a bad fall."

My veins went cold. "What kind of fall? Where?"

"Tom called on his way to the clinic. He said a neighbor was in his backyard and heard a crash. He looked over the fence and saw Miss Fizzi lying on the ground. One of the back steps off the kitchen must have rotted out."

"How is she?"

"Conscious enough to ask for Tom when the Eggheads got her to the clinic."

I remembered how the Eggheads tossed her around like a football recently. "I hope they didn't hurt her."

"Give them a little credit. At least they got her to a doctor."

We stood shaking our heads and grinding our teeth a minute. Finally, Lee said, "Are you thinking what I'm thinking?"

We hustled through the hall to the kitchen. The open door creaked in the breeze. Two curious squirrels, we crept out on the landing and peered over the edge. The top step lay broken in two, straight down the middle. Miss Fizzi must have tumbled headfirst down the next six steps.

We bent to examine the broken wood. It was not an old piece, none of the edges were jagged or soft.

"Somebody sawed this step underneath," said Lee.

I put my hand over my mouth, eyes big as doorknobs.

"We have to tell Tom about this." She straightened her back. "Roland's lost his mind. He's out of control."

"How do you know it was Roland? Suggs could've done it." Spite and envy know no boundaries.

"He could have, but he's lived here for three years. Why would he do it now?"

"I don't know. Property. Money. He's her only blood relative and stands to inherit this house if nothing else."

"Let's talk to Tom about it. Then we need to report this to the police."

"Lukzay?" My heart sank at the thought, but Lee gripped my hand.

"We'll go over his head if we have to. This is attempted murder. Come on. Let's get to the clinic and talk to Tom."

We crept back into the kitchen and closed and locked the door. Lee hurried out, saying she'd meet me at the clinic. I glanced around, making sure the oven was off and the stove cold. The lemon chess pie Miss Fizzi baked sat on a rack, cooled to room temperature. Almost in tears, I wrapped the pie pan in plastic and stuck it in the refrigerator.

On the drive to the clinic, I kept seeing Roland's icy eyes and the promise they held. Only now, he'd made good on the promise. But other eyes swirled into my mind, too—Suggs' envious eyes and Leonard's awful, black eyes, glowering from Lee's stinging rejection. Was this his way of getting back at Lee? Scaring her, using Roland's open greed to hide his own tracks?

One thing I was sure of, the Bell family Bible was mine for keeps. No matter how badly Roland Bell needed to read it or how desperately Leonard Crosswell wanted to collect it.

WHEN I ARRIVED, minutes behind Lee, Tom greeted us with encouraging news.

"She's banged up all right. Two badly sprained ankles, a gash on her temple, and a broken wrist, but it's a miracle she didn't crack her head open, break a hip, or worse."

Lee and I shuddered. Then we told him about the step.

"Tom," I spoke in a low voice, "we're afraid Roland's

gone crazy. He could have tampered with Joey's brakes. I know he's responsible for my break-in. But to try and kill a sweet old lady for inheriting a little money . . ."

A dark cloud passed over Tom's face. The ebony eyes narrowed and focused hard on the floor. His chest heaved. "There's something I have to do," he said quietly. "Tell Miss Fizzi not to worry about a thing. Don't say a word to her about what you suspect. And don't breathe a word of this to Officer Lukzay."

"Where do you think he's going?" Lee was already moving toward Miss Fizzi's room.

"I don't know." I watched Tom fling a black wool topcoat over his back and quickly stalk out of the building. A red cashmere scarf floated out of a pocket to the floor where I bent to retrieve it. I placed the scarf around my shoulders and kept it there the rest of the evening.

THERE WASN'T MUCH Lee and I could do for Miss Fizzi short of giving in to her demand for a shot of sherry with the pain pills. We simply made sure she was comfortable in mind and spirit before leaving, assuring her the oven was off and the house locked up.

I'd finished reading a couple of books from the Historical Society, so I followed Lee home to pick out two or three more. The sun had set, and a brisk wind blew through the leafless trees. Smoke poured from almost every chimney, and the streets lay empty and forlorn, no holiday decorations yet, nothing to draw people away from their warm fireplaces on a night like this. A cup of coffee at Lee's would taste awfully good.

We pulled off the street and into the cramped parking space behind the house. We walked up to the back door together. Lee fiddled in her purse for the right key, but as a course of habit I reached for the doorknob and tried it. The door slipped open.

"I could have sworn I locked it," she murmured. "Oh, well."

She started to go in, but I pulled her back. "Wait a minute." The premonition that had nagged at me earlier in the week returned in almost palpable form.

Lee didn't wait for explanations. "Damnit to hell." She bulldozed past and banged the door wide open with the heel of her hand. A light flicked on in the narrow hallway, the kitchen, the dining room.

I stood on the outside looking in, feet nailed to the ground, picturing the shambled mess of my own home only weeks before. I could hear Lee stomping from room to room, cawing damnittohelldamnittohell, a bird returning to her damaged nest.

Curiosity at last overcame fear and I inched inside, stepping lightly into the hallway. Overhead, Lee trudged through the four small rooms on the second floor, cussing. From my place in the hallway, I could see into the kitchen and dining room where Plain Jane sat undisturbed at the farmhouse table, a stoic, unperturbed expression on the Pandora face, cotton fingers dipping into the butter bean bowl as if all bad things had just now escaped into the world and she searched the wooden bottom for what was left.

I started toward her just as the broom closet door at my left creaked. Mid-step, I froze, breath cut off, eyes adjusting to the half-light of the shadowed, narrow space while the door slowly inched open toward my face. A shoe emerged from inside the shallow closet, paused, then a hand edged along the side of the door, another shoe appeared, a body in a large black overcoat and a black rain hat stepped into the hall and backed silently out.

In total quiet, the body in the black overcoat and I stood

in the same tiny square footage. A banging from Lee upstairs sent the overcoat stumbling backward into me. I whooped and the body grunted, then bounded past me into the dark night.

Within seconds, Lee came storming down the stairs. "Roland Bell! Is that you, you sonofabitch! You are going to pay for what you did to my house!"

I pointed into the night from the floor where I'd fallen flat. Lee stood in the frame of her open door, shouting after Roland, "You think you're so smart! But you didn't find them, did you, Roland? You couldn't find them! Miss Fizzi still has her trust and Flip still has the Bell family Bible! And if you had anything to do with Joey's car crash and Miss Fizzi's fall—you'll get yours, Roland, don't you worry! You'll get what you deserve!"

She slammed the door, boiling mad, immediately jerked me up by the shoulders and led me to the farmhouse table. I sat down next to Plain Jane, shaking, willing my breath back while Lee made coffee, violently clanging and banging spoons, mugs, pots. While the coffee brewed, she marched over to Jane and with a tight face unbuttoned the doll's blouse. The letters lay safe in the bosom buddy. She drew them out, gingerly lifting the three letters as if she held a poker hand that no man at her table could beat.

"Just got them back today," she said, "special delivery. They're authentic. And you know what's funny?"

"No," I rubbed the tender, bruised small of my back, shoulders, and neck. "What's funny?"

She shuffled the letters, one, two, three, three, two, one. "Even if Roland had found these letters and read them, he wouldn't get it. He wouldn't understand."

That's what she'd said to Leonard. She spread the envelopes on the table and together we stared at them.

"But that's not really the point, is it?" My finger tapped one envelope. "It doesn't matter if he gets it or doesn't get it. The important thing is he *wants* the letters, he *wants* the Bell Bible, he thought he had a right to the house, the car, the property, the money."

Lee picked up the yellowed envelopes and returned them to Plain Jane's safe keeping. "That *was* Roland, right? You saw his face? Because I'm about to call the Frederick police."

For the first time, a coldness gripped my stomach, a hard doubt. "No, I didn't see his face. I couldn't even tell if it was a man or a woman. Maybe because of the coat and hat, but whoever it was sure *seemed* bigger than Roland, now that I think about it."

Lee twisted her mouth. "Oh, come on. Who else could it be? Who else would go after you, me, and Miss Fizzi? Miss Fizzi, for God's sake! You heard Roland after Pal's car was wrecked—'One down.' It's got to be him."

I looked around at the godawful mess in Lee's house and my blood boiled. I stood, both hands holding onto either end of Tom's cashmere scarf. "You're right. It has to be Roland. It would be so easy to just let him have what he wants or hide everything away in a bank vault. But Leona wanted you to have those letters and keep them here in the Historical Society. She wanted you to figure out their importance. And she wanted me to use that Bible, keep it in my home, not stick it in a bank. I may be a Paxton, but I won't give up the Bell family history. No matter what. Call the police."

PART THREE

CHAPTER 24

❈

L OUISE LAY LIKE a doll baby in her big, king bed, supported on every side by soft, white pillows. She spoke
little as I dusted around the room, barely tapping a rag over
Marlene's many faces. She'd ask a question and I'd run on
and on, saving her the trouble of speech.

"I wanted to call you about Miss Fizzi, but Lee said she
hadn't talked to you in a while and wanted a nice visit. Did
you enjoy your time with her yesterday? Don't bother talking, just nod and smile like a good girl."

Louise barely moved her lips. It broke my heart to watch
her struggle so hard to smile.

"I tell you, Louise, when I got to the clinic, I was scared,
really scared for Miss Fizzi. I kept picturing her frail, little
old lady body slamming down those wood steps, lying there
on the ground in her flimsy housedress until the Eggheads
arrived to gawk at her. Don't you know how mortified she

was, half-conscious. Fortunately, she passed out soon after the sight of them and stayed unconscious until they got her to the clinic, into *expert* hands."

Louise's eyebrows twitched. She knew my opinion of the Eggheads.

"She asked for Tom as soon as she came to. I believe she thought she'd die. He got there right away, he's so good, and called Lee. She ran into me at Miss Fizzi's house. You know the rest."

"Tom thinks Roland did it all, doesn't he?" The words, barely audible, disappeared into the mound of pillows. I couldn't lie to Louise; she'd know it.

"He's trying to keep an open, lawyerly mind, but he was so disgusted. I've never seen him so mad. He even checked the steps himself right away and immediately called an investigator friend of his from another county to look into it. Somebody independent, you know, with higher connections and morals than dear Officer Look-away."

"You called Lukzay?" asked the small voice in a tone of incredulity.

"No. Tom said don't bother. We called the Frederick County station, though. First they referred us to Lukzay, but Lee flat out told them she'd found his investigative abilities lacking. A tactful way of saying nonexistent. They sent a couple of bodies over to have a look-see and we unloaded our whole theory on them—the car brakes, the two break-ins, Miss Fizzi's step. We pointed our fingers at Roland, but the questions they asked did make me wonder. I had to admit my doubts about the figure in the black overcoat. Anyway, they dusted around and said they'd start questioning people. So we'll see. Their professionalism satisfied me and Lee. That's what she told Sam. Her boyfriend." I shot her a coy grin and poked a finger in my cheek like a schoolgirl.

"Lee is very happy," she said. The effort drained her and she closed her eyes.

"Yes, she is. I think we can all rest comfortably in the hopes of a spring wedding."

Of course, no such word had been spoken by either Lee or Sam, but I knew the thought of a beautiful, flower-packed church event would bring Louise a measure of joy she badly needed. It would give her something to plan and imagine as she drifted in and out of sleep, picturing satin gowns, sculpted cakes, and baby showers to come.

"How is Miss Fizzi today?" she asked softly behind closed eyelids.

"Better than yesterday. She's bandaged and bruised but that little woman must have bones of steel. She'll be at the clinic another week, in high spirits and making impossible requests of the nurses."

"Sherry, of course. What about Suggs? Has he been to see her or done anything for her?" Again, the effort it took to speak drained Louise.

"You know better than to ask that. Save your strength." The comparison between Marlene and Suggs was an easy one to draw. "He doesn't think about anybody but himself. Personally, I believe she's better off if he stays completely out of it."

I dared not confide my niggling suspicions about Suggs to Louise. It would drive her crazy to imagine Miss Fizzi living under the same roof with a man who possibly tried to kill her. So I rambled on about the Thanksgiving picnic in two days, the fabulous oyster casserole I'd chosen, about Screamin' Larry grabbing C.C.'s hand and C.C. expecting me to come work for her next Monday. I told Louise I'd go at least once, if only to see what she'd done to that ramshackle old barn. It would give us something to laugh about.

She didn't answer, and when I bent to inspect her breathing, I saw she'd fallen asleep. I tiptoed out and climbed in the car. As I pulled out of Louise's driveway, I flicked on the radio. Larry announced the next song, "It Might as Well Be Spring."

Cherry, peach, and pear trees bloomed by the first of April in Solace Glen. Louise Lamm would not live to see them. The best any of us could do was give her a little springtime now.

CHAPTER 25

❊

I NEVER WORKED the Wednesday before Thanksgiving or the Friday after. That way, I had a nice little break, same as a high school student. As a result, my adrenaline rose to the freakish level of a teenager's and I zipped around, Christmas shopping nonstop over the long weekend. I zeroed in on the little towns surrounding Solace Glen in a thirty-mile radius, and the city of Frederick's downtown shopping district. Forget the big malls; I'd discovered many a Christmas knickknack in the antique stores of New Market and the odd shop here and there in Buckeystown and Urbana. I'd travel as far north as Emmitsburg, as far east as Ellicott City, as far south as Germantown, as far west as Hagerstown. Baltimore represented a whole other solar system and Washington a distant universe, if not a black hole.

After the escalating acts of violence in my own little world, getting out of town to do something as normal as

Christmas shopping offered sweet relief. All day Wednesday
I combed the eastern part of my shopping world, trudging
up and down Ellicott City's Main Street, sifting through
shelf after shelf in the town's oak-planked boutiques. You
could have lifted the town itself out of a Beatrix Potter picture book. I half-expected a porcupine dressed in a cotton
skirt and wool shawl to pop up from behind a counter and
ask, "May I help you?" Beatrix Potter's version of Melody.
When I sat down to lunch at a cafe overlooking a trickling
Tiber River, the waitress bore a peculiar likeness to one of
Tom Kitten's sisters.

I bought the oysters required for my casserole at a
seafood take-out place and drove the thirty minutes back to
Solace Glen, the back seat of my car loaded with shopping
bags. I liked to pick theme gifts at Christmas, and this year
everybody on my list could expect a present connected to
gardening. Very chic, C.C. might say, always an elegant
choice, not that she made my list. Plus, a mountain of cheap
gardening stuff filled the stores: gloves, pots, tools, books,
calendars, seeds, plants, diaries, knee pads, soap. I gave myself a hefty pat on the back for dreaming up this one.

At home by dusk, I lined the ingredients for Carolina
oysters across the kitchen counter and got busy. I covered
the finished casserole with plastic wrap and shuffled off to
bed, confident that once again my offering at the picnic
would glean some attention.

EVERY THANKSGIVING MORNING started out the same
way—agonizing over what to wear to the picnic and dancing around the house to the music from Macy's Thanksgiving Day Parade, the one day of the year lip-synching on
live television achieves cultural status. I finally decided on
black jeans, hiking boots and an over-sized sweater with a

striking design of bright pink embroidery across the chest, a gift from Louise after a trip to South America.

While the casserole heated up in the oven, I laced the hiking boots and wrapped a couple of presents. A miniature herb garden for Lee's inside windowsill. A colorful plant pot for Louise to look at lying in bed. A pie plate painted with dogwood and lilies for Miss Fizzi. A gardening diary for Margaret's meticulous approach to planting.

I crammed the casserole into a carrier and drove to the fire pond where the Thanksgiving and Fourth of July picnics had been held for more than fifty years. A small, manmade body of water built by the town behind the old brick fire department in the late nineteenth century, the fire pond proved a perfect spot for big events, bordered by acres of open, grassy meadows for kids to run wild, shade trees where the adults spread their blankets and snoozed after a big lunch, and the pond itself, which served as a miniature boat race arena on the Fourth of July. The rules were you had to make the boat yourself and could only race in one category: sail, motor driven, or animal driven. Lee won one year by harnessing a water snake that zoomed ahead like Secretariat and scared the bejesus out of all the hamsters rigged to paddlewheels.

I pulled into the grassy parking area a little after noon. People poured in toting huge round platters and bowls the size of laundry baskets. Little boys lugged lacrosse sticks and footballs; little girls did the same, although I did see two Barbie dolls—Beauty Pageant Barbie and the large head Make-Me-Up-Fix-My-Hair Barbie, no doubt birthday gifts from Sally and Tina who favored that sort of thing.

All four churches in town donated long picnic tables and paper tablecloths that flapped in the wind. Each table sagged under the weight of a different course—vegetables, meat and seafood, breads, desserts, drinks, and salads. I set my casserole on the seafood table and checked out the other dishes, a smattering of the usual fare: the turkey, the chicken, the venison, the roast beef, and the Smithfield ham. At the seafood end, a tremendous bowl of iced shrimp reigned as centerpiece to crab balls, breaded catfish fingers, fried scallops, and steamed crab legs. Nobody had done a thing with oysters. I proudly arranged a serving spoon by the casserole and stood there a minute or two.

A lady from the Methodist Church passed by and cooed, "Oh, is that oyster dish yours?"

"Why, yes." I practically shouted her ear off. "*I'm* the one who brought the oysters."

Two times a year I acted like such a showoff.

She lingered, pressing me for details about any connection between my break-in and Lee's, Miss Fizzy's fall, and what the police had come up with. Apparently, this was all anybody could talk about and I got bombarded with questions by each passerby.

"So you think the two break-ins are connected, Flip?"

"I do."

"Who do you think is responsible?"

"I have my opinion." Thanks to the beauty parlor crowd, the whole town already knew what that opinion was, but I wasn't about to give Roland ammo for a slander suit. I kept answers short and information tight to the vest.

"I heard Miss Fizzi's fall was no accident."

"True enough."

"The woman has no enemies! Who'd want to hurt her, for God's sake?"

"That's a question for the police."

I was patting myself on the back for exercising such wise discretion when Marlene appeared with her usual nasty plate of hot dogs. She said she brought hot dogs so the poor little children would have at least one thing they liked, but I knew she did it because it only required her to boil water and slap a weenie on a bun.

I expected the same questions from her as everyone else, but she simply asked, "What did you bring, Flip?" The round fish eyes scanned the table. "Those bologna sandwiches?"

"Of course not," I said down my nose. I swung her plate of weenies around, scowling, as if a different position might make them look worth eating. "I baked an oyster casserole, m'dear."

She spouted like a whale and moved away, fumes of Vicks VapoRub trailing behind. I watched her go and found myself wondering, just for an instant, if Marlene really would do anything for money.

Several other women floated by, friends from church, clients. Everybody had something nice to say before launching into the topic of the day. When I felt pumped full enough of compliments, I scouted out Lee. She was standing by the dessert table with Sam behind her, his long arms wrapped around her waist, both of them feigning interest in cakes and pies. No keeping those two a secret any longer. A steady stream of old ladies trotted by, gathering a bit of information from one, a new fact from the other, their questions on the none-too-subtle side. So you're planning on settling in Solace Glen, Sam? How long's it been since we had a wedding around here, Lee?

I stood to one side, arms crossed, watching the show. After a good ten or fifteen minutes, I made a discovery. It didn't hurt. As a matter of fact, seeing the two of them together, so openly agog with one another, gave me a pleasant sense of satisfaction. Somehow, Henry and Marie, Jake and Leona—the four of them must have had a hand in it.

"Gold Medal is best."

"How can you say that? Pillsbury's always made a better flour."

The Eggheads faced off at the bread table, one on each side. Pal dumped a tin of crusty corn muffins in the middle. "What's wrong with Wash'ton flour milled right down the road in Ell'cott City? That's what I use. Done good by us all these years."

"Gold Medal."

"Pillsbury."

Before they could give me a headache, I hurried off in the opposite direction.

"Hey, where you going?" Lee caught up with me, leaving poor Sam with two particularly persistent ladies.

"Back to the car for a blanket. You think that was a nice thing to do to your intended?"

She tried to act mad. "My intended? Come on, it's not that serious. Everybody's getting so worked up." She couldn't look me in the eye.

"I'd say the two of you were pretty worked up back there at the dessert table, having a little rub fest. Why not knock a few cakes off the table and have at it? Be more fun than listening to the Eggheads fight about what type flour to buy."

"Gold Medal," she said.

"Pillsbury."

She pushed my arm. "Why don't you come sit with us? We've already got a bedspread set out over there." She pointed to a chestnut tree and a massive red cloth.

"Ooo, a bedspread. How subtle. OK, meet you there after the prayer."

She skipped away to rescue Sam and I headed to the edge of the pond where a group of children threw pebbles in the water, making circles. One child silently handed me a couple of stones and I imitated his aim, falling into a contest.

"Don't try to out-throw Flip Paxton, Jeremy. Her aim is sure."

Tom picked up a handful of pebbles and joined us. "Yes,

siree. She's been known to bring down a moving lawyer at fifty paces."

"Ha, ha."

"Happy Thanksgiving. Heard you brung ersters."

"You hear that while you were drooling over Marlene's weenie dogs?"

"How'd you know?"

"You've always been a dog man."

"Only of the Labrador variety." Eli took this as his cue to appear and plunged into the pond, snapping his massive jaws at pebbles skimming by.

Tom tossed in a pebble and I threw one in after his. We watched our expanding circles loop into one another like magician's rings.

"So," he kicked at a small rock, dislodging it, "where are you sitting?"

"Where else? With Sam and Lee."

I expected to hear the name of the important family or client he'd been invited to sit with, but he said, "Oh, good. Mind if I join you?"

"What? No bigwig clients to entertain? No senior citizens itching to get a little free advice about their estate planning?"

His head wagged forlornly. He reached for the rock at his foot and chucked it into the water, kerplunk. "Not even a lingerie model from Baltimore."

I feigned embarrassment and watched the circles on the surface of the pond expand. "Naw. You have to settle for the domestic help."

That's when I felt his arm link through mine. "I'd say that's a step up, wouldn't you?"

For a second, I froze. I wanted to jerk my arm away and lecture him. *What do you think you're doing? You can't fool around like that! People will think we're together! Every dowager in Solace Glen will have us married, same as Sam and Lee!*

That's what I wanted to say. But Tom grinned at me with his magazine smile and started walking off, no hesitation, me on his arm. My boots dragged, weighted down with worry, but he pulled me along and my frozen smile melted into a shocked daze. Faces in the crowd blended together as we drew into the heart of the Thanksgiving gathering. He stopped, waiting with the rest of the community for Reverend Grayson from the Methodist Church to call for quiet and recite the Lord's Prayer.

Our Father which art in heaven, Hallowed be thy name.

The palm of my right hand practically gurgled with perspiration. Any moment it would squirt him in the face like the buttonhole flower of a circus clown.

Thy Kingdom come, Thy will be done in earth, as it is in heaven.

I panicked over what to do once the prayer stopped. Would he let go of my arm? Would I need a crowbar?

Give us this day our daily bread. And forgive us our trespasses/DEBTS, as we forgive those who trespass against us/OUR DEBTORS.

I opened my mouth to whoop it up with the other Presbyterians, but nothing came out. I'd lost feeling in my arm.

And lead us not into temptation, but deliver us from evil: For thine is the kingdom, and the power, and the glory, forever. Amen.

Tom shouted a hardy Amen and gracefully let my arm slip away.

"After you," he said, placing the tips of his fingers on my spine. He steered my lobster face through the crowd to a table with paper plates and utensils, sliding a place setting into my hand. "Now let's grab some of your oyster casserole before it's completely demolished."

* * *

SAM, IN TOP form, played class cutup all during the meal, reeling out story after story. Lee rolled off the bedspread more than once, holding her ribcage, laughing so hard she choked and sputtered. An unladylike exhibition, Louise would say.

Like indulgent parents, Tom and I sat gazing on the two of them, making a comment here and there, sipping coffee, the fringe grownups. I had no idea what I'd spooned onto my paper plate. The colors of the food mixed and ran together.

I avoided eye contact with Tom except to acknowledge cooking compliments, scared of what I might or might not read in his look. Lucky for me, Sam's Thanksgiving goal seemed geared to impress his lady love, and he and Lee, giddy as spring colts, provided the comic relief. In the middle of all this revelry, Ferrell T. and Hilda stumbled by, stuffing chocolate eclairs down their windpipes, whipped cream and streaks of dark goo melting down their matched faces.

There walked the seventh generation of Bells in Maryland. What a letdown.

I EXCUSED MYSELF to pick out a dessert, but when I reached the dessert table, my eyes ricocheted from plate to bowl to tin container. Too many choices and nothing made sense. Around the table spun bodies with faces and voices.

"Canola beats all."

"How can you say that? The only way to go is olive oil."

"Olive oil? Pompeian makes a good olive oil."

"Not as good as Goya."

"Crisco. That's what everybody on TV uses. I wouldn't use anything but Crisco. Makes the best crust."

I wheeled around, dizzy, and bumped into Roland.

Our eyes locked. Almost at once, I could see in that icy stare a frail old lady toppling down hard wooden steps, a boy in a coma, two ransacked homes, a basket of Spanish moss covering a secret. In that moment, I felt absolute certainty that Roland committed each crime.

"How could you?" I hissed, pulling up resolve. "How do you live with yourself?"

"What the hell are you talking about?"

"You know what I'm talking about." The doubts seeped back in; the doubts held me in check. Hadn't the body in the overcoat been bigger, taller?

A flicker of anger sparked the ice, but he curled his lip and cast me away, almost laughing, "You're a stupid, crazy broad and everybody knows it. That's what I told those two cops you and Lee tried to sic on me. I referred them to my good friend, Officer Lukzay. He set them straight."

He strutted away and I yelled after him, "You think this is over? I might be stupid and crazy but at least I'm not guilty of—"

Two hands grabbed my elbows, whirled me around, shoved me several yards down the dessert table. "Would you like some devil's food cake?"

I wrestled free of Tom. "What'd you do that for? And stop grabbing hold of my arms every time I turn around. You want people to think we're engaged?"

"I want you," he said, grabbing hold of my hands with surprising strength, "to keep your distance from Roland because somehow you've lost control of your tongue and temper. Both will be your undoing."

I let steam blow out my ears for a minute. "You think we should let him get away with trying to kill a woman? Or tampering with brakes and getting a boy almost killed?"

Tom, cool as ever, didn't appear the least ruffled. "Do you know for a fact he did any of these thing? Would you be willing to testify under oath?"

"Or breaking into two houses and tearing through like a hurricane?"

"You and Lee reported those crimes to the police. Now let them do their job. Are you so convinced the criminal is Roland? Out-of-control, crazy Roland?"

I studied my feet.

"You *are* convinced Roland did all of this, aren't you, Flip?"

I had to confess. "I'm not sure. Sometimes I think I'm sure, then I get doubtful. The person in the coat at Lee's house seemed bigger and taller than Roland. So I guess I'm not sure."

He pressed his lips together tightly and slowly nodded, as if letting something sink in. "Fair enough. We're dealing with criminal offenses, but this is a tight community. Nobody wants to see Garland or Hilda hurt. We all want to do the right thing. Do you agree with me?"

I pouted. "I guess so."

"And you will back off and let the police and my investigator do their jobs? Let experts handle this situation with Miss Fizzi, which is by far the most serious unless it is *proven* the car's brakes were tampered with?"

I chewed the inside of my mouth and mumbled, "OK."

He leaned into my ear. "And if you don't want me touching your arms, is there some other body part you suggest I hold that will attract less attention?"

My face went crimson and my mouth dropped. "I can't believe . . . you are . . . who do you . . . this is just . . ." I pulled away from him and meandered off, weaving through the crowd, the sound of his building laughter ringing in my ears.

Somewhere in the throng, C.C.'s commandant voice bugled, "Flip Paxton, don't forget! Monday! Not in the morning, I decided! Definitely not in the morning!"

Monday morning it would be, then. I careened back to

my car and drove home, completely forgetting my nice casserole dish and serving spoon laid out on the table, right by Tom Scott and his awful laughter.

EVEN BEFORE THE break-in at Lee's house, the Bell family Bible had taken on mysterious qualities and become a mission of mine. And a comfort in times of stress and doubt. I pulled the basket down from the top of the kitchen cabinet that night and lovingly took out the Bible determined to learn what facts I could and imagine the rest.

I scanned one branch of the family tree: Roland Bell (1851–1908) and Florence Openheim Bell (1859–1929). Across the way hung the other branch, Roland's contemporary, Lucinda Ann Tanner (1850–1890), his second cousin and the daughter of Lucy and Jason. Below Lucinda's name, the empty parentheses, no explanation.

Lucinda was eleven—not quite a child, not quite a young lady—when the Civil War broke out, fifteen when it ended, never married, and died at age forty, twenty-two years before her mother. She never knew a father; Jason died the year she was born, her mother, Lucy, never remarried.

Lucinda Ann marked the end of the female branch of the Bell family, going all the way back to Lucy Hanover Bell, her great-grandmother. For some reason, that saddened me, especially when I realized only one branch of the family still walked the planet and how degenerate that bloodline flowed.

Poor Lucinda Ann. Her generation of choice husbands got fairly swallowed by guns and cannon fire. Nobody much left but old men and little boys. Maybe she wasn't a looker or clung too tightly to Lucy's skirt. Maybe she suffered a disability like a clubfoot or harelip that put off men. That's how I imagined her—a pitiful sort of woman, sheltered by an independent mother, her only friend a leather-tooled diary where she poured out her heart. Perhaps there had been men she admired from afar: a widowed preacher with a bad lisp, a one-legged soldier who refused comfort, a local recluse people talked ugly about. All misfits like herself, sad and sorrowful, leading miserable lives. At least poor Lucinda Ann died before her mother. Alone, she would have drifted on a perilous sea, taken advantage of by con artists and ne'er-do-wells.

Roland and his wife, Florence, gave Lucinda two little cousins to spoil, a boy and a girl. Lucinda, no doubt, doted on the children. No matter what her impairment, they would have loved her unconditionally, as children do. When they reached a certain age, they might have asked, "Cousin Lucinda, why is your mouth so different from ours?" Or your leg, your eyes, your skin, your hands.

She might have replied, "God made me this way for a purpose. To help others develop a blind and accepting heart, and help me develop a humble and meek spirit."

Roland and Florence might have chided the children for their blunt questions, but little Roland, Jr. and Florie would have remembered Lucinda's answer all their lives, and learned from it.

When Lucinda died in 1890, it was a small funeral, only the immediate family: her mother Lucy, cousin Roland, wife Florence, ten-year-old Roland, Jr., and Florie, six. Nothing spectacular—a simple, dignified affair with a couple of hymns, a psalm read, a favorite poem. No husband looking lost and bewildered, holding a weeping toddler. No siblings, shaking their heads and commiserating with each other, asking what if.

Just Lucy, wondering if things could have turned out differently for her child, reflecting on a short, secluded life with comfort enough, but little joy. No father, no husband, no child. Not even a secret lover. Forty years, only forty years.

I pictured Lucy telling the others to go on home, back to

the house her brother John Bell Paca left her, that she needed a minute alone to say goodbye. What did she say? Thank you? I'm sorry? Forgive me?

Or something else? Something so hidden and secret, the words could not be spoken out loud for ears to hear, or written down for eyes to see.

I stared at the empty parentheses beneath Lucinda's name, and I knew what was not written there was engraved like granite on Lucy's heart.

CHAPTER 26

✻

EARLY MONDAY MORNING, I stopped by Miss Fizzi's house and got everything in order before she arrived home from the hospital later that day. The Episcopal Ladies Circle rallied to handle her food and care for the next week or two when she'd require extra attention. I knew if she had to depend on Suggs to help her, she'd be dead within forty-eight hours. Fortunately, in Solace Glen, the four church ladies circles didn't serve as mere excuses to get together and socialize. They served. The community would have been in a sorry state without those energetic bands of women, like Melody and Tina, roaming the countryside with plates of homecooked meals, visiting the sick and disabled, assisting with births, deaths, and weddings.

The Presbyterian Circle extended a yearly invitation to me to join, but I always declined. I told them they were wonderful, but unlike most of the members, I carried a full workload. Besides, I ended up doing a lot of what they did, anyway, in an unofficial capacity.

I left Miss Fizzi a note saying get well soon, this cleaning's on the house, compliments of Flip Paxton's Circle of One.

It was almost nine o'clock when I rang C.C.'s doorbell. The landscaping still needed work, but she was probably driving the local nursery insane, calling to squawk about why this and that hadn't been done and what the hell happened to her shrub delivery.

The improvement to the exterior of the house couldn't be denied. Three stories of barn now looked like three stories of *House Beautiful,* the eighteenth-century lumber rejuvenated, a new roof, a covered front porch that ran the length of the house. A line of rocking chairs creaked in the stiff breeze, waiting for summer. A gleaming oak door graced the entrance with shiny brass lamps on either side. The welcome mat held a flock of Canada geese in V-formation.

I rang the doorbell again and noticed the windows still had manufacturer's stickers glued to the glass. C.C. would no doubt want me to kill myself scrubbing them off. I stepped back and counted windows. She'd gone crazy installing them on all three floors, being such a child of the light.

After the third ring, the oak door swung open and C.C., a vision of loveliness in her leopard print bathrobe, hair net, and face cream, glared at me and lit a cigarette.

"Good God, what time is it?"

"Good morning to you, too." I walked into her hallway, set the carryall and vacuum down and closed the door. Then I took a look around. "Whooooeee. I don't know what you paid your decorator, but he was worth every penny."

C.C. inhaled her first hit of nicotine for the day and picked a speck of tobacco off her tongue. "He did what I told him to do." Her left arm draped across her waist and

propped the opposite arm up, right hand waving the cigarette. "I have a way with color. Even Leonard was impressed
and, God knows, little in life excites him except the stupid
Civil War. But he loves the entrance way, just adores it."

"I can understand why." The floors, a buttery pine, refin-
ished, buffed, and polyurethaned to a mirrorlike gloss, laid
the foundation to a soaring, three-story-high atrium. On the
yellow pine walls hung huge gilt-framed oil paintings that
probably belonged in a modern art museum in San Fran-
cisco or New York. An open stairway led to the second and
third stories, the banister sleek and simple. C.C.'s taste in
furniture ran on the Shaker side. Nothing overdone, nothing ornate. Tables, chairs, sofas—all basic lines, cool, teak
woods, no carved seat backs, no clawed feet, no feeling (as
at Miss Fizzi's house) that you'd eaten too much dinner
and needed a nap. I had to admit, C.C. nailed it. She was a
damn child of the light. The sun poured in from every direction on the simple, bare furnishings, setting the bold
colors of the paintings on fire.

"Well!" I'd drunk my fill. "I expect the workmen left an
inch of dust top to bottom. I'll start on the third floor and
work my way down. I dust, vacuum, scrub bathrooms,
empty trash, and change beds. I leave no germ untouched
in the kitchen. If you want others things done—refrigerator, oven, *windows*, that's extra." I took a breath. "I haven't
decided whether to take you on as a permanent client or
not. I'll give us a month, once a week."

Given the fact I represented the only game in town and
C.C. knew it, she bit her forked tongue and nodded, slouch-
ing off to the kitchen for espresso, the folds in her leopard-
print bathrobe hanging like loose skin.

The top two floors of the house gave the same impression
as the ground floor. Basic, stark furnishings, expensive-
looking artwork, well-placed windows, and warm, wonderful smelling pine floors and walls. Except for the workmen's

dust, an easy house to clean. The top floor contained two libraries, his and hers. I took a slow tour of Leonard's half as I dusted. His shelves bulged with thick law books and thicker Civil War histories, many volumes behind glass. Perfectly framed historical documents covered the walls, ceiling to floor at points. A letter written and signed by General Longstreet drew my interest.

"What are you doing?" A voice barked behind me. I jumped in my skin, but quickly recovered my composure.

"I was admiring your collection, Mr. Crosswell." I faced him head on. "You haven't exactly kept it a secret. In fact, you're really proud of it, aren't you?" I plastered a sweet, innocuous tourist expression across my face as my eyes swept the room. "You must have spent years putting this together."

He said nothing for a few seconds, the steel eyes reading me as if perusing the contents of a business journal. Finally, he responded gruffly, "Of course I've spent years assembling this collection. Look around you. Every major Civil War general is represented."

I didn't take my eyes off him. "Where's J.E.B. Stuart?"

The black, fox eyes gave nothing away. "He's in storage. I'm having a short note of his reframed."

"Only a short note? Don't you have any letters?"

He smiled charmingly and said, "You never know." He started to leave, but hesitated a moment to add, "Is the publication date of your Bible pre or post Civil War?"

"To tell you the truth," I lied, "I hadn't even noticed."

He blessed me with another glimpse of white teeth and headed downstairs. When I heard the BMW start, I breathed easier.

C.C.'s library contained steamy romance novels and decorating references with an exercise bike in the center. Stacks of *Architectural Digest* formed three towers against one wall. I moved down to the next floor. The master bedroom and huge bathroom took up most of the second floor, with two small guestrooms and a connecting bath on the opposite end of a hall. Nowhere did I see photographs of children, pets, or family. She kept a 4 × 6 picture of Leonard in a silver frame by her side of the bed; he kept an 8 × 10 of C.C. on his side. They were an evenly divided couple it seemed to me. I worked down to the ground floor, lugging the bed linen and a bag of trash. C.C. sat at the dining room table, sipping espresso, puffing on a cigarette, and reading the *Washington Post*. She didn't glance up.

I found the laundry room off the kitchen. The appliances in those two rooms could have come off a space ship—modern, glossy black finish with tons of computer options, no avocado greens or Acapulco golds, no unsightly buttons and knobs to twist, like my own thirty-year-old kitchen equipment. The dishwasher looked like something in which you could blast off to the moon.

I cleaned the downstairs, working hard as a beaver, then wrote out a bill to cover the two-hour job. I handed the bill to C.C. "All done."

She glimpsed the amount and pulled a blank check out of her thin robe, writing in a number that covered a whole month's cleaning. "This should take us through your little trial period," she said, shoving the check into my stomach.

"Fine by me." It was a good amount of money, just in time for Christmas. I'd charged extra for the third floor.

As I started to go, C.C. decided to strike up a conversation. "Marlene tells me the whole town turns out for a big Christmas tree lighting at the fire station. A sort of Williamsburg."

"Yes, that's right. Just like they do in Williamsburg." I wondered if she aimed to involve herself in the community now that she and Leonard were settled in.

"When is that exactly?"

"On the twelfth. At six o'clock."

"Eleven days. Doesn't leave me a lot of time."

"You need to prepare for lights to switch on?"

She looked completely bored with me. "I need time to give a party. I suggested to Marlene that after the big tree event, a select group be invited to a small cocktail party here."

"Oh." So Marlene lurked behind it. "Marlene's writing out the 'select' list?"

"She did volunteer to be in charge of the invitations. They should go out in a couple of days."

"Why are you telling me all this?" I knew I wouldn't be receiving any pretty printed invitation urging my appearance for cocktails.

"Marlene thought perhaps you could help serve."

Tom always said a good trial lawyer takes a spear to the heart without flinching so the jury never suspects he's in trouble. I struggled to do just that, to hide the humiliation she'd so blithely doled out.

"She did, did she?" Marlene would love to see me dressed in a plain black maid's uniform with a crisp, starched apron, offering her stuffed mushrooms on a silver tray and running to fetch another glass of chardonnay.

"She thought you'd jump at the chance to earn a few extra dollars."

"You can tell her there's no need to concern herself. I'm declining your offer."

C.C.'s forehead wrinkled under the coat of face cream. "Well, who else is there? Who can help me?"

"Ask Marlene," I bolted for the door, vision blurred. "She's been such a big help so far."

C.C. shrugged and mumbled something about a D.C. catering service and she'd see me next Monday, but in the afternoon, for God's sake.

I threw my stuff in the car and climbed behind the steering wheel, tears spilling over.

They wanted me at their party, all right. As the maid. As the hired help. Waiting hand and foot on the socially acceptable citizens of Solace Glen. Like C.C. and Leonard. Like Marlene. Like the Bells and Lee and Sam. Like Tom.

I imagined Tom showing up at the party and spying me in an ugly black-and-white uniform, kowtowing to the gentry.

No way! I might be the town domestic. I might clean people's houses for a living. But I was also a businesswoman, owning and controlling my own firm, doing well enough to own a home, support myself, and even indulge in luxuries now and again. My clients counted as friends and family, and I was proud of what I had accomplished all alone from the time I turned eighteen.

I drove home, skipping lunch at the Café, avoiding contact with Marlene until I'd calmed down. Wait until Louise heard about this tomorrow. She'd roll her eyes and winkle her nose over C.C.'s fine house and poor manners and how Marlene wanted to humiliate me.

Just wait until Louise heard about this.

C.C. HAD GOTTEN me so rattled, that night I took the Bell family Bible down for a therapy session. It occurred to me, glimpsing the entire tree, that the women in the Bell family had a tough time staying alive, getting married, or having children. The one female line died out with Lucinda Ann. The one remaining male line produced one or two offspring per generation, and only the male produced children.

Roland and his wife, Florence Openheim Bell, gave the world the first generation of Bells born after the Civil War, Roland Bell, Jr. and Florie O. Bell.

Florie appeared in 1884, the year Mark Twain wrote *The Adventures of Huckleberry Finn* and Chester A. Arthur was president. She probably lived a pretty fine childhood, spoiled by her parents and a big brother, her early years untouched by war and deprivation. Imagine the excitement she felt, at age fifteen, when the clock struck twelve and a whole new century dawned. She must have had the world by a string, so full of promise. Eight years later, her father died; Florie was twenty-four, old enough to be a wife and mother, but no man had attached his name to hers. She no doubt lived with her mother, Florence, and kept living with her until Florence passed away in 1929. She found herself alone, except for her brother and his family. Had she, I wondered, turned down suitors early on, a woman who rejected this man because he whistled too much, that one because she hated the way he parted his hair? By the time she started to feel desperate, in her early thirties, her luck would have run out. World War I swallowed a lot of good men beneath foreign ground. Years later, when Roland and Leona came along, she was just the old maid aunt, like her cousin before her, Lucinda Ann.

Florie O. Bell was born, she died. She left nothing behind but her name and the dates, 1884–1939. She led a spinster life—a barren, solitary moon orbiting the lush lives of others. She died at age fifty-five, probably from something like breast cancer or ovarian cancer, too embarrassed to go to a doctor.

I had at last reached fruit of the family tree that those living might remember. Unfortunately, Roland could best answer most questions. Miss Fizzi, however, might know enough to satisfy my curiosity, and I decided to ask her at our next visit.

Though studying and admiring the Bell family tree normally calmed me, doubt clouded the usual effect. I felt only depression as I pondered the lives of Lucinda Ann and Florie, the two spinster women, dead at forty and fifty-five, living their entire existences celebrating other people's weddings and births, sewing other women's trousseaux, knitting booties for babies they could only baby-sit, worrying if their time would ever come, if they'd be stuck serving the party punch, never offered a taste from the cup themselves. I knew how they felt, and I hated that I knew.

I slapped shut the Bible. How I hated that I knew.

CHAPTER 27

❈

BY TUESDAY MORNING, I'd finally calmed down from my excursion to C.C.'s house, but it took a full twenty-four hours to work the thorn out.

I drove by Miss Fizzi's house on the way to Louise's. Miss Fizzi lay propped up in bed, surrounded by flower bouquets, with Melody and Tina talking at once, filling her in on the doings at church and in town, the latest on Joey's condition, and the two break-ins.

She beamed bright when I swooped into the room with my own token of good will, a can of orange spice tea. Melody and Tina drew to the side so I could visit, holding back their insatiable curiosity about the police investigation. (Everybody had seen the flashing lights at Lee's house that night, and a few people had already been questioned.)

"You look pretty spry for a beat up old lady." I kissed Miss Fizzi on the cheek.

"I am spry," she tooted. "You could enter me in the Preakness." Both feet rested on elevated pillows along with the right wrist, which sported a splint. She'd taken three stitches over the right eye. Whoever did this should not be walking the streets a free man.

"By Preakness time, you'll be right as rain. Here's some tea."

"Thank you, dear." She whispered, "I'm sorry I have no pie to offer," and shot a meaningful glance at Tina who appeared to be licking her fingers.

"Think nothing of it. You just get better."

We talked a little more. With Melody and Tina hovering, both of whom loved to gossip, I thought it best to save the Bell family questions for another time. Instead, I filled her in on the Thanksgiving Day picnic and delivered an abbreviated version of my visit to C.C.'s house. Tina and Melody uttered "oh's" and "no's" at all the appropriate moments.

"Wait'll I tell Michael!" I knew Melody couldn't wait. She'd be out the door as soon as I left.

"Can you imagine what Margaret will say?" Tina already wrestled with the best way she'd divulge this information to her good friend.

"I'm on my way over to Louise's now to tell her about it."

Nobody spoke. I threw Melody a question in my eyes.

"She's not doing well," she answered.

"Not well at all," echoed Tina.

"She's slipping fast," sighed Miss Fizzi. "I called a couple of times this week and she couldn't speak. You run on over there and send her my love. It'll do her good to see you."

I said my good-byes before anyone could break into a long discussion of police investigations and hurried to Louise's, afraid of what I'd find. A car pulled out of the driveway as I drove in. To my surprise, I spied Garland at the wheel. She lowered her head as she drove by, as if she didn't want me to know she'd been helping Louise with the morning routine. I entered the house and went straight to the bedroom.

Louise's face, once so vibrant and expressive, showed no movement, the white skin translucent as still water. Scared, I crept closer until I recognized the tiny rise and fall of her chest. She must have heard me gulp.

Eyelids, thin as cobwebs, fluttered open. "Fli . . ."

"Don't talk. You probably wore yourself out, talking up a blue streak with that lady who just left."

"Gar-land."

So I was not mistaken. "Garland? Since when is Garland a member of a Circle? Roland keeps her chained to the kitchen. But then, I don't pretend to know everything around here."

I started dusting as I babbled. "I'll start with your bureau here, then do the bathroom. Guess I could vacuum after that and finish dusting. Those sheets look fresh. Don't tell me Garland took care of that for you."

Louise struggled to communicate with a bat of the eye, a twitch of the lip. I knocked the dust off Marlene's baby pictures and went in to clean the bathroom, shouting my one-sided conversation through the open door.

"Louise, you won't believe what happened at the picnic." I needed to tell her about Tom. Maybe she could advise me with a squeeze of the hand. So I told her everything. About the great casserole I baked, and Sam and Lee making things public. About my aborted little spat with Roland.

I finished scrubbing tile and porcelain and stepped back into the bedroom. Louise's face was turned toward the bathroom, so I knew she'd been listening. "There's something else, too, but I'll tell you after I vacuum."

The machine whirred to business and I zipped around the carpeted room. When I'd run over every strand of fiber twice, I shut the vacuum down and wrapped the cord in a neat oval. Louise turned her face to the center of the room.

"Would you like something to drink? Some water or juice?"

Her brows joined, which I took to mean no, thank you. I walked to her desk and started dusting Marlene in elementary school, an exceptionally unattractive child.

"I need to tell you about Tom," I said slowly, knowing I was about to sort through feelings out loud, very confusing feelings. "He . . . surprised me at the picnic. Maybe it didn't even start there. Maybe it started in Baltimore, at the Harbor Court. Or maybe that day on the Monocacy. Maybe it was in his office afterward. I don't know. I don't know when it happened, Louise, but he's been treating me like I was somebody special. Like I was somebody special to *him*. At the picnic, he actually took my arm and linked it with his, as if we were a courting couple in an old movie. And he looked at me differently than he ever has before, as though he really does see a different Flip Paxton. And I don't know why. I'm not different. I'm not."

When I glanced over at Louise, the pale face wore a strange smile, one tinged with mystery.

"So, the thing is, I don't know how to play this out. I'm not sure I'm reading him right. And if I am . . . if I am, God help me."

"He will," said Louise in a voice so faded, I half-expected the bed to be empty when I looked up. But there she lay, still wearing the mystery smile.

"He better because I have little else to go on. Anyway, Tom's on my schedule tomorrow. Maybe I'll get a better fix on him, who knows?" I moved to the bookshelf and to Marlene in her teen years, no improvement. "Now let me tell you about C.C. and her gorgeous home and terrible manners." I'd decided to leave out Marlene's role in the party snub. No sense adding to Louise's misery.

"I'll give C.C. the month. She did pay in full, but after

that, it's *adios, amigo*. She'd do well to buy herself a live-in slave."

I slapped the last dot of dust off Marlene, crossed over to the bed and sat on the end. "Louise," I addressed the strange smile, "I know you don't have the strength to talk and barely the strength to listen, but I want to thank you for letting me ramble on about my big questions in life. Not just today. I mean for all the times you've listened. You sort of took up where my mother left off. I hope I did the same for you, as a daughter. We've been lucky—no—*blessed* to have had each other."

I reached for her open hand and my heart lurched. The place where my fingers touched her skin—the lifeline, etched in the center of her palm—felt cold as winter. She was gone. She had left me.

All my mothers had left me.

CHAPTER 28

✳

I DIDN'T EXPECT to come away from Louise's funeral uplifted, but I did. The Episcopal minister, Reverend Farlow, a fairly young man, conducted the service as Louise requested. She'd had a good amount of time to plan and had given a written copy of her wishes to both Reverend Farlow and Tom.

She did not want her coffin in the church during the service. Instead, she'd picked out a nice photograph of herself taken ten years earlier to prop up on the altar table, the Caribbean sun beaming bright across her face, arms draped over a white fence with the sparkling, aqua blue sea in the background. She wore an orange sundress, white sneakers and red Marilyn Monroe lips. Her skin glowed pink and healthy, and the wind whipped the gray hair off her face. A picture to wipe away the cold image of her deathbed.

Sam, Lee, Tom, and I sat together in the second row on the left. Marlene took the pew opposite with C.C., her new best friend, and Leonard, whose cellular phone went off during the opening prayer. I noticed him staring at Lee before he disappeared down the aisle, nobody upset to see him go. The small church overflowed with people touched by Louise Lamm. Young children, teenagers, families starting out, middle-aged parents with kids in college, the elderly—every age and generation, male and female, all colors, all sizes, all beliefs represented in the gathering.

And almost everybody was smiling.

"What a good life she had!" I heard a lot of people say.

"What an example that woman set!"

"I remember the time Sally got sick with the scarlet fever and Louise organized everything from taking care of the twins to meals to car pools to cleaning house. She was a whirlwind when she had her health."

I also heard a lot of comments that ran in another vein. "Too bad about Marlene."

"I can't believe she even had the nerve to show up at her mother's funeral."

"Probably hoping for an inheritance. Her type never changes."

We sang the first hymn, "My Faith Looks Up to Thee."

*While life's dark maze I tread, And griefs around me
    spread, Be thou my Guide;
Bid darkness turn to day, Wipe sorrow's tears away, Nor
    let me ever stray
From Thee aside
When ends life's transient dream, When death's cold,
    sullen stream
Shall o'er me roll, Blest Saviour, then, in love, Fear and
    distrust remove;
O bear me safe above, A ransomed soul!*

Then a couple of lay readers delivered the scripture passages Louise had chosen from the King James version. She liked it best, she said, because the old English sounded soothing to the ear.

I thought her choice from the Old Testament strange and foreboding. Deuteronomy 11: 26-28.

Behold, I set before you this day a blessing and a curse;
A blessing, if ye obey the commandments of the Lord your God, which I command you this day;
And a curse, if ye will not obey the commandments of the Lord your God, but turn aside out of the way which I command you this day, to go after other gods, which ye have not known.

The New Testament passage that followed consisted of only one verse, John 13:34. "A new commandment I give unto you, That ye love one another; as I have loved you, that ye also love one another."

Then we sang "Here, O My Lord, I See Thee Face to Face" after which Reverend Farlow took the podium and preached a few words. He hadn't known Louise half as long as most of us, he said, and thought the loveliest form of tribute would be our own stories of how she'd touched our lives.

One by one, people stood and briefly recounted some tiny incident that had meant the world to them. How she'd come in the middle of the night to help their mother or child. How she secretly sent money to this person or another, only to be found out later. Her sense of humor, her love of life, her warmth. Several who stood were brave enough to say she'd been a wonderful mother, then shot Marlene a poisonous eye before taking their seats again.

None of it fazed Marlene Lamm Worthington, who sat stiff-necked the entire hour, jiggling her crossed ankle like she couldn't wait for the bell to ring and school to be over. C.C. put on a sweet show, reaching across periodically to pat Marlene's greedy hand, a strained, courageous smile on her face.

Tom stood and said a few words, hand resting comfortably on my shoulder, telling the story of how Louise got a recipe mixed-up so bad one Thanksgiving, dumping in pepper for flour and flour for pepper, that folks were on their knees slurping water out of the fire pond. Louise compensated everyone in town by hiring a catering service to bake a cake the size of a Buick and we all feasted on it during the Christmas tree lighting ceremony. The icing on top spelled out, "I'M SORRY, SOLACE GLEN!", which, Tom reflected, told you everything you needed to know about Louise Lamm. If she wronged you, she righted the wrong, but those wrongs consisted of such inconsequential things as too little flour, too much pepper. Nobody, he concluded, could accuse Louise of any real sin. Nobody could throw stones at that great lady.

I flashed a glance at Marlene, expecting her to jump up and heave a few rocks of her own, but she only coughed and unwrapped a peppermint, making as much rattle as she could. C.C. cooed and patted her hand for the hundredth time.

With stories told and everybody smiling at the happy memories, Screamin' Larry blessed us with the most beautiful, devout, reverent rendition of "Dear Lord and Father of Mankind" I had ever heard. Even C.C.'s mouth dropped at the dignity and emotion he put into that song, especially the last two verses:

> Drop Thy still dews of quietness, Till all our strivings cease;
> Take from our souls the strain and stress, And let our ordered lives confess

The beauty of Thy peace.
Breathe through the heats of our desire Thy coolness
    and Thy balm;
Let sense be dumb, let flesh retire; Speak through the
    earthquake, wind, and fire,
O still, small voice of calm!

"Well, I never," I heard C.C. mutter.

Then Larry ruined the mood by leering at her and making his tongue flick like a lizard's. She jammed on her sunglasses, high heels clicking as she left the church with Marlene.

The four of us walked out together and thanked Reverend Farlow for a service we were sure Louise would have been proud of. Sam and Lee drove off for a quiet Friday night outing in Frederick; Tom patted me on the back and said he had business to wrap up.

I watched him drive away, wondering if I'd read him wrong, after all. A linked arm at the picnic, a brief hug at his office the day after Louise's death. Nothing more.

At once, I missed Louise.

"Flip." It was Margaret. She slipped a hand under my elbow and guided me a little ways beyond the lingering crowd. She obviously wanted to say something important and private, but seemed to be struggling.

"What is it, Margaret?" I really had no idea.

She drew herself up as if preparing to deliver a long speech. But this was all she said: "You're not alone, Flip."

In her eyes, I saw loss—terrible, devastating loss. I also saw compassion and warmth and strength. Dressed in black, her smile lit the lamp of comfort, and I was transported back in time, twenty-four years before, to a grave site where my whole world lay silent and still until I raised my eyes and discovered how many mothers called me daughter.

In that instant, Margaret took all their places, those

women who'd come before, those women who'd saved my life—my saviors of Solace Glen.

We hugged each other, knowing without words what had passed between us. She squeezed my hand, a brief kiss on the temple, and walked on.

Gratitude overwhelmed me. Louise had left me, but not all my mothers had gone. Not all.

Margaret's tall, straight form disappeared around a corner just as Pal came racing up from out of nowhere, shouting, "He's awake! Joey woke up outta the coma! Everybody! He's woke up!"

Plenty of people still milled around after the funeral, sharing a story or a remembrance of Louise. The occasion quickly turned into a rally for Joey Sykes and words of thanks to the Lord were not forgotten given the ground where we stood.

"Oh, mercy, mercy, Praise the Lord!" Miss Fizzi, determined to attend the funeral in a wheelchair driven by Sally and her strapping twin boys, could hardly sit still. "Is he *himself*, Pal?"

"She means is his brain working normal or is it cracked," explained one Egghead to Pal, using his best technical jargon.

"Oh, yeah!" Pal practically rose from the sidewalk in his ecstasy. "He's himself, all right. Already ordered a pizza and a number four from the Burger Hut."

"Does he remember the accident?" Melody and Michael asked in near perfect unison.

"Yeah, pretty much. At least what led up to it. A couple of cops from the county showed up and asked about it. Joey admitted he'd been speeding, but said he tried to stop and there were no brakes."

A little gasp escaped my mouth and I searched out Roland, standing between Garland and Lukzay, all three interested in Pal's announcement.

Pal's face crumpled as if in deep pain and he whimpered, "It's my own fault. I'm the one who worked on the brakes. I musta screwed up."

"That's highly unlikely, Pal," I said in a strong voice. "You're an expert mechanic. There has to be some other explanation."

Lukzay and Roland huffed at the dirty look I sent their way and Lukzay said roughly, "Boy admitted speeding. Pal admitted being the last to touch the brakes. End of investigation."

"But was he really the last one to touch the brakes?" I asked, hoping to fan a tiny flame. The crowd began to rumble. "I hope *somebody* examined that wrecked car top to bottom."

"Did they, Pal?" An Egghead pressed. "Is the car still at that garage?"

"I-I don't know," Pal replied, blinking in confusion. "I haven't seen it since the accident, I've been so upset and busy."

I saw Roland and Lukzay slide eyes at each other and skulk away from the crowd.

Everyone refocused on Pal and congratulated him on Joey's return to consciousness, assuring him that he was not to blame.

"Maybe those other policemen will get to the bottom of this," Tina offered, and Tom's warning to let the experts do their job came back to me.

I headed for home and slowly my thoughts switched from Joey's "accident" to more reflective thoughts of Tom. Louise could have told me which end was up. Yet she did say God would help, her last words, "He will."

But were those her last words? The scripture Louise planned for her funeral she chose carefully, purposefully. A blessing and a curse. Other gods. Love one another.

A blessing and a curse.

I smiled to myself as I walked. Knowing Louise, they were one and the same. We take the bitter with the sweet, she often said whenever I got whiny, the vinegar with the honey. We take the blessing with the curse, she was saying now.

I wrapped my coat tighter against the December cold and set out to make a mental list of blessings and curses in my life. The blessings mounted—eighteen good years with two loving parents; my "mothers": Marie, Leona, Louise, and now Margaret; my deep friendship with Lee; a business that gave me independence; a network of love and support in a tight community; the precious inheritance of a family tree. Before I realized it, I was home, safe and warm, no curses yet on the list.

On my answering machine, the voice of Marlene, snippy and authoritative, instructed me to call her. I brewed a cup of tea and erased her with the press of a button.

I knew the curse in Louise's life; I dreaded discovering my own.

CHAPTER 29

❋

SATURDAY, THE DAY after Louise's funeral, I slid into my regular seat behind the register feeling a little sad for myself and everybody in town. Hilda slouched over and picked up my order. She looked similarly down in the mouth, although I knew it couldn't be because of Louise.

"What's got you so depressed, Hilda? Maybelline go out of business?"

"Naw." She'd used a heavy hand on the eyeliner and cheek blush that day, a cross between Cleopatra and Ronald McDonald. "I flunked a geometry test."

"Why don't you get a tutor?"

"I guess Ferrell T. could help me if I asked."

Guess again. "Ferrell T. wasn't so hot at math when he was in high school."

"No," she agreed, "but he did pass it at last."

"Why don't you ask the teacher to suggest somebody?"

Why was I even trying to help? She had two parents, even if one of them was Roland.

"That's what Momma said to do."

"There you go." At last. "Listen to your mother."

"I guess I could."

She guessed she could. I gave up and scrambled for my pocket atlas. Hilda shrugged and slouched back toward the kitchen. I caught a glimpse of Garland staring at me through the window of the swinging door. I smiled, but she ducked away.

Just then, C.C. and Marlene whirled in out of the wind. C.C. wore what all us ladies in Solace Glen donned on our day off: knee-length fox fur, slinky cashmere wrap dress, black suede boots, and a fur-lined hat. She spotted me and waved. Marlene did more than that. She stormed over.

"You didn't return my call."

I put on a Queen Mother accent. "Oh, did you rrrring me?"

"You know I did." Her eyes looked ready to pop out, lotto Ping-Pong balls complete with dollar signs stamped on the corneas. "You have the keys to my mother's house, don't you?"

"And Tom has the other set." Her mouth dropped. I knew she'd demanded the keys from Tom seconds after hearing of Louise's death so she could go into her mother's house and "get some things that belonged to her." Tom wouldn't hand them over, saying the estate would have to be settled first.

"You know," I admired my hideous fingernails, "I didn't get my invitation to C.C.'s party next Friday."

"DO you have the keys?"

I clapped the pocket atlas shut. "If she left the house to you, I will give you the keys. Otherwise, don't hold your breath."

"You impudent bitch."

"Gee, Marlene, that's not very Christian."

"How dare you. . . ."

She was winding up to run all day, but Tom, thank God, appeared out of nowhere. He took her arm, pulling her away from the table. "Marlene. Can you come by my office Monday afternoon, about three? We need to go over some things."

Her nostrils flared, but she nodded, throwing me a snitty look before tramping back to have a lovely lunch with C.C.

"Mind if I join you?" He pulled out the other chair and sat down hard. "What a day. What a week."

Hilda brought me a tuna sandwich and hurried off again with Tom's order.

"It's been a week, all right," I said. "Want my pickle?"

He screwed up his nose. "By the way, you need to be there, too. You're in Louise's will."

My hands fell to my lap. "Good Lord, I hope she didn't leave me a family Bible. I can't sleep at night as it is with this Bell and that one floating through my dreams."

He grinned. "I hope that's not all who floats through your dreams."

There he went again. I wanted to cuss. Instead, I bit into the sandwich and changed the subject. "Wonder who'll flip the switch this year."

Each year, the Tree Lighting Committee chose someone to light the tree and the town Christmas lights, usually someone who'd given an obscene amount of volunteer service to the community. Usually a Circle Lady.

"No idea. Who do you think?"

"Oh, probably C.C. Although she is new to our little community, she has shown extraordinary care and concern for the pitiful outcasts of society who appear to thrive in Solace Glen like termites. After all, she employed me."

"You going to her party next Friday?"

I almost choked. "No. No, I'm not going to the big shindig."

"Would you like to go with me?"

"You?" I quickly lifted a glass of iced tea to my mouth and hid behind it.

"Should be mildly entertaining. Screamin' Larry has vowed to crash it. If we're lucky, he'll arrive drunk as a skunk and sing Broadway hits all night."

Before I could respond, Ferrell T. came galloping through the door like a bloodhound on the trail, caught sight of Tom, and whisked him away, babbling something about a judge on the phone. Tom grabbed the remainder of my sandwich, told me to take home his lunch when it came, and he'd talk to me Monday.

While I waited for Hilda, someone else slipped into the chair opposite mine. I looked up to see Roland glowering at me, claws methodically tapping the top of the table.

"I was about to leave." I pulled bills out of my wallet—one's, five's, anything.

"Not just yet." He reached across the table and latched snaky fingers around my wrist. "We need to have a little talk."

I tried to pull my wrist away, but he only tightened the grip. "What do you want, Roland?"

"I want what I've always wanted, Flip Paxton." His mouth curled at the corners, not quite a smile, not quite a grimace. His eyes gleamed like the eyes of a stove slowly heating. "You see, I finally figured out the big picture and my focus has been out of whack. I've been concentrating on the money end of things, like Leona's house. I shouldn't feel angry about Lee getting that old ramshackle money pit. Mine's better, anyway. The stuff in the house—I got most of what I wanted long before Leona left this earth. Miss Fizzi's trust—she's gonna keel over dead any day at her age. Those things aren't as important, though, as the good name you leave your kids. That's where my focus has been out of whack, you see. I've come to what you call a *realization*."

I noticed he left out any mention of Pal's car. "What are you saying?"

His nails dug into my flesh and he took a sip from my water glass. "If those letters turn out to be historic, you know, elevating the Bell name in the history books, then as head of the Bell family, I'll take Lee to court to get the originals for my kids' inheritance. I'll go through the proper channels."

Somehow I doubted that, recalling Joey's coma, my torn up house, Lee's break-in, and Miss Fizzi's so-called accident. "And?"

"And you ought to think about what you want to give me for Christmas. Soon." He released his grip and flung my wrist down. "Remember, you're only the hired help. No relation. Don't fancy yourself keeper of the flame."

With that, he stalked away, disappearing through the swinging doors of the kitchen. I heard Lukzay chuckling hoarsely over his meal.

I rubbed my wrist as Hilda dropped off the wrapped plate of food.

"Can I get you anything else?" she asked.

"No," I snapped, "nobody can get me anything. I don't want any*thing*." Not a drink, not a sandwich, not a car, or a house, or a painting, or china. Not a book. Not a Bible.

Nothing that held names and dates, dreams and secrets. Nothing that began with the tree of life and ended with an apocalypse.

FOR THE REST of Saturday and most of Sunday, I moped around the house, glaring at the basket on top of the kitchen cabinet, wishing Leona had given me a bracelet or a picture frame, anything but that Bible. The irony was, if Roland had inherited the letters and the Bible, he never would have cracked open a page, but because a Jenner and a Paxton held possession, he'd gone off the deep end. What part Leonard or anybody else played in this soap opera was anyone's guess.

By Sunday night, I'd worked myself from a frenzy back into a state of resolve. I couldn't give in to Roland. For whatever reason, Leona wanted me to have the history of the Bell family—not her brother and certainly not a man like Leonard Crosswell—and I would honor her intentions, no matter what. *Let the experts do their job.*

I climbed up on the counter and pulled down the basket. Born in 1880, four years ahead of his sister Florie, Roland Bell, Jr. could have joined the navy for the Spanish–American War in 1898, but he didn't. At age 37, he wouldn't have joined up to fight in Europe, either.

No, my picture of old Roland, Jr. rang clear. I saw him as an overweight, spoiled young man who rolled contentedly into middle-age and beyond, taken care of by women, given to practical jokes, admired for his knowledge of trivia, and baffled and frustrated by the demands and responsibilities of husbandhood and fatherhood. A momma's boy who never left Momma, grateful as hell she left him her fine, big house that he poured his wife's money into collecting art, carpets, furnishings, and china.

His parents guided him in the choice of a helpmate, picking from the field a passive, plain, unremarkable woman seven years his senior with tons more money than looks. Roland, Jr., a bare eighteen years under his wide belt, consented to the union, delighted he'd have so much wealth to squander at such an early age. He could show his friends a high time at the races.

So in 1898, Roland, Jr., wed Katrina T. Chapelle. It was she, so grateful at age twenty-five to have landed a husband, who received the Bell family Bible as a wedding present and began the process of recording the generations of her young husband's family. From 1898 until 1940, Katrina

Chapelle Bell penned the births, the marriages, and the deaths of the clan. It was she, not a blood member of the family, who felt the importance of family history and tradition, who wanted her son to know his heritage and take pride in his birthright.

Young, spoiled Roland, Jr., at least gave Katrina the two things she wanted most—a Mrs. in front of her name and, in 1899, a son, Roland Bell, III. After those two unselfish acts, which required nothing more than to say "I do" and consummate the union, Roland, Jr., drifted on his merry way through life, adored by mother and sister, occasionally patted on the head by father, taken advantage of by friends ever short on cash, and tolerated by a wife who gradually ignored him and lavished all her time and attention on the son.

Poor, unwitting Katrina. She only added to the pattern of raising and nurturing the sins of the father. Men spoiled by their mothers, overprotected, handed no responsibility in life, nothing required of them. Teaching her boy early on that he equaled the sun and whatever he touched turned to gold. Materialistic, greedy, and ruthless. Like grandfather, like father, like son.

Katrina died in 1940 at age sixty-seven. Roland, Jr. lived through the Second World War, going to his reward in 1945 at age sixty-five. They left behind a son, a daughter-in-law, and two grandchildren: a girl, Leona, and a boy, Roland, IV.

They left behind a legacy of self-absorption, self-importance, and greed, greed, greed.

How Leona became the person she did remained a mystery to me. The answer probably lay with her mother, but I could wait to wrestle with that generation next time.

I closed the Bible and sipped a glass of wine. I hoped Miss Fizzi's long-term memory outshone her short-term memory. At any rate, it would be intriguing to see if my imagination hit the target or completely missed the mark.

The Bible went back to its honored place under the Spanish moss on top of the cabinet. A lamp under a bushel. I went back to my honored place, a single body in a double bed, curled tight beneath the sheets and quilt, still counting the blessings on my list, leaving the curses in darkness.

CHAPTER 30

✳

MARLENE, DRESSED IN black to resemble a sainted nun sporting a fish face, licked her lips when Tom entered the conference room and closed the door behind him.

"Is that the will?" The saucer eyes fixated on the papers in his hand.

"Yes. I have the original and two copies. One for each of you." He placed an envelope in front of both of us and sat down. "Rather than read Louise's Last Will and Testament word for word, I'll simply give you the gist of it. Then you can read through it at home, consult other counsel if you wish," he aimed this last part at Marlene, "and get back to me with any questions."

Marlene fingered the envelope suspiciously. "Well? What is the gist of it?"

Tom sucked in a gallon of air, blew it out again. "Your mother left you one thousand dollars a month for life."

The pop eyes stared at him. "A thousand a month."

"Yes."

"That's it?"

"That's it."

I squirmed in the chair; really, it was Roland all over again.

Marlene sputtered, "I've got debts to pay! What about the rest of it? What about the house?" The only reason she cared anything about the house, a modest rancher, was because the house she'd rented for nearly twenty-five years was falling in on itself and neither she nor her cheap landlord wanted to pour any money into it. "Don't tell me she left it to *her*. Haven't you inherited enough of other people's property, Flip?"

Tom and I ignored the insult. "The house," he continued, "which is unencumbered, is to be sold or rented and the proceeds placed in trust with the remainder of the estate. The personal property in the house goes to Flip, who is named Personal Representative of the estate, to do with as she chooses."

Her breathing came hard and fast. She leaned forward. "You said the estate, the bulk of the estate is to be put in a trust?"

"That's right."

"Who's the beneficiary?"

"Several named charities, plus, the trustees are given wide latitude in distributing income to entities or individuals who fall under certain specified categories."

Marlene stopped breathing altogether. "Who are the trustees?"

"I am one. Flip is the other."

I felt an electric shock and Marlene toppled backward in her chair.

"Me?" Now it was my turn to sputter. "What do I know about being a trustee?"

"You might be surprised," said Tom. "All it takes is good judgment."

"A thousand dollars a month." Marlene spat the words. "From a three-million-dollar-plus estate?"

I stared at Tom, eyes wide as Marlene's.

Marlene turned on Tom and spoke in a superior tone. "I *know* that's what the sale of my father's business brought her. She told me when I was eighteen. Plus, she inherited tons from her own family. Old money." She sneered at me like I was a caterpillar she had a mind to squish. "Very old money."

Tom listened patiently to the ranting tinged with accusation. "You're right. It is more than three million. Your mother invested wisely. I put it more in the neighborhood of nine or ten million."

"And I get the grand sum of A THOUSAND DOLLARS A MONTH!" She went so scarlet in the face, I thought we'd have to call the Eggheads.

I was fool enough to say, "A thousand bucks is nothing to sneeze at, Marlene. You can save up and buy a condo."

"Shut up! Shut up! You did this! Both of you did this! You influenced her to write me out! I was her only kin!"

I bolted up and crossed to the window, needing a whiff of cold air. "Now you really do sound like Roland."

She turned on Tom. "You wrote this will, didn't you?"

"As a matter of fact, Louise used a Baltimore law firm, then advised them when the time came that I was to handle the trust. If you fight this, Marlene, you will be fighting a losing battle. Don't believe me, though, take the will to another attorney. Please."

"You better believe I will! I bet Leonard Crosswell would *love* to take you on. Ten million—you *know* I'll fight this!" She sat in the chair, one hand tugging at her black sweater, glaring at the envelope in front of her. "Why should I let you and Flip have a high time blowing ten million on cancer patients who are going to die, anyway. Just like my mother." She reared up, snatched the envelope off the table, and stomped to the door. "In the meantime, you can mail me my first check. I wouldn't be caught dead stopping by here once a month to grovel from the likes of you. As for you, Flip Paxton, you'll get what's coming to you soon enough."

She blew out, slamming the door.

"Nice doing business with you, too," murmured Tom. He tossed an ink pen on the table.

I turned away from the window and faced him. "So," I said.

"So," he said, stretching his legs out, causing Eli to switch positions. He remained quiet for a time, then said, "Your hair has a blondish halo to it in the sun."

"That's called gray." My finger wrapped around a piece of hair and made a curl. "Anyway, you're only flattering me because I'm almost a hot-shot trustee. Subject to legal wrangling, of course."

"You're right. The very word *trustee* has a certain sex appeal, don't you think?"

I started to laugh, but there was something in his eyes that caused me to hold my breath. He parted his lips to speak, but Ferrell T., such an efficient little secretary, burst through the door.

"Tom, circuit court just called."

"Thank you." Tom didn't move or take his eyes off mine. "You may go now."

Ferrell T. stood rigid as the king's guard. Tom turned to dismiss him again, but I cut them both off.

"What should we do about Louise's house while Marlene drags this thing out?"

The moment vanished. Ferrell T. picked up a pile of books from the conference table and busied himself shelving.

Tom rubbed the back of his neck a long minute, eyes downcast. "OK. The house. We'll need a professional appraisal of the real and personal property. You can still go over there and make your own inventory of what you would want to eventually keep, give to charity, sell, hand over to friends. We can discuss whether to sell or rent later on, as soon as Marlene discovers she doesn't have a leg to stand on."

"OK." I nodded and swallowed hard. "Thanks." I scooped up my coat.

"I'll walk you out."

"No, no, you're busy, and I've got a lot to think about now with this house and getting ready for Christmas. I got behind this past week."

He stood up, took the coat from me and wrapped it around my shoulders. I stuck a hand in the pocket, searching for the car keys. The red cashmere scarf felt soft and warm. "Oh, this is yours. You dropped it at the clinic."

"There it is." He unfurled the scarf and gently placed it around my neck, the touch of his fingertips against my throat. "It looks better on you. Keep it."

I didn't know what to say, so I said, "Yes, I'll go with you."

"Good," he whispered, and smiled. "Let's hope Larry shows up."

I flew down the street to my car, talking to Louise as if she was hurrying along right beside me. "Did you know, Louise? Is that why you bound us together as equals in your will? You planned this. You planned this as a blessing."

Marlene would never understand that the curse in her life at her mother's death had nothing to do with the inheritance, or that the blessings she could have had during her mother's life had nothing to do with riches.

I drove straight home, the copy of Louise's will tight in my hand. Whether I ever got around to reading it or not, I knew what Louise would have wanted.

* * *

TWO DAYS LATER, I walked through the empty house into
the bedroom. A little more than a week before, Louise had
lain in that bed and quietly slipped away from me, nothing
more than a mysterious smile as her good-bye. Now I had a
job to do, and I didn't want to attend to it. I carried a clipboard and started jotting notes.

The books could be divided between Lee's Historical
Society and the school system. The clothes, which filled
two closets and two chests, everything good quality, could
go to friends or charity. Melody certainly matched Louise's
size and Sally would eventually, after the baby arrived. The
furniture, too, stood as a testament to Louise's good taste,
most of it fine antiques. I hoped to keep a Martha Washington chair I'd always admired and picked out a couple of
things for Lee and Margaret, but most of the furnishings
should go to auction and the money used for one of Louise's
worthy causes.

I continued through the house. Linen, silver, china, a
couple of oil paintings, kitchenware, rugs, an old upright
piano I knew the Methodists could use. Nothing lavish,
nothing ostentatious. Louise lived a simple life for a woman
with nine or ten million reasons to go berserk. Outside I
listed garden tools, hoses, a new lawn mower, a Blue Mar-
tin birdhouse, stone figures of St. Francis and three rabbits,
a birdbath, and a fountain. A car.

The idea hit me like thunder—Pal's new car. Not a
Cadillac, but a perfectly decent Chevrolet. I skipped inside,
toothy as a game show host giving away the big prize behind door number three. My eyes skimmed around the
rancher. I'd covered everything but one small concern and
for that I'd brought along a box.

In Louise's bedroom, I walked methodically from corner to corner, clearing shelves and tables and bureaus of a

baby, a toddler, a girl, a teenager, a young woman. With the room stripped bare of pictures and the box filled to the top, I taped the cardboard tight and wrote in black ink, TO MARLENE FROM MARLENE.

The Gift and Flower Shoppe was closed when I left the box on the front door steps with all the other UPS shipments of tacky, hollow trinkets and cheap merchandise.

I hoped she'd be very happy with herself.

CHAPTER 31

❈

FRIDAY MORNING, SOLACE Glen woke to the first snow-fall of the season. I opened my bedroom window and leaned out, face to heaven, mouth open to catch the fat flakes. Workmen clambered up and down the linen white streets, stringing lights, preparing for the big tree lighting ceremony that night. People smiled and opened shops. Children's voices grew louder by the hour, tuning up for Christmas morning. Peace on Earth seemed real enough to wrap your hands around and bring inside by the fire.

I closed the window and got dressed, humming, coaxing last winter's thermal underwear onto my body. When I caught a glimpse of myself in the mirror, the woman in the glass fairly shimmered.

* * *

SAM'S HOUSE WAS a mess, and I scolded him up and down as he sat at Leona's huge dining table wrestling with scotch tape and Christmas wrapping.

"Two weeks! You made all this mess in two weeks?" I kicked at a plastic mixing bowl, leftover popcorn kernels, yellow and gloppy, stuck inside. "Has Lee seen this place? No, I know she hasn't or she'd have torn up the lease and kicked your butt out in the street."

He jerked a rectangle of tape off his finger and stuck it on a present. "I'd sue. Right after I told her how much I adore the ground she walks on." He reached up and unzipped another inch of tape off one of his eyebrows. "Owww. And it's been four weeks. You didn't come the day after Thanksgiving. Then last Friday we buried Louise."

I counted in my head. "You're right. Now I feel bad. Good God, you're a victim."

"I am. But," he brightened, the boy who caught the prettiest salamander, "Lee loves me even though she agrees I'm a slob."

I started picking up dirty plates and T-shirts with my fingertips. "You and Lee going to the tree lighting?"

"Wouldn't miss it."

"How about C.C.'s party afterward?"

"Yeah, that, too. Lee's making me go. She wants to see the house. Speaking of the Crosswells . . ."

He paused dramatically, forcing me to stop cleaning and look him in the eye. "Yeeesss?"

"I had an interesting visit from Leonard yesterday."

My forehead wrinkled. "Leonard? What in the world would he want to talk to you about? Oh, wait. Let me guess. Letters."

Sam lifted one brow. "Letters. And lawsuits."

The pit of my stomach fluttered and I sat down hard in a chair, giving Sam my full attention. "Tell me."

"He came on the pretext of seeking advice about adding to his Civil War document collection."

I pictured the Longstreet letter on the wall of Leonard's study, so perfectly framed. "What kind of advice?"

"Whether Lee's letters are authentic and written by J.E.B. Stuart. What the contents of the letters are. If I think they're worth anything. If I've stumbled across any other historical documents while living here in Leona's house. If I might like to make a few bucks."

My skin blazed. "What did you tell him?"

Sam shrugged. "I told him what Lee already told everybody who asked at the Thanksgiving picnic—the letters are authentic and Stuart wrote them. I couldn't tell him the exact contents because Lee hasn't let me read them. She feels protective because of the way Leona and the Bell women kept the letters secret all these years. I know they're love letters, but I don't know who they're written to or what they're worth. No, I haven't seen any other valuable Civil War memorabilia floating around this house because I don't snoop. And thanks, but no thanks, I'm happy with my salary at the college."

"Anything else?"

"Only one thing. I assured him Lee would never sell, not to him, not to anybody. Those letters are part of her heritage and a part of the history of Solace Glen."

I glowed at Sam. I had a feeling he was going to make himself a part of Lee's heritage and history before too long. But Leonard's snooping bothered me, especially after Roland's threat of a lawsuit to take the letters away from Lee. Two fireballs building in opposite corners. "You said, 'Letters and *lawsuits*.'"

"Oh, that." Sam stacked a couple of gifts he'd wrapped. "He asked me what I could tell him about you and Tom."

My eyes popped. "Me and Tom?"

Sam's own eyes narrowed and he grinned slyly. "You and

Tom. You *know*. The cotrustees of Louise's estate. Seems he's been retained by Marlene. He was just fishing. Didn't catch anything. Probably thought I'd be more receptive to questions as a relative newcomer."

"He didn't say anything about Roland? Roland and the letters?"

Sam shook his head, apparently growing bored with the subject. "Nope. No Roland. No more letter talk. How's Miss Fizzi doing? I hear Tom has hired a private investigator."

I confirmed as much, and we rambled on about Miss Fizzi's health, Joey's awakening, and our own conclusions about who caused her fall and the failed brakes. I stuck to the notion Roland did it, but admitted room for doubt because of the figure in the black overcoat. Sam couldn't decide between Suggs and Leonard based solely on the fact he didn't like either one. We moved on to the weather, Marlene, and Louise. Like any secret in Solace Glen, Sam said word of the cotrusteeship had leaked out, except that the Eggheads, who probably heard it from Marlene or Roland, buttered the truth with a coat of acid.

"The Eggheads told me, along with about fifty other intimates, that you and Tom plugged Louise with a bottle of Johnnie Walker Red one night and she changed her will to exclude Marlene. Said Tom slid one thin dime across the table and told Marlene, 'Meet your inheritance.' Did you know you and he are running off to live in Mexico?"

"To escape winter or our criminal past?"

Sam chewed on it a minute. "I'd do it for both. Cover the bases, that's my motto."

"Sounds good to me." I set him straight with the unvarnished story. "Marlene got more than she deserved. Frankly, I wouldn't have been as charitable as Louise."

"She'll still have to work for a living."

"Yeah, too bad. Like the rest of us."

Sam finished a gift he'd been struggling with and held it up proudly.

"A four year old could do better," I commented. "What are you getting Lee for Christmas?"

"I'm getting her a surprise. What are you getting Tom?"

The question caught me off guard. "Tom? I don't usually get him anything."

"But isn't this year . . ." Sam danced a little tap dance, throwing his arms out. "*Special?*"

"Not. Really."

"Oh?" He stood there grinning like an idiot then kissed my cheek. "I hear Tom likes jazz and owns a herd of boring ties."

Late that afternoon, I gift-wrapped a Ramsey Lewis CD and a tie featuring Hogarth barristers in curly white wigs. I placed both wrapped presents in the basket under the Bell Bible, certain I'd never have occasion to take them out again.

THE DOORBELL RANG at exactly five thirty, and my skin flushed hot and cold. I opened the door, and for the first time since I'd known him, Tom Scott stepped into my home.

"Hello. How are you? This is lovely." The ebony eyes scanned the living room. "Really lovely. Reminds me of an English country cottage."

"Thank you." I closed the door behind him. "That's what I was aiming for. I used to ride up to York to shop at the outlets, and I'd always grab a few yards of material." Why in the world would he care about that?

He turned to me in wonder. "You sewed all this upholstery yourself?"

"God, no. I'm worthless with a needle. Louise did most of it, and Leona helped." Shoot. I should have lied.

"Well," he rocked back on his heels, snow drifting off his shoulders and bare head, "I am still impressed."

We stood silent for a minute. "Would you like a cup of coffee or something?" I croaked.

"No, thank you. There's still a light snow falling. It's beautiful, the first snow. Let's get out there and enjoy it. Have a walk around before the ceremony."

"Fine." I couldn't resist. I reached up and brushed a patch of snow off his hair. "Do you want a hat?"

"And miss another opportunity to have you run your fingers through my youthful locks? I don't think so."

I flung on my old down coat, wrapped his red scarf around my neck and we waded out into the first snow.

A lot of people had the same idea. The town streamed with unrecognizable children, bundled toe to crown in snowsuits, screaming with excitement, adults shivering behind, calling out not to run too far ahead, almost time for the tree lighting. We plunged into the center of the street, taking advantage of the scarcity of cars, and swam up and down the white-capped roads of our town, winding closer and closer to the fire station. Homes twinkled with Christmas lights. Trees, loaded with silver, red, gold, and green balls, framed window after window. A few front yards staged manger scenes, often side by side with Santa and the reindeer, as though he'd skidded in on his sleigh to lay a skateboard or an action figure by the Christ child.

"No tree yet, Flip?" He caught me as I stumbled over a mound of snow.

"I never get one before the fifteenth and out it goes January first."

"No fire hazards for you, eh? Smart lady."

I looked at him quick, to see if his face wore a touch of sarcasm, but no. He'd called me smart.

We walked on and it occurred to me something was missing—a wagging tail. "Where's Eli?"

"Arthritic hip. He hates the cold. I hope I'm in better shape in my dotage."

You're certainly in good shape now, I thought, admiring his profile on the sly.

The fire station loomed ahead, surrounded by a large crowd of mittened and scarfed citizens. Our mayor rubbed his mitts together and cheerfully introduced the master of ceremonies for the year, Reverend McKnight.

The Presbyterians managed a *whoop*, and the rest of the crowd applauded politely. Reverend McKnight, nose and cheeks as fiery as his hair, took the podium and adjusted the microphone to match his significant height. In the old days, he'd have made a fine champion log hurler.

"Mayor Cummings, fellow clergy, citizens, and visitors of Solace Glen." His voice matched his height. "Welcome, one and all, to the annual tree lighting ceremony! We will open with the youth choirs of our four town churches—Presbyterian, Methodist, Episcopalian, and Catholic—joining together to lead us in song. Please sing along. Sing!" He commanded, lifting both hands, wrists flapping upward.

A drove of preteens invaded the platform erected for the occasion. They banded as one unit and, under the direction of the high school music teacher, launched into a familiar round of seasonal tunes. We all sang and made sure Reverend McKnight saw our lips moving.

God Rest Ye Merry, Gentlemen. The Eggheads, with Pal, lolled against the ambulance, front end sticking out of the station garage, a wreath roped to the shiny grill.

Frosty the Snowman. Roland glared around at the crowd and snarled whenever somebody bumped into him. Garland, enjoying the kids on stage, sang every other word, often tripping up and twittering at herself. Ferrell T. and Hilda stood beside their parents, the son silent and sour, a replica of the old man, the daughter singing without the vaguest idea of the words.

You're All I Want for Christmas. Sam and Lee huddled together, giggling, knocking into each other's hips like thirteen year olds. Melody and Michael watched them, laughing.

Little Jack Frost Get Lost. Marlene stomped her big feet in the snow, impatient for the ceremony to end so she could run play cohostess with C.C.

Deck the Halls. C.C. and Leonard flanked Marlene, the two of them draped in dueling minks. C.C. kept glancing at her diamond watch while Leonard must have made three calls on his cell phone in the span of two minutes.

I Love the Winter Weather. "I love the win-ter wea-ther, so the two of us can get to-ge-ther." Screamin' Larry, a deadly glint in the eye, boomed the words at the top of his inebriated lungs, trying to catch C.C.'s attention, waving a bottle of Peppermint Schnapps in her direction.

Angels We Have Heard on High. I glanced over the crowd at the little house down the block. Through the treetops, I spied Miss Fizzi at her bedroom window, singing along with Tina and Margaret. Sally's pregnant silhouette swayed in the background as she pinned a finishing touch to Miss Fizzi's hair—a pink rose. Suggs probably brooded in his dank basement apartment, occasionally sticking a pin in a Santa voodoo doll.

And finally, *Winter Wonderland*. I sang, tapping my foot, getting into the bop of the rhythm, swinging my shoulders. "A beautiful sight, we're happy tonight, walking in a winter wonderland."

Tom sang, too, louder and louder, snapping his fingers like Frank Sinatra, "In the meadow, we can build a snowman . . ." A wide grin on his face melted into laughter at the sound of his own terrible, off-key voice. "And pretend that he is Parson Brown."

We belted it out. "He'll say, 'Are you married?' We'll say, 'No, man. But you can do the job when you're in town.' Later on . . ." A beautiful sight. We're happy tonight.

Reverend McKnight took the podium again. "Splendid! Splendid! I heard some . . . marvelous voices in the crowd. And now, the moment we've been waiting for, the name of the person who has the honor this year of turning on the lights of Christmas for the town of Solace Glen." He opened a small, folded piece of paper. "This year's honor goes to a woman in my own congregation. A quiet, thoughtful, behind-the-scenes kind of person who uses her kitchen to fill the mouths of those in need, unbeknownst to many, including, I believe, her own family. Our hats off to Mrs. Garland Bell."

I zoomed in on Garland. She'd gone white as the snow at her feet, hunching her shoulders to shrink smaller. Hands and arms around her pushed and shoved the poor woman onto the platform. Hilda and Ferrell T. gaped. And Roland. Her supportive spouse. His face went crimson, lips curved into a scythe.

Tom whispered, "That was the best kept secret in town, now shot to blazes. It should have stayed secret—for a very good reason."

At once, I understood why Tom hired Ferrell T. as his secretary. He'd done it as a favor to Garland. I stared at her, a shaking leaf in front of the crowd, in front of her husband. I remembered her kindness to Louise and my heart went out to her.

Garland tried to put on a brave face, but it was obvious she was scared to death. She'd been discovered. Now Roland could rant, "I'd be a rich man but for you flushing away the profit. You. You. You." Always somebody else hindering him from Greatness.

Garland reached the center podium, propelled by the gratitude of neighbors and strangers into the spotlight. Reverend McKnight heartily shook her hand and placed a mobile light switch in her palm.

"As Christ was the Light of the World, may you, kind lady, light the night and officially begin our holiday season in Solace Glen."

The crowd shouted huzzah, huzzah, with Screamin' Larry's huzzah's loudest of all, piercing the cold air. Garland lost sight of her horrible, depressing family and only heard the cheers of the audience, the encouragement of the Circle Ladies, felt the pats on her back from Mayor Cummings and her strong-willed pastor. She held high the 3×5 card Reverend McKnight pressed into her hand and read, haltingly, the words printed out for her. " 'With mortal hand, I light these symbols of Life, Spirit, Happiness, and Redemption. May we hold in our hearts the true fires that warm the human condition: love, joy, peace, gentleness, goodness, faith, meekness, and temperance.' "

With a nervous hand, Garland lifted the switch and clicked on the lever.

White, twinkling lights starred the streets of Solace Glen, the stores, the businesses, the courthouse, the fire station, the landscaping, the town council building, the telephone poles, and, of course, the official town tree, a newly cut blue spruce. It was beautiful, spectacular, wondrous—the snow providing the perfect postcard effect.

Not three seconds later, as we all *oooo*'ed and *ahhhh*'ed at the change in scenery, the fireworks went off. Only we never set off fireworks at Christmas.

We turned, faces east, drawn to the roar and boom, the flash and fire of a huge explosion in the distance, on the far hill, in the center of the O'Connell property. The Leonard and C.C. property.

Between sonic booms and fiery blasts, C.C. moaned, "No, no, no, no, no, no."

"My God! Is that your house?" Marlene saw her big role as party cohostess explode into thin air.

Leonard started punching numbers into the cell phone and struck out toward his car.

"Damn," Lee hissed in my ear. "I never got to see inside the house."

"Look at Larry." Sam gawked at the platform, the only one of the four of us who didn't know Screamin' Larry's special history of insanity and shady criminal inclinations.

Larry, inspired, leaped to the stage beside poor, pitiful Garland who still held the light switch clamped tight in her palm. She stared off in the distance, convinced, no doubt, that her innocent flick of a plastic lever caused the greatest fireball in Maryland since Antietam.

Larry pranced and danced around her. "This goes out to you-know-who!" he shouted, and started belting out "Smoke Gets in Your Eyes." He threw off his coat and earmuffs, boots and socks. He stripped off his shirt and tossed it into the crowd, and he would have given them his pants, squirming on his back to rip them off, but Reverend McKnight summoned the aid of the Eggheads and Pal. The four of them dragged Larry, kicking and screaming, off the stage and into the back of the ambulance for safe-keeping.

"If I didn't know better," reasoned Sam, shaking a raised index finger, "I'd say Larry had something to do with this explosion business."

We moved away from the fire station, firefighters jumping into action, half the crowd jumping into cars to go watch the action. The four of us drifted toward Lee's Historical Society, the little munchkin house crammed attic to cellar with books, a large, stuffed doll, and a good coffee machine. From that inviting vantage point, we could attempt to solve the puzzle of how Larry managed to pull this one off—a pinpoint of destruction, the cherished home of the town's least favorite new residents, and Larry's hated obsession.

"Yes." Sam bobbed his head, serious, and veered into

Lee, who snorted, hysterical, tugging at his coat. "I'm certain that brilliant disc jockey is behind all this fire in the sky."

With the two of them cavorting ahead of us, Tom and I fell into their parade. He linked his arm with mine and as we stumbled in the snow past hundreds of white lights, the serious, incisive, aristocratic attorney of Solace Glen sang and sang and sang.

CHAPTER 32

❈

T HE SATURDAY LUNCH crowd buzzed with talk of last
night's tree lighting explosion. A couple of new customers thought Garland really did set it off, but they didn't
know Garland. The silent majority, protective of one of their
own (no matter how criminally insane), agreed she had
nothing to do with it. Then they turned away and whispered knowingly that our very own Screamin' Larry had finally rigged it so C.C. got her just desserts for denting the
Big Orange Volkswagon Beetle. After all, years before when
Larry fell under suspicion for blowing up a gas line, the
town gratefully watched the disappearing tailpipe of an unsavory slumlord. Pending Officer Lukzay's energetic investigation, Larry walked free.

I smirked when I heard that. If Larry could blow up a
gas line and get away with it, one exploding house wasn't
going to put an end to his shenanigans, either, especially if

"investigated" by Officer Look-away. Fortunately, no one had been inside the Crosswell's house since the caterers mysteriously received two phone calls with conflicting timetables. So, no lives lost, only the presence of two unwanted new residents, C.C. and Leonard.

The Eggheads blabbed that Larry had confessed everything to them, but Pal, stopping by the Café for a rare store-bought sandwich, refuted their account saying Larry passed out once they got him in the back of the ambulance. His last words before oblivion were, " 'Something deep inside, cannot be denied.' "

Word was, C.C. and Leonard suffered well, mourning at the Willard in Washington, this particular dream of a country home smoldering in the melting snow of Frederick County. Rumors ran that they would sell the O'Connell property and start anew, farther out of town.

Hilda came around to take my order and proudly informed me she had a tutor lined up to help her pass geometry. She stood there, waiting, until I realized she expected a word of approval from me. So I gave her one.

"Good," I said. Approval probably counted as a rare commodity in her life with a father like Roland and a brother like Ferrell T. "How's your mother?" I slipped the pocket atlas back in my pocket.

"OK," she said slowly, eyes flashing in her father's direction. "She's OK."

Roland's gray eyes fixed on us, monitoring every movement. I lowered my voice. "Is she here today?"

"No. She didn't feel well this morning."

"You just told me she was OK."

"OK but for that." She turned on her heel and scampered into the kitchen, as much the scared rabbit as her mother. It was the first time Hilda had ever shied away from conversation and I knew why. Roland watched his daughter hurry away, his expression set firm and hard as an executioner's.

* * *

From the time I left Roland's Café on Saturday afternoon until Thursday night, I barely had a moment's rest. Everybody needed a house cleaning before the holidays, there were still people to cover on my Christmas list, and the church needed an extra pair of hands with the baking.

All the while, I didn't see or hear from Tom. Though impressed with my living room decor, the admiration apparently didn't cross over to me as a date. Immediately after coffee at Lee's, he'd walked me home and acted so much the gentleman, I was insulted.

Since I'd promised Miss Fizzi a Friday visit, I put aside some time Thursday night to study the Bell family tree. The basket came down from the top of the cabinet, hardly an ounce heavier with Tom's CD and tie wrapped up in the bottom. The CD could always fit in my stereo, but the tie wouldn't match anything I had to wear.

I opened the Bible and out sprang another generation.

Roland's daddy, Roland Bell, III, was born in 1899, ignored by his father and spoiled to death by his mother, Katrina. In 1930, at the start of the Great Depression, Roland, III, married Penelope Higgins. He was thirty-one, she a mere twenty. The following year, Leona was born. Ten years later, Penelope gave birth to a son, Roland Bell, IV.

A history of sweet women marrying spoiled, awful Bell men. What is it in a woman's background or character, I wondered, that leads her to make such a poor choice?

I thought of Garland who fit the family pattern perfectly—a sweet, passive, giving soul who made a terrible choice in a life mate. She actually had to sneak food to the needy because her husband wouldn't approve. For the first time, I didn't question that Roland beat her.

I remembered Roland's mother, Penelope. She was much like Garland, physically, spiritually, mentally. A woman who tried to emulate her husband against her nature. A mouse. A scared, cornered mouse who simply did the best she could, pouring herself into family.

Both Roland, III, and Penelope died in a plane crash in 1971 when I was a teenager. People whispered he'd been drinking, showing off and flying low down a country road, treating the expensive new Cessna like a toy. He lost control and the plane sailed into a huge oak tree. They were killed instantly. I attended the funeral with my parents who would die three years later, only my father wasn't drunk in an airplane. The other driver was drunk in an eighteen wheeler.

Nobody mourned her husband, but Penelope's name appeared later, etched in a special stained glass window with the words, IT IS MORE BLESSED TO GIVE THAN TO RECEIVE, a tribute paid for by her circle of friends, the Presbyterian Circle Ladies.

Beside Penelope's window was the window dedicated to my parents, Garrett Joseph and Julia Reed Paxton, with the words, HE MAKETH HIS SUN TO RISE ON THE EVIL AND THE GOOD, AND SENDETH RAIN ON THE JUST AND UNJUST.

I closed the Bell Bible. It had taken me a long time to comprehend the meaning of those words and why they were chosen. My parents were the kind of people who would have forgiven the driver who ended their lives and his, but I had always struggled with forgiving anyone I didn't know or love. I struggled with it every day, and it galled me yet that God allowed the sun to rise on a man like Roland Bell, and comforted me none that He sent rain to fall on both my parents' graves and the grave of the man who made me an orphan.

CHAPTER 33

✳

"JUST LOOK," WHINED Miss Fizzi. "I need a hair job so
bad even the Circle Ladies are talking ugly about me."

"Can't you get Sally to come here again?" I fluffed the
pillows behind her back. She'd moved from the bed to the
Victorian love seat by the bedroom window, sprained ankles
propped high on a stack of soft blankets. "If she can't do it, I
will."

"No, you won't, either." The bottom lip poked out.
"You'd make a mess of it. Sally's the only one can fix my
hair right, the way I like it. But would you call her for me?
It keeps slipping my mind."

"Sure I will." I hoped remembrance of things past
hadn't slipped her mind as well. "Miss Fizzi, I've been reading the Bell family Bible Leona left me."

"I'm so glad to hear it." She laid her good hand on my

arm. "Are you a New Testament person or an Old Testament person?"

"No, I don't mean the book. I mean the family part. The Bell family tree that's written out in the first couple of pages."

"Oh." She let that sink in.

"You're almost eighty-five, aren't you, Miss Fizzi?"

"Is it May already?" Her glance skimmed over my shoulder to the trees outside.

"No, you're still eighty-four." I pulled a carved chair from under a dressing table and sat down beside the love seat. "I want to ask you about some of the Bells. Are you up to a little trip down memory lane?"

"My favorite vacation spot." The blue eyes twinkled. She set her shoulders square, ready for the journey.

"OK, do you remember Florence Openheim Bell?"

"Florie?"

"No, not Florie." At least we were on the same track. "Her mother. She died in 1929."

Miss Fizzi's nose wrinkled. "Vaguely. I was just a child. I know she was real big on getting the Presbyterian Church started. The Bells were staunch Episcopalians. But Florence always hated her husband's church and as soon as old Mr. Bell died she banded with her mother-in-law, what was her name?"

"Gretal Stubing Bell."

"Yes! You see, another German Lutheran. Those two hated being Church of Englanders. Anyway, they got together with some others who wanted to go Presbyterian. Florence couldn't persuade them to go Lutheran, but she was satisfied with the end product and spent the last twenty-five years of her life the most devout member of that congregation. Quite a pillar of the community, upright and stern as a telephone pole, except where her son was concerned, Roland, Jr."

I brightened at testing a theory. "Did she spoil him?"

"Lord! You've never seen the like. Except Katrina, his wife. She was worse with her child."

"What about Florie?"

"Florie I remember better. My mother said Florie had all the promise of a beauty as a girl, but once she hit her early twenties, two or three years before her father died, something happened to her. Changed her. She got old overnight. It was rumored some man had forced himself on her and the experience left her scarred."

"Wouldn't her parents have had the man arrested?" Poor Florie. My theory that she'd been too picky flew out the door.

"Well, dear. Under certain circumstances, the family might have wanted to keep it hush-hush. People had more secrets in those days. He might have been a family friend or a relative. To make Florie's tragedy public would have ruined her chances for a husband, and she did have suitors."

"For all the good it did. She never married."

"No, she withdrew from the world, became a recluse, never left Florence's side. When Florence died, Florie depended wholly on her brother. She shot herself."

"Shot herself!"

Miss Fizzi brought her small hand to a cheek and shook her head sadly. "The family couldn't cover up that truth, even if they tried. She did it in front of the Presbyterian Church, ten years to the day after her mother died, as people came filing in for services."

"No!"

"It was in the papers." As if that made it true as the turning of the tide.

"What happened?"

"Well, they buried her, of course. What was left. Katrina had to handle everything because Florie's brother was so 'upset,' she said. But everybody knew he'd gone on a drinking binge in some bar. You know, that's how the family acquired half their lovely things. Roland, Jr., was a big rum-runner during prohibition. Heavy drinker, heavy gambler, heavy womanizer, and just plain heavy. He liked making money the easy way, the way of the devil."

So I'd pretty much nailed him, too. "Did Katrina have money of her own?"

"Oh, I'm sure she brought Roland, Jr., a handsome dowry when they married and, of course, she inherited her father's estate, a right well-off gentleman as I recall."

My guesses proved so on target that we could have been playing bingo, with Miss Fizzi calling out all the right numbers. "What about Roland's parents, Roland, III, and Penelope?"

She closed her eyes and smiled as if conjuring them up. "Penelope was a dear woman. Can't say the same for her husband."

I recounted what little I could of the two of them.

"You remember correctly, dear," Miss Fizzi agreed. "Penelope gave her heart out to all who knew her, and she was married to the cheapest, lowest backstabber in Maryland. Nothing she did suited him. He treated her like a dirty doormat. What little money he gave her, she sent to people in need or bought toys to spoil Roland. Even the clothes on Penelope's back were given to her by friends who couldn't stand to see the poor thing traipse around in rags. Roland, III, didn't care. He spent money only on himself and his precious namesake. And look how Roland turned out!"

Yes, I thought, *look how Roland turned out.*

"What I can't understand, Miss Fizzi, is why some perfectly normal, respectable women end up with such jerks. Why is that?"

"I don't know. *C'est l'amour.*" She knitted her brow.

"Garland. Penelope. Katrina. And for all we know, Florence, Gretal, Sara, back to Lucy Hanover Bell. Maybe all the Bell wives were sweet little doormats."

"Was she the first one? Lucy? Lucy Hanover Bell," she repeated thoughtfully. "I remember some story about a Lucy."

I ran through the female side of the Bells for Miss Fizzi: Lucy Hanover begat Lucinda who begat Lucy Bell who begat Lucinda Ann. And there it ended.

"What was that story Leona told me?" she asked herself. "It was definitely about a Lucy. Well!" She threw up her hands, the bad wrist mending nicely. "If I think of it, I'll let you know."

"You do that. You've already told me so much. Can I get you anything before I go?"

"No, thank you. Just don't forget to call Sally."

With a work day crammed full with cleanings, I kissed Miss Fizzi's cheek and hurried off, leaving her on the love seat, a book of religious poetry in her lap and the question on her lips, "What was that story? What was that story?"

THAT NIGHT, EXHAUSTED, but my mind teaming with Miss Fizzi's recollections, I opened the Bell family Bible and stared at the final two generations squeezed on the page: Leona Bell Jenner, born 1931, and her younger brother, Roland Bell, IV, born 1941; Ferrell T. Bell, born 1977, and his younger sister, Hilda Higgins Bell, born 1986.

A chill prickled my skin. No one had filled in Leona's date of death. Then it hit me—it was up to me. That was my job.

I took a fine point black ink pen and wrote in the month, day, and year of Leona's death, a complete life in the space of two inches. Jake Jenner's name rested beside hers, the life dates filled in, as if two tombstones from the Episcopal graveyard had chiseled their way into the pages of the Bell family Bible.

Leona and Jake married in 1952, and though no children blessed the union, they were an extremely happy couple, devoted to each other and their families. Leona tried her best to dote on Ferrell T. and Hilda, but as they grew up and their personalities emerged, the doting switched to Lee, the daughter of her husband's brother. When Lee lost Henry and Marie, Leona and Jake stepped right in, and no child could have wanted more for parents.

Leona was a blessing to everyone she met. Like her mother, Penelope, Leona Bell Jenner was a giver. She inherited none of the traits so rampant among the Bell males—selfishness, greed, immorality, cruelty—and spared herself the misery of marrying a copy of her father.

On the other hand, Roland fit the Bell mold exactly. He even found an exact replica of Penelope in Garland Day. They married in 1968; I remembered the wedding. Garland's parents blew the wad, hiring a big band and setting up tents with tables of fabulous foods. I heard more than one guest speculate on how long it would last, given Roland's stingy ways and his need to control the tiniest details in life.

"She'll be sorry," clucked one old lady. "And she's pretty enough to snag almost any man in the state."

"She's pretty, but she's got jelly for a backbone," replied another lady. "That's the attraction, you know. He needs to be in charge. She needs somebody to tell her what color checkbook to pick out."

Those two ladies knew their stuff. Garland must have had regrets, but no strength to act on them until she'd been beaten so low, she'd almost disappeared. Like the line of Bell brides before her, she doted on her two children, spoiling Ferrell T. beyond repair. Though, maybe hope hadn't run dry for Hilda.

As for Ferrell T., I knew the path he would take. Like his

daddy before him and his daddy's daddy and on and on, he would zero in on some wealthy girl with a low opinion of herself, some passive, sweet, yielding creature who would not understand, until too late, that when you boil it down, our choices are life-giving or life-threatening. And she would have made a terrible choice.

I covered the pages of the tree with my ten fingers, the tips touching every generation. So many lives, so many years, so many choices. They were all gone now, but for the last four names on the tree. No doubt Ferrell T. and Hilda would marry in the not-too-distant future, and I would be the one to pen new names onto the spreading branches.

I would be the one because Leona chose me.

I closed the Bible, looking forward to reading each little envelope, poem and scrap of paper scattered throughout its pages, happy at the thought of new discoveries. I hugged the precious treasure to my chest and knew I could never give it up to Roland. One day, though, one day I would hand it over to some other woman, maybe even Hilda, a woman who would appreciate these faceless scratches of ink that took shape, lived and breathed, loved, gave birth, suffered, and died, not only in my imagination, but here in this real place of ground and sky and seasons where she and I would someday rest, a stone above our heads telling nothing of our lives to those who passed by but a name, a date of birth, a death.

CHAPTER 34

※

CHRISTMAS SHOPPERS AND the usual crew packed the Café Saturday afternoon. I shoved bags of gifts under my table and collapsed in the chair to wait for Lee. That morning she'd hatched a plan that might douse Roland's obsession with the letters. I wasn't so sure.

I wrote a lunch order and opened my date book, frowning at the packed cleaning schedule ahead of me, the last job not until five o'clock Tuesday, Miss Fizzi's house.

Hilda swooped down and snatched up the order, not a word. Not herself. I squinted at the kitchen door window, hoping for a glimpse of Garland, but she was nowhere to be found. I closed the date book, crossed my legs, and sat back, my eyes skimming the room while I waited for Lee to show up.

Pieces of conversation rose and fell at each table like drifting confetti—amazement at Joey coming out of the coma; Was the accident a brake failure or brake tampering?; Who broke into my house and Lee's? Teenagers? (And in a murmur) Roland?; Who would want to hurt Miss Fizzi?; Would Screamin' Larry (as dearly hoped) get away with gutting C.C. and Leonard's happy home?

There sat Pal and the Eggheads, in between talk of Joey, voices rising in a crescendo over the best brand of kitty litter. There sat Larry, consuming his three lunches, looking all the world as guiltless and guileless as a choirboy on Christmas Eve. There sat Tina, Melody, and Margaret, debating all the latest gossip plus the questionable taste of Tina's new fashion purchase and the success of her latest diet. There sat Officer Lukzay, smirking at me over his menu as if he knew something I didn't. There sat Marlene, glum and morose, her artsy, rich friends vamoosed. She sighed heavily, more a groan than a sigh, distracting the Eggheads.

"Hey, Marlene," one of them yelled, "where's C.C. these days? Conferring with her decorator?" The two sniggered into their shirtsleeves and Larry let out a little whoop.

Marlene huffed and clanged a spoon around her teacup, eyes boring into Larry. She recognized his handiwork when she saw it, but bowed to the protective, impenetrable veil the community wrapped around their vigilante DJ hero.

"No plans to rebuild? Nice property. Handsome view. Gonna sell the property, are they?"

"You can ask Mr. Crosswell yourselves, morons. Here he comes now." Marlene sat up straight and brightened at the sight of her legal Galahad swooping into the Café.

Leonard, ever on his way to something more important, didn't bother to take his coat off when he spotted Marlene and scraped a chair up to hers. She leaned eagerly toward him. I could practically see the dollar signs in her pupils.

Leonard, all business, got right down to it. He did all the talking in a discreet, high-priced attorney's voice. Marlene's face fell after the first thirty seconds and the dollar signs in her eyes visibly faded. She stuttered out a question or two and at the end of Leonard's speech, barely five minutes, her whole body seemed to shrink. I saw Leonard pat her hand paternally and pull out a fat envelope that he presented to her matter-of-factly, probably a bill.

As our Mr. Crosswell rose to leave, one of the Eggheads found the courage, based solely on incurable curiosity, to ask him if he and C.C. were, in fact, going to rebuild the house.

"No," he answered curtly, peering intently over his spectacles on the long, fox snout. "The house is history. The property will be sold."

Too stupid to realize he was pressing his luck, the other Egghead piped up, "You lose everything? Even your expensive Civil War collection?"

Leonard came to a halt midstep and slowly rotated, glaring at the entire room. You could practically hear his teeth grind when he said, "Yes. Everything. The collection was . . . irreplaceable. But I *will* start over." The black, canine eyes briefly caught hold of mine, and he disappeared.

A minute later, a whiff of cold air blew in and I turned to see Tom in the entranceway, stomping ice and dirt off his boots. He wasn't anywhere near, yet a rush like warm, mulled wine raced through my limbs and left me nearly drunk. He glanced up just as I felt the need to peel off a layer of clothes, and appeared at the table in time to help pull one arm out of a coat sleeve.

"Thanks."

He plopped into the chair beside me. "Always willing to help a lady undress."

I hadn't heard from him in a week and trying to read the man was wearing me out. "Well. What have you been up to, counselor?"

Roland slid behind the register close by, helping himself to a customer's money. Tom removed his coat, leaned forward, and whispered, "There's something you need to know."

"There's something you need to know, too. Lee is going to give Roland the letters."

He cocked a brow. "Oh?"

"Not the originals. She's keeping those at the Historical Society as a Civil War exhibit because they really were written by J.E.B. Stuart. But she ran off some copies this morning and she's bringing them in any minute. Her theory is once Roland reads the letters himself and sees what they're all about, he'll lose interest and we won't hear anymore lawsuit talk. Also," I peered beyond his shoulder into the street, "we're in luck today. Leonard Crosswell made his exit a minute ago."

Tom rubbed two index fingers down the bridge of his nose, thinking. Finally he said, "Good. That's a smart thing to do. Stem the tide and quell the fire. I suggest you do the same with the Bell Bible."

I scowled at him. "What are you talking about?"

"Lee has a point. Give Roland what he wants—or at least a modified version thereof—and his fire will burn itself out. Give him a copy of any personal writings, family memorabilia, whatever is in that Bible. Let him have it." He leaned back, problem solved. "Why do you look so shocked?"

I shook my head. "No."

"No? No what? You don't want him to even have a copy of what's in that Bible?"

"No, *Leona* didn't want him to have what's in that Bible. And frankly, I'm not so sure Lee should hand him copies of the Stuart letters because no male in the Bell family has ever seen them and there must be a very good reason for that."

"Perhaps at one time there was. But, Flip, we're talking about something that occurred over a hundred and thirty years ago. What possible difference could it make now?"

My stomach tightened. "I don't know. I don't know." He was making me so mad and disoriented, I turned on him abruptly, "What are you doing about Miss Fizzi?"

"Miss Fizzi?"

I hissed, one eye on Roland. "About you-know-who's attack on her! What the hell have you been doing about it?"

He dropped his voice, keeping the tone quiet and soothing as though speaking to a mental patient. "We still don't know if you-know-who is the culprit. My investigator had a look at the site but could draw no conclusions, and Suggs has been less than cooperative. No surprise there. I might also add, Pal said that when he went to the Frederick garage to check on the Cadillac, they told him it had been ordered to the scrap yard, apparently a day or two after Miss Fizzi's fall."

My glance flew to Officer Lukzay. That's what he knew that I didn't.

Tom continued. "But . . . as a precaution, I went to Garland and told her everything. I laid it on the line, told her Roland was a prime suspect and may need some kind of help soon or he'd end up in jail. I gave her a week to come up with viable suggestions."

"You're kidding." The idea of the rabbit snaring the wolf didn't cut it.

"No, I'm not kidding and you'd be surprised at Garland's good sense."

"What did she come up with?"

"Family counseling with Reverend McKnight. He came for Sunday supper at their home two weeks ago with Hilda and Ferrell T. present. It didn't go well. Roland was in complete denial."

The image crossed my mind: a hulking six foot six Reverend McKnight hovering over Roland, the minister's fiery hair on end.

Our foreheads practically touched now as we whispered

behind Roland's back. Tom leaned even closer. "What I meant when I said there is something you need to know is this—that first Sunday of family counseling was the last. The Friday after McKnight came to the house, Garland made headline news at the tree lighting ceremony for giving away Roland's 'hard-fought earnings.' He got her home and beat her to a pulp."

"Oh, my God." I spied Hilda across the room, face drawn, concentrating hard on work. "That's why Hilda's been acting the way she has. She told me her mother wasn't feeling well."

"She doesn't even know where her mother is. Garland did what I thought she'd never do. She left Roland a week ago."

Like a horror movie, the memory of Roland twisting my arm reeled through my mind. If he'd beat the hell out of his wife, why not twist the arm of a woman he really hated?

"How do you know all this?"

"Garland called me from a safe house in Baltimore. One of the Circle Ladies drove her down there."

"God bless her whoever she is. Does McKnight know?"

"Not yet, but I intend to tell him."

So. The answer seemed simple now. "When's Roland going to be arrested?"

Tom removed his glasses and rubbed dark eyes. "He's not. Garland won't cooperate."

My face fell. "Don't tell me that."

"She won't be persuaded. Believe me, I tried. She's going to let me know in a day or two what she wants done."

"What she wants *done*? Before or after the body count?" Hilda dropped off my lunch order and spun away. "And what about her? If he'd beat his wife, he'll go after the daughter soon enough."

"Don't you think I'm worried about that, too?!" All pretense at whispering fell away. Roland turned to stare at us.

Just then, a singsong voice chimed, "Oh, Roooolaaaand."

Roland's eyes swiveled to lock on Lee. "What the hell do you want?"

"I have something for you," she cooed. "Copies of the letters Leona left me. You know, the letters you've been so anxious to study for their historical value."

She stood there, a sticky sweet expression on her face and Sam behind her back. The hard glaze of Roland's demeanor melted into confusion. He jumped back when Lee offered him the papers.

"If you don't believe they're the same as the originals, feel free to check it out yourself down at Tom's office sometime—neutral territory."

"What is this?" he mumbled. "What are you trying to pull?"

"Nothing," Lee spoke loud enough for all to hear. "Absolutely nothing. This is no trick. These are bona fide copies of the Stuart letters."

"Read 'em, Roland!" Neither one of the Eggheads could keep still.

"Whudothey say? Whudothey say?"

I couldn't stand it. "Lee," I pleaded, "don't let *him* read them out loud, for God's sake!" The image I bore at that moment was of one of my mothers, Leona, stretched out on the floor of the majestic Bell house, telling me where to find these beautiful, almost sacred letters.

The second Lee caught the look in my eyes, she knew. She dropped the cavalier style and faced the audience who gathered round. This was their history, too. It was time to gift the letters to the town of Solace Glen.

Sam took a seat next to Tom and me. Lee waited for people to quiet down. Everyone opened their ears.

"Some time ago, as you all know, my Aunt Leona asked Flip to retrieve some letters for me that she said were written by General J.E.B. Stuart. I didn't think that possible, since all three letters were signed 'K.G.S.' Sam here helped me find an expert at the Smithsonian who examined the contents and paper. All the tests checked out."

Somebody called out, "If Stuart wrote them, what does 'K.G.S.' mean?"

"Knight of the Golden Spurs." Lee held up one of the copies and pointed to the signature. "Stuart used to sign his personal letters like that after an unknown lady from Baltimore sent him a pair of golden spurs. Pretty romantic, huh?"

"Who's the woman he wrote to, Lee? Did the expert know who she was? Was she from Solace Glen?"

"Was she a Bell?" snapped Roland. "Because if so, I'm filing suit tomorrow. *Was* she a Bell?"

Lee held a rein on her temper; I don't know how. "No clue. This is the only known correspondence between the two of them, no mention of her to his wife or friends—big surprise. No mention of her by anyone else associated with Stuart at the time. I'm not familiar with the name, and the expert said we'd have to research local records of births, deaths, marriages, church membership, that sort of thing, to find her. It would take an awful lot of time." She shook her head at the letters and sighed. "I don't know if it's that important we know who she was."

"Not important?!" I had to throw in my two cents. If Lee chose to divulge the Bell women's secret, we ought to at least try to find all the pieces of the puzzle. "Of course it's important. Leona said so herself. These letters make Solace Glen important. Historical. Here is a famous Civil War general—dashing, brave, known for his daring cavalry escapades, raids into enemy territory, unbelievable escapes. The love his men had for him. The plumed hat. His reputation as a ladies' man."

Lee stuck a hand on her hip. "I think you should run the Historical Society."

"Seriously." I addressed my comments to everyone.

"Find out who that woman was and we find out why, for more than one hundred and thirty-five years, the Bell family women passed these letters down to one another and shared the secret with *no one*. How is that not important?"

Forehead creased, Lee picked up the first letter and began to read. No one in the room made a sound.

September 9, 1862

Dearest Ellby,

Only two days ago I first set eyes upon you, strolling arm and arm with your friend, Miss Marsh, down the main thoroughfare of Urbana. I admit to you now, I had never seen a face so stirring. If the wind had not blown your bonnet off at that precise moment, I do not doubt that some other twist of fate would have conspired to join us together. Yet, I despaired, for no sooner had I presented you with the miscreant blue bonnet than duty called, and I was forced to part without introduction, carrying with me only the memory of your russet hair, your sunlit face, and your thanks. I thought never to see you again. How kind the Fates in our regard! The very next night, at the ball I gave in the female academy in Urbana, imagine my unbounded delight when your cousin presented you and you left his arm and took mine for the Virginia reel! I regret my little party was twice interrupted, once by a skirmish at the pickets, and again, by the wounded carried into the vacant academy rooms at dawn. You and the other ladies in your white dresses were only a little less than angels, administering to the poor fallen.

As Blackford, my adjutant, says, "One hour's acquaintance in war times goes further toward good feeling and acquaintanceship than months in the dull, slow

period of peace." Could I have imagined an attach-
ment and admiration so instantaneous and yet so deep,
the poetry I deign to write would have taken quite a
different turn in my youth. I dare say, I would have
given up all early attempts entirely, knowing pure po-
etry walked this earth, and one day I would have the
joy of dancing the Virginia reel with her.

Think me not a trifling man, Ellby, given to rhap-
sodies at the sight of any pretty face. I am, I assure
you, in earnest. Yet time flows in a narrow stream for
us, condensed to boundaries too paltry and contained.

Allow me to call on you and your cousin tomorrow
in Solace Glen.

I lay my heart before you. Only you, dear Ellby,
know the weight of it.

Your Most Obedient Servant,
K.G.S.

Lee handed me the second letter to read out loud.

September 11, 1862

My Darling Ellby

When we stand before our God, we can but confess
that among our many tiny sins, our great weakness was
brought about by overpowering human emotion, for
nothing base passed between us. I know this as I know
my life and your heart. You remain a Lady of Esteem
and I, your worshipful admirer.

We both painfully acknowledged the paths of our
circumstances. My road is clear and laid out before
me, a road I must advance upon, regardless of per-
sonal complaints or satisfactions. I take no satisfac-
tion, though, Ellby, in leaving you. I know not when or

if we shall meet again, except the sureness of our facing the same Maker and answering identical issues.

Know that I loved you, a deep, profound, and sorrowful love that tore the firmaments and ripped the recesses of my being.

I had known only faithfulness before you. Now I meet in combat, not only a mortal enemy on the field of battle, but the ghostly foe of my Immortal Soul, and each day and hour I must face the contest.

Will we, dearest Ellby, look upon our time and denounce it or cherish it? Will you confine the memory of me to the chamber in your being designed for guilt and regret? Of that, I pray not. For you will hold that kind place in my heart where only the most beautiful things of this earth reside. But you, dearest Ellby, will shame all other beauties and shine—the brightest jewel in my crown of remembrance!

> *Your Most Obedient Servant,*
> *K.G.S.*

Lee ironed the last letter with the palm of her hand and read.

November 1862

Dearest Ellby,

I thought my last letter to you before Sharpsburg would be the final correspondence between us, but I find myself turning urgently to one who knows my heart. Ellby, I fear the Almighty is a harsh judge, indeed, to punish mortal man in such a terrifying fashion as He has admonished this lowly servant. Dearest Ellby, my firstborn, my darling little daughter, Flora, has been taken from us. I could not, because of duty to country and to

*all our mothers and children, leave my post on the field
of battle and hasten to the mother of my child to comfort her. Nor could I share in that grief in the final
hours when the angels transported our little one, but
five years old in September, to the heaven where she belonged.*

*I have a son, little more than two years of age, and I
pray my wife and I will have the blessing of more children, but the loss of this one goes hard with me, Ellby. I
cannot help but believe this is a punishment for our
weakness and I have sought forgiveness at every turn.*

*I write to tell you of this affliction and to ask your
own forgiveness for a sin I know I am solely responsible for, though you have protested that account. You
need not write in response. What words leave your lips
in silent prayer will reach the One who requires such
an answer. Pray for me and keep this repentant soul
alive in that kind chamber of your heart where the
beautiful things of this earth reside and are remembered for their honor and their worth.*

> *In Humble Gratitude, Your Obedient Servant,*
> *K.G.S.*

Lee folded the copies of the three letters together and
handed them to Roland.

"You're right," she said to me quietly. "It is important to
know."

WHEN I ARRIVED home that night after a long afternoon
of work, two messages blinked on my answering machine.
The first voice was Tom's, assuring me we'd have no further trouble with Marlene and adding, wouldn't it be a
great idea to let Garland and Hilda stay in Louise's house?

I grinned and clapped my hands together at his brilliance. Then I heard the second voice.

"Flip Paxton, Keeper of the Flame. Don't think this stuff Lee did with the letters will satisfy me. So what if the Bell women saved a bunch of stupid love letters written to some fool friend of theirs. You have a Bell original. An original. J.E.B. Stuart and his soppy love drool can go to blazes for all I care." He added in a loud farewell, "Don't you forget me at Christmas time, you hear? Because I won't forget *you*."

CHAPTER 35

※

I WORKED SO hard the next three days that Roland's bla-
tant threats hung in the shadows, but on Tuesday, with
Christmas fast approaching, the message he left on my machine replayed in my head louder and louder. By the time I
arrived at Miss Fizzi's house late Tuesday, my vacuum and I
had covered almost every floor in Solace Glen, and Roland's
voice traveled with us. Three days of bleach and ammonia
clung so tight to my skin that the aroma of Miss Fizzi's fresh
lemon chess pie could barely get through. I stood over a hot
pie and breathed deep, the next best thing to a spa treatment.

The road to recovery neared the end for Miss Fizzi, and
she hobbled around her heavy, dark antiques with newly
minted hair, sprayed to the hilt with stuff the EPA probably
banned years ago. With Sally, all was fair in love and hair.
Miss Fizzi's bright pink lips dipped into a glass of sherry
on the kitchen counter now and again.

"I baked one specially for you," she crowed, proud as a peacock.

"You are a wonder." I set my carryall and vacuum on the kitchen floor. "You look ready to run the Preakness."

"Less than five months away! I'll be there with bells on!" She twittered and sipped at the sherry. "Flip." A sparkle lit her beautiful eyes. "You'll be happy to hear I remembered something."

"That is news. What did you remember?"

"I remembered the story Leona told me. The Lucy story."

"You did?" She had my full attention.

Miss Fizzi backed into a Windsor chair, so old its mahogany skin peeled, and propped her healing feet on a stool. "Years ago, Leona and I got hooked on that game, Clue. We couldn't get enough of it. Played every spare moment until we got hooked on Spades."

"Uh-huh." What all this had to do with the Lucy story, I could only guess.

"One rainy afternoon, we were going at it, guessing how the character got killed off, with what instrument, in what room, and we got on the subject of secrets."

"Secrets."

"Yes. And we agreed to tell each other our most private secret. I went first." She blushed. "I told her I was in love with Jake, had been for years, but if I couldn't have him, I was glad she was the one."

"When was this?" It touched me to think of Miss Fizzi carrying a torch for Jake all those years.

"Oh, I fell in love with him in my teens, even though he was a couple of years younger. I waited and waited, through my twenties, into my thirties. We maintained a lovely friendship, but one day he came back home from his traveling job, was sitting in church, and he spied Leona, about twenty years old. The thing hit him like a tidal wave. They married within a year."

"Goodness. And you never met anyone else who interested you?"

She sighed sweetly. "No one could compare to Jake."

"Was Leona surprised when you told her?"

"Not at all. Knew all the time, she said. Big deal. Do you want him now, she asked me, because the fool gave me a bird dog for my birthday. They named him Ruckus because that's what Leona raised with Jake. She'd wanted a diamond brooch."

I remembered Ruckus, a completely untrainable Springer. Leona used to hurl her fine china at him. "And what was Leona's secret?"

Miss Fizzi's robin's egg eyes widened. "An illegitimate child."

My head jerked back in surprise. "Leona had a baby before she married Jake?"

"Oh, no, dear heart! Bite your tongue! No." She shook her white head emphatically. "It wasn't Leona's baby. It was Lucy's baby."

I drew closer. "Lucy who?"

"Lucy Bell . . ."

"Paca Tanner."

"Yes," she bobbed her head. "That's right. You remember from the Bible. And the man was . . ."

"J.E.B. Stuart." The Knight of the Golden Spurs writing to Ellby. Lucy Bell. L.B.

She beamed at me. "Isn't that something? And all those years later, the Bell women still kept the secret, handing down letters, she said, that proved the affair."

"That's right. Leona's letters. She left them to Lee." I shook my head. "What I don't understand is why keep the secret for so long, and in such a way, with only the women in the family knowing."

"Consider the Bell men, Flip." We exchanged a knowing glance. "You know, only very recently has illegitimacy taken on a kind of vogue. I find it deeply disturbing and bizarre," she fluttered a little hand up to her heart. "But during the Civil War, such a circumstance warranted not only the ruination of a woman, but her entire family. Lucy Bell apparently made some excuse and left town before the birth. She gave up the child to friends for adoption."

I pictured the whole family tree in my mind with the empty parentheses under Lucinda Ann's name—the baby Lucy gave up. "Lucy must have confided in Gretal and Gretal's daughter-in-law, Florence Openheim. It was Florence who got the letters when Lucy passed away in 1912."

"And they've been handed down by the Bell women ever since."

"That's right." So Florence inherited the secret and passed it on to Katrina Chapelle Bell who gave the letters to Penelope who gave them to Leona who left them to Lee. "But I still don't understand why Penelope and Leona kept the secret all those years later."

Miss Fizzi shook her head. "I don't know, either, but what an unusual testament to the love Lucy inspired. Gretal and Florence must have held her in very high esteem. As did, of course, the General."

"Who never knew he'd fathered a child," I said sadly, thinking of his letters to Lucy and the loss of his little daughter, Flora. I'd read that he did have another child with his wife, a girl, less than a year after Flora's death, and five months later he was wounded at Yellow Tavern and died. "Lucy didn't tell him. He never knew."

"She didn't tell the child either."

I wrinkled my forehead. "I guess not since she gave the baby up for adoption."

"But the girl knew Lucy was her mother."

I stared at her. "How do you know that?"

"From the letter she wrote Lucy. The granddaughter wrote one, too, I remember."

"What letters?"

"The letters Lee has. I have no idea what is in them. Didn't you read them?"

I gaped at her. "Lee only has three letters, all from Stuart to Lucy."

Her face went quizzical and one shoulder lifted. "I know Leona said something about the girl writing Lucy after she married and had a baby, then the baby grew up and wrote Lucy when she married." Miss Fizzi concentrated, tapping a finger against pursed lips. "Maybe those two letters are in the big house somewhere. Where would Leona have put them?"

The answer knocked me erect. I flew out of the room and into the car so fast, Miss Fizzi must have wondered what came over me and if I ever intended to come back for the carryall and vacuum left lying on her kitchen floor.

IT DIDN'T HIT me until I saw his face that I'd run right through an open front door and into a house that had been locked tight. Ferrell T. stood in the center of my kitchen, the Bell family Bible in his hands. The basket of Spanish moss lay on the floor, Tom's gifts spilling out.

I screeched to a halt in the doorway, breathing fast, eyes fastened on the Bible. "What do you think you're doing, Ferrell T.?" Through my mind raced four things: Joey's car crash, my torn-apart house, Lee's break-in, Miss Fizzi's horrible fall. Was Ferrell T. really capable of such crimes?

"What's it look like? I'm collecting Daddy's Christmas present a little early, that's all." He stuck the Bible possessively under one arm and slid his hand into a pocket, a defiant grin spreading across his face.

He might just as well have ignited the pages for the effect that small gesture had on me. The names of every Bell woman swept through my being, but the most important names were the two I did not know. The letters they left behind lay almost within reach, under the arm of a Bell man not five feet away. "Over my dead body."

He sniggered. "That's your choice, Miss Paxton."

From his pocket, I caught the gleam of something shiny and instantly grasped Ferrell T.'s capabilities. His father's son, after all.

"Roland put you up to this."

"Like I can't do anything on my own. Guess again." He snapped the blade open with the flick of a wrist and jabbed the knife in the air, close to my throat.

I flinched, surprised. "You wouldn't dare."

"Call my bluff, then. I'd just as soon carve you up as a Christmas turkey to keep what's rightfully mine."

One choice causes one domino to fall; another choice downs them all. My choices lined up against me in a wall so tall and thick, I had no inkling which one to knock over.

Ferrell T. stood there, grinning at my indecision. I took so long, he snapped the blade closed again. "Jeez. I don't have all night." He slid the knife back into his pocket, convinced I posed no threat. "Anyway, it's not like you don't have another Bible."

"But I don't have a *family* Bible, Ferrell T. Don't you get it? Leona left that Bible to me so I'd feel like I had a family. She left it to *me*. Not Roland. And certainly not to you."

He huffed. "This isn't your family. It's mine. It's *my* inheritance, like the house and the car and the letters—everything. It was all supposed to go to *me*. I'm the rightful heir, and if I can't get it all back, I can at least get this back." He turned toward the door.

"No!" I sprang forward and wrenched the Bible out of his arm. Dried flower petals, scraps of paper, small envelopes floated to the floor.

Ferrell T. whirled around, grabbed the book and jerked it away. "It's mine!"

"No, it's not!" I lunged for the Bible, but a fist struck me dead center in the chest. I reeled backward onto the floor, breathless.

Two arms scized my waist from behind, yanked me off the floor and stayed securely coiled around my body. A large form flashed past and in one sudden motion, Ferrell T. lay stretched out, unconscious.

"When he comes to, I hope he gives me a crack at the other cheek." Reverend McKnight bent over his parishioner, wiping his huge paws.

"Don't soil your knuckles again." Tom slowly uncoiled his arms from around my waist and led me to a chair. "Are you all right?"

I nodded, unable to speak, gasping for the breath Ferrell T. knocked out.

Anguish drenched Tom's face. "I wish we'd gotten here sooner."

Ferrell T. groaned and rolled to a sitting position.

"If you thought I lit into your father a couple of weeks ago, wait'll you hear what's in store for *you*, heathen." Reverend McKnight plucked Ferrell T. off the floor as he might a stringed puppet. "You're coming with me and we're going to straighten you out down at the Frederick police station. And by God, if you don't get in line and make a good confessional, you'll not see the light of day till the next millennium."

Ferrell T. staggered out of my house at last, his minister shepherding the path ahead.

My lungs gradually took in air. "How did you know to come?"

"We dropped by to check on Miss Fizzi and found her with the two police officers you and Lee talked to. They'd traced the order to scrap Pal's car to Lukzay who admitted to doing a favor for 'the Bell boy.' When they couldn't find Ferrell T. at home or at my office, they headed to Miss Fizzi's for safety's sake. She told us her only visitor today was you and that you'd bolted away after discovering something about the Bell's. So we came here, thank God, with the police right behind us." Tom pulled up a chair and sank into it. "Also, Garland called Sunday, and yesterday McKnight and I picked her up in Baltimore. She's at Louise's house with Hilda. All Roland and Ferrell T. know is that Garland left and Hilda disappeared last night."

I rubbed my chest. "So they're safe. I hope they stay that way."

He placed a gentle hand on my knee, but every muscle in his face tensed. "If I'd acted sooner, maybe I could have kept you safe, too."

I wanted to take a fingertip and iron out each tight place along his jaw. "I don't know that he would have killed me, but I know now he's capable of it, Tom. And all he wanted was this."

I reached down and picked up the Bell family Bible. Tom bent to retrieve the dried flower petals, scraps of paper, and small, yellowed envelopes scattered across the kitchen floor. He placed the stack on the table before me and I lightly raked three fingers across the pile, spreading everything out. Two envelopes addressed to Lucy Bell Paca Tanner jumped out at me. I opened the first one, overwhelmed with curiosity, and began to read.

September 2, 1893

Dear Madam:

Although I have always known, since ever I could remember, that my kind parents adopted me, only of late did my mother reveal to me the name of that lady who showed me into this world, and through her own unhappy circumstance made my parents' situation most happy and complete. I know my mother, an old friend of

*yours from childhood, promised you from my birth that
she would send news of my upbringing and did faith-
fully record my modest achievements, sending you brief
accounts over the years. I know, too, that you destroyed
those letters, having told my mother you would do so.*

   *I have set before me two tasks, the reasons I write to
you today. One is quite painful for us both. My mother,
your dear friend, died not one week ago, and it was
while she lay at death's door that she divulged your
name and implored me to send this note. The second
task is one of great joy and I only wish my mother had
lived but a little longer and she could have shared in it,
also. She, and you, have a granddaughter.*

   *My fondest wish is that this child grow to be the
adoring mother my own sweet mother was to me, and I
have you to thank for placing me in such capable and
loving arms.*

   I hope, Madam, this letter finds you in good health.

I am, most sincerely yours,
Flora Ellby Stockard

Flora Ellby. Flora, for Stuart's dead child. Ellby, for the
secret name he gave Lucy. Lucy herself must have named
the baby before handing her to the friend to raise. The
poignancy of it brought me close to tears.

   The second envelope, postmarked from Baltimore, addressed Lucy in a different hand. The date at the top of the
letter was only a few days before Lucy's death.

March 10, 1912

Dear Grandmother,

*I hope you do not mind me calling you Grandmother.
Mother assures me you will not. I only recently learned*

that I have a living grandparent. Mother explained everything, now that she says I am old enough to understand and will be marrying in a few weeks.

The purpose of my note is to invite you to my wedding. You would not have to reveal the relation if you do not wish to. We could simply refer to you as Mrs. Tanner from Solace Glen. Your presence would mean the world to both me and Mother, and I am quite positive my deceased grandmother, your good friend, would smile down from Heaven at the sight of us, all three, reunited. The wedding date is May 12 of this year. Please try to come. We both look forward to your response, as does my fiancé, Mr. George Reed.

> *Lovingly, Your Granddaughter,*
> *Lila Ann Stockard*

My heart leapt into my throat. I knew little of my father's family, even less of my mother's background. But I did know the names of her parents, my grandparents.

George and Lila Ann Reed.

CHAPTER 36

✵

S HE RESPECTED THE decisions and feelings of the
women of her past; she respected the right of another
generation to know the truth. To accomplish both ends,
Leona bound Lee and me together, each with a part of the
secret, each with different pieces of the puzzle. Without
Lee's letters, I never would have grasped the whole picture. Without the letters in the Bell Bible, Lee may never
have discovered the identity of Ellby, and I would never
have known my true heritage.

> *I leave this Bible in your care, Flip, knowing your deep
> appreciation of books, your love of this community
> and its history, and your own aloneness since the loss,
> so many years ago, of your family. May this old book,
> with its words of wisdom and inspiration, its pages*

filled with Bell family mementos, give you what I believe you long for most.

Leona Bell Jenner indeed knew what I longed for most. Family was her gift to me.

Leona knew, and her mother Penelope knew. It was Penelope who put it together, who befriended my mother, Julia Reed Paxton, when she arrived in Solace Glen as a twenty-four-year-old bride in 1948. She and Leona probably even met my grandmother, Lila Ann, before she died in Baltimore ten years later. Penelope harbored the letters, holding the secret dear, not for the sake of Lucy Bell, resting in peace, reunited at last with daughter and granddaughter, but for the sake of my mother who, if the truth were known, would have been stigmatized even then, most especially by the Bell men, for sins repented of long ago.

The sins of the mother, equal to, if not more grievous, than the sins of the father.

CHAPTER 37

✻

CHRISTMAS EVE'S DUSK glowed as pink and rosy as Miss Fizzi's favorite lipstick. I dropped off her present, the botanical pie dish, and drove to Louise's house to deliver a special gift: the painted plant pot with a fresh poinsettia planted inside. Louise could no longer enjoy it, but Garland and Hilda would appreciate a touch of brightness in their lives this Christmas, especially after the sickening revelation of Ferrell T.'s evil acts. Following a confession that he later recanted, he sat in the Frederick County jail awaiting trial on brake tampering, breaking and entering, burglary, and the attempted murder of Miss Fizzi.

Garland and Hilda invited me in and we shared a cup of eggnog. Garland exercised her funny bone, laughing in a free and easy manner that lit her face bright and reminded me of her wedding and the old ladies talking about how pretty she was. Even Hilda relaxed, comfortable in the new

setting of Louise's modest rancher, so different from
the crowded, cramped Victorian house she'd grown up in,
crammed with things, things, things.

Before I departed, Tina, Melody and Michael, Margaret,
and Sally converged on the house bearing gifts and pure-
from-the-heart laughter. I closed Louise's door behind me,
Garland and Hilda chattering with their guests about silly,
happy, mundane things, scrounging through suitcases to
get at proper clothes for the evening church service.

Tom, Sam, Lee, and I devoured the whole enchilada for
Christmas Eve—twenty minutes at each of the four Solace
Glen church services—Catholic for Sam, Methodist for
Tom, Episcopalian for Lee, and Presbyterian for me. We
began our rounds at the tiny dollhouse of St. Francis of As-
sisi of Solace Glen, where from five o'clock to five-twenty,
we knelt and crossed ourselves and got mixed up between
prayer books and hymnals. Then we ran two blocks down
the street to Tom's Methodist Church and listened to
Reverend Grayson deliver a children's sermon that nobody
could hear for all the screeching and wailing and shouting
of the children. After that, we whisked into the Episcopal
Church and bobbed like corks in the water up and down on
our knees again. Finally, we capped the marathon off with
the Presbyterian service, my favorite part, where the whole
congregation lit candles, held them skyward, and sang
"Silent Night, Holy Night" until every eye watered.

"I'm feeling extremely forgiven," declared Sam as we
walked arm and arm back to Lee's house to get good and
snockered on hot spiced wine. "If I keeled over dead right
now, I might actually find myself in heaven."

"Dream on," Lee jabbed his chest. "It'll take more than
an hour and a half of Christmas carols to usher you through
the pearly gates."

Lee had decorated the Historical Society to beat
the band—greenery, flowers, red apples and cranberries,

popcorn, lemons. Even Plain Jane wore a festive air, her tomato red hair sporting a halo of baby's breath, a pair of papier-mâché wings crowning her shoulders.

"She's my guardian angel." Lee tweaked a wing. "Isn't she pretty?"

We dipped into the wine and settled around the old pine table to listen to Tom and Sam trade lawyer jokes, but the joking stopped when I drew the two yellowed envelopes out of my pocket that completed Lucy's saga and read them. Lee started to cry.

"I can't believe it." She stumbled to the kitchen sink to wipe her eyes on a dish towel. "Those women."

"So what all this boils down to is," Sam set his wine cup on the table and pointed at me, "you are related to Roland Bell."

"Thank you, Sam," I said. "Thank you so very, very much and Merry Christmas."

Tom sat quietly, a bemused expression across his face.

"Merry Christmas to you, too," said Sam, popping up. "But it won't really be merry until I present Miss Jenner with her Christmas present."

With that, Sam disappeared outside for a few minutes. When he returned, he carried over his shoulder what looked like a dead body. He flung it into a chair beside Plain Jane. "Plain Jane," he announced proudly, "meet Dear John!"

Lee crept from the sink to the life-size doll. His hair matched Jane's, tomato red. He donned black boots made from blown out tires, pants stitched from tobacco burlap, a belt of bottle caps, a shirt of roofing shingles, Mickey Mouse-sized cotton glove hands, a mouth made of rubber worms, and a nose of bottle glass. And the eyes, the eyes stared back at us neon green. Neon IUDs.

"You outdid yourself." Tom wore a lopsided grin.

"No," Sam replied. "Not quite yet."

He moved behind Dear John and raised the cotton glove hands. "John has something to say. He's a talkative sort." He maneuvered the dummy to kneel down in front of Plain Jane and cleared his throat. "Jane, my darling angel. Will you marry me?"

Lee hopped behind Plain Jane, her mouth broad. "John, you mad, impetuous fool. This is so sudden. I have to consult my personal psychic."

"OK," said Dear John, "but I don't want to lug this thing back to Connolly's Jewelry Store, so would you wear it until your personal psychic can figure out the future?"

"Sure thing," burbled Plain Jane. "A doll can never have enough jewelry."

"So I'm told," said Sam, and he took a shiny object from his shirt pocket and slipped it on Lee's finger.

"Omigod. You're serious." Lee sputtered and started to cry again.

An elbow gently nudged my ribs and Tom and I slipped gracefully out of the Historical Society, Dear John collapsed in a heap on the floor from his big dramatic scene, Plain Jane slumped in her chair in shock.

I BALANCED MYSELF on top of the kitchen counter and pulled the basket off the cabinet, pushed the Spanish moss aside and took out the Bell family Bible—*my* family Bible— the wrapped CD and the tie. I handed the gifts to Tom.

"Merry Christmas."

He helped me down. "You didn't have to do that."

He must not have gotten me anything. "Oh, it's not much. Just a little something for the trouble I've put you through this year."

"Is that what you've done?" Those eyes could melt a steel door. "A client/lawyer gift?"

"Well. Not exactly. A business lady/ lawyer gift."

He unwrapped the presents, delighted with both. He threw the tie around his neck. "I bet you think I didn't get you anything."

"No!" Too much protest. "I mean, I hadn't thought about it. It doesn't matter."

He paused, smiling, then said, "I couldn't find frankincense and myrrh, but . . ." From a very deep pocket in his overcoat, Tom withdrew a sparkling, gold-ribboned bottle of Taittinger champagne. From another pocket, a gold half-pound box of Godiva chocolates met the kitchen light and gleamed. Glittering. Gold. Blinding.

I had to turn away. My eyes rested on the Bell family Bible and remained there, focused on the familiar, worn leather binding.

Behind me, a voice in my ear, his breath on my hair, then the rush of the warm mulled river of wine heating every vein in my body. "If you don't want the champagne and the chocolate, what do you want?"

A smile broke across my face and I slowly turned to face him.

"I want you," I said, inching my way along untested territory, "to ply me with wit and champagne, fruit, bread and cheese, a box of Godiva." I took the bottle and the box from his hands and set them on the counter. "Then I want you to recite one of your favorite poems. Something by Walt Whitman would be nice. And I want you to kiss me. Lightly. Insistently."

The dark eyes drew close, clasped onto mine. He placed one hand on either side of my face and slowly, quietly, softly, gently lulled me into his world.

Are you the new person drawn toward me?
To begin . . .

POSTSCRIPT

✳

THE LADYBUGS LEAVE in the spring, disappearing as suddenly as they appeared in September. The ceiling in the corner of my bathroom is bare, like the rest of the house. Bare, cleaned, culled of nearly twenty-five years of living alone, collecting the things one person collects.

I gave a lot of my little trinkets to Hilda to use in her dorm room in college in a year or so, knickknacks, old kitchen utensils, big sweaters never worn. She loves getting gifts, as if she never got any growing up. More important, she and Garland are both discovering each other's gifts.

They live in the same town as Roland, Ferrell T.'s most ardent supporter—the family split into two gender camps—attend the same church, shop the same grocery store, stop at the same stop signs. But that's where it ends. Garland opened her own restaurant, Garland's Bistro, which serves beer and wine, a first in Solace Glen. All of Roland's kitchen help switched to the other side of the street and his business, like his life, is falling apart, nothing left soon but the Victorian house packed with relics from the past.

Marlene stomps through the days of the week, adding Garland and Hilda to her list of people to blame for her problems, glaring holes into Louise's house with cold, fish eyes whenever she drives by.

Miss Fizzi, healthy as the racehorse she put her two dollars on at the Preakness, took center stage at her eighty-fifth birthday bash in May and danced a jig. The Eggheads stood by, ready to administer expert assistance if she jigged off the platform and broke a hip, but Miss Fizzi disappointed them and they got into a big argument with each other and Pal about the best car stereo systems. They tried to drag Screamin' Larry into it, calling on his fame as a radio personality to settle the issue, but he yawned in their faces and sauntered off, draining another longneck beer.

The next big event was Sam and Lee's wedding, and Louise would have loved the flowers. Tom and I stood as best man and best woman and Miss Fizzi sat in the front pew of the Episcopal Church as honorary grandmother, Plain Jane on her right, Dear John on her left. I glimpsed her at one point in the service, whispering a secret in Jane's ear.

The pear trees outshone themselves this year, along with the cherry and peach blossoms. They pepper the O'Connell property, and every window in the new house going up contains a view of a spring or autumn tree.

Trees are important, Tom says, and he plans to plant more around the house and down the drive. In twenty or thirty years, when we sit rocking on the porch, those new trees will be tall, their branches sweeping out to shelter Tom and me. Only to shelter.

National bestselling author
EARLENE FOWLER

Sunshine
and Shadow

Spirited ex-cowgirl, quilter, and folk-art expert Benni Harper is investigating the connection between her favorite author, the murder of a family friend, and a crazy quilt.
When she starts receiving strange phone calls and anonymous letters telling her she'll be the next victim, Benni's interest in the case becomes even more urgent.

"BEGUILING...INGENIOUS."
—*PUBLISHERS WEEKLY* (STARRED REVIEW)

"WARMHEARTED." —*BOOKLIST*

Available wherever books are sold or to order call 1-800-788-6262

PC002

SUSAN
WITTIG
ALBERT

A DILLY OF
A DEATH

BERKLEY